KELLEY ARMSTRONG

the Darkest Powers trilogy

The Summoning

The Awakening

The Reckoning

Doubleday Canada

This edition contains the complete texts of the original trade paperback editions.

Doubleday Canada edition published 2010

Library and Archives of Canada Cataloguing in Publication has been applied for.

ISBN: 978-0-385-67051-7

Printed and bound in the USA

Published in Canada by Doubleday Canada,
a division of Random House of Canada Limited

Visit Random House of Canada Limited's website: www.randomhouse.ca

10 9 8 7 6 5 4 3 2 1

For Julia

Contents

the Summoning

BOOK ONE

twelve years earlier

MOMMY FORGOT TO WARN the new babysitter about the basement.

Chloe teetered on the top step, chubby hands reaching up to clutch both railings, her arms shaking so much she could barely hang on. Her legs shook, too, the Scooby Doo heads on her slippers bobbing. Even her breath shook, puffing like she'd been running.

"Chloe?" Emily's muffled voice drifted up from the dark basement. "Your mom said the Coke's in the cold cellar, but I can't find it. Can you come down and help me?"

Mommy said she'd told Emily about the basement. Chloe was sure of it. She closed her eyes and thought hard. Before Mommy and Daddy left for the party, she'd been playing in the TV room. Mommy had called, and Chloe had run into the front hall where Mommy had scooped her up in a hug, laughing when Chloe's doll poked her eye.

"I see you're playing with Princess—I mean, *Pirate* Jasmine. Has she rescued poor Aladdin from the evil genie yet?"

Chloe shook her head, then whispered, "Did you tell Emily about the basement?"

"I most certainly did. No basements for Miss Chloe. That door stays closed." When Daddy came around the corner, Mommy said, "We really need to talk about moving, Steve."

"Say the word and the sign goes up." Daddy ruffled Chloe's hair. "Be good for Emily, kiddo."

And then they were gone.

"Chloe, I know you can hear me," Emily yelled.

Chloe peeled her fingers from the railing and stuck them in her ears.

"Chloe!"

"I c-can't go in the basement," Chloe called. "I-I'm not allowed."

"Well, I'm in charge and I say you are. You're a big girl."

Chloe made her feet move down one step. The back of her throat hurt and everything looked fuzzy, like she was going to cry.

"Chloe Saunders, you have five seconds or I'll drag you down here and lock the door."

Chloe raced down the steps so fast her feet tangled and she tumbled into a heap on the landing. She lay there, ankle throbbing, tears burning her eyes as she peered into the basement, with its creaks and smells and shadows. And Mrs. Hobb.

There'd been others, before Mrs. Hobb scared them away. Like old Mrs. Miller, who'd play peek-a-boo with Chloe and call her Mary. And Mr. Drake, who'd ask weird questions, like whether anyone lived on the moon yet, and most times Chloe didn't know the answer, but he'd still smile and tell her she was a good girl.

She used to like coming downstairs and talking to the people. All she had to do was not look behind the furnace, where a man hung from the ceiling, his face all purple and puffy. He never said anything, but seeing him always made Chloe's tummy hurt.

"Chloe?" Emily's muffled voice called. "Are you coming?"

Mommy would say "Think about the good parts, not the bad." So as Chloe walked down the last three steps, she remembered Mrs. Miller and Mr. Drake and she didn't think about Mrs. Hobb at all . . . or not very much.

At the bottom, she squinted into the near darkness. Just the night lights were on, the ones Mommy had put everywhere when Chloe started saying she didn't want to go downstairs and Mommy thought she was afraid of the dark, which she was, a little, but only because the dark meant Mrs. Hobb could sneak up on her.

Chloe could see the cold cellar door, though, so she kept her eyes on that and walked as fast as she could. When something moved, she forgot about not looking, but it was only the hanging man, and all she could see was his hand peeking from behind the furnace as he swayed.

She ran to the cold cellar door and yanked it open. Inside, it was pitch black.

"Chloe?" Emily called from the darkness.

Chloe clenched her fists. Now Emily was being *really* mean. Hiding on her—

Footsteps pattered overhead. Mommy? Home already?

"Come on, Chloe. You aren't afraid of the dark, are you?" Emily laughed. "I guess you're still a little baby after all."

Chloe scowled. Emily didn't know anything. Just a stupid, mean girl. Chloe would get her Coke, then run upstairs and tell Mommy, and Emily would never babysit her again.

She leaned into the tiny room, trying to remember where Mommy kept the Coke. That was it on the shelf, wasn't it? She darted over and stood on her tiptoes. Her fingers closed around a cool metal can.

"Chloe? Chloe!" It was Emily's voice, but far away, shrill. Footsteps pounded across the floor overhead. "Chloe, where are you?"

Chloe dropped the can. It hit the concrete with a crack, then rolled against her foot, hissing and spitting, soda pooling around her slippers.

"Chloe, Chloe, where are you?" mimicked a voice behind her, like Emily's, but not quite.

Chloe turned slowly.

In the doorway stood an old woman in a pink housecoat, her eyes and teeth glittering in the dark. Mrs. Hobb. Chloe wanted to squeeze her eyes shut, but she didn't dare because it only made her madder, made everything worse.

Mrs. Hobb's skin rippled and squirmed. Then it went black and shiny, crackling like twigs in a campfire. Big chunks fell off, plopping onto the floor. Her hair sizzled and burned away. And then there was nothing left but a skull dotted with scraps of blackened flesh. The jaws opened, the teeth still glittering.

"Welcome back, Chloe."

one

I BOLTED UP IN BED, one hand clutching my pendant, the other wrapped in my sheets. I struggled to recapture wisps of the dream already fluttering away. Something about a basement . . . a little girl . . . me? I couldn't remember ever having a basement—we'd always lived in condo apartments.

A little girl in a basement, something scary . . . weren't basements always scary? I shivered just thinking about them, dark and damp and empty. But this one hadn't been empty. There'd been . . . I couldn't remember what. A man behind a furnace . . . ?

A bang at my bedroom door made me jump.

"Chloe!" Annette shrieked. "Why hasn't your alarm gone off? I'm the housekeeper, not your nanny. If you're late again, I'm calling your father."

As threats went, this wasn't exactly the stuff of nightmares. Even if Annette managed to get hold of my dad in Berlin, he'd just pretend to listen, eyes on his BlackBerry, attention riveted to something more important, like the weather forecast. He'd murmur a vague "Yes, I'll see to it when I get back" and forget all about me the moment he hung up.

I turned on my radio, cranked it up, and crawled out of bed.

A half hour later, I was in my bathroom, getting ready for school.

I pulled the sides of my hair back in clips, glanced in the mirror, and shuddered. The style made me look twelve years old . . . and I didn't need any help. I'd just turned fifteen and servers still handed me the kiddie menu in restaurants. I couldn't blame them. I was five foot nothing with curves that only showed if I wore tight jeans and a tighter T-shirt.

Aunt Lauren swore I'd shoot up—and out—when I finally got my period. By this point, I figured it was "if," not "when." Most of my friends had gotten theirs at twelve, eleven even. I tried not to think about it too much, but of course I did. I worried that there was something wrong with me, felt like a freak every time my friends talked about their periods, prayed they didn't find out I hadn't gotten mine. Aunt Lauren said I was fine, and she was a doctor, so I guess she'd know. But it still bugged me. A lot.

"Chloe!" The door shuddered under Annette's meaty fist.

"I'm on the toilet," I shouted back. "Can I get some privacy maybe?"

I tried just one clip at the back of my head, holding the sides up. Not bad. When I turned my head for a side view, the clip slid from my baby-fine hair.

I never should have gotten it cut. But I'd been sick of having long, straight, little-girl hair. I'd decided on a shoulder-length, wispy style. On the model it looked great. On me? Not so much.

I eyed the unopened hair color tube. Kari swore red streaks would be perfect in my strawberry blond hair. I couldn't help thinking I'd look like a candy cane. Still, it might make me look older . . .

"I'm picking up the phone, Chloe," Annette yelled.

I grabbed the tube of dye, stuffed it in my backpack, and threw open the door.

I took the stairs, as always. The building might change, but my routine never did. The day I'd started kindergarten, my mother held my hand, my Sailor Moon backpack over her other arm as we'd stood at the top of the landing.

"Get ready, Chloe," she'd said. "One, two, three—"

And we were off, racing down the stairs until we reached the bottom, panting and giggling, the floor swaying and sliding under our unsteady feet, all the fears over my first school day gone.

We'd run down the stairs together every morning all through kindergarten and half of first grade and then . . . well, then there wasn't anyone to run down the stairs with anymore.

I paused at the bottom, touching the necklace under my T-shirt, then shook off the memories, hoisted my backpack, and walked from the stairwell.

After my mom died, we'd moved around Buffalo a lot. My dad flipped luxury apartments, meaning he bought them in buildings in the final stages of construction, then sold them when the work was complete. Since he was away on business most of the time, putting down roots wasn't important. Not for him, anyway.

This morning, the stairs hadn't been such a bright idea. My stomach was already fluttering with nerves over my Spanish midterm. I'd screwed up the last test—gone to a weekend sleepover at Beth's when I should have been studying—and barely passed. Spanish had never been my best subject, but if I didn't pull it up to a C, Dad might actually notice and start wondering whether an art school had been such a smart choice.

Milos was waiting for me in his cab at the curb. He'd been driving me for two years now, through two moves and three schools. As I got in, he adjusted the visor on my side. The morning sun still hit my eyes, but I didn't tell him that.

My stomach relaxed as I rubbed my fingers over the familiar rip in the armrest and inhaled chemical pine from the air freshener twisting above the vent.

"I saw a movie last night," he said as he slid the cab across three lanes. "One of the kind you like."

"A thriller?"

"No." He frowned, lips moving as if testing out word choices. "An action-adventure. You know, lots of guns, things blowing up. A real shoot-'em-down movie."

I hated correcting Milos's English, but he insisted on it. "You mean, a shoot-'em-up movie."

He cocked one dark brow. "When you shoot a man, which way does he fall? Up?"

I laughed, and we talked about movies for a while. My favorite subject.

When Milos had to take a call from his dispatcher, I glanced out the side window. A long-haired boy darted from behind a cluster of businessmen. He carried an old-fashioned plastic lunch box with a superhero on it. I was so busy trying to figure out which superhero it was, I didn't notice where the boy was headed until he leaped off the curb, landing between us and the next car.

"Milos!" I screamed. "Watch—"

The last word was ripped from my lungs as I slammed against my shoulder belt. The driver behind us, and the one behind him, laid on their horns, a chain reaction of protest.

"What?" Milos said. "Chloe? What's wrong?"

I looked over the hood of the car and saw . . . nothing. Just an empty lane in front and traffic veering to our left, drivers flashing Milos the finger as they passed.

"Th-th-th—" I clenched my fists, as if that could somehow force the word out. *If you get jammed, take another route*, my speech therapist always said. "I thought I saw some-wha-wha—"

Speak slowly. Consider your words first.

"I'm sorry. I thought I saw someone jump in front of us."

Milos eased the taxi forward. "That happens to me sometimes, especially if I'm turning my head. I think I see someone, but there's no one there."

I nodded. My stomach hurt again.

two

BETWEEN THE DREAM I couldn't remember and the boy I couldn't have seen, I was spooked. Until I got at least one question out of my head, focusing on my Spanish test was out of the question. So I called Aunt Lauren. When I got her voice mail, I said I'd phone back at lunch. I was halfway to my friend Kari's locker when my aunt called back.

"Did I ever live in a house with a basement?" I asked.

"And good morning to you, too."

"Sorry. I had this dream and it's bugging me." I told her what bits I could recall.

"Ah, that would have been the old house in Allentown. You were just a tyke. I'm not surprised you don't remember."

"Thanks. It was—"

"Bugging you, I can tell. Must have been a doozy of a nightmare."

"Something about a monster living in the basement. Very cliché. I'm ashamed of myself."

"Monster? What—?"

The PA system on her end cut her off, a tinny voice saying, "Dr. Fellows, please report to station 3B."

"That'd be your cue," I said.

"It can wait. Is everything okay, Chloe? You sound off."

"No, just . . . my imagination's in overdrive today. I freaked Milos out this morning, thinking I saw a boy run in front of the cab."

"What?"

"There wasn't a boy. Not outside my head, anyway." I saw Kari at her locker and waved. "The bell's going to ring so—"

"I'm picking you up after school. High tea at the Crowne. We'll talk."

The line went dead before I could argue. I shook my head and ran to catch up with Kari.

School. Not much to say about it. People think art schools must be different, all that creative energy simmering, classes full of happy kids, even the Goths as close to happy as their tortured souls will allow. They figure art schools must have less peer pressure and bullying. After all, most kids there are the ones who *get* bullied in other schools.

It's true that stuff like that isn't bad at A. R. Gurney High, but when you put kids together, no matter how similar they seem, lines are drawn. Cliques form. Instead of jocks and geeks and nobodies, you get artists and musicians and actors.

As a theater arts student, I was lumped in with the actors, where talent seemed to count less than looks, poise, and verbal ability. I didn't turn heads, and I scored a fat zero on the last two. On a popularity scale, I ranked a perfectly mediocre five. The kind of girl nobody thinks a whole lot about.

But I'd always dreamed of being in art school, and it *was* as cool as I'd imagined. Better yet, my father had promised that I could stay until I graduated, no matter how many times we moved. That meant for the first time in my life, I wasn't the "new girl." I'd started at A. R. Gurney as a freshman, like everyone else. Just like a normal kid. Finally.

That day, though, I didn't feel normal. I spent the morning thinking about that boy on the street. There were plenty of logical explanations. I'd been staring at his lunch box, so I'd misjudged where he'd been running. He'd jumped into a waiting car at the curb. Or swerved at the last second and vanished into the crowd.

That made perfect sense. So why did it still bug me?

"Oh, come on," Miranda said as I rooted through my locker at lunchtime. "He's right there. Ask him if he's going to the dance. How tough can that be?"

"Leave her alone," Beth said. She reached over my shoulder, grabbed my bright yellow lunch bag from the top shelf, and dangled it. "Don't know how you can miss this, Chloe. It's practically neon."

"She needs a stepladder to see that high," Kari said.

I banged her with my hip, and she bounced away, laughing.

Beth rolled her eyes. "Come on, people, or we'll never get a table."

We made it as far as Brent's locker before Miranda elbowed me. "Ask him, Chloe."

She mock-whispered it. Brent glanced over . . . then quickly looked away. My face heated and I clutched my lunch bag to my chest.

Kari's long, dark hair brushed my shoulder. "He's a jerk," she whispered. "Ignore him."

"No, he's not a jerk. He just doesn't like me. Can't help that."

"Here," Miranda said. "I'll ask him for you."

"No!" I grabbed her arm. "P-please."

Her round face screwed up in disgust. "God, you can be such a baby. You're fifteen, Chloe. You have to take matters into your own hands."

"Like phoning a guy until his mother tells you to leave him alone?" Kari said.

Miranda only shrugged. "That's Rob's mother. *He* never said it."

"Yeah? You just keep telling yourself that."

That set them off for real. Normally, I'd have jumped in and made them quit, but I was still upset over Miranda's embarrassing me in front of Brent.

Kari, Beth, and I used to talk about guys, but we weren't totally into them. Miranda was—she'd had more boyfriends than she could name.

So when she started hanging with us, it suddenly became really important to have a guy we liked. I worried enough about being immature, and it didn't help that she'd burst out laughing when I'd admitted I'd never been on a real date. So I invented a crush. Brent.

I figured I could just name a guy I liked and that would be enough. Not a chance. Miranda had outed me—telling him I liked him. I'd been horrified. Well, mostly. There'd also been a little part of me that hoped he'd go "Cool. I really like Chloe, too." Not a chance. Before, we used to talk in Spanish class sometimes. Now he sat two rows away, like I'd suddenly developed the world's worst case of BO.

We'd just reached the cafeteria when someone called my name. I turned to see Nate Bozian jogging toward me, his red hair like a beacon in the crowded hall. He bumped into a senior, grinned an apology, and kept coming.

"Hey," I said as he drew near.

"Hey yourself. Did you forget Petrie rescheduled film club for lunchtime this week? We're discussing avant-garde. I *know* you love art films."

I fake gagged.

"I'll send your regrets, then. And I'll tell Petrie you aren't interested in directing that short either."

"We're deciding that today?"

Nate started walking backward. "Maybe. Maybe not. So I'll tell Petrie—"

"Gotta run," I said to my friends and hurried to catch up with him.

The film club meeting started backstage as always, where we'd go through business stuff and eat lunch. Food wasn't allowed in the auditorium.

We discussed the short, and I *was* on the list for directors—the only freshman who'd made the cut. After, as everyone else watched scenes from avant-garde films, I mulled through my options for an audition tape. I snuck out before it ended and headed back to my locker.

My brain kept whirring until I was halfway there. Then my stomach started acting up again, reminding me that I'd been so excited about making the short list that I'd forgotten to eat.

I'd left my lunch bag backstage. I checked my watch. Ten minutes before class. I could make it.

Film club had ended. Whoever left the auditorium last had turned out the lights, and I didn't have a clue how to turn them on, especially when finding the switch would require being able to *see* it. Glow-in-the-dark light switches. That's how I'd finance my first film. Of course, I'd need someone to actually *make* them. Like most directors, I was more of an idea person.

I picked my way through the aisles, bashing my knees twice. Finally my eyes adjusted to the dim emergency lights, and I found the stairs leading backstage. Then it got tougher.

The backstage dissolved into smaller areas curtained off for storage and makeshift dressing rooms. There were lights, but someone else had always turned them on. After feeling around the nearest wall and not finding a switch, I gave up. The faint glow of more emergency lights let me see shapes. Good enough.

Still, it was pretty dark. I'm afraid of the dark. I had some bad experiences as a child, imaginary friends who lurked in dark places and scared me. I know that sounds weird. Other kids dream up playmates—I imagined bogeymen.

The smell of greasepaint told me I was in the dressing area, but the scent, mingled with the unmistakable odor of mothballs and old costumes, didn't calm me the way it usually did.

Three more steps and I did let out a shriek as fabric billowed around me. I'd stumbled into a curtain. Great. Exactly how loud had I screamed? I really hoped these walls were soundproof.

I swept my hand over the scratchy polyester until I found the opening and parted the curtains. Ahead, I could make out the lunch table. Something yellow sat on the top. My bag?

The makeshift hall seemed to stretch before me, yawning into darkness. It was the perspective—the two curtained sides angled inward, so the hall narrowed. Interesting illusion, especially for a suspense film. I'd have to remember that.

Thinking about the corridor as a movie set calmed my nerves. I framed the shot, the bounce of my step adding a jerkiness that would make the scene more immediate, putting the viewer in the head of our protagonist, the foolish girl making her way toward the strange noise.

Something thumped. I started, and my shoes squeaked and *that* noise made me jump higher. I rubbed the goose bumps on my arms and tried to laugh. Okay, I did say *strange noise*, didn't I? Cue the sound effects, please.

Another noise. A rustling. So we had rats in our spooky corridor, did we? How clichéd. Time to turn off my galloping imagination and focus. *Direct* the scene.

Our protagonist sees something at the end of the corridor. A shadowy figure—

Oh, please. Talk about cheap thrills. Go for original . . . mysterious . . .

Take two.

What's that she sees? A child's lunch bag, bright yellow and new, out of place in this old, condemned house.

Keep the film rolling. Don't let my mind wander—

A sob echoed through the silent rooms, then broke off, dissolving into a wet snuffling.

Crying. Right. From my movie. The protagonist sees a child's lunch bag, then hears eerie sobs. Something moved at the end of the hall. A dark shape—

I flung myself forward, racing for my bag. I grabbed it and took off.

three

"CHLOE! HOLD UP!"

I'd just dumped my uneaten lunch in my locker and was walking away when Nate hailed me. I turned to see him edging sideways through a group of girls. The bell sounded and the hall erupted, kids jostling like salmon fighting their way upstream, carrying along anything in their path. Nate had to struggle to reach me.

"You took off from film club before I could grab you. I wanted to ask if you're going to the dance."

"Tomorrow? Um, yeah."

He flashed a dimpled grin. "Great. See you there."

A swarm of kids engulfed him. I stood there, staring after him. Had Nate just tracked me down to ask if I was going to the dance? It wasn't the same as asking me *to* the dance, but still . . . I was definitely going to need to rethink my outfit.

A senior whacked into me, knocking off my backpack and muttering something about "standing in the middle of the hall." As I bent to grab my bag, I felt a gush between my legs.

I snapped upright and stood frozen before taking a tentative step.

Oh God. Had I actually wet myself? I took a deep breath. Maybe I *was* sick. My stomach had been dancing all day.

See if you can clean up and if it's bad, take a cab home.

In the bathroom, I pulled down my pants and saw bright red.

For a couple of minutes, I just sat there, on the toilet, grinning like an idiot and hoping that the rumor about school bathroom cams wasn't true.

I balled up toilet paper in my panties, pulled up my jeans, and waddled out of the stall. And there it was, a sight that had mocked me since fall: the sanitary napkin dispenser.

I reached into my back pocket and pulled out a five-dollar bill, a ten, and two pennies. Back into the stall. Scavenge through my backpack. Find . . . one nickel.

I eyed the machine. Drew closer. Examined the scratched lock, the one Beth said could be opened with a long fingernail. Mine weren't long, but my house key worked just fine.

A banner week for me. Getting short-listed for the director spot. Nate asking me about the dance. My first period. And now my first criminal act.

After I fixed myself up, I dug into my backpack for my brush and emerged instead with the tube of hair color. I lifted it. My reflection in the mirror grinned back.

Why not add "first skipped class" and "first dye job" to the list? Coloring my hair at the school bathroom sink wouldn't be easy, but it would probably be simpler than at home, with Annette hovering.

Dyeing a dozen bright red streaks took twenty minutes. I'd had to take off my shirt to avoid getting dye on it, so I was standing over the sink in my bra and jeans. Luckily no one came in.

I finished squeezing the strands dry with paper towel, took a deep breath, looked . . . and smiled. Kari had been right. It did look good. Annette would freak. My dad might notice. Might even get mad. But I was pretty sure no one was going to hand me a twelve-and-under menu anymore.

The door creaked. I shoved the towels in the trash, grabbed my shirt, and dashed into a stall. I barely had time to latch the door before the other girl started crying. I glanced over and saw a pair of Reeboks in the next stall.

Should I ask whether she was okay? Or would that embarrass her?

The toilet flushed and the shadow at my feet shifted. The stall lock clicked open. When the taps started, though, her sobs got even louder.

The water shut off. The towel roll squeaked. Paper crumpled. The door opened. It shut. The crying continued.

A cold finger slid down my spine. I told myself she'd changed her mind, and was staying until she got things under control, but the crying was right beside me. In the next stall.

I squeezed my hands into fists. It was just my imagination.

I slowly bent. No shoes under the divider. I ducked farther. No shoes in any of the stalls. The crying stopped.

I yanked my shirt on and hurried from the bathroom before it could start again. As the door shut behind me, all went silent. An empty hall.

"You!"

I spun to see a custodian walking toward me, and I breathed a sigh of relief.

"Th-the bathroom," I said. "I was using the bathroom."

He kept coming. I didn't recognize him. He was maybe my dad's age, with a brush cut, wearing our school janitorial uniform. A temp, filling in for Mr. Teitlebaum.

"I—I'm heading to c-class now."

I started walking.

"You! Get back here. I want to talk to you."

The only other sound was my footsteps. *My* footsteps. Why couldn't I hear *his*?

I walked faster.

A blur passed me. The air shimmered about ten feet ahead, a figure taking form in a custodian's shirt and slacks. I wheeled and broke into a run.

The man let out a snarl that echoed down the hall. A student rounded the corner, and we almost collided. I stammered an apology and glanced over my shoulder. The janitor was gone.

I exhaled and closed my eyes. When I opened them, the blue uniform shirt was inches from my face. I looked up . . . and let out a shriek.

He looked like a mannequin that had gotten too close to a fire. Face burned. Melted. One eye bulged, exposed. The other eye had slid down near his cheekbone, the whole cheek sagging, lips drooping, skin shiny and misshapen and—

The twisted lips parted. "Maybe now you'll pay attention to me."

I ran headlong down the hall. As I flew past one classroom door, it opened.

"Chloe?" A man's voice.

I kept running.

"Talk to me!" the horrible, garbled voice snarled, getting closer. "Do you know how long I've been trapped here?"

I flew through the doors into the stairwell and headed up.

Up? All the stupid heroines go up!

I veered across the landing and hit the next set of stairs. The custodian limped up the flight below, fingers clutching the railing, melted fingers, bone peeking through—

I barreled through the doors and raced along the main hall.

"Listen to me, you selfish brat. All I want is five minutes—"

I swerved into the nearest empty classroom and slammed the door. As I backed into the center of the room, the custodian stepped through the door. Right *through* it. That awful melted face was gone, and he was normal again.

"Is that better? Now will you stop screaming and talk to—"

I darted to the window and started looking for a way to open it, then saw how far down it was. At least thirty feet . . . onto pavement.

"Chloe!"

The door flew open. It was the vice principal, Ms. Waugh, with my math teacher, Mr. Travis, and a music teacher whose name I couldn't remember. Seeing me at the window, Ms. Waugh threw out her arms, blocking the two men.

"Chloe?" she said, voice low. "Honey, you need to step away from that window."

"I was just—"

"Chloe . . ."

Confused, I glanced back toward the window.

Mr. Travis shot past Ms. Waugh and tackled me. As we hit the floor, the air flew out of my lungs. Scrambling off, he accidentally kneed me in the stomach. I fell back, doubled over, wheezing.

I opened my eyes to see the custodian standing over me. I screamed and tried to get up, but Mr. Travis and the music teacher held me down while Ms. Waugh babbled into a cell phone.

The custodian leaned through Mr. Travis. "Now will you talk to me, girl? Can't get away."

I thrashed, kicking at the custodian, trying to pull away from the teachers. They only held me tighter. I vaguely heard Ms. Waugh calling that help was on the way. The custodian pushed his face into mine and it changed to that horrible melted mask, so close I was staring into his one bulging eye, almost out of its socket.

I chomped down on my tongue so I wouldn't scream. Blood filled my mouth. The more I fought, the harder the teachers restrained me, twisting my arms, pain stabbing through me.

"Can't you see him?" I shouted. "He's right there. Please. Please, please, please. Get him away from me. Get him away!"

They wouldn't listen. I continued to struggle, to argue, but they held me still as the burned man taunted me.

Finally, two men in uniforms hurried through the door. One helped the teachers restrain me while the other moved behind, out of my sight. Fingers tightened on my forearm. Then a needle prick. Ice slid through my veins.

The room started to sway. The custodian faded, blinking in and out.

"No!" he yelled. "I need to speak to her. Don't you understand? She can hear me. I only want to . . ."

His voice faded as the paramedics lowered me onto a stretcher. It rose, swaying. Swaying . . . like an elephant. I'd rode one once, with my mom, at the zoo, and my mind slipped back there, Mom's arms around me, her laughter—

The custodian's howl of rage sliced through my memory. "Don't take her away. I need her!"

Swaying. The elephant swaying. Mom laughing . . .

four

I SAT ON THE EDGE of my hospital bed and tried to persuade myself I was still asleep. That was the best explanation for what I was hearing. I could also chalk it up to *delusional*, but I preferred *dreaming*.

Aunt Lauren sat beside me, holding my hand. My eyes went to the nurses gliding past in the corridor. She followed my gaze, rose, and shut the door. Through a glaze of tears, I watched her and pictured Mom instead. Something inside me crumpled, and I was six years old, huddled on the bed, crying for my mother.

I rubbed my hands over the covers, stiff and scratchy, catching at my dry skin. The room was so hot every breath made my parched throat tighten. Aunt Lauren handed me my water, and I wrapped my hands around the cool glass. The water had a metallic taste, but I gulped it down.

"A group home," I said. The walls seemed to suck the words from my mouth, like a sound stage, absorbing them and leaving only dead air.

"Oh God, Chloe." She pulled a tissue from her pocket and wiped her nose. "Do you know how many times I've had to tell a patient he's dying? And somehow, this seems harder."

She shifted to face me. "I know how badly you want to go to UCLA for college. This is the only way we're going to get you there, hon."

"Is it Dad?"

She paused, and I knew she'd like to blame him. She'd wanted to raise me after my mom passed away, spare me a life of housekeepers and empty apartments. She'd never forgiven my father for refusing. Just like she'd never forgiven him for that night my mother died. It didn't matter that they'd been sideswiped in a hit-and-run—he'd been driving, so she held him responsible.

"No," she said finally. "It's the school. Unless you spend two weeks undergoing evaluation in a group home, it will go on your permanent record."

"What will go on my record?"

Her fist clenched around the tissue. "It's that da—" She caught herself. "It's the zero-tolerance policy." She spit the words with more venom than the curse.

"Zero tolerance? You mean violence? B-b-but I didn't—"

"I know you didn't. But to them, it's simple. You struggled with a teacher. You need help."

In a home. For crazy kids.

I awoke several times that night. The second time, my father was in the doorway, watching me. The third, he was sitting beside my bed. Seeing my eyes open, he reached over and awkwardly patted my hand.

"It's going to be all right," he murmured. "Everything will be all right."

I fell back to sleep.

My father was still there the next morning. His eyes were bleary, the wrinkles around his mouth deeper than I remembered. He'd been up all night, flying back from Berlin.

I don't think Dad ever wanted kids. But he'd never tell me that, even in anger. Whatever Aunt Lauren thinks of him, he does his best. He just doesn't seem to know what to make of me. I'm like a puppy left to him by someone he loved very much, and he struggles to do right by it even if he isn't much of a dog person.

"You changed your hair," he said as I sat up.

I braced myself. When you run screaming through the school halls after dyeing your hair in the girls' bathroom, the first thing people say—well, after they get past the screaming-through-the-halls part—is "you were doing *what*?" Coloring your hair in a school bathroom isn't normal. Not for girls like me. And bright red streaks? While skipping class? It screams *mental breakdown*.

"Do you like it?" my father asked after a moment.

I nodded.

He paused, then let out a strained chuckle. "Well, it's not exactly what I would have chosen, but it looks all right. If you like it, that's what counts." He scratched his throat, peppered with beard shadow. "I guess your aunt Lauren told you about this group home business. She's found one she thinks will be okay. Small, private. Can't say I'm thrilled with the idea, but it's only for a couple of weeks. . . ."

No one would say what was wrong with me. They had me talk to a bunch of doctors and they ran some tests, and I could tell they had a good idea what was wrong and just wouldn't say it. That meant it was bad.

This wasn't the first time I'd seen people who weren't really there. That's what Aunt Lauren had wanted to talk to me about after school. When I'd mentioned the dream, she'd remembered how I used to talk about people in our old basement. My parents figured it was my creative version of make-believe friends, inventing a whole cast of characters. Then those friends started terrifying me, so much that we'd moved.

Even after that, I'd sometimes "seen" people, so my mom bought me my ruby necklace and said it would protect me. Dad said it was all about psychology. I'd believed it worked, so it had. But now, it was happening again. And this time, no one was chalking it up to an overactive imagination.

They were sending me to a home for crazy kids. They thought I was crazy. I wasn't. I was fifteen and had finally gotten my period and that had to count for something. It couldn't just be coincidence that I'd started seeing things the same day. All those stockpiled hormones had exploded and my brain misfired, plucking images from forgotten movies and tricking me into thinking they were real.

If I was crazy, I'd be doing more than seeing and hearing people who weren't there. I'd be acting crazy, and I wasn't.

Was I?

The more I thought about it, the more I wasn't sure. I felt normal. I couldn't remember doing anything weird. Except for dyeing my hair in the bathroom. And skipping class. And breaking into the napkin dispenser. And fighting with a teacher.

That last one didn't count. I'd been freaked out from seeing that burned guy and I'd been struggling to get away from him, not trying to hurt anyone. Before that, I'd been fine. My friends had thought I was fine. Mr. Petrie thought I was fine when he put me on the director short list. Nate Bozian obviously thought I was fine. You wouldn't be happy that a crazy girl was going to a dance.

He had been happy, hadn't he?

When I thought back, it all seemed fuzzy, like some distant memory that maybe I only dreamed.

What if none of that happened? I'd *wanted* the director spot. I'd *wanted* Nate to be interested in me. Maybe I'd imagined it all. Hallucinated it, like the boy on the street and the crying girl and the burned janitor.

If I was crazy, would I know it? That's what being crazy was, wasn't it? You thought you were fine. Everyone else knew better.

Maybe I was crazy.

My father and Aunt Lauren drove me to Lyle House on Sunday afternoon. They'd given me some medicine before I left the hospital and it made me sleepy. Our arrival was a montage of still shots and clips.

A huge white Victorian house perched on an oversized lot. Yellow trim. A swing on the wraparound porch.

Two women. The first, gray haired and wide hipped, coming forward to greet me. The younger one's dour eyes following me, her arms crossed, braced for trouble.

Walking up a long narrow flight of stairs. The older woman—a nurse, who introduced herself as Mrs. Talbot—chirping a guided tour that my fuzzy brain couldn't follow.

A bedroom, white and yellow, decorated with daisies, smelling of hair gel.

On the far side of the room, a twin bed with a quilt yanked over the bunched-up sheets. The walls over the bed decorated with pages ripped from teen magazines. The dresser covered with makeup tubes and bottles. Only the tiny desk bare.

My side of the room was a sterile mirror image—same bed, same dresser, same tiny desk, all wiped clean of personality.

Time for Dad and Aunt Lauren to go. Mrs. Talbot explained I wouldn't see them for a couple of days because I needed time to "acclimate" to my new "environment." Like a pet in a new home.

Hugging Aunt Lauren. Pretending I didn't see the tears in her eyes.

An awkward embrace from Dad. He mumbled that he'd stay in town, and he would come to visit as soon as they let him. Then he pressed a roll of twenties into my hand as he kissed the top of my head.

Mrs. Talbot telling me they'd put my things away, since I was probably tired. Just crawl into bed. The blind closing. Room going dark. Falling back to sleep.

My father's voice waking me. Room completely dark now, black outside. Night.

Dad silhouetted in the doorway. The younger nurse—Miss Van Dop—behind him, face set in disapproval. My father moving to my bedside and pressing something soft into my arms. "We forgot Ozzie. I wasn't sure you'd sleep without him." The koala bear had been on a shelf in my room for two years, banished from my bed when I'd outgrown him. But I took him and buried my nose in his ratty fake fur that smelled of home.

I awoke to the wheezy sleep breathing of the girl in the next bed. I looked over but saw only a form under the quilt.

As I turned onto my back, hot tears slid down my cheeks. Not homesickness. Shame. Embarrassment. Humiliation.

I'd scared Aunt Lauren and Dad. They'd had to scramble to figure out what to do with me. What was wrong with me. How to fix it.

And school . . .

My cheeks burned hotter than my tears. How many kids had heard me screaming? Peeked in that classroom while I'd been fighting the teachers and babbling about being chased by melted custodians. Seen me being taken away strapped to a stretcher.

Anyone who'd missed the drama would have heard about it. Everyone would know that Chloe Saunders had lost it. That she was nuts, crazy, locked up with the rest of the loonies.

Even if they let me return to school, I didn't think I'd ever have the guts to go back.

five

I WOKE TO THE *CLINK-CLINK* of metal hangers. A blond girl flipped through clothes that I was pretty sure were mine, hung up yesterday by Mrs. Talbot.

"Hello," I said.

She turned and smiled. "Nice stuff. Good labels."

"I'm Chloe."

"Liz. Like Lizzie McGuire." She waved at an old and faded magazine cutout on her wall. "Except, I don't go by Lizzie, 'cause I think it sounds kind of" —she lowered her voice, as if not to offend the picture Lizzie—"babyish."

She continued talking, but I didn't hear it because all I could think was, What's wrong with her? If she was at Lyle House, there was something wrong with her. Some "mental condition."

She didn't look crazy. Her long hair was brushed into a gleaming ponytail. She wore Guess jeans and a Gap T-shirt. If I didn't know better, I'd think I'd woken up in a boarding school.

She kept talking. Maybe that was a sign.

She seemed harmless enough, though. She'd have to be, wouldn't she? They wouldn't put anyone dangerous in here. Or *really* crazy.

Oh no, Chloe. They don't put any really crazy people in here. Just the ones who hear voices and see burned-up janitors and fight with teachers.

My stomach started to ache.

"Come on," she said. "Breakfast's in five minutes, and they get real snippy if you're late." Liz put out a hand as I opened a dresser drawer. "You can wear your pajamas down to breakfast. The guys eat lunch and dinner with us, but they have breakfast later, so we get some privacy."

"Guys?"

"Simon, Derek, and Peter."

"The house is coed?"

"Uh-huh." She pursed her lips in the mirror and picked off a dry flake. "We all share the bottom floor, but the top one is divided."

She leaned out the door and showed me how short the hall was. "They get the other side. There's not even a joining door. Like we'd sneak over there at night if we could." She giggled. "Well, Tori would. And I might, if there was someone worth sneaking over for. Tori has dibs on Simon." She scrutinized me in the mirror. "You might like Peter. He's cute but way too young for me. He's thirteen. Almost fourteen, I think."

"I'm fifteen."

She bit her lip. "Oh, geez. Um, anyway, Peter won't be around much longer. I heard he's going home soon." She paused. "Fifteen, huh? What grade?"

"Ninth."

"Same as Tori. I'm in tenth, like Simon, Derek, and Rae. I think Simon and Rae are still fifteen, though. And did I say I love your hair? I wanted to do that, with blue streaks, but my mom said . . ."

Liz kept up the commentary as we headed downstairs, moving on to the whole cast of characters. There was Dr. Gill, the psychologist, but she only came for her office hours, as did the tutor, Ms. Wang.

I'd met two of the three nurses. Mrs. Talbot—the older woman, whom Liz proclaimed "really nice," and the younger Miss Van Dop, who was, she whispered, "not so nice." The third nurse, Mrs. Abdo, worked weekends, giving the others each a day off. They lived in and looked after us. They sounded more like the housemothers I'd heard boarding school kids talk about, but Liz called them nurses.

At the bottom of the stairs, the overpowering stink of lemon cleaner hit me. It smelled like Gran's house. Even Dad never seemed comfortable in his mother's immaculate house, under the glare that said you'd better not expect any birthday money if you spilled your soda on the white leather sofa. One look in this living room, though, and I breathed a sigh of relief. It was as clean as Gran's—the carpet spotless, the wood gleaming—but it had a worn, comfortable look that invited you to curl up on the sofa.

It was also painted the favored color for Lyle House—a pale yellow this time. Pillows covered the dark blue sofa and two rocking chairs. An old grandfather clock ticked in the corner. Every end table held a vase of daisies or daffodils. Bright and cheerful. Too bright and cheerful, really, like this bed-and-breakfast near Syracuse where Aunt Lauren and I stayed last fall—so desperate to be homey that it seemed more a stage set than someone's house.

No different from this, I guess—a business eager to convince you it *wasn't* a business, to make you feel at home. To make you forget you were in a place for crazy kids.

Liz stopped me outside the dining room so we could peek in.

On one side of the table sat a tall girl with short dark hair. "That's Tori. Victoria, but she likes Tori. With an *i*. She's my best friend. She gets moody, and I've heard that's why she's here, but I think she's fine." She jerked her chin toward the other person at the table—a pretty, copper-skinned girl with long dark curls. "That's Rachelle. Rae. She has this 'thing' for fire."

I stared at the girl. Thing for fire? Did that mean she *set* fires? I thought this place was supposed to be safe.

What about the boys? Were any of them violent?

I rubbed my stomach.

"Someone's hungry, I see," chirped a voice.

I glanced up to see Mrs. Talbot coming through what I guessed was the kitchen door, milk pitcher in hand. She smiled at me.

"Come in, Chloe. Let me introduce you."

———

Before breakfast, Miss Van Dop gave us all pills, then watched as we took them. It was creepy. No one said a word, just held out their hands, gulped their pill down with water, and returned to their conversations.

When I stared at mine, Miss Van Dop said the doctor would explain everything later, but for now, I should just take it. So I did.

After we'd eaten, we trooped upstairs to dress. Rae was in the lead, followed by Liz and Tori. Then me.

"Rachelle?" Tori called.

Rae's shoulders tightened and she didn't turn. "Yes, Victoria?"

Tori climbed two more steps, closing the gap between them. "You did get the laundry done, right? It's your turn, and I want to wear that new shirt my mom bought me."

Rae slowly turned. "Mrs. T. said I could do laundry today, since we had to take off while"—her gaze lit on me, and she offered a tiny, almost apologetic smile—"Chloe got settled."

"So you didn't do the laundry."

"That's what I said."

"But I want—"

"Your shirt. Got that part. So wear it. It's brand-new."

"Yeah, and other people probably tried it on. That's gross."

Rae threw up her hands and disappeared down the hall. Tori shot a scowl over her shoulder, as if this were my fault. As she turned, something flashed between us, and I stumbled back a step, grabbing the railing.

Her scowl twisted. "Geez, I'm not going to *hit* you."

Over her shoulder, a hand appeared, pale fingers wriggling like worms.

"Chloe?" Liz said.

"I—I—I—" I peeled my gaze from the disembodied hand. "I t-tripped."

"Listen—girl—" A man's voice whispered in my ear.

Liz came down the two steps between us and laid her fingers on my arm. "Are you okay? You're all white."

"I j-j-just thought I h-h-heard something."

"Why is she talking like that?" Tori asked Liz.

"It's called a stutter." Liz squeezed my arm. "It's okay. My brother stutters, too."

"Your brother is *five*, Liz. Lots of little kids do it. Not teenagers." Tori peered down at me. "Are you slow?"

"What?"

"You know, do you ride the looong bus"—she pulled her hands apart, then brought them together again—"or the short one."

Liz flushed. "Tori, that's not—"

"Well, she talks like a little kid, and she looks like one so . . ."

"I have a speech impediment," I said, enunciating carefully, as if she were the slow one. "I'm working to overcome it."

"You're doing great," Liz chirped. "You said that whole sentence without stuttering."

"Girls?" Mrs. Talbot peered around the hall doorway below. "You know you aren't supposed to fool around on the stairs. Someone could get hurt. Class is in ten minutes. Chloe, we're still waiting for notes from your teachers, so you won't be in class today. When you're dressed, we'll discuss your schedule."

Lyle House liked schedules the way a boot camp likes discipline.

We rose at 7:30. Ate, showered, dressed, and were in class by 9:00, where we did independent work assigned by our regular teachers, supervised by the tutor, Ms. Wang. Break at 10:30 for a snack—nutritious, of course. Back to class. Break for lunch at noon. Back to class from 1:00 until 4:30 with a twenty-minute break at 2:30. At some point during classes—the timing would vary—we'd have our individual hour-long therapy session with Dr. Gill; my first would be after lunch today. From 4:30 until 6:00, we had free time . . . kind of. In addition to classes and therapy, we had chores. A lot of chores from the looks of the list. These had to be done during our free time before and after dinner. Plus we had to squeeze in thirty minutes of physical activity every day. Then after a snack, it was off to bed at 9:00, lights-out at 10:00.

Nutritious snacks? Therapy sessions? Chore lists? Mandatory exercises? Nine o'clock bedtime?

Boot camp was starting to look good.

I didn't belong here. I really didn't.

After our talk, a phone call sent Mrs. Talbot scurrying off, calling back promises to return with my job list. Oh joy.

I sat in the living room trying to think, but the unrelenting cheerfulness was like a bright light shining in my eyes, making it hard to concentrate. A few days of yellow paint and daisies and I'd turn into a happy zombie, like Liz.

I felt a pang of shame. Liz had made me feel welcome and been quick to defend me against her friend. If being cheerful was a mental illness, it wasn't such a bad one to have—certainly better than seeing burned-up people.

I rubbed the back of my neck and closed my eyes.

Lyle House wasn't so bad, really. Better than padded rooms and endless hallways filled with *real* zombies, shambling mental patients so doped up they couldn't be bothered to get dressed, much less bathe. Maybe it was the illusion of home that bothered me. Maybe, in some ways, I'd be happier with ugly couches and white walls and bars on the windows, so there'd be no false promises. Yet just because I couldn't see any bars didn't mean it was as open as it seemed. It couldn't be.

I walked to the front window. Closed, despite the sunny day. There was a hole where there'd probably been a latch for opening it. I looked out. Lots of trees, a quiet street, more older houses on big lots. No electric fences. No sign on the lawn proclaiming LYLE HOUSE FOR CRAZY KIDS. All very ordinary, but I suspected if I grabbed a chair and smashed the window, an alarm would sound.

So where was the alarm?

I stepped into the hall, glanced at the front door, and saw it, blinking away. No attempt to hide it. A reminder, I guess. This might look like your house, but don't try walking out the front door.

What about the back?

I went into the dining room and looked out the window into a large yard with as many trees as the front. There was a shed, lawn chairs, and gardens. The soccer ball on one wooden chair and the basketball hoop over a cement pad suggested we were allowed out—probably for that "thirty minutes of physical activity." Was it monitored? I couldn't see any cameras, but there were enough windows for the nurses to keep an eye on anyone in the yard. And the six-foot-high fence was a good deterrent.

"Looking for a way out?"

I spun to see Miss Van Dop. Her eyes glittered with what looked like amusement, but her face was solemn.

"N-no. I w-was just looking around. Oh, and while I was getting dressed, I noticed I don't have my necklace. I think I might have left it in the hospital, and I want to make sure I get it back. It's kind of special."

"I'll let your father know, but he'll have to hold it for you while you're here. We don't like our girls wearing jewelry. Now, as for looking around . . ."

In other words, nice try on the distraction, but it hadn't worked. She pulled out a dining room chair and motioned for me to sit. I did.

"I'm sure you saw the security system at the front door," she said.

"I—I wasn't—"

"Trying to escape. I know." The smile touched her lips. "Most of our residents aren't the sort of teenagers who run away from home, unless it's to make a statement. They're bright enough to know that whatever is out there is worse than what's in here. And what's in here isn't so bad. Not Disney World, but not prison either. The only escape attempts we've ever had are from kids trying to sneak out to meet friends. Hardly serious, but parents expect better security from us; and, while we pride ourselves on providing a homelike environment, I think it's important to point out the limits early."

She waited as if for a response. I nodded.

"The windows are armed with a siren, as are the exterior doors. You are allowed out the back only, and there is no gate. Because of the alarm, you must notify us before going out, so we can disable it and, yes, watch you. If you have any questions about what you can and cannot do, come to me. I won't sugarcoat it for you, Chloe. I believe honesty is the first step to establishing trust, and trust is critical in a place like this."

Again her gaze pierced mine, probing, making sure I understood the other side of that statement—that honesty went both ways and I was expected to keep up my end.

I nodded.

six

Mrs. Talbot set me up to peel carrots for lunch. I didn't dare tell her I'd never peeled one in my life. After hacking my thumb, I got the hang of it.

As I peeled, my mind started to wander . . . into places I'd rather not visit. So I called in my best defense: turn it all into a movie.

As traumatic experiences went, the last few days were my best film fodder ever. But what genre would it be? Straight horror? Or psychological suspense? Maybe a combination of elements, surprising the viewer with—

"Peeling duty already?" a voice whispered. "What'd you do to deserve that?"

This time, when I wheeled around, I didn't see a disembodied hand but a whole body. A guy, in fact, maybe a year older than me, a half foot taller and slender, with high cheekbones and dark blond hair worn in short, messy spikes. His almond-shaped brown eyes danced with amusement.

"You must be Chloe."

He reached out. I jumped back. The carrot leaped from my hands and bounced off his arm. A real arm. Attached to a real guy.

"I—I—"

He put a finger to his lips, then pointed at the dining room door. Beyond it, Mrs. Talbot was talking to Liz.

"I'm not supposed to be in here," he whispered. "I'm Simon, by the way."

I was suddenly aware that he was standing between me and the exit. His smile was friendly, and he was definitely cute, but cute didn't count with a guy who had you cornered in a group home.

He backed up to the walk-in pantry, lifted a finger telling me to wait, then disappeared inside. I could hear him rooting around in the shelves. When I peeked in, he was taking down a box of graham crackers.

A kitchen raid? I couldn't help smiling. Guess it didn't matter whether it was a group home or summer camp, guys and their stomachs didn't change. Simon pulled out an unopened sleeve of crackers.

"The other one's already open," I whispered, pointing.

"Thanks, but he'll want the whole thing. Right, bro?"

I followed his gaze over my shoulder, and let out a yelp. The guy standing behind me had to be six feet tall, with shoulders as wide as the door. Though he was as big as an adult, he'd never be mistaken for one. His face could be used as the "before" picture for acne cream. Dark hair hung in his eyes, lank and dull.

"I—I—I—" I swallowed. "I didn't see you there."

He reached past me and took the crackers from Simon. When he started to retreat, Simon grabbed the back of his shirt.

"We're still teaching him manners," he said to me. "Derek, Chloe. Chloe, my brother, Derek."

"Brother?" I said.

"Yeah." Derek's voice was a low rumble. "Identical twins."

"He's my foster brother," Simon said. "So I was just about to tell Chloe—"

"We done here?" Derek said.

Simon waved him away, then rolled his eyes. "Sorry. Anyway, I was just going to say welcome—"

"Simon?" Tori's voice echoed through the kitchen. "Aha. I thought I heard you." Her fingers closed around the pantry door. "You and Derek, always raiding the—"

She spotted me and her eyes narrowed.

"Tori?" Simon said.

Her expression flipped from simmering to simpering. "Yes?"

He jabbed a finger toward the dining room door. "Shhh!"

As she babbled apologies, I made my escape.

After I finished the carrots, Mrs. Talbot said I could have free time until lunch and directed me to the media room. If I was hoping for a big-screen TV with surround sound and a top-of-the-line computer, I was out of luck. There was a twenty-inch TV, a cheap DVD/VCR combo, an old Xbox, and an even older computer. One flip through the movie collection and I knew I wouldn't be spending much time here . . . unless I was suddenly nostalgic for the Olsen twins. The only movie rated above PG was *Jurassic Park*, and it was labeled "Please ask before viewing," like I had to show my school ID card to prove I was over thirteen.

I turned on the computer. It took five minutes to boot up. Windows 98. I spent another five minutes trying to remember how to use Windows. We had Macs at school and I'd used that as an excuse to finally persuade my dad to buy me an Apple laptop—complete with all the upgraded movie editing programs.

I searched for a browser. I hoped for Firefox, but wasn't getting anything better than plain old IE. I typed in a URL and held my breath, expecting to get a "cannot connect to the Internet message." Instead, the page popped up. Guess we weren't as cut off from the outside world as I'd feared.

I flipped through my favorite sites, killing time until I worked up the nerve to check my in-box. A few minutes checking the weekend box office figures cleared my mind, then I typed in the URL to access my MSN account.

The browser chugged away for a minute, then brought up a "Page cannot be displayed" message. I tried Hotmail. Same thing.

"Chloe, there you are."

I turned as Mrs. Talbot walked in.

"I was just . . ." I waved at the screen. "I wanted to check my e-mail, but I keep getting this."

She walked over, glanced at the screen and sighed. "It's that Net Nanny software or whatever they use. It does more than block some Web sites, I'm afraid. You can send and receive e-mail through our account. You need to use the e-mail program that came with the computer, and get Miss Van Dop to type in the password so you can send it. A pain, I know, but we had a problem last year with a young man accessing sites he shouldn't have and when the board of directors found out . . ." She shook her head. "We're punishing everyone because of one bad apple, I'm sorry to say. Now, it's time for lunch."

I met the last housemate, Peter, over lunch. He said hello, asked how things were going, then turned his attention to his PSP as he ate. Like everything else at Lyle House, it was all very normal. Too normal. Every time someone moved, I tensed, waiting for her to start speaking in tongues or screaming about bugs crawling over his plate. No one did.

The food was decent enough. A homemade casserole, chock-full of vegetables and meat. Healthy, I was sure, like the milk and whole wheat rolls we had to go with it. For dessert we'd been promised Jell-O. Oh joy.

The sirens and screeching tires from Peter's game provided most of the meal's soundtrack. Rae was a no-show. Tori and Liz twittered together, too low for me to join in. Derek was too busy inhaling his food to talk.

So it was left to Simon to play host. He asked what part of the city I was from. When I admitted I hadn't been in any neighborhood very long, he said they'd moved around a lot, too—him and Derek. We started comparing worst-move-ever stories, and Tori jumped in with her own tale of moving horror—from her upstairs bedroom to her basement. Simon let her ramble for about two minutes before asking what grade I was in and at what school.

I knew he was just being polite—including the new girl in conversation—but if Tori had been a cartoon character, smoke would have billowed from her ears. I'd met girls like that. Territorial, whether it was about a hairbrush, a best friend, or a boy they had their eye on.

"Art school," she breathed. "Isn't that just *fascinating*. Tell me, Chloe. What do you study there? Ghost photography? Ghost writing?"

I choked on a chunk of meat.

"Oh." Tori turned doe eyes on Simon. "Didn't Chloe tell you why she's here? She sees dead people."

Peter lifted his head from his game. "Really? Cool."

When I looked up, Derek's fork was stopped halfway to his mouth, green eyes piercing the curtain of hair as he stared at me, his lip curled, as if to say *What kind of freak thinks she sees ghosts?*

"It's not like that. I—I—I—"

"There she goes." Tori sighed. "Liz, slap her back. See if you can restart her."

Simon glared at her. "Stop being such a bitch, Tori."

She froze, mouth open, a still shot of humiliated horror. Derek returned to his lunch.

"I didn't mean it that way," Tori said, words tumbling out. "Like Peter said, it's kinda cool. If she does see ghosts, maybe she could help Liz with her, you know, poltergeist."

"Tori!" Liz shrieked, dropping her fork.

"Here we go," Derek grumbled.

Liz's eyes filled as she screeched back her chair. Tori retreated into stumbling apologies again. Simon grabbed Liz's glass before she knocked it flying. Peter hunched over his game. Derek took advantage of the chaos to scoop up the last of the casserole.

The kitchen door flew open and Mrs. Talbot appeared, but her words were beat back by the cacophony.

Rae appeared in the other doorway holding a basket of dirty laundry. "Last call," she mouthed. "Any more?"

No one else noticed, much less heard her. I glanced around, and realized with all the commotion no one would notice if I left. So I did.

They knew. Everyone knew.

I was a freak. A crazy girl who saw ghosts. I belonged here.

Lunch churned in my stomach. I hurried up the stairs, thinking of my bed with its thin mattress that smelled of chemical vanilla, suddenly so inviting. Pull the blinds down, curl up under the covers with my iPod, and try to forget—

"Can I help you, Chloe?"

Two steps from the top, I stopped and turned to see Miss Van Dop below.

"I—I was just going to lie down for a minute. My head hurts and—"

"Then come and get some Tylenol."

"I—I'm kind of tired. I don't have classes, so I thought—"

"Come down, Chloe."

She waited until I was almost there then said, "At Lyle House, bedrooms are for sleeping."

"I—"

"I know you're probably tired and feeling overwhelmed, but you need activity and interaction, not isolation. Rae's getting a head start on the laundry before afternoon classes. If you've finished lunch, you can go help her."

I braced myself as I opened the basement door, expecting a descent down creaky wooden steps into a dark, damp basement, the kind of place I hated. Instead, I saw gleaming stairs, the passage brightly lit, the walls painted pale green with a flowery border. For the first time that day, I was glad of the too-bright cheeriness.

The laundry room had a tile floor, an old recliner, a washer and dryer, and a bunch of cupboards and shelves. Zero "old basement" creep factor.

The washing machine was running, but there was no sign of Rae.

I looked across the room, toward a closed door. As I walked to it, I picked up an acrid smell.

Smoke?

If Rae was smoking down here, I wasn't going to be the one to catch her. I turned to go back upstairs, and saw Rae squeezed between two towers of shelves.

Her lips formed a silent oath as she shook her hand, putting out a match. I looked for a cigarette. There wasn't one—just the smoldering match.

I heard Liz's voice again: *She has this "thing" for fire.*

My reaction must have shown because Rae jumped forward, getting between me and the door, hands flying up.

"No, no, it's not like that. I wasn't going to do anything. I don't—" She slowed, seeing she had my attention. "I don't start fires. They wouldn't let me stay here if I did. Ask anyone. I just like fire."

"Oh."

She noticed me staring at the matchbook and pocketed it.

"I, uh, noticed you didn't get lunch," I said. "Can I bring you something?"

Her face brightened. "Thanks. But I'll grab an apple before class. I use any excuse to avoid eating with Queen Victoria. You saw what she's like. With me, it's food. If I take a big helping or seconds or dessert, she gets her jabs in."

I must have looked confused, because she waved a hand down her body.

"Yes, I could stand to lose a few pounds, but I don't need her as my personal dietitian." She moved to a pile of unsorted laundry. "My advice? Steer clear of her. She's like these monsters I saw in an old sci-fi film, vampires from space, only they didn't drink blood, they sucked out all your energy."

"*Lifeforce*. Tobe Hooper. Psychic vampires."

She grinned, showing a crooked canine. "Psychic vampires. I'll have to remember that one."

Earlier I'd thought I didn't belong here because I didn't feel crazy. I bet none of them did either. Maybe mental illness was like stuttering. I'd spent my life trying to convince people that just because I stammered didn't mean there was anything else wrong with me. I just had a problem that I was working hard to overcome.

Like seeing people who weren't there.

Like being attracted to fire.

It didn't mean you were schizo or anything.

The sooner I got over myself, the better off I'd be at Lyle House. The sooner I'd *get* better . . . and get out.

I looked at the piles of laundry. "Can I help?"

She showed me how—another thing I'd never done. Even at camp, someone did it for us.

After a few minutes of working together, she said, "Does it make sense to you?"

"What?"

"Putting a girl in a place like this because she likes fire."

"Well, if that's all . . ."

"There's more, but it's small stuff, related to the fire thing. Nothing dangerous. I don't hurt myself or anyone else."

She returned to her sorting.

"Do you like manga?" she asked after a minute. "Anime?"

"Anime's cool. I'm not really into it, but I like Japanese movies, animated or not."

"Well, I'm into it. I watch the shows, read the books, chat on the boards, and all that. But this girl I know, she's completely into it. She spends most of her allowance on the books and DVDs. She can recite dialogue from them." She caught my gaze. "So would you say *she* belongs here?"

"No. Most kids are that way about something, right? With me, it's movies. Like knowing who directed a sci-fi movie made before I was born."

"But no one would say that makes you crazy. Just crazy about movies. Fascinated by them. Just like—" she took the matchbook from her pocket and waggled it "—me and fire."

The door at the top of the stairs clicked.

"Girls?" Mrs. Talbot called. "Are you still down there?"

Her footsteps tapped down before we could answer. As her shadow rounded the corner, I snatched the matchbook from Rae's outstretched hand and hid it under the shirt I'd been folding.

"Rae?" Mrs. Talbot said. "Your classes are starting. Chloe—"

"I'll finish here, then come up."

Mrs. Talbot left. I passed Rae back her matchbook and she mouthed her thanks, then followed the nurse up the stairs. And I was left alone in the basement.

seven

I TOSSED A PAIR OF pink underwear marked *Liz* into her pile, then stopped. Did we wash the guys' underwear, too? I really hoped not. I sifted through the pile, finding only ones for Rae, Liz, and Tori, and exhaled in relief.

"Girl . . ."

A man's voice over my head. I stiffened but forced myself to keep sorting. No one was here. Or, if someone was, he wasn't real. This was how I needed to handle it. Not jump like a scorched cat. Tough it out. Hear the voices, see the visions, and ignore them.

". . . come here . . ."

The voice had moved across the room. I lifted a red lace thong marked *Tori* and thought of my little girl cotton undies.

". . . over here . . ."

I tried to focus on how I could get better underwear before anyone else washed mine, but my hands started to tremble from the effort of ignoring the voice. Just one look. Just one—

I glanced across the room. No one there. I sighed and returned to sorting.

". . . door . . . closed . . ."

I looked at the closed door. The one I'd noticed earlier, which was proof that the voice was really just my overactive imagination.

Why do you need proof? What else would it be?

Great. Two voices to ignore.

"Open the door . . . something . . . show you . . ."

Ha! Now there was a classic movie scene: *Just come look behind the closed door, little girl.* I laughed, but the sound quavered, squeaking at the end.

Get a grip. Toughen up or they'll never let you out.

My gaze snuck to the door. It looked like an ordinary closet. If I really believed the voice was in my head, then what was stopping me from opening it?

I strode to the door, forcing myself to put one foot in front of the other, knowing if I stopped, I'd lose my nerve.

"Good . . . come . . ."

I grasped the doorknob, the metal cold under my fingers.

". . . open . . ."

I turned the handle slowly. It went a quarter turn, then stopped. I jiggled it.

"Locked." My voice echoed through the laundry room.

I jangled it again, then twisted sharply. The door didn't budge.

"Key . . . find . . . unlock . . ."

I pressed my fingers to my temples. "The door is locked and I'm going upstairs," I answered.

As I turned, I smacked into a wall of solid flesh and for the second time that day gave a girlie yelp. I looked up to see the same face that had made me shriek the last time.

I stumbled back and would have fallen if the door wasn't right behind me. Derek made no move to catch me, just stood there, hands in his pockets as I recovered.

"Who were you talking to?" he asked.

"Myself."

"Huh."

"Now, if you'll excuse me . . ."

When he didn't budge, I sidestepped to get around him. He moved into my path.

"You saw a ghost, didn't you?" he said.

To my relief, I managed to laugh. "Hate to break it to you, but there's no such thing as ghosts."

"Huh."

His gaze traveled around the laundry room, like a cop searching for an escaped convict. When he turned that piercing look on me, its intensity sucked the backbone out of me.

"What do you see, Chloe?"

"I—I—I don't s-s-s—"

"Slow down." He snapped the words, impatient. "What do they look like? Do they talk to you?"

"You really want to know?"

"Yeah."

I chewed my lip, then lifted onto my tiptoes. He bent to listen.

"They wear white sheets with big eye holes. And they say 'Boo!' " I glowered up at him. "Now get out of my way."

I expected him to sneer. Cross his arms and say, *Make me, little girl.*

His lips twitched and I steeled myself, then I realized he was smiling. Laughing at me.

He stepped aside. I swept past him to the stairs.

Dr. Gill was a small woman with a long rodent nose and bulging ratlike eyes that studied me as if *I* were the rat—one whose every twitch had to be scribbled into her notebook. I'd had therapists before. Two of them, both after my mom died. I'd hated the first one, an old man with bad breath who'd closed his eyes when I talked, like he was taking a nap. When I complained, I got the second one, Dr. Anna, a woman with bright red hair who'd joked with me and reminded me of my mom and helped me get on with my life. After ten minutes with Dr. Gill, I knew she fell somewhere in the middle. She seemed nice enough, and listened carefully, but she wasn't going to start cracking jokes anytime soon.

We talked about how I'd slept; how I was eating; what I thought of the others; and, mostly, how I felt about being here. I lied about the last. I wasn't stupid. If I wanted to get out, I couldn't moan that I didn't belong or complain that someone made a horrible mistake.

So I said that I knew my dad and aunt had done the right thing by putting me in Lyle House, and that I was determined to get better, whatever it took.

Dr. Gill's rat face relaxed. "That's a very mature attitude. I'm glad to hear it."

I nodded, and tried to look sincere.

"Now, Chloe, have you ever heard of schizophrenia?"

My heart stopped. "Sch-schizophrenia?"

"Yes. Do you know anything about it?"

My mouth opened and closed, brain refusing to fill it with words.

"Chloe?"

"Y-you think I'm schizo?"

Her mouth tightened. "We don't use that word, Chloe. In fact, we prefer not to use labels at all. But a diagnosis is a necessary part of the process. A patient must know her condition, understand and accept it before we can begin treatment."

"B-but I just got here. How c-can you know already—"

"Do you remember at the hospital? The doctors you spoke to? The tests they ran?"

"They found schizophrenia?"

She shook her head. "While scientists are working on a way to definitively diagnose schizophrenia, we don't have anything conclusive yet. Those tests, though, ruled out other possibilities, such as tumors or drug use. Taking those results and combining them with your symptoms, the most likely diagnosis is schizophrenia."

I stared at the floor. "You think I have schizophrenia."

"Do you know what it is?" She spoke slowly, like she was starting to question my intelligence.

"I've seen *A Beautiful Mind*."

More lip pursing. "That's Hollywood's version, Chloe."

"But it's based on a true story, right?"

"*Based*." Her voice softened. "I know from your file that you enjoy movies, and that's wonderful. But they aren't a good place to learn about mental illness. There are many forms and degrees of schizophrenia and yours isn't the same as that one."

Wasn't it? I saw people who weren't there, just like the guy in the movie.

Dr. Gill continued. "What you are experiencing is what we'd call undifferentiated schizophrenia, meaning you're displaying a limited number of the primary symptoms—in your case, seeing visions and hearing voices. Visual and auditory hallucinations."

"What about paranoia?"

"We see no evidence of that. You show no signs of disorganized behavior or disorganized speech patterns—"

"What about stuttering?"

She shook her head. "That's unrelated. You display none of the other symptoms, Chloe."

"Will I? Eventually?"

"Not necessarily. We'll have to be vigilant, of course, but we've caught this early. Usually a diagnosis isn't made until a patient is in her late teens or twenties. It's like catching a disease in its early stages, when we have the best chance to minimize its progression."

"And get rid of it."

A moment of silence as she fingered a long corded necklace. "Schizophrenia . . . is not like the flu, Chloe. It is permanent."

Blood thundered in my ears, drowning out her next words. She leaned forward, touching my knee.

"Chloe, are you listening to me?"

I nodded.

She moved back. "Schizophrenia is not a life sentence. But it is a lifelong condition. Like having asthma. With lifestyle changes and medication, it can be controlled and you can lead an otherwise normal life, to the point where no one will realize you have it unless you choose to tell them." She leaned back, meeting my gaze. "Earlier you said you were determined to do whatever it took to get through this. I know you were hoping for a quick fix, but this is going to require that same level of maturity and determination. Are you still prepared to do that, Chloe?"

I had more questions. Did it usually happen this fast, with no warning? One day you're walking around, totally normal, and the next you're hallucinating and running screaming through the halls? Then, bang, you get told you have schizophrenia, case closed?

It all seemed too sudden. But when I looked at Dr. Gill, watching me expectantly, waiting to get on to the next phase, I was afraid if I said anything, it would sound like I was still in denial; and if I did that, I'd never get out of Lyle House.

So I nodded. "I just want to get better."

"Good. Then we'll begin."

Dr. Gill explained about the medication. It was supposed to stop my hallucinations. Once they had the dose adjusted, there shouldn't be any significant side effects, but at first I might experience partial hallucinations, depression, and paranoia. Great. Sounded like the cure was as bad as the disease.

Dr. Gill assured me that by the time I left the group home, taking the pills would be no different than taking daily asthma medicine. "That's how you need to think of schizophrenia, Chloe. As a medical condition. You did nothing to cause it."

And could do nothing to cure it.

"You'll go through a period of depression, anger, and even denial. That's natural, and we'll deal with that in our sessions. You'll meet with me for an hour a day."

"Are there group sessions, too?" I asked.

"No. Someday you may decide you want to explore the dynamics of group therapy and we can discuss that later, but at Lyle House, we believe that privacy is critical. You need to fully accept your condition before you'll be comfortable sharing it with others."

She laid her notebook on the desk and crossed her hands on her knee. "And that leads to our final topic for today. Privacy. As I'm sure you've guessed, all the residents here are coping with mental issues. But that is all anyone needs to know. We will not share details of your condition, your symptoms, or your treatment with anyone here. If anyone pressures you for details, you are to come to us right away."

"They already know," I murmured.

"What?"

The outrage blazing from her eyes told me I should have kept my mouth shut. I knew from past therapy that it was important to share anything that was bothering me, but I didn't need to start my stay at Lyle House by tattling.

"N-not about the schizophrenia. Just . . . someone knew about me seeing things. Ghosts. Which I *never* said. To anyone."

"Who was it?"

"I—I'd rather not say. It was no big deal."

She unfolded her hands. "Yes, it is a big deal, Chloe. But I also appreciate that you don't want to get anyone into trouble. I have a good idea who it was. She must have been eavesdropping when we were discussing your hallucinations and jumped to her own conclusions about . . ." A dismissive wave of her hands. "Ghosts. I'm sorry this happened, but I promise it will be handled discreetly."

"But—"

"She won't know you told us anything, but it must be dealt with." She eased back into her seat. "I'm sorry this happened on your first day. Young people are, by nature, curious, and as hard as we strive to provide privacy, it isn't always possible in such tight living quarters."

"It's okay. No one made a big deal of it."

She nodded. "We have a very good group of young people here. In general, they are very respectful and accepting. That's important at Lyle House. You have a difficult road ahead and we're all here to make that journey as smooth as possible."

Schizo.

It didn't matter how many times Dr. Gill compared it to a disease or physical disability, it wasn't the same thing. It just wasn't. I had schizophrenia.

If I saw two guys on the sidewalk, one in a wheelchair and one talking to himself, which one would I rush to open a door for? And which would I cross the road to avoid?

Dr. Gill said it was just a matter of taking my meds and learning to cope. If it was that easy, why *were* there people wandering the streets talking to themselves? Crazy-eyed homeless people shouting at thin air?

Seeing people who weren't there. Hearing voices that didn't exist.

Schizo.

Just like me.

After my session, I ducked into the media room to think. I was curled up on the love seat, hugging a pillow to my chest, when Simon sailed in.

Not seeing me, he crossed the room and grabbed a baseball cap from the computer desk. Humming under his breath, he tossed the hat in the air and caught it.

He looked happy.

How could he be happy here? Comfortable, maybe. But happy?

He flipped the cap over in his hand and tugged it on. He stopped, gaze fixed on the window. I couldn't see his expression, but he went very still. Then a sharp shake of his head. He turned and saw me. A flash of surprise, then a broad grin.

"Hey."

"Hi."

He stepped closer, smile fading. "You okay?"

I'm fine sprang to my lips, but I couldn't force it out. I wasn't fine. I wanted to say I wasn't. I wanted it to be okay to say I wasn't. But the concern in his voice went no deeper than his grin, neither touching his eyes. They stayed distant, like he was making an effort to be nice because he was a nice guy and it was the right thing to do.

"I'm fine," I said.

He twisted the bill of his cap, watching me. Then he shrugged. "Okay. But a word of advice? Don't let them catch you holing up in here. It's like going to your room during the day. You'll get a lecture on moping around."

"I'm not—"

He lifted his hands. "Their words, not mine. I'm just warning you. You can get away with turning on the TV and pretending you're watching it, but they'll be happier if you're up and about, hanging with us. We're not such a bad bunch. Not too crazy."

He gave a blazing grin that made my stomach flip. I sat up, struggling for something to say, something to keep him here. I did want to talk. Not about Dr. Gill. Not about schizophrenia. About anything *but* that. Simon seemed normal and I desperately needed normal.

But his gaze had already shunted to the door. Sure, he thought I should hang out . . . with someone else. He was just giving advice to the new girl.

The doorway darkened and Simon's smile flashed fresh.

"Hey, bro. Don't worry. I didn't forget you. Just talking to Chloe."

He waved my way. Derek looked in, so expressionless you'd think Simon was gesturing at the furniture.

The scene in the basement flashed back—Derek accusing me of talking to ghosts. Had he told Simon? Probably. I bet they had a good laugh at the crazy girl.

"We're heading out back," Simon said. "Kick around the ball for our break. You're welcome to join us."

The invitation came lightly, automatically, and he didn't even wait for a response before he brushed past Derek with, "I'll get Talbot to disarm the door."

Derek stayed where he was. Still watching me.

Staring at me.

Like I was a freak.

Like I was schizo.

"Take a picture," I snapped. "It'll last longer."

He didn't so much as blink. Didn't leave either. Just kept studying me, as if I hadn't said a word. He'd leave when he was ready. And he did, walking out without a word.

———

When I left the media room, only Mrs. Talbot was around. The other kids had returned to class after their break. She sent me into the kitchen to peel—potatoes this time.

Before I started, she gave me another pill. I wanted to ask when I could expect them to start working, but if I did, then I'd have to admit I was still hearing voices. I wasn't seeing anything, though. Just that hand this morning, right after I took the pills. So maybe they *were* working. Maybe it didn't get any better than this. What would I do then?

Fake it. Block the voices and pretend I wasn't hearing them. Learn to—

A scream echoed through the house.

I jumped, the peeler clattering into the sink. As my heart thumped, I listened for a reaction. No reaction would mean the voice had been in my head. See, I was learning already.

"Elizabeth Delaney! Get back here!"

A door slammed. Footsteps raced down the hall, punctuated by sobs. The hairs on my neck rose as I thought of the crying girl at school. But I forced myself to the door and cracked it open just in time to see Liz lurch up the stairs.

"Enjoying the show?"

I jumped and caught Tori's glower before she hurried after her friend. Miss Van Dop strode from the living room into the hall.

"I have had it!" the other voice boomed from the classroom. "I expect some behavioral problems tutoring in a place like this, but that girl needs professional help."

"Ms. Wang, please," Miss Van Dop said. "Not in front of—"

"She threw a pencil at me. Whipped it. Like a weapon. Another half inch and she'd have taken my eye out. She broke the skin. Blood. From a pencil! All because I dared to suggest that a tenth grade student should be able to understand basic algebra."

Miss Van Dop tugged her into the hall, but the woman broke away and stormed into another room.

"Where's the director's number? I'm quitting. That girl is a menace. . . ."

A shadow glided past me and I turned to see Derek at my shoulder.

As the dining room door swung shut behind him, I caught a glimpse of books and a calculator spread across the table. He must have been there the whole time, doing independent work.

As he looked down at me, I expected some sarcastic comment about eavesdropping, but he only muttered, "Welcome to the madhouse," then brushed past me into the kitchen to swipe an extra snack.

eight

AFTER THAT, CALM DESCENDED. Like the calm before the storm, only in reverse. The nurses put dinner in the oven, then sequestered themselves in Dr. Gill's office, on a conference call, not to be disturbed.

No one had disagreed with Ms. Wang's explanation of events. No one tried to say it had been an accident. No one even seemed surprised that Liz had almost put someone's eye out.

When dinner time came, Mrs. Talbot served the food, then retreated into the office again. Liz joined us, wan and quiet. Simon snuck her a juice box, though we were supposed to be having milk. Tori hovered over her, coaxing her to eat. Even Rae and Peter made efforts at conversation, as if to distract her. Only Derek and I didn't participate.

After dinner Tori reminded Liz it was movie night, when they could get a DVD delivered. She gave Liz the honor of choosing, but Liz seemed overwhelmed by the responsibility and looked to us for help. Simon made suggestions, but said he wouldn't be watching it—he and Derek had a project due the next day. Liz finally settled on a romantic comedy. While she and Tori went to tell the nurses, Rae announced she had to fold the now-clean laundry. I offered to help.

We each carried a basket to the room Rae shared with Tori. I could tell neither was pleased with the arrangement. I swore I saw pencil marks on the windowsill to divide the room in half.

Tori's side was so clean it looked like mine when I'd first walked in. Nothing on the walls. Nothing on the bed or the floor. Every surface was bare, except two picture frames on the dresser. One held a shot of Tori and her parents and the other of a huge Siamese cat.

Rae's half had enough clutter for both of them. Hooded sweatshirts on the bedposts, textbooks balancing precariously on the desk, makeup left open on the dresser, drawers leaking clothing. The room of someone who didn't see why she had to put things away when she'd only be using them again the next day. Her walls were covered with taped photos.

Rae set her basket on Tori's bed, then closed the door. "Okay, I could beat around the bush, but I hate that, so I'm going to come right out and ask. Did I hear right? That you're here because you see ghosts?"

The words *I don't want to talk about it* rose to my lips. But I *did* want to talk about it. I longed to pick up the phone and call Kari or Beth, but I wasn't sure how much they'd heard about what happened and whether they'd understand. The person who seemed least likely to make fun of me or gossip about my problem was right here, asking for my story. So I gave it to her.

When I finished, Rae knelt there, holding up a shirt for at least thirty seconds before realizing what she was doing and folding it.

"Wow," she said.

"No wonder I'm in here, huh?"

"And it started right before you got your first period? Maybe that's it. Because you were kinda late, all that stuff built up, and then . . . bam."

"Super PMS?"

She laughed. "So have you looked it up?"

"Looked what up?"

"The custodian."

When I frowned, she went on. "You got chased by a guy in a custodian's uniform, right? And he was burned, like he died in some fire or explosion. If it really happened, it would have made the papers. You could look it up online."

I won't say the thought hadn't occurred to me, but I'd only given it permission to flit through my brain, like a streaker at a football game, moving too fast for me to get a good look.

What if I was *really* seeing ghosts?

My brain flashed *don't go there* neon warnings, but some deeper part was fascinated, *wanted* to go there.

I rubbed my temples.

Ghosts aren't real. Ghosts are for crazy people. What I saw were hallucinations, and the sooner I accepted that, the sooner I'd get out of here.

"It'd be cool if it was," I said carefully. "But Dr. Gill said seeing visions is a clear sign of a mental illness."

"Ah, the label. God, they love their labels here. Can't even let a girl get through her first day without slapping one on. Mine's pyromania." She caught my look. "Yeah, I know. We aren't supposed to share. Protecting our privacy. I think that's crap. They just don't want us comparing notes."

She lined up socks and started matching them. "You don't agree."

"Maybe with something like pyromania. It sounds almost . . . cool. But there are other things, labels, that we might not want to share."

"Like what?"

I concentrated on mating the socks for a minute. I wanted to tell her. Like the stuff about the ghosts. As scared as I was of sounding like a freak, I wanted to tell someone, to see what she said, get a second opinion.

"They say I have schizophrenia."

I studied her reaction. Just a small frown of confusion.

"Isn't that multiple personality?" she asked.

"No. Schizophrenia is, like, you know, schizo."

Her expression didn't change. "So it's seeing things and stuff?"

I lifted a white sail of a T-shirt, with faintly dingy armpits. No need to check the name. I folded it and added it to Derek's pile. "There's a whole lot of other symptoms, but I don't have them."

"None of them?"

"Guess not."

She eased back, uncrossing her legs. "See, that's my problem with it. You have one weird episode and they slap on a label, even if you just have the one problem. It's like coughing and they decide you've got pneumonia. I bet there are a lot more symptoms to pyromania, too. Ones I don't have."

Her gaze fixed on a red and a blue sock, and she stared intently at them, as if she could will them to turn purple and match. "So what else comes with schizophrenia?"

"Dr. Gill didn't say exactly."

"Huh."

"I guess I could look it up on the Internet. I should."

"*We* should. Schizophrenia and pyromania. I'd like to know more. To be sure, you know? Especially with the way things are going with Liz . . ." She rubbed her mouth with the back of her hand, still staring at the mismatched socks. "I think you're going to have the room to yourself soon. Maybe real soon."

"They're transferring her?"

"Probably. They've been talking about it for a while. This place is for kids who have problems, but they're not too bad and they're getting better. A couple weeks after I got here, they transferred a guy named Brady. He wasn't getting worse or anything. Not like Liz. He just didn't want to get better. He didn't think there was anything wrong with himself. So off he went. . . . Taught me a lesson. I might not like their labels and their meds, but I'll keep my mouth shut, play the game, and get out of here the *right* way."

"And go home."

A moment of silence, neither of us moving. Then she yanked a blue sock from my hand and waved it in front of my face.

"Whoops." I hadn't even realized I'd been holding it.

She folded the blue pair together, then shoved the lone red sock under Tori's bed. "Done. It should be movie time soon." She piled folded laundry into one basket. "Notice how quick Simon was to get out of watching the movie? Couple of real scholars, those two. Anything to avoid hanging out with the crazy kids."

"I got that impression. Simon seems nice but . . ."

She handed me one basket and took the other. "He's as much of a diva as Tori. They'd be a great pair. Derek might be a jerk, but at least he's honest about it. Simon makes nice during the day when he has to hang with us, then bolts the minute he can escape with his brother. Acts like he doesn't belong here. Like he doesn't have any problems and it's all a huge mistake."

"What *is* he in here for?"

"Believe me, I'd love to know. Him and Derek, both. Simon never goes to therapy, but Derek gets more than anyone. No one ever comes to visit them, but sometimes you'll hear them going on about their dad. Simon's dad, I think. If he's so great, why'd he dump them here and take off? And how do two guys from the same family, but not blood brothers, both have mental problems? I'd love to see their files."

I'd be lying if I said I wasn't curious about Simon. And maybe Derek, if only because I had the feeling I might need some ammunition against him. But I wouldn't want anyone reading *my* file and I wasn't going to help Rae read theirs.

"We couldn't risk taking a peek tonight anyway," she said. "With what's going on with Liz, they'll be on high alert. I don't want to get kicked out for corrupting the new kid."

"Maybe I'd get tossed out for corrupting you."

She caught my grin and laughed. "Oh, yeah, you're trouble, girl. I can tell."

She scooted me from the room and shut the door behind us.

nine

I'M NOT KEEN ON ROMANTIC COMEDIES. This may be like a guy admitting he doesn't like car chases, but Rae nodded off a few times, too, so I guessed this wouldn't have been her choice either.

I stayed awake by deconstructing the screenplay, which was so predictable I'd bet my college fund the writer was a student of screenwriting guru Robert McKee.

But as I watched the silly movie and munched popcorn, I finally relaxed. Talking to Rae had helped. She'd didn't think I was crazy. She didn't even think I was schizophrenic.

For the first time since my breakdown, things didn't look so bad. Maybe life as I knew it hadn't really ended in that classroom. Maybe I was overreacting and going all drama queen.

Did the kids at school know what had happened to me? A few saw me run down a hall. More saw me carried out on a stretcher, unconscious. Big deal. I could return in a few weeks and most probably wouldn't even notice I'd been gone.

Tomorrow, I'd e-mail Kari, tell her I was sick, and see what she said. That's probably exactly what she heard, that I had something like mono.

I'd get through this. Whatever I thought of their diagnosis, now wasn't the time to argue. I'd take my meds, lie if I had to, get released from Lyle House, and get on with my life.

"Chloe? Chloe?"

Liz's voice echoed through the deep caves of dreamland, and it took me a few minutes to find the way out. When I opened my eyes, she was leaning over me, bathing me in toothpaste breath, her long hair tickling my cheek. The hand clutching my arm kept trembling even after she stopped shaking me.

I pushed up on my elbows. "What's wrong?"

"I've been lying here for hours, trying to think of some way to ask you, some way that won't sound weird. But I can't. I just can't."

She backed away, her pale face glowing in the darkness, hands tugging at her nightshirt neckline, like it was choking her.

I scrambled up. "Liz?"

"They're going to send me away. Everyone knows they are, and that's why they're being so nice to me. I don't want to go, Chloe. They'll lock me up and—" She hiccuped deep breaths, hands cupped over her mouth. When she looked at me, her eyes were so wide the whites showed around her dark irises. "I know you haven't been here long, but I really need your help."

"Okay."

"Really?"

I stifled a yawn as I sat up. "If there's anything I can do—"

"There is. Thank you. Thank you." She dropped to her knees and pulled a bag from under her bed. "I don't know what all you need, but I did one at a sleepover last year, so I gathered up everything we used. There's a glass, some spices, a candle—" Her hand flew to her mouth. "Matches! Oh, no. We don't have any matches. They keep them locked up because of Rae. Can we do it without lighting the candle?"

"Do what?" I rubbed my hands over my face. I hadn't taken a sleeping pill but still felt that weird fogginess, like I was swimming through a sea of cotton balls. "What exactly are we doing, Liz?"

"A séance, of course."

The sleep fog evaporated, and I wondered if this was a prank. But I could tell by her expression that it wasn't. I remembered Tori's words at lunch.

"The . . . poltergeist?" I said carefully.

Liz flew at me so fast I smacked backward into the wall, hands flying up to ward her off. But she only pounced down beside me, eyes wild.

"Yes!" she said. "I have a poltergeist. It's so obvious, but they won't see it. They keep saying it's me doing all this stuff. But how would I throw a pencil that hard? Did anyone see me throw it? No. I get mad at Ms. Wang and the pencil flies and hits her and everyone says 'Oh, Liz threw it,' but I didn't. I never do."

"It's the . . . poltergeist."

"Right! I think it's trying to protect me because every time I get mad, things start flying. I've tried to talk to it, to make it stop. But it can't hear me because I can't talk to ghosts. That's why I need you."

I struggled to keep my expression neutral. I'd seen a documentary on poltergeist activity once. It usually *did* happen around girls like Liz—troubled teens desperate for attention. Some people thought the girls were playing pranks. Others believed the energy the girls gave off—hormones and rage—actually made things move.

"You don't believe me," she said.

"No, I didn't say—"

"You don't *believe* me!" She rose to her knees, eyes blazing. "Nobody believes me!"

"Liz, I—"

Behind her, the hair gel bottles rocked. Empty hangers in the closet chattered. I dug my fingers into the mattress.

"O-o-okay, Liz. I s-s-see—"

"No, you *don't*!"

She slammed her hands down. The bottles jetted into the air, smashing against the ceiling with such force the plastic exploded. Hair gel rained down.

"Do you see?"

"Y-y-yes."

Her hands flew up again, like a conductor hitting the crescendo. A picture leaped from the wall. It smashed onto the hardwood floor, glass spraying. Another fell. Then a third. A sliver of glass shot into my knee. A button of blood welled up and streamed down my leg.

Out of the corner of my eye, I saw the picture above my bed quaver. It sprang from its moorings.

"No!" Liz cried.

I dove. Liz hit my side, shoving me out of the picture's path. It struck her shoulder. She twisted. We both rolled from the bed, hitting the floor hard.

I lay on my side, catching my breath.

"I'm so sorry," she gasped. "I didn't mean— Do you see what happens? I can't control it. I get mad and everything . . ."

"You think it's a poltergeist."

She nodded, her lip quivering.

I had no idea what was going on. Not a poltergeist though—that was nuts—but if she thought it was, then maybe if she thought I'd told it to stop, it really *would* stop.

"Okay," I said. "Get the candle and we'll—"

The door shot open. Mrs. Talbot's bathrobed form stood silhouetted in the doorway. She flipped on the light. I drew back, blinking.

"Oh my God," she breathed, barely above a whisper. "Elizabeth. What have you done?"

I jumped to my feet. "It wasn't her. I—I—I—"

For once, I wasn't stammering. I just couldn't think of more words. Her gaze swept across the room, taking in the glass littering the floor, the hair gel dripping from the ceiling, the exploded makeup painting the wall, and I knew there was no reasonable explanation.

Her gaze fell to my leg and she let out a squeak.

"It's okay," I said, drawing my leg up and swiping the blood. "It's nothing. I cut myself. Shaving. Earlier."

She picked her way past me, eyes fixed on the glass-carpeted floor.

"No," Liz whispered. "Please no. I didn't mean it."

"It's okay, hon. We're going to get you help."

Miss Van Dop strode in, carrying a needle. She sedated Liz as Mrs. Talbot tried to calm her, telling her they were only transferring her to a better hospital, one more suitable, one that could help her get well faster.

When Liz was unconscious, they shooed me from the room. As I backed into the hall, a hand walloped me in the back, slamming me into the wall. I turned to see Tori looming over me.

"What did you do to her?" she snarled.

"Nothing." To my shock, the word came out clear, defiant even. I pulled myself up straight. "*I'm* not the one who told her I could help."

"Help?"

"By contacting her poltergeist."

Her eyes went wide, with that same horrified expression as when Simon told her to stop acting like a bitch. She turned away and stumbled into her room.

ten

THE PARAMEDICS CAME FOR LIZ. I watched her go, asleep on the stretcher, just like I'd been taken from school. Deluxe transportation for crazy kids.

Miss Van Dop insisted I take half a sleeping pill. I gave in, but when she tried to follow it with an extra dose of my antihallucination medicine, I hid that pill under my tongue.

I hadn't seen or heard anything since lunchtime. While that might have been the meds kicking in, I couldn't help hoping Rae's wild theory was right—that my "break with reality" was only a temporary mental vacation, brought on by stress and hormones. With any luck, I was already making the return trip to sanity.

I had to test that theory. So I'd save the pill and, if I saw anything, I'd take it.

I offered to help clean the room, but Mrs. Talbot took me downstairs for a glass of milk, then settled me on the sofa. I drifted off, waking when she came to trundle me back to bed, and was asleep again before I could pull up the covers.

I awoke to the fruity smell of Liz's hair gel. I floated there, dreaming I was trapped in a vat of cotton candy, the sweet smell making my stomach churn as I fought through the sticky strands. Finally I broke free, eyes flying open, gulping air.

"Chloe?"

I blinked. It sounded like Liz's voice, timid and wavering.

"Are you awake, Chloe?"

I rolled onto my side. Liz sat on the edge of her bed, wearing her Minnie Mouse nightshirt and gray socks covered with purple and orange giraffes.

She wiggled her toes. "Funky, huh? My little brother got them for me last Christmas."

I pushed up, blinking harder. The cotton candy from the sleeping pill still encircled my brain, sticky and thick, and I couldn't seem to focus. Sunlight streamed through the venetian blind, making the giraffes on Liz's socks dance as she waggled her toes.

"I had the weirdest dream last night," she said, gaze fixed on her feet.

You and me both, I thought.

"I dreamed they took me away and I woke up in this hospital. Only I wasn't in a bed but on a table. A cold, metal table. And there was this woman there, like a nurse, wearing one of those masks. She was bending over me. When I opened my eyes, she jumped."

Her gaze shot my way, and she managed a tiny smile. "Kinda like you do sometimes. Like I startled her. She calls this guy over, and I ask where I am, but they just keep talking. They're mad because I wasn't supposed to wake up and now they don't know what to do. I try to sit, but I'm tied down."

Liz bunched her nightshirt in her hands, kneading it. "All of a sudden I couldn't breathe. I couldn't move, couldn't yell, and then . . ." She shuddered, arms wrapping around herself. "I woke up here."

I sat up. "I'm going to help you, Liz. Okay?"

She scuttled back on the bed, pulling her knees up. She opened her mouth, but she was shaking too badly to form words. I stood, the wood floor icy beneath my feet, and crossed over to sit beside her.

"Do you want me to try talking to your poltergeist?"

She nodded, chin drumming against her chest. "Tell it to stop. Tell it I don't need its help. I can look after myself."

I reached out to lay my hand on her arm. I saw my fingers make contact, but they kept moving. Kept going. Through her arm.

As I stared in horror, Liz looked down. She saw my hand pass through her. And she started to scream.

eleven

I TUMBLED OFF HER BED, hitting the floor so hard pain jolted through my spine. When I scrambled up, Liz's bed was empty, the comforter wrinkled only where I'd been sitting.

I took a slow look around the bedroom. Liz was gone.

Gone? She'd never been here. They'd taken her away last night. I hadn't dreamed that part—hair gel still freckled the ceiling.

I pressed my palms to my eyes and backed up until I hit my bed, sitting down on it and inhaling deeply. After a moment, I opened my eyes. Sticky strands of sleep were still woven around my brain.

I'd been dreaming.

No, not dreaming. Not imagining things. Hallucinating.

Dr. Gill was right. I had schizophrenia.

But what if it wasn't? What if Rae was right, and I was seeing ghosts?

I shook my head sharply. No, that was crazy talk. That would mean Liz was dead. That was nuts. I was hallucinating, and I had to accept it.

I reached under my mattress, pulled out the pill I'd stuffed there the night before, and swallowed it dry, gagging in protest.

I had to take my meds. Take them and get better or I'd be shipped off to a real mental hospital, like Liz.

Only Rae joined me for breakfast. Tori was still in her room, and the nurses seemed content to leave her there.

I picked at my cereal, scooping one Cheerio at a time so it looked like I was eating. I kept thinking of how scared Liz had been. Terrified of being sent away. Then talking about her dream of being tied down, unable to breathe . . .

A hallucination. In real life, things like that don't happen.

And in real life, teenage girls can't make bottles explode and pictures fly off the walls. . . .

"Miss Van Dop?" I said when she came in to lay the breakfast table for the boys. "About Liz . . ."

"She's fine, Chloe. She's gone to a better place."

Those words sent a shiver through me, my spoon clattering against the bowl.

"I'd like to talk to her if I could," I said. "I didn't get a chance to say good-bye. Or thank her for helping me my first day."

Miss Van Dop's severe face softened. "She needs to settle in, but we'll call her in a few days and you can speak to her then."

See? Liz was fine. I was being paranoid.

Paranoia. Another symptom of schizophrenia. I pushed back the stab of dismay.

The nurse turned to go.

"Miss Van Dop? Sorry. I, um, I was talking to Mrs. Talbot yesterday, about e-mailing a friend. She said I needed to speak to you."

"Just use the e-mail program to write your letter and click send. It'll sit in the out-box until I enter the password."

Some instructions from my school had arrived, so after breakfast, I showered and dressed as the guys ate, then headed off to class with Rae.

Tori stayed in her room and the nurses let her. That surprised me, but I guessed it was because she was upset over Liz. I remembered Liz saying Tori was here because she was moody. There'd been a girl at drama camp a couple years ago whom I'd overheard counselors calling "moody." She'd always seemed to be either really happy or really sad, with no in-between.

With Tori absent, I was the only ninth grader. Peter was in eighth; Simon, Rae, and Derek in tenth. It didn't seem to matter much. Kind of like running a one-room schoolhouse, I guess. We shared a room with eight desks and we all worked on our separate assignments as Ms. Wang went around, helping and quietly giving short lessons.

Maybe knowing Ms. Wang had been partly responsible for Liz's leaving influenced my opinion of her, but she seemed to be one of those teachers who trudges through her job, watching the clock, waiting for the day to end . . . or a better job to come along.

I didn't get much work done that morning. I couldn't concentrate, couldn't stop thinking about Liz, what she'd done, what had happened to her.

The nurses hadn't seemed at all surprised by the damage in our room. That's just what Liz did, like with the pencil. She got mad and threw things.

But she hadn't thrown that stuff. I'd seen pictures fly from the wall when she'd been nowhere near them.

Or had I?

If I *was* schizophrenic, how was I supposed to know what I'd really seen or heard? And if paranoia was another symptom, how could I even trust my own gut feeling that said something bad had happened to Liz?

Rae was in session with Dr. Gill for the first part of the morning. When she returned, I spent the rest of the class eagerly awaiting break time, so I could talk to her. Not about Liz and my fears. Just talk to her. About class, last night's movie, the weather . . . anything that would clear Liz from my head.

But she was having problems with a work sheet, and Ms. Wang made her stay through the break. So I promised to grab her a snack, then trudged out, heading for the kitchen, sentenced to another hour or two trapped in my own head, thinking about Liz.

"Hey." Simon jogged up beside me in the hall. "You okay? You seem quiet this morning."

I managed a wan smile. "I'm always quiet."

"Yeah, but after last night, you have an excuse. Probably didn't get much sleep, huh?"

I shrugged.

Simon reached for the kitchen door. A hand appeared over my head and grabbed it for him. I didn't jump this time, just glanced back, and murmured a good morning to Derek. He didn't answer.

Simon headed into the pantry. Derek stayed in the kitchen, watching me. Studying me, again, with that spookily intense look of his.

"What?" I didn't mean to snap, but the word came out harsh.

Derek reached for me. I stumbled back . . . and realized he was reaching for the fruit bowl, which I was blocking. My cheeks burned as I darted out of the way, mumbling an apology. He ignored that, too.

"So what happened last night?" he asked as he grabbed two apples in one big hand.

"Hap-p-p-?"

"Slow down."

My face heated more—with anger now. I didn't like it when adults told me to slow down. From another kid, it was worse. Rude with a grating edge of condescension.

Simon stepped from the pantry, a box of granola bars in hand.

"You should have an apple," Derek said. "That's not—"

"I'm good, bro."

He flipped one granola bar to Derek, then held out the box for me. I took two, with thanks, and turned to leave.

"Might help if you talk about it," Simon called after me.

I turned back. Simon was unwrapping his granola bar, gaze averted, trying to look casual. Derek didn't bother. He leaned back against the counter, chomping into his apple, staring at me, expectant.

"Well?" Derek said when I stayed silent. He gestured for me to hurry up, spill all the gory details.

I'd never been one for gossip. Maybe that's not what they wanted—maybe they were just curious, concerned even. But it felt like gossip, and Liz deserved better.

"Rae's waiting for me," I said.

Simon stepped forward, raising a hand as if to stop me. Then he glanced at Derek. I didn't catch the look that passed between them, but it made Simon pull back, nod a good-bye to me, and busy himself unwrapping the rest of his bar.

The door was still swinging shut behind me when Simon whispered, "Something happened."

"Yeah."

I let the door close, and stood there. Derek said something else, but his low rumble swallowed the words.

"I don't know," Simon said. "We shouldn't—"

"Chloe?"

I wheeled as Mrs. Talbot stepped into the hall from the living room.

"Is Peter around?" she asked. Her broad face beamed.

"Uh, in class I think."

"Could you tell him I need to see him in the living room? I have a surprise for him."

I glanced at the kitchen door, but the guys had gone silent. I nodded to Mrs. Talbot and hurried off.

Peter's parents had come to take him home.

He'd known it would be coming soon, but they'd wanted to surprise him, so we had a little party, complete with cake. Low-fat, organic, frosting-free carrot cake. Then his parents went upstairs to help him pack, while Simon, Derek, and Rae returned to class and I had my session with Dr. Gill.

Twenty minutes later, from her office window, I watched his parents' minivan back out the drive and disappear down the street.

Another week and I'd be doing the same. I just had to stop thinking about Liz and ghosts and concentrate on getting out.

twelve

AFTER LUNCH, IT WAS time for math. That was one class where the tutor needed to know exactly where I was in the program and my math teacher hadn't sent over my work yet, so I was allowed to skip it for now. Math was also the class Derek had been sitting out the day before, and he did so again, taking his course work into the dining room as Ms. Wang gave a short lesson. I guessed he was doing remedial work and needed the quiet. He went his way and I went mine, into the media room to write that e-mail to Kari.

Getting the words right took time. The third version finally seemed vague but not like I was obviously avoiding anything. I was about to hit Send when I stopped.

I was using a communal account. What would come up in the sender field? Lyle Group Home for Mentally Disturbed Teens? I was sure it wouldn't be *that*, but even just "Lyle House" would throw Kari off, maybe enough for her to look it up.

I switched to the browser and searched for "Lyle House." Over a million hits. I added "Buffalo" and that cut my hits in half, but a scan of the first page showed they were all just random hits—a mention of a house on Lyle in Buffalo, a list of Lyle Lovett songs including the words "house" and "buffalo," a House representative named Lyle talking about Buffalo Lake.

I moved my mouse over the Send button again, and stopped again.

Just because Lyle House didn't have a cheerful Web site with a daisy border didn't mean Kari couldn't find it in the phone book.

I saved the e-mail as a text document with an obscure name. Then I deleted the message. At least with a phone call, I could probably block call display. There were no telephones in the common area, so I'd have to ask to use the nurses' phone. I'd do that later, when Kari would be home from school.

I shut down Outlook and was about to turn off the browser when a search result caught my eye—one about a Buffalo man named Lyle who'd died in a house fire.

I remembered what Rae had said last night about looking up my burned custodian. Here was my chance to settle the battle between the side that said *you're hallucinating—take your meds and shut up* and the side that wasn't so sure.

I moused to the search field, deleted the words, then sat there, fingers poised over the keys, every muscle tensed, as if bracing for an electric shock.

What was I afraid of?

Finding out I really did have schizophrenia?

Or finding out I didn't?

I lowered my fingers to the keys and typed. *A. R. Gurney school arts Buffalo death custodian.*

Thousands of hits, most of them random matches to A. R. Gurney, the Buffalo playwright. Then I saw the words *tragic accident* and I knew.

I forced my mouse up the screen, clicked, and read the article.

In 1991, forty-one-year-old Rod Stinson, head custodian at Buffalo's A. R. Gurney School of the Arts, had died in a chemical explosion. A freak accident, caused by a part-time janitor refilling a container with the wrong solution.

He'd died before I'd been born. So there was no way I could have ever heard about the accident.

But just because I couldn't remember hearing about it didn't mean I hadn't caught a snatch of it, maybe someone talking in class, and stored it deep in my subconscious, for schizophrenia to pull out and reshape as a hallucination.

I scanned the article. No picture. I backed out to the search page and went to the next. Same basic information, but this one did have a picture. And there was no question it was the man I'd seen.

Had I seen the photo somewhere?

You have an answer for everything, don't you? A "logical explanation." Well, what would you think if you were seeing this in one of your movies?

I'd run to the screen and smack this silly girl who was staring the truth in the face, too dumb to see it. No, not too dumb. Too stubborn.

You want a logical explanation? String the facts together. The scenes.

Scene one: girl hears disembodied voices and sees a boy who disappears before her eyes.

Scene two: she sees a dead guy with some kind of burns.

Scene three: she discovers that the burned custodian is real and died in her school, just the way she saw it.

Yet this girl, our supposedly intelligent heroine, doesn't believe she's seeing ghosts? Give yourself a shake.

Still I resisted. As much as I loved the world of cinema, I knew the difference between reality and story. In movies, there are ghosts and aliens and vampires. Even someone who doesn't believe in extraterrestrials can sit in a movie theater, see the protagonists struggling with clues that suggest alien invasion, and want to scream "Well, duh!"

But in real life, if you tell people you're being chased by melted school custodians, they don't say "Wow, you must be seeing ghosts." They put you someplace like this.

I stared at the picture. There could be no question—

"Is that who you saw?"

I spun in my chair. Derek was there at my shoulder. For someone his size, he could move so quietly I'd almost think *he* was a ghost. Just as silent . . . and just as unwelcome.

He pointed to the headline over the janitor's article. "A. R. Gurney. That's your school. You saw that guy, didn't you?"

"I don't know what you're talking about."

He fixed me with a look.

I clicked off the browser. "I was doing schoolwork. For when I go back. A project."

"On what? 'People who died at my school'? You know, I always heard art schools were weird. . . ."

I bristled. "Weird?"

"You want something to research?" As he leaned over to take the mouse, I caught a whiff of BO. Nothing flower wilting, just that first hint that his deodorant was about to expire. I tried to move away discreetly, but he noticed and glowered, as if insulted, then shifted to one side, pulling in his elbows.

He opened a fresh browser session, typed a single word, and clicked *Search*. Then he straightened.

"Try that. Maybe you'll learn something."

I'd been staring at the search term for at least five minutes. One word. *Necromancer.*

Was that even English? I moved the cursor in front of the word and typed "define." When I hit Enter, the screen filled.

Necromancer: one who practices divination by conjuring up the dead.

Divination? As in foretelling the future? By talking to dead people . . . from the past? That made no sense at all.

I skipped to the next definition, from Wikipedia.

Necromancy is divination by raising the spirits of the dead. The word derives from the Greek nekrós *"dead" and* manteía *"divination." It has a subsidiary meaning reflected in an alternative and archaic form of the word,* nigromancy *(a folk etymology using Latin* niger, *"black"), in which the magical force of "dark powers" is gained from or by acting upon corpses. A practitioner of necromancy is a necromancer.*

I reread the paragraph three times and slowly deciphered the geek talk, only to realize it didn't tell me anything more than the first definition. On to the next one, also from Wikipedia.

In the fictional universe of Diablo 2, the Priests of Rathma . . .

Definitely not what I was looking for, but I ran a quick search and I discovered a role-playing game class called necromancers, who could raise and control the dead. Was that where Derek got it? No. He might be creepy, but if he'd misplaced the boundary between real life and video games, he'd be in a real mental hospital.

I returned to Wikipedia, skimmed the rest of the definitions, and found only variations on the first. A necromancer foretells the future by talking to the dead.

Curious now, I deleted *define* and searched on *necromancer*. The first couple of sites were religious ones. According to them, necromancy was the art of communicating with the spirit world. They called it evil, a practice of black magic and Satan worship.

Did Derek think I was involved in black magic? Was he trying to save my soul? Or warn me that he was watching? I shivered.

Aunt Lauren's women's health clinic had once mistakenly been the target of a militant prolife group. I knew firsthand how scary people could get when they thought you did something that crossed their beliefs.

I flipped back to the list of search results and picked one that seemed more academic. It said that necromancy was another—older—name for mediums, spiritualists, and other people who could talk to ghosts. The meaning came from an ancient belief that if you could talk to the dead, they could predict the future because they could see everything—they'd know what your enemy was doing or where you could find buried treasure.

I switched to the next site on the list, and a horrible painting filled my screen—a mob of dead people, rotting and hacked up, being led by a guy with glowing eyes and an evil grin. The title: *The Army of the Dead.*

I scrolled down the page. It was filled with stuff like that, men surrounded by zombies.

I quickly switched to another page. It described the "art of necromancy" as the raising of the dead. I shuddered and flipped to another. A religious site now, quoting some old book ranting about "foul necromancers" who committed crimes against nature, communicating with spirits and re-animating the dead.

More sites. More old engravings and paintings. Grotesque pictures of grotesque men. Raising corpses. Raising spirits. Raising demons.

Fingers trembling, I turned off the browser.

thirteen

I STEPPED CAUTIOUSLY FROM THE media room, expecting to find Derek lurking around the corner, waiting to pounce.

The rumble of his voice made me jump, but it came from the dining room, where he was asking Mrs. Talbot when Dr. Gill would be ready to see him. I hurried into class. They weren't done with math yet, and Ms. Wang waved for me to take the seat next to the door.

When the lesson finally ended, Derek lumbered in. I struggled to ignore him. Rae waved me to the desk beside hers. I bolted for it. Derek never even looked my way, just took his regular seat beside Simon, their heads and voices lowering as they talked.

Simon laughed. I strained to hear what Derek was saying. Was he telling Simon about his "joke"? Or was I getting paranoid?

After English, school was done for the day. Derek disappeared with Simon, and I followed Rae to the dining room, where we did our homework.

I could barely finish a page on sentence diagramming. It was like deciphering a foreign language.

I was seeing ghosts. Real ghosts.

Maybe it would be different for someone who already believed in ghosts. I didn't.

My religious training was limited to sporadic church and Bible school visits with friends, and one brief stint at a private Christian school when my dad hadn't been able to get me into a public school. But I believed in God and in an afterlife the same way I believed in solar systems I'd never seen—that matter-of-fact acceptance that they existed even if I'd never thought much about the specifics.

If ghosts existed, did that mean there was no heaven? Were we all doomed to walk the earth forever as shades, hoping to find someone who could see or hear us and . . . ?

And what? What did the ghosts want from me?

I thought of the voice in the basement. I knew what that one wanted—a door opened. So this spirit had been wandering for years, finally finds someone who can hear him and his earth-shattering request is "Hey, could you open that door for me?"

What about Liz? I must have dreamed that. Anything else . . . I couldn't wrap my head around it.

But one thing was certain. I needed to know more, and if the pills were stopping me from seeing and hearing the ghosts clearly, then I had to stop taking them.

"It's not going to happen to you."

I turned from the living room window as Rae walked in.

"What happened to Liz, getting transferred, that won't happen with you." She sat on the couch. "That's what you're worried about, right? Why you haven't said ten words all day?"

"Sorry. I'm just . . ."

"Freaked out."

I nodded. This was true, even if it wasn't about what she thought. I sat in one of the rocking chairs.

"Like I said last night, Chloe, there's a trick to getting out of here." She lowered her voice. "Whatever you think? About their labels? Just nod and smile. Say 'Yes, Dr. Gill. Whatever you say, Dr. Gill. I just want to get better, Dr. Gill.' Do that, and you'll be following Peter out that front door any day now. We both will. Then I'll send you a bill for my advice."

I struggled to smile. From what I'd seen so far, Rae was a model patient. So why was she still here?

"How long is the average stay?" I asked.

She reclined on the sofa. "A couple months, I think."

"M-months?"

"Peter was here about that long. Tori a bit more. Derek and Simon, about three months."

"Three months?"

"I think so. But I could be wrong. Before you, Liz and I were the newbies. Three weeks for each of us, me a few days more than her."

"I—I was told I'd only be in for two weeks."

She shrugged. "I guess it's different for you then, lucky girl."

"Or did they mean two weeks was the *minimum*?"

She stretched her foot to nudge my knee. "Don't look so glum. The company's good, isn't it?"

I managed a smile. "Some of it."

"No kidding, huh? With Peter and Liz gone, we're stuck with Frankenstein and the divas. Speaking of which, Queen Victoria is up and about . . . relatively speaking."

"Hmm?"

She lowered her voice another notch. "She's stuffed full of meds and totally out of it." I must have looked alarmed because she hurried on. "Oh, that's not normal. They don't do that to anyone but Tori, and she wants it. She's the pill princess. If she doesn't get hers on time, she *asks* for them. Once, on the weekend, they ran out and had to page Dr. Gill for a refill and whoa boy—" She shook her head. "Tori ran to our room, locked the door, and wouldn't come out until someone brought her the medication. Then she tattled to her mom and there was this huge uproar. Her mom's connected to the people who run Lyle House. Anyway, she's totally doped up today, so she shouldn't give us any trouble."

When Mrs. Talbot rounded us up for dinner, I realized I hadn't told Rae about taking her advice and looking up the dead janitor.

Tori joined us for dinner—in body, at least. She spent the meal practicing for a role in the next zombie movie, expressionless, methodically moving fork to mouth, sometimes even with food on it. I was torn between feeling sorry for her and just being creeped out.

I wasn't the only one left uncertain. Rae tensed with every mouthful, as if waiting for "old Tori" to leap out and jab her about her eating. Simon gamely tried to carry on a conversation with me and tentatively slanted questions Tori's way, as if afraid she was just playing possum, looking for sympathy.

After that endless meal, we all fled, gratefully, to our chores—Rae and me on dinner cleanup, the guys on garbage and recycling detail. Later Rae had a project to work on, and Ms. Wang had warned the nurses that she wanted Rae to do it without help.

So after telling Miss Van Dop that I'd be right back, I headed up to my room for my iPod. When I opened the door, I found a folded note on the floor.

Chloe,

We need to talk. Meet me in the laundry room at 7:15.

Simon

I folded the note into quarters. Had Derek put Simon up to this when I didn't freak out over him calling me a necromancer? Did he hope I might give a more gratifying response to his brother?

Or did Simon want to resume our discussion from the kitchen, when they'd asked about Liz? Maybe I wasn't the only one worried about her.

I went downstairs just past seven, and used the extra time to ghost hunt, prowling the laundry room, listening and looking. The one time I wanted to see or hear a ghost, I didn't.

Could I contact it? Or was it a one-way street, and did I have to wait until one chose to speak to *me*? I wanted to test that by calling out, but Derek had already caught me talking to myself. I wasn't taking that risk with Simon.

So I just wandered, my mind automatically sliding behind a camera lens.

". . . here . . ." a voice whispered, so soft and dry it sounded like the wind through long grass. ". . . talk to . . ."

A shadow loomed over my shoulder. I braced myself to see a vision of horror as I looked up into . . . Derek's face.

"You always this jumpy?" he said.

"Wh-where did you come from?"

"Upstairs."

"I'm waiting for some—" I stopped and studied his expression. "It's you, isn't it? You had Simon send—"

"Simon didn't send anything. I knew you wouldn't come for me. But Simon?" He glanced at his watch. "For Simon, you're early. So did you look it up?"

So that's what this was about. "You mean that word? *Nec*—" I pursed my lips, testing it. "*Necromancer*? Is that how you say it?"

He waved the pronunciation off. Unimportant. He leaned against the wall, trying for casual, uninterested maybe. His flexing fingers betrayed his eagerness to hear my answer. To see my reaction.

"Did you look it up?" he asked again.

"I did. And, well, I don't quite know what to say."

He rubbed his hands against his jeans, as if drying them. "Okay. So, you searched for it and . . ."

"It wasn't what I expected."

He brushed his jeans again, then closed his hands. Crossed his arms. Uncrossed them. I looked around, drawing it out, making him rock forward, almost bouncing with impatience.

"So . . ." he said.

"Well, I have to admit . . ." I took a deep breath. "I'm not really into computer games."

His eyes closed to slits, face screwed up. "Computer games?"

"Video games? RPGs? I've played some, but not the kind you're talking about."

He looked at me, wary, as if suspecting I really did belong in a home for crazy kids.

"But if you guys are into them?" I flashed a bright smile. "Then I'm certainly willing to give them a shot."

"Them?"

"The games. Role playing, right? But I don't think the necromancer is for me, though I do appreciate the suggestion."

"Suggestion . . ." he said slowly.

"That I play a necromancer? That's why you had me look it up, right?"

His lips parted, eyes rounding as he understood. "No, I didn't mean—"

"I suppose it could be cool, playing a character who can raise the dead, but it's just, you know, not really *me*. A little too dark. Too emo, you know? I'd rather play a magician."

"I wasn't—"

"So I don't have to be a necromancer? Thanks. I really do appreciate you taking the time to make me feel welcome. It's *so* sweet."

As I fixed him with a sugary smile, he finally realized I was having him on. His face darkened. "I wasn't inviting you to a game, Chloe."

"No?" I widened my eyes. "Then why would you send me to those sites about necromancers? Show me pictures of madmen raising armies of rotting zombies? Is that how you get your kicks, Derek? Scaring the new kids? Well, you've had your fun, and if you corner me again or lure me into the basement—"

"Lure you? I was trying to talk to you."

"No." I lifted my gaze to his. "You were trying to scare me. Do it again and I'll tell the nurses."

When I scripted the lines in my head, they'd been strong and defiant—the new girl standing up to the bully. But when I said them, I sounded like a spoiled brat threatening to tattle.

Derek's eyes hardened into shards of green glass and his face twisted into something not quite human, filling with a rage that made me stumble back out of its path and bolt for the stairs.

He grabbed for me, fingers clamping around my forearm. He yanked so hard I yelped, shoulder wrenching as I sailed off my feet. He let go and I crashed to the floor.

For a moment, I just lay there, crumpled in a heap, cradling my arm and blinking hard, unable to believe what had just happened. Then his shadow fell across me, and I scrambled to my feet.

He reached for me. "Chloe, I—"

I staggered back before he could touch me. He said something. I didn't hear it. Didn't look at him. Just ran for the stairs.

I didn't stop until I was in my room. Then I sat cross-legged on my bed, gulping oxygen. My shoulder burned. When I rolled up my sleeve, I saw a red mark for each of his fingers.

I stared at them. No one had ever hurt me before. My parents had never struck me. Never spanked me or even threatened to. I wasn't the kind of girl who got into fistfights or catfights. Sure, I'd been pushed, jostled, elbowed . . . but grabbed and thrown across a room?

I yanked down my sleeve. Was I surprised? Derek had made me nervous from that first encounter in the pantry. When I realized he'd sent the note, I should have gone upstairs. If he'd tried to stop me, I should have screamed. But no, I had to be cool. Be clever. Bait him.

Yet I had no proof except marks on my arm that were already fading. Even if I still had them when I showed the nurses, Derek could say I'd lured him into the basement and flipped out, and he'd had to grab my arm to restrain me. After all, I was a diagnosed schizophrenic. Hallucinations and paranoia went with the territory.

I had to handle this myself.

I *should* handle this myself.

I'd led the proverbial sheltered life. I'd always known that meant I lacked the life experience I'd need to be a screenwriter. Here was my chance to start getting it.

I'd handle this. But to handle it, I needed to know exactly what I was up against.

I took Rae aside.

"Do you still want to see Simon and Derek's files?" I asked.

She nodded.

"Then I'll help you get them. Tonight."

fourteen

We found Mrs. Talbot setting out the evening snack. Carrot sticks and dip. Yum. Whatever complaints I had about Annette, at least I could always count on brownies at home.

"Hungry, girls? I'm not surprised. No one ate very much at dinner."

She held out the plate. We each took a stick and dipped it.

"Chloe and I were thinking, Mrs. T," Rae said. "About Tori."

She set the plate on the table, eyes downcast as she nodded. "I know, dear. She's taking Liz's leaving very hard. They were close. I'm sure she'll feel better once they can talk, but until then she may feel a little down while we get her . . . medication adjusted. We'll need you girls to be extra nice to her."

"Sure." Rae licked dip off her finger. "We were wondering, though, whether it might be easier for her if she had the room to herself. I could sleep in Chloe's."

Mrs. Talbot handed Rae a napkin. "I don't want to isolate her too much but, yes, she'd probably be happier alone for now."

"Just for now?"

The nurse smiled. "No, you can move in with Chloe permanently, if that's what you'd both like."

While Tori was downstairs watching television, Rae started to move, as if afraid Miss Van Dop or Dr. Gill would veto the change.

She handed me a stack of T-shirts. "It's Simon, isn't it?"

"Hmm?"

"You want to know what Simon is in for."

"I don't—"

She draped her jeans over her arms and waved me out. "You two have been chatting every meal. At first, I thought maybe he was using you to throw Tori off his trail, but she wasn't paying any attention today, and he kept talking."

"I'm not—"

"Hey, you like him. That's fine." She opened Liz's bottom drawer. It was empty—every trace of her cleaned out while we'd been in class. "I don't care for the guy, but that's just my opinion. Maybe he's just stuck up with me because I'm not in his league."

"League?"

She held up a pair of jeans and pointed to the label. "You see anyone else in this place wearing jeans from Wal-Mart? It's a private home. You gotta pay for it, and I bet it costs more than Motel 6. I'm the designated charity case."

"I—"

"It's cool. You treat me fine. So did Peter and"—a somber look around her new room—"Liz. Derek's a jerk to everyone, so I don't take it personally. If I'm only getting the cold shoulder from Simon and Tori, I can live with it. That's why I think those two are perfect for each other, but if you like him and he likes you? None of my business. But you're smart to run a background check."

She headed back to her old room, me at her heels. "My friend's mom did that with a guy she was supposed to marry. Found out he had three kids he'd never mentioned." She grinned over her shoulder. "I'm pretty sure Simon doesn't have kids, but you never know."

As we finished clearing out her drawers, I considered letting it go at that. But I didn't want her thinking I was the kind of girl who gets into a new place and immediately starts scoping out the guys. If I wasn't ready to tell the nurses about Derek, I should tell someone. That way, I'd have backup for my story if I needed it later.

"It's not Simon," I said as we returned to her room, clothing finished. "It's Derek."

She'd been in the middle of plucking a photo from the wall and fumbled it, cursing as I rescued the fallen photograph.

"Derek? You like—"

"God, no. I meant Derek's the one I'm checking out—and not *that* way."

She exhaled and leaned against the wall. "Thank God. I know some girls go for the jerks, but that's just nasty." She flushed as she took the picture from me and reached for another. "I shouldn't say that. It's not his fault, the whole . . ." She faltered for a word.

"Puberty smackdown."

A grin. "Exactly. I should feel sorry for the guy, but it's hard when his attitude is as ugly as his face." She stopped, photo in hand, and glanced over her shoulder at me. "Is that it? Did he . . . do something?"

"Why? Does he have a history of that?"

"Depends on what *that* is. Being rude, yes. A jerk, yes. He ignores us except when he doesn't have a choice and, believe me, no one complains. So what did he do?"

I considered my words. I didn't want her to insist I talk to the nurses, so I left out the throwing-me-across-the-room part and just said he'd been following me, popping up when I was alone.

"Ah, he likes you." She handed me a photo to hold.

"No, it isn't like that."

"Uh-huh. Well, you'd probably rather it *wasn't* like that, but it sure sounds like it. Maybe you're his type. At my school, there's this guy I like, on the basketball team. He's even taller than Derek, but he always goes for tiny girls like you."

I took another photo from her. "That's not it. I'm absolutely certain of it."

She opened her mouth and I felt a flash of annoyance. Why is it that every time a girl says a guy is bothering her, it's fluffed off with *oh, he just likes you*, as if that makes it okay?

Seeing my expression, Rae snapped her mouth closed and took down another picture.

I said, "He freaks me out and I want to see what his file says. Whether there's any reason to be spooked. Whether he has, you know, a problem."

"That's smart. And I'm sorry. If he scares you, that's serious. I don't mean to make jokes. We'll get the facts tonight."

fifteen

BEDTIME AT LYLE HOUSE was nine, with the lights out and the no-talking rule coming into effect an hour later when the nurses retired.

Each side of the upper level had a bedroom for its assigned nurse. Liz had said there was no door linking the boys' and girls' areas, but according to Rae, there was one between the nurses' rooms, which gave them quick access to the whole upper floor in an emergency.

So while Rae swore Mrs. Talbot was a quick and sound sleeper, we had to take Miss Van Dop into account, too. An early break-in was too risky. Rae set the alarm on her sports watch for 2:30 and we went to sleep.

At 2:30, the house was still and silent. Too still and too silent. Every creaking floorboard sounded like a gunshot. And in an old house, *most* boards creak.

Rae followed me into the kitchen, where we took two juice boxes from the fridge and set them on the counter. Then I opened the pantry door, turned on the light, and returned to the hall, leaving both doors half open.

Dr. Gill's office was at the west end, near the boys' stairs. Rae had checked out the lock a week ago. It was only a regular interior key lock, not much tougher than the kind you can pick with a coin. Or so she said.

I'd never had any reason to open a household lock—probably because I didn't have siblings. So I watched and took mental notes. All part of gaining life experience.

Rae had watched Dr. Gill get her file out once, during her session, so she knew where they were kept. The office had an all-in-one printer, which made things easy. I stood guard. The only hitch came when she copied the pages, the *swoosh-shoosh* of the scanner head loud enough to make me nervous. But the files must have been short because by the time I looked in, she was returning them to the folder, copies made.

She passed me two sheets, folded in half, then she returned the file to the drawer. We backed out of the room. As she reengaged the lock, the unmistakable sound of a creaking floorboard made us both freeze. A long moment of silence passed. Then a fresh creak. Someone was coming down the boys' stairs.

We took off, padding barefooted down the hall. At the half-open kitchen door, we darted inside, then into the open pantry.

"Come on," I stage-whispered. "Just pick something already."

"I can't find the Rice Krispie bars. I know there were some last week."

"The guys probably—" I stopped, then hissed. "Someone's coming. Get the light!"

She flipped the switch as I closed the door all but a crack. As I peered through the gap, Derek stopped inside the kitchen door. He left the light off as he looked around, moonbeams from the window casting a glow on his face. His gaze swept the kitchen and came to rest on the pantry door.

I pushed it open and stepped out.

"Cracker?" I said, holding up a box.

He looked at me and, in a flash, I was back in the basement, sailing through the air. My smile fell away and I shoved the box into his hands.

"We were getting a snack," Rae said.

He kept watching me, eyes narrowing.

"I'll get the juice," Rae said, squeezing past.

Derek looked over at the boxes we'd left on the counter. Proof that we'd only been raiding the kitchen. It had been my plan, and I thought it was so clever, but as his gaze swung back my way, the hairs on my neck rose and I knew he didn't buy it.

I stepped forward. For a second, he didn't move and all I could hear was his breathing, feel the sheer size of him, looming there.

He stepped aside.

As I passed, he took a cracker sleeve from the box and held it out. "Forgot these."

"Right. Thanks."

I took one and fled into the hall, Rae behind me. Derek followed us out but headed the other way, toward the boys' side. When I turned to go up the stairs, I glanced down the hall. He'd stopped outside Dr. Gill's office and stood looking at the door.

We lay in bed with the lights out for fifteen minutes, long enough for Derek to either tell the nurses on us or just go back to bed. My fingers kept brushing the pages I'd stuffed in my pajama waistband. Finally, Rae scooted over to my bed, flashlight in hand.

"That was a close call," she said.

"Do you think he'll tell the nurses?"

"Nah. He was getting a snack himself. He wouldn't dare tattle."

So Derek had just happened to get up for a snack while we were breaking into Dr. Gill's office? I hated coincidence, but surely the printer hadn't made enough noise for him to hear it upstairs.

I pulled the sheets out and smoothed them on the mattress.

"That's Derek's," Rae whispered as she turned on the flashlight.

I tugged the second page free and held it out. "You want Simon's?"

She shook her head. "That's Derek's second page. There wasn't one for Simon."

"You couldn't find it?"

"No, there *wasn't* one. The dividers in the drawer are marked with our names, then the file folders are marked again. There wasn't a divider or a file for Simon."

"That's—"

"Weird, I know. Maybe they keep it someplace else. Anyway, you wanted Derek's, so I figured I shouldn't waste time searching for Simon's. Now, let's see what Frankenstein is in for." She moved the beam to the top of the page. "Derek Souza. Birth date, blah, blah, blah."

She shifted the light to the next section. "Huh. He was brought to Lyle House by a children's services agency. No mention of that father they're always talking about. If child services is involved, then you can bet he's no dad of the year. Oh, here it is. Diagnosis . . . antisocial personality disorder." She snorted a laugh. "Yeah? Tell me something I didn't know. Is that really an illness? Being rude? What kind of meds do they give you for that?"

"Whatever it is, they aren't working."

She grinned. "Got that right. No wonder he's been stuck here so long—"

The hall light clicked on. Rae dove for her bed, leaving the flashlight behind. I turned it off as the bathroom door closed. When I made a motion to toss it to her, she shook her head, then leaned out and whispered, "You finish up. Find anything interesting? Tell me in the morning."

Whoever was in the bathroom—Tori or Mrs. Talbot—seemed to take forever. By the time the toilet flushed, Rae was asleep. I waited a few minutes, then turned on the flashlight and read.

With each sentence, the ball of dread in my stomach grew. Antisocial personality disorder had nothing to do with being rude. It meant someone who showed a complete disregard for others, who lacked the ability to empathize—to put himself in another person's shoes. The disorder was characterized by a violent temper and fits of rage, which only made it worse. If you didn't understand that you were hurting someone, what would make you stop?

I flipped to the second page, labeled "background."

> Performing a standard background check on DS has proved difficult. No birth certificate or other identifying records could be found. They likely exist, but the lack of concrete information on his early life makes a proper search impossible. According to DS and

his foster brother, SB, Derek came to live with them at approximately five years of age. DS does not recall—or refused to share—the details of his life before this, though his responses suggest he may have been raised in an institutional setting.

Simon's father, Christopher Bae, appears to have taken de facto custody of DS, with no record of a formal adoption or fostering arrangement. The boys were enrolled in school as "Simon Kim" and "Derek Brown." The reason for the false names is not known.

School records suggest DS's behavioral problems began in seventh grade. Never an outgoing or cheerful child, he became increasingly sullen, his withdrawal punctuated by bouts of misplaced anger, often culminating in violent outbursts.

Violent outbursts . . .

The bruises on my arms throbbed and I absently rubbed them, wincing.

No incidents have been properly documented, making a complete forensic study of the disorder's progression impossible. DS seems to have avoided expulsion or other serious disciplinary action until an altercation described by witnesses as "a normal school yard fight." DS violently attacked three youths in what officers suspected was a chemically fueled rage. An adrenaline surge may also explain the display of extraordinary strength reported by witnesses. By the time authorities interceded, one youth had suffered spinal fractures. Medical experts fear he may never walk again.

The single-spaced page of background detail continued, but the words vanished, and all I could see was the floor whipping past as Derek flung me across the laundry room.

Extraordinary strength . . .

Violent outbursts . . .

May never walk again . . .

They'd taken Liz away for throwing pencils and hair gel bottles, and they kept Derek? A huge guy with a history of violent rages? With a disorder that meant he didn't care who he hurt or how badly?

Why hadn't someone warned me?

Why wasn't he locked up?

I shoved the pages under my mattress. I didn't need to read the rest. I knew what it would say. That he was being medicated. That he was being rehabilitated. That he was cooperating and had shown no signs of violence while at Lyle House. That his condition was under control.

I shone the flashlight on my arm. The finger marks were turning purple.

sixteen

EVERY TIME I DRIFTED OFF, I'd get stuck in that weird place between sleep and waking, where my mind sifted through the memories of the day, confusing them and twisting them. I'd be back in the basement, Derek grabbing my arm and throwing me across the room. Then I'd wake up in a hospital, with Mrs. Talbot at my side, telling me I'd never walk again.

When the wake-up rap came at the door, I buried my head under my pillow.

"Chloe?" Mrs. Talbot opened the door. "You need to get dressed before you come down today."

My stomach seized. With Liz and Peter gone, had they decided we should all eat breakfast together? I couldn't face Derek. I just couldn't.

"Your aunt is coming by at eight to take you out to breakfast. You need to be ready for her."

I released my death grip on the pillow and got up.

"You're mad at me, aren't you, Chloe?"

I stopped moving my scrambled eggs around my plate and looked up. Worry clouded Aunt Lauren's face. Dark half-moons under each eye said she hadn't been getting enough sleep. I'd missed those smudges earlier, hidden under her makeup until we got under the fluorescent lights of Denny's.

"Mad about what?" I asked.

A short laugh. "Well, I don't know. Maybe because I dumped you in a group home with strangers and disappeared."

I set down my fork. "You didn't 'dump' me. The school insisted I go there and the home insisted you and Dad stay away while I adjusted. I'm not a little kid. I understand what's going on."

She exhaled, the sound loud enough to be heard over the roar of the busy restaurant.

"I have a problem," I continued. "I have to learn to deal with it, and it isn't your fault or Dad's."

She leaned forward. "It isn't yours either. You understand that, too, right? It's a medical condition. You didn't do anything to cause it."

"I know." I nibbled my toast.

"You're being very mature about this, Chloe. I'm proud of you."

I nodded and kept nibbling. Seeds from the raspberry jam crackled between my teeth.

"Oh, and I have something for you." She reached into her purse and pulled out a sandwich bag. Inside was my ruby necklace. "The nurses called from the home and told me you were missing it. Your dad forgot to take it from the hospital when you left."

I took it, fingering the familiar pendant through the plastic, then passed it back. "You'll have to keep it for me. I'm not allowed to have jewelry at the home."

"Don't worry, I've already spoken to the nurses. I told them it was important to you, and they've agreed to let you have it."

"Thanks."

"Make sure you wear it, though. We don't want it going missing again."

I took the necklace out of the bag and put it on. I knew it was a silly superstition, but it did make me feel better. Reassured, I guess. A reminder of Mom and something I'd been wearing so many years that I'd felt a little odd without it.

"I can't believe your father left it at the hospital," she said, shaking her head. "God only knows when he would have remembered, now that he's jetted off again."

Yes, my dad was gone. He'd called me on Aunt Lauren's cell phone to explain that he'd had to leave for Shanghai last night on an emergency business trip. She was furious with him, but I couldn't see how it mattered when I was living at the group home. He'd already arranged to take a month off when I got out, and I'd rather he was around then.

My aunt talked about her plan for a "girls' New York trip" when I was released. I didn't have the heart to tell her I'd rather just go home, see Dad, hang with my friends. Getting back to my normal life would be the best post–Lyle House celebration I could imagine.

My normal life . . .

I thought of the ghosts. Would my life ever be normal again? Would *I* ever be normal again?

My gaze tripped over the landscape of faces. Was anyone here a ghost? How would I know?

What about that guy in the back wearing a heavy metal shirt, looking like he'd just stepped off the set of VH1's *I Love the 80's*? Or the old woman with long gray hair and a tie-dyed shirt? Or even the guy in a suit, waiting by the door? Unless someone smacked into them, how did I know they weren't ghosts, just waiting for me to notice them?

I lowered my gaze to my orange juice.

Oh, there's a plan, Chloe. Spend the rest of your life avoiding eye contact.

"So how are you adjusting? Getting along with the other kids?"

Her words were a slap, reminding me I had bigger problems than ghosts.

She was smiling, the question meant as a joke. *Obviously*, I would be getting along with the kids. I might not be the most outgoing girl, but I could be counted on not to make waves or cause trouble. As I looked up, her smile faded.

"Chloe?"

"Hmm?"

"Is there a problem with the other kids?"

"N-no. Everything's f-f-f—" My teeth clicked as I snapped my jaw shut. To anyone who knew me well, my stutter was a stress-o-meter. There was no sense saying everything was fine if I couldn't even get the lie out.

"What happened?" Her hand gripped her fork and knife, as if ready to wield them against whoever was responsible.

"It's noth—"

"Don't tell me it's nothing. When I asked about the other kids, you looked like you were going to be sick."

"It's the eggs. I put too much hot sauce on them. The other kids are fine." Her eyes bored into mine, and I knew I wasn't getting away with that. "There's just this one, but it's no big deal. You can't get along with everyone, right?"

"Who is it?" She waved off the server tentatively approaching with her coffeepot. "Don't roll your eyes at me, Chloe. You're at that home to rest, and if someone's bothering you—"

"I can handle it."

She released her death-grip on the cutlery, set them down, and smoothed her place mat. "That's not the point, hon. You have enough to worry about right now. Tell me who this boy is and I'll make sure he doesn't bother you anymore."

"He won't—"

"So it is a boy. Which one? There are three—no, only two now. It's the big boy, isn't it? I saw him this morning. I tried to introduce myself, but he walked away. Darren, Damian . . ."

I stopped myself before correcting her. She'd already tricked me into admitting my tormentor was a boy. I really wished that, for once, she'd just listen to my problems, maybe offer some advice, not leap in trying to fix everything.

"Derek," she said. "That's his name. When he ignored me this morning, Mrs. Talbot said he was like that. Rude. Am I right?"

"He's just . . . not very friendly. But that's fine. Like I said, you can't get along with everyone, and the other kids seem okay. One girl's kind of stuck up, like my roommate at camp last year. Remember her? The one who—"

"What did this Derek do to you, Chloe?" she said, refusing to be distracted. "Did he touch you?"

"N-no, of c-course n-not."

"Chloe." Her voice sharpened, my stuttering giving me away. "This is not something you hide. If he did anything inappropriate, I swear—"

"It wasn't like that. We were talking. I tried to walk away and he grabbed my arm—"

"He *grabbed* you?"

"For, like, a second. It just freaked me out. I overreacted."

She leaned forward. "You did not overreact. Anytime someone lays an unwanted hand on you it is your right to object and to complain and . . ."

And so it went, through the rest of breakfast. A lecture on "inappropriate touching," like I was five years old. I didn't know why she was so upset. It's not like I'd even shown her the bruises. The more I argued, though, the madder she got, and I started thinking maybe this wasn't really about a boy bothering me or grabbing my arm. She was angry at my dad for taking off and at my school for making me go to this group home, and because she couldn't go after them, she'd found someone she *could* go after, a problem she *could* fix for me.

"Please don't," I said as we sat in the car, idling in the driveway. "He didn't *do* anything. Please. It's hard enough—"

"Which is why I'm not going to make this any harder for you, Chloe. I'm not stirring up trouble; I'm settling it down." She smiled. "Preventative medicine."

She squeezed my knee. When I looked out the window, she sighed and turned off the engine. "I promise I will be discreet. I've learned how to handle problems like this delicately, because the last thing a victim needs is to be blamed for tattling."

"I'm not a vic—"

"This Derek boy will never know who complained. Even the nurses won't know you said a word to me. I'm going to carefully raise concerns based on my own professional observations."

"Just give me a couple of days—"

"No, Chloe," she said firmly. "I'm talking to the nurses and, if necessary, to the administrators. It would be irresponsible of me not to."

I turned to face her, mouth opening to argue, but she was already out of the car.

When I returned, Tori was back. Back in class and back in attitude.

If I'd been scripting this scene, I'd have been tempted to go for a character reversal. The young woman sees her only friend taken away, partly because of a snide remark she made. When her housemates rally around, trying to lift her depression with support and concern, she realizes she hasn't lost her only friend and vows to be a kinder, gentler person.

In real life, though, people don't change overnight.

Tori started the first class by informing me that I was sitting in Liz's seat, and I'd better not act like she wasn't coming back. Afterward, she followed Rae and me into the hall.

"Did you have a good breakfast with your auntie? Parents too busy for you, I guess?"

"I'm sure Mom would have made it. But it's kind of hard for her, being dead and all."

A great slap-down comeback. Tori didn't even blink.

"So what did you do to deserve a pass already, Chloe? Was that your reward for helping them get rid of Liz?"

"She didn't—" Rae began.

"Like you're any better, *Rachelle*. You couldn't even wait until Liz's bed was cold before you bunked down with your new buddy. So, Chloe, what's with the special treatment?"

"It's not special," Rae said. "Your mom takes you out all the time. In Chloe's case, it's probably a reward for good behavior. With you, it's just because your mom's on the board of directors."

At our age, being "well behaved" isn't exactly a goal to strive for. But Tori's nostrils flared, her face twisting, as if Rae had lobbed the worst possible insult.

"Yeah?" she said. "Well, we don't see your parents coming around, do we, Rachelle? How many times have they visited or called since you've been here? Let's see . . . oh, right, zero." She made an O with her thumb and forefinger. "And it has nothing to do with bad behavior. They just don't care."

Rae shoved her into the wall. Tori let out an ear-shattering shriek.

"She burned me!" she said, clutching her shoulder.

"I *pushed* you."

Ms. Wang hurried from the classroom, followed by Simon and Derek, who'd stayed behind to discuss an assignment.

"Rae burned me. She has matches or something. Look, look . . ." Tori pulled down the collar of her T-shirt.

"Leave your clothes on, Tori," Simon said, raising his hands to his eyes. "Please."

Derek let out a low rumble that sounded suspiciously like a laugh.

Rae held up her hands. "No matches. No lighters. Nothing up my sleeve . . ."

"I see a very faint red mark, Tori, from being pushed," Ms. Wang said.

"She burned me! I felt it! She's hiding matches again. Search her. *Do* something."

"How about you do something, Tori?" Simon said as he brushed past us. "Like get a life."

She wheeled—not on him but on Rae—lunging at her before being grabbed by Ms. Wang. The nurses came running.

Yep, Tori was back.

seventeen

I'D SPENT THAT FIRST CLASS braced for Miss Van Dop or Dr. Gill to stride in and yank Derek out for a "conference." I should have trusted my aunt. When we'd come back from breakfast, she'd quietly taken Mrs. Talbot aside, saying only that she wanted to discuss my progress. No one thought anything of it. And no one had burst into the class and dragged Derek out.

Tori's episode was the only bump in an otherwise quiet morning. Derek attended classes and ignored me. He went to his session with Dr. Gill before lunch. When he came out, I was in the hall, waiting to use the bathroom. Simon was inside, as he always was before a meal. I'd never known a guy to be so conscientious about washing up before eating.

I was considering running upstairs to the girls' bathroom when Dr. Gill's door opened, and Derek's dark form filled it. I braced myself. He stepped out and looked at me. My heart pounded so hard I was sure he could hear it, just as sure as I was that he'd just gotten bawled out. Our eyes met. He nodded, grunted something that sounded like "hi," and was about to brush past me when the bathroom door opened.

Simon walked out, head down. He saw me and shoved something into his back pocket. "Whoops. Guess I'm hogging the bathroom again, causing lines."

"Just Chloe." Derek pushed open the door for me. He didn't seem angry at all. Nicer than normal, even. My aunt must have handled it fine. I should have known she would.

As I went inside, Simon said to Derek, "Hey, lunch is this way."

"Start without me. I gotta get something from our room."

A pause. Then "Hold up," and Simon's footsteps followed Derek's up the stairs.

After lunch, it was my turn to take out the trash. Life experience, I kept telling myself as I wheeled the wagon to the shed, swatting away flies buzzing in for a closer look. All life experience. You never know when I'd need a critical scene with the protagonist hauling trash.

My laugh fluttered across the yard. The sun was shining, heat beating down on my face, tree and daffodils blossoming, the faint smell of newly cut grass almost masking the stink of rotting garbage.

A pretty good start to my afternoon. Better than I'd expected—

I stopped. There, in the yard behind ours, was a ghost. A little girl, no more than four.

She had to be a ghost. She was alone in the yard, playing outside in a frilly dress—a wedding cake confection of bows and ribbons, with more ribbons wound in her corkscrew curls and more bows on her shiny patent leather shoes. She looked like Shirley Temple off an old movie poster.

I tossed the bags into the shed, where they'd be safe from marauding raccoons and skunks. The bags thumped as they hit the wooden floor, but the girl, only twenty feet away, didn't look up. I closed the shed, walked behind it to the fence, and crouched, getting closer to her level.

"Hello," I said.

She frowned, as if wondering who I was talking to.

I smiled. "Yes, I can see you. That's a pretty dress. I had one like that when I was about your age."

One last hesitant glance over her shoulder, then she sidled closer. "Mommy bought it for me."

"My mom bought mine, too. Do you like it?"

She nodded, her smile lighting up her dark eyes.

"I bet you do. I loved mine. Do—?"

"Amanda!"

The girl jumped back, landing on her rear and letting out a wail. A woman in slacks and a leather coat broke into a run, keys jangling in her hand, the back door whooshing shut behind her.

"Oh, Amanda, you got your pretty dress all dirty. I'm going to have to reschedule your special photos." The woman shot me a glare, scooping up the little girl and carrying her toward the house. "I told you not to go near that fence, Amanda. Never talk to the kids over there. *Never*, do you hear me?"

Don't talk to the crazy kids. I longed to shout back that we weren't crazy. I'd mistaken her kid for a ghost, that's all.

I wondered whether they had books about this sort of thing. *Fifty Ways to Tell the Living from the Dead Before You Wind Up in a Padded Room*. Yep, I'm sure the library carried that one.

I couldn't be the only person in the world who saw ghosts. Was it something I'd inherited, like blue eyes? Or was it something I'd contracted, like a virus?

There had to be others. How would I find them? Could I? Should I?

The thump of footsteps told me someone was coming. A living person. That was one lesson I'd already learned: ghosts can yell, cry, and talk, but they don't make any noise when they move.

I was still behind the shed, hidden from view. Like being in the basement, only here, no one would hear me scream for help.

I dashed forward just as a shadow rounded the shed. Simon.

He strode toward me, his face dark with anger. I stiffened, but stood my ground.

"What did you say?" His words came slow, deliberate, as if struggling to keep his voice steady.

"Say?"

"To the nurses. About my brother. You accused him of something."

"I didn't tell the nurses any—"

"Your aunt did, then." His fingers drummed against the shed. "You know what I'm talking about. You told her, she told the nurses, then Dr. Gill took Derek into a special conference before lunch and warned him not to bother you. If he does, they're sending him away."

"Wh-what?"

"A word from you, and he's gone. Transferred." A vein in his neck throbbed. "He's been *perfect* since he got here. Now, all of a sudden, after one problem with you, he's put on notice. If he so much as *looks* at you funny, he's gone."

"I—I—I—"

"Something happened with you two last night, didn't it? Derek came upstairs completely freaked out. Said he was talking to you and screwed up. That's all he'd tell me."

I considered the truth—that I hadn't meant to tattle on Derek. I'd been quiet at breakfast and my aunt had figured out I was upset. But that might sound as if I'd been sulking, wanting her to drag it out of me.

And Simon's attitude pissed me off. He'd all but accused me of making up stories, unfairly targeting his poor, misunderstood brother.

"It was hot at the restaurant," I said. "So I rolled up my sleeves."

"What?"

I pushed my left one up, showing four bruises, dark as ink spots. Simon paled.

"My aunt wanted to know what happened. When I wouldn't tell her, she tricked me into admitting it was a boy. She met Derek this morning and he was rude, so she decided it had to be him. I never confirmed it. If he's in trouble, it is *not* my fault. I had every right to tell someone and I didn't."

"Okay, okay." He rubbed his mouth, still staring at my arm. "So he grabbed your arm. That's what it looks like. Right? He just grabbed harder than he thought."

"He threw me across the room."

Simon's eyes widened, then he lowered his lids to hide his surprise. "But he didn't *mean* to. If you saw how freaked out he was last night, you'd know that."

"So that makes it okay? If I lose my temper and smack you, it's all right, because I didn't mean to, didn't *plan* to."

"You don't understand. He just—"

"She's right." Derek's voice preceded him around the corner.

I shrank back. I couldn't help it. As I did, a look passed through Derek's eyes. Remorse? Guilt? He blinked it away.

He stopped behind Simon's shoulder, at least five feet from me.

"I wanted to talk to you last night. When you tried to leave, I pulled you back and . . ." He trailed off, gaze shunting to the side.

"You *threw* me across the room."

"I didn't— Yeah, you're right. Like I said. No excuse. Simon? Let's go."

Simon shook his head. "She doesn't understand. See, Chloe, it's not Derek's fault. He's superstrong and—"

"And you weren't wearing your kryptonite necklace," Derek said. His mouth twisted in a bitter smile. "Yeah, I'm big. I got big fast. Maybe I don't know my own strength yet."

"That's not—" Simon began.

"No excuse, like you said. You want me to stay away from you? Wish granted."

"Derek, tell her—"

"Drop it, okay? She's not interested. She's made that very, very clear. Now let's go before someone catches me with her and I get stomped again."

"Chloe!" Mrs. Talbot's voice rang through yard.

"Perfect timing," Derek muttered. "Must have ESP."

"Just a second," I called back, moving sideways so she could see me.

"Go on," Derek said when the back door banged shut. "You don't want to be late for your meds."

I glowered, then turned away, circling wide around them as I started for the door. Simon murmured something under his breath, as if to Derek.

Smoke rose in my path. I stumbled back. It hovered over the ground, like a low patch of fog.

"Simon!" Derek hissed.

I turned, pointing at the fog. "What is that?"

"What's what?" Derek followed my finger. "Huh. Must be a ghost. No, wait, you don't see ghosts. You hallucinate. Guess it's a hallucination then."

"That's not—"

"It's nothing, Chloe." He pushed his hands in his pockets, rocking back on his heels. "Just your imagination, like everything else. Now run along and take your meds and be a good girl. Don't worry, I'll stay out of your way from now on. Seems I made a mistake. A *big* mistake."

He meant he misjudged me. That I wasn't worthy of his interest. My fists clenched.

"Watch it, Chloe. You wouldn't want to hit me. Then *I'd* have to tattle on *you*."

Simon stepped forward. "Cut it out, Derek. She didn't tattle—"

"He knows that," I cut in, holding Derek's gaze. "He's baiting me. He's a jerk and a bully and whatever 'secrets' he's taunting me with, he can keep them. He's right. I'm not interested."

I wheeled, strode to the wagon, and grabbed the handle.

"Here," Simon called. "I'll take that—"

"She's got it."

I turned to see Derek's hand on Simon's shoulder.

Simon shrugged his brother off. "Chloe—"

I wheeled the wagon back to the house.

eighteen

WHEN I CAME IN THE back door, I almost mowed down Tori.

"Have fun putting out the trash?" she asked.

I glanced back through the frilly curtains to see Simon near the shed. I could have said he'd been helping or, better yet, point out that Derek was there, too, if she looked closer.

But I didn't much see the point.

Derek blamed me for getting him into trouble. Simon blamed me for getting Derek into trouble.

If Tori was going to blame me for poaching her non-boyfriend, so be it. I couldn't work up the energy to care.

Rae was quiet all afternoon. Tori's comments about her parents not visiting seemed to have brought her down. At break, we got permission to go upstairs before classes and move the rest of her photos to our room.

"Thanks for helping with this," she said. "I know, I don't have to clear out right now, but if I leave one of these, Tori's liable to toss it out and say she thought I didn't want it anymore."

I looked at the top photo, one of a blond girl about three years old and a slightly older boy, who looked Native American. "Cute. Friends? Kids you babysit?"

"No, my little brother and sister."

I'm sure my face turned bright red as I stammered an apology.

Rae laughed. "No need to be sorry. I'm adopted. My mother was from Jamaica. Or so I'm told. She was just a kid when she had me, so she had to give me up. That"—she pointed to a photo of a Caucasian couple on the beach—"is my mom and dad. And that"—she pointed to a Hispanic girl mugging for the camera with Donald Duck—"is my sister, Jess. She's twelve. That"—She waved to a solemn-faced boy with red hair—"is my brother, Mike. He's eight. A very multicultural family, as you can tell."

"Five kids? Wow."

"Jess and I were adopted. The others are fosters. Mom likes kids." She paused. "Well, in theory anyway."

We walked to my room. She took the stack of photos from me and put them on her new dresser.

As she moved her Nintendo DS aside, her fingers tapped the scratched plastic. "You know how some kids are when they get a new gizmo? For weeks or even months, it's the coolest, best, most interesting whatsit they've ever owned and they can't stop talking about it. They carry it everywhere. Then, one day, they're all hyped up over some new gadget. There's nothing wrong with the old one. It just isn't cool and new anymore. Well, that's how my mom is." She turned and walked to the bed. "Only with her, it isn't gadgets. It's kids."

"Oh."

"When they're little, they're great. When they get older . . . not so much." Rae sat on the bed and shook her head. "Yeah, I'm probably being too hard on her. You know how it is. When you're little, your mom is so cool and she can't do anything wrong and then you get older—" She stopped and blushed. "No, I guess you wouldn't know what that's like, would you? Sorry."

"It's okay." I sat on my bed.

"Your dad never got married again?"

I shook my head.

"So who looks after you?"

As we headed down to class, I told her about Aunt Lauren, and the endless succession of housekeepers, making her laugh with my impressions, and forgot everything else . . . at least for a little while.

That afternoon, during my session with Dr. Gill, I put on an Oscar-worthy performance. I admitted that, as she'd suspected, I *had* thought I might be seeing ghosts. Now, after hearing her diagnosis and letting my medication take effect, I understood that I'd been hallucinating. I was a schizophrenic. I needed help.

She totally bought it.

All I had to do now was keep up the act for a week or so, and I'd be free.

When classes ended, Rae and I did our homework together in the media room. Simon passed the door a couple of times and I thought maybe he wanted to talk to me, but when I stuck my head out the door, he'd disappeared upstairs.

As I worked, I thought about that patch of fog in the yard. If Derek hadn't seen it, too, I might have mistaken it for a ghost.

Why had he shushed Simon? Was Simon somehow causing my "hallucinations"? Some kind of special effects?

Sure, that would explain the ghosts I'd seen at school—holographic projections created by a guy I'd never met. Right.

But something was going on.

Or, at least, that's what Derek wanted me to believe.

By refusing to explain and making a big deal of refusing, Derek wanted me to do exactly what I was doing right now—driving myself nuts wondering what he wasn't telling me. He wanted me to go to him, begging for answers, so he could taunt and torment me some more.

There was no way Simon or Derek could have created the ghosts at school, but that fog would be a simple effect to pull off. Maybe Derek had done it. That's why Simon had protested, and Derek had shut him up.

Was Simon afraid of his brother? He pretended to defend him and act like best buds, but what choice did he have? He was stuck with Derek until his father returned.

Where was his father?

Why had he enrolled Simon and Derek in school under false names?

Why was Simon even here, if he didn't have a file?

Too many questions. I needed to start finding answers.

We were clearing the table after dinner when Mrs. Talbot came into the dining room with a man she introduced as Dr. Davidoff, the head of the board that ran Lyle House. With only a thin circle of hair and a huge, sharp nose, he was so tall that he seemed to be permanently leaning down to hear better. With the hair and the nose, he bore an unfortunate resemblance to a vulture, head tucked down, eyes beady behind his glasses.

"This must be little Chloe Saunders." He beamed with the false heartiness of a middle-aged guy who doesn't have kids and never stops to think that a fifteen-year-old girl might not like being called "little" Chloe Saunders.

He awkwardly clapped me on the back. "I like your hair, Chloe. Red stripes. Very cool."

He said "cool" like I say a Spanish word when I'm not sure of the pronunciation. Rae rolled her eyes behind his back, then came around front.

"Hey, Dr. D."

"Rachelle. Oh, sorry, *Rae*, right? Are you keeping out of trouble?"

Rae flashed a perky smile, one custom-made for adults she had to suck up to. "Always, Dr. D."

"That's my girl. Now, Chloe, Dr. Gill tells me you had quite a breakthrough today. She's very pleased with your progress and how quickly you've fit into the therapeutic routine and accepted your diagnosis."

I tried not to squirm. He meant well, but being a good patient wasn't something I wanted to be publicly congratulated on. Especially when Derek had stopped eating to watch.

Now run along, take your meds and be a good girl.

Dr. Davidoff continued. "Normally, I don't meet with our young people until they've been here at least a week, but since you're speeding right along, Chloe, I don't want to hold you back. I'm sure you're eager to get back to your friends and school as soon as possible."

"Yes, sir." I copied Rae's perky smile, ignoring Derek's heavy gaze.

"Come along then and we'll chat in Dr. Gill's office."

He put his hand on one shoulder to propel me out.

Tori stepped in front of us. "Hello, Dr. Davidoff. That new medicine you have me on is working great. I'm really doing well."

"That's good, Victoria."

He absently patted her arm, then led me out.

The session was similar to the first one I'd had with Dr. Gill, filling in background. Who was Chloe Saunders? What had happened to her? How did she feel about it?

I'm sure he could get all this from Dr. Gill's notes, and she'd stayed late today to sit in, but it was like in a cop movie, where the detective interviews the suspect, asking all the same questions as the last guy. It's not the information that's important, but how I tell it. What's my emotional reaction? What extra details did I add this time? What did I leave out?

For all his false heartiness, Dr. Davidoff was Dr. Gill's supervisor, meaning he was here to check her work.

Dr. Gill had sat stiff and tense, leaning forward, squinting at me as she raced to capture every word, every gesture, like a student afraid to miss a key point for the exam. Dr. Davidoff took his time, getting a coffee for himself and a juice box for me, relaxing in Dr. Gill's chair, chatting me up before we started.

When he asked whether I'd had any hallucinations since I'd been here, I said yes, I'd seen a disembodied hand the second morning and heard a voice later that day. I didn't mention yesterday but said honestly that all had been fine today.

I sailed through the session without a hitch. At the end, he told me I was doing "fine, just fine," patted me on the back, and led me from the office.

As I passed the open media room door, I glanced inside. Derek was at the computer, his back to me as he played what looked like a war strategy game. Simon was also playing a game, on his Nintendo DS, as he sprawled sideways in the recliner, legs draped over the arm.

He noticed me and straightened, lips parting as if ready to call after me.

"If you're going for a snack, grab me a Coke," Derek said, attention fixed on the screen. "You know where they're hidden."

Simon paused, gaze shunting between us. His brother was giving him the perfect excuse to sneak out and talk to me, but he still hesitated, as if sensing a setup or a test. There was no way Derek knew I was here, behind his back. Yet Simon slouched in his chair.

"You want a Coke, get it yourself."

"I didn't *ask* you to get me one. I said *if* you were going."

"I'm not."

"Then say so already. What's with you tonight?"

I continued down the hall.

I found Rae in the dining room, homework spread across the table.

"You've got a DS, don't you?" I asked.

"Yep. Only Mario Karts on it, though. You want to borrow it?"

"Please."

"It's on my dresser."

I walked past the media room doorway again. The guys were still there, looking like they hadn't budged since I last passed. Again Simon glanced up. I waved Rae's DS and gestured. He grinned and shot me a discreet thumbs-up.

Now to find a place within range . . . I had a DS at home and knew I should be able to connect with another one within fifty feet. The media room was sandwiched between the front hall and the classroom, both off-limits for hanging out. But it was also right under the bathroom. So I went up, started PictoChat and prayed I could connect to Simon.

I could.

I used the stylus to write my message: *u want to talk?*

He drew a check mark, then wrote *D* followed by a picture that, after a moment I realized was an eye. Yes, he wanted to talk, but Derek was keeping an eye on him.

Before I could reply, he sent another. *D 8?* a box with "soap" drawn in it, surrounded by bubbles. It took a moment, but I finally interpreted that as "Derek has a shower around eight."

He erased it and drew an *8* followed by *yard*. Meet him outside at eight.

I sent back a check mark.

nineteen

At 7:50, I WAS HELPING Rae empty the dishwasher. From the hall, I heard Simon ask if he could go out back and shoot hoops while Derek showered. Mrs. Talbot warned that it was getting dark, and he couldn't stay out for long, but she turned off the alarm and let him go. Once the dishwasher was empty, I told Rae I'd catch up with her later, then slipped out after him.

As Mrs. Talbot warned, dusk was already falling. Huge shade trees bordered the deep yard, casting even more shadow. The basketball net was on a patch of concrete beyond the reach of the porch light, and I could see only the white flash of Simon's shirt and hear the *thump-thump-thump* of the dribbled ball. I circled the perimeter.

He didn't see me, just kept dribbling, gaze fixed on the ball, face solemn.

Keeping to the shadows, I moved closer and waited for him to see me. When he did, he jumped, as if startled, then waved me to an even darker spot on the other side of the net.

"Everything okay?" I asked. "You looked . . . busy."

"Just thinking." His gaze swept the fence line. "Can't wait to get out of here. Just like everyone else I guess, but . . ."

"Rae said you've been here awhile."

"You could say that."

A shadow passed behind his eyes, like he was scanning his future, seeing no sign of release. At least I had someplace to go. They'd been in child services. Where would they go from here?

He bounced the ball hard and managed a smile. "Wasting our time, aren't I? I've got about ten minutes before Derek tracks me down. First off, I wanted to say I'm sorry."

"Why? You didn't do anything."

"For Derek."

"He's your brother, not your responsibility. You can't help what he does." I nodded toward the house. "Why didn't you want him seeing us talking? Will he get mad?"

"He won't be happy, but—" He caught my expression and let out a sharp laugh. "You mean, Am I afraid he'll beat the crap out of me? No way. Derek isn't like that at all. If he gets mad, he just treats me the same way he treats everyone else—ignores me. Hardly fatal but, no, I don't *want* to piss him off if I can help it. It's just . . ." He bounced the ball, gaze fixed on it. After a moment, he stopped and flipped it into his hands. "He's already mad that I defended him—he hates that—and now if I'm talking to you, trying to explain things, when he doesn't want them explained . . ."

He twirled the ball on his fingertip. "See, Derek's not really a people person."

I tried not to look shocked.

"When he decided you might really be seeing ghosts, I should have said, *Sure, bro, let me talk to her.* I'd have handled it . . . well, different. Derek doesn't know when to back off. To him, it's as simple as adding two plus two. If you can't figure it out yourself and you don't listen when he tells you the answer, he'll keep slamming you until you wake up."

"Running away screaming doesn't help."

He laughed. "Hey, if Derek kept coming at me, I'd be screaming, too. And you didn't run anywhere today. You stood up to him, which, believe me, he's not used to." A grin. "Good on ya. That's all you have to do. Don't take his crap."

He took another shot. This one dropped gracefully through the hoop.

"So Derek thinks I'm a . . . necromancer?"

"You're seeing ghosts, right? A dead guy who talked to you, chased you, asked for your help?"

"How did you—?" I stopped myself. My heart thumped, breath coming hard and fast. I'd just convinced Dr. Gill that I'd accepted my diagnosis. As much as I longed to trust Simon, I didn't dare.

"How did I know? Because that's what ghosts do to necromancers. You're the only person who can hear them, and they all have something to say. That's why they're hanging out here, in limbo or whatever." He shrugged as he tossed the ball. "I'm not real clear on the specifics. Never actually met a necromancer. I just know what I've been told."

I inhaled and exhaled before saying, as casually as I could, "I guess that makes sense. That's what you'd expect ghosts would do to people who think they can talk to the dead. Mediums, spiritualists, psychics, whatever."

He shook his head. "Yes, mediums, spiritualists, and psychics *are* people who *think* they can talk to the dead. But necromancers *can*. It's hereditary." He smiled. "Like blond hair. You can cover it up with red streaks, but underneath, it's still blond. And you can ignore the ghosts, but they'll still come. They know you can see them."

"I don't understand."

He flipped the ball and caught it on his open palm. Then he murmured something. I was about to say I couldn't hear him when the ball rose. Levitating.

I stared.

"Yeah, I know, it's about as useless as that patch of fog," he said, gaze fixed on the levitating ball, as if concentrating. "Now, if I could lift it more than a couple of inches, maybe to the top of that hoop, and slam-dunk it every time, that'd be a trick. But I'm not Harry Potter and real magic doesn't work that way."

"That's . . . magic?" I said.

The ball dropped into his hand. "You don't believe me, do you?"

"No, I—"

He cut me off with a laugh. "You think it's some kind of trick or a special effect. Well, movie girl, get your butt over here and test me."

"I—"

"Get over here." He pointed at the spot beside him. "See if you can find the strings."

I slid closer. He said some words, louder now, so I could hear them. It wasn't English.

When the ball didn't move, he cursed. "Did I mention I'm not Harry Potter? Let's try that again."

He repeated the words, slower, his gaze glued to the ball. It rose two inches.

"Now check for strings or wires or whatever you think is holding it up."

I hesitated, but he prodded and teased me until I moved closer and poked a finger between the ball and his hand. When I didn't hit anything, I slid all my fingers through, then waggled them. Simon's fist closed, grabbing my hand and I yelped as the ball bounced off across the concrete pad.

"Sorry," he said, grinning, his fingers still holding mine. "I couldn't resist."

"Yes—I'm skittish, as your brother has probably pointed out. So how did you . . ." I looked at the ball, coming to rest on the grass. "Wow."

His grin grew. "You believe me now?"

As I stared at the ball, I struggled for other explanations. None came.

"Can you teach me how to do that?" I said finally.

"Nah. No more than you can teach me how to see ghosts. Either you have it or you—"

"Playing basketball in the dark, Simon?" asked a voice across the yard. "You should have called me. You know I'm always up for a little—"

Tori stopped short, seeing me now. Her gaze moved to my hand, still in his.

"—one-on-one," she finished.

I yanked my fingers away. She kept staring.

"Hey, Tori," Simon said as he retrieved the ball. "What's up?"

"I saw you playing and thought maybe you could use a partner." Her gaze swung my way, expression unreadable. "I guess not."

"I should get inside," I said. "Thanks for the pointers, Simon."

"No, hold up." He took a step after me, then glanced at Tori. "Uh, right. You're welcome. And it is getting dark, isn't it? It must be snack time by now . . ."

He hurried into the house.

I lay in bed, unable to sleep again. This time, though, it wasn't bad dreams that kept me awake but thoughts pinging through my head, so shrill and insistent that by midnight, I was seriously considering a real kitchen raid—to grab the travel tube of Tylenol I'd seen there.

I was a necromancer.

Having a label should have come as a relief, but I wasn't sure this one was any better than *schizophrenic*. At least schizophrenia was a known and accepted condition. I could talk to people about it, get help coping with it, take my meds, and make the symptoms go away.

Those same meds might cover the symptoms of necromancy, but as Simon said, it would be like coloring my hair—I'd still be the same underneath, my true nature waiting to pop up as soon as the medication wore off.

Necromancy.

Where had it come from? My mother? If so, why didn't Aunt Lauren know about it? From my father? Maybe he hadn't worked up the nerve to warn me and that's why he'd seemed so guilty in the hospital, so eager to make me happy and comfortable. Or maybe neither of my parents or my aunt knew anything about it. It could be a recessive gene, one that skipped generations.

Simon was lucky. His dad must have told him about the magic, showed him how to use it. My envy evaporated. Lucky? He was stuck in a group home. His magic didn't seem to be doing him any good here.

Magic. The word came so casually, as if I'd already accepted it. Had I? *Should* I?

I'd spent days denying that I saw ghosts, and now, suddenly, I had no problem believing in magic? I should be demanding more demonstrations. Coming up with alternate explanations. But I'd done that with myself, and now, having realized that I really did see the dead, there was almost a comfort in accepting that I wasn't the only one out there with weird powers.

And what about Derek? Simon said Derek was unnaturally strong. Was that magical? I'd felt that strength. I'd read his file, and I knew even the authorities had been stumped for a cause.

As bizarre as it sounded, the explanation that made the most sense was the most far-fetched one. There were people out there with powers found only in legends and movies. And we were part of that.

I almost laughed. It was like something out of a comic book. Kids with supernatural powers, like superheroes. Superheroes? Right. Somehow, I didn't think seeing ghosts and levitating basketballs was going to help us save the world from evil anytime soon.

If both Derek and Simon had powers, is that how they'd ended up together, as foster brothers? What had their dad told them? Did his disappearance have something to do with being magical? Was that why the guys had enrolled in school under fake names and kept moving around? Is that what our kind had to do? Hide?

The questions crowded my brain, none of them willing to leave without answers . . . answers I couldn't get at two in the morning. They bounced around like Simon's basketball. After a while, I swore I could see them—orange balls bouncing through my head, back and forth, back and forth, until I fell asleep.

A voice sliced through the heavy blanket of sleep, and I bolted up, fighting my way to consciousness.

I gulped air as I surveyed the room, ears and eyes straining. All was still and silent. I glanced over at Rae. She was sound asleep.

A dream. I started lying back down.

"Wake up."

The whisper floated through the half-open door. I lay down, resisting the urge to pull the covers higher.

I thought you weren't going to cower anymore? That's the plan, right? Not to ignore the voices but get answers, take control.

A deep breath. Then I slipped out of bed and walked to the door.

The hall was empty. I could hear only the *tick-tick-tick* of the grandfather clock downstairs. As I turned, a pale shape flickered near a closed door down the hall. A closet, I'd presumed earlier. What was it with ghosts and closets in this house?

I crept down the hall and eased the door open. Dark stairs led up.

The attic.

Uh-uh, this was as bad as a basement, maybe even worse. I wasn't following some ghost up there.

Good excuse.

It's not an—

You don't want to talk to them. Not really. You don't want to know the truth.

Great. Not only did I have to deal with Derek's taunts and jibes but now even my inner voice was starting to sound like him.

I took a deep breath and stepped inside.

twenty

I SLID MY HAND ALONG the wall, searching for a light switch, then stopped. Was that a good idea? With my luck, Tori would head to the bathroom, see the attic light on, and investigate . . . only to find me up there talking to myself.

I left the light off.

One hand on the railing, the other gliding along the opposite wall, I climbed the stairs, ascending into blackness.

My hand slipped off the end of the railing, and I pitched forward. I'd reached the top. A trickle of moonlight came from the tiny attic window, but even after I paused to let my eyes adjust, I could only make out vague shapes.

I walked with my hands out, feeling my way. I smacked into something, and it sent up a cloud of dust. My hands flew over my nose to stifle a sneeze.

"Girl . . ."

I stiffened. It was the ghost from the basement, the one who kept insisting I open the locked door. I took a deep breath. Whoever he was, he couldn't hurt me. Even that janitor, as hard as he tried, couldn't do anything more than scare me.

I had the power here. I was the necromancer.

"Who are you?" I asked.

". . . contact . . . get through . . ."

"I can't understand you."

". . . blocked . . ."

Something was blocking him from making contact? Leftover meds in my system?

". . . basement . . . try . . ."

"Try that door again? Forget it. No more basements. No more attics. If you want to talk to me, do it on the main level. Got it?"

". . . can't . . . block . . ."

"Yes, you're blocked. I think it's something I was taking, but it should be better tomorrow. Talk to me in my room. When I'm alone. Okay?"

Silence. I repeated it, but he didn't answer. I stood there, shivering, for at least five minutes before trying one last time. When he didn't respond, I turned toward the stairs.

"Chloe?"

I wheeled so fast I knocked into something at knee level, my bare legs scraping against wood, hands hitting the top with a thud, enveloping me in a cloud of dust. I sneezed.

"Bless you." A giggle. "Do you know why we say that?"

Blood pounded in my ears as I recognized the voice. I could make out Liz, a few feet away, dressed in her Minnie Mouse nightshirt.

"It's because when we sneeze, our soul flies out our nose and if no one says 'bless you,' the devil can snatch it." Another giggle. "Or so my nana always said. Funny, huh?"

I opened my mouth but couldn't force words out.

She looked around, nose wrinkling. "Is this the attic? What are we doing up here?"

"I—I—I—I—"

"Take a deep breath. That always helps my brother." Another look around. "How did we get up here? Oh, right. The séance. We were going to do a séance."

"Séance?" I hesitated. "Don't you remember?"

"Remember what?" She frowned. "Are you okay, Chloe?"

No, I was pretty sure I wasn't. "You . . . never mind. I—I was just talking to a man. Can you see him? Is he here?"

"Um, no. It's just us." Her eyes went round. "Are you seeing ghosts?"

"Gh-ghosts?"

"Chloe?"

This voice was sharp and I spun to see Mrs. Talbot feeling her way over to me. I turned back to Liz. No one was there.

"Chloe, what are you doing up here?"

"I—I—I—I thought I heard . . . a mouse. Or a rat. Something was moving around up here."

"And you were talking to it?" Tori stepped through the attic doorway.

"N-no, I—I—"

"Oh, I'm pretty sure I heard you say *ghost*. And you were definitely talking to someone. It seems you aren't quite as cured as you said you were."

Mrs. Talbot brought me a sleeping pill and waited while I took it. The whole time, she didn't say a word to me, but as I heard her feet tapping double time down the stairs, I knew there would be a lot of words for Dr. Gill and Dr. Davidoff.

I'd blown it.

Tears burned my eyes. I swiped them back.

"You really can see ghosts, can't you?" Rae whispered.

I said nothing.

"I heard what happened. You aren't even going to admit it to me now, are you?"

"I want to get out of here."

"News flash. We *all* do." An edge crept into her voice. "It's fine to lie to *them*. But I thought you were seeing ghosts even before you did. Who gave you the idea of looking up that guy you saw at your school? You looked him up, didn't you? You just didn't bother to tell me."

"That's not—"

She rolled over, her back to me. I knew I should say something, but I wasn't sure what.

When I closed my eyes, I saw Liz again and my stomach clenched.

Had I really seen her? Talked to her? I struggled for some other explanation. She couldn't be a ghost because I'd seen and heard her clearly—not like the ghost who'd called me up there. And she couldn't be dead. The nurses had promised we could talk to her.

When could we talk to her?

I struggled to get up, suddenly needing to know now. But I was so tired that I couldn't think straight and hovered there, propped up on my elbows, as the sleeping pill kicked in.

Something about Liz. I wanted to check. . . .

My head fell back to the pillow.

twenty-one

THE NEXT MORNING WHEN I was called into a meeting with the doctors, I did my best damage control. I claimed I really had gotten past the I-see-dead-people stage and accepted my condition, but had woken up hearing a voice in the night, calling me to the attic. I'd been confused, sleep drunk, *dreaming* of seeing ghosts, not really seeing them.

Dr. Gill and Dr. Davidoff didn't fully appreciate the distinction.

Then Aunt Lauren arrived. It was like when I'd been eleven, caught peeking at test scores, egged on by the new classmates I'd been eager to impress. Being hauled to the principal's office had been bad enough. But the disappointment on Aunt Lauren's face had hurt worse than any punishment.

That day, I saw the same disappointment, and it didn't hurt any less.

In the end, I managed to persuade them all that I'd had a minor setback, but it was like the little boy crying wolf. The next time I said I was improving, they'd be a lot slower to believe me. No quick track to release now.

"We're going to need you to provide urine samples for the next week," Dr. Gill said.

"Oh, that's ridiculous," Aunt Lauren said. "How do we know she wasn't sleepwalking and dreaming? She can't control her dreams."

"Dreams are the windows to the soul," Dr. Gill said.

"That's the eyes," my aunt snapped.

"Anyone versed in psychiatry will tell you it's the same for dreams." Dr. Gill's voice was level, but her look said she was sick of parents and guardians questioning her diagnoses and defending their children. "Even if Chloe is only dreaming she sees ghosts, it suggests that, subconsciously, she hasn't accepted her condition. We need to monitor her with urine tests."

"I—I don't understand," I said. "Why do I need urine tests?"

"To ensure you're receiving the proper dosage for your size, activity level, food intake, and other factors. It's a delicate balance."

"You don't believe—" Aunt Lauren began.

Dr. Davidoff cleared his throat. Aunt Lauren pressed her lips into a thin line and started picking lint from her wool skirt. She rarely backed down from an argument, but these doctors held the key to my future.

I already knew what she'd been going to say. The urine tests weren't to check my dosage. They were to make sure I was taking my pills.

Since I'd missed morning classes, I was assigned lunch duty. I was setting the table, lost in my thoughts, when a voice said, "I'm behind you."

I spun to see Derek.

"I can't win," he said. "You're as skittish as a kitten."

"So if you sneak up and announce yourself, that's going to startle me less than if you tap me on the shoulder?"

"I didn't sneak—"

He shook his head, grabbed two rolls from the bread basket, then rearranged the others to hide the theft. "I just wanted to say that if you and Simon want to talk, you don't need to do it behind my back. Unless you want to."

"We were just—"

"I know what you were doing. Simon already told me. You want answers. I've been trying to give them to you all along. You just have to ask."

"But you said—"

"Tonight. Eight. Our room. Tell Mrs. Talbot you'll be with me for math tutoring."

"Your side is off-limits. Is she going to let me go up there, alone, with a boy?"

"Just tell her it's for math. She won't question it."

Because he had problems with math, I supposed.

"Will that be . . . okay? You and I aren't supposed to—"

"Tell her Simon will be there. And talk to Talbot, not Van Dop."

twenty-two

RAE AND I DIDN'T SPEAK much all day. She wasn't nasty; Rae wasn't like that. She sat beside me in class and asked questions, but there was no chatter, no giggling or goofing off. Today we were classmates, not friends.

Before dinner, when we'd normally hang out or do homework together, she took her books, retreated to the dining room, and closed the door.

After dinner, I followed her into the kitchen with my dirty plates.

"It's my turn to do laundry," I said. "Would you have a minute to show me how to use the machine?" I lowered my voice. "And I'd like to talk to you."

She shrugged. "Sure."

"I'm sorry I didn't tell you," I said as she demonstrated the dials on the washer. "I'm . . . I'm having a hard time with it."

"Why? You can talk to the dead. How cool is that?"

It wasn't cool at all—it was terrifying. But I didn't want to sound like I was whining. Or maybe I just didn't want to sound like a wimp.

I dumped in the first load and added soap.

"Whoa, whoa! You'll give this place a bubble carpet." She took the soap box from me and scooped some of the detergent back out of the machine. "If you can prove you're seeing ghosts, why not just tell them?"

A perfectly logical question, but at the thought, some deep-rooted instinct screamed *Don't tell! Never tell!*

"I—I don't want to tell anyone the truth. Not yet. Not here."

She nodded and set the box aside. "Gill is a pencil pusher with all the imagination of a thumbtack. She'd keep you locked up in here until you stopped this 'ghost nonsense.' Better to save the spooky stuff for when you get out."

We sorted a basket of laundry in silence, then I said, "The reason I asked to talk to you down here is, well, there's a ghost."

She took a slow look around, wrapping a T-shirt around her hand like a boxer taping up for a fight.

"Not right now. I mean, there *was* a ghost in here. The same one I heard upstairs last night." Before Liz showed up. All day I'd been struggling not to think of Liz. If I was seeing her, didn't that mean . . .

Why hadn't I asked Mrs. Talbot when I could talk to Liz? Was I afraid of the answer?

"—he say?"

I shook it off and turned to Rae. "Hmm?"

"What did the ghost say?"

"It's hard to tell. He keeps cutting out. I think it's the meds. But he said he wanted me to open that door."

I pointed. Her head whipped around so fast she winced and rubbed her neck.

"That door?" Her eyes glittered. "The *locked* basement door?"

"Yes, cliché, I know. Whoooo, don't go into the locked room, little girl."

Rae was already striding to the door.

I said, "I thought maybe, we could, you know, check it out. Like open it."

"Duh, *of course*. I'd have done that days ago." She jiggled the handle. "How can you live with the suspense?"

"For starters, I'm pretty sure there's nothing in there."

"Then why's it locked?"

"Because it's for storing stuff they don't want us messing with. Lawn furniture. Winter bedding. Christmas decorations."

"The bodies of Lyle House kids who never went home . . ."

She grinned, but I froze, thinking of Liz.

"Geez, I'm *kidding*. You are such a girl."

"No, I've just seen too many movies."

"That, too." She walked back to the laundry shelves and rooted through a box. "Another crappy lock, so easy a six-year-old with a credit card can pick it."

"Not many six-year-olds have credit cards."

"I bet Tori did. That's who this house is made for." She lifted a sponge, shook her head, and dropped it back into the box. "Rich kids whose only use for a credit card is buying a new pair of Timbs. They stick cheap locks on the doors, knowing you guys will turn the handle and say 'huh, locked' and walk away."

"That's—"

She stopped me with a look. "Unfair? Uh, that's exactly what you did, girl." She brandished a stiff piece of cardboard, a tag ripped off a new shirt.

"It's not perfect," she murmured as she slid it between the door and the frame. "But it'll"—She jiggled the cardboard and swore. "Or maybe it"—she swiped it down sharply, a ripping sound as it tore in half—"won't."

More curses, some of them quite creative.

"There's a piece caught . . . Here, let me."

I grabbed the edge between my fingernails, which would have been much easier if I had any. When I'd woken in the hospital, my nails had been filed to the pink, like they'd been worried I'd commit suicide by scratching. I managed to get hold of the cardboard, pulled . . . and ripped out another chunk, leaving the rest wedged in where no nails, however long, could reach it.

"Get the feeling someone doesn't want us going in there?" Rae said.

I tried to laugh, but ever since she'd mentioned "bodies," there'd been a sour taste in my mouth.

"We're going to need the key," she pronounced, straightening. "It might be on the ring with the one for the shed in the kitchen."

"I'll get it."

When I slipped into the kitchen, Derek was pawing through the fruit basket. The door hadn't made any noise opening and he had his back to me. The perfect chance for payback. I took three slow, silent steps toward him, barely daring to breathe—

"The key you want isn't on that ring," he said, not looking my way.

I froze. He dug out an apple, took a bite, then walked to the fridge, reached behind it, and pulled off a magnetized set of keys.

"Try these." He dropped them in my hand and walked past me to the kitchen door. "I have no idea what you guys are doing down there, but next time you want to secretly open a locked door, don't whale on it hard enough to bring down the house."

When I brought the keys downstairs, I didn't tell Rae that Derek knew what we were up to. She might have decided to abort the plan. Anyway tattling wasn't Derek's style. Or so I hoped.

As Rae tried the keys, I rubbed the back of my neck, grimacing against the dull throb of a threatening headache. Was I really that anxious about what lay behind the door? I rolled my shoulders, trying to shake it off.

"Found it," she whispered.

She swung open the door to reveal . . .

An empty closet. Rae stepped inside. I followed. We were in a space so small we could both barely fit.

"Okay," Rae said. "This is weird. Who builds a closet, doesn't put anything in it, then locks it? There's gotta be a catch." She rapped on the wall. "Yow! It's concrete. Painted concrete. Scraped my knuckles good." She touched the adjoining walls. "I don't get it. Where's the rest of the basement?"

I rubbed my temple, now throbbing. "It's a half basement. My aunt lived in an old Victorian place before she got sick of the renovations and moved into a condo. She said when her house was built, it didn't have a basement at all, just a crawl space under the house. Then someone dug out a room for the laundry. She used to have real bad problems with flooding and stuff. Maybe that's why this is empty and locked. So no one uses it."

"Okay, so what does your spook want you to see? Overlooked storage space?"

"I told you it was probably nothing."

The words came out more sharply than I intended. I rolled my shoulders and rubbed my neck again.

"What's wrong?" Rae laid her hand on my arm. "God, girl, you're covered in goose bumps."

"Just a chill."

"Maybe it's a cold spot."

I nodded, but I didn't feel cold. Just . . . anxious. Like a cat sensing a threat, its fur rising.

"There's a ghost here, isn't there?" she said, looking around. "Try contacting it."

"How?"

She shot me a look. "Start with 'hello.' "

I did.

"More," Rae said. "Keep talking."

"Hello? Is anyone there?"

She rolled her eyes. I ignored her. I felt foolish enough without having my dialogue critiqued.

"If someone's here, I'd like to talk to you."

"Close your eyes," Rae said. "Focus."

Something told me it had to be a lot more complicated than "close your eyes, focus, and talk to them." But I didn't have a better idea. So I gave it a shot.

"Nothing," I said after a moment.

When I opened my eyes, a figure flashed past so fast it was only a blur. I wheeled, trying to follow, but it was gone.

"What?" Rae said. "What'd you see?"

I closed my eyes and struggled to pull a replay tape from memory. After a moment, it came. I saw a man dressed in a gray suit, clean shaven, wearing a fedora and horn-rimmed glasses, like someone out of the fifties.

I told her what I'd seen. "But it was just a flash. It's the meds. I had to take them today and they seem to . . . block transmission. I only get flashes."

I turned slowly, eyes narrowing as I concentrated as hard as I could, looking for even the faintest shimmer. As I circled, my elbow hit the door, knocking it against the wall with an oddly metallic clank.

Motioning Rae aside, I pulled the door forward to peek behind it. She squeezed in to take a look.

"Seems we missed something, huh?" she said, grinning.

The closet was so small that when the door opened, it had blocked the left wall. Now, looking behind it, I saw there was a metal ladder fastened to that wall. It led up a few steps to a small wooden door halfway up the wall, the gray paint blending with the concrete. I stepped onto the ladder. The door was secured only with a latch. One hard push and it swung open into darkness.

A musty stink billowed out.

The smell of the moldering dead.

Right. Like I knew what the dead smelled like. The only body I'd ever seen had been my mother's. She hadn't smelled dead. She'd smelled like Mom. I shook the memory off.

"I think it's a crawl space," I said. "Like at my aunt's old place. Let me take a look."

"Hey." She plucked at the back of my shirt. "Not so fast. It looks awfully dark in there . . . too dark for someone who sleeps with the blinds open."

I ran my hand over the floor. Damp, packed dirt. I felt along the wall.

"A dirt crawl space," I said. "With no light switch. We're going to need a flashlight. I saw one—"

"I know. My turn to get it."

twenty-three

When Rae got back, she spread her empty hands wide and said, "Okay, guess where I hid it."

She even turned around for me, but I could see no bulge big enough to hide a flashlight. With a grin, she reached down the front of her shirt into the middle of her bra, and pulled out a flashlight with flourish.

I laughed.

"Cleavage is great," she said. "Like an extra pocket."

She smacked the flashlight into my hand. I shone it into the crawl space. The dirt floor extended through the darkness as far as the beam pierced. I waved the flashlight. The beam bounced off something to my left. A metal box.

"There's a box," I said. "But I can't reach it from here."

I climbed the remaining two steps and crawled in. The space stunk of dirt and stale air, as if no one had been there in years.

The ceiling was really low, so I had to waddle hunched over. I maneuvered to the box. It was dull gray metal with the kind of lid that lifted off, like a gift box.

"Is it locked?" Rae whispered. She had climbed the ladder and was peering in.

I passed the light around the perimeter of the lid. No sign of a lock.

"Well, open it," she said.

Kneeling, I gripped the flashlight between my knees. My fingertips slid under the lid's rim.

"Come on, come on," Rae said.

I ignored her. This room was what the ghost had wanted me to see. I was sure of it. And this box was the only thing I could see in this barren, dark space.

I'd seen boxes like this in movies, and what lay inside was never good. Body parts were usually involved.

But I had to know. The lid started coming off, then stopped. I jiggled it. One side came up, but the other caught. I slid my fingertips around the edge, trying to find what it was catching on. It was a piece of paper.

I tugged, and the paper ripped, leaving me with a corner. There was handwriting on it, but only fragments of words. I found the part of the paper still stuck in the box and pulled, prying the lid with my other hand. One sharp tug, and the paper came free . . . and so did the lid, flying off and landing in my lap. Before I could think about whether I wanted to look, I *was* looking, staring straight down into the box.

"Papers?" Rae said.

"It looks like . . . files."

I reached into a folder marked *2002* and pulled out a sheaf of papers. I read the first.

"Property taxes." I flipped through the other pages. "It's just records of stuff they needed to keep. They put them into a fireproof box and stored it here. The door's probably only locked so we don't snoop."

"Or this isn't what the ghost was telling you about. That means there must be something else down here."

We spent ten minutes crawling around, and finding nothing more than a dead mole that stunk so bad I nearly puked.

"Let's go," I said, crouched on my heels with my arms crossed. "There's nothing here, and it's freezing."

Rae shone the flashlight in my face. I swatted it out of the way.

"No need to get snippy," Rae said. "I was just going to say it's not cold."

I took her hand and wrapped it around my arm. "I'm *cold.* Those are goose bumps, all right? Feel them?"

"I didn't say you weren't—"

"I'm going. Stay if you want."

I started crawling away. When Rae grabbed my foot, I yanked hard, almost toppling her over.

"What's with you?" she said.

I rubbed my arms. Tension strummed my nerves. My jaw ached, and I realized I was clenching my teeth.

"I just—I was okay before but now . . . I just want to get out."

Rae crawled up beside me. "You're sweating, too. Sweat and goose bumps. And your eyes are all glittery, like you have a fever."

"Maybe I do. Can we just—?"

"There's something here, isn't there?"

"No, I—" I stopped and looked around. "Maybe. I don't know. It's just— I need to go."

"Okay." She handed me the flashlight. "Lead the way."

The moment my fingers closed around the flashlight, the light started to dim. Within seconds, it was giving off only a faint yellowish glow.

"Tell me that's the batteries going," Rae whispered.

I quickly handed it back to her. The light surged, but only for a second. Then it went out, plunging us into darkness. Rae let out an oath. A swish. Light flared. Rae's face glowed behind the match flame.

"Knew these things would come in handy someday," she said. "Now . . ."

She stopped, her gaze going to the flame. She stared at it like a child mesmerized by a campfire.

"Rae!" I said.

"Oh, uh, sorry." A sharp shake of her head. We were almost at the door when I heard the distant sound of the basement door opening.

"The match!" I whispered.

"Right."

She extinguished it. Not by waving it or blowing it, but by cupping the flame in her hand. Then she tossed the dead match and the matchbook over her shoulder.

"Girls?" Mrs. Talbot called from the top of the stairs. "Is your homework done?"

Homework. Simon and Derek. I checked my watch. 7:58.

I scrambled out of the crawl space.

twenty-four

I KNEW RAE WAS DISAPPOINTED by what we'd found—or hadn't. I felt a weird kind of guilt, like a performer who failed to entertain. But she never doubted I'd seen a ghost or that he'd told me to open that door, and I was grateful for that.

I returned the key, washed, then found Mrs. Talbot and told her I was going upstairs for math tutoring with Derek and that Simon would be there. She hesitated but only for a moment, then sent me off.

I retrieved my newly arrived math text from my room and went around to the boys' side. The door was open. Simon sprawled on the bed, reading a comic. Derek was hunched over the too-small desk, doing homework.

The room was a reverse image of ours, set at the back of the house instead of the front. Simon's walls were covered in what looked like pages ripped from a comic book, but when I squinted, I realized they were hand drawn. Some were black-and-white, but most were in full color, everything from character sketches to splash panels to full pages, done in a style that wasn't quite manga, wasn't quite comic book. More than once Simon had gotten in trouble for doodling in class. Now I could see what he'd been working on.

Derek's walls were bare. Books were stacked on his dresser and magazines lay open on the bed. Shoved to the back corner of his desk was some kind of contraption full of wires and pulleys. A school project, I supposed, but if I had to build anything that complicated next year, I was doomed.

I rapped on the doorframe.

"Hey." Simon slapped down the comic as he sat up. "I was just going to tell Derek we should go downstairs, make sure the nurses weren't giving you a hassle. They didn't, did they?"

I shook my head.

Derek set his math text on the bedside table, as a prop, then put his binder over it. "I'll be in the shower. Start without me."

"Won't the nurses hear the water running?"

He shrugged, and shoved back his hair, lank and stringy now, the dull sheen of oil glistening under the lights. "Tell them I was already in there. I'll only be a few minutes."

He headed for the door, circling as wide around me as he could manage, which made me wonder how badly he *needed* that shower. I wasn't about to sniff and find out.

If he was showering at night, that might be part of his problem. Kari said she always used to have a bath in the evening, but she'd had to switch to morning showers or her hair would be gross by dinner. I wouldn't dare suggest this to Derek, but as he passed, I couldn't resist an innocent, "Why don't you just shower in the morning?"

"I do," he muttered as he left.

Simon put away his comic. "Come on in. I don't bite."

He lay back in the middle of his bed, springs squeaking, then patted a spot at the edge.

"I'd say this is the first time I've had a girl in my bed . . . if I didn't mind sounding like a total loser."

I reached over to put my books on the beside table, hiding my blush. As I opened my text, to look like we were working on it, I knocked the binder off Derek's. I glimpsed the cover and did a double take.

College Algebra with Trigonometry.

I flipped through the pages.

"If you can understand any of that, you're way ahead of me," Simon said.

"I thought Derek was in tenth grade."

"Yeah, but not in algebra. Or geometry. Or chemistry, physics, or biology, though he's only in twelfth grade in the sciences."

Only twelfth . . . ?

When he said that no one would question us working on math together, he hadn't meant that *he* needed help. Great. It was bad enough Derek thought I was a flighty blond, jumping at every noise. Apparently he figured I wasn't too bright, either.

I put the binder back on top of Derek's text.

"Tori . . . she didn't give you a hard time or anything, did she?" he asked. "About yesterday."

I shook my head.

He exhaled and crossed his arms behind his head. "Good. I don't know what her problem is. I've made it clear that I'm not interested. At first, I tried being nice about it, brushing her off. When she didn't take a hint, I told her I wasn't interested. Now, I'm downright rude to her and she still won't back off."

I twisted around to see him better. "I guess that would be hard—having someone really like you and you aren't interested back."

He laughed. "The only person Tori really likes is Tori. I'm just a stand-in until she can get back to her football captains. Girls like Tori need to have a guy—any guy—and here I'm her only option. Peter was way too young and Derek's—Derek's not her type. Trust me, if another guy walks in here, she'll forget I exist."

"I don't know about that. I think she might really—"

"Puh-lease. Do I look like diva bait to you?" He turned onto his side, head propped on his arm. "Oh, sure, when Derek and I start at a new school, I'll get some attention from the clique girls. Like"—he raised his voice to a falsetto—" 'Hey, Simon, I was, like, wondering if you could maybe, you know, help me with my homework after school? 'Cause it's, like, math and, like, you're Chinese, right? I bet you're sooo good at it.' "

He rolled his eyes. "First, my Dad's Korean and my mom was Swedish. Second, I totally suck at math. I don't like cuckoo clocks or skiing or fancy chocolate either."

I sputtered a laugh. "I think that's Swiss."

"Huh. So what's Swedish?"

"Um, I don't know. Meatballs?"

"Well, I kind of like those. But probably not Swedish ones."

"So what do you like?"

"In school? History. Don't laugh. And I'm not bad in English. I write mean haiku, which, by the way, is Japanese."

"I knew that." I glanced up at the drawings on his walls. "You must ace art, though. Those are amazing."

His eyes lit up, amber glinting in the deep brown.

"Not sure about *amazing*, but thanks. Actually, I don't ace art. Last year, I barely passed. I pissed off the teacher because I kept handing in my comics. I was doing the assignments, just taking the techniques and using them for my stuff. She thought I was being a smart-ass."

"That's not fair."

"Well, when I kept handing in my stuff even after the first couple of warnings, I probably *was* being a smart-ass. Or just stubborn. Anyway, I'm not that great in school overall—a solid B minus student. Derek's the genius. My best class is gym. I'm into cross-country, hurdles, B-ball, soccer . . ."

"Oh, I played soccer." I stopped. "Well, a while ago. A long while ago. Like back when we'd all chase the ball like a swarm of bumblebees."

"I remember those days. I'll have to give you some brushup lessons, so we can start a team. The Lyle House soccer club."

"A very small club."

"No, a very *exclusive* club."

I leaned back on my elbows, reclining on the bed. The last time I'd talked one-on-one like this with a guy was . . . well, probably back before I stopped thinking of them as "other kids" and started thinking of them as "boys."

"Speaking of exclusive clubs," I said, "I hope you asked me up here planning to answer some questions."

"My company isn't enough?" His brows shot up in mock outrage, ruined by the gleam in his eyes. "Okay, you've been patient long enough. What do you want to know?"

"Everything."

We grinned at each other.

"Okay, you're a necromancer and I'm a sorcerer. You speak to the dead and I cast spells."

"Is that why you're here? You did something?"

"Nah." He paused, a shadow crossing his face. "Well, kind of, but not magic. Something happened. With Der—" He cut himself short. From Derek's file, I knew why *he* was here, though I wasn't about to admit it. "Anyway, something happened, and then my dad disappeared and it's a very long story, but the short version is that we're stuck here until someone figures out what to do with us."

And until Derek was "cured," I supposed. That's why Simon didn't have a file or go to therapy. He wasn't here for any problem. When their dad left, the authorities must have brought Derek here, and decided to leave Simon with him.

"So what else is there? What other kind of . . ." I struggled for a word.

"Supernaturals. The different types are called races. There aren't very many. The biggies would be necros, sorcerers, witches—which are the girl spellcasters. Similar, but a different race, and not as strong as sorcerers, or so everyone says. What else? Half-demons, but don't ask me about them because I know next to nothing. Derek knows more. Oh, and shamans. They're good healers and they can astral project."

"Astral . . .?"

"Leave their bodies. Move around like a ghost. Cool for cheating on tests or sneaking into the girls' locker room . . . for guys who'd do that kind of thing . . ."

"Uh-huh. You said Derek knows more about half-demons. Is that what he is?"

He glanced toward the hall, head turning as if making sure he could still hear the water running.

"You dragged it out of me, okay?"

"Huh?"

He turned onto his side, moving close enough to brush my leg. His voice dropped. "About Derek. What he is. If he asks, you dragged it out of me."

I straightened, annoyance flickering. "So Derek doesn't want me to know what he is? The same guy who threw *necromancer* in my face and demanded I accept it. If he doesn't want—"

"He does. He will. It's just . . . complicated. If you don't ask, he won't tell you. But if you ask . . ."

His eyes lifted to mine, pleading with me to make this easy.

I sighed. "Fine, I'm asking. What's Derek? One of these half-demon things?"

"No. There's not really a name for what he is. I guess you could call it the superman gene, but that's really cheesy."

"Uh-huh."

"Which is why they don't call it that. Guys like Derek have . . . physical enhancements, you might say. Extra strong, as you saw. Better senses, too. That kind of thing."

I glanced at the math text. "Smarter?"

"Nah, that's just Derek. Or so my dad says."

"Your dad's a . . . sorcerer, too, then, I guess. So he knows others . . . like us?"

"Yeah. Supernaturals have a kind of community. Maybe *network* is a better word. You know others so you can talk to them, get things you can't get from the regular world, whatever. My dad used to be right into it. These days, not so much. Stuff . . . happened."

He went quiet for a moment, plucking at a loose thread on the comforter, then he dropped it and flopped onto his back again. "We'll get into all that later. Huge story. Short answer is, yes, Dad used to be into the whole supernatural network. He worked for this research company, supernatural doctors and scientists trying to make things easier for other supernaturals. Dad's a lawyer, but they needed people like that, too. Anyway, that's how we got Derek."

"*Got* Derek?"

Simon made a face. "That didn't come out right. Sounds like Dad brought home a stray puppy. But that's kind of how it was. See, Derek's type? It's rare. We're all rare, but he's really, really rare. These people, the ones my dad worked for, they were raising him. He'd been orphaned or abandoned or something when he was just a baby, and they wanted to make sure he didn't end up in some human foster home, which would be bad when he hit, like, twelve and started throwing people across the room. Only, my dad's company wasn't really equipped to raise a kid. Derek doesn't talk much about living there, but I think it was like growing up in a hospital. My dad didn't like that, so they let him bring Derek home. It was . . . weird. Like he'd never been out before. Things like school or a shopping mall or even a highway totally freaked him out. He wasn't used to people, all that noise—"

He went still, head turning toward the hall. The pipes clanked as the water shut off.

"Later," he mouthed.

"He just got out. He can't hear—"

"Oh yes, he can."

I remembered what Simon said about Derek's "enhanced senses." Now I understood why Derek always seemed to be able to hear things he shouldn't have been able to. I made a mental note to be more careful.

I cleared my throat, pitching it to normal. "Okay, so we've got sorcerers, witches, half-demons, necromancers, shamans, and other really rare types, like Derek. That's it, right? I'm not going to run into any werewolves or vampires, am I?"

He laughed. "That'd be cool."

Cool, maybe, but I was happy to leave werewolves and vampires to Hollywood. I could believe in magic and ghosts and even spirit travel, but turning into an animal or sucking blood stretched disbelief farther than I cared to.

A dozen questions leaped to my lips. Where was their father? What about the people his dad worked for? Why'd he leave them? What about Simon's mother? But Simon said he'd "get into that later." To demand their personal story now would be prying.

"So there are three of us? In one place? That has to mean something."

"Derek thinks it's because some supernatural powers—like yours and his—can't be explained, so humans chalk them up to mental illness. Some kids in homes could be supernatural. Most aren't. You have to talk to him about that. He explains stuff better."

"Okay, back to me, then. What do these ghosts want?"

He shrugged. "Help, I guess."

"With what? Why me?"

"Because you can hear them," Derek said as he walked in, towel-drying his hair. "Not much sense in talking to someone who can't hear you."

"Well, duh."

"I wasn't going to say it."

I glared at him, but he had his back to me, neatly folding the towel and hanging it on the desk chair.

He continued. "How many necromancers do you think are walking around out there?"

"How would I know?"

"Well, if the answer was 'a whole lot,' don't you think you'd have heard of them?"

"Ease up, bro," Simon murmured.

"We're talking hundreds in the whole country." Derek yanked a comb through his hair. "Have you ever met an albino?"

"No."

"Statistically speaking, you're about three times more likely to bump into an albino than a necromancer. So, imagine you're a ghost. If you see a necro, it's like being stranded on a desert island, then spotting a plane overheard. Are you going to try to get their attention? Of course. As for what they want?" He turned the desk chair around and straddled it. "Who knows? If you were a ghost and you bumped into the one living being who could hear you, I'm sure you'd want *something* from her. To know what they want, you're going to need to ask them."

"Easier said than done," I muttered.

I told them about the ghost in the basement.

"There could still be something back there. Something you didn't find. Something important to him." He idly scratched his cheek, winced, and pulled his hand back. "Maybe a paper or an object he'd like you to pass on to his family."

"Or clues to his murder," Simon said. "Or buried treasure."

Derek fixed him with a look, then shook his head. "Moving right along . . . it's probably something stupid, like a letter he forgot to give to his wife. Meaningless."

That didn't sound stupid to me. Or meaningless. Kind of romantic, really. The ghost lingers for years, wanting to pass along that undelivered letter to his wife, now an old woman in a nursing home . . . Not my kind of movie, but I wouldn't call it stupid.

"Whatever it is," I said, "the point is moot because as long as I'm on these pills, I can't make contact to ask."

Derek swiped at a drop of blood on his cheek, where he'd scratched a zit. He scowled with annoyance, letting it bubble over into his voice as he snapped, "Then you need to stop taking the pills."

"Love to. If I could. But after what happened last night, they're giving me urine tests now."

"Ugh. That's harsh." Simon went quiet, then snapped his fingers. "Hey, I've got an idea. It's kinda gross, but what if you take the pills, crush them and mix them with your, you know, urine."

Derek stared at him.

"What?"

"You did pass chem last year, didn't you?"

Simon flipped him the finger. "Okay, genius, what's your idea?"

"I'll think about it. We should get her off those meds. I don't really care what that ghost wants, but he could be useful. As long as we have a willing subject, Chloe should take advantage of it, so she can learn. It's not like she's going anywhere soon . . . unless they ship her off."

Simon shot him a look. "Not funny, bro."

Derek raked his fingers through his wet hair. "Not trying to be funny. Seeing ghosts isn't easy to hide. It's not like casting spells. After this morning, with Dr. Davidoff and Gill, I caught some of their conversation later—" Derek glanced at me. "I was walking by and heard—"

"She knows about your hearing, bro." Derek scowled at Simon, who only shrugged and said, "She figured it out. She's not stupid. Anyway, you overheard . . ."

He stopped, head lifting. "Someone's coming."

"Boys? Chloe?" Mrs. Talbot called from the stairs. "Snack time. Come on down."

Simon called back that we were coming.

"Just a sec," I said. "You heard the doctors talking. What about?"

"You. And whether Lyle House is the right place for you."

twenty-five

WAS DEREK TRYING TO scare me? A few days ago I would have said yes, without hesitation. But now I knew it was only honesty. He'd heard it, so he passed it on, with no attempt to soften the blow because the thought wouldn't cross his mind.

But it did make me all the more determined to get at least one question answered when the nurse popped her head in to announce lights-out.

"Mrs. Talbot?"

"Yes, dear?" she said, peeking back in.

"Can we call Liz yet? I'd really like to talk to her. To explain about that last night."

"There's nothing to explain, dear. Liz is the one who feels horrible about it, frightening you like that. I'm sure you can call her on the weekend."

"This *weekend*?"

She slipped into the room, shutting the door behind her. "The other doctors tell me Liz is having some difficulty adjusting."

Rae popped up from bed. "What's wrong?"

"It's called post-traumatic stress. That last night here was very difficult for her. The doctors in her new hospital don't want her reminded of it."

"What if I don't mention it?"

"Even talking to you will be a reminder, dear. By Sunday, they say she should be fine. Next week at the latest."

Fingers of dread plucked at me.

Not now, dear.

Maybe next weekend.

Maybe next week.

Maybe never.

I glanced at Rae, but pictured Liz instead, perched on the edge of the bed, wriggling her toes, purple and orange giraffes dancing.

Dead Liz.

Ghost Liz.

That was ridiculous, of course. Even if I could dream up a reason why Lyle House would want to kill kids, what about their families? These weren't street kids and runaways. They had parents who would notice if they vanished. Notice and care.

Are you so sure? What about Rae's parents? So attentive, always calling and coming by to see her? And Simon and Derek's dad? The Invisible Man?

I rolled onto my side and wrapped my pillow around my ears, as if that could stifle the voice.

Then I remembered what Simon had said earlier. Astral projecting. There was a race of supernaturals who could leave their bodies and teleport. Could necromancers see those teleporting spirits, too? I bet they could—that spirit would be the part that left the body, at death or during this astral projecting.

So that's what Liz was. A . . . what did he call it? Shaman. She was astral-projecting here and I was seeing her. That could explain why I could see and hear her, but not the ghosts. It might also explain the poltergeist. Liz was doing that projecting stuff without realizing it, and throwing things around.

That had to be the answer. It *had* to be.

"Here," Derek whispered, pressing an empty Mason jar into my hand. He'd pulled me aside after class and we were now standing at the base of the boy's staircase. "Take this up to your room and hide it."

"It's a . . . jar."

He grunted, exasperated that I was so dense I failed to see the critical importance of hiding an empty Mason jar in my room.

"It's for your urine."

"My what?"

He rolled his eyes, a growl-like sound sliding through his teeth as he leaned down, closer to my ear. "Urine. Pee. Whatever. For the testing."

I lifted the jar to eye level. "I think they'll give me something smaller."

This time he definitely growled. A quick glance around. Then he reached for my arm before stopping short and waving me onto the steps. He took them two at a time and was on the landing in a flash, then glowered back at me, as if I was dawdling.

"You took your meds today, right?" he whispered.

I nodded.

"Then use this jar to save it."

"Save . . . ?"

"Your urine. If you give them some of today's tomorrow, it'll seem like you're still taking your meds."

"You want me to . . . dole it out? Into specimen jars?"

"Got a better idea?"

"Um, no, but . . ." I lifted the jar and stared into it.

"Oh, for God's sake. Save your piss. Don't save your piss. It's all the same to me."

Simon peeked around the corner, brows lifted. "I was going to ask what you guys were doing, but hearing that, I think I'll pass."

Derek shooed me down the stairs. I tucked the jar into my knapsack. I'd really rather not use it, but if I squirmed at the thought of stockpiling urine, it would only prove I was the flighty girlie girl he expected.

twenty-six

I DID USE THE JAR, as gross as it was. I'd already provided my "sample" for that day, so the next time I had to go, I did it in the upstairs bathroom, in the jar, hiding it behind the cleaning stuff under the sink. Cleaning the bathroom was one of our chores, so I hoped that meant the nurses never went under there.

We didn't do much work in class that day. We tried, but Ms. Wang wasn't cooperating. It was Friday and she saw the weekend looming, so she just set us up with our assignments, then played solitaire on her laptop.

Rae spent most of the morning in therapy, first with Dr. Gill, then in a special session with Dr. Davidoff, while Tori went for hers with Dr. Gill. That meant when Ms. Wang let us out early for lunch, I was left to pass the time with Simon and Derek, which was just fine by me. There was still so much I wanted to know. Asking wasn't nearly so easy, especially since it wasn't stuff we could discuss in the media room.

Going outside would have been the obvious choice, but Miss Van Dop was working in the garden. So Simon offered to help me finish the laundry. Derek said he'd sneak down later.

"So this is where our resident ghost lurks," Simon said, circling the laundry room.

"I think so but—"

He held up a hand, then lowered himself to the floor and started sorting the last basket. "You don't need to tell me there might not be a ghost here, and I'm not going to make you try to contact it. When Derek comes down, he might. Don't let him push you around."

"I don't push her anywhere." Derek's voice preceded him around the corner.

"If I tell someone to do something and they do it?" Derek said, rounding the corner. "That's not my problem. All she has to do is say no. Her tongue works, doesn't it?"

Great. The guy can manage to make me feel stupid even when he's telling me I don't have to let him make me feel stupid.

"So if they decide to transfer you, what are you going to do about it?"

Simon balled up a shirt. "For God's sake, Derek, they're not—"

"They're thinking about it. She needs a plan."

"Does she?" Simon pitched the shirt into the colored pile. "What about you, bro? If word comes down that you're next to go, do you have a plan?"

They exchanged a look. I couldn't see Simon's face, but Derek's jaw set.

I stood and gathered a load for the washer. "If they do, I don't see that I have a lot of options. I can't exactly refuse."

"So you'll just give in? Go along like a good girl?"

"Ease up, bro."

Derek ignored him, scooped up the laundry I'd missed, and dropped it into the washer, moving beside me as he did. "They won't let you talk to Liz, will they?"

"Huh—what?"

"Tori asked this morning. I heard. Talbot told her no and said she'd told you the same thing when you asked last night." He grabbed the soap box from my hands, lifted the measuring cup from the shelf, and waggled it. "This helps."

"They said I can call Liz on the weekend."

"Still, seems a little odd. You barely knew the girl, and you're the first one wanting to call her?"

"It's called being considerate. Maybe you've heard of it?"

He batted my hand from the dials. "Darks, cold. Or you'll end up with the dye bleeding." A glance back at me. "See? I'm considerate."

"Sure, when it's mostly *your* stuff in there."

Behind us, Simon snorted a laugh.

"As for Liz," I continued, "I just wanted to be sure she was okay."

"Why wouldn't she be?"

He'd scoff at my stupidity, thinking Liz was dead, murdered. Oddly enough, that's exactly what I wanted. Reassurance that my head was stuffed too full of movie plots.

I got as far as the part about waking to see Liz on the bed, chattering away.

"So . . ." Derek cut in. "Liz returned from the great beyond to show you her really cool socks?"

I told them about her "dream" and her attic appearance.

When I finished, Simon sat there, staring, a shirt dangling from his hands. "That sure sounds like a ghost."

"Just because she's a ghost doesn't mean she was murdered," Derek said. "She could have had a completely unrelated accident on the way to the hospital. If that happened, they wouldn't want to tell us right away."

"Or maybe she's not dead at all," I said. "Could she be astral projecting? Shamans do that, right? It might also explain how she was moving stuff around. It wasn't a poltergeist spirit—it was *her* spirit or however it works. You said our powers kick in around puberty, right? If we don't know what we are when that happens, this is just the kind of place we'd end up. A home for teens with weird problems."

He shrugged. But he didn't argue.

"Would being a shaman explain what she was doing? Throwing stuff around? Could she have been popping out of her body without knowing it?"

"I . . . don't know." The admission came slowly, reluctantly. "Let me think about it."

We were halfway through dessert when Mrs. Talbot reappeared.

"I know you kids have free time after lunch, and I hate to interfere with that, but I'm going to have to ask you to spend it in this end of the house, and give Victoria and her mother some privacy. Please stay out of the classroom until it's time for classes, and don't play in the media room. You can go outside or in the living room."

Now, last week, if anyone told me to give someone privacy, I'd make sure I stayed away. That was only polite. After a few days at Lyle House, though, when someone said "Don't go there," I didn't say "okay," but "why?" . . . and decided to find out. In this house, knowledge was power, and I was a quick learner.

The question was: How to get close enough to Dr. Gill's office to overhear Tori and her mom, and learn why we had to give them privacy for a friendly mother-daughter chat. I could ask the guy with the supercharged hearing, but didn't want to owe Derek any favors.

Mrs. Talbot said the girls were allowed upstairs, but not the boys, because getting to their rooms meant passing Dr. Gill's office. That gave me an idea. I went upstairs, crept into Mrs. Talbot's room, through the adjoining door into Miss Van Dop's, then down the boys' hall to the stairs.

My daring move was rewarded the moment I crouched on the stairs.

"I cannot believe you did this to me, Tori. Do you have any idea how much you've embarrassed me? You overheard what the nurses said about Chloe Saunders when I was here Sunday, and you couldn't wait to tell the other kids."

It took me a moment to realize what Tori's mom was talking about. So much had happened this week. Then it hit—Tori telling the others I thought I saw ghosts. Rae had said Tori's mom had some business connection with Lyle House, so when she'd dropped off that new shirt for Tori on Sunday, the nurses must have mentioned the new girl and her "hallucinations." Tori had been eavesdropping.

"If that wasn't enough, they tell me you've been sulking over that girl's transfer."

"Liz," Tori whispered. "Her name is Liz."

"I know her name. What I don't know is why it would send you off the deep end."

"Deep end?"

"Sulking in your room. Bickering with Rachelle. Gloating over that new girl's setback yesterday. Is your medication not working right, Victoria? I told you, if that new prescription doesn't help, you're to let me know—"

"It *is* helping, Mom." Tori's voice was thick, muffled, like she'd been crying.

"Are you still taking them?"

"I always take them. You know that."

"All I know is that if you're taking them, you should be getting better and this week proves you aren't."

"But that doesn't have anything to do with my problem. It's—it's the new girl. She's driving me nuts. Little Miss Goody Two-shoes. Always trying to show me up. Always trying to prove she's better." She switched to a bitter falsetto. "Oh, Chloe's such a good girl. Oh, Chloe's going to be out of here in no time. Oh, Chloe's trying so hard." She switched back to her normal voice. "I'm trying hard. Way harder than her. But Dr. Davidoff already came to visit her."

"Marcel only wants to motivate you kids."

"I *am* motivated. Do you think I like being stuck here with these losers and freaks? But I don't just want to get out—I want to get better. Chloe doesn't care about that. She lied, telling everyone she doesn't think she sees ghosts. Chloe Saunders is a two-faced little bi—" She swallowed the rest of word and said, "—witch."

I'd never been called anything like that, probably not even behind my back.

But I *had* lied. I'd said one thing while believing another. That was the definition of two-faced, wasn't it?

"I understand you don't care for this girl—"

"I *hate* her. She moves in, gets my best friend here kicked out, shows me up with the nurses and doctors, steals my guy—" She stopped short, then mumbled. "Anyway, she deserved it."

"What's this about a boy?" Her mother's words came sharp, brittle.

"Nothing."

"Are you involved with one of the boys here, Tori?"

"No, Mom, I'm not *involved* with anyone."

"Don't take that tone with me. And blow your nose. I can barely understand you through all that blubbering." A pause. "I'm only going to ask you one more time. What's this about a boy?"

"I just—" Tori inhaled loudly enough for me to hear. "I like one of the guys here, and Chloe knows that, so she's been chasing him to show me up."

Chasing him?

"Which boy is it?" Her mother's voice was so low I had to strain to hear it.

"Oh, Mom, it doesn't matter. It's just—"

"Don't you 'oh, Mom' me. I think I have the right to be concerned—" Her voice dropped another notch. "Don't tell me it's Simon, Tori. Don't you dare tell me it's Simon. I warned you to stay away from that boy—"

"Why? He's fine. He doesn't even take meds. I like him and— Ow! Mom! What are you doing?"

"Getting your attention. I told you to stay away from him and I expect to be obeyed. You already have a boyfriend. More than one if I recall. Perfectly nice boys who are waiting for you to get out of here."

"Yeah, like that's going to happen anytime soon."

"It will happen when you decide to make it happen. Do you have any idea how embarrassing it is for a member of the board to have her own daughter sent to this place? Well, let me tell you, Miss Victoria, it's nothing compared to the humiliation of having her still here almost two months later."

"You've already told me that. And told me. And told me."

"Not often enough or you'd be doing something about it. Like trying to get better."

"I am trying." Tori's voice rose in a wail of frustration.

"It's your father's fault—he spoils you rotten. You've never fought for anything in your life. Never known what it was to want anything."

"Mom, I'm trying—"

"You don't know what trying is." The venom in her mother's voice made my skin creep. "You're spoiled and lazy and selfish and you don't care how much you're hurting me, making me look like a lousy mother, damaging my professional reputation . . ."

Tori's only answer was a gut-wrenching sob. I hugged my knees, rubbing my arms.

"You don't worry about Chloe Saunders." Her mother's voice lowered to a hiss. "She's not getting out nearly as fast as she thinks she is. You worry about Victoria Enright and about me. Make me proud, Tori. That's all I ask."

"I'm try—" She stopped. "I will."

"Ignore Chloe Saunders and ignore Simon Bae. They aren't worth your attention."

"But Simon—"

"Did you hear me? I don't want you near that boy. He's trouble—him and his brother. If I hear of you two ever being seen together, alone, he's gone. I'll have him transferred."

Life experience. I can talk it up, vow to broaden my horizons, but I'm still limited to the experiences within my life.

How can a person understand an experience that lies completely outside her own? She can see it, feel it, imagine what it would be like to live it, but it's no different from seeing it on a movie screen and saying "Thank God that's not me."

After listening to Tori's mother, I vowed never to bad-mouth Aunt Lauren again. I was lucky to have a "parent" whose biggest fault was that she cared about me too much. Even when she was disappointed in me, she'd come to my defense. To accuse *me* of embarrassing *her* would never enter my aunt's mind.

Calling me lazy for not trying hard enough? Threatening to send away a boy I liked?

I shivered.

Tori *was* trying to get better. Rae had called her the queen of meds. Now I could see why. I could only imagine what life was like for Tori, and even my imagination wasn't good enough to stretch that far.

How could a parent blame her child for not overcoming a mental illness? It wasn't like pushing a reluctant student to get a passing grade. It was like blaming one with a learning disorder for not getting As. Whatever Tori's "condition" was, it was like schizophrenia—not her fault and not entirely within her control.

Tori skipped class that afternoon, not surprisingly. The rule about not hiding out in your room apparently didn't apply to her, maybe because of her condition or maybe because of her mother's position. Between periods, I slipped upstairs to find her. She was in her bedroom, her sobs barely muffled by the closed door.

I stood in the hall, listening to her cry, yearning to do something.

In a movie, I'd go in there, comfort her, and maybe even become her friend. I'd seen it on the screen a dozen times. But again, that wasn't the same as experiencing it in real life, something I couldn't really appreciate until I was there, outside the door.

Tori hated me.

The thought made my stomach hurt. I'd never been hated before. I was the kind of kid that, if someone asked others what they thought of me, they'd say "Chloe? She's okay, I guess." They didn't love me, didn't hate me, just didn't think much about me either way.

Whether I'd earned Tori's hate was another matter, but I couldn't argue with her experience of events. To her, I *had* barged in and taken her place. I'd become the "good patient" she desperately needed to be.

If I walked into her room now, she wouldn't see a sympathetic face. She'd see a victor come to gloat, and she'd hate me all the more. So I left her there, crying in her room, alone.

When afternoon break ended, Mrs. Talbot announced classes were over for the day. We were going to make a rare trip into the outside world. We weren't going far—just to an indoor community pool a block away, within walking distance.

A great idea. If only I had a bathing suit.

Mrs. Talbot offered to call Aunt Lauren, but I wasn't about to interrupt my aunt for that, especially after she'd been dragged away for my misbehavior yesterday.

I wasn't the only one being left behind, though. Derek had to go to his session with Dr. Gill. That didn't seem fair, but when I said so to Simon, he said Derek wasn't allowed on the outings. I guess that made sense, considering what he was in here for. The day I arrived, when they'd taken the others to lunch while I settled in, he must have been confined to his room.

After everyone left, I took advantage of the nurses being gone and hung out in my room, listening to music. I'd been up there only a few minutes when I thought I heard a rap at my door. I pulled out one earbud. Another rap. I was pretty sure ghosts couldn't knock, so I called a greeting.

The door swung open. There stood Tori, looking . . . very un-Tori-like. Her dark hair stood in spikes, as if she'd been running her hands through it. Her shirt was wrinkled, the back untucked from her jeans.

I sat up. "I thought you went swimming."

"I have cramps. That okay with you?" Her words were clipped, with an undertone of her usual snottiness, but forced. "Anyway, I didn't come to borrow your eyeliner. Not like you have any. I just came to say you can have Simon. I've decided . . ." Her gaze slid away. "I'm not interested. He's not my type anyway. Too . . . young." A twist of her lips. "Immature. Anyway. Take him. He's all yours."

I'd have been tempted to shoot back a "Gee, thanks" if it wasn't obvious how much this was hurting her. Simon was wrong. Tori did really like him.

"Anyway"—she cleared her throat—"I've come to declare a truce."

"Truce?"

With an impatient wave, she stepped into the room, closing the door behind her. "This silly feud of ours. You aren't worth my . . ." She trailed off, shoulder slumping. "No more fighting. You want Simon? Take him. You think you see ghosts? That's your problem. All I want is for you to tell Dr. Gill that I apologized for telling everyone you saw ghosts the first day. They were going to let me out Monday, but now they aren't. And it's your fault."

"I didn't—"

"I'm not done." A touch of her old attitude gave the words a snarky lilt. "You'll tell Dr. Gill that I apologized and maybe you blew the whole thing out of proportion. I thought it was cool you saw ghosts and you took it the wrong way, but that I've been nice to you ever since."

"About 'giving' me Simon . . . I'm not—"

"That's part one of the deal. Part two? I'll show you something you want to see."

"What's that?"

"In that"—a flip of her hand—"filthy crawl space. I was going downstairs to see when you were finally going to get my jeans washed, and I heard you and Rae looking for something."

I wiped any expression from my face. "I don't know what—"

"Oh, stuff it. Let me guess. Brady told Rae there was something in there, didn't he?"

I had no idea what she meant but nodded.

"It's a jewelry box full of old stuff." Her lips curled in distaste. "Brady showed me. He thought I might actually be interested in it. It's, like, antiques, he said. Gross." She shivered. "When I wasn't all 'Oh, wow, that's so sweet and romantic. I just love rotting necklaces and filthy crawl spaces,' he must have mentioned it to Rae. If you want, I can show you."

"Sure, I guess. Maybe tonight—"

"You think I'm going to risk getting into more trouble? I'll show you now, when I'll have time to shower after. And don't think you'll find it on your own, because you won't."

I hesitated.

Her mouth tightened. "Fine. You don't want to help me? That's just peachy." She headed for the door.

I swung my legs over the side of the bed. "Hold up. I'm coming."

twenty-seven

I CLIMBED ONTO THE LADDER, pushed open the door, and peered inside—into the pitch blackness. I pulled back and looked down at Tori.

"Rae had a flashlight. We need to get it."

An exasperated sigh. "Where is it?"

"I don't know. I thought you'd—"

"Why would I know where they keep flashlights? Do you think I sneak around at night? Read dirty books under the covers? Just go—" She stopped, lips curving in a mocking smile. "Oh, that's right. You're afraid of the dark, aren't you?"

"Where did you hear—"

She plucked at my pant leg. "Get down, little girl. I'll lead the way . . . and fend off all the nasty ghosts."

"No, I've got it. Just give me a sec so my eyes adjust."

Where was Rae and her matches when you needed them? Wait. Matches. She'd thrown them in here. I felt around, but the dark earth floor camouflaged the matchbook.

"Hello?" Tori said. "Petrified with fear already? Move or get out of my way."

I started forward.

"Head left," Tori said as she crawled in behind me. "It's about halfway to the wall."

We'd gone around twenty feet when she said, "Swing right. See that pillar?"

I squinted and could make out a support post.

"It's right behind that."

I crawled to the pillar and started feeling around the base of it.

"*Behind*, not *beside*. Can't you do anything? Here, let me."

She reached for my arm, hand wrapping around my forearm and yanking me off balance.

"Hey!" I said. "That—"

"Hurts?" Her fingers dug in harder. When I tried to wrench back, she kneed me in the stomach, and I doubled over. "Do you know how much trouble you got me in, Chloe? You come here, get Liz sent away, steal Simon, ruin my chance to get out. Well, you're about to get out yourself. A one way ticket to the loony bin. Let's see just how scared of the dark you really are."

She lifted a ragged rectangle. A broken brick? She swung. Pain exploded in the back of my head and I pitched forward, tasting dirt before everything went black.

Several times I woke, groggy, some deeper part of me screaming, "You have to get up!" before the sleepy, confused part muttered, "It's just the pills again" and I drifted back into unconsciousness.

Finally I remembered I wasn't taking the pills and I did wake. To the sound of labored breathing. I lay there, my brain still fuddled, heart racing, as I tried to call "Who's there?" But my lips wouldn't move.

I rocked wildly, unable to get up, unable to move my arms, scarcely able to breathe. Then, as I struggled to inhale, I realized where the sound of heavy breathing came from. Me.

I forced myself to lay still, to calm down. Something was tight across my cheeks, pulling the skin when I moved. Tape. I had tape over my mouth.

My hands were tied behind my back, and my legs . . . I squinted into the dark, trying to see my feet, but with the door closed and no light coming in, I couldn't see anything. When I moved my legs, I could feel something holding them together near the ankles. Tied.

That crazy bitch!

I never thought I'd call someone that, but with Tori, no other word fit.

She hadn't just lured me into the crawl space and knocked me out. She'd bound and gagged me.

She was nuts. Absolutely nuts.

Well, duh, that's why she's locked up in this place. Mentally disturbed. Read the label, Chloe. You're the idiot who forgot.

Now I was stuck here, gagged and bound in the dark, waiting for someone to find me.

Will anyone find you?

Of course. They wouldn't just leave me here to rot.

You've probably been unconscious for hours. Maybe they've stopped looking. Maybe they think you've run away.

It didn't matter. Once Tori'd had her fun—and her revenge—she'd find a way to let someone know where I was.

Will she? She's crazy, remember. All she cares about is getting rid of you. Maybe she'll decide it's better if you're never found. A few days without water . . .

Stop that.

They'll think someone broke in. Tied poor Chloe up and left her in the crawl space. That would make a good story. Chloe's last story.

Ridiculous. They'd find me. Eventually. But I wasn't going to lie here and wait for rescue.

I flipped onto my back and tried using my hands to push myself up. When I couldn't get a grip, I rolled onto my side, then twisted and squirmed until I was on my knees.

There. At least I could inch forward. If I could make it to the other side of the crawl space, I could bang on the door, get someone's attention. It would be slow going, but—

"Chloe?"

A man's voice. Dr. Davidoff? I tried to answer, but could only make a muffled "uh-uh" sound.

". . . your name . . . Chloe . . ."

As the voice drew near, and I recognized it, the hairs on my arms went up. The basement ghost.

I braced myself and looked around, knowing even as I did that I couldn't see anything in this blackness.

This complete dark.

". . . relax . . . come for you . . ."

I shifted forward and smacked nose-first into a post. Pain exploded behind my eyes and they filled with tears. When I lowered my head, wincing, I smacked my skull into the post, and toppled sideways.

Get up.

What's the use? I can barely move. I can't see where I'm going. It's so dark.

I lifted my head but, of course, saw nothing. Ghosts could be all around me, everywhere—

Oh, stop that! They're ghosts. They can't do anything to you. They can't "come for you."

". . . summon them . . . you *must* . . ."

I closed my eyes and concentrated on breathing. Nothing but breathing, blocking that voice.

". . . *help* you . . . listen . . . this house . . ."

As terrified as I was, the moment I heard the words "this house" spoken with such urgency, I had to listen.

". . . good . . . relax . . . concentrate . . ."

I struggled against my bonds, trying to push myself up.

"No, relax . . . come for you . . . use the time . . . make contact . . . I can't . . . must get . . . their story . . . urgent . . ."

I strained to pick up more, struggling to understand. Relax and concentrate? Sounded like what Rae suggested. It had worked when I was with her, at least enough for me to see a flash.

I closed my eyes.

". . . good . . . relax . . . summon . . ."

I squeezed my eyes shut and imagined myself making contact with him. Pictured him. Visualized pulling him through. Strained until my temples began to throb.

". . . child . . . not so . . ."

His voice was louder. I balled up my hands, willing myself to pass through the barrier, to contact the dead—

"No!" the ghost said. "Don't—!"

My head jerked up, eyes flying open to blackness.

Are you there? I thought the words, then tried saying them, an "uh-uh-uh" against the gag.

I ticked off two minutes of complete quiet. So much for pulling the ghost through. I must have shoved him farther out of reach.

At least the interlude gave me a moment to calm down. My heart had stopped its scared-rabbit pattering, and even the dark didn't seem so bad. If I could inch toward the door and bang on it . . .

And what direction is the door?

I'd just have to find out.

I started toward a sliver of light that probably came from around the door. The ground trembled, and I pitched forward.

As I straightened, the bindings around my hands moved, loosening. I twisted my arms, pulling my wrists apart. Whatever knot Tori had tied was poorly done, and slipping.

Rich girls, I thought. That's what Rae would say.

I worked my hands free. When I reached for my legs, the tremor came again, stronger now, and I had to brace myself to keep from falling over.

An earthquake?

With my luck, I wouldn't doubt it. I waited it out, then started fumbling with the rope around my feet. It was twisted and knotted in several places, as if it had knots before Tori found it. Finding the right knot in the dark was—

A *crunch* cut my thought short. It sounded like someone stepping onto the dirt floor. But ghosts didn't make any noise when they moved. I listened.

It came again, a shifting, crackling sound, like someone dropping a handful of pebble-filled dirt.

I swallowed and kept working on the knot.

What if there's a real person down here with me? Someone who could *hurt me?*

A scraping noise behind me. I jumped, wrenching my side. The gag stifled my yelp, and I searched the darkness, heart pounding so loud I swore I could hear it.

Thump-thump-thump.

That's not my heartbeat.

The sound came from my left, too soft to be footsteps. Like someone's hands hitting the dirt. Like someone crawling toward me.

"Stop that!"

I only meant to think the words, but I heard them rip from my raw throat, muffled by the gag. The thumping stopped. A guttural noise, like a growl.

My God, there isn't someone down here, there's some thing, *some animal.*

A mole. Rae and I had seen a dead mole yesterday.

A mole? Growling? Making a thumping loud enough to be heard across the room?

Just stay still. If you stay still, it can't find you.

That's sharks! You idiot, sharks and dinosaurs can't find you if you stay still. This isn't Jurassic Park!

Hysterical laughter bubbled up in my throat. I swallowed it, twisting the sound into a whimper. The thumping grew louder, closer, underscored now by a new noise. A . . . clicking.

Click-clack-click-clack.

What was that?

Are you going to sit here and find out?

I reached for my gag but I couldn't get a grip on the tape, so I gave up and fumbled for the rope around my feet again, fingertips whizzing along it so fast it cut into my skin. At every knot, I felt for loose ends and, finding none, kept going until—

There it was. A loose end.

I worked at the knot, tugging this bit, then that bit, searching for the one that would yank out an end. I put all my concentration into it, blocking the sounds.

I was trying to get my fingers under a section of knot when something rattled right beside me. A rustle, then a *click-clack*.

A thick musty smell filled my nostrils. Then icy fingertips brushed my bare arm.

Something in me just . . . let go. A small rush of wetness trickled down my leg, but I barely noticed. I sat there, frozen, holding myself so still and tight that my jaw started to ache.

I tracked the thumping, rustling, clicking thing as it seemed to circle me. Another sound rose. A long low whimper. My whimper. I tried to stop it, but couldn't, could only huddle there, so terrified my mind was an absolute blank.

Then it touched me again. Long, dry, cold, fingerlike things tickled across the back of my neck. An indescribable smacking, cracking, rustling sound set my every hair on end. The sound repeated until it became not a sound but a word. A horrible mangled word that couldn't come from any human throat, a single word endlessly repeated.

"Help. Help. Help."

I lunged forward, away from the thing. Ankles still tied, I flopped face-first to the floor, then pushed up on all fours, moving as fast as I could to that distant door.

A hissing, thumping, clicking sound came from my other side.

Another one.

Oh God, what were they? How many were there?

It doesn't matter. Just go!

I dragged myself until I was at the door. My fingertips brushed the wood. I pushed. It didn't budge.

Locked.

I backed up and slammed my fists against it, screaming, banging, calling for help.

Cold fingers wrapped around my bare ankle.

twenty-eight

MY HAND BRUSHED SOMETHING lying in the dirt. The matchbook.

I snatched it up and fumbled with the cover. I pulled out a match, then turned the book over, fingers searching for the strike strip. There.

"Help. Help. Me."

I backpedaled, shimmying and kicking my bound feet to get away, match falling. I stopped, and ran my hand over the dirt, searching for it.

Get another one!

I did. Found the strike strip again. Pinched the match between my fingers and . . . realized that I had no idea how to light it. Why would I? At camp, only counselors started fires. I'd never smoked a cigarette. I didn't share other girls' fascination with candles.

You must have done this before.

Probably, but I didn't remember . . .

Who cares! You've seen it in movies, haven't you? How hard can it be?

I pinched the match again, struck it . . . and it folded on impact. I pulled out another. How many were there? Not many—it was the same pack Rae had used the first day I'd caught her lighting matches.

This time, I held the match lower, near the head. I struck it. Nothing. I struck again and the match head flared, singeing my fingertips, but

I didn't let go. The flame burned bright, but gave off very little light. I could see my hand, but beyond that—darkness.

No, there was something to the right, moving on the dirt. I could make out only a dark shape, dragging itself toward me. Big and long. Something reached out. It looked like an arm, splotchy, the hand almost white, long fingers glowing against the earth.

The hands reached forward, clawing the dirt, then pulling the body along. I could see clothes, ripped clothing. The smell of dirt and something dank filled my nostrils.

I lifted the match higher. The thing raised its head. A skull stared at me, strips of blackened flesh and dirty encrusted hair hanging from it. Empty eye sockets turned my way. The jaw opened, teeth clacking as it tried to speak, uttering only that horrible, guttural groan.

"Help. Help me."

I screamed into the gag so loud I thought my head would explode. Anything left in my bladder gave way. I dropped the match. It sputtered on the ground, then went out, but not before I saw a bony hand reaching for my leg and a second corpse slithering up beside the first.

For a second, I just sat there, nearly convulsing with fear, my screams little more than rasps. Then that hand wrapped around my leg, cold bone biting in, scraps of ragged cloth brushing my bare skin. Even if I couldn't see it, I could visualize it, and that image was enough to stop the screams in my throat and jolt me back to life.

I yanked free, kicking, shuddering as my foot made contact, and I heard a dry, snapping sound. As I scuttled away, I heard someone saying my name, telling me to stop.

I tried to pull the gag off, but my shaking fingers still couldn't find an edge. I gave up, crawling as fast as I could, until the thumps and clicks and enraged hisses grew distant.

"Chloe! Stop." A dark shape loomed above me, illuminated by a dim light. "It's—"

I kicked as hard as I could. A sharp hiss of pain and a curse.

"Chloe!"

Fingers clamped down on my arm. I swung. Another hand grabbed that arm, and yanked me off balance.

"Chloe, it's me. Derek."

I don't know what I did next. I think I might have collapsed into his arms, but if I did, I prefer not to remember it that way. I do remember feeling the gag rip away, then hearing that awful *thump-thump* and scrambling up.

"Th-th-there's—"

"Dead people, I know. They must have been buried down here. You accidentally raised them."

"R-r-raised—"

"Later. Right now, you need to—"

The thumping sounded again, and I could see them—in my mind—pulling their limp bodies along. The rustle of their clothing and dried flesh. The clatter and clicks of their bones. Their spirits trapped inside. Trapped in their corpses—

"Chloe, focus!"

Derek grabbed my forearms, holding me still, pulling me close enough to see the white flash of his teeth as he talked. From behind him came that faint light I'd seen earlier. The door had been left open, letting in just enough light to make out shapes.

"They won't hurt you. They aren't brain-eating movie zombies, okay? They're just dead bodies with their spirits returned to them."

Just dead bodies? With their spirits returned to them? I'd sent people—ghosts—back into their corpses? I thought of what that would be like, shoved back into your decomposed body, trapped there—

"I—I—I need to send them back."

"Yeah, that'd be the general idea."

Strain sapped the sarcasm from his words; and when I stopped shaking, I could feel the tension running through him, vibrating through the hands gripping my arms, and I knew he was struggling to stay calm. I rubbed my hands over my face, the stink of dirt filling my nostrils.

"O-okay, so how do I send them back?"

Silence. I looked up.

"Derek?"

"I . . . I don't know." He shook it off, rolling his shoulders, the gruffness returning to his voice. "You summoned them, Chloe. Whatever you did, undo it. Reverse it."

"I didn't do—"

"Just *try*."

I closed my eyes. "Go back. Back to your afterlife. I release you."

I repeated the words, concentrating so hard sweat trickled down my face. But the thumping kept coming. Closer. Closer.

I closed my eyes and made myself a movie, starring a foolish young necromancer who needs to send spirits back to the netherworld. I forced myself to picture the corpses. I saw myself calling to their ghosts, freeing them of their earthly bonds. I imagined their spirits lifting—

"Help. Help."

My throat went dry. The voice was right behind me. I opened my eyes.

Derek let out an oath and his hands tightened around my forearms.

"Keep your eyes closed, Chloe. Just remember, they won't hurt you."

A bony fingertip touched my elbow. I jumped.

"It's okay, Chloe. I'm right here. Keep going."

As I held myself still, the fingertips poked my arm, then slid along it, stroking, testing, feeling, like the blind man with the elephant. Bone scraped over my skin. A rustling clatter as the corpse pulled itself closer. The smell of it—

Visualize.

I am!

Not like that!

I closed my eyes—meaningless since I could see nothing with them open, but it made me feel better. The fingers crept and poked over my back, plucking my shirt, the corpse making *gah-gah-gah* noises as if trying to talk.

I gritted my teeth and blocked it out. Not easy, knowing what was touching me, pressing up against my side—

Enough already!

I concentrated instead on Derek's breathing. Slow, deep breaths through his mouth, as he struggled to stay calm.

Deep breaths. Deep breaths. Find a quiet spot. The creative place.

Slowly the sounds and touches and smells of the real world faded. I squeezed my eyes shut, and let myself free-fall into my imagination. I focused on the bodies, imagining myself tugging out their spirits, setting them free, like caged doves, winging their way into the sunlight.

I repeated the images—freeing the spirits, wishing them well, apologizing as I sent them on their way. Dimly I heard Derek's voice, telling me I was doing fine, but it seemed to float, dreamlike on the edge of consciousness. The real world was here, where I was undoing my mistake, reversing the—

"They're gone, Chloe," he whispered.

I stopped. I could still feel bony fingers, now on my leg, a body resting against mine, but it wasn't moving. When I twisted sideways, the corpse fell, an empty shell, collapsing at my feet.

Derek let out a long, deep breath, running his hands through his hair. After a moment, he asked, as if in afterthought, whether I was okay.

"I'll live."

Another shuddering deep breath. Then he looked at the body.

"Guess we've got some work to do."

twenty-nine

BY "WORK," HE MEANT cleanup. As in, reburying the bodies. All I'll say about that is that I was glad even with the door open it was still too dark to see those corpses very well.

The graves were shallow, barely more than a few inches of dirt over the bodies, enough for them to claw through when their spirits were slammed back into their corpses. But I didn't want to think about that.

I could tell the bodies had been buried quite a while, probably before Lyle House had become a group home. And they were adults. For now, that was all I needed to know.

As we worked, I asked Derek how he'd found me. He said that when he realized Tori had stayed behind, he knew she was up to something, so he went to check on me. How exactly he found me, he didn't say, only shrugged and mumbled something about checking "the obvious places" when I seemed to be missing.

The question now was: What to do about Tori?

"Nothing," I said, wiping my trembling hands after smoothing over the second grave.

"Huh?"

Nice to hear *him* say that for a change.

"I'm going to act like nothing happened."

He considered it, then nodded. "Yeah. If you blame her, things will only escalate. Better to ignore her and hope she gives up."

"*Pray* she gives up," I muttered as I crawled for the door.

"Is there still clean clothing down here?" Derek asked.

"One load in the dryer. That's it. Why—? Oh, right. Better not to go upstairs covered in dirt." I climbed down the ladder. "Most of what's in the dryer was yours so—"

"Chloe? Derek?" Mrs. Talbot stood in the laundry room. "What are you two doing together? Derek, you know you're not supposed to—" Her gaze traveled over my filthy clothing. "Dear Lord, what happened to you?"

There was no sense denying we'd been in the crawl space, since she caught us stepping from the closet, me caked in dirt. I moved my legs together, hoping it hid the wet mark. The blow to the back of my skull throbbed and I struggled to speak, praying Derek would jump in. He didn't. One rescue a day must have been his limit.

"I was doing laundry, and D-Derek came down, looking for—"

Dr. Gill stepped into the room. My gaze shot to her.

"Go on, Chloe."

"H-he wanted his shirt. I—I asked about stain stuff, because I couldn't find any and I opened the closet to look, and Derek said it was usually l-locked. We f-found the ladder and the crawl sp-space and we were curious."

"Oh, I bet you were curious," Dr. Gill said, crossing her arms. "Kids your age are very curious, aren't they?"

"I—I guess so. We were exploring—"

"I bet you were," Dr. Gill cut in.

I realized what she thought Derek and I had been doing.

Even as I denied it, I saw she'd given us the perfect out. If I just dropped my gaze sheepishly and said "Yep, you caught us," they'd have their explanation, with no reason to go into the crawl space and discover those hastily reburied corpses.

If it had been Simon, I'd have done it in a second. But Derek? I wasn't that good a liar.

It didn't matter. The more I denied it, the more certain they were that we'd been fooling around. Dr. Gill had already made up her mind. If you find a teenage boy and girl in a dark, private place, was there really any question what they'd been up to?

Even Mrs. Talbot seemed convinced, her mouth tight with disapproval as I blathered.

And Derek? He didn't say a word.

Once we were released, I hurried upstairs to change my jeans before anyone noticed the pee mark. When I checked my head, I had two goose eggs, one from Tori and one from hitting that pillar.

Back downstairs, I showed the smaller one to Dr. Gill, hoping it would support my story that we'd been exploring—see, I even bopped my head. She just took a cursory look, handed me Tylenol, and told me to lie down in the media room. Aunt Lauren was on the way.

"I don't know what to say, Chloe."

Aunt Lauren's voice was barely above a whisper. These were the first words she'd said to me since arriving at Lyle House. I'd heard her arguing with Dr. Gill and the nurses earlier, demanding to know why they weren't making sure Derek stayed away from me, as she'd been promised. But now, with me, that anger had disappeared.

We were alone in Dr. Gill's office. Just like Tori and her mother had been. While I knew this meeting wouldn't end in threats and bruises, I imagined I'd leave feeling no better than Tori had.

Aunt Lauren sat ramrod straight, her hands cupped in her lap, fingers twisting her emerald ring.

"I know you're fifteen. Even if you haven't really dated yet, you're curious. In a place like this, isolated from your friends and family, living with boys, the temptation to experiment—"

"It wasn't like that. It wasn't *anything* like that." I twisted to face her. "We found the crawl space and Derek wanted to check it out and I thought that'd be cool."

"So you followed him in there? After what he'd done to you?" She'd gone still, the disappointment in her eyes changing to horror. "Oh, Chloe, I can't believe— Did you think harassing and hurting you the other day meant he liked you?"

"What? No, of course not. Derek isn't— He made a mistake. He didn't really hurt me and he didn't mean to do it. It was a misunderstanding."

She reached forward and gripped my hand. "Oh, Chloe. Sweetheart, no. You can't fall for that. You can't make excuses for him."

"Excuses?"

"Maybe this is the first boy who's ever said 'I like you,' and I know that feels good, but this will not be the only boy who likes you, Chloe. He's just the first with the nerve to say so. He's older. He took advantage of the situation. At school, I imagine girls won't look at him twice and here he is, with a pretty girl, young, impressionable, trapped—"

"Aunt Lauren!" I yanked from her grasp. "God, it's not—"

"You can do better, Chloe. Much better."

From the distaste on her face, I knew she wasn't talking about how Derek treated me. I felt an odd surge of outrage. Sure, I couldn't bring myself to pretend that I'd been fooling around with him. But I'd felt bad about thinking that way.

How Derek looked wasn't his fault. He was obviously aware of it—and how others reacted to it—and it certainly wasn't like he tried to be repulsive. An adult should know better. Aunt Lauren should be the one giving me the you-can't-judge-a-book-by-its-cover speech.

Any notion I'd had of confessing the truth to Aunt Lauren evaporated. She looked at Derek and she saw a creep who'd attacked her niece. Nothing I could say would convince her otherwise, because he *seemed* like a creep. And nothing I could say would convince her I was really seeing ghosts, because I *seemed* like a schizophrenic.

"Aren't you going to say anything, Chloe?"

"Why?" I heard the chill in my voice. "I've tried. You've already made up your mind."

She shifted in her seat, inching to the edge, closing the gap between us. "I'd like to hear your side."

"Just because I'm in this place, just because I'm 'sick,' doesn't mean I'm any different than I was a week ago. Back then, you'd know something was wrong with this story. You'd have asked for my explanation *before* accusing me of anything. But now?" I stood. "Now I'm just the crazy girl."

"Chloe, I don't think—"

"I know exactly what you think," I said, and walked out.

Aunt Lauren tried to follow, but I wouldn't listen. I was too angry. Too hurt. To think I'd fool around in a basement crawl space with the first boy who showed an interest in me? That really stung.

God only knew what she thought we'd been doing. I was pretty sure her imagination had taken her way past the sweet first-kiss stage. To think I'd go from "never been on a date" to "rolling around in the dirt with a stranger"? That was insulting. No, more than insulting. It made me furious.

Did Aunt Lauren know the first thing about me? And if *she* didn't, who did?

When it was clear I wasn't going to "calm down" and talk to my aunt, it was time for the next phase. The trial. I was summoned back into the office, with Derek as my codefendant and Dr. Gill and Dr. Davidoff as judge and jury. It was a closed court. Even Aunt Lauren wasn't allowed in.

I didn't bother to argue about why we'd been in the crawl space. I'd moved well past the "Oh, my God, I don't want anyone to think I'm that kind of girl" stage. If they thought Derek and I had been grappling in the dirt, then at least it meant they wouldn't go into the crawl space and see the signs of disturbance . . . or, if they did, they'd figure they knew what caused it.

Despite what Aunt Lauren believed, I was sure Derek was as horrified by the thought as I was. When Dr. Gill tried to get a confession from him, he only shrugged, and muttered "whatever," arms crossed, big frame slumped in his seat, defiance in the set of his chin. Like me, he'd realized there was no use arguing, but he wasn't about to confess either.

"This isn't the first time you two have . . . tangled," Dr. Gill said finally. "And I have a feeling it won't be the last. We need to nip this in the bud, and the only way we're going to do that is with a transfer. One of you will have to go."

"I will." I heard the words and it took a moment to realize they'd come from me.

Was I crazy? Volunteering to be transferred when I was already worried about what such a transfer meant?

But I didn't take it back. If one of us had to leave, it should be me. As frightened as I was of being shipped out, I wouldn't separate Simon and Derek.

Still, I expected Derek to jump in. I don't know why—certainly not chivalry. But, it seemed only right to at least raise a token protest. The polite thing to do . . . which I supposed should explain why he didn't say a word.

"No one's going anywhere," Dr. Davidoff said softly. "For now, I'm putting you both on notice. But don't give me any reason to revisit this discussion. Is that understood?"

It was.

thirty

WHEN THE DOCTORS DISMISSED US, Derek and I headed into the hall together. I tried to dawdle, fussing with an imaginary spot on my shirt and giving him time to walk ahead, avoiding any awkwardness. He parked himself in front of me, arms crossed, fingers rapping his biceps with impatience.

I reminded myself of how he'd rescued me. I should be grateful. I was. Right then, though . . . I don't know. My head hurt and I was still smarting over my aunt's rejection, and when I'd offered to be sent away and he didn't argue, it stung. I didn't want it to. But it did.

"What are you wiping at?" he whispered finally.

"A spot."

"There's no spot."

I straightened, tugging my shirt down and adjusting it. "That's because I fixed it."

I tried to step past him. He didn't budge.

"We need to talk," he whispered.

"Do you really think that's a good idea?"

"Simon'll be there," he said. "Five minutes. Out back."

———

I really didn't think it was wise for me to be seen hanging out with Derek, even if Simon was there. So five minutes, later, I was in the media room, lying on the love seat, listening to my iPod, trying to lose myself in my music.

When a shadow passed over my head, I jumped up.

Rae stood there, hands out. "Down, girl. It's just me."

I pulled out my earbuds.

She draped her sweatshirt over a chair. "So what happened?"

"Not what everyone thinks."

"Well, duh."

She settled in at the other end, feet pulled up under her, throw pillow on her lap, getting comfortable, waiting for the real story. She'd known me less than a week, and *she* knew I hadn't been fooling around in a crawl space with Derek.

"I'll tell you later," I murmured, "when we're in our room."

"But you *will* tell me, right?"

I nodded.

"Good. So, how'd it go?"

I told her about the meeting with the doctors and about Aunt Lauren. "It's one thing when strangers think you'd do stuff you wouldn't. They don't know you. But when it's someone who should? Someone you thought *did*?" I shook my head.

"Yeah, I've had my share of that. At school, if I did anything wrong, I got hauled in to the counselor, who lectured me on the temptations of the street and the importance of staying in school. It's, like, excuse me? Is there anything in my record that says I've ever been near a gang? Or that I don't think school's important? I get straight Bs, and I never skip class—go lecture someone else."

She hugged the pillow to her chest. "I tell myself that's cool—they don't know me. But I get the same crap from my mom. Every time we get into it, she reminds me about my friend Trina. Ran away at fourteen, got mixed up in a gang, and killed in a drive-by shooting. Hello? What does that have to do with me? There's a reason Trina and I weren't friends anymore. I'm not like that."

"They mean well, I guess. But it stings."

"The worst of it—" Her gaze rose above my head. "What do you want?"

Derek circled in front of me and tapped his watch. "Did I say five minutes?"

"Yes, you did. And I said it wasn't a good idea."

"We need to talk to you."

Rae started to rise. "Should I get the nurses?"

I waved her down, then turned to Derek. "No."

He pushed his hands into his jean pockets, rocked back on his heels, then said, "Simon wants to talk to you."

"Does Simon have feet?" Rae asked. "A mouth? What are you? His faithful Saint Bernard, lumbering around, bearing your master's messages?"

He swiveled, putting his back to Rae. "Chloe?" There was a note of pleading in his voice that made my resolve falter. "Chloe, pl—" He held the *l*, stretching it; and for a second, I thought he was actually going to say "please," and if he had, I'd have given in, despite my reservations about being seen together. But after a second, he snipped the syllable off and stalked out.

"Bye!" Rae called after him. "Always a pleasure chatting with you!" She turned to me. "You *are* going to tell me what all this is about, right?"

"I promise. So how did swimming go?"

"Okay, I guess. Nice to get out, but not much fun. Simon swam laps, I can barely dog-paddle, so we went our separate ways. Nothing new there. They have a cool slide, though, and—"

She looked behind me again and offered a cautious nod.

"Hey," Simon said.

He perched on the love seat arm. I moved over to give him room, but Rae was on the other side, so I couldn't go far, and his hip brushed my shoulder.

"I—" I began.

"Don't want to go outside," he finished for me. "That's cool. We can both hide out from Derek in here, see how long it takes him to find us."

"I'll leave you two—" Rae began, pushing up from the sofa.

"No, stay," Simon said. "I didn't mean to butt in."

"You didn't. I hear chores calling my name, though, so I'll take off."

When she was gone, I moved over. Simon slid down beside me. I gave him plenty of room, but he stayed close, not touching but almost, and I gazed at the gap between us, that scant inch of bare sofa, staring at it because, well, I didn't know what else to do, to say.

The horror in the crawl space had been hovering over my head, cushioned by the shock and confusion and stress of dealing with the doctors and Aunt Lauren, but now that cushion began to sag, the weight sliding down, the memories returning.

"I feel awful," he said. "About Tori. I knew she was mad about seeing us together, so I tried setting her straight, but I think I only made it worse."

"It's not your fault. She has problems."

A small, sharp laugh. "Yeah, that's one way of putting it." After a minute, he glanced over at me. "You okay?"

I nodded.

He leaned over, his shoulder rubbing mine, breath warm against my ear. "If it was me, I wouldn't be okay. I'd have been scared out of my mind."

I dipped my head, and a strand of my hair fell forward. He reached over with his free hand, as if to brush it back, then stopped. He cleared his throat, but didn't say anything.

"It was pretty interesting," I said after a moment.

"I bet. The kind of thing that's really cool in the movies, but in real life . . ." Our eyes met. "Not so much, huh?"

I nodded. "Not so much."

He twisted, backing into the corner of the couch. "So, what's your favorite zombie movie?"

I sputtered a laugh and as it bubbled up, the weight eased. I felt my thoughts shift, settling into a place where I could make some sense of them. I'd been trying to forget what happened, to push past it, be strong, be tough, be like Derek. Raising the dead? No biggie. Send 'em back, bury the bodies, next problem please.

But I couldn't do it. I kept seeing them, smelling them, feeling their touch. My gut kept seizing up with remembered horror, then thinking about what I'd done to them, *their* horror. The best way for me to handle it right now was to get some distance. Don't forget it—just shift it aside with safe images of celluloid.

So we talked about zombie movies, debating and discussing the merits of films that, according to the ratings board, neither of us should have seen.

"It has the best special effects," Simon said, "hands down."

"Sure, if you make enough things blow up, you can hide plot holes big enough to drive a truck through."

"Plot? It's a zombie movie."

He was now sprawled on the floor, having moved there to demonstrate a particularly lame zombie "death scene." I lay on the couch, looking down at him.

"Let me guess," he said. "You're going to write the world's first art-house zombie movie to premiere at Sundown."

"Sun*dance*. And, no. If I ever have to direct any art-house film?" I shuddered. "Shoot me now."

He grinned and sat up. "I'll second that. No art flicks for me. Not that I'm going to ever write or direct *any* film. So which is it you want to do? Write or direct?"

"Both if I can. Screenwriting's where the story's at, but if you want to see that story come to life, you've got to direct, because in Hollywood, the director is king. Screenwriters? Barely even register on the radar."

"So the director is at the top of the heap."

"No, that's the studio. The director is king. The studio is God. And they just want something they can sell, something that'll fit their four little quadrants."

"Quadrants?"

"The four main demographic groups. Guys and girls, divided by young and old. Hit all four, and you've got a blockbuster . . . and a very happy studio. That is not, however, going to happen with a zombie movie, however cool it is."

He flipped onto his stomach. "How do you know all this?"

"I might be stuck in Buffalo, but I'm wired. I subscribe to *Variety*, *Creative Screenwriting*, a whack of industry loops, bookmark the blogs . . . If I want to be in this business, I have to know this business. The sooner the better."

"Oh, *man*. I don't even know what I want to be yet."

"I can hire you to do all my fog effects."

He laughed, then looked behind me. "Hey, bro. Get enough fresh air?"

"I wanted to talk to you." Derek swung his glare to include me. "Both of you."

"Then pull up a chair. The current topic of conversation is zombie movies." Simon glanced at me. "Are we still on zombie movies?"

"I think so."

"Zombie movies?" Derek said, slowly, as if he'd misheard. His face darkened and he lowered his voice. "Have you two forgotten what happened today?"

"Nope. That's why we're talking about it." Simon tossed a grin my way. "Kinda."

Derek lowered his voice another notch. "Chloe is in danger. Serious danger. And you're lounging around, yapping about zombie movies?"

"Lounging? Yapping? Good word choices. Very evocative. You making a point? I know perfectly well what happened and what it could mean for Chloe. But the sky isn't going to fall if we don't discuss it this very minute, Chicken Little." He stretched. "Right now, I think we could all use some time to just chill."

"Chill? You do a lot of that, don't you?" Derek walked over to Simon. "In fact, that's pretty much all you do."

I stood. "I—I'd better see if Rae needs help. With her chores."

Simon sat. "Hold up. We're almost done here." He turned to Derek. "Right?"

"Sure. Go ahead. Take it easy. I'm sure Dad will walk in that door any minute and rescue us. And if he's in trouble? If he needs help? Well, too bad, 'cause that would require effort and you're too busy . . . chilling."

Simon sprang to his feet. Derek stood his ground. They faced off for a moment, then Simon nudged me toward the door.

"Let's go."

When I hesitated, he mouthed "please." I nodded and we left.

thirty-one

AS WE WALKED DOWN THE HALL, I glanced at Simon. His face was hard, expressionless. When he caught me looking, he managed a smile as if to reassure me he wasn't mad at me.

"Mrs. Talbot?" he called. "Can I go out back? Shoot some hoops before dark?"

"Of course, dear."

We waited at the door. She stepped from the kitchen, drying her hands on a towel, and punched in the security code. Only then did she look over and realize Simon wasn't alone.

"Oh, Chloe . . . I'm not sure you two should . . ."

"It's basketball, Mrs. Talbot." He pushed open the screen door and held it for me. "You can watch from the window if you need to."

"Just . . . just don't go anywhere I can't see you."

He slammed the screen door shut behind us and marched into the yard so fast I had to jog to keep up. I glanced over my shoulder. The door was closed, no sign of Mrs. Talbot.

He looked around. "You see the ball?"

"I think it's in the shed. I'll go get—"

He touched my elbow. "No. Unless you really want to play."

I shook my head and he led me toward the stone bench near the central garden. "Talbot can still see us from there." He exhaled. "Derek sure knows how to push my buttons. Worst of it? I *know* he's pushing my buttons, trying to get a rise out of me, and I rise anyway. Stupid, stupid, stupid."

For a moment, he said nothing, gaze moving across the yard.

"Derek wants me to go looking for our dad."

"How? Like, break out? You can't—"

"That's no big deal." He settled back on the bench. "When you're raised like us, as supernaturals, it's . . . different. The rules are different. They have to be. If there's trouble, you have to run."

"But you don't want to go?"

"Oh, I *want* to. I've been chomping at the bit since we got here. My dad's out there—somewhere—maybe in trouble and I'm sitting around in a group home? Going to class? Hanging with Derek? Acting like nothing's wrong? It's *killing* me, Chloe. Derek knows how bad I want out. Like I said, he's pushing my buttons."

"Where is your dad?"

He shook his head. "We don't know. He just— Things went wrong and he disappeared and we ended up here. It's a long story . . ."

"Then it can wait."

"Thanks. Point is, he's gone and I'm sure he didn't leave willingly. So we're stuck here, supposedly waiting to get released, but then what? Where would we go? There's no grandma or great-uncle or family friend waiting to take us. We'd go into foster care and then we'd need to escape from there, so what's the point of waiting?"

"You want out now, but you can't *get* out."

"We *can* get out. Derek's got a plan." A small laugh. "Trust me, the man's always got a plan. But it's an escape plan for one—for me. He won't go. Flat-out refuses."

"*What?* He's making you feel guilty about staying when he won't go himself? Where does he get off?"

"Yeah, I know, and I don't want to sound like I'm defending him, but he has a reason for not wanting to go. It's a stupid reason, but it's a big deal to him and there's no sense trying to change his mind. He just . . . freaks."

"Freaks?"

Simon flexed his hand, staring down at it. "It's complicated. Derek's idea, though, is for me to get out and find Dad. Dad taught me ways to get in touch with him. Spells and stuff. But I can't leave Derek."

"Can't?"

"Won't, I guess. I'm worried about Dad, but he can take care of himself, way better than Derek can."

I must have looked skeptical, because he went on, "I know Derek seems like he can and in most ways he can, but in others . . ." He shook his head. "It's complicated. If I take off and something goes wrong, I'm afraid he'll just . . . let it."

"I don't understand."

"I know." He stared down at his hands. "I know I'm not making any sense, but . . ."

"It's complicated."

"Yeah. But—" He inhaled. "I'm starting to think I need to take that chance. Derek's right. Sitting on my butt isn't getting us anywhere. Now there's you to consider. You really need to get out."

"I do?" The words escaped as a squeak.

"Derek's right. It doesn't matter how hard we work to hide your powers, they aren't like mine. They *can't* be hidden. Not when you're living under a microscope."

"If I get transferred to a hospital, I'll get through it."

"But what if it's *not* a transfer?" He glanced over, worry in his eyes. "What you said about Liz keeps gnawing at me. Maybe she is a shaman. Or if she is dead, maybe it was an accident. Why would they kill kids who don't get better? It sounds nuts, but even Derek's worried."

"Derek? But he said—"

"I know what he said. But when I talked to him later, he wasn't so quick to brush it off. Even raised some questions himself. With Derek, that's as close to agreement as you can get. But you still need help. Say everything goes fine and you get released, what will you do? Who will you talk to? How will you learn how to get back to normal?"

Normal. Such a simple, boring word. Funny how it shone now, like a brass ring on a merry-go-round, bright with promise, just out of reach.

Getting out wouldn't solve my problems. Aunt Lauren would always be watching, misinterpreting every "abnormal" thing I did as a sign that I needed to return to Lyle House . . . or worse.

But to run away?

I knew what Derek would say. I could even picture his expression, that scowl of disdain and frustration. I wasn't Chloe Saunders, sheltered art-school girl anymore. I wasn't even Chloe Saunders, schizophrenic. If Chloe Saunders, necromancer, followed the old rules, she could wind up in a padded cell, ranting about voices no one else could hear.

I wasn't naive. I read the news. I knew what happened to kids who ran away, and it wasn't the wonderful life of freedom they imagined. How long would it take to find Simon's dad? How would we live in the meantime? What would we eat? Where would we sleep? I had some money, but how long would that last? What would happen when our pictures were splashed across the news? When every cop and concerned citizen was looking for us?

I could hole up here, screw my eyes shut, and pray nothing bad happened. Or I could take matters into my own hands. Take action.

Getting help from Simon's missing father wasn't exactly my idea of a firm plan. But if I got out of here, I could track down Liz. That would be easy. There were a limited number of hospitals in Buffalo. And if she wasn't safe in a hospital, what did that mean for the rest of us? Were we in danger? I couldn't keep plugging my fingers in my ears and pretending everything was fine.

"If you're getting out of here, I'll go with you," I said.

"You don't have to. I just meant that *I* need to leave, for me and Derek and, now, for you. When I find Dad, he can help us."

"Who will help *you*? Out there?"

A twist of a smile. "I've got my killer fog spell."

"You need backup. Derek would be a lot better at that, but you're going to be stuck with me. I'm going."

thirty-two

I WAITED IN THE BOYS' bathroom, tucked in beside the storage tower. With every noise from the hall, my heart thudded, telling me I was about to make the biggest fool of myself yet.

But I wasn't wrong. Like Derek, I could add two plus two and see the answer. I wiped my sweaty palms against my jeans, glanced at my watch, and prayed I'd come to the proper conclusion. And, in some ways, prayed I hadn't.

When my watch hit 8:00, the bathroom door swung open. Derek flipped the light on and shut the door. As he turned toward the mirror, he saw me and he let out a yelp of surprise that would have been very satisfying under any other circumstances.

"Are you nuts?" he hissed. "What are you doing here?"

I walked past him and locked the door.

"If you want to discuss the plan, this really isn't the place," he said.

He pivoted, gaze following me as I crossed to the shower and turned on the cold water, so it would drown out our conversation without steaming up the room.

"Great," he muttered. "Now they're going to think we're showering together. Maybe we can just tell them we were washing off the crawl space dirt and trying to conserve water."

I planted myself in front of him. "You set me up."

He opened his mouth, but, for once, nothing came out and he settled for a token scowl.

"All this time, I've been trying to figure out why you want to help me. Why do you care if I know I'm a necromancer? Why do you care if I get booted out? Why stick your neck out for me, like you did this afternoon?"

"I just want—"

"To help. Sure, you're obnoxious and arrogant, but underneath, there's a decent guy who wants to help a fellow supernatural. Yeah, right. There has to be another reason. Today I found it. Simon."

He crossed his arms. "Yeah, Simon wanted me to be nice to you. Okay? Can I have my shower now? Alone?"

"You want Simon to run away. To find your dad. But he won't go without you. He needs a reason to go right now. So you gave him one. The designated damsel in distress."

"I don't know what you're talking about," he muttered, but his gaze wouldn't quite meet mine. My remaining doubts vanished in a fresh surge of anger.

"Here I was, a real necromancer, naive and lost. Perfect bait. Just keep pushing us together, make a big deal out of how helpless I am, and eventually he'll pull on his shining armor. Great plan. But it still lacks something. Stakes. In any great thriller, your hero needs three things. Goal, motivation, and stakes. Goal: find your missing dad. Motivation: help the poor necromancer chick. The stakes were missing, though. You needed to put your damsel in actual distress. What if she was about to be transferred to a real mental hospital? Where she'd be out of Simon's reach and beyond help? Or, worse, where she might die, the victim of some evil plan. So you get Tori to—"

"No!" He raised his hands, genuine shock in his eyes. "I did not have anything to do with that. Even if Tori would get close enough to me to carry on a conversation—which you may have noticed, she won't—I wouldn't do that. I did nothing to *make* them transfer you."

"Okay, so you just took advantage of the situation."

I gave him a moment to respond. He didn't, which was all the answer I needed.

"When I first told you about seeing Liz, you brushed it off. But then you realized this could work in your favor, so you changed your tune with Simon. You planted the seeds of doubt, then waited for them to sprout. That's why you didn't argue when I offered to be the one transferred. That's exactly where you wanted me. You manipulated the situation and you lied—"

"I never lied."

I fixed him with a look. "You really heard the doctors talking about transferring me yesterday?"

He shoved his hands in his pockets. "I heard them talking about you and they seemed to be suggesting—"

"Okay, you didn't lie. You exaggerated."

He scowled. "You *are* in danger. The more I think about Liz—"

"Cut the crap, okay, Derek? You got your wish. Simon's going. I'm going with him. You're right. He needs to get out and find his father. Of course, you could have saved us all this trouble by just going with him yourself. But that might be dangerous. And he's not your father so it's not really your problem—"

He shot toward me so fast I stumbled back, but managed to catch myself and stand my ground. It wasn't easy with him looming over me, eyes blazing.

"Is that what I think, Chloe?"

I locked my knees, refusing to break eye contact.

"I don't know what you think, Derek," I said, calmly—or so I hoped. "Simon says there's a reason you won't go. A stupid reason, according to him. So maybe it's an excuse. Maybe you just don't want to bother."

"An excuse?" A bitter laugh. Then he backed away from me slowly, as if forcing himself. "You read my file, right?"

"I—"

"I know you read it that night when you and Rae pretended to be raiding the kitchen."

"Only because of what you did. I had to know—"

"How dangerous I was. I don't blame you. But you got your answer, right? You know *exactly* how dangerous I am."

I swallowed. "I—"

"You know what I did, and you think I should be walking the streets?" His lip curled. "I'm exactly where I belong."

Something in his eyes, in his voice, in his face, made the back of my throat ache. I glanced over at the shower, watching the water dapple the doors as the harsh pounding filled the silence.

After a moment, I looked back at him. "You must have had a reason for doing it."

"Did I?" When I tried looking away again, he sidestepped and snagged my gaze. "Is that what you want, Chloe? To hear my reason? My excuse? That the guy pulled a gun on me and if I hadn't thrown him into a wall, I'd be dead? Well, that's not how it happened. There's a kid out there who'll never walk again and I have no excuse. It's my fault. *All* my fault. Our dad disappearing. Simon being thrown in here. I—"

He snapped his mouth shut, hands going into his pockets as he stared out over my head, the muscles in his jaw working.

After another moment, he said, "So, yeah, I want Simon out, and I'll do anything to get him out, but it's not like I'm putting you in danger. You're getting something out of it. You don't have any reason to complain."

I could only stare, any sense that maybe I understood him evaporating as it always did. I'd glimpse something underneath, and he'd snatch it away so fast it left bruises that called me a fool for hoping for more.

"No danger?" I said slowly. "I'm running away. From the home. From my family. From my *life*."

"You'll be with Simon. Don't pretend that's any big hardship."

"What?"

"You know what I mean. A few days alone with Simon? That'll be tough. And it means a lot to him. A *lot*. Running away to help him find his dad? He'll never forget that."

I widened my eyes. "Oh my God, do you think so? Really? That's so cool. I bet he'll ask me to go steady and everything. We can send love letters between my juvenile detention center and his, and maybe they'll let us meet at the coed dances. . . ."

He glowered down at me.

"You really think I'm an idiot, don't you?" I said, then shot up my hand. "No, don't answer that. *Please.* News flash: getting a boyfriend is not at the top of every girl's priority list. Right now, it ranks about as low on mine as you can get—way below such trivial concerns as getting my life back together."

"All right—"

"After this is over, I wouldn't be surprised if Simon wanted to never see me again. Just put this all behind him. You know what? That's fine. Because I need to find out what happened to Liz. And I want to help Simon because it's the right thing to do, not because I think he's sooo cute. I might not be a genius like you—"

The glower returned. "I'm not—"

"But I'm smart enough to know this isn't going to be some grand romantic adventure. I'm running away. I'll be living on the streets. Even if we find your dad, I'm not sure he's going to be able to fix my life." I thought of Aunt Lauren and felt a pang of grief. "I'm not sure it can be fixed."

"So I'm supposed to be grateful to you for going?"

"I never said—"

He shifted back into looming mode. "You need to get out of here just as much as Simon does, maybe more. You might not see the danger you're in, but I do. And I'm worried."

"Worried? About me?"

He shrugged. "Sure. Concerned. You know." He couldn't even look me in the eye when he said it. "Yeah, we need you, but I *do* want to help a fellow supernatural." He snuck a glance my way. "We gotta stick together."

"Don't you dare."

"What?"

His gaze broke away, started roaming the bathroom.

"You're right," I said. "I do need help. My life is falling apart and maybe someday I'll look back on this as the biggest, stupidest mistake I've ever made, but at this moment, it's the only solution I see. You need me to be your designated damsel in distress? Okay. But don't *ever* say you're doing this for me. This has nothing to do with me. Don't you dare pretend it does."

I turned and walked out.

thirty-three

I WONDERED WHETHER, AFTER OUR ESCAPE, I'd find time to sleep. Because I certainly hadn't been getting much at Lyle House.

That night I was so exhausted I didn't even have a chance to lie there, raging about Derek or fretting about the step I was about to take. I hit the bed and fell straight into dreams of wailing police sirens and baying tracking dogs. Of a boy trapped in a hospital bed and a boy trapped in a group home and ghosts trapped in rotting corpses. Of zombies screaming for mercy and a girl screaming, "But I didn't mean it," and a boy saying, "I didn't mean it either. Doesn't matter."

The dreams spun and melted together until one slid free. An image buried by the stronger, louder ones, separating and saying, "What about me?"

I bolted awake and sat there, suspended in the dark, reeling in that tangled memory, the questions it raised, the answers it promised.

Then I leaped from bed.

I tapped at the bedroom door.

"Derek?"

Rough snores answered.

I rapped at the door again, raising my voice as loud as I dared.

"Derek?"

My toes curled against the icy hardwood and I rubbed the goose bumps on my arms. I should have grabbed a sweater. And socks.

I shouldn't even be here. I'd told the guy off, made the perfect exit . . . and was now creeping back, begging him to talk to me.

Talk about ruining a scene.

As I lifted my hand to knock, the doorknob clicked. When the door creaked open, I lifted my gaze to eye level, an apology on my lips, and found myself staring at a chest. A bare chest . . . and not a boy's chest. Broad and muscular, a scattering of angry red acne dots the only sign that it *wasn't* attached to a grown man.

Around the house, Derek always wore oversized sweatshirts and baggy jeans. If I'd pictured what he looked like under them—which I hadn't—I would have guessed stocky, bordering on overweight. All that food he scarfed down had to go somewhere. And, apparently, it did—just not to fat.

My cheeks heated and my gaze dropped from Derek's chest . . . only to see he was wearing nothing but boxers.

"Chloe?"

My gaze shot—gratefully—to his face.

He peered at me. "Chloe? What—?"

"You owe me."

"Huh?" He rubbed his eyes with his thumb and forefinger, snarled a yawn, and rolled his shoulders. "What time is it?"

"Late. Or early. It doesn't matter. I need your help and you owe me. Get dressed and be downstairs in five minutes."

I turned on my heel and headed for the stairs.

Would Derek follow me? Probably not, considering I'd ignored his "meet me in five minutes" command that afternoon.

I'd planned to not leave his doorway until he agreed to help me. But I hadn't expected him to be nearly naked during the conversation. It also reminded me that I was wearing only pajama pants and a tank top. When I got downstairs, I found the sweatshirt Rae had shucked in the media room earlier. I was pulling it on as I walked into the hall, and nearly smacked into Derek.

He wore sweatpants and a T-shirt and had stopped in the middle of the hall, furiously scratching one bare forearm.

"Fleas?" I said.

The joke was an admittedly lame attempt to lighten the mood from earlier, and I didn't think it deserved the glower he gave me.

"Let's just get this over with," he said. "I'm not in a good mood."

I could have asked how that was different from normal, but bit my tongue, motioned him into the media room and closed the door. Then I cocked my head, listening.

"We're fine here," he said. "Just keep it down. Someone comes, I'll hear."

I moved across the room and stopped in a patch of moonlight. When he followed, I got my first good look at him in the light. His face was pale, his cheeks flaming red, and not from the acne. Sweat plastered his hair around his face and his red-rimmed eyes glittered, struggling to focus.

"You've got a fever," I said.

"Maybe." He raked his hair back. "Something I ate, I guess."

"Or some bug you picked up."

He shook his head. "I don't . . ." He hesitated, then pushed on. "I don't get sick. Not often anyway. Part of my . . . condition. This seems to be a reaction." He scratched his arms again. "No big deal. I'm just off. Crankier than usual, Simon would say."

"You should go back to bed. Forget this—"

"No, you're right. I owe you. What do you need?"

I wanted to argue but could tell he'd made up his mind.

"Hold on," I said, and hurried into the hall.

He whispered an exasperated, "Chloe!" after me, followed by a half-hearted string of profanity, as if he couldn't work up the energy to even curse properly.

I returned with a glass of cold water and handed it to him, along with four Tylenol.

"Two for now, two for later, in case you—"

He tossed all four in his mouth and drained half the water.

"Or you could just take them all now."

"I've got a high metabolism," he said. "Another part of my condition."

"I know a lot of girls who wouldn't mind that."

He grunted something unintelligible and drained the glass. "Thanks, but . . ." He met my gaze. "You don't need to be nice to me just because I'm not feeling great. You're mad. You've got a right to be. I used you and I made it worse by pretending I hadn't. If I were you, I wouldn't be bringing water unless it was to dump over my head."

He turned away to set the empty glass on the table, and I'm glad he did, because I was pretty sure my jaw had dropped. Either that fever had gone straight to his brain or I was still asleep, dreaming, because that had sounded suspiciously like an admission of guilt. Maybe even a roundabout apology.

He turned back. "Okay, so you need . . . ?"

I waved him to the love seat. Annoyance flickered across his face—getting comfortable was a distraction he couldn't be bothered with—but when I sat on the opposite chair, he lumbered to the couch. If I couldn't get him to return to bed, at least he could rest while I talked.

"You know something about necromancy, right?" I began.

He shrugged. "I'm no expert."

"But you know more than me, Simon, or anyone else I can talk to at this moment. So how do necromancers contact the dead?"

"You mean like the guy in the basement? If he's there, you should see him. Then you'd just talk, like we are right now."

"I mean contacting a specific person. Can I do that? Or am I restricted to those I just stumble across?"

He went quiet. When he spoke, his voice was uncharacteristically soft. "If you mean your mom, Chloe—"

"No." The word came sharper than I intended. "I haven't even thought— Well, yes, I've considered it, for someday maybe, of course I'd like to, love to—" I heard myself rambling and took a deep breath. "This is connected to our situation."

"You mean Liz?"

"No. I—I should try to contact her, I guess. J-just to be sure. But that's not it. Forget why I want to know."

He leaned back into the sofa pillows. "If I knew why, I could answer a lot easier."

Maybe, but I wasn't telling him until I had enough facts to confidently lay out my theory.

"If I *can* contact a specific person, how would I do it?"

"You can, but it's not easy and it's not guaranteed at your age. Like Simon and his spells, you're at the . . . apprenticeship level."

"Where I can do things by accident, like raising the dead."

"Well, no." He absently scratched his arm, the *skritch-skritch* filling the silence. "From what I heard, raising the dead is the toughest thing to do, and it needs this complicated ritual." He shook his head and stopped scratching. "I must have heard wrong. Like I said, I'm not an expert."

"Back to *how*, then. How do I call up a specific ghost?"

He slouched, head resting on the sofa back, staring at the ceiling before nodding, as if to himself. "If I remember right, there are two ways. You could use a personal effect."

"Like with a tracking dog."

A small noise that sounded like a laugh. "Yeah, I guess so. Or like one of those psychics you see in movies, always asking for something that belonged to the person."

"And the second way?" I tried not to show how much I wanted this answer, how much I hoped I'd already guessed it.

"You need to be at the grave."

My heart hammered, and it was a moment before I could speak. "At the grave. Presuming that's where the body is buried. It's the body that's important, not the grave site."

He waved off my petty distinction, the old Derek sliding back. "Yeah, the body. The ultimate personal effect."

"Then I think I know what that ghost in the basement wanted."

I explained how the ghost had urged me to "make contact" to "summon them" and "get their story."

"He meant the buried bodies. That's why he wanted me to go into the crawl space. So I could get close enough to the bodies to contact those ghosts."

Derek reached back to scratch between his shoulders. "Why?"

"From what he seemed to say, it's about Lyle House. Something they can tell me."

"But those bodies have been down there way longer than Lyle House has been a group home. And if this ghost knows something, why not just tell you himself?"

"I don't know. He said . . ." I strained to remember. "He seemed to be saying he couldn't make contact with them himself."

"Then how would he know they had anything important to tell you?"

Good questions. This was why I'd gone to Derek. Because he'd challenge my assumptions, show me where the holes were and what I had to learn before jumping to any conclusions.

"I don't know," I said finally. "However they got there, I'm pretty sure they didn't die of natural causes. You're probably right, and it's completely unconnected to us, and this ghost is confused, losing track of time. Or maybe he wants me to solve their murder." I stood. "But, whatever he wants me to hear, I'm going to listen. Or at least try."

"Hold up."

He lifted a hand, and I braced for more arguments. It was a waste of time. Dangerous, too, after we'd been caught down there earlier. And, don't forget, last time I tried to contact these ghosts, I'd returned them to their corpses. Do that again, and I'd better not call him for reburial duty.

He pushed to his feet. "We should take a flashlight. I'll grab that. You get our shoes."

thirty-four

I WASN'T SETTING FOOT—BARE, STOCKINGED, OR SHOED—in that crawl space until I'd talked to the first ghost and asked all the questions Derek had raised.

We went down to the laundry room. Derek took up a position at the side, leaning back against the dryer. I sat cross-legged in the middle of the floor, closed my eyes, and focused.

It didn't take long, as if the ghost had been waiting for me. I still couldn't catch more than phrases and glimpses. I told Derek this, then said, "I stopped taking the meds after you gave me that jar. But they must still be in my system."

". . . not medic . . ." the ghost said. ". . . block . . ."

"What's blocked?"

"Spell . . . ghosts . . . blocking . . ."

"A spell to block ghosts?" I guessed.

That got Derek's attention and he shifted forward, arms uncrossing. "Did he say a spell's blocking him? What kind?"

I was about to translate, but the ghost could obviously hear and answered. "Magic . . . ritual . . . important."

"It's important?"

"Not . . . *not* important," he said emphatically.

I related this to Derek who grumbled about the imperfection of this mode of communication as he furiously scratched his forearm, then said, "Tell him to say one word at a time. Repeat it until you get it and you say it back. It'll be slow, but at least we won't miss—"

He stopped, his gaze following mine to his forearm. His skin was . . . moving. Rippling.

"What the—?" he began, then growled in frustration and gave his arm a fierce shake. "Muscle spasms. I've been getting them a lot lately."

He peered down at the rippling skin again, made a fist, and pumped his arm, trying to work it out. I was about to suggest he see a doctor, then realized that might not be so easy for someone like Derek. I could see now that it *was* his muscles, expanding and contracting on their own. A side effect of his condition, I guess, muscles developing in overdrive. Like the rest of him, slamming through puberty.

"Just as long as you don't rip through your clothing and turn green," I said.

"What?" His face scrunched up, then he got it. "*The Incredible Hulk*. Ha-ha. *Incredibly Stupid Movie*, more like." His rubbed his forearm. "Ignore me and get back to your ghost."

The ghost had heard Derek's suggestion about taking it one word at a time, and that's what we did. It worked much better, though it felt a bit like charades, him saying a word over and over, and me excitedly repeating it when I finally understood.

I started with questions about the ghost himself, and learned he was a necromancer. He'd been at the hospital when I'd been admitted. Something about stopping ghosts from harassing the mental patients, which I didn't really understand, but it wasn't important.

Ghosts recognize necromancers, so he'd known that's what I was. Realizing that *I* didn't know what I was, he knew I needed help. But before he could make contact, they moved me. So he'd followed me to Lyle House. Only it was somehow blocked against ghosts. He thought it was a spell, though when Derek challenged that assumption, the ghost admitted that it could be anything from the construction materials to the geographic location. All he knew was that the only places he could make even partial contact with me were the basement and the attic.

As for the bodies in the crawl space, he knew two things. One, they'd been murdered. Two, they were supernaturals. Put those together and he was convinced their stories would be important. He couldn't get them himself because he couldn't contact the dead as easily as he could *before* he became one of them himself.

"But they were just skeletons and dried up flesh," Derek said. "Like mummies. Whatever happened to them wouldn't have anything to do with us, here, now."

"Maybe," was the ghost's only answer.

"Maybe?" Derek threw up his hands and started pacing. He muttered under his breath, but there was no anger in it, just frustration, trying to work through this problem and see a connection when he really should be in bed, nursing a fever.

"Samuel Lyle," the ghost communicated next. "Original owner. Know him?"

I said I didn't and asked Derek.

"How would I know the guy who built this place a hundred years ago?"

"Sixty," the ghost said, and I relayed it.

"Whatever." Derek resumed pacing. "Does he even know what year this is?"

I could have pointed out that if the ghost knew how long ago the house had been built, he obviously knew the current year, but Derek was just grouching, his fever making it hard to concentrate on this puzzle.

"Supernatural," the ghost said. "Lyle. Sorcerer."

That made Derek stop when I relayed it.

"The guy who built this place was a sorcerer?"

"Dark magic. Alchemist. Experimented. On supernaturals."

A chill ran up my arms and I crossed them. "You think that's how those people in the cellar died? This sorcerer, Lyle, experimented on them?"

"How does he know so much about this guy?" Derek said. "He followed you here, didn't he?"

"Everyone knew," the ghost replied. "In Buffalo. All supernaturals. Knew where he lived. And stayed away. Or didn't."

Derek shook his head. "I *still* don't see how any of this is connected to us."

"Maybe," the ghost replied. "Maybe not. Need to ask."

Derek hissed a curse and smacked his hand into the wall hard enough to make me wince. I walked over to him.

"Go to bed. You're probably right. I'm sure it's nothing—"

"I'm not saying that. I'm just saying . . . A sorcerer built this place sixty years ago; there are supernaturals buried in the cellar; and now we're here, three supernatural kids. The group home is named after him. Is that significant? Or is it just named after the guy who built it? It seems too much to be a coincidence, but I'm just not getting the connection."

"I can do this. Go back—"

"No, he's right. We need to ask. I just . . ." He shoved his hand up the back of his shirt, scratching. "I feel like crap and it's making me cranky. But we need to do this."

The ghost followed us into the crawl space.

"How do I avoid what I did earlier?" I asked. "Returning them to their bodies?"

Silence. I counted to sixty, then said, "Hello? Are you still there?"

"Stay calm. Focus. But go easy. Soft. Your power. Too strong."

"My powers are too strong?"

I couldn't suppress a smile. I might not be certain I wanted these powers, but it was kind of cool to hear that I had more than the average necromancer. Like taking an IQ test and finding out you're smarter than you thought.

"Your age. Should never be able to . . ."

Silence. I waited patiently to catch the next word. And waited.

"Hello?"

He started again, word by word. "Too soon. Too much. Too . . ."

A longer pause.

"Something's wrong," he said finally.

"Wrong?"

Derek crawled from the shadows, where he'd been silently watching. "What's he saying?"

"Something about my powers. That they're . . . wrong."

"Too strong," the ghost said. "Unnatural."

"Unnatural?" I whispered.

Derek's eyes blazed. "Don't listen to him, Chloe. So you're powerful. Big deal. You're fine. Just take it slow."

The ghost apologized. He gave a few more instructions, then said he'd watch from the "other side," in case his presence had boosted my powers earlier. If I needed him, he'd come back. One last warning against trying too hard, and he was gone.

thirty-five

DEREK RETURNED TO THE SHADOWS, leaving me alone, sitting cross-legged again, the flashlight lying in front of me. As much as I'd have liked to use it as a candle, pushing back the dark, I'd set it on its side, the beam directed at the spot where the bodies were buried in hopes that, if the ground so much as quivered, Derek would warn me before I raised the dead.

To free the ghosts from their corpses, I'd used visualization, so I did that again. I imagined myself tugging the ghosts from the ether, drawing them out like a magician pulling an endless scarf from his sleeve.

A few times I caught a flicker, only to have it vanish again. I kept working, slowly and steadily, resisting the urge to concentrate harder.

"What do you want?" a woman's voice snapped, so close and so clear I grabbed the flashlight, certain one of the nurses had discovered us.

Instead, I shone the beam on a woman dressed in a sweater set. Or that's what her top half was wearing. She was standing, her head brushing the low ceiling, meaning she was "buried" to mid-thigh under the dirt floor. She was maybe thirty, with a blond bob. Her sharp features were rigid with annoyance.

"Well, necromancer, what do you want?"

"Tell her to leave us be," a man's voice whined from the darkness.

I shone the beam in his direction but could make out only a faint form by the farthest wall.

“I just w-want to talk to you,” I said.

“That much is obvious,” the woman snapped. “Calling and pulling and pestering until you drag us out against our will.”

“I didn’t m-mean—”

“Can’t leave well enough alone, can you? It wasn’t enough to shove us back into our bodies. Do you know what that’s like? Sitting down, enjoying a nice afternoon, and all of a sudden you’re back in your corpse, buried, clawing your way to the surface, terrified you’ve been trapped by some demented necromancer looking for zombie slaves?”

“I didn’t mean—”

“Oh, do you hear that, Michael? She didn’t *mean* it.” The woman moved toward me. “So if I accidentally unleash a storm of hellfire on your head, it’ll be all right, as long as I didn’t really *mean* it? You have a power, little girl, and you’d better learn to use it properly before someone decides to teach you a lesson. Summon me again and *I’ll* do it.”

She started to fade.

“Wait! You’re”—I struggled to remember what Simon had called a female spellcaster—“a witch, right? What happened to you here?”

“I was murdered, in case that isn’t perfectly obvious.”

“Was it because you’re a witch?”

She surged back so fast I jumped. “You mean, did I bring this on myself?”

“N-no. Samuel Lyle—the man who owned this house—did he kill you? Because you’re a witch?”

Her lips curled in an ugly smile. “I’m sure my being a witch added a little extra dash of pleasure for him. I should have known better than to trust a sorcerer, but I was a fool. A desperate fool. Sam Lyle promised us an easier life. That’s what we all want, isn’t it? Power without price. Sam Lyle was a seller of dreams. A snake oil salesman. Or a madman.” That twist of a smile again. “We could never figure out which, could we, Michael?”

"A madman," came the whisper from the back. "The things he did to us . . ."

"Ah, but we were willing subjects. At least, in the beginning. You see, little girl, all scientific advancement requires experimentation, and experimentation requires subjects, and that's what Michael and I were. Lab rats sacrificed to the vision of a madman."

"What about me?"

She sneered. "What about you?"

"Does this have anything to do with me being here? Now? There are more of us. Supernaturals. In a group home."

"Are they experimenting on you? Tying you to beds and prodding you with electrical wires until you bite off your tongue?"

"N-no. N-nothing like that."

"Then you count your blessings, little girl, and stop pestering us. Sam Lyle is dead and—if the Fates are just—rotting in a hell dimension."

She started fading again.

"Wait! I need to know—"

"Then find out!" She surged back again. "If you think you're here because of a dead sorcerer, then you're as mad as he was, but I don't have your answers. I'm a shade, not an oracle. Why are you brats here, where I died? How should I know? Why should I care?"

"Am I in danger?"

Her lip twisted. "You're a supernatural. You're always in danger."

"Mission accomplished, but nothing gained. Except more questions," I said as we brushed off our clothing in the laundry room. "Now you can finally get back to bed."

Derek shook his head. "Doesn't matter. I won't sleep."

"Because of this? I'm sorry. I didn't mean—"

"I wasn't sleeping before you got me up." He tugged off his shoe and dumped a trickle of dirt down the sink. "This fever or whatever. It's making me edgy. Restless." As if on cue, his forearm muscles started twitching. "Part of the problem is I'm not getting enough exercise.

Tossing a ball around with Simon just doesn't cut it. I need more . . . space. More activity. I think that's what's causing this." He rubbed harder at the rippling muscles.

"Could you ask for workout equipment? They seem pretty good about stuff like that."

He slanted a look my way. "You've seen my file. You really think they're going to buy me a set of dumbbells and a punching bag?" He looked around the laundry room. "You tired?"

"After that? No."

"How about some fresh air? Get out, go for a walk?"

I laughed. "Sure, if there wasn't the small matter of an alarm system standing in our way."

He raked his hand through his hair, shaking out dirt he'd brushed from the crawl space ceiling. "I know the code."

"What?"

"You think I'm going to push Simon to leave and not know the security code? I can get us out, and we really should do a walk around, check out escape routes, hiding places. I don't get to go on many field trips, so I haven't gotten a look at the neighborhood."

I crossed my arms. "You can walk out anytime? Get that exercise you need? But you never have?"

He shifted his weight. "Never thought of it—"

"Of course you have. But there could be an alert when the alarm is turned off. Or a record of it being disabled. So you've never taken the chance. But now we should. If we get caught, well, everyone already thinks we're fooling around. We'd get in trouble for sneaking off, but not like Simon and I would if we were caught running away."

He scratched his chin. "That's a good idea."

"And it never crossed your mind."

He said nothing. I sighed and headed for the stairs.

"Chloe," he said. "Hold on. I—"

I glanced back. "Coming?"

thirty-six

FIVE MINUTES LATER, we were walking down the sidewalk, the lights from Lyle House fading behind us. We circled the block and mapped out all routes from the house. We were in a section of Buffalo I didn't recognize, one filled with old houses on big lots, where you'd expect to find a Mercedes or Cadillac in every drive. But I could see why it didn't—the billowing smokestacks a few blocks to the east.

After two blocks walking west, the light pollution ahead suggested a business district, which Derek confirmed. Like this neighborhood, it was older and decent enough, but not fancy. No pawn- and porn shops, but no bistros and baristas either. On Simon's rare outings, he'd told Derek he'd seen lots of older, ordinary businesses with plenty of alleys and dark corners.

"When you get to that business area," Derek said, "you'll be home free. If you can't go that way?" He waved east, toward the factory. "Go there. It's all industrial. I'm sure you'd find an abandoned warehouse or two, if you needed to hole up for a while." He looked around, scanning the neighborhood, nostrils flaring as he drank in the chill night air, probably a welcome relief from his fever. "Will you remember all that?"

"Can you say it again? Slower? Maybe write it out for me? With pictures?"

He scowled. "I'm just checking, okay? It's important."

"If you're worried we can't handle it, there's an obvious solution. Come with us."

"Don't."

"I'm just saying . . ."

"Well, don't."

He walked faster, leaving me jogging to keep up. I could tell Simon was right—the subject was closed to discussion—but I couldn't help myself.

"Simon's worried about you."

"Yeah?" He stopped, turned, and spread his arms. "Do I look okay to you?"

"No, you look like a guy who should be in bed, nursing a fever, not prowling—"

"I'm not prowling," he snapped, harsher than necessary. "I mean, where am I? On the street, right? Blocks from Lyle House. No cop cars are ripping down the road after me. If anything goes wrong, I can get out. Do you really think Talbot and Van Dop could stop me?"

"The question isn't whether you *can* escape. It's whether you *will*."

He paused. While I was gratified to know he wasn't just going to tell me what I wanted to hear, I didn't like seeing how much thought the answer required. Simon had said he was afraid that if something went wrong, Derek might just let it. He'd already decided he belonged at Lyle House. Would he leave even if he was in danger? Or could he see only the danger he posed . . . or thought he did?

"Derek?"

He shoved his hands in his pockets. "Yeah."

"Yeah what?"

He yanked one hand out and scratched his arm, nails digging in until they left red marks. "If I'm in danger, I'll get away and find you guys. Okay?"

"Okay."

I woke to see a figure on my bed and sat up, Liz's name on my lips. But it was Rae, leaning against the wall, knees up, eyes sparkling with amusement.

"Thought you saw a ghost?" she said.

"N-no. Maybe." I rubbed my eyes and yawned.

"I suppose it's not a good idea to surprise someone who sees spooks, huh?"

I peered around the bedroom, blinking hard. Early morning light poured in. I glanced at Rae's bed and pictured Liz there, toes wiggling in the sunlight.

"Did Liz leave anything behind?" I asked.

"What?"

I pulled myself up, shoving the covers back. "When you moved in, did you find anything?"

"Just a shirt of Tori's. I didn't bother giving it back yet. Not like Tori's in any rush to return that green hoodie she borrowed from Liz. I saw her wearing it the other day. Why? Did Liz finally call?"

I stretched. "No. I was just . . ." Another yawn. "It's early and half my brain is still in dreamland. Did I miss Mrs. Talbot's knock?"

"No, we have a few minutes yet. I wanted to talk to you before everyone got up."

"Sure, what's—" I jerked upright. "Yesterday! We were supposed to talk. I totally forgot."

"You've been busy." She plucked at the hem of her baby doll nightdress. "So am I going to get an invite?"

"Invite?"

"On the great escape. That's what you were going to talk to me about last night, right? What you and Simon and Derek have been scurrying around planning for the past few days."

I don't want to imagine the look on my face at that moment. Shock, horror, disbelief—I'm sure it was all there, writ large enough to erase her doubts.

"I d-don't—"

"—know what I'm talking about?" She twisted a loose thread between her fingers and ripped it off, gaze fixed on it. "So what were you going to tell me? Make up a story to throw me off the trail?"

"N-no. I was going to tell you what happened in the crawl space. With Derek. I contacted that ghost again."

"Oh."

Her gaze dropped. As fascinating as my zombie story would normally have been, it wasn't what she'd been hoping to hear. She let the thread fall to the bed.

"So I'm not invited, am I?"

"Th-there's no—"

She held up her hands. "I overheard Simon and Derek arguing about escaping once. Now, with all this talk of transferring you or Derek, and you guys suddenly hanging out together . . ."

"It's not—"

"Last night, I woke up and you were gone. I went downstairs just as you and Derek were sneaking in and I caught enough to know you weren't taking a moonlight stroll."

"Derek isn't running away." Which was true, if not exactly what she meant.

She eased back against the wall again, drawing her knees up. "What if I met the club requirement? Would that snag me an invite?"

"What?"

"Your club. The special kids. The ones with superpowers."

I let out a laugh that sounded more like the yip of a startled poodle. "Superp-powers? I wish. My powers aren't winning me a slot on the Cartoon Network anytime soon . . . except as comic relief. *Ghost Whisperer Junior.* Or *Ghost Screamer*, more like. Tune in, every week, as Chloe Saunders runs screaming from yet another ghost looking for her help."

"Okay, *superpower* might be pushing it. But what if you could shove a kid out of your way with a flick of your fingers? Bet that would come in handy."

I swung out of bed and walked to the dresser. "Sure, but that's not what Derek did. He grabbed me. Believe me, I felt physical contact."

"I'm not talking about Derek. A few days before Brady got shipped out, he and Derek got into it. Or Brady was trying to. Derek wasn't having any of it, so Brady kept razzing him, trying to get a rise, and when he got in Derek's face, Simon flicked his fingers and, *wham,* Brady flew into the wall. I was there. Derek and Simon never touched him. That's why I wanted to see Simon's file."

"Well, as you saw, Simon doesn't have a file. He's here because of Derek. Their dad disappeared and Derek was sent here because of his problem, so they put Simon in the same place."

"How'd their dad disappear?"

I shrugged and pulled out a shirt. "They haven't said much about it. I don't want to push."

A thump. When I looked over my shoulder, Rae had thudded back onto the bed.

"You're too nice, girl," she said. "I'd have been all over them for that story."

I shook my head. "I think I hear Mrs. Talbot—"

"You don't. It's Saturday. We can sleep in, and you aren't getting off that easily. I know Simon's got some magic power, like you. And I'm pretty sure Derek does. That's why they're so tight. That's why Simon's dad took Derek in, I bet."

I looked in the mirror and ran the brush through my hair.

"What makes me so sure of all this?" Rae continued. "Remember when I told you about my diagnosis? How it didn't fit? I didn't tell you the whole story. You didn't read *my* file, did you?"

I slowly turned, brush still raised.

She went on. "According to the report, I got into a fight with my mom and burned her with a lighter. Only I wasn't holding a lighter. I just grabbed her arm and gave her first-degree burns."

"Why didn't you—?"

"Tell you?" she cut in. "I was waiting until I knew you better. Until you'd believe me. But then you figured out you were seeing ghosts and I knew how it would sound. Like a little kid jealous 'cause his friend's going to Disney World—gotta show that he's special, too. And my power isn't like yours. I can't make it happen. It just *does,* when I get mad."

"Like with Tori. You *did* burn her, didn't you?"

She hugged my pillow to her chest. "I think so. But where's the proof? She *felt* like she'd been burned and there was a red mark, but it wasn't like I set her shirt on fire." She grinned. "As fun as *that* might be. So with my mom I lied and said I had been playing with a lighter and, when I went at her, I forgot I was still holding it. No one cared that there *wasn't* a lighter. They see what they want to see. Stick a label on it; medicate it; and, if you're lucky, it'll just go away. Only what we've got doesn't go away."

My brain struggled to take it all in. I knew I should say something, but what? Admit? Deny?

Rae rolled off the bed to her feet, twisted her long curls back, and held out her hand. When I didn't move, she said, "Elastics? Behind you?"

"Right."

I tossed her one. She wrapped it around her ponytail and headed for the door.

"Wait," I said.

She shook her head. "You gotta talk to the guys first."

"I don't—"

She turned to face me. "Yes, you do. You should. Would you want them blabbing your secrets before checking with you? Talk to them. Then get back to me. Not like I'm going anywhere."

thirty-seven

I ATE BREAKFAST WITH TORI. I'm sure, yesterday, she'd been hoping to see me carried from the house, tied to a stretcher, ranting, driven mad after hours bound and gagged in the dark. Yet this morning, she just sat there and ate, eyes forward, expression empty, like she'd given up.

If I'd told the doctors what she'd done, she'd have been booted out, no matter how important her mom was. Maybe, when I came out of the crawl space and didn't tattle, she'd realized how close she'd been to getting transferred. Maybe she'd realized her stunt could have been fatal.

Maybe she even felt bad about it. That was probably too much to hope for, but from the look on her face this morning, any feud between us was over. She'd gotten it out of her system and seen how close she'd come to making a very big mistake. As hard as it was for me to be near her, thinking of what she'd put me through, I wasn't giving her any satisfaction. So I sat down and struggled to eat like nothing was wrong.

Every mouthful of oatmeal I forced down sank to the pit of my stomach and congealed into a lump of cement. Not only did I have to eat with someone who could have gotten me killed but also now I had to figure out what to do about Rae. How would I tell the guys? Derek would blame me for sure.

I was so wrapped up in my thoughts that it wasn't until I was coming back down after my shower and heard the weekend nurse, Ms. Abdo, talking about a "door" and a "new lock" that I remembered our dry run the night before. Had we been caught?

"Dr. Davidoff wants a deadbolt," Mrs. Talbot replied. "I don't know whether they make them for interior doors, but if you can't find one at the hardware store, we'll call Rob to replace the door. After yesterday, Dr. Davidoff doesn't want the kids getting into that crawl space."

The *basement* door. I breathed a sigh of relief and continued down. I reached the bottom just as Simon peeked from the dining room.

"Thought I heard you. Catch." He tossed me an apple. "I know you like the green ones. Derek's been hoarding them." He beckoned me in. "Sit and eat with us. You'll need your energy. It's Saturday and around here, that means all chores, all the time."

As I passed, he leaned down to whisper. "You okay?"

I nodded. He closed the door. I looked at the empty table.

"How's Derek?" I asked, keeping my voice low.

"He's in the kitchen, loading up. I hear you guys had a little adventure last night."

Derek had insisted on telling Simon that contacting the zombie ghosts had been his idea, so if Simon was put out by being excluded, the blame would fall on him. I thought he'd been trying to grab the glory—pretend *he'd* figured out what my ghost wanted. But Simon's expression told me he felt he *had* missed out on something. So I was kind of glad he didn't think I'd been the one who left him sleeping.

As I settled at the table, Derek came in, glass of milk in one hand, juice in the other. Simon reached out for one, but Derek set them both down at his plate with a grunted, "Get your own." Simon pushed to his feet, slapped Derek's back, and sauntered into the kitchen.

"Are you okay?" I whispered.

Derek's gaze shot to the closing kitchen door. He didn't want Simon knowing he'd been sick. I wasn't sure I liked that, and we locked glares, but the set of his jaw told me it wasn't open for discussion.

"I'm fine," he rumbled after a moment. "Tylenol finally kicked in."

His eyes were underscored with dark circles and were faintly bloodshot, but so were mine. He was pale, his acne redder than normal. Tired, but recovering. There was no fever in his eyes and by the way he attacked his oatmeal, he hadn't lost his appetite.

"Do I pass, Dr. Saunders?" he murmured under his breath.

"I guess so."

A grunt as he spooned more brown sugar into his bowl. "Some kind of reaction, like I said." He ate three heaping spoonfuls of porridge. Then, gaze still on his breakfast, he said, "What's wrong?"

"I didn't say a word."

"Something's up. What is it?"

"Nothing."

His head turned, gaze going to mine. "Yeah?"

"Yes."

A snort and he returned to his bowl as Simon came back.

"Anyone see the chore list for this morning?" he said, handing me a glass of orange juice. He sat down and reached for the sugar bowl. Derek took it from him, paused, then spooned more onto his oatmeal. A look passed between them. Simon gulped his orange juice and said, "We're on leaf-raking duty. Van Dop wants the dead leaves from last fall cleared . . ."

As he talked, Derek's gaze lifted to mine again, studying. I glanced away and bit into my apple.

Saturday was indeed chore day. Normally, I'd have been groaning at the thought—and wishing for school instead—but today it worked out perfectly. With Dr. Gill, Ms. Wang, and Miss Van Dop gone, Ms. Abdo out running errands, and Mrs. Talbot doing paperwork, we had the run of the house and I had an excuse for getting Simon outside alone, by offering to help him with the raking while Derek was upstairs changing the bedding.

"You're having second thoughts," Simon said when we were far enough from the house to not be overheard.

"What?"

He bent and retied his sneakers, face down. "About running away. You're afraid to tell Derek because he'll give you a hassle, get up in your face."

"That's not—"

"No, that's okay. I was surprised you offered in the first place. Surprised in a good way but— If you've changed your mind, that's totally cool and I don't blame you."

I continued toward the shed. "I am coming . . . unless *you're* having second thoughts about taking me."

He swung open the shed door and motioned for me to stay as he vanished in its dark depths, dirt and dust swirling in his wake. "I should probably say I don't *need* any help. But honestly?" His words were punctuated by rattles and clanks as he hunted for the rakes. "Though I don't expect trouble, a second pair of eyes would really come in handy if I'm on the run."

"I'd rather be that second set of eyes than sit here waiting for rescue," I said as he emerged holding two rakes.

"Like Derek you mean?"

"No, that wasn't a slam." I shut the shed door and fastened the latch. "Last night he told me why he was staying. Because of what he did. Which I already knew about because I kind of—"

"Read his file?"

"I—I was—"

"Checking up on him after he grabbed you in the basement. That's what he figured. Smart move." He motioned for us to start in the farthest corner, where a layer of decomposing leaves from last year blanketed the ground. "Don't let him razz you about it. He read yours."

I shrugged. "Fair is fair, I guess."

"He read yours *before* you read his. Bet he didn't mention that when you confessed."

"No, he didn't."

We started raking. For at least a minute, Simon said nothing, then he glanced over at me. "I bet he didn't mention how it happened either. The fight, that is."

I shook my head. "He just said the guy didn't pull a gun on him. He wouldn't discuss it."

"It happened last fall. We'd moved to some hick town outside Albany. No offense to small towns, I'm sure they're very nice places to live . . . for some people. Hotbeds of multiculturalism, they are not. But my dad hooked a job in Albany and this was the only place he could snag a sublet before the school year started."

He raked his leaves into the pile I'd started. "I was hanging out behind the school, waiting for Derek to finish talking to the math teacher. They were trying to come up with a special curriculum for him. Small school; not used to guys like Derek. Or, like me, as it turned out."

A mouse scampered from under a tree root, and Simon crouched to squint into the hole, making sure there weren't any more coming out before he raked around it. "I was shooting hoops when these three senior guys came strolling over. They're wearing Docs and beaters, and they're sauntering my way and I smell redneck trouble. I'm not going to bolt, but if they want the hoop, I'll get out of their way, you know?"

A blast of wind scattered the top layer of our pile. He sighed, shoulders slumping. I motioned for him to continue while I tidied it up.

"Only they didn't want the court. They wanted me. Seems one guy's mom worked at this 7-Eleven before it was bought by a Vietnamese family who gave her the boot. This was, like, a year before but, naturally, I must be related to them, right? I pointed out that, shockingly, not all Asians are related and we don't all own convenience stores."

He stopped raking. "When I say I'm not Vietnamese, one guy asks what I am. I say American, but eventually I give them what they want, and say my grandfather came from South Korea. Well, wouldn't you know it, one guy's uncle was killed in the Korean War. If this guy ever took a history class, he slept through it. He thought Koreans declared war on Americans. So I set him straight. And, yeah, I was a bit of a smart-ass about it. My dad always says if I can't learn to keep my mouth shut, I'd better work on my defensive spells. And that day"—he resumed raking, voice dropping—"that day, he was right.

"I'm smart-mouthing but keeping it light, you know? Goofing. Next thing I know, one guy pulls a switchblade. It's closed, though, and I'm staring at it like an idiot wondering what it is. Cell phone? MP3 player? Then, flick, out comes the blade. I tried to make a break for it, but it was too late. Another guy kicks out my feet and down I go. The guy with the blade is standing over me, and I'm readying a knock-back spell when Derek comes ripping around the corner. He grabs the guy with the knife, throws him aside, punches a second guy, and the third runs. Second guy gets up—he's fine—runs after his buddy. But the first guy? The one he threw off me?"

"Doesn't get up," I whispered.

Simon speared a leaf on the tines of his rake. "Derek was right. There was no gun. But you know what?" He lifted his gaze to mine. "If a guy came at Derek with a gun, he'd have kept his cool and handled it smart. But *he* wasn't the one in danger. I was. With Derek, that's a whole different thing. It's in his nature, my dad says, the—" He started raking hard, tearing through new grass and dirt. "So that's how it happened. I was a smart-ass and I couldn't back down from a bunch of rednecks and now Derek . . ."

He trailed off, and I knew Derek wasn't the only one who blamed himself for what had happened.

"Anyway," he said after a moment, "you didn't bring me out here to talk about that, and if I keep yapping, Derek will track us down. I get the feeling this isn't something you want to discuss with him."

"It's not."

I told him about Rae. "I didn't know what to say and that only made it worse, but she caught me completely off guard. Now Derek's going to think I let something slip or I was chatting with my girlfriend, telling her my secrets, which I didn't do, I swear—"

"I know. You aren't like that." He leaned on his rake. "Rae's right about Brady. I used a knock-back spell on him. It was careless and stupid, but after what happened with those other guys, I wanted to be quicker on the draw, you know? When I saw Brady was trying to get into it with Derek, I just . . . reacted."

"You wanted to diffuse the situation."

"Yeah. And if Rae caught you guys coming in last night, that's Derek's fault. He should have been on the lookout. He's got the ears and the—" he stopped, "the eyes. He can see pretty good in the dark, better than us. Normally, he'd have noticed Rae, but he must have been busy thinking about the escape."

Not preoccupied—sick and feverish. But I couldn't say that.

Simon went on. "He's been in a mood, too. Crankier than usual. He broke our shower. Did you hear about that?" He shook his head. "Snapped the handle right off, so I had to tell Talbot it had been loose. But as for Rae, we're going to have to tell him."

"Do you think she's one of us? A supernatural?"

"Could be half-demon. If she is, though, what does that mean, for us, being here? Four out of five kids? Maybe Liz, too, if she's a shaman? That's no coincidence. It can't be." He paused, thinking. "We'll worry about that later. For now, I'm more concerned with her knowing about our plan."

"She doesn't just know. She wants to sign up."

He cursed under his breath.

"She'd be useful," I said. "She's way more street smart than me."

"And me. It's just . . ." He shrugged. "I'm sure Rae's cool, but I wouldn't have argued about it just being the two of us."

He glanced over at me. My heart started pounding double time.

"There's a lot I want to talk to you about." He touched the back of my hand, leaning so close I could feel his breath against my hair.

"What's this about Rae?" a voice demanded. We turned to see Derek crossing the lawn.

Simon swore. "Anyone ever tell you your sense of timing really sucks."

"That's why I don't play the drums. Now what's up?"

I told him.

thirty-eight

SIMON DOUBTED RAE HAD supernatural powers. There were fire half-demons, but by fifteen she should have been doing more than leaving marks that barely qualified as first-degree burns. He didn't think she was lying. She was just too eager to believe.

I suspected he was right. Given up at birth, displaced by younger siblings, tossed into Lyle House with strangers and forgotten, it would mean so much to Rae to be special. I'd seen it in her face that morning, glowing with excitement.

The person slowest to dismiss the idea was Derek. He didn't say he believed Rae was a half-demon, but his silence said he was considering the possibility. Last night was still bugging him—and me—our failure to find or dismiss a connection between us, Samuel Lyle, and those supernatural bodies in the cellar. If Rae *was* a half-demon and Liz might be a shaman, then the possibility we were here by chance plummeted.

You could argue that a group home for disturbed teens isn't an unusual place to find teenage supernaturals, especially those who don't know what they are. Our symptoms could be massaged to fit known psychiatric disorders, and, since everyone knew it was impossible to contact the dead or to burn people with your bare hands or toss a kid aside and break his neck—the obvious solution would be that we were mentally ill. Hallucinating, obsessed with fire, uncontrollably violent . . .

But there was nothing paranormal about Tori's mood swings. Peter had apparently been in for some kind of anxiety disorder and that didn't fit the pattern either.

Still, I couldn't shake the feeling I was missing something, that the connection was there and my brain was too distracted by other problems to see it. I suspected Derek felt the same.

Whether Rae was a supernatural or not, we all agreed, she should come with us. To Derek, it wasn't so much a matter of *should we let her come* as *do we dare let her stay*. What if she retaliated by telling the nurses? I couldn't see that, but after we were gone, if they came down hard on her, she'd cave before Derek did.

Derek's only condition was that we'd keep the details about our powers and our plans vague, at least for now.

I told Rae, and then Derek dropped the bomb none of us expected. We had to leave that night.

Since it was Saturday, we'd have all day to prepare, and chores gave us an excuse for poking around the house, gathering supplies. Tonight Miss Van Dop was off and the weekend nurse was much less likely to realize we were up to something. It was better to go now, before anything else went wrong.

Once I got past the initial "OMG, you mean *tonight*!" panic, I had to agree the sooner we left, the better.

So, while Rae stood guard cleaning the girls bathroom, I packed.

I'd packed for camp many times but, in comparison, this was agonizing. For every item I put in, I had to consider how badly I needed it, how much room and weight it would add, and whether I'd be better off picking it up on the road.

The brush was out, and the comb was in. Deodorant, definitely in. My iPod and lipgloss might not be essential for daily life, but they were tiny enough to keep. Soap, a toothbrush, and toothpaste would need to be bought later because I couldn't afford to have anyone notice them missing from the bathroom now.

Next came clothing. It was still cool, especially at night. Layering would be the key. I packed as Aunt Lauren taught me when we'd spent a week in France. I'd wear a sweatshirt, long-sleeved pullover, and T-shirt with jeans. In the bag, I'd have two more T-shirts, another pullover, and three pairs of socks and underwear.

Would that be enough? How long would we be on the run?

I'd been avoiding that question since I'd first offered to go. Simon and Derek seemed to think we'd find their dad pretty quickly. Simon had spells and just needed to travel around Buffalo, casting them.

It sounded easy. Too easy?

I'd seen the looks in their eyes. Derek's barely concealed worry. Simon's stubborn conviction. When pressed, they'd both admitted that, if they couldn't find their dad, there were other supernaturals they could contact.

If it took longer than a few days, I had a bank card and the money from my dad. Simon and Derek had a bank card, too, with emergency funds their dad had stashed for them, at least a thousand dollars each, they thought. We'd need to withdraw as much as we could immediately, before anyone knew we were gone and started tracking us. Derek would keep his card and cash in case he needed it, but we'd have Simon's money plus mine. That would get us through.

Whatever happened, we'd be fine. Another shirt, though, might not be a bad idea.

Shirt . . . That reminded me . . .

I shoved my backpack under the bed, slipped down to Tori's room. The door was ajar. Through it, I could see that Tori's bed was empty. I gave a gentle push.

"Hello?" She sprang up from Rae's old bed, ripping out her earbuds. "Knock much?"

"I—I thought you were downstairs."

"Oh, so you were going to take advantage of that, were you? Set your little scheme in motion?"

I opened the door and stepped inside. "What scheme?"

"The one you and your gang have been planning. I've seen you skulking around, plotting against me."

"Huh?"

She wound the earbud wire around her MP3 player, yanking it tight, as if imagining it going around my neck instead. "You think I'm stupid? You're not as sweet and innocent as you seem, Chloe Saunders. First, you seduce my boyfriend."

"Boy— *Seduce?*"

"Then you bat your baby blues at tall, dark, and gruesome, and next thing you know, he's trailing you like a lost puppy."

"*What?*"

"And now, to make sure *everyone* in the house is against me, you pull in Rachelle. Don't think I missed your powwow this morning."

"And you think we're . . . plotting against *you*?" I sputtered a laugh and leaned back against the dresser. "How do you get that ego through the door, Tori? I'm not interested in revenge. I'm not interested in you at all. Get it?"

She slid to the edge of the bed, feet touching down, eyes narrowing. "You think you're clever, don't you?"

I slumped back against the dresser with an exaggerated sigh. "Don't you ever quit? You're like a broken record. Me, me, me. The world revolves around Tori. No wonder even your mom thinks you're a spoiled—"

I stopped myself, but it was too late. For a moment, Tori froze in mid-rise. Then, slowly, she crumpled back onto the bed.

"I didn't mean—"

"What do you want, Chloe?" She tried to put some bite in the words, but they came out quiet, weary.

"Liz's shirt," I said after a moment. "Rae says you borrowed a green hoodie from Liz."

She waved toward the dresser. "It's in there. Middle drawer. Mess it up and you can refold everything."

And that was it. No "Why do you want it?" or even "Did she call asking for it?" Her gaze had already gone distant. Doped up? Or beyond caring?

I found the shirt. An emerald green Gap hoodie. A personal effect.

I shut the drawer and straightened.

"You got what you came for," Tori said. "Now run along and play with your friends."

I walked to the door, grasped the handle, then turned to face her.

"Tori?"

"What?"

I wanted to wish her luck. I wanted to tell her I hoped she got what she was looking for, what she needed. I wanted to tell her I was sorry.

With everything that went on at Lyle House, and the discovery that at least three of us didn't belong here, it was easy to forget that some kids did. Tori had problems. Expecting her to behave like any normal teenage girl, then shunning and insulting her when she didn't, was like mocking the slow kids at school. She needed help and support and consideration, and she hadn't gotten it from anyone but Liz.

I clutched Liz's shirt in my hands and tried to think of something to say, but anything I did say would come out wrong, condescending.

So I said the only thing I could. "Good-bye."

thirty-nine

I STUFFED LIZ'S HOODIE INTO my bag. It took up more room than I could afford, but I needed it. It could answer a question I really needed to answer . . . just as soon as I worked up the courage to ask.

When Derek had announced we'd be leaving that night, my first thought had been *there's not enough time*, but there was too much time. We did homework we'd never submit, helped Mrs. Talbot think up meals we'd never eat, all the while fighting the urge to slip away and plan some more. Both Rae and Tori had noticed my "powwows" with the guys, and if we kept it up, the nurses might suspect it was more than teen hormones at work.

I warned the others about Tori, but no one seemed concerned. It was like I told her—she was totally out of our minds. Insignificant. I wondered whether that hurt her most of all.

We spent the evening watching a movie. For once, I paid so little attention that if I was asked for a log line ten minutes after the credits rolled, I couldn't have given one.

Derek didn't join us. Simon said his brother was wiped from the night before and wanted to rest up so he'd be clear-headed for helping us tonight. I wondered whether his fever was coming back.

When Mrs. Talbot asked after Derek, Simon said he "wasn't feeling great." She tut-tutted and withdrew to play cards with Ms. Abdo, not even going upstairs to check on him. That's how it always was with Derek. The nurses seemed to leave him to his own devices, like his size made them forget he was still a kid. Or maybe, given his file and his diagnosis, they wanted as little contact with him as possible.

Did he notice how they treated him? I'm sure he did. Nothing escaped Derek, and I suspected it only reinforced that he needed to be in here.

As the movie droned on, I fretted about him. He'd been so careful not to let Simon know he'd been sick. If Simon could tell he "wasn't feeling great," that had to mean he was too sick to hide it.

I slipped from the media room, got four Tylenol and a glass of water, and took it upstairs.

I tapped on the door. No answer. Light shone under it, but he could have fallen asleep reading.

Or be too sick to answer.

I rapped again, a little louder.

"Derek? It's me. I brought water and Tylenol."

Still nothing. I touched the doorknob, cold under my fingertips. He was probably asleep. Or ignoring me.

"I'll leave it here."

As I bent to set the glass on the floor, the door opened, just enough for me to see Derek's bare foot. I straightened. He was in his boxers again, and my gaze shot to the safety of his face, but not before noticing the sheen of sweat on his chest. Sweat plastered his hair around his face, and his eyes were feverish, lips parted, breath coming hard, labored.

"Are y-you—?" I began.

"Be fine."

He ran his tongue over his parched lips and blinked hard, as if struggling to focus. When I held out the glass, he reached for it through the gap and took a long gulp.

"Thanks."

I handed him the Tylenol. "Are you sure you're okay?"

"Good enough."

He braced the door with his foot and reached around his back, scratching.

"Maybe you should take a bath," I said. "A cold bath, for your fever. Baking soda would help the itching. I could get—"

"Nah, I'm okay."

"If you need anything . . ."

"Just rest. Go on back down before someone notices."

I headed for the stairs.

"Chloe?"

I glanced back. He was leaning out the door.

"Nothing to Simon, okay? About how bad I am?"

"He knows you're not feeling well. You really should tell—"

"I'm fine."

"You're not fine. He's going to figure that out—"

"He won't. I'll take care of it."

He withdrew and the door clicked shut.

That night in bed, Rae couldn't keep quiet. She wanted to talk about her backpack and what she'd packed and whether she'd made the right choices and should she take anything else . . .

I hated to shush her. She was as excited as a kid getting ready for her first overnight camp, which was weird because after what had happened to her friend, Rae should know that life on the street wasn't going to be some fabulous, unchaperoned adventure.

I suppose, to her, this wasn't the same thing. She was going with Simon and me, and there were few kids less likely to turn Bonnie and Clyde. This wasn't an act of delinquency; it was a mission. And, besides, like Simon and Derek said, old rules didn't apply to us anymore.

" 'Cause we're special." She gave a bubbling laugh. "That sounds so lame. But it's what everyone wants, isn't it? To be special."

Do they? There were a lot of things I wanted to be. Smart, sure. Talented, definitely. Pretty? Okay, I'll admit it. But special?

I'd spent too much of my life being special. The rich girl who lost her mother. The new kid in class. The drama major who didn't want to be an actor. For me, special meant different, and not in a good way. I'd wanted to be normal, and I guess the irony is that, the whole time I was dreaming of a normal life, I already had one . . . or a whole lot closer to it than I'd ever have again.

But now I watched Rae lying on her stomach, matches in hand, struggling to light one with her bare fingertips, the tip of her tongue sticking through her teeth, determination bordering on desperation, and I could see how badly she wanted a supernatural power. I had one, and I cared so little for it that I'd gladly give it to her.

It was like in school, when other girls drooled over designer jeans, counting the babysitting hours until they could buy a pair, and I sat there wearing mine, four other pairs in the closet at home, no more meaningful to me than a pair of no-names. I felt guilty for not appreciating what I had.

But necromancy wasn't a pair of expensive jeans, and I was pretty sure my life would be better without it. Definitely easier. And yet, if I woke tomorrow and couldn't talk to the dead, would I be disappointed?

"I think it's getting warm," she said, pinching the match head between her fingers.

I crawled out of bed. "Let me see."

"No." She pulled it back. "Not yet. Not until I'm sure."

Was Rae half-demon? Derek said they did burn things with their hands. By her age, Rae should have been lighting that match no problem. But then he'd never heard of a necromancer who woke up one morning and suddenly started seeing ghosts everywhere. Usually it was a gradual process.

Wasn't that typical for development in general? A book might say "at twelve, children begin a process of puberty, ending at eighteen," but that's a generalization. You get girls like me and guys like Derek, neither of us fitting the norm.

Maybe Rae's supernatural powers were late blooming, like me and my period. And maybe my powers were like Derek's puberty, the changes hitting all at once.

Apparently half-demons had a human mother and a demon father, who'd taken human form to impregnate her. That fit Rae's history, with a mother who'd given her up at birth, no father in the picture.

"Smoke!" she squealed before slapping a hand over her mouth. She waved the match. "I saw smoke. I swear it. Yes, I know, I need a life, but it was just so cool. Here, watch."

She pulled another match from the book.

Was Rae a half-demon?

I really hoped so.

forty

RAE'S WATCH ALARM was set to go off at three. According to Derek, that was the quietest time of night, when we'd be least likely to be spotted. At 2:45 we shut the alarm off, and by 2:50 we were out of our room, backpacks in hand.

When I eased our door shut, the hall fell to pitch-black. The ticking of the grandfather clock guided us to the stairs.

I swore this time *every* step creaked, but as hard as I strained for sounds of Tori or Mrs. Talbot stirring, I heard only the clock.

At the bottom of the stairs, the moon peeked in around the drawn curtains, lifting the darkness just enough so I could make out chairs and tables before I crashed into them. I was turning into the hall when a dark shape stepped from the shadows. I bit back a yelp and scowled, ready to blast Derek. But it was Simon, and one look at his ashen face killed the words in my throat.

"What's—?" I began.

"Is Derek with you?"

"No, wh—"

"He's gone." He lifted something that glinted and it took a moment for me to recognize it as Derek's watch. "He had the alarm set for 2:45. When it went off, I woke up and found it on my pillow. His bed was empty."

Rae's fingers closed on my arm. "But Derek's not coming, right? Let's just go."

"Did he say anything to you last night?" I whispered.

Simon shook his head. "He was asleep. I didn't wake him."

"Maybe he's in the bathroom," Rae whispered. "Come on, guys, we have to—"

"I checked the bathrooms. And the spare room. And the kitchen. Something's wrong. Something happened to him."

"If it did, would he have left you the watch? Maybe . . ." I struggled for a reasonable explanation, fighting the rising panic that said there wasn't one. "Maybe he's afraid we'll try to drag him along at the last minute and we'll wake someone up."

"Speaking of which . . ." Rae said with a pointed look at the ceiling.

Simon and I looked at each other and I knew, as logical as my explanation was, Derek would know Simon couldn't leave without making sure he was okay.

"Guys . . ." Rae said.

"You two go," said Simon. "I'll find—"

"No," I said. "I will."

"But—"

I lifted my hand to cut him short. "What good will it do if I get away and you don't? It's your dad. You know how to find him."

Simon's gaze slid to the side.

"What?" Rae turned to me. "Forget Derek, Chloe. He's not coming, remember? He'll be fine. We have to go."

"I'll find him and come after you," I said. "We'll meet behind the factory, okay?"

Simon shook his head. "He's my responsibility—"

"Right now, your *dad* is your responsibility. You can't help Derek—or me—if you can't find him."

Silence.

"Okay?"

His brows knitted, and I could tell that it *wasn't* okay, that he hated to run.

"You have to go," I said.

He took my hand, wrapped his fingers around it, and squeezed. I'm sure I turned as red as if he'd scooped me up in a kiss.

"Be careful?" he said.

"I will. I'll find him, then I'll find you."

"I'll be waiting."

Simon took my backpack. It'd be a dead giveaway if I was caught carrying it. If I stashed it someplace, I might not get a chance to retrieve it.

We had the security code—Derek had written it out for us, together with instructions and hand-drawn maps. I could take that as proof that he hadn't planned to be here when we left, but I knew it was just Derek being Derek, leaving nothing to chance.

So why take off and risk Simon not going? My last memory of Derek flashed past—standing in his bedroom doorway, bathed in sweat, barely able to focus—and I knew what had happened.

If Simon saw him like that, he'd know how sick Derek was. If Simon knew, Simon would stay. No question. So Derek had done the only thing he could—holed up someplace, left the alarm on, and prayed Simon would go. A slim chance versus no chance.

So where was he? I headed to the basement first. The door was closed, light off, but he wouldn't leave any sign if he was hiding. The laundry room was empty. The door to the closet was locked.

Last night, when we'd gone on our walk, he'd gulped down the cold air. When we'd returned, his fever seemed gone and I'd chalked it up to the Tylenol kicking in, but maybe the cold air had been enough. If he was desperate for a quick fix, he'd go outside, in hopes of cooling down enough to see Simon off.

I stepped onto the back porch. The quarter moon had slid behind clouds and it was as dark as the upstairs hall. I could make out the glimmer of lights at a neighbor's, but the towering trees blocked all but that faint glow.

My gaze swept the black yard, seeing only the pale box that I knew was the shed. It was colder than the night before, and my breath hung in the air. The only sound was the creak of branches, as steady and monotonous as the ticking of the grandfather clock.

I took three tentative strides across the deck. By the time I climbed down the steps to the concrete pad, I could make out more pale shapes in the yard—the bench, a lawn chair, the garden angel, and a soccer-ball-sized blob near the shed.

An engine revved and I froze, but it was only a car passing. Another two slow steps. I glanced over my shoulder and considered dashing back in for a flashlight, but Simon had taken the only one I knew about.

I peered around. My lips parted to whisper Derek's name, then closed. Would he answer? Or hide?

When I drew closer to the presumed ball, I saw it was a big white sneaker. Derek's. I scooped it up, looking about wildly now.

A blast of wind struck me, so cold it made my eyes water. I rubbed the icy tip of my nose as the wind moaned through the trees. Then the wind died down . . . and the moaning continued, a long, low sound that made the back of my neck prickle.

I turned slowly. The sound stopped. Then came a stifled cough, and as I wheeled toward it, I saw a white sock peeking from behind the shed.

I dashed over. Derek was there, deep in the shadows, on all fours, his head and upper body barely visible. The stink of sweat rolled off him, and the breeze brought a sharp, bitter smell that made the back of my throat constrict, reflexively gagging.

His body tensed as he retched, a dry, ragged heave.

"Derek?" I whispered. "It's Chloe."

He went rigid. "Go away." The words were a guttural growl, barely intelligible.

I stepped closer, dropping my voice another notch. "Simon's gone. I convinced him to go on ahead while I found you."

His back arched, arms stretched out, pale fingers digging into the soil. A low moan, cut short by a grunt.

"You found me. Now go."

"Do you really think I'd leave you like this?" I took another step forward. The stink of vomit made me clap my hand to my nose. I switched to breathing through my mouth. "If you're throwing up, that's more than a fever. You need—"

"Go!" The word was a snarl and I staggered back.

His head dropped. Another moan, this one ending in a high-pitched sound, almost like a whimper. He wore a T-shirt, bare muscles bunching as he gripped the ground again. His arms darkened, as if a shadow passed over them, then reappeared, pale against the surrounding shadow.

"Derek, I—"

His back arched, stretching so high I could see the rigid line of his spine, T-shirt pulled tight, muscles writhing and rippling. Then he sagged, his panting breaths as ragged as the rustling leaves.

"Please. Go." The words were a deep mumble, like he wasn't opening his mouth.

"You need help—"

"No!"

"Simon, then. I'm getting Simon. I'll be right—"

"No!"

He twisted and I caught a glimpse of his face, contorted, misshapen . . . wrong. He whipped his head down before I could process what I'd seen.

He gagged, the sound horrible and raw, like he was coughing up his insides. His back shot up again, limbs stretching to the very limits, bones crackling. His arms went dark, then lightened, the muscles and tendons rippling. The moon chose that moment to peek from the cloud and when his arms darkened, I could see it was hair sprouting, just enough to break the surface, then sliding back under his skin. And his hands . . . His fingers were long and twisted like talons, digging into the earth as his back arched.

In my mind, I heard Simon again. "Guys like Derek have . . . physical enhancements, you might say. Extra strong, as you saw. Better senses, too. That kind of thing."

That kind of thing.

Then my own voice asking lightly, "I'm not going to run into any werewolves or vampires, am I?"

And Simon's answer, coupled with a laugh. "That'd be cool."

Not an answer at all. Avoiding a reply he couldn't give.

Derek convulsed, his head flying back, jaw clenched, an awful moaning howl hissing through his teeth. Then his head whipped down and he gagged, strings of saliva dripping.

"Derek?"

He retched, his whole body racked with heaves. When they subsided, I inched forward. He tilted his head away.

"Is there anything I can do?"

A voice inside my head said, "Sure. Run for your life!" But it was a small warning, not even serious, really, because there was no question of running. This wasn't a matinee monster. Even now, with hair sprouting on his arms, fingers twisted into claws, when he looked away and growled at me to leave, I knew that whatever was happening, he was still Derek.

"Is there anything I can do?"

A ridiculous question. I could imagine the response he'd make any other time—the curl of his lip, the roll of his eyes.

But after one halfhearted "go away," he crouched there, head turned, body trembling, each breath a rasp ending in a quaver.

"Don't." His fingers dug into the ground, arms stiffening, then relaxing. "Go."

"I can't leave you here. If there's anything I can do . . ."

"Don't." A sharp intake of breath, then he expelled the words. "Don't go."

His head lifted my way, just enough for me to see one green eye, wide with terror.

His arms and legs went rigid, back shooting up as he heaved. Vomit sprayed the grass, a fresh wave with every spasm. The sickly smell filled the air.

And I sat there, doing nothing, because there was nothing I could do. My brain raced through ideas, discarding each as fast as it came. I inched over and put my hand on his arm, feeling the coarse hair push through red-hot skin that writhed and pulsed. That was all I could do—stay and tell him I was there.

Finally, with one last heave, one last spray of vomit dappling the fence three feet away, it stopped. Just stopped.

The muscles under my hand went still, the coarse hair receded. Slowly, he relaxed, his back dropping, hands releasing their grip on the earth. He crouched there, panting, hair hanging around his face.

Then he slumped onto his side, hands going over his face, fingers still long, misshapen, the nails thick, like claws. He curled up on his side, knees drawn in, and moaned.

"Should I—? Simon. Should I get Simon? Will he know what to—?"

"No." The word was hoarse, guttural, as if his vocal cords weren't quite human.

"It's over," he said after a minute. "I think. Pretty sure." He rubbed his face, still shielded behind his hands. "Shouldn't have happened. Not yet. Not for years."

In other words, he knew perfectly well what he was, he just hadn't expected the . . . transformation until he was older. I felt a spark of anger that he'd misled me, made Simon lie to me, but I couldn't sustain it, not after what I'd seen, not sitting there, watching him, shirt soaked with sweat as he struggled to breathe, his body shaking with exhaustion and pain.

"Go," he whispered. "I'll be fine now."

"I'm not—"

"*Chloe*," he snapped, the old Derek back in his voice. "Go. Help Simon. Tell him I'm fine."

"No."

"Chloe . . ." He drew my name out in a low growl.

"Five minutes. I want to make sure you're okay."

He grunted, but settled into silence, relaxing onto the grass.

"See, you *did* rip out of your clothes," I said, trying to keep my tone light. "Hope you didn't like that shirt, 'cause it's toast."

It was a weak joke, but he said, "Least I didn't turn green."

"No, just . . ." I was going to say "hairy," but I couldn't get the word out, couldn't wrap my head around what I'd seen.

The back door banged. Derek shot up, his hands falling from his face. His nose looked crushed, wide and flat, cheekbones jutting as if rising to meet it, his brows thick and heavy. Not monstrous, more like an artist's reconstruction of Neanderthal man.

I tore my gaze away and crawled toward the corner of the shed. He caught my leg.

"I'll be careful," I whispered. "I'm just getting a look."

I slid on my belly, creeping to the corner and peeking around it. A flashlight beam swept the yard.

"A woman," I whispered, as low as I could. "I think it's Rae—no, too skinny. Ms. Abdo, maybe?"

He tugged my ankle. My jeans had hiked up, and his hand was wrapped around bare skin above my sock. I could feel his palm, rough, like the pads on a dog's feet.

"Go," he whispered. "I'll boost you over the fence. Climb the next one and—"

The flashlight beam cut a swath across the back of the yard.

"Who's out there?" The voice was high, sharp, with a faint accent.

"Dr. Gill," I whispered to Derek. "What's she—?"

"Never mind. Go!"

"I know someone's out here," she said. "I heard you."

I glanced at Derek, his face still deformed. Dr. Gill couldn't find him like this.

I grabbed the shoe of his that I'd dropped, and kicked off one of my own, and that confused him enough for me to wrench from his grasp and dart to the side fence, squeezing between it and the shed. At the last second, he scrambled up and lunged at me, but I was wedged in too far to reach, and he couldn't follow.

"Chloe! Get back here! Don't you dare—"

I kept going.

forty-one

I SQUEEZED THROUGH THE GAP between the fence and shed, with Derek's shoe clutched in one hand, while the other tugged the shirt from my jeans, and mussed my hair. When I reached the end of the shed, I peeked out. Dr. Gill had her back to me, her flashlight scanning the other side of the yard.

I darted behind the shrubs and continued along the fence until I reached the porch. Then I crouched in the bushes there, daubed dirt on my cheek, and stumbled out, twigs crackling.

"D-Dr. Gill." I fumbled to shove my shirt back into my jeans. "I—I was just out g-getting some air."

I hopped on one foot, trying to put on Derek's shoe.

"I don't think that's yours, Chloe," she said as she approached, flashlight in my eyes.

I shielded my face from the light and lifted the shoe, squinting at it. Then I let out a nervous laugh. "Whoops. Guess I grabbed the wrong one when I came outside."

"Where is he?"

"Who?" I squeaked.

She pointed at the shoe. "Derek."

"Derek? Is this his?" I cast a surreptitious glance over my shoulder, into the bushes, drawing her attention there. "I—I haven't seen Derek since dinner. Is h-he out here, too?"

"Oh, I'm sure he is. Long gone, I suppose, with Simon and Rae. Making their escape while you stand guard and provide a diversion."

"Wh-what?" That time the stammer wasn't faked. "E-escape? N-no. Derek and I were . . ." I gestured at the bushes. "He knew the code so we came outside to be alone and . . . you know."

She stepped closer, beam right in my eyes. "Pick up where you left off Friday afternoon?"

"Right." I tugged down my shirt and tried to look embarrassed.

"Do you really think I'm going to buy that, Chloe? Girls like you wouldn't give boys like Derek Souza the time of day, much less roll around in bushes and crawl spaces with them."

My head shot up. "B-but you caught us. Friday. You're the one who said—"

"I know what I said, Chloe. And I know what you were really doing in that crawl space. I found your new friends."

I stood, feet rooted, unable to believe what I was hearing.

"What did they tell you?" Her fingers went around my arm. "They were his, weren't they? Samuel Lyle's subjects." She leaned toward me, eyes glittering, as feverish as Derek's but with a glimmer of madness behind them. "Did they tell you his secrets? His discoveries? I'll make sure no one knows you ran away. I'll say I found you asleep in the TV room. Just tell me everything those ghosts said."

"I—I can't talk to ghosts."

I tried to pull away, but her fingers clamped down tighter. I went limp, as if giving in, then threw myself in the other direction. Her hand fell from my arm, but I'd pulled too hard and stumbled, off balance. She plunged toward me. I dove, hitting the ground. As I clambered out of her way, a dark shape vaulted over the deck railing.

Dr. Gill only had time to see a shadow passing over her. She turned, mouth opening. Derek landed right in front of her. Her arms flew up, and she let out a shriek, falling back, but she was still in mid-turn and tripped over her own feet. As she went down, she fumbled for something in her pocket. Derek dove and pinned her arm as she pulled out a two-way radio. It flew onto the grass. Her skull smacked into the cement pad.

I ran forward. Derek was already crouching at her side, checking her pulse.

"She's fine," he said, exhaling with relief. "Just unconscious. Come on. Before she wakes up."

His fingers closed around my arm. Dirty, but very human fingers, his face and hands back to normal, the ripped and sweaty shirt the only sign of his ordeal. I brushed him off, jogged over to his shoe and picked it up, then turned to see him holding the sneaker I'd discarded.

"Trade?"

We pulled our shoes on.

"Simon's waiting at the factory," I said. "We have to warn him. They know about the escape."

He pushed me toward the side fence. "The road won't be safe. Cut through the yards."

I glanced over my shoulder.

"I'm right behind you," he said. "Now *go*!"

At the first fence, I started climbing, but I was too slow for Derek, who grabbed me and swung me over, then vaulted like it was a hurdle. Two doors down, the wail of a siren sent us diving behind a child's playhouse.

"Police?" I whispered.

"Can't tell."

After a moment, I said, "Dr. Gill knows about the bodies. When I raised them, she must not have been holed up in her office like we thought. She knows I can contact the dead, and about Samuel Lyle, and—"

"Later."

He was right. I squeezed the thought from my head and concentrated on the siren. It whipped past, heading back the way we came, then disappeared.

"Did it stop at the house?" I asked.

He shook his head. "I can still hear it. Now go."

According to Derek, there were seven backyards between Lyle House and the end of the block. Trust him to have counted. We were racing through the fifth when his hand shot out like a railway guard and I plowed into it. When I turned, he had his head cocked, listening. Ten seconds passed. I plucked at his shirt, but he ignored me for another ten. Then he lowered his head and whispered, "I hear a car idling. Someone's out there."

"Where?"

An impatient wave. "*There.* On the street we need to cross." He held up a finger. "Footsteps. Someone's talking. A woman. She's whispering. I can't make it out."

"Do you recognize the voice?"

He shook his head. "Stay here. I'll get closer, see if that helps."

He loped closer to the house, stopping behind a cluster of bushes.

I looked around. I was standing in the middle of the yard, exposed to anyone who heard a noise and glanced out the window. His spot looked a whole lot safer. When I approached, he whirled, pinning me with a glare.

"Sorry," I whispered, and moved slower, quieter.

He waved me back. When I didn't stop, he glared again, then turned away. I crept up behind him and went still. His head moved slowly, tracking the voices, I presumed. But when his head swiveled my way, I noticed the lift of his chin, the flare of his nostrils, and realized he was sniffing the air.

When he noticed me watching, I got a full-blown scowl.

"Can you recognize the, uh . . . ?"

"Scents." He spat the word. "Yes, I can track scents. Like a dog."

"I didn't mean—"

"Whatever."

He looked away again, scanning the fence line. "I suppose you figured out what I am."

"A werewolf."

I tried to say it casually, but I wasn't sure I succeeded. I didn't want to sound freaked out because that was exactly what he expected—why he hadn't told me the truth. I told myself it was no different than being a necromancer or a sorcerer or a half-demon. But it was.

As the silence stretched, I knew I should say something. If he'd told me he was a half-demon, I'd be peppering him with questions, and when I didn't now, my silence damned him as something different than us, something less natural, something . . . worse.

"So what . . . happened back there? You were, uh . . ."

"Changing." He stepped to the right, leaning out for a better listen, then pulled back. "It's not supposed to start until I'm at least eighteen. That's what Dad thought. Last night, the itching, the fever, the muscle spasms—that must have been a warning. I should have figured it out."

His head tilted as a breeze fluttered past. He took a deep breath, then shook his head. "No one I recognize." He pointed to the back of the yard. "We'll climb the back fence, go through that way, and loop around. Hopefully, they'll have driven off by then."

We dashed over the rear fence, and through the next yard to the drive. Derek scanned the street, looking and listening and, I guess, sniffing, then waved me across the street. We slipped into the first yard and continued heading east, cutting through yards.

When we reached the road, I saw the car he'd been talking about. It was a silver SUV, a block down. The headlights were off, but someone stood at the driver's window, leaning in, as if talking.

"We'll have to make a run for it," Derek said. "Hope they don't notice us."

"You think they're looking for us?"

"No, but—"

"Then if we run, it'll look suspicious."

"It's three-thirty in the morning. We're going to look suspicious anyway." He looked at the car for a moment. "Fine. But any sign of trouble? Follow my lead."

"Yes, sir."

forty-two

WE CLIMBED THE FENCE under a weeping willow, letting its branches and shadows hide us. Then Derek positioned me on his left, away from the car. From this distance, they'd only see what looked like a grown man and maybe a woman beside him.

"We're going to walk and talk, okay? Normal couple, late night walk. Not hiding anything."

I nodded, and his hand closed around mine. We moved quickly to the sidewalk, then slowed as we cut to the curb.

"Okay, talk," he murmured.

"So when you . . . change . . ."

A short laugh, this obviously not being what he'd had in mind. But I was keeping my voice low, and if I couldn't hear them talking, they wouldn't hear more than the murmur of my voice.

"You change into . . ." I struggled to think of the right word for the image that came to mind—a Hollywood werewolf, half human, half beast.

"A wolf." He steered us to the left, away from the car.

"Wolf?"

"You know. Large wild canine. Commonly seen in zoos."

"You change into . . . ? But that's not—" I stopped myself.

"Physically possible?" Another short laugh. "Yeah, my body was screaming the same thing. No idea how it works. I guess I'll find out later. Much later, if I'm lucky. We're heading for the street to the left. The factory is just up—"

He stopped short, turning sharply at the same moment that the headlights from the idling car flicked on. His hand tightened around mine and he broke into a run, dragging me along.

"They spotted us," he said.

"But they aren't looking for us."

"Yes, they are."

He yanked my arm, propelling me toward the next yard. As we neared the fence, he grabbed me around the waist and threw me over. I hit the ground on all fours, leaped up, and ran for the nearest cover—a metal shed.

Derek dove in behind me and, for a moment, I just stood there, leaning my blazing cheek against the cool metal, gulping the icy air. Then I straightened.

"How—?"

"I heard them say 'It's them' and 'Call Marcel.' "

"Marcel? Isn't that Dr. Davidoff's name?"

"Yeah, and something tells me it's not common enough to be a coincidence."

"But how—"

He clamped his hand over my mouth and I tasted dirt. He leaned down to my ear. "They're circling the block. I hear voices. They must have the windows down, listening for us."

But who were they? Where had they come from? Simon and Rae hadn't been gone more than forty minutes. How had they gotten here so fast?

"Tori," I whispered.

"What?"

"Tori found out about our escape. That's why she was so quiet. She didn't give up; she was—"

"Doesn't matter. They're heading down that road," Derek said, pointing. "Come on."

He prodded me in the opposite direction.

"The factory is at the end. We just need to make it that far. Run on the grass—it's quieter."

We raced along the strip between the sidewalk and the road, our shoes slapping the driveway pavement, then silent on the grass between. We were three houses from the end, the factory looming, when Derek let out a curse. Within three strides, I knew why: there was an eight-foot-high chain-link fence around the factory parking lot, and the gate was padlocked.

"Up," he said.

I grabbed the links and started to climb. He tried to boost me, but I waved for him to forget that and follow. I was almost to the top when the side of the factory lit up in two circles of light. I glanced over my shoulder. The SUV's engine roared as it accelerated.

"Go, go, go!" Derek whispered.

The car slammed to a halt, brakes squealing. I flipped over the top and started scrambling down. Beside me, Derek crouched on the fence top, then jumped. He landed square on his feet and wheeled as the car door was flung open.

"Jump! I've got you."

I was already halfway down, but I let go. He caught me and spun me around onto my feet with a push toward the factory.

"Derek! Chloe!"

It was a woman's voice. I kept running, but had to glance back, hearing my name. A small gray-haired woman gripped the links. A stranger.

A man hurried around the front of the car. He carried a long, dark object, and as he lifted it, my heart stuttered.

"Gun!" I shouted, still running.

Derek glanced over at me, eyes wide.

"They have a—"

He tackled me just as something whooshed past. We slid into a pile of wooden pallets. They clattered down around us, bouncing hard off my back and shoulders. I scrambled up and dove behind the next stack, then ran, hunched over, until we reached the factory wall.

We raced along the north side and ducked into a delivery dock bay. Derek pulled me behind a rusted metal bin.

"Th-they sh-shot at us," I whispered, barely able to get the words out. "No. I m-must have— A radio maybe. Or a cell phone. I made a mistake."

"You didn't." He twisted, reaching around his back.

"B-but they *sh-shot* at us. They tried to kill us. Th-that doesn't make any sense."

He plucked something from the bottom folds of his T-shirt. A long narrow metal tube with a pointed end.

"It caught in my shirt. It nicked me, but it shouldn't matter. It'd take a lot to knock me out."

"Knock you out?" I stared at it. "It's a tranquilizer dart?"

"I think so. Never seen one outside a nature show."

But we weren't animals. People didn't hunt kids with tranquilizer guns.

"I d-don't understand."

"Neither do I. Point is, they want us back. *Bad.* All the more reason to keep going." He dropped the dart and moved past me to the edge of the bin and inhaled, making no effort to hide it now. "Simon's here. He's not close, but he's been past recently."

"You can find him?"

"Yeah. Right now, though, I'm going to trust he can look after himself and worry about us. He'll lie low until he sees you. We should find a place to do the same until they move on."

He strode to the delivery doors, but they were locked and solid, the handles on the inside. I crept along the bin and scanned the factory yard.

"It looks like a warehouse back there. You mentioned something about that Friday? That it'd make a good place to hide?"

He glanced over my shoulder. "That one's too near the factory to be abandoned." He studied it. "But it'll do for now. I should be able to break in."

He surveyed the yard, then he hustled me along the dark wall, and we dashed across to the warehouse. A sharp wrench on the door and we were inside.

Derek was right: it wasn't abandoned. It was packed with rolls of steel, giving us lots of hiding places. I had to move slowly, feeling my way and following in Derek's tracks, testing each footstep for noise.

When we'd gone about twenty paces, he found a crevice and wedged us inside. We barely got in when a voice outside boomed.

"Derek? I know you're here. It's Dr. Davidoff."

I glanced at Derek, but he had his head turned toward the voice.

"Derek? I know you don't want to do this. You want to get better. You can't do that by running away."

The voice was moving, as the doctor walked through the factory yard. Derek cocked his head, listening, then whispered, "Four—no, five sets of footsteps. All separate. Searching."

Hoping we'd give ourselves away.

"Derek? You know you shouldn't be out here. It's not safe. We've talked about this, remember? You don't want to hurt anyone. I know that, and you know you need our help to get better."

I looked up. Derek's jaw worked, his gaze distant.

"I could go," he whispered. "Create a distraction so you can escape. Simon's around. You just need to find—"

"You're going *back*? After they shot at you?"

"Just tranquilizers."

"Just? *Just?*" My voice rose and I fought to keep it down. "They're hunting us, Derek. Dr. Gill knows what I am."

"*She* knew. That doesn't mean *they* do."

"Are you sure?"

He hesitated, his gaze lifting toward the voice.

"Derek?" Dr. Davidoff continued. "Please. I want to make this easy for you, but you need to make it easy for us. Come out now and we'll talk. That's it. Just talk. No disciplinary action will be taken and we won't transfer you."

Derek shifted against me. Considering.

"You can't—" I began.

"If you don't come out, Derek, we will find you, and you *will* be transferred . . . to a juvenile detention center for kidnapping Chloe."

"Kid—" I squawked.

He clapped his hand over my mouth until I motioned I'd be quiet.

Dr. Davidoff continued. "You already have a documented history of inappropriate behavior toward her. When the police see that, and hear our corroborating statements, you will be in a lot of trouble, Derek, and I know you don't want that. Even if she defends you, it won't matter to the police. You're a sixteen-year-old boy running away with a fourteen-year-old girl." He paused. "You do realize she's only fourteen, don't you, Derek?"

I shook my head vehemently and whispered, "He's lying. I turned fifteen last month."

Dr. Davidoff said, "To the police, it will be a clear case of kidnapping and interference, possibly even sexual assault."

"Sexual—!" I squeaked.

Derek's glare shut me up as effectively as his hand had.

"It's your choice, Derek. Make this hard, and you'll only hurt yourself."

Derek snorted and with that, Dr. Davidoff lost him. Prey on Derek's fears of hurting others, and he might be convinced to surrender. But threaten Derek himself? Like Simon said, it was a whole different matter.

"Stay here," he whispered. "I'm going to find a way out."

I wanted to argue, insist on helping, but I didn't have his night vision. If I started stumbling around looking for an exit, I'd bring Dr. Davidoff and the others running.

I stayed put.

forty-three

AFTER A FEW MINUTES, Derek returned and wordlessly led me to the back wall, where a window had been broken. It must have been boarded over, but the board was now resting on the floor.

"Hold on."

He swept the broken glass from the lower sill, then laced his fingers into a step for me. As I crawled through, my sleeve snagged on a left-over shard.

A nearby door banged.

"Chloe? Derek? I know you're in here. The door was broken."

I yanked my sleeve free, feeling a sharp sting. The shard tinkled to the pavement below as I scrambled through.

I tumbled to the ground, recovered, and broke into a run, aiming for the nearest cover—a tarp over a lumber pile. I dropped and crawled under it, Derek shoving me in farther. I found a spot where the tarp tented and stretched out on my stomach. The moment I caught my breath, my upper arm started to throb, telling me the glass had done more than scrape my skin.

"You're hurt," Derek whispered as if reading my mind.

"Just a scratch."

"No, it's not."

He grabbed my arm and pulled it straight. A stab of pain. I stifled a gasp. It was too dark to see, but the sleeve felt wet against my skin. Blood. He'd smelled it.

He gingerly rolled up my sleeve and swore.

"Bad?" I whispered.

"Deep. Gotta stop the bleeding. We need a bandage."

He released my arm. A flash of white, and I realized he was pulling off his T-shirt.

"Hold on," I said. "That's all you've got. I'm layered up."

He turned his head away. I stripped off all three shirts, gritting my teeth as the fabric brushed my wound. I reminded myself that I'd barely felt it before he told me it was bad.

I put the top two shirts back on and handed him my tee. He ripped it, the sound echoing. I must have looked alarmed, because he said, "No one's around. I can hear them searching the warehouse."

He wound the strips around my arm. Then his head lifted, tracking something, and I caught the faint sound of a voice calling, then an answer.

"They're all in the warehouse now," he whispered. "Time to move. I'll try picking up Simon's scent. Follow my lead."

Derek zigged and zagged through the obstacle course of debris, never slowing. Luckily, I was behind him, where he couldn't see how many times I rapped my knees or elbows swerving past some obstacle.

Finally, he slowed. "Got him," he whispered, and jabbed a finger at the south side of the factory. We steered that way. When we neared the corner, a figure leaned from a recessed doorway, then retreated fast. Simon. A moment later, Rae stepped out and waved wildly before being yanked back, presumably by Simon.

We raced over and found them in a deep narrow alcove that reeked of cigarette smoke and looked like a main entrance.

"What are you doing here?" Rae whispered, staring at Derek as if in alarm. "You're supposed to be—"

"Change of plans."

"Good to see you, bro," Simon said, slapping Derek's back. "I was worried Chloe'd never find us. There's a whole bunch of people looking for us."

"I know."

Simon moved to the edge, looked out, then walked over to me, handing me my backpack. "You okay?"

I nodded, keeping my injured arm out of sight. "They have guns."

"What?" Rae's eyes rounded. "No way. They'd never—"

"Tranq guns," Derek corrected.

"Oh." She nodded, as if tranquilizer guns were standard issue for tracking runaway kids.

"Who've you seen?" Derek asked Simon.

"Van Dop, Davidoff, and, I think, Talbot, but I'm not sure. No sign of Gill."

"She's back at the house," I said. "But there are two more we didn't recognize. A man and a woman." I looked at Derek. "Undercover cops, you think?"

"No idea. We'll worry about that later. Right now, we're sitting ducks. We need to get out of here."

As Derek moved to look out, Simon leaned down to my ear. "Thanks. For finding him. Was everything okay?"

"Later," Derek said. "There's another warehouse farther back, with broken windows. It's probably abandoned. If we can get to that—"

"Chloe?" Rae said, staring down at my arm. "What's all over your sleeve? It looks like . . ." She touched the fabric. "Oh, my God. You're bleeding. You're *really* bleeding."

Simon ducked around to my other side. "It's soaked. What—?"

"Just a cut," I said.

"It's deep," Derek said. "She needs stitches."

"I don't—"

"She needs stitches," he repeated. "I'll figure something out. For now—" He swore and jumped back from the opening. "They're coming." He looked around, scowling. "This is the lousiest hiding place . . ."

"I know," Simon said. "I wanted to find a better one, but . . ." A pointed look at Rae said she'd refused to leave.

"What's wrong with here?" she said. She backed up against the wall. "It's completely dark. They won't see me."

"Until they shine a flashlight on you."

"Oh."

Derek strode to the door, grabbed the handle, and gave it a test pull. Then he braced his feet, took the handle in both hands, and heaved until the tendons in his neck bulged. The door quivered, then flew open with a crack as loud as a gunshot.

He frantically waved us inside. "Find cover!" he whispered as I hurried past.

We raced through into a wide hall flanked with doors, some open, some closed. Rae headed for the first. Derek shoved her past.

"Keep going!" he whispered.

He loped by her and led us to a second hall. Then, he motioned for silence as he listened, but even without super senses, I heard the whoosh of the door and the clamor of footsteps.

"It's open!" a man yelled. "They came through here."

"We've got to get out," Derek whispered. "Split up. Find an exit. Any exit. Then whistle, but softly. I'll hear you."

forty-four

AROUND THE NEXT CORNER, we split up to search for an exit.

The first door I tried opened into a long, narrow room filled with worktables. No sign of a way out.

Back in the hall, I could hear voices, but distant, searching the rooms nearest the entrance, presuming we'd ducked into the first one we saw.

Hurrying toward the next door, I spotted a figure in the room across the hall. I stopped short, but too late. I was already standing in plain sight.

As I pulled my heart from my throat, I realized the man had his back to me. Dressed in jeans and a plaid shirt, he was the same size as the man with the gun, and had the same dark hair. I didn't remember the plaid shirt, but he'd been wearing a jacket.

He stood on a raised platform, gripping the railing, looking down at a big industrial saw. He seemed intent on whatever had caught his attention.

I took one careful step forward. When the man shifted, I froze, but he only seemed to be readjusting his grip on the railing. I lifted my foot. The man did the same—stepping onto the lower bar of the barrier.

He climbed onto the railing and crouched there, hands gripping the bar. Something moved below him and my gaze shot to the saw. The blades were turning—spinning so fast that the glint of a distant emergency light bounced off like a strobe. But there was no sound, not even the motor's hum.

The man tested his grip on the railing. Then, suddenly, he pitched forward. I saw him hit the blades, saw the first spray of blood, and I fell back against the wall, my hand flying to cover my mouth but not before the first note of a shriek escaped.

Something—some part of him—flew from the saw, landing in the doorway with a splat. I ripped my gaze away before I could see what it was, staggering back as running footsteps sounded behind me.

Arms grabbed me. I heard Simon's voice at my ear. "Chloe?"

"Th-there was a man. He—" I balled my hands into fists, pushing the image back. "A ghost. A man. He j-jumped onto a saw."

Simon pulled me against him, his hand going to the back of my head, burying my face against his chest. He smelled of vanilla fabric softener with a trace of perspiration, oddly comforting. I lingered, catching my breath.

Derek wheeled around the corner. "What happened?"

"A ghost," I said, pulling away from Simon. "I'm sorry."

"Someone heard. We gotta go."

As I was turning, I saw the ghost again, standing on the platform. Derek followed my gaze. The ghost stood in exactly the same position, gripping the railing. Then he stepped up.

"It's r-repeating. Like a film loop." I shook it off. "Never mind. We—"

"Have to *go*," Derek said, pushing me. "Move!"

As we started down the hall, Rae let out a piercing whistle.

"Did I say softly?" Derek hissed under his breath.

We veered into Rae's hall to see her standing at a door marked EXIT. She reached for the handle.

"Don't!" Derek strode past her and cracked the door open, listening and sniffing before pushing it wide. "See that warehouse?"

"The one, like, a mile back there?" Rae said.

"Quarter mile, tops. Now go. We're right behind—" His head whipped up, tracking a sound. "They're coming. They heard the whistle. You guys go. I'll distract them, then follow."

"Uh-uh," Simon said. "I've got your back. Chloe, take Rae and run."

Derek opened his mouth to argue.

Simon cut him off. "You want distractions?" He whispered a spell and waved his hand, fog rising. "I'm your guy." He turned to me. "Go. We'll catch up."

I wanted to argue but, again, there was nothing I could offer. My powers had already proved more hindrance than help.

Rae was already twenty feet across the lot, dancing in place like a boxer, waving for me to hurry up.

As I turned to go, Derek shouldered past Simon. "Get in the warehouse and don't leave. For one hour, don't even peek out. If we don't come, find a place to hole up. We'll be back."

Simon nodded. "Count on it."

"Don't stay in the warehouse if it's dangerous, but that'll be our rendezvous point. Keep checking in. If you can't stay, find a way to leave a note. We *will* meet you there. Got it?"

I nodded.

"They must be back here," someone called. "Search every room."

Derek shoved me through the doorway.

Simon leaned out, mouthing "I'll see you soon," with a thumbs-up, then he turned to Derek. "Show time."

I started to run.

forty-five

WE WAITED IN THE WAREHOUSE for one hour and forty minutes.

"They caught them," I whispered.

Rae shrugged. "Maybe not. Maybe they saw their chance to get away and they took it."

A protest rose to my lips, but I swallowed it. She was right. If they had the opportunity to escape and no easy way of alerting us, I'd want them to take it.

I lifted my numb rear off the ice-cold cement. "We'll wait here a bit longer, then we'll go. If they got away, they'll hook up with us later."

Rae shook her head. "I wouldn't count on it, Chloe. It's like I said, the way they act, the way they behave, it's always us against them, and 'us' means the two of them. No one else, except maybe that missing dad of theirs." She shifted into a crouch. "Did they even give you any idea where they think he is? Or why he hasn't come for them?"

"No, but—"

"I'm not arguing, I'm just saying . . ." She crawled to the opening and peeked out. "It's like last year, when I went out with this guy. He was part of a clique at school. The 'cool kids.' " She added the quotes with her fingers. "And, sure, I kinda liked getting to hang with them. I thought it'd make me one of them. Only it didn't. They were nice enough, but they'd been friends since, like, third grade. Just because I had an in didn't mean I'd ever be one of them. You've got these superpowers. That gives you cred with Simon and Derek. But . . ." She turned my way. "You've only known them for a week. When push comes to shove . . ."

"Their first priority is each other. I know that. And I'm not saying you're wrong, just—"

"Simon's nice to you and all, sure. I see that. But—" She nibbled her lip, then slowly lifted her gaze to mine. "When you were back there, looking for Derek, it wasn't you Simon was worrying about. He didn't even mention you. It was all about Derek."

Of course he was worried about Derek. Derek was his brother; I was some girl he met a week ago. But it still stung a little that he hadn't mentioned me at *all*.

I'd been about to tell Rae about the part of the plan she missed, to make this our permanent rendezvous point, and keep checking back. But now it would sound like I was trying to prove the guys hadn't turned their backs on me. How pathetic was that?

I still thought they'd come back after things died down. It had nothing to do with whether Simon liked me or not. They'd come back because it was the right thing to do. Because they said they would. And maybe that makes me a silly girl who's watched too many movies where the good guy always comes back to save the day. But it's what I believed.

That did not, however, mean I was sitting here like an action-flick girlfriend, twiddling her thumbs waiting for rescue. I might be naive, but I wasn't stupid. We'd set a rendezvous point, so there was no need to stick around any longer.

I crawled from our cubbyhole, looked, and listened. I waved Rae out.

"First thing I need to do is get money," I said. "I've got my dad's but we might need more. There's a daily withdrawal limit, and that's probably all I'll get, so I have to act fast, before they put a trace on it or freeze the account. Derek said the nearest ATM was—"

"What are you doing?" Rae asked.

"What?"

She took hold of my arm and pointed at the blood. "You don't need money; you need a doctor."

I shook my head. "I can't go to a hospital. Even if they haven't put out an APB on me yet, I'm too young. They'd call my Aunt Lauren—"

"I *meant* your Aunt Lauren. She's a doctor, isn't she?"

"N-no. I can't. She'd just take us back—"

"After they shot at us? I know you're mad at her right now, but you've told me how she's always worrying about you, always looking out for you, defending you. If you show up at her front door and say that Davidoff and his buds *shot* at you, even with tranquilizers, do you really think she'll march you back to Lyle House?"

"That depends on whether she believes me. A week ago, yes. But now?" I shook my head. "When she was talking to me about Derek, it was like I wasn't even Chloe anymore. I'm a schizophrenic. I'm paranoid and I'm delusional. She won't believe me."

"Then tell me exactly what the gun and the dart looked like, and I'll say I saw it, too. No, wait! The dart. Derek pulled one out of his shirt, right? Do you know where it is?"

"I—I think so." I thought back, pictured him dropping it in the delivery bay. "Yes, I know exactly where it is."

"Then let's go get it."

It wasn't that easy. For all we knew, the factory yard was swarming with cops searching for two teen runaways. But when we looked out, the only people we saw were a half-dozen factory workers, heading in to work Sunday overtime, laughing and talking, lunch pails swinging, takeout coffees steaming.

I took off my blood-soaked sweatshirt and swapped it for Liz's hoodie. Then we crept out, moving from cover to cover. No sign of anyone looking for us. That made sense. How many teenagers run away in Buffalo every day? Even escaping from a home for disturbed kids wouldn't warrant a full-out manhunt.

Last night, it had probably been only Lyle House employees chasing us. Maybe board members, like Tori's mother, more worried about the home's reputation than our safety. If they wanted to keep our escape quiet, they'd be gone before any factory employees arrived. By now they were probably in a meeting, deciding what to do and when to notify our parents—and the police.

I found the dart easily, and put it into my backpack. Then we headed for the business district, looping three blocks past Lyle House and keeping our eyes open. Nothing happened. We found a pay phone, I called for a cab, and gave the driver Aunt Lauren's address.

Aunt Lauren lived in a duplex near the university. When we walked up her steps, the *Buffalo News* was still there. I picked it up and rang the bell.

After a minute, a shadow passed behind the curtain. Locks clanked and the door flew open. Aunt Lauren stood there in a short bathrobe, hair wet.

"Chloe? Oh my God. Where—" She pulled the door open. "What are you doing here? Are you okay? Is everything all right?"

She tugged me inside by my injured arm and I tried not to wince. Her gaze shot to Rae.

"Aunt Lauren, this is Rae. From Lyle House. We need to talk to you."

As we went inside, I did a proper introduction. Then I told her the whole story. Well, the edited version. Very edited, with no mention of zombies, magic, or werewolves. The boys had been planning to run away and they'd invited us. We'd gone along just for fun—to get out, goof off, then go back later. Knowing Aunt Lauren didn't care for Dr. Gill, I included the part about her attacking me in the yard with her wild accusations. Then I told her about the gun.

She stared down at the dart, lying on her coffee table, on top of a stack of *New Yorker* magazines. She picked it up, gingerly, as if it might detonate, and turned it over in her hands.

"It's a tranquilizer dart," she said, voice barely above a whisper.

"That's what we thought."

"But— They shot this at you? At *you*?"

"At us."

She slumped back, leather squeaking under her.

"I was there, Dr. Fellows," Rae said. "Chloe's telling the truth."

"No, I—" She lifted her gaze to mine. "I believe you, hon. I just can't believe— This is so completely . . ." She shook her head.

"Where did you find Lyle House?" I asked.

She blinked. "Find?"

"How did you find it for me? In the yellow pages? Through a recommendation?"

"It came highly recommended, Chloe. *Very* highly. Someone at the hospital told me about it and I did all my research. Their recovery rate is excellent and they had glowing reports from patients and their families. I can't believe this happened."

So I hadn't randomly arrived at Lyle House. It'd been recommended. Did that mean anything? I fingered Liz's hoodie and thought about us—all of us. No ordinary group home would track runaways with tranquilizer guns. The ghost had been right. There was a reason we'd been at Lyle House and now, withholding the truth from Aunt Lauren, I could be putting her into danger.

"About the ghosts . . ." I began.

"You mean what that Gill woman said?" Aunt Lauren slapped the dart back onto the magazines with such force that the pile fell, magazines sliding across the glass tabletop. "The woman is obviously in need of mental help herself. Thinking you can communicate with ghosts? One whiff of that to a review board and her license will be revoked. She'll be lucky if she isn't committed. No sane person believes people can speak to the dead."

Okay, forget the confession . . .

Aunt Lauren rose. "I'm going to start by calling your father, then my lawyer, and *he* can contact Lyle House."

"Dr. Fellows?"

Aunt Lauren turned to Rae.

"Before you do that, you'd better take a look at Chloe's arm."

forty-six

AUNT LAUREN TOOK ONE LOOK and freaked out. I needed stitches, immediately. She didn't have the supplies at home, and I had to have full medical attention. Who knew what I might have severed or what filth or germs might have been on that glass? While she was rebandaging me, she made me drink a bottle of Gatorade to replace any fluids I'd lost from bleeding. Within ten minutes, Rae and I were in the back of her Mercedes, tearing from her garage.

I dozed off before we reached the first traffic light. I supposed all those sleepless nights had something to do with that. Being in Aunt Lauren's car helped, with its familiar smell of berry air freshener and its soft beige leather seats and the faded blue spot where I'd spilled a slushie three years ago. Back home. Back to normal.

I knew it wasn't that simple. I wasn't back to normal. And Derek and Simon were still out there and I was worried about them. But even that worry seemed to fade as the car bumped along, like I was leaving it behind in another life. A dream life. Part nightmare, part . . . not.

Raising the dead, escaping from the clutches of an evil doctor, tearing through abandoned warehouses with people shooting at me. It all seemed so unreal in this familiar car, the radio station tuned to WJYE, my aunt laughing at something Rae said about her choice of music, saying I complained, too. So familiar. So normal. So comforting.

And, yet, even as I drifted off, I clung to the memories of that other life, where the dead came to life and fathers disappeared and sorcerers conducted horrific experiments and buried the bodies under the house and boys could make fog appear from their fingertips or turn into wolves. Now it was over and it was like waking up to discover I couldn't see ghosts anymore. The feeling that I'd missed out on something that would make my life tougher but might also make it different. An adventure. Special.

I woke to Aunt Lauren shaking me.

"I know you're tired, hon. Just come on inside and you can go back to sleep."

I stumbled out of the car. She caught me, Rae diving in to help.

"Is she okay?" Rae asked my aunt. "She lost a lot of blood."

"She's exhausted. You both must be."

When the cold air hit, I yawned and gave my head a sharp shake. I could make out a building in front of me. I blinked hard and it came into focus. A yellow brick rectangle with a single, unmarked door.

"Is this the hospital?"

"No, it's a walk-in clinic. I called Buffalo General and Mercy and their emergencies are packed. A typical Sunday morning. Between the Saturday night gunshot wounds and the drunk drivers, it's a zoo. I know a doctor here and we'll get you straight in."

She looked up as a small, gray-haired woman rounded the corner. "Oh, there's Sue. She's a nurse here. Rae, Sue's going to take you over to the waiting room, get you some breakfast, and check you over."

I peered at the woman as I struggled to focus. She looked familiar. When she stopped to talk to my aunt, I realized she must be her friend. But even after she walked away, it niggled at the back of my foggy brain, some connection I wasn't getting.

It wasn't until we were inside that I remembered where I'd seen her. Just last night, clutching the chain-link fence, calling my name.

I wheeled on Aunt Lauren. "That woman—"

"Sue, yes. She's a nurse here. She'll take good care of—"

"No! I saw her last night with the man who shot at us."

Aunt Lauren's face crumpled and she put her arm around me. "No, honey, that's not the same woman. You've been through a lot and you're confused—"

I pushed her away. "I'm not. I saw her. Is she the one who recommended Lyle House? We need to get out of here."

I ducked out of her grasp and raced back to the door. I grabbed the handle, but she caught up, holding it shut.

"Chloe, listen to me. You need to—"

"I need to get out." I pulled on the door with both hands, but she held it fast. "Please, Aunt Lauren, you don't understand. We have to get out of here."

"Would someone please help Dr. Fellows?" a voice echoed down the hall. I turned to see Dr. Davidoff striding toward us.

A man hurried past him, coming at me with a syringe.

"That won't be necessary, Marcel," Aunt Lauren snapped. "I've already given her something."

"And I can see it's working very well. Bruce, sedate Chloe, please."

I looked up at Aunt Lauren. "Y-you drugged me?"

Her arms went around me. "You'll be okay, hon. I promise."

I lashed out, hitting her so hard she stumbled back. Then she turned on Dr. Davidoff.

"I told you this wasn't the way to handle it. I told you to leave it to me."

"Leave what to you?" I said, taking a slow step back and hitting the door.

She reached for me, but my hands flew up, warding her off.

"Leave what to you?"

The man with the syringe caught my arm. I tried to yank away, but the needle went in. Aunt Lauren stepped toward me, mouth opening. Then a woman hurried down the hall, calling to Dr. Davidoff.

"The team just called in a report, sir. There's no sign of the boys."

"Surprise, surprise," Aunt Lauren said, turning to Dr. Davidoff. "Kit taught them well. Once they're gone, they'll keep running. I warned you."

"We'll find them."

"You'd better, and when you do, I expect that brute to be handled the way he should have been handled years ago. Put down like a rabid dog. Wait until you see what he did to Chloe's arm."

"D-Derek?" I struggled against the pull of the sedative. "Derek didn't do this. I cut myself—"

Aunt Lauren caught me as I slid down the wall. I tried to push her away, but my arms wouldn't respond. She shouted for them to hurry with the stretcher, then leaned over me, holding me steady.

"You don't need to cover for him, Chloe," she whispered. "We know what he is." A glare back at Dr. Davidoff. "A monster. One that didn't belong in the . . ."

I didn't catch her next few words. The hall flickered, fading.

When I focused, I saw her face over mine. "But we won't let him hurt Simon, Chloe. I promise you that. When you wake up, you're going to help us find Simon and bring him home. I know he's important to you. He's important to all of us. You all are. You and Rachelle and Simon and Victoria. Very special. You're—"

Everything went dark.

forty-seven

I LAY AWAKE, STARING AT the wall. I couldn't bring myself to roll over and look around. Couldn't even bother lifting my head from the pillow. I could feel the pull of the sedative, luring me back into sleep, but I kept my eyes open, gaze fixed on the green painted wall.

Aunt Lauren had betrayed me.

When she'd thought I'd been fooling around with Derek, I'd felt betrayed. Now I looked back on how furious I'd been and my throat tightened as I prayed I could go back there, to where that was the worst thing I could ever imagine her doing.

It was all a lie.

She was a lie. Our relationship was a lie.

Even when I was a child seeing bogeymen in the basement, she'd known perfectly well I was seeing ghosts. My mother knew it—that's why she'd insisted we move.

I fingered my necklace. Was this more than a silly talisman to convince me I was safe? Did my mother really think it would protect me? Is that why Aunt Lauren had insisted I wear it at Lyle House? Simon said necromancy was hereditary. If both my mother and my aunt had known about the ghosts, it must run in their blood.

Did my father know? Was that why he stayed away from me? Because I was a freak?

I thought about my mother. About the accident. The hit-and-run driver had never been found. Had it really been an accident? Or had someone killed—?

No. I squeezed the thought from my brain as I clutched the pillow tighter. I couldn't let my mind start running away like that or I'd go crazy.

Crazy.

Aunt Lauren knew I wasn't crazy, and she let me think I was. Shipped me off to a group home.

A group home filled with other supernatural kids.

When Aunt Lauren said we were special, she'd included Rae. So she must really be one of those half-demons. What about Tori? What was she? Did her mother know? If her mother worked for them, she must know, and if she did, and blamed Tori for not getting better . . .

What kind of parent would do that?

But hadn't my aunt done the same thing? Only she sweetened it with smiles and hugs and maybe that was worse. Right now, it felt worse.

Was Lyle House where they sent us when things went wrong? Put us there and medicated us and tried to tell us we had a mental illness? But why? Wouldn't the truth be easier? Why not tell us when we were young and prepare us, and teach us how to control it?

From what Simon said, that's the way it was supposed to work. You told your kids and you trained them how to use and hide their powers *before* they lost control.

What was Lyle House?

I remembered what Simon said about his dad.

He worked for this research company, supernatural doctors and scientists trying to make things easier for other supernaturals.

Then I heard the ghost of the witch buried in the basement.

Sam Lyle promised us an easier life. That's what we all want, isn't it? Power without price . . . You see, little girl, all scientific advancement requires experimentation, and experimentation requires subjects, and that's what Michael and I were. Lab rats sacrificed to the vision of a madman.

I leaped up, heart thudding so hard I couldn't breathe.

Aunt Lauren said we were special. All of us. Rae and Simon and Tori and me.

But not Derek.

I expect that brute to be handled the way he should have been handled years ago. Put down like a rabid dog.

I had to find Derek before they did.

I turned around, seeing my surroundings. A double bed with big pillows and a thick comforter. Carpet on the floor. A desk. An armchair. A private bathroom through a half-open door. Like a fancy hotel room.

Across the room was a door, painted white. It looked like any interior door, but when I walked over and put my hands against it, it was cold steel. A thick steel door with no window, not even a peephole.

And no doorknob.

Wherever I was, it wasn't a fake group home where I had the run of the house and yard, had chores, classes, and field trips. I was in this room, and I wasn't getting out.

I backed up to the bed.

I was trapped. I'd never escape, never—

Oh, that's great. You've been awake five minutes, taken a quick look around, and given up. Why don't you just lie back and wait for them to come and strap you to a table? What did that witch say? Something about being prodded with electrical wires until she bit off her tongue?

I let out a whimper.

And what about Derek? He got you out of Lyle House and now you aren't even going to try to warn him? Just let them catch him? Kill him?

Derek wouldn't get caught. He was too smart for that. He got out of Lyle House—

He got you out of Lyle House? He didn't plan to go. That was a total fluke. Remember when Dr. Davidoff tried to call him back? He almost went. What happens if they do that again? Maybe he'll have had second thoughts, decide he really is better off locked away.

Not as long as he has to protect Simon.

Ah, Simon. Derek will never turn in Simon. But what about distracting them so Simon can escape, like he did for you and Rae? If he thinks turning himself in will let Simon escape, he'll do it. You know he will.

I had to warn him. But to warn him, I had to get out of here. This time, I couldn't just sit back and let someone else make the plans. I had to do it myself.

Maybe I was locked in here for now, but I'd be let out eventually. I wasn't exactly a high-risk prisoner. They'd take me out—for exercise, to eat, to experiment on me . . .

I tried not to think about the last.

Point was, I'd get out, and when I did, I needed to be ready to escape. First, though, I had to get a good look around and plan. But how was I going to do that locked in this room? Pray for a convenient blueprint stuffed under the mattress? Astral-project out the door and look around?

I stopped and slowly looked down at the sweater I wore. Liz's green hoodie.

If she was dead, maybe I could summon her, get her to scout the building and—

If she's dead*? So you're hoping she's dead now?*

I clenched the comforter and took a deep breath. For days now, I'd refused to believe Liz had died. No matter how much proof I had, I couldn't believe it because the very idea was insane.

But now, sitting here, locked in this room, betrayed by my aunt, waiting for them to track down and kill Derek like some kind of animal . . .

Liz was dead.

They'd killed her.

She'd been a supernatural of some kind, and her powers were out of control, so they executed her. They must have or they would have included her in that list. And what about Peter? Had his parents pretended to pick him up only to let these people kill him? Or maybe because he got better, he got out. Liz didn't get better . . . so she didn't get out.

Some tiny part of me still clung to the hope that I was wrong about Liz. But I knew I wasn't.

I pulled off the hoodie. I saw my arm, rebandaged. Stitched up, while I'd been unconscious. If they were fixing me, at least that meant they didn't plan to kill me yet.

I stared at the hoodie, thinking of Liz and of dying. Of what it would be like to be dead at sixteen, the rest of your life gone—?

I squeezed my eyes shut. No time for that.

I searched my room for cameras. I didn't find any, but that didn't mean there wasn't one. If they saw me talking to myself, they'd figure out what I was doing, maybe decide my powers were out of control, like Liz's.

Either I did this or I didn't. My choice.

I sat cross-legged on the bed, holding Liz's hoodie, and called her as I'd done the other ghosts. I didn't need to worry about overdoing it and raising the dead. There were no corpses here. Or so I hoped. But I had no idea what was outside my door, maybe a laboratory, maybe the bodies of other failures, like Liz—

No time for that.

The ghost necromancer had said Lyle House was protected by a spell blocking ghosts. That meant this place probably was, too, which meant I needed all that extra power he said I had.

I concentrated so hard my temples hurt, but nothing happened.

I closed my eyes to visualize better, but I kept peeking and breaking my focus. Finally I shut them and kept them shut, putting everything I had into imagining myself pulling Liz out of the ether and—

"Whoa. Where am I?"

I opened my eyes and there she was, still wearing her Minnie Mouse nightshirt and giraffe socks.

Liz.

No, Liz's ghost.

"Hello?" She waved a hand in front of my eyes. "What's wrong, Chloe? There's nothing to be scared of. I know, Lyle House isn't exactly Disneyland but—" She looked around, brow furrowing. "This isn't Lyle House, is it? Where—? Oh my God. We're in the hospital. They put you in here, too. When?"

She blinked hard, shaking her head. "They have some funky meds here. I keep sleeping and having these dreams, and when I wake up, I'm totally confused. Did they give you those, too?"

So where had Liz been all this time? Stuck in limbo? One thing was for sure. She didn't know she was dead. And now I had to tell her.

Tell her? No way. She was happy. If she didn't know, that was better.

And how long do you think it'll be before she figures it out? Shouldn't you be the one to tell her?

I didn't want to. I really, really didn't want to. But I needed her to help me escape and rescue Rae and warn Simon and Derek. It was all on me this time, and to help them, I needed to do something awful.

Fingers trembling, I clutched her hoodie and took a deep breath.

"Liz? There's something I need to tell you."

the Awakening

BOOK TWO

one

When the door to my cell clicked open, the first thought that flitted through my doped-up brain was that Liz had changed her mind and come back. But ghosts don't open doors. They will, on occasion, ask me to open one, so I can raise and interrogate the zombies of supernaturals killed by a mad scientist, but they never need one opened for themselves.

I sat up in bed and rubbed my bleary eyes, blinking away the lingering fog of the sedative. For a moment, the door stayed open only a crack. I slid from the bed, tiptoeing across the thick carpet of my fake hotel room, praying the person on the other side had been called away and I could escape before these people started whatever experiments they'd brought me here to—

"Hello, Chloe." Dr. Davidoff beamed his best kindly-old-man smile as he pushed the door wide. He wasn't that old—maybe fifty—but in a movie, I'd cast him as the doddering absentminded scientist. It was an act I'm sure he'd worked on until he got it just right.

The woman behind him had chic blond hair and a New York suit. I'd cast her as the mother of the nastiest girl in class. Which was cheating, because that's exactly who she was. Mother of Victoria—Tori—Enright, the one housemate we'd left out of our plans when we'd escaped from Lyle

House, and for good cause, considering she was one of the reasons I'd needed to escape.

Tori's mom carried a Macy's bag, like she'd just been out shopping and popped in to conduct a few horrific experiments before heading to lunch.

"I know you have a lot of questions, Chloe," Dr. Davidoff said as I sat on the edge of the bed. "We're here to answer them for you. We just need a little help from you first."

"Simon and Derek," Mrs. Enright said. "Where are they?"

I looked from her to Dr. Davidoff, who smiled and nodded encouragingly, like he fully expected me to turn in my friends.

I'd never been an angry kid. I'd never run away from home. Never stamped my feet and screamed that life was unfair and I wished I'd never been born. Whenever my dad told me we were moving again and I needed to transfer schools, I'd swallowed a whiny "but I just made new friends," nod, and tell him I understood.

Accept your lot. Count your blessings. Be a big girl.

Now, looking back at a life of doing what I was told, I realized I'd bought into the game. When adults patted me on the head and told me I was so grown-up, what they really meant was that they were glad I wasn't grown-up enough yet to question, to fight back.

Looking at Dr. Davidoff and Mrs. Enright, I thought of what they'd done to me—lying to me, locking me up—and I *wanted* to stamp my feet. Wanted to scream. But I wasn't going to give them that satisfaction.

I widened my eyes as I met Mrs. Enright's gaze. "You mean you haven't found them yet?"

I think she would have slapped me if Dr. Davidoff hadn't lifted his hand.

"No, Chloe, we haven't found the boys," he said. "We're very concerned for Simon's safety."

"Because you think Derek might hurt him?"

"Not intentionally, of course. I know Derek's fond of Simon."

Fond? What a strange word to use. Derek and Simon were foster brothers, tighter than any blood brothers I knew. Sure, Derek was a werewolf, but that wolf part of him was what would *stop* him from ever hurting Simon. He'd protect him at all costs—I'd already seen that.

My skepticism must have shown on my face, because Dr. Davidoff shook his head, as if disappointed in me. "All right, Chloe. If you can't spare any concern for Simon's safety, maybe you can for his health."

"W-what ab-bou—" My stutter cropped up most when I was nervous, and I couldn't let them know they'd struck a nerve. So I tried again, slower now. "What about his health?"

"His condition."

Apparently I wasn't the only one who watched too many movies. Now they would tell me that Simon had some rare medical condition and if he didn't get his medicine within twelve hours, he'd spontaneously combust.

"What condition?"

"He has diabetes," Dr. Davidoff said. "His blood sugar levels need to be monitored and regulated."

"With one of those blood testing things?" I said slowly, thinking back. Simon had always disappeared into the bathroom before meals. I'd thought he just liked to wash up. I'd bumped into him once coming out as he'd been shoving a small black case into his pocket.

"That's right," Dr. Davidoff said. "With proper care, diabetes is easily managed. You weren't aware of it because you didn't need to be. Simon leads a normal life."

"Except for one thing," Tori's mom said.

She reached into the Macy's bag and took out a backpack. It looked like Simon's, but I wasn't falling for that—they'd probably bought a matching one. Sure, she pulled out a hoodie I recognized as Simon's, but he'd left behind a whole closet of clothing at Lyle House. Easy enough to grab stuff from there.

Next came a pad of paper and pouch of colored pencils. Simon's room was filled with his comic book sketches. Again, easy enough to—

Mrs. Enright flipped through the sketch pad, holding up pages. Simon's work in progress. He'd never have left that behind.

Finally, she laid a flashlight on the table. The flashlight from Lyle House—the one I'd watched him put into his bag.

"Simon slipped going over the fence," she said. "He had his backpack over one shoulder. It fell. Our people were right behind him so he had to leave it. There's something in here that Simon needs much more than clothing and art supplies."

She opened a navy nylon pouch. Inside were two penlike vials, one filled with cloudy liquid, the other clear. "The insulin to replace what Simon's body can't produce. He injects himself with these three times a day."

"What happens if he doesn't?"

Dr. Davidoff took over. "We aren't going to scare you and say that if Simon skips a single shot, he'll die. He's already missed his morning one, and I'm sure he only feels a bit out of sorts. But by tomorrow, he'll be vomiting. In about three days, he'll lapse into a diabetic coma." He took the pouch from Tori's mom and set it in front of me. "We need to get this to Simon. To do that, you need to tell us where he is."

I agreed to try.

two

IN A GOOD DRAMA, the protagonist never takes the straight line to the prize. She must set out, hit an obstacle, detour around it, hit another, take a longer detour, another obstacle, another detour. . . . Only when she has built up the strength of character to *deserve* the prize does she finally succeed.

My story was already fitting the time-honored pattern. Fitting, I guess, for a film student. Or, I should say, former film student. Chloe Saunders, fifteen-year-old Steven Spielberg wannabe, her dreams of writing and directing Hollywood blockbusters shattered on the day she got her first period and started living the kind of life she'd once imagined putting on the screen.

That's when I started seeing ghosts. After freaking out at school, I was taken away by the men in the white jackets and shipped off to a group home for mentally disturbed teens. Problem is, I really *did* see ghosts. And I wasn't the only kid at Lyle House with supernatural powers.

Simon could cast spells. Rae could burn people with her bare fingers. Derek had superhuman strength and senses and, apparently, soon would be able to change into a wolf. Tori . . . well, I didn't know what Tori was—maybe just a screwed-up kid put in Lyle House because her mom helped run it.

Simon, Derek, Rae, and I realized it was no coincidence we were in the same place, and we escaped. Rae and I got separated from the guys and, after running to my aunt Lauren—the person I had trusted most in the world—I ended up here, in some kind of laboratory run by the same people who owned Lyle House.

Now they expected me to help them bring in Simon and Derek?

Well, it was time to introduce a few obstacles of my own. So, in the spirit of proper storytelling, I told Dr. Davidoff where to find Simon and Derek.

Step one: establish the goal. "Rae and I were supposed to hide while the guys stayed behind to distract you with Simon's magic," I told Dr. Davidoff. "Rae ran on ahead so she didn't hear, but at the last second Simon pulled me back and said, if we got separated, we'd meet at the rendezvous point."

Step two: introduce the obstacle. "Where is the rendezvous point? That's the problem. I don't *know* where it is. We talked about needing one, but everything was so crazy that day. We'd only just decided to escape, and then Derek was saying it had to be that night. The guys must have picked a rendezvous point, and forgot they never told me where it was."

Step three: map out the detour. "But I do have some ideas—places we talked about. One of them must be the rendezvous point. I could help you find it. They'll be looking for me, so they might hide until they see me."

Rather than escape this place, I'd let them take me out by using me as bait. I'd list places I'd never discussed with Simon or Derek, and there would be no chance they'd get captured. A brilliant plan.

The response?

"We'll keep that in mind, Chloe. But for now, just tell us the locations. We have ways to find the boys once we get there."

Obstacles. An essential part of the storytelling process. But in real life? They suck.

After Dr. Davidoff and Tori's mom had gotten my list of fake rendezvous points, they left, giving me nothing in return—no answers, no clues about why I was here or what would happen to me.

I sat cross-legged on my bed, staring down at the necklace in my hands as if it were a crystal ball that could provide all those answers. My mom had given it to me back when I was seeing "bogeymen"—ghosts, as I now knew. She said the necklace would stop them from coming, and it did. I'd always figured, like my dad said, that it was psychological. I believed in it, so it worked. Now, I wasn't so sure.

Had my mom known I was a necromancer? She must have, if the blood ran in her family. Was the necklace supposed to ward off ghosts? If so, its power must have faded. It even looked faded—I swore the bright red jewel had gone a purplish color. One thing it didn't do, though, was answer my questions. That I had to do for myself.

I put the necklace back on. Whatever Dr. Davidoff and the others wanted from me, it wasn't good. You don't lock up kids you want to help.

I certainly wasn't going to tell them how to find Simon. If he needed insulin, Derek would get it, even if it meant breaking into a drugstore.

I had to concentrate on getting Rae and me out. But this wasn't Lyle House, where the only thing standing between us and freedom was an alarm system. This room might look like it belonged in a nice hotel—with a double bed, a carpeted floor, an armchair, desk, and private bathroom—but there were no windows and no knob on the inside of the door.

I'd hoped to get Liz's help escaping. My roommate at Lyle House, Liz hadn't made it out alive, so when I first got here, I'd summoned her ghost, hoping she could help me find a way out. Only problem? Liz didn't realize she was dead. As gently as I could, I'd broken the news. She'd flipped out, accusing me of lying, and disappeared.

Maybe she'd had enough time to cool off. I doubted it, but I couldn't wait. I had to try summoning her again.

three

I PREPARED FOR A SÉANCE. As set pieces went, this one was so lame I'd never put it in a movie. No sputtering candles to cast eerie shadows on the walls, no moldy skulls forming a ritual circle, no chalices filled with what the audience would suppose was red wine but secretly hope was blood.

Did experienced necromancers use stuff like candles and incense? From the little I'd learned about the supernatural world, I knew some of what we see in movies is true. Maybe, way back in history, people had known about necromancers and witches and werewolves, and those stories are based, if very loosely, on old truths.

My method—if I can call it a method since I've only used it twice—came from trial and error and a few grudging tips from Derek. As a guy who was taking college-level courses at sixteen, being confident of his facts is important to Derek. If he isn't sure, he'd rather keep his mouth shut. But when I'd pushed him, he'd told me that he'd heard that necromancers summoned ghosts either by being at a graveside or by using a personal effect, like Liz's hoodie, so I was sitting cross-legged on the carpet, clutching it.

I pictured Liz and imagined myself pulling her out of limbo. At first, I didn't try very hard. The last time I'd focused all my power into summoning a ghost, I'd summoned two right back into their buried corpses. I wasn't near a grave this time, but that didn't mean there weren't bodies around somewhere. So I kept the voltage low at first, gradually ramping it up, focusing harder and harder until . . .

"What the—? Hey, who are you?"

My eyes flew open. There stood a dark-haired boy about my age with the build, looks, and arrogant chin tilt of a star quarterback. Finding the ghost of another teenager in this place wasn't a coincidence. A name popped into my head—that of another Lyle House resident who'd been taken away before I arrived, supposedly transferred to a mental hospital, like Liz.

"Brady?" I said tentatively.

"Yeah, but I don't know you. Or this place."

He pivoted, scanning the room, then rubbed the back of his neck. I stopped myself before asking if he was okay. Of course he wasn't okay. He was dead. Like Liz. I swallowed.

"What happened to you?" I asked softly.

He jumped, as if startled by my voice.

"Is someone else here?" I asked, hoping he sensed Liz, beyond the pale where I couldn't see her.

"I thought I heard . . ." He studied me, frowning. "You brought me here?"

"I—I didn't mean to. But . . . since you *are* here, can you tell me—?"

"Nothing. I can't tell you anything." He squared his shoulders. "Whatever you want to talk about, I'm not interested."

He looked away, *determined* not to be interested. When he started to fade, I was ready to let him go. Rest in peace. Then I thought about Rae and Simon and Derek. If I didn't get some answers, we might all join Brady in the afterlife.

"My name's Chloe," I said quickly. "I'm a friend of Rae's. From Lyle House. I was there with her, after you—"

He kept fading.

"Wait!" I said. "I c-can prove it. Back at Lyle House. You tried getting into a fight with Derek, and Simon shoved you away. Only he didn't touch you. He used magic."

"Magic?"

"It was a spell that knocks people back. Simon's a sorcerer. All the kids in Lyle House—"

"I knew it. I *knew* it." He swore under his breath as he rematerialized. "All that time, they kept trying to shove their diagnosis down my throat, and I told them where else they could shove it, but I couldn't prove anything."

"You told the nurses what happened with Simon, didn't you?"

"Nurses?" He snorted. "Glorified security guards. I wanted to speak to the real boss: Davidoff. They took me to see him at this other place, looked like a warehouse."

I described what I'd seen of this building when we'd arrived.

"Yeah, that's it. They took me inside and . . ." His face screwed up in thought. "A woman came to talk to me. A blonde. Said she was a doctor. Bellows? Fellows?"

Aunt Lauren. My heart battered my rib cage. "So this woman, Dr. Fellows . . ."

"She wanted me to say Derek started the fight. That he threatened me, punched me, shoved me, whatever. I considered it. A little payback for all the attitude I had to put up with from that jerk. I'd just been goofing around with him when Simon got all up in my face and smacked me with that spell."

In the version I'd heard, Brady had been the one getting in Derek's face. Simon had a good reason for interfering, too—the last time Derek took a swing, he'd broken a kid's back.

"So Dr. Fellows wanted you to say Derek started the fight. . . ."

"I wouldn't. I'd have to deal with the fallout when I went back to Lyle House and I didn't need that grief. That's when Davidoff came in. He hauled her out of the room, but I could still hear him chewing her out in the hall. She kept saying Derek was a menace and the only reason Davidoff kept him was because he couldn't admit he made a mistake by including Derek's type."

"Type?"

"In the experiment."

A chill settled in my gut. "Ex-experiment?"

Brady shrugged. "That's all she said. Davidoff told her to shove off. He said he made a mistake with the others, but Derek was different."

Others? Did he mean other werewolves? Or other subjects in this experiment? Was I *a subject in this experiment?*

"Did they say any—?" I began.

His head whipped to the side, as if seeing something out of the corner of his eye.

"What is it?" I asked.

"Don't you hear that?"

I listened. "What is it?"

"Whispering."

"It could be Liz. She—"

Brady went rigid. His eyes rolled. Then his head flew back, the tendons in his neck popping out, bones crackling. His throat convulsed and he gurgled. Instinctively I reached out to help. My hands passed through him, but I could feel the heat of his body, a scorching heat that made me fall back in surprise.

As I recovered, Brady went still again. His chin lowered and he rolled his shoulders, as if working out the kinks. Then he looked down at me. His dark eyes were now a glowing yellowish-orange. The chill in my gut slunk up my spine.

"Frightened, child?" The voice coming out of Brady's mouth was a woman's, so high and light it was almost girlish. "Your instincts are excellent, but you have nothing to fear from me."

"W-where's Brady?"

She looked down at the body she was possessing. "Do you like him? He *is* pretty, isn't he? All of dear Dr. Lyle's creations are so very pretty. Perfect balls of perfect energy, waiting to explode."

In a blink, "Brady" was in front of me, his face coming down to mine, bathing me in scorching hot breath that smelled strangely sweet. Those orange eyes met mine, the pupils slitted like a cat's.

"The boy can't help you, child. But I can. You just need to—"

Her eyes rolled back, darkening to Brady's brown, then back to orange as she snarled.

"They're pulling him back to the other side. Call me, child. Quickly."

"C-call—"

"Call me forth. I can—"

Her eyes rolled again, her snarl deepening into something inhuman, a sound that made the chill in my veins harden to ice. I stepped back and smacked into the wall.

"Call me forth," she said, voice going ragged, deepening into Brady's. "I can answer all your questions. Call me—"

Brady's image wavered, then popped, like a TV screen after the power cord is pulled. One flash of white light and he was gone. I thought I heard a knock at the door but couldn't move, just stared at the spot where Brady had been.

The door opened, and Dr. Davidoff stepped in to find me plastered to the wall.

"Chloe?"

I staggered forward, rubbing my arms.

"Chloe?"

"S-spider," I said, pointing to the bed. "It r-ran under there."

Dr. Davidoff struggled against a smile. "Don't worry. I'll get someone to take care of it, while we're gone. We're going to go for a walk. It's time you got a proper tour and a proper explanation."

four

As I followed Dr. Davidoff down the hall, I tried to shake off thoughts of whatever had been in my room. I was a necromancer: ghosts were my one and only specialty. So it had to be a ghost, no matter how strongly every instinct in me insisted it wasn't. All I knew for sure was that I was in no hurry to go back in there.

"Now, Chloe—" Dr. Davidoff stopped, noticing me rubbing the lingering goose bumps on my arms. "Cold? I'll have them turn up the heat in your room. Your comfort is important to us."

We started walking again.

"But comfort isn't just physical, is it?" he continued. "Equally important, perhaps even more, is mental comfort. A sense of security. I know you're upset and confused, and it didn't help when we refused to answer your questions. We were eager to start checking those places you listed."

He hadn't been gone long enough to visit spots miles away. I knew what he'd really been checking: whether Rae corroborated my story. She would. She didn't know the real rendezvous point, only that I'd said the guys would meet up with us.

Dr. Davidoff opened a door at the end of the hall. It was a security station, the wall lined with flat-screen monitors. Inside, a young man spun in his chair, like he'd been caught surfing porn sites.

"Why don't you go grab a coffee, Rob," Dr. Davidoff said. "We'll take over."

He turned to me as the guard left. "You'll be seeing more of the building later. For now"—he waved at the screens—"consider this the one-stop tour."

Did he think I was stupid? I knew what he was really doing: showing me how well guarded this place was, in case I was planning another escape. But he was also giving me a chance to study what I was up against.

"As you can see, there's no camera in your room," he said, "nor in any of the bedrooms. Just in the hallway."

Two hall cameras, one at each end. I scanned the other screens. Some flipped between cameras, giving multiple angles of halls and entryways. Two showed laboratories, both empty, the lights dim, probably because it was Sunday.

An older model monitor was propped on the desk, cords every which way, like it had been quickly set up. The tiny picture screen was black-and-white and showed what looked like a storage room, all the boxes shoved along the walls. I could see the back of a girl in a beanbag chair.

She was slumped, sneakers stretched next to a game console, long curls spilling over the beanbag, the controller held between dark hands. It looked like Rae. Or maybe it was an impostor set up to convince me that she was okay, playing games, not locked up, screaming for—

The girl in the chair reached for her Diet 7UP and I saw her face. Rae.

"Yes, as Rae has informed us, that GameCube is terribly outdated. But once we promised to replace it with the latest model, she resigned herself to playing it."

As he spoke, his eyes never left the screen. The expression on his face was . . . fond. Weirdly, the very word he'd used earlier for Derek seemed to fit here.

When he turned to me, his expression rearranged itself, as if to say *I like you well enough, Chloe, but you're no Rachelle.* And I felt . . .

bewildered. Maybe even a little hurt, like there was still part of me that wanted to please.

He waved at the screen. "As you can see, we weren't prepared to have you kids with us here, but we're adjusting. While it will never be as cozy as Lyle House, the five of you will be comfortable here, perhaps more so, with all those unfortunate misrepresentations corrected."

Five of us? That must mean he didn't plan to put Derek "down like a rabid dog," as Aunt Lauren wanted. I breathed a soft sigh of relief.

"I won't apologize, Chloe," Dr. Davidoff continued. "Perhaps I should, but we thought setting up Lyle House was the best way to handle the situation."

He waved me to a chair. There were two, the one the security guard had vacated and a second, pushed against the wall. As I stepped toward the second one, it rolled from the shadows and stopped right in front of me.

"No, that's not a ghost," Dr. Davidoff said. "They can't move objects in our world—unless they happen to be a very specific kind, namely the ghost of an Agito."

"A what?"

"Agito. It's Latin roughly translating to 'put into motion.' Half-demons come in many types, as you'll discover. An Agito's power, as the name might suggest, is telekinesis."

"Moving things with the mind."

"Very good. And it is an Agito who moved that chair, though one who is still very much alive."

"You?"

He smiled and, for a second, the mask of the doddering old fool cracked, and I caught a glimpse of the real man beneath. What I saw was pride and arrogance, like a classmate flashing his A+ paper as if to say *top that.*

"Yes, I'm a supernatural, as is almost everyone who works here. I know what you must have been thinking—that we're humans who've discovered your powers and wish to destroy what we don't understand, like in those comic books."

"The *X-Men*."

I don't know what was more shocking, that Dr. Davidoff and his colleagues were supernaturals or the image of this stooped, awkward man reading *X-Men*. Had he pored over them as a boy, imagining himself in Xavier's School for Gifted Youngsters?

Did that mean Aunt Lauren was a necromancer? That she saw ghosts, too?

He continued before I could ask anything. "The Edison Group was founded by supernaturals eighty years ago. And as much as it has grown since those early days, it's still an institution run by supernaturals and for supernaturals, dedicated to bettering the lives of our kind."

"Edison Group?"

"Named after Thomas Edison."

"The guy who invented the lightbulb?"

"That's what he's best known for. He also invented the movie projector, which I'm sure *you're* grateful for. Yet you, Chloe, have accomplished something he dreamed of but never succeeded in doing." A dramatic pause. "Contacting the dead."

"Thomas Edison wanted to talk to the dead?"

"He believed in an afterlife and wanted to communicate with it not through séances and spiritualism but through science. When he died, it's thought he was working on just such a device—a telephone to the afterlife. No plans for it were ever found." Dr. Davidoff smiled conspiratorially. "Or, at least, not officially. We adopted the name because, like Edison, we take a scientific approach to matters of the paranormal."

Improving supernatural lives through science. Where had I heard something like that? It took me a moment to remember, and when I did, I shivered.

The ghosts I'd raised in the Lyle House basement had been subjects of experiments by a sorcerer named Samuel Lyle. Willing subjects, at first, they'd said, because they'd been promised a better life. Instead, they'd ended up lab rats sacrificed to the vision of a madman, as one ghost had put it. And that thing in my room had called Brady—and me, I think—Samuel Lyle's "creations."

"Chloe?"

"S-sorry. I'm just—"

"Tired, I imagine, after being up all night. Would you like a rest?"

"No, I-I'm fine. It's just— So how do we fit in? And Lyle House? It's part of an experiment, isn't it?"

His chin lifted, not much, just enough of a reaction to tell me I'd caught him off guard and that he didn't like it. A pleasant smile erased the look and he eased back in his chair.

"It *is* an experiment, Chloe. I know how that must sound, but I assure you, it's a noninvasive study, using only benign psychological therapy."

Benign? There was nothing benign about what had happened to Liz and Brady.

"Okay, so we're part of this experiment. . . ." I said.

"Being a supernatural is both a blessing and curse. Adolescence is the most difficult time for us, as our powers begin to manifest. One of the Edison Group's theories is that it might be easier if our children don't know of their future."

"Don't know they're supernatural?"

"Yes, instead allowing them to grow up as human, assimilating into human society without anxiety over the upcoming transition. You and the others are part of that study. For most, it has worked. But for others, such as you, your powers came too quickly. We needed to ease you into the truth and ensure you didn't harm yourselves or anyone else in the meantime."

So they put us into a group home and told us we were crazy? Drugged us? That made no sense. What about Simon and Derek, who'd already known what they were? How could they be part of this study? But Derek clearly was, if what Brady said was right.

What about that thing calling us Dr. Lyle's creations? What about Brady and Liz, permanently removed from this *study*? Murdered. You don't kill a subject when he doesn't respond well to your "benign psychological therapy."

They'd lied all along—did I really think they'd fess up now? If I wanted the truth, I needed to do what I'd been doing. Search for my own answers.

So I let Dr. Davidoff blather on, telling me about their study, about the other kids, about how we'd be "fixed" and out of here in no time. And I smiled and nodded and started making my own plans.

five

When Dr. Davidoff was done with the propaganda, he took me to see Rae, who was still in that makeshift game room playing Zelda. He opened the door and waved me in, then closed it, leaving us alone.

"Game time over?" Rae said, turning slowly. "Just let me finish—"

Seeing me, she leaped up, controller clattering to the floor. She hugged me, then pulled back.

"Your arm," she said. "Did I hurt—?"

"No, it's all bandaged up. It needed some stitches."

"Ouch." Rae took a long look at me. "You need some sleep, girl. You look like death."

"That's just the necromancer genes kicking in."

She laughed and gave me another hug before plunking back down in her beanbag chair. Despite our long night on the run, Rae looked fine. But then Rae was one of those girls who always looked fine—perfect clear copper skin; copper eyes; and long curls that, if they caught the light right, glinted with copper, too.

"Pull up a box. I'd offer you a chair, but decorators these days?" She rolled her eyes. "So slow. When the renovations are done, though, you won't recognize the place. Stereo system, DVD player, computer . . . chairs. And, as of tomorrow, we're getting a Wii."

"Really?"

"Yep. I said, 'People, if I'm helping you with this study of yours, I need a little love in return. And a GameCube ain't gonna cut it.'"

"Did you ask for a bigger TV, too?"

"I should have. After the whole Lyle House screwup, they're tripping over themselves to make us happy. We are going to be so spoiled here. Of course, we deserve it."

"We do."

She grinned, her face glowing. "Did you hear? I'm a half-demon. An Exhaust—Exustio. That's the highest kind of fire demon you can be. Cool, huh?"

Being a half-demon *was* cool. But being a half-demon lab rat, teetering on the brink of extermination? Definitely not cool. As much as I longed to tell her the truth, though, I couldn't. Not yet.

Just last night, Rae had been lying on her bed at Lyle House, trying to light a match with her bare fingers, desperate for proof she had a supernatural ability. Now she'd discovered she was a special kind of half-demon. That was important to Rae in a way I couldn't understand—in a way that I just had to accept until I had more proof that this wasn't the best thing that ever happened to her.

"And you know what else?" she said. "They showed me pictures of my mom. My *real* mom. None of my dad, of course, being a demon. Kind of freaky when you think about it. Demons aren't exactly . . ." For the first time, worry clouded her eyes. She blinked it back. "But Dr. D. says that it doesn't make you evil or whatever. Anyway, my mom? Her name was Jacinda. Isn't that pretty?"

I opened my mouth to agree, but she kept rambling excitedly.

"She used to work here, like Simon's dad. They have pictures of her. She was gorgeous. Like a model. And Dr. D. said they might even know where to find her, and they're going to try. Just for me."

"What about your adoptive parents?"

The clouds descended again, lingering longer, and I felt bad, being the one to bring her down. First telling Liz she was dead, then making Brady relive his final evening, now reminding Rae of her parents . . . I was trying to get answers to help all of us. But it felt cruel.

After a moment, Rae said, "They aren't supernaturals."

"Oh?"

"Nope, just humans." She gave the word an ugly twist. "They said when my mom left here, she cut off all ties with the group. Somehow I got put up for adoption. Dr. D. says that must have been a mistake. Jacinda loved me. She'd never have given me up. He says that story my adoptive parents told me, about her not being able to keep me, was a lie, and if the Edison Group had known about the adoption, they'd have found me parents like us. By the time they tracked me down, though, it was too late, so all they could do was monitor me. When they found out I was having problems, they contacted my adoptive parents and offered me a free stay at Lyle House. I bet it'll probably be weeks before my folks even notice I'm not there anymore, and then they'll just breathe a big sigh of relief."

"I can't see—"

"I was at Lyle House for almost a month. Do you know how many times my parents came to visit? Called?" She held up her thumb and forefinger in an O.

"Maybe they weren't allowed to visit. Maybe they left messages that you never got."

Her nose scrunched. "Why wouldn't I get them?"

"Because your adoptive parents aren't supernaturals. Having them interfering would complicate things."

Her eyes grew distant as she considered this. A spark flickered through them—hope that she'd been mistaken, that the only parents she'd ever known hadn't abandoned her.

She gave her head a sharp shake. "No, I was trouble, and Mom was glad to get rid of me." Her hands gripped the beanbag tight, then released it and patted out the creases. "It's better this way. *I'm* better this way."

Better a special half-demon embarking on a new life than a regular girl, sent back to her regular life with her regular parents. I reached over and took her game controller.

"How far have you gotten?" I asked.

"You set on beating me, girl?"

"Absolutely."

I had lunch with Rae. Pizza. Unlike Lyle House, here they seemed more concerned with keeping us happy than keeping us healthy.

Maybe because they aren't planning on keeping us alive?

Talking to Rae, hearing her excitement, I had enough distance from the pain and betrayal to face a very real, very disturbing possibility.

What if I was wrong? About everything?

I didn't have any evidence that the people here had actually killed Liz and Brady. Liz had "dreamed" of being in some kind of hospital room, restrained. For all I knew, she'd died in a car crash when they were bringing her here. Or she'd committed suicide that night. Or, in trying to restrain her, they'd accidentally killed her.

Liz and Brady just happened to both die accidentally after leaving Lyle House?

Okay, that was unlikely.

Rae's birth mom and Simon's dad both happened to have a falling-out with the Edison Group and fled, taking their study subject kids with them?

No, there was definitely something wrong here. I needed answers and I wasn't going to find them locked in my cell. Nor was I eager to meet that thing in my room again.

Just as I thought that, Dr. Davidoff arrived to take me back there. As I followed him down the hall, I scrambled for an excuse to go someplace else in the building, any way to add details to my mental map of the place.

I considered asking to speak to Aunt Lauren. I'd have to pretend I'd forgiven her for lying to me my entire life, betraying me, and tossing me to the mercy of the Edison Group. I wasn't that good an actor. And Aunt Lauren wasn't that stupid. There was a reason she hadn't tried to see me.

She was biding her time, waiting until I got lonely for a familiar face, desperate for excuses. Until then, she'd stay away.

There was one other person I could ask to speak to. . . .

The thought made my skin crawl almost as much as the thought of seeing Aunt Lauren. But I needed answers.

"Dr. Davidoff?" I said as we approached my door.

"Yes, Chloe."

"Is Tori here?"

"She is."

"I was thinking . . . I'd like to see her, make sure she's all right."

six

DR. DAVIDOFF DECLARED that a "splendid idea," meaning he had no clue I'd figured out that Tori was the one who'd tipped them off to our escape. As for getting a better look at the place—that plan didn't work so well. Her cell turned out to be only a few doors from mine.

The doctor ushered me in, then locked the door. When the bolt slid home, I inched back, ready to scream at the first sign of trouble. At my last up-close-and-personal encounter with Victoria Enright, she'd knocked me out with a brick, tied me up, and left me alone in a pitch-black basement crawl space. So I could be forgiven if that locked door made me nervous.

The only light in the room came from the bedside clock. "Tori?"

A figure rose from the mattress, her short hair a halo of spikes. "Huh. I guess if stern lectures don't work, they can always resort to torture. Tell them I surrender, as long as they take you away. Please."

"I came to—"

"Gloat?"

I stepped toward her. "Sure. I came to gloat. Get a good laugh at you, locked in a cell, just like I am down the hall."

"If you say 'we're in this together,' I'm going to hurl."

"Hey, we wouldn't be in this at all if it wasn't for you telling the nurses on us. Only you didn't count on getting locked away yourself. That's what we call dramatic irony."

A moment of silence. Then she gave a harsh laugh. "You think I ratted you out? If I'd known you were running away, I would have packed your bag."

"Not if I was leaving with Simon."

She swung her legs over the side of the bed. "So in a fit of jealous rage, I spill your plans, getting you and the guy who rejected me sent away to a mental hospital? What movie is that from?"

"The same one where the cheerleader knocks out the new girl with a brick and leaves her in a locked crawl space."

"I am not a cheerleader." She spat the word with such venom, you'd think I'd called her a slut. "I was going to let you out after dinner, but Prince Not-So-Charming got to you first." She slid from the bed. "I liked Simon, but no guy is worth humiliating myself over. You want someone to blame? Check the mirror. You're the one who stirred things up. You and your ghosts. You got Liz sent away, got Derek in trouble, got me in trouble."

"*You* got you in trouble. I didn't do anything."

"Of course you didn't."

She stepped closer. Her skin looked yellow, and purple underscored her brown eyes. "I've got a sister just like you, Chloe. *She's* the cheerleader, the cute little blonde, bats her eyelashes and everyone comes running. Just like you at Lyle House, with Simon tripping over himself to help you. Even Derek rushed to your rescue—"

"I didn't—"

"Do anything. That's the point. You can't do anything. You're a silly, useless Barbie, just like my sister. I'm smarter, tougher, more popular. But does that matter? No." She towered a head above me, staring down. "All anyone cares about is the helpless little blonde. But being helpless only works when there's someone around to save you."

She lifted her hands. Sparks leaped from her fingers. When I fell back, she grinned.

"Why don't you call Derek to help you now, Chloe? Or your little ghost friends?" Tori advanced, the sparks swirling into a ball of blue light between her raised hands. She whipped her hands down. I dove. The ball shot over my shoulder, hit the wall, and exploded into a shower of sparks that singed my cheek.

I got to my feet, backing toward the door. Tori raised her hands and swung them down, and an invisible force knocked me over again. The room shook, every piece of furniture rocking and chattering. Even Tori looked surprised.

"Y-you're a witch," I said.

"Am I?" She bore down on me, her eyes as wild as her hair. "Nice for someone to tell me. My mother insisted it was all in my head. She shipped me off to Lyle House, had me diagnosed as bipolar, and gave me a cartload of meds. And I gulped them because I didn't want to disappoint her."

She slammed down her hands. Lightning bolts flew from her fingertips, heading straight for me.

Tori's eyes went wide with shock, her lips parting in a silent *no*!

I tried to scramble out of the way, but I wasn't fast enough. As those crackling bolts came at me, a figure materialized—a girl in a nightgown. Liz. She shoved the dresser, and it shot from the wall and into the bolt's path. Wood splintered. The mirror glass shattered, raining shards down on me as I crouched, head down.

When I lifted my head, the room was silent and Liz was gone. The dresser lay on its side with a smoldering hole through it, and all I could think was: *That could have been me.*

Tori sat huddled on the floor, her knees pulled up, her face buried against them as she rocked. "I didn't mean it, I didn't mean it. I get so mad, so *mad.* And it just happens."

Like Liz, making things fly when she got angry. Like Rae, burning her mom in a fight. Like Derek, throwing a kid and breaking his back. What would happen if I got mad enough?

Uncontrollable powers. That wasn't normal for supernaturals. It couldn't be.

I took a slow step toward Tori. "Tori, I—"

The door whacked open, and Tori's mom barreled in. She stopped short when she saw the destruction.

"Victoria Enright!" The name came out in a snarl worthy of a werewolf. "What have you done?"

"I-it wasn't her," I said. "It was me. We argued and I—I . . ."

I stared at the hole blasted through the dresser and I couldn't finish the sentence.

"I know very well who's responsible for this, Miss Chloe." Tori's mom turned that snarl on me. "Though I don't doubt you played your role. You're quite the little instigator, aren't you?"

"Diane, that's enough," Dr. Davidoff snapped from the doorway. "Help your daughter clean up her mess. Chloe, come with me."

Instigator? Me? Two weeks ago, I would have laughed at the thought. But now . . . Tori said this all started with me, with the guys wanting to save the helpless little girl. I hated that idea. Yet she had a point.

Derek had wanted Simon to leave Lyle House and find their dad. Simon wouldn't leave Derek, who refused to go because he was afraid he'd hurt someone else. When Derek figured out I was a necromancer, he found his weapon to beat down Simon's defenses. One damsel in distress, to go.

I was the poor girl who didn't know anything about being a necromancer, who kept making mistakes, getting closer and closer to being shipped off to a mental hospital. *See her, Simon? She's in danger. She needs your help. Take her, find Dad, and he'll fix everything.*

I'd been furious with Derek, and I'd called him on it. But I hadn't refused to go along with the plan. We needed Simon's dad—all of us did. Even Derek, who'd eventually joined us when our escape had been uncovered and he had no choice.

If I'd known what was going to happen, would I have stopped searching for answers back at Lyle House? Would I have accepted the diagnosis, taken my meds, shut up, and gotten released?

No. Harsh truth was better than comfortable lies. It had to be.

Dr. Davidoff took me back to my room, and I told myself I was fine with that. I needed to be alone so I could try again to contact Liz, now that I knew she was still around.

I started slowly, gradually increasing my efforts until I heard a voice so soft it could have been a hiss from the vent. I looked around, hoping to see Liz in her Minnie Mouse nightshirt and giraffe socks. But there was only me.

"Liz?"

A soft, hesitant "Yes?"

"I'm sorry," I said, getting to my feet. "I know you're angry with me, but it didn't seem right not to tell you the truth."

She didn't answer.

"I'm going to find out who killed you. I promise."

The words flew to my lips like I was reading a script, but at least I'd had the sense to shut my mouth before promising to avenge her death. That was one of those things that made perfect sense on the screen, but in real life, you think *Great . . . and how exactly would I do that?* Liz stayed silent, like she was holding out for more.

"Can I see you?" I said. "Please?"

"I can't . . . come through. You need to try harder."

I sat back on the floor, hands wrapped in her hoodie and concentrated.

"Harder," she whispered.

I squeezed my eyes shut and imagined myself pulling Liz through. Just one huge yank and—

A familiar tinkling laugh sent me scrambling to my feet. Warm air slid along my unbandaged forearm.

I yanked my sleeve down. "*You.* I didn't call you."

"You didn't need to, child. When you summon, spirits must obey. You called to your friend and the shades of a thousand dead answered, winging their way back to their rotted shells." Her breath tickled my ear. "Shells buried in a cemetery two miles away. A thousand corpses ready to become a thousand zombies. A vast army of the dead for you to control."

"I—I didn't—"

"No, you didn't. Not yet. Your powers need time to mature. And then?" Her laugh filled the room. "Dear Dr. Lyle must be dancing in Hell today, his agonies borne away on the thrill of his triumph. Dearly departed, scarcely lamented, deeply demented Dr. Samuel Lyle. Creator of the prettiest, sweetest abomination I have ever seen."

"Wh-what?"

"A bit of this, a bit of that. A twist here, a tweak there. And look what we have."

I squeezed my eyes shut against the urge to ask what she meant. Whatever this thing was, I couldn't trust her, no more than I could trust Dr. Davidoff and the Edison Group.

"What do you want?" I asked.

"The same thing you do. Freedom from this place."

I settled onto the bed. As hard as I looked, though, I couldn't see any sign of her. There was only the voice and the warm breeze.

"You're trapped here?" I asked.

"Like a fairy under a bell jar, metaphorically speaking. Fairies are a product of the human imagination. Little people flitting about on wings? How positively quaint. A more fitting simile would be to say that I am trapped like a lightning bug in a bottle. For magical energy, nothing quite compares to a soul-bound demi-demon. Except, of course, a soul-bound *full* demon, but to summon one and attempt to harness its power would be suicide. Just ask Samuel Lyle."

"He died summoning a demon?"

"The summoning is usually a forgivable offense. It's soul binding that rather annoys them. Lyle should have been content with me, but humans are never satisfied, are they? Too arrogant to contemplate the possibility of failure, he neglected to pass along the true secret of his success: me."

"Your magic powers this place. And they don't even realize it?"

"Lyle guarded his secrets to the grave and beyond, though taking them into the afterlife was not his intention. I'm sure he meant to tell them about me . . . had he not died before he got around to it. Even a necromancer as powerful as you would have difficulty contacting a spirit in a hell dimension, so now I am bound here, my power enhancing the magics cast in this place. The others—this Edison Group—think it's built on the junction of ley lines or some such foolishness."

"So if I freed you . . . ?"

"The building would collapse into a pile of smoldering rubble, the evil souls within sucked into Hell, to be tormented by demons for eternity." She laughed. "A pleasant thought, but no, my departure would merely hamper their efforts. Significantly hamper, though—putting an end to their most ambitious projects."

Release the demon under promise that I'd be repaid handsomely, my enemies destroyed? Hmm, where had I seen this before? Oh, right. Every demon horror movie ever made. And the horror part started right after the releasing part.

"I don't think so," I said.

"Ah, yes. Set me free and I shall take my revenge on the world. Start wars and famines, hurl thunderbolts, raise the very dead from their graves . . . Perhaps you could help with that?"

The voice slid to my ear again. "You are still such a child, aren't you? Believing in bogeymen. Of all the wars and massacres in the last century, demons are responsible for perhaps a tenth; and that, some would say, gives us too much credit. Unlike humans, we are wise enough to know that destroying the world that sustains us is hardly in our best interests. Free me and, yes, I will have my fun, but I'm no more dangerous out there than I am in here."

I considered it . . . and imagined the audience screaming. "You stupid twit! It's a *demon*!"

"I don't think so."

Her sigh ruffled my shirt. "There is no sight sadder than a desperate demi-demon. After decades alone in this place, beating the bars of my cage, howling to deaf ears, I'm reduced to begging favors from a child. Ask me your questions, and I shall play schoolteacher, answering them at no cost. I *was* a schoolteacher once, you know, when a foolish witch summoned me and invited possession, which is never wise, even if you're trying to destroy the dreadful little Puritan village that accused you of—"

"I don't have any questions."

"None?"

"None."

Her voice snaked around me. "Speaking of witches, I could tell you a secret about the dark-haired one you visited. Her mother—too ambitious by far—heard of another witch bearing a sorcerer's child, so she had to do the same. Now she's paying the price. A mixed-blood spellcaster is always dangerous."

"Tori's dad is a sorcerer?" I said in spite of myself.

"The man she calls Daddy? No. Her real father? Yes."

"So that is why—" I stopped. "No, I don't want to know."

"Of course you do. How about the wolf boy? I heard them talking to you about him. I remember the pups. They lived here, you know."

"They?"

"Four pups, cute as could be. Perfect little predators, flashing fangs and claws even before they could change forms—all but the biggest of the litter. The lone wolf. The smart wolf. When his Pack brothers flashed those fangs and claws one time too many, those who'd opposed the inclusion of the beasties got their way."

"What happened?"

"What happens to pups that bite their owner's hand? They were killed, of course. All but the clever one who didn't play their wolfie games. He got to go away and be a real boy." Her voice tickled my ear again. "What else can I tell you . . . ?"

"Nothing. I want you to leave."

She laughed. "Which is why you're lapping up my every word like sweet mead."

Fighting my curiosity, I found my iPod, stuck in my earbuds, and cranked up the volume.

seven

LATER THAT AFTERNOON, Dr. Davidoff knocked at my door again. Time for a history lesson, apparently. He led me to his office and entered the code to a closet-sized vault lined with bookshelves.

"We have more reference books than this, naturally. The rest are in the library, which you'll visit soon. However, this"—he waved at the closet—"is what a public library would call its special collection, containing the rarest and most prized volumes."

He slid a red leather-bound one from the shelf. Silver letters spelled out *Nekromantia*.

"The early history of the necromancer race. This is an eighteenth-century reproduction. There are only three known copies, including this one."

He lowered it into my hands with all the ceremony of passing over the crown jewels. I didn't want to be impressed, but when I felt the worn leather, smelled the mustiness of time, a thrill rippled through me. I was every great fantasy hero raised in ignominy, then handed the magic book and told "this is who you really are." I couldn't help falling for it—the story was hardwired in my brain.

Dr. Davidoff opened a second door. Inside was a surprisingly cozy sitting room with leather chairs, a jungle of plants, and a skylight.

"My secret hiding spot," he said. "You can read your book in here while I work in my office."

After he left, I checked out the narrow skylight, but even if I could manage to climb twenty feet to get to it, I'd never fit through. So I settled into the chair with the book.

I'd just opened it when he returned.

"Chloe? I need to leave. Is that all right?"

Leave me alone in his office? I tried not to nod too enthusiastically.

"If you need anything, dial nine for front reception," he said. "This door will be locked."

Of course . . .

I waited until I heard the outer door close. I was sure he'd locked my door, as promised, but I had to check.

It was a rich girl lock, Rae would say—the kind that keep out only kids who've never had to share a bathroom and, occasionally, break in to grab a hairbrush while their sister hogs the shower.

A side table held a stack of paperbacks. I found one with a cover sturdy enough to do the job, then copied Rae by wriggling it in the door crack until the lock clicked.

Voilà, my first break-in. Or break*out*.

I stepped into Dr. Davidoff's office. What I needed was a file cabinet, stuffed with records on the study, but all I could see was a desktop computer.

At least it was a Mac—I was more familiar with those than PCs. I jiggled the mouse and the computer popped out of sleep mode. The user login screen appeared. There was only one user account—Davidoff, with an eight ball as the graphic. I clicked it and got the password box. Ignoring it, I clicked on "Forgot password." The hint appeared: *usual.* In other words, his usual password, I supposed. That really helped.

At the password prompt, I typed *Davidoff.* Then *Marcel.*

Uh, do you really think it could be that easy?

I tried every variation on Lyle House and Edison Group, then, in what I considered a stroke of insight: Agito, with several possible spellings.

After my third wrong guess, it had again prompted me with the hint: *usual.* A few more tries and it asked me to enter the master password so I could reset the user account password. Great. If I knew what the master password was . . .

I remembered reading that most people kept their password written near their computer. I checked under the keyboard, under the mouse pad, under the monitor. As I peered under the desk, a voice whispered, "It's Jacinda."

I jumped so fast I banged my head.

A tinkling laugh. "Careful, child." It was the demi-demon. Again.

"The password is Jacinda?" I said as I backed out from under the desk. "That's Rae's mom's name. Why would he—?" I stopped myself.

"What connection does Dr. Davidoff have with Rae and her mother? Another delicious secret. All these scientists, so proud and lofty, pretending they are above mere human frailties. Foolishness. They are prey to them all—greed, ambition, pride, lust. I'm particularly fond of lust. Very amusing."

As she prattled, I typed in *Jacinda.* The password box vanished and Dr. Davidoff's desktop began to load.

I opened a Finder window and searched on my name. The window began filling with hits. I tried clicking on one in a folder labeled "Genesis II subjects," but misjudged and instead opened a file called simply "Genesis II" in the root folder of the same name.

The first paragraph looked like something out of Aunt Lauren's medical journals—the summary of an experiment. I read:

> The blessing of supernatural powers is tempered by two serious disadvantages: dangerous or unpleasant side effects and the constant struggle to assimilate into human society. This study attempts to reduce or eliminate these disadvantages through genetic modification.

Genetic modification? The hairs on my scalp prickled.

> The DNA of five subjects from five of the major races was modified in vitro. This modification was primarily designed to reduce the side effects of supernatural powers. It was expected that reducing these effects would aid assimilation, but this was further tested by raising twenty of the children in ignorance of their heritage. The remaining five served as a control group and were raised as supernaturals. During the intervening years, the study experienced some subject attrition (Appendix A), though contact has been reestablished with most.

Attrition? They must mean kids they lost track of—like Rae, Simon, and Derek. Did that mean there were others like us out there, ones they hadn't found?

> As the remaining subjects proceed through puberty, side effects have been drastically reduced in nine (Appendix B). However, in those subjects who did not improve, the genetic modification itself has had serious and unexpected side effects (Appendix C).

Fingers shaking, I typed "Appendix C" into the Find box. The document scrolled down.

> One problem noted in the nine successful subjects was a general reduction in powers, which may be an unavoidable consequence of reducing negative side effects. It appears, however, that with the unsuccessful subjects, the reverse occurred. Their powers were heightened, as were the negative side effects, particularly sudden onset of these powers and, more seriously, their uncontrollable nature, apparently emotion based.

Uncontrollable powers. Emotion based.

I remembered Tori sobbing that she couldn't help it, that when she got mad, things just happened. Like Liz. Like Derek. Like Rae. Like me?

I skimmed over the next page. It detailed how they'd handled these "unsuccessful" subjects—put them into a group home, tried to medicate their powers and convince them they were mentally ill. When that failed . . .

The powers of supernaturals increase through puberty, meaning the powers of these failed subjects will continue to grow. It can be reasonably hypothesized that their powers will become more volatile and uncontrollable, threatening the lives of the subjects; the lives of innocents around them; and, perhaps most important, posing an immense exposure risk to the entire supernatural world.

We undertook this experiment in hopes of bettering the lives of all supernaturals. We cannot, through our actions, endanger that same world. As responsible scientists, we must accept responsibility for our failures and deal with them decisively to minimize the damage. While the decision was not unanimous, it was agreed that if the predetermined rehabilitation process fails, the subject must, with deep regret, be terminated quickly and humanely.

At the bottom was a list of names. Beside each was their current status.

Peter Ricci—rehabilitated
Mila Andrews—rehabilitated
Amber Long—terminated
Brady Hirsch—terminated
Elizabeth Delany—terminated
Rachelle Rogers—rehabilitation progressing
Victoria Enright—rehabilitation progressing

And finally, at the bottom, two names.

Derek Souza—???
Chloe Saunders—???

I don't know how long I stared at that list—and those question marks—before something hit my skull. I spun as a stapler bounced onto the carpet.

"Café mocha," said Dr. Davidoff, right outside the door. "Decaf, nonfat."

As I logged off, my gaze flipped between the reading room door and the kneehole under the desk. The kneehole was closer, but then I'd be trapped. A spurt of courage sent me lunging for the door. I made it—*to* the door, not through it into the reading room—as the hall door clicked open. I wheeled and pressed myself against the wall, beside a tall bookcase. I was out of sight but just barely.

I reached for the reading room doorknob. If I opened it wide enough to get through, though, he'd notice.

Go to the desk, I pleaded. *Check your e-mail. Check your voice messages. Just please, please, please, don't check on me.*

His footsteps headed straight for me. I plastered myself to the wall and held my breath. His arm appeared. Then his knee. Then—

He stopped. The arm and knee turned toward the desk. He bent and picked up the stapler.

Oh, God. He knew. I had to come clean. Make up a story and turn myself in before I was caught. I stepped forward. A chattering broke the silence. My teeth? No, the pen holder on his desk was shaking, pens and pencils rattling.

Dr. Davidoff stared at it, his head tilting as if to say, *Am I doing that?* He caught the pen holder. It stopped shaking. As he pulled back his hand, the mouse rolled across the pad.

"Well?" a voice said by my ear. "Are you just going to stand there?"

Liz stood at my shoulder. She jabbed her finger at the door.

"Go!"

I made sure Dr. Davidoff had his back to me, then eased through the door.

"Lock it!" she whispered.

I reached around and turned the lock. The pens chattered again, covering the click of the door latch.

Liz stepped through the wall and waved me to the chair like she was shooing a cat. I'd barely settled in with the book when the door opened.

Dr. Davidoff took a slow look around the room. I followed his gaze, frowning, like I was wondering what he was searching for. I forced myself to look past Liz perched on the side table.

"Dr. Davidoff?"

He said nothing, just looked around.

"Did you forget something?" I asked.

He murmured about checking on dinner, then left after pausing at the door for one last, slow look around.

"Thank you," I said to Liz after Dr. Davidoff had locked me in again. "I know you're mad at me, for saying you're dead—"

"Because I'm obviously not dead, am I? You said the reason I couldn't touch stuff or move it was because I was a ghost." She smiled smugly, pulling her knees up and hugging them. "So I worked really hard at moving stuff. If I concentrate, I can. That means I must be a shaman."

Earlier I'd tried to explain why I hadn't told her sooner that she was a ghost. I'd said I'd thought she might be a shaman, because Derek said they could astral-project—appear without their bodies.

"They've got me drugged up," she continued. "That's why I keep getting all confused. I can't wake up, so my spirit is moving around instead."

She dangled her legs again and made figure eights with her feet, watching the giraffes on her socks dance. She didn't believe what she was saying. She knew she was dead. But she wasn't ready to face it.

As for being able to move objects, Dr. Davidoff had said one kind of ghost could: a telekinetic half-demon. When Liz got mad, objects had attacked whoever she was angry at. Now, as a ghost, she'd finally learned to harness her power.

In life, Liz thought she had a poltergeist. In death, she was one. She just couldn't accept that yet. And I wasn't going to force her.

eight

WE HAD SPAGHETTI AND MEATBALLS for dinner. Rae's favorite. I couldn't eat, only sipping at a glass of flat Coke, but she didn't notice my loss of appetite. She was like a kid on her first day back from camp, with so much to tell that it burbled out in one endless stream.

She'd had a training session, a demonology lecture, and a long talk with Dr. Davidoff, who told her all about her mother and their hopes of contacting her. And as she talked, all I could think was, *We've been genetically modified. We're Frankenstein monsters*—failed *Frankenstein monsters. And I have no idea how I'm going to break it to you.*

"I saw Brady today," I finally blurted.

Rae stopped, fork raised, dangling spaghetti strands swaying. "Brady? Seriously? He's here. Oh my God, that is so cool." Her grin blazed. "And you know what the first words out of that boy's mouth are gonna be? 'I told you so.' He kept saying there was nothing wrong with him, that something weird was going on—"

"He's dead Rae. I contacted his ghost."

She blinked. One slow blink, and then it was like someone paralyzed every muscle in her face, and it went completely still, her eyes empty, expressionless.

"I-I'm sorry. I didn't mean to blurt it out like—"

"Why would you make up such a"—she seemed to chew over her words, searching for the best, before spitting out—"*vicious* lie."

"Lie? No! I'd never—"

"Why are you doing this, Chloe?"

"Because we're in danger. We've been genetically modified and it didn't work. The Edison Group killed Liz and Brady and—"

"And it's only a matter of time before they kill us all. *Mwah-ha-ha!* You really do watch too many movies, don't you? And now those boys have brainwashed you with their conspiracy theory crap."

"Conspiracy theory?"

"All their talk about Lyle House and the evil people Simon's dad worked for. Those guys have you so brainwashed, you need to make the Edison Group into the bad guys. So don't tell me stories about Liz and Brady being dead."

My voice went as cold as hers. "You don't believe me? Fine. I'll summon Liz and you can ask her a question only she could answer."

"Don't bother."

I stood. "No, really. I insist. It'll only take a sec."

When I closed my eyes, her chair squealed. Fingers clamped around my forearm. I opened my eyes to see her face, inches away.

"Don't play games, Chloe. I'm sure you can make me think Liz is here."

I looked into her eyes and saw a glimmer of fear. Rae wouldn't let me summon Liz because she didn't want to know the truth.

"Just let me—" I began.

"No."

She gripped my arm tighter, her fingers scorching hot. I gasped and yanked back. She let go quickly and a stricken look crossed her face. She started to apologize, then stopped herself, marched across the room, called reception, and said we were done with dinner.

I was actually glad to get back to my cell. I needed to figure out how I could convince Rae that we needed to escape . . . and what I'd do if I couldn't.

I had to get out. Those question marks beside Derek's name meant they hadn't decided what to do with him, and I'd already known that. Now I'd seen the same marks beside my name.

I needed to come up with an escape plan fast. But the moment I stretched out on my bed to start thinking, I discovered that my Coke at dinner hadn't been just flat. It had been drugged.

I fell into a dreamless sleep and didn't wake until someone touched my shoulder. I opened my eyes to see Sue, the gray-haired woman who'd chased us at the factory yard. She stood there, smiling down at me like a kindly nurse. My stomach twisted and I had to glance away.

"Time to get up, honey," she said. "Dr. Davidoff let you sleep in today, but we have a full afternoon of lessons that I'm sure you don't want to miss."

"A-afternoon?" I said, sitting up. "What time is it?"

"Almost eleven thirty. Rachelle and Victoria are finishing up their morning lessons and they'll meet you in the dining room for lunch."

nine

LUNCH WAS VEGGIE WRAPS, salad, and bottled water. Tori's choice apparently. Rae said a polite hello to me, then not another word. At least she'd made eye contact, though, which was more than I could say for Tori.

We were finishing up when Dr. Davidoff came in.

"I apologize for the interruption, girls," he said, "but I need to speak to Chloe."

I rose. "Sure. Where—?"

"Here's fine."

He took his time settling into a chair. Sweat trickled down the back of my neck, like a kid singled out in front of the class.

"We appreciate the help you've given us to try finding Simon, Chloe. We're very worried, as you girls know."

"Sure," Rae said. "He needs that medicine. If I had any idea where to find him, I'd tell—"

She stopped and looked at me. Tori did the same, and I understood why I wasn't getting this lecture in private.

"I gave you that list of places," I said quickly. "That's all I have."

"They weren't there, Chloe," Dr. Davidoff said. "So we've reconsidered your offer. We'd like to take you along on our search this afternoon."

That crash I heard? The collision of clichés. One: never look a gift horse in the mouth. Two: if it sounds too good to be true, it probably is. I'd been lied to and misled often enough in the last few days that I wasn't just questioning this horse's dental health—I was examining him from nose to tail.

"You want me to go with you . . ."

"Yes, and, with luck, the boys will see you and come out. There's just one problem."

Oh, I was sure there were *lots* of problems with this scenario.

"The places you've given us don't seem right," he said. "The boys are clever, and their dad taught them well. They'd either choose a private spot or a very public one, and the possibilities you've provided are neither. We think there might be one you forgot to mention." He paused, meeting my gaze. "If there isn't, then we don't see the point of taking you along."

That second crash? The sound of the other shoe dropping. Dr. Davidoff knew why I wanted to go with them, and he'd decided to play my game. Did I dare play along?

"Come on, Chloe," Rae whispered.

"You'd better not think you're protecting them by keeping your mouth shut," Tori said. "Simon's sick, Chloe. If he dies, I hope he haunts you until—"

"That's enough, Tori," Dr. Davidoff said.

"I . . . might have another idea," I said. Oh God, I'd *better* have another idea. As hard as I thought, though, I needed time to come up with something good, and I wasn't going to get that time. So I stumbled through a lame story about Derek and me running through that factory yard, until we found a hiding spot. Maybe that's where he meant for our rendezvous spot. Only it had been dark, and we'd run through so many buildings that I wasn't sure exactly which one we'd hidden in, but I'd recognize it when I saw it.

Dr. Davidoff smiled, and I braced for him to call me on it, but he just said, "Then it's a good thing you're coming, isn't it?"

"And me," Tori said. "I've barely been out of my room since we got here, and I haven't been *outside* since Chloe arrived at Lyle House. I want to go, too."

"It isn't a field trip," Rae muttered.

"Your help, while appreciated, won't be necessary," Dr. Davidoff said.

"You think I want to *help*? Sure, I'll look around, for Simon's sake. But I need to go shopping."

"Shopping?" Dr. Davidoff stared at her like he must have misheard. We all did.

"Do you know how long it's been since I got new stuff? It's spring, and everything I have is from last year."

"The *tragedy*. Someone call Amnesty International." Rae looked at Tori. "You'll survive. I'm sure it all still fits you."

"Which is more than we can say for your wardrobe. Like another wrap, Rachelle? You've only had two so far."

Rae lifted her hand, fingers splayed at Tori. "Like third-degree burns, Queen Victoria? You've only had first-degree so far."

"Girls, that's enough. Victoria—"

"And when my mom locked me away at Lyle House, she made me a deal. If I got better, she'd buy me a new laptop. Best on the market."

"Why?" Rae said. "So you can IM your friends faster?"

"No, so I can work on my entrance package for software design camp at MIT."

Rae laughed, and Tori glared. She was serious. Tori the computer geek? I tried to picture it, but even my imagination wasn't that good.

Tori turned to Dr. Davidoff. "Obviously I *can't* get better, and my mother knew it when she made that promise. So she owes me a laptop."

Dr. Davidoff frowned, as if trying to follow her logic. Then he shook his head. "All right, Victoria. We'll order you—"

"I know what I need and I'll pick it out myself."

Dr. Davidoff stood. "As you wish. Tomorrow we'll—"

"Today. And I want a spring wardrobe, too."

"Fine. I'll ask someone to take you—"

"You think I'm letting some middle-aged dweeb help me choose clothes? I'm going today so Chloe can give me a second opinion."

"You want Chloe to help you shop?" Rae said.

"Well, I sure don't want you, skater girl. Chloe may be a loser, but she's a loser with money, and someone has taught her some small degree of fashion sense."

"No, Victoria," Dr. Davidoff said. "You are not going—"

She walked over to him, rose onto her tiptoes, and whispered in his ear. A look passed over his face, one part shock, two parts sheer terror.

"I see," he said. "Yes, now that I think about it, perhaps you could help us find the boys."

"I thought so."

She sauntered back to her chair. Blackmail? Two weeks ago, I'd have been horrified. Today, I was impressed.

It's a classic movie moment. Our hero, trapped in a jungle prison, plots and schemes until finally he breaks free . . . to find himself miles from civilization with no idea how to get home. Likewise, my ploy to "help" find Simon and Derek had paid off, and I had only the faintest notion of how to use the opportunity.

And Dr. Davidoff didn't give me time to plot my next move. He called Sue and told the others to meet us at the front door. I asked for a pit stop at my room, to grab something warmer, but he said they'd do it for me. I had the foresight to specify which sweatshirt I wanted—Liz's green Gap hoodie.

As Tori and I waited up front with Sue, I felt a now familiar warm current tickling across the back of my neck.

"Leaving without saying good-bye?" the demi-demon whispered in my ear. "And leaving me trapped here, after all I've done for you?"

There was no menace in her voice, just a teasing lilt.

"I'm sorry," I said automatically.

"An apology? My, my, such a polite child. No need to apologize. I didn't expect you to free me now. You'll be back when you're ready, and when you are, I'll be waiting."

"Girls?" Dr. Davidoff said, striding toward us. "Our car is here."

As we followed him out, that warm breeze ruffled my hair. "Good-bye, child. And do be careful, you and your little band of magic makers and monsters. Keep those lovely powers of yours in check. I'd hate for the apocalypse to start without me."

ten

WE RODE IN A MINIVAN with Dr. Davidoff, Tori's mom, and a driver I didn't recognize—a blond security guy. Behind us, in another car, was Sue, a balding driver, and the dark-haired man who'd had the gun the night we'd escaped Lyle House.

There was a fourth person in that car: Aunt Lauren. I hadn't seen her—I knew only because Dr. Davidoff said she would be. When he did, I'd scrambled into the van as fast as I could, so I wouldn't see her come out.

How was I going to face Aunt Lauren? Even thinking about it made my stomach ache. I'd spent the last twenty-four hours trying hard not to think about her, about what she'd done.

My mom died when I was five. Aunt Lauren was her younger sister. In all the years of moving around with my dad, who was always away on business, leaving me with a succession of nannies and housekeepers, Aunt Lauren had been the one sure thing in my life. The person I could count on. So after I escaped, when I got hurt, and Rae and I were separated from the guys, we'd gone to her for help.

And Aunt Lauren took me back to Dr. Davidoff. If she'd thought she was sending her delusional niece back to the nice folks who could help her, then as angry and hurt as I'd have been, I'd have understood. But Aunt Lauren hadn't been tricked by these people. She was one of them.

She'd put me—or my mom, I guess—in their experiment. She'd let them kill Brady and Liz and the other girl, had maybe even helped them do it. And now, knowing all this, I had to face her and pretend it was okay.

The minivan had a middle seat that could turn around, and that's where Tori's mom sat. For the first part of the trip, she read her *Wall Street Journal*, gaze lifting now and then to be sure we hadn't vanished. Tori and I rode, staring out our respective side windows, as if they weren't too darkly tinted for us to see more than shapes outside.

There'd been no chance to grab my backpack. Even Tori hadn't been allowed to bring her purse, as much as she'd argued. At least I had money. I'd arrived at Lyle House with my wad of twenties and my bank card stuffed in my shoe, and they were still there. I wore jeans, a long-sleeved shirt, and sneakers. A change of underwear and socks would have been nice, but right now, my bigger concern was how thin my shirt was.

"Dr. Davidoff?" I leaned as far as my seat belt would allow. "Did you get that sweatshirt for me?"

"Oh, yes. And you'll need it. It's chilly out. Diane? Could you pass this to Chloe?"

When I saw the green hoodie coming over the seat, I let out a sigh of relief.

"Isn't that Liz's?" Tori said.

"I don't think so."

"No?" She snatched it from me and read the tag. "Since when do you wear a ladies' medium? I bet you aren't even out of the kid's department yet."

"Very funny. Yes, I usually wear a small—"

"*Extra*small."

"But I like my sweatshirts big, okay?"

"You think I'm stupid? This is the same hoodie I borrowed from Liz—the one you came into my room and asked about the other day."

Tori's mom lowered her newspaper.

"I—I thought Liz might want it back. Rae mentioned that you still had it so—"

"So you appointed yourself keeper of *my* friend's stuff?"

Tori's mom folded the paper onto her lap, her long red finger-nails ironing the crease. "Is that Liz's sweatshirt, Chloe?"

"M-maybe. When we left Lyle House, I grabbed clothes in the dark. I have one that looks like it. I'll wear it today, then give it to you, so you can get it to Liz."

"You better." Tori started handing it back to me.

Her mother plucked it from Tori's fingers and folded it onto her lap. "I'll see that Liz gets it."

"C-can I wear it today? Dr. Davidoff said it's c-cold—"

"You'll be fine."

Tori rolled her eyes. "It's no big deal, Mom. Just give it to her."

"I said, no. What part of that isn't clear, Victoria?"

Tori grumbled under her breath and turned back to her window.

Her mom looked at me, her expression unreadable. "I'm sure you'll be just fine without it."

When the driver dropped us off on the street behind the factory complex, my teeth were chattering, and not just from the cold. Tori's mom knew why I'd had that sweatshirt—and that I had realized Liz was dead. Why else would a necromancer make a point of getting a personal article from her?

First Dr. Davidoff, now Tori's mom. Did anyone *not* see through my schemes?

Maybe one person. The one who might still see me as sweet little Chloe. The one who thought I hadn't really meant to run away from Lyle House but just got caught up in the plots of those boys.

"Aunt Lauren?"

I walked over as she got out of the car with Sue. I felt like I was looking at a stranger who'd taken my aunt's form.

"You're freezing." She rubbed my arms, being careful with the injured one. "Where's your coat?"

I saw Tori's mom watching. If I tattled to Aunt Lauren, she'd tell her why I wanted Liz's hoodie.

"I forgot it. It was warmer last week."

She looked around. "Does anyone have an extra—?"

The dark-haired man from Saturday night climbed from the front seat and held out a nylon jacket.

"Thanks, Mike," Aunt Lauren said, and helped me into it.

The sleeves dangled six inches past my fingertips. I rolled them up, hoping the extra folds would keep me warmer, but the jacket was so thin it didn't even seem to stop the wind.

"Do you have the insulin?" I asked.

"I do, hon. Don't worry."

As the group prepared for the search, I stayed close to Aunt Lauren. She liked that, and kept her arm around me, rubbing my shoulder, as if to keep me warm. I gritted my teeth and let her.

"Now, Chloe," Dr. Davidoff said when everyone was ready, "tell us where to look."

The real rendezvous point was the warehouse nearest the factory. So the goal was to keep them as far from that as possible, in case the guys decided now was a good time to check in.

"We started in the warehouse where you guys tracked us and I did this—" I lifted my injured arm.

"Climbing out the window," Dr. Davidoff said.

I nodded. "I didn't know I'd hurt myself, so we ran. Derek wanted to get us as far from that warehouse as possible. We seemed to run and run, going around all these storage buildings, trying to find a good hiding spot. I—I wasn't paying much attention. It was dark and I couldn't see. Derek could, so I followed him."

"A werewolf's enhanced night vision," Dr. Davidoff murmured.

"We finally found a spot that Derek said would make a good place to hide and we should stay there until you guys left. But then he smelled the blood—"

Aunt Lauren's hand tightened on my shoulder, as if imagining me seconds away from being devoured.

"So he *helped* me," I continued. "He bandaged it up. But he said it was bad and I needed stitches. Then he smelled Simon. That's why we left—because of my arm and Simon—but before we did, he said the spot would make a good hiding place, that we should remember it."

"And you didn't," Tori said. "Nice going."

"It was dark and I was confused. I figured he meant *he'd* remember it—"

"We understand, Chloe," Dr. Davidoff said. "And you're right. It certainly sounds more promising than your other suggestions. As for whether you'll know it when you see it, though . . ."

"We had to rip up my T-shirt to bandage my arm. The rest of my shirt should still be there."

"All right, then. Chloe, you go with Mrs. Enright—"

Aunt Lauren's hands gripped my shoulders. "I'll take Chloe."

"No, you'll take Victoria."

"But—"

Tori's mom cut her off. "Do you have blur spells, Lauren?"

"No, but—"

"Do you have any powers at all?"

Aunt Lauren's grip on my shoulder tightened. "Yes, Diane. I have the power of medicine, which is why I should be the first on the scene when Simon is found—"

"You'll be nearby," Dr. Davidoff said. "I need Chloe to have an escort, but we can't let the boys *see* her escort. Diane will take care of that."

eleven

A BLUR SPELL TURNED OUT to be like something you see in sci-fi movies, where the villain all but disappears, camouflaged behind a magical force field. As an effect, it's easily done. Apparently, it's just as easy in real life, if you're a witch.

Tori's mom walked right beside me, nearly invisible. With no chance to take off, I had to play my role, searching for the rendezvous spot, which gave me the excuse to look for an escape opportunity. Maybe a hole in the wall too small for Tori's mom to follow me through or a precarious stack of boxes I could topple onto her head or an abandoned hammer I could brain her with.

I'd never "brained" anyone in my life, but with Tori's mom, I was willing to try.

From the front road, the place looked like a regular factory with a few outbuildings. Once you got back here, though, there were buildings everywhere, a lot of them not even being used. Prime real estate. Or it would be . . . without the smog-spouting factory to bring down the neighborhood.

Those spewing stacks were the only sign the factory was operational. Probably running well below capacity, barely hanging on, like a lot of industry in Buffalo. I had no idea what they made. Metal stuff, it looked like from the stock in the warehouses. Once, when we were darting between buildings, we had to duck behind some barrels as a trucker drove through the lot, but that was the only employee we saw.

The third building we checked was open, so Tori's mom didn't need to cast a spell to unlock it. As we stepped in, I thought, *This looks promising.* The last two had been filled with equipment and rolls of metal. This one seemed unused, and was scattered with crates. They weren't stacked precariously, but there was a whole warehouse to search.

As we moved in deeper, I saw what looked like an off-balance stack. Near it was a pile of small metal pipes, the perfect size for braining someone.

I headed toward the pipes, my gaze on the ground, as if searching for my torn shirt.

"I think we can stop this charade now, Chloe," Tori's mom said.

I turned slowly, taking a moment to plaster on my best wide-eyed look.

"There's no shirt here," she said, "or rendezvous point. Perhaps there is, somewhere in this complex, but not here."

"Let's try the next—"

She caught my arm as I walked past. "We all know you're trying to escape again. Marcel only hopes the real rendezvous point is nearby and that you're laying a trail right now, one that will entice Derek back to investigate once he thinks we're gone."

Laying a trail? Oh, no. Why hadn't I thought of that? I didn't need to be here to get Derek's attention. If he smelled that I'd been near the factory . . .

"I-I'm not trying to escape. I want to help Simon. We need to find—"

"The boys don't interest me. You do."

"Me?"

Her grip on my arm tightened. "All those kids had been at Lyle House for months, behaving themselves, working so hard to get better. Then you arrive and suddenly we have a full-scale mutiny on our hands. Within a week, four residents are on the run. Quite the little instigator, aren't you?"

I'd been the catalyst, not the instigator. But it wouldn't win me any brownie points to correct her.

She continued. "You took action while the rest swallowed our lies and prayed for rescue. My daughter didn't even have the guts to join you."

Umm, because you crushed any fight left in her? Because you made her think she had to play perfect patient to please you?

"The Fates played us a nasty twist, Chloe Saunders. They stuck you with dear Aunt Lauren, always fretting and wringing her hands. A perfect match for my spineless daughter. But where fate wrongs us, free will can make things right. I think you and I can reach an agreement that will benefit us both." She released my arm. "Dr. Gill tells me you contacted spirits from Lyle's early experiments."

I said nothing, my gaze steady.

"I know she confronted you," Tori's mom continued. "Something of a fanatic, our Dr. Gill, as I'm sure you noticed. She's obsessed with Lyle's secrets. Ambition is healthy. Obsession is not." She eyed me. "So what did these spirits tell you?"

"Nothing. I'd accidentally raised them from the dead, so they weren't too interested in chatting with me."

She laughed. "I suppose not. But for you, at your age, to raise the dead . . . ?" Her eyes glittered. "Remarkable."

Okay, that was dumb. I just confirmed I'd raised the dead. A lesson in playing it cool—don't.

"Could you contact them again?" she asked.

"I could try."

"Resourceful and reasonable. That's a combination that will take you far. Here's what we'll do, then. I'll tell Dr. Davidoff we found the spot here. The shirt was gone, likely taken by the boys. But they left this." She pulled a page from her pocket. It was from Simon's sketch pad, carefully torn out. On one side was a partial drawing, clearly Simon's work. On the other side, she'd written in block letters: BSC CAFE 2 PM.

"Meet at the Buffalo State cafeteria at two," I said. "The page is too clean, though. They'll know it wasn't left here."

I took it, walked over by the metal pipe, crouched, and brushed the note across the dirty floor. Then I paused, still hunched over, and looked up at her.

"What about the insulin?"

"I'm sure those boys have already found some."

"Can we leave it here, just in case?"

She hesitated. She didn't want to bother, but if it would win my trust . . .

"I'll get the vials from Lauren later and bring them back," she said. "Now, though, we need to report that note."

She turned to leave. I wrapped my fingers around a metal pipe, then sprang up, swinging it at the back of her head.

She spun, fingers flicking. I sailed backward into a stack of boxes, the pipe flying from my hands and clanging to the floor. I scrambled for it, but she was faster, snatching it up and brandishing it.

Her mouth opened, but before she could get out a word, a crate shot from the stack over my head. She sidestepped as it whizzed past. Behind it stood Liz.

I lunged for the pile of pipes, but Mrs. Enright hit me with another spell. My feet sailed out, my outstretched hands hitting the floor, pain blasting through my injured arm. As I looked around, I caught a glimpse of Liz's nightshirt behind the stacks of crates.

"Elizabeth Delaney, I presume." Mrs. Enright moved back against a wall, her gaze flitting from side to side, ready for the next flying object. "So it seems, in death, you've finally mastered your powers. If only it had been sooner. Such a waste."

Liz froze between stacks, her face stricken as Mrs. Enright confirmed her death. Then she squared her shoulders and, eyes narrowing, fixed them on a stack of crates.

"Even in death, you can be useful, Elizabeth," Mrs. Enright said. "A poltergeist is a rare find, one that will help Dr. Davidoff overcome his disappointment at losing dear Simon and Derek."

The crates shuddered and cracked as Liz pushed, tendons popping with the strain. I frantically motioned for her to concentrate on just the top one. She nodded and pushed it . . . but Mrs. Enright simply stepped out of range.

"Enough of that, Elizabeth," she said calmly as the crates crashed behind her.

Liz grabbed a loose board and hurled it at her.

"I said, *enough*."

She hit me with another spell, this one a jolt of electricity that left me on the floor, gasping and shaking. Liz crouched over me. I whispered I was okay and pushed up until I was sitting. My whole body throbbed.

Mrs. Enright looked around, unable to see Liz unless she was moving something. "I can't hurt you, Elizabeth, but I can hurt Chloe. If so much as a scrap of wood flies, I'll hit her with another energy bolt. Is that clear?"

I struggled to my feet, then raced for the door. I made it five feet before I froze. Literally.

"It's called a binding spell," Mrs. Enright said. "Very useful. Now, Elizabeth, you are going to behave while Chloe and I—"

The spell broke. I stumbled, twisting to regain my balance, and looked up to see *her* frozen instead. A dark figure stepped from the shadows.

"A binding spell?" Tori strolled over. "Is that what you call it, Mom? You're right. It *is* useful."

She walked in front of her mother's still form. "So I'm a disappointment, am I? Chloe is the daughter you wish you'd had? You know, I'd be really hurt by that . . . if I thought you actually knew her. Or me." She stepped closer. "Shopping, Mom? I'm locked in a cell, my life is falling apart, and you really believed I wanted to go shopping? You don't know me any better than she does." She waved at me. "You—"

Tori staggered back with a gasp as her mother broke free and hit her with a spell.

"You've got a lot of learning to do, Victoria, if you think you can hurt me."

Tori met her mother's gaze. "You think I came here for revenge? This is called an escape."

"Escape? So you're going to run off and live on the streets? Daddy's princess sleeping in alleys?"

Tori's eyes flashed, but she only said calmly, "I'll be fine."

"With what? Did you bring money? A bank card?"

"And how would I get that, when you locked me up?"

"I bet Chloe has some. I bet she never left her room without it, just in case."

They both looked at me. I didn't say a word, but my answer must have shown on my face. Mrs. Enright laughed.

"Oh, I'm going to get money, Mom," Tori said. "I'll take it from you."

She slammed her arms down and a wave of energy smacked into her mother and me, tottering us backward. Tori waved her hands over her head. Sparks flew, caught in a gust of wind that wailed around us in a whirlwind of dirt and sawdust. I squeezed my eyes shut and covered my nose and mouth.

"You call that powerful magic, Victoria?" her mother shouted over the wind. "It's a temper tantrum. You haven't changed at all. Only now, you call on the forces of nature to howl and stomp for you."

"You think that's all I can do? Just watch—"

Tori froze in a binding spell. The wind stopped. The dust and sparks fluttered to the floor.

"I'm watching," Mrs. Enright said, "and all I see is a spoiled brat with a fancy new car, tearing around, not caring who gets hurt. As selfish and inconsiderate as ever."

Tori's eyes glistened with tears. As her mother advanced on her, I eased back toward the pile of metal pipes.

"Now, Victoria, if you're done throwing tantrums, I'm going to call Lauren to come and get you, and hopefully she can manage to *keep* you this time."

Liz was circling toward Mrs. Enright, her gaze on another pile of crates. I shook my head. The angle was wrong and she'd see it falling. I bent and lifted a bar.

"Lauren Fellows won't be the only person reprimanded for this little escapade," Mrs. Enright continued. "You've just earned yourself a week in your room, alone, no classes, no visitors, no MP3 player. Just a lot of time to think about—"

I swung the pipe. It hit the back of her head with an ugly *thwack*. The weapon flew from my hands. She teetered and I thought I hadn't hit her hard enough. I tripped over my feet to get to the pipe, now rolling away.

Then she fell.

Tori broke from the spell and raced to her mother, dropping beside her. I did the same and checked her pulse.

"I think she's okay," I said.

Tori just knelt there, staring down at her mother.

I touched her arm. "If we want to go, we have—"

She shook me off. I leaped to my feet, ready to leave her. Then I realized what she was doing—checking her mother's pockets.

"Nothing," she said through her teeth. "Not even a credit card."

"I've got money. Come on."

One last look at her mother, and she followed.

twelve

TORI AND I HUDDLED under the tarp covering a trailer bed. There wasn't a cab attached, so we were in no danger of our hiding place rolling away. I thought that made it the perfect spot. Tori disagreed.

"We're sitting ducks here," she hissed, crouching. "All they have to do is lift this cover and they'll see us."

"If they get close, we'll run."

"And how will we know that? We can't *see* anything."

"Liz is scouting." I uncrossed my legs. "About Liz—"

"She's dead." Her voice was a harsh rasp. "I heard my mother. She killed Liz, didn't she? Her and those people."

"I-I'll explain later. We need to be quiet. Someone could hear—"

"No one's around, remember? Because Liz—my *friend* Liz—is a ghost and she's standing watch. Apparently, she's been helping you for God knows how long, and you didn't even bother to tell me she was dead, that they *murdered* her."

"I told Rae—"

"Of course. Rachelle. How's that working out for you?" Tori met my gaze. "If you want to know who betrayed you guys, look in that direction."

"Rae? No. She'd never—"

"Well, *someone* told. If it wasn't me or you, or the guys, who does that leave?"

"W-we should be quiet. Sound travels."

"Really? Wow. Now you give science lessons, too. Did Derek teach you that?"

"Tori?"

"What?"

"Shut it."

She did, for about five seconds, then said, "Shouldn't Liz have checked in by now? How do you know she's still out there?"

"She comes and goes. That's why I needed that sweatshirt to—"

Liz dashed through the tarp and stooped over us. "Tell her to *shhh*!"

"I already did," I whispered. "Repeatedly."

"Well, they've heard, and they're on their way. It's your aunt and a guy with a gun."

I relayed this to Tori in whispers.

"What? Why are we sitting here then?" She darted for the side.

I grabbed her arm.

"Hey!" she said, loud enough to make Liz wince.

"Which way are they coming from?" I asked Liz.

She pointed left. I crawled to the right side and lifted the tarp.

Liz hurried out. "I don't see them now."

I squinted against the sun. There was a building about twenty feet away, but I couldn't see a door. I leaned out for a better look. To my left was a cluster of rusty barrels. We could hide between—

"Chloe!" Liz yelled. "He's right—"

A *thump-thump* on the trailer bed cut her off.

"Back up!" Liz said. "Back up!"

"What's going on?" Tori whispered. "Move!"

When I tried to back up, Tori shoved me and I flew out from under the trailer, doing a face plant in the dirt.

"Well, that made it easy," said a voice.

I rolled onto my back. There, on the trailer bed, stood Mike—the man who'd shot at us Saturday night.

"Lauren?" he said. "Better give me that gun. I'll handle this."

Gaze still fixed on me, he jumped to the ground. He put out his hand as Aunt Lauren came around the back of the trailer, rifle in her hands.

"I'm sorry, Chloe," she said.

She aimed the gun at me and I scuttled back.

"N-no. I—I won't fight. I—"

She swung the gun and fired at Mike. The dart hit his arm. He stared at it. Then his knees gave way.

Aunt Lauren ran over and helped me up. "Tori, get out of there. He radioed the others when we heard you."

I backed away, my gaze on Aunt Lauren as I motioned for Tori to be ready to run. Aunt Lauren grabbed my arm; but when I pulled away, she released her grip and stepped back.

"Why do you think I shot him?" she said. "Why did I let Tori get away from me so easily? I'm trying to help. We'll find the boys, then we'll find Kit—Simon's dad."

A weird ringing sounded in my ears. I think it was my heart, shouting for joy. Aunt Lauren had realized she was wrong. She still loved me. She was going to make it up to me, fix my problems like she always did, and make everything okay.

Could I have imagined anything more perfect?

No, and that's why I took another slow step back, fingers at my side, waving for Tori to get ready to bolt. I'd been tricked too often to fall for a fairy-tale ending now.

"Chloe, please." Aunt Lauren held out the insulin pouch. As I reached for it, she caught my hand. "I made a mistake, Chloe. A huge mistake. But I'm going to fix it." She handed me the pouch. "Now head that way." She pointed toward the factory. "Stick to the shadows. I need to hide him under the truck."

Aunt Lauren caught up and we circled the warehouses, heading toward the front gates. She swore no one from the Edison Group was covering the front. Though we hadn't seen employees wandering around outside, the group wouldn't risk getting too close to the factory.

And if she was lying and leading us into a trap? I hoped Tori's spells would get us through.

At the far side of the yard, we paused behind a warehouse to catch our breaths.

"Okay, girls," Aunt Lauren said. "There's a delivery gate over there. It's closed, but you both should be able to squeeze through. Head right two blocks, then along the street to the end. You'll see a 7-Eleven."

I nodded. "I know where it is."

"Good. Go around the back of the store and wait. I'll meet you there."

Tori sprinted off, but I stood there, looking at Aunt Lauren.

"Chloe?"

"Tori didn't turn us in, did she?"

"No. Now—"

"It was Rae, wasn't it?"

Aunt Lauren paused, and I saw the answer in her eyes. "I'm not the only one who mistakenly thought she was doing the right thing, Chloe."

I started to turn away. She caught my arm and held out a folded envelope.

"An explanation and some money." When I didn't take it, she leaned around and put it into my back pocket. "If you decide to keep running, I won't blame you. But, please, give me a chance. One last chance."

I nodded. She pulled me into a hug and kissed my cheek, then let me go. Tori had already rounded the corner of the building, disappearing from sight when Liz shrieked behind me.

"Chloe!"

I spun so fast I lost my balance. Aunt Lauren gestured for me to keep going, but I saw only the figure behind her. Tori's mom.

I shouted a warning, but Mrs. Enright's hand flew out. A bolt shot from her fingertips. It hit Aunt Lauren with a horrible sizzling pop, knocking her off her feet. Blood flew from her lips, spraying the concrete as she fell.

thirteen

I STARTED TO RUN TO Aunt Lauren. I made it a few feet before Tori's mom locked me in a binding spell. I dimly heard her say something, but I didn't know what it was. My ears were filled with my own silent screams as I stared at Aunt Lauren, motionless on the ground. Finally Mrs. Enright's voice came through.

"I should probably ask where my darling daughter is."

"Right here," said a voice behind me.

Mrs. Enright's head lifted. Her brow furrowed. Her lips parted. Then she jolted backward, hit by a spell from Tori. My binding broke. I lurched toward Aunt Lauren, but Tori grabbed my arm.

"We have to go," she said.

"No. I—"

Mrs. Enright recovered, hands flying as she launched a spell. Tori yanked me out of the way and it hit the wall, blasting a blackened crater.

"You can fight her," I said. "Stop her, and I'll get the gun—"

"I can't."

Tori heaved on my arm. I pulled away. She muttered "Fine," let go, then raced off, disappearing around the corner. Tori's mom lifted her hands again. Then a voice shouted, distracting her, "They're over here!"

I took one last look at Aunt Lauren and ran.

There was no way we were getting to that delivery gate now. I soon realized why Aunt Lauren had sent us ahead—so she could watch our backs because we'd be exposed to any employees entering the side yard and we couldn't afford to raise any alarms.

We peered around the corner of the next building, saw that open expanse, heard voices coming, and knew we'd never make it.

"Now what?" Tori said.

I didn't answer.

"Come on!" she whispered. "What's the plan?"

I wanted to grab her and shake her and tell her there was no plan. I couldn't even wrap my head around the concept. My aunt might be dead. *Dead.* That's all I could think about.

"Chloe!" she whispered. "Hurry! What are we going to do?"

I longed to tell her to leave me alone. Come up with her own plan. Then I saw her eyes, bright with fear fast turning into panic, and the words died in my throat.

She'd just learned Liz was dead. She'd seen my aunt possibly killed by her mother. Neither of us was in any shape to think, but one of us had to.

"Your aunt said the Edison Group won't come close to the front," she said. "If we run for it—"

"They'll make an exception. Or find a way to cut us off. But . . ." I looked around. My gaze stopped on the huge building dominating the yard. "The factory."

"What?"

"Stay close to me."

I knew of two doors—the emergency exit we'd escaped from Saturday night and the main entrance Derek had broken into. The main doors were closest. As we headed for them, I whispered to Liz, asking her to run ahead and scout the way. If someone was coming, she'd whistle.

The door was in an alcove. I darted in and I pressed against the wall while Liz zipped through the door. She was back in a second.

"There's a guard dead ahead," she said. "I'll distract him. You open the door a crack and listen for my whistle. You know a place to hide, right?"

I nodded. When we were here Saturday, Derek had us opening all the doors, searching for an exit, and I remembered a storage room that would be perfect.

When Liz gave the all clear, I eased open the door. Tori danced impatiently behind me, though I'd asked her to watch for anyone approaching.

Inside, Liz was at a closed door twenty feet away. The guard stood beside her, staring down at the knob as it slowly turned one way, then the other.

We slipped past. I could hear the distant rumble and thump of machinery and the laughs and shouts of workers. This section, though, was quiet.

We made it to the side hall easily, as the guard stood transfixed by that mysterious turning doorknob.

Liz raced up behind us. "Where to?"

I gestured to the adjoining hall. She sprinted ahead, turned the corner, and whistled the all clear. Our luck held, and we made it safely into the storage room. As its door closed, the guard's voice echoed down the empty halls.

"Hey, Pete, come here! You gotta see this. The knob was turning by itself. I tell you, ever since Dan did a nosedive into the saws, this place has been haunted."

He was right. Saturday night, I'd seen the ghost of a man jump into those saws. Then he'd reappeared and done it again. Was that some kind of penance? Aunt Lauren had done bad things, maybe even committed murder. If she was dead, would she go to Hell? Was she—?

I swallowed hard.

"What now?" Tori whispered.

I looked around. The room was the size of a classroom and full of boxes.

"Find a place in the back," I said. "There's lots of dust, which means they don't come in here very often. We'll hide—"

Liz ran through the door.

"They're coming!"

"Wha—?"

"Dr. Davidoff and Sue. She saw you by the doors."

Thanks to Tori, who'd kept such a good watch . . .

"Are they inside?" I asked.

"Not yet."

"Is who inside?" Tori asked as Liz took off. "What's going on? What'd she say?"

I told her, then opened the door a crack.

"What are you doing?" she said, tugging my sleeve. "Are you nuts? Close that!"

Tell her to be quiet, and she got louder. Tell her to stay back, and she pushed me into the line of fire. Tell her to watch for our pursuers, and she hovered at my shoulder instead. Open the door to listen, and she wanted to drag me back inside.

Ah. The beginning of a beautiful friendship.

Friendship? We'd be lucky if we survived a temporary partnership.

I told her I was trying to listen. When she argued, I glared; and for once in my life, it actually worked. Her mouth shut and she backed into the room, sulky and glowering, but silent.

"Can I help you?" the guard's voice echoed down the hall.

"Yes, we're looking for two teenage girls," Dr. Davidoff replied. "We believe they came in here. They're runaways from a nearby group home. They're fifteen years old. One's about five six, short dark hair. The other is five feet, reddish-blond hair."

"With red streaks," Sue added. "Painted red streaks."

The guard chuckled. "Sounds like my kid, only hers are blue. Last week they were purple."

"Teenagers," Dr. Davidoff said with a fake laugh. "These two of ours are always slipping away. You know what girls are like. Running off to see their boyfriends and buy new lip gloss. They don't mean any harm, but we worry about them."

"Sure. If I see them, I'll give you a shout. You got a card?"

"We're quite certain they're in here."

"Nope. This is the only door that opens from the outside, and I've been at my post all shift."

"I understand. But perhaps if we could take a look—"

A chair squeaked and I pictured the beefy man rising. "This is a factory, folks. Do you have any idea how many safety regulations I'd be breaking if I let you poke around?"

"We'll wear hard hats and safety glasses."

"This isn't a public building. You can't come in here without an appointment and an escort."

"May we speak to the plant manager, then?"

"He's out. Meeting. All day. I told you, no one got past me. Your girls aren't in here. But if you really want to check, that's fine. Get the cops and I'll let you in."

"We'd prefer not to involve the police."

"Well, you're gonna have to, 'cause it's the only way you're getting past me."

After the guard chased them off, we holed up to wait for dark. We each found a separate spot, far enough apart that we had an excuse for not chatting. That was fine with me at first. Like Tori and I would have anything to chat about. But after a while, even bickering would have been better than this silent waiting with nothing to do but think. And cry. I did a lot of that, as quietly as I could. I'd taken out the envelope so often it was covered in tearstains. I wanted to open it, but I was terrified that whatever was in it wouldn't be a good enough explanation, that it *couldn't* be good enough, and I so desperately needed it to be.

Finally, I couldn't take it anymore. I ripped it open. Inside was money, but I shoved that into my pocket without counting it, then unfolded the letter.

Aunt Lauren started by explaining how necromancy worked. In necromancer families, not everyone saw ghosts. Most didn't. Aunt Lauren didn't. Nor had my mom or their parents. But my uncle had. My mother's twin brother, Ben—I'd never known she'd even had a twin. Aunt Lauren wrote.

> Ben died long before you were born. Your mom would have showed you pictures, but you were too young to understand. After she was gone . . . there just didn't seem any point in bringing it up. He started seeing ghosts when he was a little older than you are now. He went away to college with your mom, but it was too much for him. He came home. Your mom wanted to quit and come back, too, to keep an eye on him. He insisted she stay at school. I said I'd watch over him, but I didn't really understand what he was going through. When he was nineteen, he died in a fall. Whether he jumped or whether he was running from ghosts, we never knew.

Did it matter? Either way, his powers had killed him. I kept telling myself ghosts couldn't hurt me, but in my gut I knew I was wrong, and here was the proof. Just because you can't reach out and push someone off a roof, doesn't mean you can't kill him.

> Your mom had been looking for help for Ben before he died. Our family had some connections in the necromancer world, and eventually someone gave her a contact name for the Edison Group. Only Ben went off the roof a month before she got the message. Later, when I started med school, I contacted them. If they were scientists, they could use doctors; and if I could help people like Ben, that's what I wanted to do. Your mom wasn't involved. Not then. That didn't come until she wanted to have a child.

She'd planned to have kids even after what happened to her brother? As if in answer to my question, Aunt Lauren wrote:

> You have to understand, Chloe, it's like any other genetic disorder. It's a risk we accept. If we have a child and she has the power, then

we deal with that. Your mother wouldn't take that risk, though. Not after Ben. She wanted to adopt, but with your father, that wasn't an option. There were . . . things in his past. The agencies didn't consider him a suitable parent. Your mother was miserable. She wanted children so badly. She looked into other alternatives, but they all cost money and at that time, your parents were living in a rat-infested hole downtown. Every penny they earned went to your father's new business. Then I told her about a breakthrough with the Edison Group. A team had isolated the genes that conferred powers for necromancers. By testing the potential carrier of that gene code and the proposed human parent, we could determine the likelihood that a child of that union would be a necromancer. Jenny was so excited. I ran the tests on her and your dad . . . and it was almost certain that any child they had would be a necromancer. I tried to persaude her to consider other options, maybe artificial insemination with another biological father. But she was so tired and so *crushed* that she just didn't have the energy to consider alternatives. And she suspected I was trying to come between her and your dad, because I'd made it clear I didn't think he was right for her. We didn't talk for almost a year. Then, I called her with the most amazing news. A breakthrough, here at the lab. We couldn't give her a child who wasn't a necromancer, but we could eliminate the dangers that killed our brother. She could have a child who could speak to the dead on her own terms.

But it hadn't worked out that way, as I knew. When I started seeing ghosts so abruptly, Aunt Lauren said she'd told herself nothing was wrong. I wasn't one of the failures—I just needed time to adjust to my new powers. The Edison Group had insisted I go to Lyle House, though, and she'd agreed, still expecting they'd discover I was fine, and then I could be told the truth.

She'd kept believing that until she learned that I'd raised zombies at Lyle House. Still, she told herself it was okay—we'd deal with it. The group had promised that no matter what happened, I wouldn't be killed. A necromancer wasn't dangerous, they told her, so there was no reason to terminate me.

Still worried, she'd started digging for answers, just like I had, and she learned the same thing I had—that they'd lied. Apparently, they'd lied about a lot of things, she said, though she didn't go into detail.

> That's what changed everything for me, Chloe. I know it's horrible to admit I only realized my mistakes when my own niece's life was in danger. Until then I'd done what I thought was right—the greater good and such. But, in doing that, I forgot my oath as a doctor, to first do no harm. I did harm and I'm sure I'll pay the price, but I won't let you pay it with me. That's why I had to get you out.

Three final paragraphs. In the first, she said that if I was reading this letter, then she hadn't gotten away with me. If I'd left her behind, she understood. If she'd been killed, that was the price she'd paid. And if she'd been taken by the Edison Group, I wasn't to go back for her. I was to keep going and find Simon and his dad, Kit. She had no idea what had happened to Kit. She'd searched the Edison Group files and she was convinced they weren't involved in his disappearance, but that was it.

She also told me to make sure I wore my necklace—always. I remembered how quick she'd been to get it back for me when I went to Lyle House without it. In the letter, she didn't say much about it, only that it was supposed to ward off ghosts. But it didn't. Or maybe it *was* working, and if I lost it, I'd start seeing a lot more ghosts, my powers running unchecked.

The next bit was about my dad. He didn't know anything, not even about me being a necromancer. So if I escaped and she didn't, I needed to stay away from him.

Then came the final paragraph. Three more sentences.

> She wanted a child so badly, Chloe. And you are just as wonderful as she imagined. You were the center of her world.

Tears burned my eyes, that old never-quite-healed ache flaring. I took a deep, shuddering breath, folded the letter, and put it back in my pocket.

We'd been there over an hour when Liz came racing in with the news. "She's not dead. Your aunt. She's okay."

From the excitement on Liz's face, you'd think she'd just learned her own aunt had survived. It didn't matter that Aunt Lauren was part of the group that murdered her. All she cared about was that this news would please me. Looking at her glowing face, I realized that as good as I tried to be, I could never be as selfless as Liz.

My relief was cut short by a fresh worry. What would they do to Aunt Lauren now that she'd helped us escape? Now that she'd betrayed them. Thinking of that reminded me of another betrayal. Rae's.

I'd trusted her. I'd vouched for her to the guys, persuaded them to let her join us, and she'd turned us in.

Rae was the one who'd insisted that the boys weren't coming back. She was the one who suggested I go to Aunt Lauren, who'd talked me into it when I'd hesitated.

I remembered the night we'd left, lying in our beds trying to sleep. She'd been so excited about her powers and not the least concerned about what lay ahead of us. Now I knew why she hadn't been worried.

Aunt Lauren said Rae honestly thought she was helping me. Betrayal as tough love, forcing me onto the path chosen for me, certain she was right and I was just too stubborn to see it.

Now both she and my aunt were trapped with the Edison Group. Once the glow over her new life faded, Rae would see the cracks and pick away at them until she realized the truth. I hoped she didn't. I prayed both of them would just hold tight and do whatever the Edison Group wanted until I could return. And I *would* return.

Finally Liz popped in to tell me that Dr. Davidoff and his crew had given up, assuming Tori and I had snuck past the front gates and were long gone. They'd left a guard behind, keeping watch from some hidden spot, in case Derek showed up, following my trail.

At five, the whistle blew, the workday ending. By five thirty, the building was empty. Still we waited. Past six, past seven . . .

"It must be dark out by now," Tori whispered, crawling over to me.

"Dusk, not dark. We'll give it another hour."

At eight, we left.

fourteen

WE SNUCK PAST THE NIGHT GUARD, who was busy reading *Playboy* in the lunchroom. Liz stayed with him to make sure he didn't hear us. He didn't.

Luckily Tori and I had the good fortune to dress in dark clothes that morning—Tori in a navy American Eagle sweat suit and leather jacket, me in jeans and a green shirt. I only wished I had more than this thin jacket. With the sun gone it was freezing, made worse by an icy blast that had to be coming straight across the river from Canada.

Once inside the warehouse, we wouldn't have to worry about the wind. Getting there, though, was taking forever. Liz was having trouble finding the Edison Group guard, so we had to go the long way around, scooting from hiding place to hiding place, to reach the real rendezvous point—the warehouse where Rae and I had waited for Derek and Simon.

As it had been the other night, the warehouse door was latched but not locked. Unless you knew a hot black market in cardboard boxes, crates, and wooden pallets, there was nothing inside to steal. All that worthless junk made it the perfect place to hide . . . and meant there were a million spots for the guys to leave a note.

After a few minutes of banging around in the dark, I gave up.

"We'll have to wait until morning," I said.

No response. I squinted around for Tori.

"This is my stop," she said, somewhere to my left.

"Hmm?"

"This is where I get off." Her voice was oddly monotone, like she was too tired to put any bite into the words. "My adventure, as fun as it's been, ends here."

"Just hold on until morning. If there isn't a note, we'll figure something out."

"And if there is a note? I wanted to join your escape, Chloe, not your crusade to find Simon's dad."

"B-but he'll—"

"Save the day?" She managed a sarcastic lilt. "Rescue us from the mad scientists, cure us, and take us to a land of lollipops and unicorns?"

My voice hardened. "Finding him might not solve anything, but right now, we're a little short on options. What are you going to do instead? Go back to the Edison Group and say you're sorry, it was all a mistake?"

"I'm doing what I planned all along. We needed each other to get out. But that's all I wanted from you. I'd help you find the note, but I won't stay until morning to do it. I'm going home, to my dad."

That shut me up, if only because I was afraid I'd say something I'd regret, like ask if she meant her dad or her father. Did she know there was a difference? I doubted it.

"So your dad. . . . He's human?"

"Of course. He doesn't know anything about this. But I'm going to tell him."

"Is that such a good idea?"

"He's my *dad*," she snapped. "When he hears what my mom did . . . ? Everything's going to be okay. My dad and me get along great. Better than him and my mom. They hardly even talk. I'm sure they only stay together because of us kids."

"Maybe you should wait a day or two. See what happens."

She laughed. "And join your band of superheroes? Sorry, but I'm allergic to spandex." Her sneakers scuffed on the concrete as she turned away. "Say bye to Liz for me."

"Wait!" I tugged off my shoe. "Take some money."

"Save it. I don't plan to ever get the chance to repay you."

"It's okay. Just take—"

"Keep your money, Chloe. You'll need it more than I will." She took a few steps, then stopped. For a moment, she stood there, then she said quietly, "You could come with me."

"I need to get Simon his insulin."

"Right. Okay then."

I waited for a good-bye but heard only the slap of her sneakers, then the creaking of the door as she left.

When Liz returned from patrol, she said she'd seen Tori leaving. I explained, then braced for a chewing out. Why had I let Tori take off? Why hadn't I gone after her? But all Liz said was, "I guess she didn't want to hang around," and that was that.

We were both quiet for a while, then Liz said, "I'm sorry I didn't believe you. About me being dead."

"I handled it wrong. I should have made it easier for you."

"I don't think there's any way to make that easier."

We sat side by side in the darkness on a piece of cardboard I'd dragged over. My back rested against a crate. I'd stacked more around me, like a play fort. A small, dark, cold fortress.

"Why'd they kill me?" Liz asked.

I told her about the experiment and the genetic manipulation and what the file said about terminating us if we couldn't be rehabilitated.

"But I *could* have been rehabilitated," she said. "If they'd just *told* me what was going on, I wouldn't have been freaking out about poltergeists. I would have taken lessons, pills, whatever they wanted."

"I know."

"So why? *Why?*"

The only answer I had was that we didn't matter to them. We were subjects in an experiment. They'd try rehabilitation because we weren't animals, but Lyle House had been only a token effort, to prove to themselves that they'd made some attempt to save us.

They said they killed us because we were dangerous. I didn't believe that. I wasn't dangerous. Brady wasn't dangerous. Maybe Liz and Derek, but they weren't monsters. Derek had been willing to stay at Lyle House just so he wouldn't hurt anyone else.

They played God and they failed, and I think what they were really scared of wasn't that we'd hurt people but that other supernaturals would find out what they'd done. So they killed their failures, leaving only the successes.

That's what I thought. "I don't know" was what I said, and we sat quietly for a while longer.

Next time, I was the one to break the silence. "Thank you. For everything. Without you, Tori and I would never have gotten away. I want to help you in return—help you cross over."

"Cross over?"

"To the other side. Wherever ghosts are supposed to go. The afterlife."

"Oh."

"I'm not sure why you haven't gone. Have you . . . seen anything? A light maybe?"

A small laugh. "I think that's only in movies, Chloe."

"But you vanish sometimes. Where do you go?"

"I'm not sure. I still see everything here, but you can't see me. It's like being on the other side of a force field, where I can see— Well, I guess they must be other ghosts, but they seem to be just passing through."

"Where do they come from?"

She shrugged. "I don't talk to them. I thought maybe they were other shaman spirits, but I . . ." Her gaze dropped. "I didn't want to ask. In case they weren't."

"Can you ask them now? Find out where you're supposed to be?"

"I'm fine."

"But—"

"Not yet. Just not yet, okay?"

"Okay."

"When you do find Simon and Derek, I'm going to take off for a while. I want to visit my nana, see how she's doing, and my brother, maybe my friends, my school. I know they can't see me. I'd just like to see them."

I nodded.

Liz wanted me to sleep. I closed my eyes to make her feel better, but there was no chance of drifting off. I was too cold, too hungry.

When she slipped out to patrol, I stretched and shifted. The chill of the concrete came right through my cardboard mat. I was crawling over to grab more layers when Liz reappeared.

"Good, you're awake."

"What's wrong? Is someone coming?"

"No, it's Tori. She's in front of the warehouse. She's just sitting there."

I found Tori crouched between the warehouse and a Dumpster, staring at the rusty bin, not even blinking.

"Tori?" I had to touch her shoulder before she looked at me. "Come inside."

She followed me without a word. I showed her the spot I'd made, and she settled in, crouching in her strange way.

"What happened?" I asked.

It took a moment for her to answer. "I called my dad. I told him everything. He said to stay where I was, and he'd come and get me."

"And you changed your mind. That's okay. We'll—"

"I went across the street to wait," she said, as if I hadn't spoken. "I was in an alley, so no one would see me before he got there. The car pulled up and I started to step out and—and I didn't. I kept telling myself I was being stupid, that I'd been around you too long, getting all paranoid, but I needed to see him first, to be sure. It was his car—my dad's. It stopped right where I said I'd be. It idled there, all the windows up, too dark to see through. Then a door opened and . . ." Her voice dropped. "It was my mom."

"She must have intercepted the call," I said. "Maybe they switched cars. Or she got to his car first, knowing you'd be looking for it. He was probably on his way, in *her* car and—"

"I snuck away and called my house again, collect. My dad answered, and I hung up."

"I'm sorry."

More silence. Then, "Not even going to say 'I told you so'?"

"Of course not."

She shook her head. "You're too nice, Chloe. And I don't mean that as a compliment. There's nice, and then there's *too* nice. Anyway, I'm back." She reached into her pocket, and pulled out something. "With food."

She handed me a Snickers bar.

"Thanks. I thought you didn't have any money."

"I don't. Five-finger discount." Her sneakers squeaked on the concrete as she shifted farther onto the cardboard mat. "I've watched my friends do it plenty of times. But I never did. Know why?" She didn't wait for an answer. "Because I was afraid of getting caught. Not by the store or the cops. I didn't care about that. All they do is give you a lecture, make you pay it back. I was afraid of my mom finding out. Afraid she'd be disappointed in me."

A crackle as she unwrapped her candy bar, then broke off a piece. "Not really an issue now, is it?" She popped the chunk into her mouth.

fifteen

ONCE MY STOMACH had something in it—even a candy bar—exhaustion took over. I wasn't asleep long before the dreams came—nightmares of never finding the guys, of Mrs. Enright killing Aunt Lauren, of Tori hog-tying me and leaving me for the Edison Group to find. . . .

I awoke to the sound of voices. I leaped up, breath jamming in my throat, searching the darkness for men with guns.

Beside me, Tori was snoring.

"Liz?" I whispered.

No answer. She must have been out on patrol.

After a moment, I decided I'd dreamed the voices. Then the sound came again—a *psst-psst-psst,* too faint to make out the words. I strained to hear but could only catch that papery whisper. I blinked hard. The unending darkness became a landscape of black jagged rocks—boxes and crates. Only a pale moonglow made it through the thick grime coating the windows.

I caught a whiff of something musky, animal-like. Rats? I shivered.

The sound came again. A papery rustling, like the wind through dry leaves. Maybe that's what it was.

Dry leaves in April? When the nearest tree is hundreds of feet away?

No, it sounded like a ghost. Like the scary movie version, where all you hear is a wordless whispering that creeps down your spine and tells you there's something lurking just around—

I shook myself, then stood and stretched my legs. I scuffed my sneakers against the cardboard carpet a little more than necessary, hoping Tori might stir. She didn't.

I exhaled, cheeks ballooning. I'd been doing well so far, facing my fears and taking action. This wasn't the time to bury my head and plug my ears. If my powers were abnormally strong . . .

Uncontrollable . . .

No, not uncontrollable. Dad would say that everything can be controlled if you have the willpower and the will to learn.

The whisper seemed to come from the next room. I picked my way through the maze of boxes and crates. As careful as I was, I kept knocking my knees against them, and each rap made me wince.

With every step I took, the whispering seemed to move farther away. I was clear across the warehouse before I realized the sound *was* moving away. A ghost was luring me.

I stopped short, my scalp prickling as I peered through the darkness, boxes looming in every direction. The whisper snaked around me. I whirled and crashed into a stack of crates. A sliver jabbed into my palm.

I took a deep breath, then asked, "Do you w-want to talk to me?"

The whispers stopped. I waited.

"No? Fine, then I'm going back—"

A giggle erupted behind me. I spun, smacking into the crates again, dust flying into my mouth, my nose, my eyes. As I sputtered, the giggle turned to a snicker.

I could see enough to know no living person was attached to that snicker.

I marched back the way I'd come.

The whispers followed, right at my ear now, escalating to a guttural moan that made goose bumps rise on my arms.

I remembered what the necromancer's ghost at Lyle House had said—that he'd followed me from the hospital, where he'd been dealing with ghosts pestering mental patients. I guess if you're a sadistic moron who's been stuck in limbo for years, haunting mental patients—or young necromancers—might seem like a fun way to pass the time.

The moaning turned to a weird keening, like the wailing souls of the tormented dead.

I wheeled toward the noise. "Are you having fun? Well, guess what? If you keep it up, you're going to find out that I'm a lot more powerful than you think. I'll yank you out of there whether you want to show yourself or not."

My delivery was pitch-perfect—strong and steady—but the ghost just gave a derisive snort, then resumed keening.

I felt my way to a crate, brushed dust off the top, and sat. "One last chance or I'm pulling you through."

Two seconds of silence. Then the moaning again, right at my ear. I almost toppled off the crate. The ghost snickered. I closed my eyes and summoned, careful to keep my power on low, just in case his body was nearby. I might get some satisfaction from slamming him back into his rotting corpse, but I'd regret it later.

The moaning stopped. At a grunt of surprise, I smiled and amped it up, just a little.

The figure started to materialize—short, chubby guy old enough to be my grandfather. He twisted and writhed like he was caught in a strait-jacket. I pulled harder. . . .

A dull thump nearby made me jump.

"Liz?" I called. "Tori?"

The ghost snarled. "Let me go, you little—"

Another thump drowned out the nasty name he called me—or most of it. Then came a weird skittering noise.

"Let me go or I—"

I closed my eyes and gave the ghost one big mental shove. He gasped and sailed backward through the wall, like he'd been thrown out of a spaceship air lock. I waited to see if he'd return. He didn't. I'd cast him to the other side, wherever ghosts live. Good.

Another thump. I scrambled to my feet, the ghost forgotten. I crept past a stack of crates and listened. Silence.

"Tori?" I whispered. "Liz?"

Um, if it's not *them, maybe calling their names isn't such a bright idea.*

I eased along the crates until I reached a gap. Through it, I saw the pale rectangle of a window. The grime was smudged, like someone had haphazardly rubbed it away.

The scratching sound came again. Then the smell hit, like that musky odor in the other room, only ten times worse. The skittering came again—like tiny claws on concrete.

Rats.

As I pulled back, the window darkened. Then *thump.* I looked up too late to see what it was. Was someone throwing stuff at the window? Maybe the boys, trying to get my attention.

I hurried forward, forgetting the rats, until I saw a dark blob on the shadowy floor, moving slow, like it was dragging something. That must be what I smelled—a dead animal that the rat was taking back to the nest.

When something brushed the top of my head, I yelped, clapping my hands over my mouth. A shadow flew past and hit the window with that familiar thump. As it fell, I noticed thin, leathery wings. A bat.

The dim shape flapped its wings against the concrete, making a scratchy, rustling noise. Weren't bats supposed to fly by echolocation? It shouldn't hit a window trying to escape.

Unless it was rabid.

The bat finally launched itself again. It fluttered away, weaving and bobbing like it was still dazed. It headed for the ceiling, then turned and came straight at me.

As I stumbled back my foot slipped, and I fell with a bone-jarring crack that set my injured arm on fire. I tried to leap up, but whatever I'd stepped on was stuck to my sneaker, sending me skidding again.

The thing on my sneaker was slick and cold. I pulled it off and raised it into the moonlight. Pinched between my fingers was a rotting wing. The bat I'd seen still had both of its wings, so there must be another one in here, dead.

I threw the wing across the room and frantically wiped my hand on my jeans. The bat swooped again. I ducked, but my foot slid out and I fell. As I hit the floor, a horrible smell enveloped me, so strong I coughed. Then I saw the bat, less than a foot away, teeth bared, long fangs white against the dark.

The cloud cover shifted, the light streaming into the room, and I realized I wasn't looking at fangs but at white patches of skull. The bat was decomposing, one eye shriveled, the other a black pit. Most of the flesh was gone; only hanging bits remaining. The bat had no ears, no nose, just a bony snout. The snout opened. Rows of tiny jagged teeth flashed, and it started to shriek, a horrible garbled squeaking.

My shrieks joined it as I scrambled back. The thing pulled itself along on one crumpled wing. It was definitely a bat—and I'd raised it from the dead.

With my gaze fixed on the bat creeping toward me, I forgot about the other one until it flew at my face. I saw it coming—then saw its sunken eyes, bloody stumps of ears, and bone showing through patchy fur. Another zombie bat.

I slammed back into the crates. My hands sailed up to ward the bat off, but too late. It hit my face. I screamed then, really screamed as the rotted wings drummed me. The cold body hit my cheek. Tiny claws caught in my hair.

I tried to smack it away. It dropped. As I clapped my hands to my mouth, I felt something tugging at my shirt. I looked down to see the bat clinging to it.

Its fur wasn't patchy at all. What I'd mistaken for spots of bone were wriggling maggots.

I pressed one hand to my mouth, stifling my screams. With my free hand, I swatted at it, but it clung there, rows of teeth opening and closing, head bobbing like it was trying to see me.

"Chloe? Chloe!" Liz raced through the outside wall. She stopped short, eyes going huge. "Oh my God. Oh my God!"

"G-get it off. P-please."

I whirled, still swatting at the bat. Then I heard a sickening crunch as I stepped on the other one. When I wheeled, the one clinging to me fell off. As it hit the floor, Liz shoved the top crate off a stack and it fell on the fallen bat, the thud drowning out that horrible bone-crunching noise.

"I—I—I—"

"It's okay," she said, walking toward me. "It's dead."

"N-n-no. It's . . ."

Liz stopped. She looked down at the bat I'd stepped on. It lifted one wing feebly, then let it fall. The wing twitched, claw scratching the concrete.

Liz hurried to a crate. "I'll put it out of its misery."

"No." I held out my hand. "That won't work. It's already dead."

"No, it's not. It's—" She bent for a closer look, finally seeing the decomposing body. She stumbled back. "Oh. Oh, it's— It's—"

"Dead. I raised it from the dead."

She looked at me. And her expression . . . She tried to hide it, but I'll never forget that look—the shock, the horror, the disgust.

"You . . . ," she began. "You can . . . ?"

"It was an accident. There was a ghost pestering me. I—I was summoning him and I must have a-accidentally raised them."

The bat's wing fluttered again. I dropped beside it. I tried not to look, but of course I couldn't help seeing the tiny body crushed on the concrete, bones sticking out. And still it moved, struggling to get up, claws scraping the concrete, smashed head rising—

I closed my eyes and concentrated on freeing its spirit. After a few minutes, the scratching stopped. I opened my eyes. The bat lay still.

"So what was it? A zombie?" Liz tried to sound calm, but her voice cracked.

"Something like that."

"You . . . You can resurrect the dead?"

I stared at the crushed bat. "I wouldn't call it resurrection."

"What about people? Can you . . . ?" She swallowed. "Do that?"

I nodded.

"So that's what Tori's mom meant. You raised zombies at Lyle House."

"Accidentally."

Uncontrollable powers . . .

Liz continued. "So it's . . . like in the movies? They're just empty, re-re— What's the word?"

"Reanimated." I wasn't about to tell her the truth, that necromancers didn't reanimate a soulless body. We took a ghost like Liz and shoved her back into her rotting corpse.

I remembered what the demi-demon said, about me nearly returning the souls of a thousand dead to their buried shells. I hadn't believed her. Now . . .

Bile filled my mouth. I turned away, gagging and spitting it out.

"It's okay," Liz said, coming up beside me. "It's not your fault."

I looked at the box she'd shoved onto the other bat, took a deep breath, and walked to it. When I reached to move it, she said, "It's dead. It must be—" She stopped and said in a small, shaky voice. "Isn't it?"

"I need to be sure."

I lifted the box.

sixteen

THE BAT WASN'T DEAD. It was— I don't want to remember it. By that point, I'd been so stressed out that I couldn't concentrate, and freeing the bat's spirit had taken . . . a while. But I did it. And I was glad I'd checked. Now I could relax . . . or so I thought.

"You should sleep," Liz said after I'd lain there with my eyes open for almost an hour.

I glanced at Tori, but she was still snoring—hadn't even stirred since I'd come back.

"I'm not tired," I said.

"You need to rest. I can help. I always helped my nana sleep when she couldn't."

Liz never talked about her parents, only her grandmother, and I realized how little I knew about her.

"You lived with your nana?"

She nodded. "My mom's mom. I didn't know my dad. Nana said he didn't stick around."

Considering he'd been a demon, I supposed that was how it worked.

Liz was silent a moment, then said quietly, "I think she was raped."

"Your mom?"

"I heard stuff. Stuff I wasn't supposed to hear, Nana talking to her sisters, her friends, and later to social workers. She said Mom was wild when she was young. Not *really* wild, just smoking and drinking beer and skipping classes. Then she got pregnant, and that made her different. She got older. Pissed off. Things I heard—I think she was raped."

"That's awful."

She pulled her knees up and hugged them. "I never told anyone that. It's not the kind of thing you share. Kids might look at you funny, you know?"

"I'd never—"

"I know. That's why I told you. Anyway, for a few years, everything was okay. We lived with Nana, and she looked after me while Mom worked. But then Mom had this accident."

My gut chilled as I thought of my own mother, killed in a hit-and-run. "What kind of accident?"

"The cops said she was at this party, got drunk, and fell down the stairs. She hit her head really hard and when she got out of the hospital, it was like she was a whole different person. She couldn't work, so Nana did and Mom stayed home with me, but sometimes she'd forget to feed me lunch or she'd get really mad and hit me and say it was all my fault. Blaming me because she wasn't happy, I guess."

"I'm sure she didn't—"

"Mean it. I know. Afterward she'd cry and tell me she was sorry and buy me candy. Then she had my little brother, and she started getting into drugs and getting arrested for stealing stuff. Only she never went to jail. The court always sent her to a mental hospital. That's why, at Lyle House, I was so scared—"

"Of being sent to one. I should have helped. I—"

"You tried. It wouldn't have mattered. They'd already made up their minds." She went quiet for a moment. "Mom tried to warn me. Sometimes she'd show up at my school, high on dope, going on about experiments and magic powers, and saying I had to hide before they found me." Another pause. "I guess she wasn't so crazy after all, huh?"

"No, she wasn't. She was trying to protect you."

She nodded. "Okay, enough of that. You need to rest up so you can find the guys. Nana always said I was good at helping people fall asleep. Better than any pills. You know why?"

"Why?"

She grinned. "'Cause I can talk your ear off. Now, let's see, what can I talk about that'll bore you to sleep? Oh, I know. Guys. Hot guys. I have this list, see? The ten hottest guys ever. Actually, it's two lists, ten each, 'cause I needed one for real guys—guys I actually know—and one make-believe list, for guys in movies and bands. Not that they aren't real guys, because of course they're real . . ."

I finally drifted off and didn't wake until the roar of a truck sent me jerking up, limbs flailing.

Light streamed through the windows. I checked my watch. Eight thirty. No sign of Liz. Was she on patrol? Or had she left already?

Tori was still sound asleep, snoring softly.

I shook her shoulder. "It's morning. We need to search for the note."

Tori opened her eyes, muttered that there probably wasn't any note, the guys were long gone, and we were screwed. A ray of sunshine, our Victoria.

But after moaning about not having lifted breath mints or a hairbrush or breakfast she did rise and help me.

We'd been searching for about a half hour when Tori said, loud enough to be heard by anyone walking past the windows, "The taggers in this town really have too much time on their hands."

I hurried over to shush her. "Taggers?"

She waved at the surrounding stacks of crates and I saw what she meant. A crate in every stack had been tagged with graffiti. "My dad's store gets hit every month, but he never had one this fancy."

She pointed to one almost hidden in shadow. Where the others were typical tags—nicknames and symbols—this was a sketch in black marker of a teenage guy with a paw print tattoo on his cheek, brandishing Wolverine-like claws.

I grinned. "Simon." When Tori gave me a *huh?* look, I said, "It's Simon."

"Uh, no. It's a guy with a paw on his face."

"It's Simon's *work*. This is one of his comic-book characters."

"I knew that."

"Help me lift the crate."

She didn't move. "Why?"

"Because the note"—I heaved the top crate off by myself—"will be under it."

"Why would he put—?"

Sure enough, under the crate was a folded piece of paper. We both grabbed for it. I won.

Simon had drawn three pictures. In the top left corner, like a salutation, was a ghost. The middle had a big sketch of Arnold Schwarzenegger as the *Terminator*. The third, in place of a signature, was a lightning bolt surrounded by fog. Beside the drawing, someone had scrawled in inch-high letters *10 A.M.*

Tori snatched it from me and turned it over. "So where's the message?"

"Right there." I pointed from picture to picture. "It says: Chloe, I'll be back, Simon."

"Okay, that's just weird. And what's that mean?" She pointed to the time.

"That would be Derek, making sure I know *when* they'll be back."

"Only once a day?"

"Every time they sneak in here, it's a big risk. Anyway, the time isn't really important. If I pick up the message, Derek will smell me. He can follow my trail."

Her nose wrinkled. "Like a dog?"

"Cool, huh?"

"Uh, no." She made a face. "So they weren't kidding about him being a werewolf. Explains a lot, don't you think?"

I shrugged and checked my watch. "We've got just over an hour to wait, so—" I swore under my breath, making Tori arch her brows in mock-surprise.

"We can't let the guys come back," I said, "not with that Edison Group guard patrolling."

There wasn't an Edison Group guard patrolling. There were two. I sent Liz to check all possible entry points. She returned, naming four: the main gate, the front delivery gate, the back delivery gate, and the entire surrounding fence.

I doubted Derek would climb the fence again. He'd be exposed up there where anyone could see him. If I were him, I'd pick the same entry point as the Edison Group had yesterday—that rear gate.

But I also knew Derek well enough to admit that I *didn't* know him well enough to guess his strategy with any real confidence. So we had to split up and cover all three entrances. I needed to stay close to Liz, so she could communicate with me. That meant Tori got the back. I could only pray she'd actually remember to watch.

By nine thirty we were in position. The factory yard was at the edge of a residential area—a neighborhood of older homes including, a block away, Lyle House. Derek and I had come this way Saturday night when we escaped and I still remembered the general layout. The roads ran north-south, with the factory yard down at the southern end.

My spot was across the street from the factory, behind one of the end houses. No one was home—the driveway was empty and the windows dark.

I crouched behind a shed watching the front delivery gate, ready to whistle at the first sign of the guys. At 9:45 an SUV passed in front of the factory, moving at a crawl: it was the same Edison Group vehicle Derek and I had run from on Saturday night.

As it rolled past, I saw Mike in the driver's seat. Beside him sat Tori's mom, watching out the side window. The SUV continued to the corner, then made a right, heading for the back of the factory yard.

I waited until it was out of sight, then leaped up. As I moved, a shadow loomed over me. My fists flew up, but before I could turn, hands grabbed me, one clamping over my mouth, the other around my waist, yanking me back behind the shed.

"It's me," a deep voice rumbled.

The hands released me and I turned. There stood Derek, all six foot something of him. Maybe it was just the thrill of seeing him, but he looked better than I remembered. His black hair was still lank, and his face was still dotted with acne. But he looked . . . better.

"I am so glad to see you," I said, grinning up at him.

His snort said the feeling wasn't necessarily mutual. Maybe I should have been a little disappointed, but I was too relieved to care. At this moment, Derek's trademark scowl was better than any smile.

"I am so glad—"

"Got that," he said. "Stop bouncing, Chloe, before they notice you."

"They're gone. That's why—" I looked behind him and my grin faded. "Where's Simon? H-he's okay, isn't he?" I fumbled to pull out the insulin pouch. "I know he needs this. It was—"

"That's his backup. He had another one in his pocket."

"Oh. Right. Um, good. So where—?"

"Around back. I smelled Tori so I thought it was a trap and—"

"Tori! Her mom— The car— We have to warn her."

"What?"

I wheeled, motioning for him to follow. I crossed the yard, darting from hiding place to hiding place as I headed for the road the SUV had taken. Derek tried to keep up, his harsh whispers of "Chloe, get back here!" mingled with harsher curses when I slid into spots he couldn't fit.

Finally, as I dashed along a row of hedges, he caught me by the jacket collar and swung me off my feet, letting me dangle there like a puppy.

"I know a better route. I've been here for two days, checking things out as I waited for you." He plunked me down but kept his grip on my collar so I couldn't take off. "Now what's this about Tori and her mom?"

"No time. Just— Liz. We need Liz."

"Liz is alive?"

I hesitated, reminding myself how much he'd missed. "No. I mean . . . her ghost. I was right about her being dead. She's been helping me, though, and we need her to scout the way."

I broke from his grip and dashed to a break in the hedge. I slid sideways into it and peeked out. Liz stood in the middle of the road two blocks down. I gave a whistle that I thought was just fine, but Derek sighed, put his fingers in his mouth, and whistled loud enough to make my ears ring. I couldn't tell whether it got Liz's attention—he made me duck while he listened, in case it got anyone else's attention. After a moment, he let me peek around the hedge.

"She's coming," I said.

Derek nodded. He scanned the yards around us, making sure all was clear.

"You wanted to lead," I said. "So lead. She'll catch up."

He didn't move. When I tried to walk away, he caught my sleeve.

"I gotta know what I'm walking into."

"Two Edison Group guards discreetly patrolling the yard—"

"Edison Group?"

"And Tori's mom, plus the guy who shot at you Saturday night. But of all of them, Tori's mom is the one to watch."

"Tori's mom? Edison Group? What's—?"

"Derek?"

"What?"

I looked up, meeting his gaze. "Do you trust me?"

I honestly had no idea what the answer would be, but he didn't hesitate, just grunted, "Course."

"Then, yes, I know you want details. But we don't have time. Not if Simon's back there and Tori's mom's on her way. She's a witch, and she's not afraid to use her spells. Good enough?"

He looked off across the yard. Maybe he did trust me, but for Derek, not having all the facts was like sticking a blindfold on him and telling him to follow.

"Stay behind me," he said, and we took off.

seventeen

LIZ SCOUTED THE WAY, running ahead and whistling us onward. Derek's mouth stayed set in that way that let me know he wasn't happy . . . which was pretty much his normal expression, so I ignored it.

The SUV had gone down a service road beside the factory. Along it were smaller industrial buildings, with more at the back, which is where we'd entered with the Edison Group yesterday and where Tori now waited. It was also where the SUV had headed.

We were still in the residential blocks to the north of the factory yard, now standing behind a minivan at the neighborhood's edge. As we peered around it, we could see the SUV parked behind another vehicle. Tori's mom, Mike, and the balding driver stood beside it, talking.

"Where's Simon?" I whispered.

"On the other side of them. Tori?"

"I left her over there—" I pointed. "She went around back to watch the rear entrance. Hopefully, she's lying low and staying put."

"If it was you, yeah. Tori?" A derisive snort. I'd have basked more in the compliment if I didn't know Derek considered Tori only slightly smarter than plankton.

"We can slip across this road and cut through the next yard," I said. "Then we can circle—"

Derek caught my arm again as I started to move—at this rate, it was soon going to be as sore as my injured one.

"Dog," he said, jerking his chin toward the fenced yard. "It was inside earlier."

Expecting to see a Doberman slavering at the fence, I followed his gaze to a little puff of white fur, the kind of dog women stick in their purses. It wasn't even barking, just staring at us, dancing in place.

"Oh, my God! It's a killer Pomeranian." I glanced up at Derek. "It's a tough call, but I think you can take him."

A glare. "That's not—"

The wind changed and the dog went rigid. Derek swore, and pulled me backward. The dog gave one low, piercing whine. Then it went nuts, jumping and twisting and barking, a whirlwind of white fur battering itself against the fence.

Derek yanked me behind the minivan. We were out of the dog's sight, but it continued yelping and snarling, the wire fence twanging with each hit.

"It smelled me," Derek said. "The werewolf thing."

"Do they always do that?"

He shook his head. "I used to just make them nervous. They'd steer clear, maybe bark a bit. Now?" He waved toward the racket. "I get this. We need to shut it up."

"I'll— Wait. Liz!"

She was already running over.

"Could you distract that dog?" I asked her. "I think he wants to play fetch."

Her brow furrowed. Then she smiled. "Right. I can do that."

"Play *fetch*?" Derek whispered as she took off. "What—?"

I motioned him to the end of the van and pointed. There, on the other side of the fence, a stick levitated, then shook. Liz was holding it, but Derek could see only the stick. The dog watched it fly, then spun back to the fence, barking and jumping again. Liz retrieved the stick, and tapped it on the dog's back. Once she had his attention, she threw it. This time, he chased.

I looked up at Derek, who was staring at the dog.

"Remember Liz thought she had a poltergeist? Turned out she is the poltergeist. She's a half-demon with the power of telekinesis."

"Huh." He turned to stare again, slowly shaking his head, as if wondering why *he* hadn't figured that out. Probably because he didn't know half-demons could be telekinetic, but for Derek, that wouldn't be an excuse.

"Coast is clear!" Liz shouted. "And this pooch is getting bored!"

Derek and I got across the street. We headed for the service road on the other side, leading through the industrial buildings bordering the factory. Then Derek stopped.

"Tori," he said.

I peered past him. "Where? I don't see . . ." I noticed his face lifted to the breeze. "Not see, smell, right?"

He nodded and led me to where she was huddled behind a wall, peeking around the other side.

"It's us," I whispered.

She saw Derek and without so much as a hello, leaned to look behind him. "Where's Simon?"

"He's—"

"Is he okay? Why isn't he here?" She glared up at Derek. "Where'd you leave him?"

"Passed out in an alley." Derek frowned in thought. "Not sure where, though . . ."

"He's kidding," I said as Tori sputtered.

"We need to get moving." Derek hooked a thumb at Tori while looking at me. "She's your responsibility."

"Excuse me?" Tori said.

Derek didn't even glance her way. "Make sure she keeps up. And shuts up."

As we headed out, Liz returned to say the Edison Group was in the factory yard, having slipped in the rear way again. We found the spot where Derek had left Simon, behind a building with faded For Sale signs on the boarded-up windows.

"Well, where is he?" Tori demanded.

"Huh. Must have broken his chain."

"He means Simon's a big boy and he's free to move around." I turned to Derek. "Can you track him?"

"Yeah."

He dropped to a crouch. It was a long way from stooping to sniff the ground, but Tori still stared.

"Please tell me he isn't doing what I think he's doing," she said.

Derek scowled—not at Tori but at me. "There'd better be a good explanation for this," he said with a pointed look her way.

"Not really," I murmured.

He took a deep breath and pushed to his feet. "Stay here."

Tori waited until he was gone, then shuddered. "Okay, Derek always weirded me out, but that wolf man stuff is seriously creepy. Suits him, I suppose. A creepy power for a creepy guy."

"I thought he looked better."

She stared at me.

"What? He does. Probably because he's starting his wolf changes and he's not stressed out about being in Lyle House. That must help."

"You know what would really help? Shampoo. Deodorant—"

I raised my hand to cut her off. "He smelled fine, so don't start that. I'm sure he's wearing deodorant and—for once—it's working. As for showers, they're a little hard to come by on the street, and we won't look much better soon."

"I'm just saying—"

"Do you think he doesn't *know* what you're saying? News flash—he's not stupid."

Derek was all too aware of the impression he made. At Lyle House, he'd showered twice a day, and it still hadn't fixed the puberty smackdown.

She went back to watching for Simon. I stayed where I was, ten feet away, better hidden, while keeping an eye on her *and* on that corner, waiting for—

A soft poke at my shoulder blade startled me.

"Still jumpy, I see."

I spun to see Simon, Derek hanging back behind him.

Simon grinned, the sight as familiar as Derek's scowl. "Got my note, I hear," he said.

I pulled it out and waved it.

He plucked it from my fingers and tucked it into my jacket pocket. Then he caught my hand, his thumb rubbing my knuckles, and the back of my throat ached with the relief of seeing him, finally actually seeing *both* of them after all the worry and the nightmares . . .

If I'd had the courage, I would have hugged him. Instead, I just said, "I'm really glad you found us," my voice cracking.

Simon squeezed my hand. His lips lowering to my ear, whispering, "I—"

He went rigid, head lifting.

"Hey, Simon," Tori said behind me.

"What is she doing here?"

Derek jabbed his thumb at me. "Ask her. I'm not getting any answers."

"It's a long story," I said.

"Then it'll have to wait," Derek said. "We need to get away from here."

Simon whispered to me, "But is everything okay?"

"No," Tori said. "I kidnapped her and forced her to escape with me. I've been using her as a human shield against those guys with guns, and I was just about to strangle her and leave her body here to throw them off my trail. But then you showed up and foiled my evil plans. Lucky for you, though. You get to rescue poor little Chloe again and win her undying gratitude."

"Undying gratitude?" Simon looked at me. "Cool. Does that come with eternal servitude? If so, I like my eggs sunnyside up."

I smiled. "I'll remember that."

"Enough yapping," Derek said. "Move out."

eighteen

IN THE MOVIE VERSION of our flight, we'd have run straight into a trap. Everyone would have been taken captive . . . except me, being the heroine. I'd be smart enough to avoid capture, so I could plot a daring rescue to free my friends. But it wouldn't be easy. Or quiet. Tori and Simon would blow up a city block with magic. Derek would throw a few trucks at our pursuers. I would recruit a platoon of zombies from a conveniently located cemetery.

But as cool as all that would have looked on the big screen, I was really more in the mood for a quiet getaway. And that's exactly what we got. The Edison Group never left the factory yard.

We walked at least three miles. When we were far enough from the factory to stop skulking, Derek led us into the commercial section on the other side of the neighborhood, where four teens wouldn't look so out of place on a school day.

"I know you guys love this cloak-and-dagger stuff," Tori said finally, "but can't we just grab a taxi?"

Derek shook his head.

I cleared my throat. "A cab would be risky, but if there's a shorter route to where we're going, my feet would really appreciate it."

Derek stopped short. I smacked into his back—not for the first time, since he insisted on walking in front of me. I'd been tripping on his heels and mumbling apologies the whole way. When I'd slow down to let him get farther ahead, he'd snap at me to keep up.

"We're almost there," Simon said.

He was beside me—sticking to the curbside, walking as close as Derek. While normally I wouldn't complain about Simon being so close, I had the weird sensation of being blocked in.

As we started forward again, I tried dropping back with Tori, who lagged behind, but Simon put his fingers on my elbow and steered me back into place.

"Okay," I said. "Something's up. What's with the walking blockade?"

"They're protecting you," Tori said. "Shielding you from the big bad world."

Neither of the guys said a word. Whatever it was, they weren't telling me. Not yet.

Our destination was some kind of unused industrial building in a neighborhood so rundown that even the gangbangers and the homeless seemed to steer clear.

Just as we were about to go inside, Liz called to me. She stood by the missing front door like she couldn't cross the threshold. I asked whether there was magic keeping her out, but she said no, she just needed to talk to me. So I waved Derek and Simon on, telling them I had to speak to Liz.

She'd been quiet since I'd met up with the others, staying out of sight. Now she crouched on the dirt patch beside the building to tug up one purple and orange sock.

"You know, I really loved these socks, but another day of having to look at them, and I'm going barefoot for eternity." She tried to smile, but after a moment's struggle, gave up and straightened. "I'm taking off now. You don't need me anymore."

"No, I—I mean, if you want to, sure, but—"

"That came out wrong. I just . . ." She lifted her foot, adjusting the sock again. "I should go. But I'll be back."

"I don't have your shirt. We'll need to set up a rendezvous point or something."

She laughed, almost genuine now. "No more rendezvous points. I'll find you. I always do. It just . . . might be a while. I've got stuff to do. And you . . ." She looked toward the building, and the wistfulness in her eyes stabbed through me. "You've got stuff to do. You and the others."

"Liz, I—"

"It's okay. You do your thing, and I'll catch up."

"I'll miss you."

She reached out, and I swore I felt her fingers brush mine. "You're sweet, Chloe. Don't worry about me. I'll be back." Then she disappeared.

The others were waiting just inside the door. We picked our way through the debris, walking single file in the near dark behind Derek.

As we moved, the hairs on my neck rose, and a dull throbbing started in the back of my skull. I slowed. Now it was Tori's turn to smack into me.

"Come on, *move*," she said. "Oh, that's right. Chloe's afraid of the dark. Simon, you'd better hold her hand or—"

"Knock it off." Simon pushed past Tori and came up beside me. "You okay?"

"There's . . . something here. I can feel it."

"Ghosts?"

"I don't think so. It's like what I felt in the crawl space at Lyle House."

Derek swore.

I turned to peer at him in the darkness. "What?"

"There's a body."

"*What?*" Simon said, with Tori echoing, shriller.

"There's a dead body somewhere in here. I smelled it yesterday, after we'd settled in."

"And you didn't bother telling me?" Simon said.

"It's a body. Long dead. Some homeless guy. It's a good place otherwise."

"*Otherwise?* A pitch-black hideaway filled with trash, dead bodies, and rats. You know how to pick 'em, bro."

"R-rats?" I said, thinking of the bats.

"Great," Tori muttered. "She's scared of rats, too."

"As long as I'm here, they're staying away," Derek said.

It wasn't the *live* rats I was worried about.

He continued. "But I didn't think about the body. Chloe? Is it a problem?"

It was. I should say something about the bats, how I'd accidentally raised them while dealing with that ghost. But I looked at everyone, how tired they seemed, all impatiently waiting to find a place to rest and talk, find out what I knew. I could handle this. As long as I didn't try summoning Liz, I wouldn't raise this body.

So that's what I said.

"But it bothers you being near it," Simon said. "We should—"

"I'm sure safe places aren't easy to find." I forced a smile. "It'll be good experience. I need to learn to recognize the feeling."

"Oh, of course," Tori said. "Chloe's going to *learn* from it. Do you ever quit? You're like a perky little Energizer bunny—"

Simon turned to snap something at her, but Derek waved us on. We reached a room in the middle, with no windows. Derek turned on a lantern. It cast enough wavering light to see by. Earlier, the guys had set up crates to sit on, and laid newspaper over the filthy floor. Two new backpacks were hidden behind the crates alongside a neat stack of cheap blankets. Not exactly the Hilton—or even Lyle House—but a lot better than where we'd slept last night.

As we sat, Derek pulled a handful of energy bars from his pocket, and gave one to me.

"Oh, right. You must be starving." Simon reached into his pockets. "I can offer one bruised apple and one brown banana. Convenience stores aren't the place to buy fruit, as I keep telling someone."

"Better than these. For you, anyway, Simon." Derek passed a bar to Tori.

"Because you aren't supposed to have those, are you?" I said. "Which reminds me . . ." I took out the insulin. "Derek said it's your backup."

"So my dark secret is out."

"I didn't know it was a secret."

"Not really. Just not something I advertise."

In other words, if kids knew he had a chronic illness, they might treat him differently. He had it under control, so there was no reason for anyone to know about it.

"Backup?" Tori said. "You mean he didn't need that?"

"Apparently not," I murmured.

Simon looked from her to me, confused, then understanding. "You guys thought . . ."

"That if you didn't get your medicine in the next twenty-four hours, you'd be dead?" I said. "Not exactly, but close. You know, the old 'upping the ante with a fatal disease that needs medication' twist. Apparently, it still works."

"Kind of a letdown, then, huh?"

"No kidding. Here we were, expecting to find you minutes from death. Look at you, not even gasping."

"All right, then. Emergency medical situation, take two."

He leaped to his feet, staggered, keeled over, then lifted his head weakly.

"Chloe? Is that you?" He coughed. "Do you have my insulin?"

I placed it in his outstretched hand.

"You saved my life," he said. "How can I ever repay you?"

"Undying servitude sounds good. I like my eggs scrambled."

He held up a piece of fruit. "Would you settle for a bruised apple?"

I laughed.

"You guys are weird," Tori said.

Simon sat on the crate beside me. "That's right. We are totally weird and completely uncool. Your popularity is plummeting just by being near us. So why don't you—"

"Chloe?" Derek interrupted. "How's your arm?"

"Her—?" Simon swore under his breath. "Way to keep showing me up. First, food. Now her arm." He turned to me. "How is it?"

"Fine. All stitched and bandaged."

"We should take a look," Derek said.

Simon helped me pull off the jacket.

"Is that all you're wearing?" Derek said. "Where's your sweater?"

"They didn't give us a chance to grab anything. I have money. I'll buy one."

"Two," Simon said. "It's freezing after the sun goes down. You must have been a Popsicle last night."

I shrugged. "I had other things on my mind."

"Her aunt and Rae," Tori said.

"W-we'll get to that," I said, as Simon looked at me. "There's a lot to catch up on. You guys start."

nineteen

"BACK TO THE BEGINNING, then," Derek said, settling onto his crate. "The last time we saw you, you were running for the warehouse with Rae. Our distraction worked and we got away, but we couldn't go back for a while, in case they were watching. When we got there, you guys were gone."

"Rae convinced me to leave." She'd said that when she was alone with Simon, Simon hadn't mentioned me at all—only worried about his brother. I knew now that wasn't true—she'd known it would make me feel bad, maybe bad enough to leave with her, and now I was embarrassed that it had worked. "She . . . said stuff. She got me to leave to get my arm checked by Aunt Lauren, and then . . ."

I took them through the last two days, step by step, revelation by revelation. When I finally finished, they all sat there, silent, even Tori.

"So Brady and Liz are dead," Simon said slowly. "And, I guess, that other girl—the one who was shipped out earlier."

"Amber," Tori said. "Her name was Amber."

I nodded. "She was on the list. All three of them."

Another moment of silence.

"Rae and Aunt Lauren are still there," I said finally. "I know Rae betrayed us, and my aunt was one of them, but I—I need to get them out. I don't expect any help with that—"

"No, you're right," Simon said. "Rae screwed up, but she sure doesn't deserve to die for it."

"I know we can't rescue them alone." I snuck a look at Derek. When he nodded, I felt a pinch of disappointment, like I'd been hoping he'd say that we could handle it. He was right, of course. We couldn't.

"Once we find your dad, I want to go back," I said. "I guess now we know why he took you guys and ran."

"Because he decided genetically engineering his son hadn't been such a bright idea after all?" There was a bitterness in Simon's voice that surprised me. All this time, I hadn't thought of that—I'd been too focused on Simon's father as "the good guy." But he'd put his son in the experiment, like all the other parents.

"They tried to do the right thing," I said, remembering my aunt's letter. "They thought it would make our lives easier. The Edison Group sold them this dream, and when it started to go wrong, your dad got out. Aunt Lauren tried, too." I touched the letter in my pocket. "Just too late."

"And then there are those of us whose parents never regretted it," Tori said. "Whose mothers have turned out to be total evil bitches. But, hey, at least now no one can say I don't come by it honestly." She ripped the last bit of wrapper from her energy bar. "I don't buy this crap about us being failures, though. They wanted stronger supernaturals. That's what we are. They just need to teach us how to control it."

"You go back and tell them that," Simon said.

"What about you?" Tori waved at Simon. "Your powers work fine. You didn't even get counseling at Lyle House."

"Simon isn't on the list. They consider him a success."

"Whatever that means." Simon shifted on his crate. "The experiment's so-called successes seem to have weaker powers, but maybe they just haven't kicked in yet. When they do, we could have the same problems."

Tori nodded. "Ticking time bombs."

Exactly what the demi-demon had said . . .

I hadn't mentioned the demi-demon. An unnecessary complication and a chance for Derek to tell me I'd been stupid even to listen to her. As for what she said, about going back, freeing her? Not something I wanted to consider right now. If we did go back, we'd have Simon's dad and he'd find a way to stop the Edison Group *without* freeing any demons.

"My dad will fill in the blanks," Simon said.

"Great," Tori said. "We can save Chloe's aunt and Rae and get all our questions answered . . . just as soon as you find your missing dad. How's that going?" She looked at our surroundings. "Not so well, I see."

Anger flared in Simon's eyes, but he blinked it away. "We're working on it."

"How?"

"Later," Derek said. "Right now, we need to get Chloe warmer clothes—"

"Chloe, Chloe, Chloe. Stop worrying about poor little Chloe. She hasn't frozen yet. What about your dad? Any clues? Hints?"

"Not yet," Simon said.

"So what have you been doing for the last two days?"

His anger flared, and this time he let it, turning on her so fast she shrank back. "We've spent every waking minute of them on three things: surviving, finding Chloe, and finding our dad. What have *you* been doing?"

"I was locked up."

"So? That didn't stop Chloe. What do you have to add, Tori? Did you find out *anything*? Or just piggyback on her escape?"

"Tori helped me," I said. "Without her—"

She whipped around to face me. "Don't you defend me, Chloe Saunders."

Silence. Then Derek said, "Where can we take you, Tori? To a grandparent? Friend? You're out now and you're safe, so I'm sure there's someplace you'd rather be."

"No."

I opened my mouth to tell them what had happened with her dad, but her glare shut me up.

"She doesn't have any place to go," I said. "Like me."

"There must be someone," Derek said, "maybe not in Buffalo, but we'll buy you a bus ticket."

"Preferably on one leaving in the next hour?" she said. "I'm not going anywhere. I'm joining your little gang of baby heroes on the quest to find Superdad."

Simon and Derek exchanged a look.

"No," Derek said.

"No? Excuse me, it was *Rae* who betrayed you guys. Not me. I helped Chloe."

"And was it Rae who tormented her at Lyle House?"

"Tormented?" A derisive snort. "I didn't—"

"You did everything you could to get Chloe kicked out," Simon said. "And when that didn't work, you tried to kill her."

"Kill her?" Tori's mouth hardened. "I'm not my mother. Don't you dare accuse—"

"You lured her into the crawl space," Derek said. "Hit her over the head with a brick, bound and gagged her, and locked her in. Did you even check to make sure she was okay? That you hadn't cracked her skull?"

Tori sputtered a protest, but from the horror in her eyes, I knew the possibility hadn't occurred to her.

"Derek," I said, "I don't think—"

"No, *she* didn't think. She could have killed you with the brick, suffocated you with the gag, given you a heart attack from fright, not to mention what would have happened if you hadn't gotten out of your bindings. It only takes a couple of days to die from dehydration."

"I would *never* have left Chloe to die. You can't accuse me of that."

"No," Derek said. "Just of wanting her locked up in a mental hospital. And why? Because you didn't like her. Because she talked to a guy you *did* like. Maybe you're not your mother, Tori. But what you *are* . . ." He fixed her with an icy look. "I don't want it around."

The expression on her face . . . I felt for her, whether she'd welcome my sympathy or not.

"We don't trust you," Simon said, his tone softer than his brother's. "We can't have someone along that we don't trust."

"What if I'm okay with it," I cut in. "If I feel safe with her . . ."

"You don't," Derek said. "You won't kick her to the curb, though, because it's not the kind of person you are." He met Tori's gaze. "But it's the kind of person I am. Chloe won't force you to leave because she'd feel horrible if anything happened to you. Me? I don't care. You brought it on yourself."

Now that was too harsh. Simon squirmed, mouth opening.

I beat him to it. "Where is she going to go? She doesn't have any money. Anyone she runs to will almost certainly call her parents."

"I don't care."

"We can't do that," Simon said. "It's not right."

I knew Derek didn't lack empathy—he couldn't forget what he'd done to that kid who attacked Simon. But it was like he held some weird list of checks and balances, and if you got on the wrong side, like Tori had, he had no problem "kicking you to the curb," to face whatever fate waited.

"No," I said.

"It isn't up for negotiation. She's not coming."

"Okay." I stood and brushed off my jeans. "Come on, Tori."

When Simon rose, I thought he was going to stop me. Instead, he followed me to the door. Tori caught up, and we made it into the next room before Derek jogged out, catching my arm with a wrench that yanked me off my feet.

I winced and peeled off his fingers. "Wrong one."

He dropped my arm quickly, realizing he'd grabbed my injured one. A long minute of silence, then, "Fine." He turned to Tori. "Three conditions. One, whatever your problem is with Chloe, get over it. Go after her again, you're gone."

"Understood," Tori said.

"Two, get over Simon. He's not interested."

She flushed and snapped, "I think I've figured that out. And number three?"

"Get over yourself."

twenty

ONCE THAT BIT OF ugliness was over, I was—for the first time in my life—excited about going shopping. I couldn't wait to get out of this damp, dark, cold place, reminding me too much of the basements I hated. Get away from that dead body, the vibes from it keeping my nerves on edge. Get warm clothing, get real food, and a real *bathroom*, with soap and running water and a toilet. Don't ask what I'd been doing about "bodily needs" until now—the answer is really better left unsaid.

"If we get far enough from here that it's safe, I want to try using my bank card," I said. "My account is probably locked, but it's worth a shot. We can always use more money."

"We have some," Derek said.

"Okay. If you don't think it's safe for me to try."

"You aren't going out, Chloe. We are. You're staying here."

"Where you'll be safe," Tori said. "We wouldn't want you to break a nail using your card."

"Tori . . ." Derek said, turning. "You've been warned. Leave her alone."

"That slam was directed at you, wolf boy."

His voice dropped another octave, almost a growl. "Don't call me that."

"Please. Can we stop the bickering?" I stepped between them. "If I haven't proven by now that I'm careful and can look after myself—"

"You have," Simon said. "*This* is the problem." He handed me a newspaper clipping. I read the headline, then slowly lowered myself onto a crate, gaze fixed on the article.

My father was offering a half-million-dollar reward for information leading to my safe return. There was a picture of me—last year's school photo. And there was one of him, at what looked like a news conference.

The night after my breakdown at school, my father came to see me in the hospital. He'd flown back from Berlin, and he'd looked awful—exhausted and unshaven and worried. He looked even worse in the newspaper article, circles under his eyes, lines etched in his face.

I had no idea what the Edison Group had planned to tell my dad about my disappearance. They must have fed him a story, maybe said I'd been transferred and he couldn't visit me yet. They meant to cover up my disappearance, but they'd been too slow.

They were trying to cover their tracks, though. According to the nurses and my roommate, Rachelle Rogers—interviewed for the story—I'd run away.

Did my dad believe that? I guess he did. The article quoted him as saying he'd handled my situation badly—that he'd handled a lot of things with me badly—and he desperately wanted the chance to start over. When I read that, tears plopped onto the paper. I shook them off it.

"Half a million?" Tori read over my shoulder. "The Edison Group must be footing the bill, to get us back."

Simon pointed to the date. Yesterday morning, when we'd still been in their custody.

"Okay," Tori said. "They told her dad to make this big deal of her being gone so no one asks questions. He offers money he'll never have to pay, because he knows where she is."

I shook my head. "My aunt said he doesn't know anything about the Edison Group." I stared at the article, then folded it quickly. "I have to warn him."

Derek stepped into my path. "You can't do that, Chloe."

"If he's doing this"—I waved the paper—"he's putting himself in danger and he doesn't know it. I have to warn—"

"He's not in danger. If they could have beat him to the media, maybe. But now, if anything happened to him, it would only attract more attention. He's obviously not questioning their story about you running off so they'll leave him alone . . . as long as he doesn't find out the truth."

"But I have to let him know I'm okay. He's worried."

"And he's going to have to worry a little longer."

"Do we know for sure he's not in on it?" Tori said. "What did your aunt say? Did she trick your mom into the genetic modification? Or was your mom involved?"

I took out the letter and ran my fingers over it. Then I told them what it said—the parts that would matter to them.

"Anything about your dad?" Derek asked.

I hesitated, then nodded.

"What did she say?"

"That he wasn't involved, like I said."

"Which means it should be safe for Chloe to contact him, right?" Simon said.

Derek searched my face. Then said, in a low voice, "Chloe . . ."

"She said— My aunt said to stay away from him."

I guess Derek trusted me not to run to the nearest pay phone and call my dad because all three went shopping after that.

Both my aunt and Derek thought I should stay away from my dad. Derek said it would endanger him; Aunt Lauren probably figured it would endanger me.

I loved my dad. Maybe he worked too much, wasn't home enough, didn't quite know what to do with me, but he tried his best. He'd said he'd stick around while I was at Lyle House, but when a business emergency called him away, I hadn't been mad at him for leaving. He'd made arrangements to take a month off after my release instead, and that was more important to me. He thought I was safe at Lyle House, under my aunt's care.

He must think that I'd been so hurt and angry that I'd run away. Now his schizophrenic daughter was wandering the streets of Buffalo. I wanted to call him, just to say "I'm okay." But Derek and Aunt Lauren were right. If I did that, it might not be okay . . . for either of us.

To distract myself from thoughts of my father, I decided to check out the dead body. After what happened with the bats, if there was a way of honing my corpse-sense, I needed to start training now, so I'd know about nearby dead bodies *before* I accidentally slammed their ghosts back into them.

It did seem to work like radar. The closer I got, the stronger the feeling got. Which made finding the body sound easy, but it wasn't. The "feeling" was only a vague sense of unease, a prickle on the back of my neck and a dull headache; and when it seemed to increase, it was impossible to tell whether I was detecting the body, my nerves, or a draft.

I couldn't tell what kind of business had once run out of this place. Buffalo is full of abandoned buildings and houses. Drive down I-90 and you see them—crumbling buildings, boarded-up windows, empty yards. This one was no bigger than a house, with rooms like a house, though the outside didn't look like one. The inside was filled with junk—moldy cardboard boxes, pieces of wood, broken furniture, piles of garbage.

I'm sure I could have found the body without using my powers—there were only eight rooms. But I used them anyway, for practice. I finally found it in one of the back corners. From the doorway, it just looked like a pile of rags. When I got closer, I saw something white sticking out from under those rags—a hand, the flesh nearly rotted away, leaving only bone. The closer I got, the more I saw—a leg, then a skull, the corpse mostly skeletonized. Whatever smell it gave off, my human nose wasn't good enough to detect it.

The rags, I realized, were actually clothes, and not all that ragged, just crumpled around what remained of the body. The corpse wore boots, gloves, jeans, and a sweatshirt with a faded logo. A few strings of graying hair hung below the hat, and the clothes and body didn't identify it as male or female, but I instinctively thought of it as "him."

At some point last winter, this person had crawled in here to escape the cold, curled in this corner, and never gotten up. We couldn't have been the first ones to find him. Had everyone else just steered clear, like we were doing? No thought of informing the authorities, getting him out and identified and buried?

Was he on a missing person's list? Was someone waiting for him to come home? Had they offered a reward, like my dad?

Not quite as much, I was sure. A *half-million* dollars. That would bring out every crank in Buffalo. What was Dad thinking?

He wasn't thinking. He just wanted me home safe.

I blinked away tears. Great. Even examining a corpse couldn't stop me from worrying about my dad.

What about this guy? Someone had to be concerned about him. If I could contact his ghost, maybe I could relay a message. But I couldn't risk accidentally summoning him back into his corpse, like I had with the bats.

A tap on my shoulder sent me spinning.

"Sorry," Simon said. "I thought you heard me coming. I see you found our roomie. Trying to communicate?"

"Trying *not* to communicate."

"Looks like he's been here awhile." He crouched beside the corpse. "We could play CSI, figure out how long he's been dead. I don't see any bugs."

"Wrong time of year."

He winced. "Duh, right. It's still too cold in here. He definitely died a few months ago, meaning no bugs. I should have known that. Derek did a science fair experiment a couple years ago on bugs and decomposition." He caught my look. "Yeah, gross. Kind of interesting, too, but I wouldn't ask Derek about it. He was pissed. Only placed second in the city finals."

"Slacker." I backed up as he straightened. "I'm done here, though, so I'd better get farther away. Me and corpses don't mix." I considered telling him about the bats. I wanted to tell someone, talk it over, get advice, but . . . "I was just seeing whether I could use my powers to find it."

"I'm guessing the answer is yes."

I nodded and we left the room.

"We can find another place to stay," he said. "Derek's fine with that. Really."

"I'm okay. Speaking of Derek, where is he?"

"Still shopping. He sent me back to hang with you." He leaned down to my ear. "I think he just wanted to spend more time with Tori."

I laughed. "Want to take bets on who makes it back alive?"

"Derek. No contest. Last I saw, he was ordering her to go find more blankets. By now, he's probably on his way here, leaving her to find her own way and hoping she doesn't."

"How mad is he? About her being with us?"

"Mad? I'd rate it a five. Annoyed? An eleven. He'll get over it. We all have to. At least until she gets bored and remembers a long-lost aunt in Peoria."

When we got back to our spot, Simon set out a spread of the best a convenience store had to offer—juice, milk, yogurt, apples, wheat crackers, and cheese slices.

"All the food groups . . . except one." He handed me a candy bar. "Dessert."

"Thanks."

"Now, if you'll excuse me a moment, I'll spare you the sight of blood and needles before dining."

"It's okay. That stuff doesn't bother me."

He still turned around, to test his blood, then give himself a shot.

"And I thought annual flu shots were bad," I said. "Do you have to do that every day?"

"Three times for the needle. More for the testing."

"Three needles?"

He put the pouch away. "I'm used to it. I was diagnosed when I was three, so I don't ever remember not getting them."

"And you'll always have to do that?"

"There's a pump I can use. Stick it on my leg and it monitors my blood sugar and injects insulin. I got one when I turned thirteen. But . . ." He shrugged. "I had a deal with my dad, that I could only have one if I didn't use it as a license to eat whatever I wanted. Too much insulin isn't good. I screwed up."

"Too many of these?" I waved the candy bar.

"Nah. Too many carbs in general. I'd go out for pizza with the team, and I wouldn't want to have only two slices if everyone else was scarfing down six. You get razzed about being on a diet, being such a girl . . ."

"Now there's an insult."

"Hey, I was thirteen. I know it was stupid, but when you're always the new kid, you just want to fit in. I guess you know what that's like. You've probably been in as many schools as we have."

"Ten . . . no, eleven."

"It's a tie. Cool." He took a bite of his apple. "Now that I'm approaching the very mature age of sixteen, though, I've gotten over that. Dad and I were negotiating for me to get the pump back again when he disappeared."

"Simon?" Tori's voice echoed through the building.

"So much for peace and quiet," he muttered, then called, "We're back here."

twenty-one

DEREK RETURNED BEARING SHOPPING bags and cash. I'd given him my bank card and PIN, and he'd found an ATM without a camera. My card still worked. He'd withdrawn my limit of four hundred dollars. We couldn't do this again—every time I used it, the bank would know I was still in Buffalo, and Derek was afraid the Edison Group might be able to find that out.

He handed me the cash and receipt, discreetly folded. Tori snatched the receipt and opened it.

"My God, is this your bank account or college fund?"

I took it back. "My dad direct-deposits my allowance. After fifteen years, it adds up."

"And he just lets you access it?"

"Why wouldn't he?"

"Um, because you could spend it. No, wait. Let me guess. You're too responsible for that."

"She's smart," Simon said.

"Is that what you call it? I was thinking more . . ." She yawned.

My cheeks heated.

"Enough," Derek growled.

"Yeah, don't forget who gave you money for this." Simon nudged Tori's shopping bag.

Tori's jaw twitched. "It was twenty bucks for food and a blanket, and I'm keeping tabs. I'll pay her back. I'm responsible, too. Just not"—she waved at my receipt—"disgustingly responsible."

I took my bag from Derek. "So what did I get?" I reached inside. "A backpack. Two sweaters. Thank—"

The sweaters unrolled, and Tori choked on her mouthful of soda, laughing.

I turned, slowly and calmly, to her. "Your choices?"

She lifted her hands. "Uh-uh. I offered to pick something out, but Derek insisted." She turned to him. "No wonder you were gone so long. Must have had a hard time finding ones that ugly."

He'd bought me two identical gray hooded sweatshirts, made from the tacky polyester found only in the cheapest discount stores, the kind that shimmers like plastic and picks at your skin.

"What?" Derek said.

"They're fine. Thanks."

Tori reached out and caught the tag, then laughed. "I thought so. They're *boys'*. Size twelve boys."

"So? The women's cost more. I figured it wouldn't make a difference with Chloe."

Tori looked at me. Then she looked at my chest and started to laugh.

"What?" Derek said.

"Nothing," Tori sputtered. "You're just being honest, right?"

"Tori?" Simon said. "Shut up. Chloe, we'll grab something else for you tomorrow."

"No, Derek's right. These will fit. Thanks." Cheeks burning, I mumbled something about trying them on and fled the room.

When dusk began to fall, we settled in for the night. It was only eight o'clock and Tori complained bitterly. Derek told her she was free to stay awake, as long as she didn't use the lantern batteries and could still wake up at dawn. We weren't living in a world of light switches anymore. We had to use the sun when we could and sleep when we couldn't.

That was fine by me. I wasn't in the mood for a slumber party. Simon had tried cheering me up, but that only brought me down all the more. I didn't want to *need* to be cheered. I wanted to roll with the punches, bounce back smiling.

I couldn't stop thinking about Aunt Lauren. I thought of Rae, too, and my dad, but most of all I thought of Aunt Lauren. I could tell myself Dad and Rae were safe for now. The Edison Group wouldn't bother my father as long as he knew nothing about them. And Rae was well on her way to "rehabilitation," according to that file. But with Aunt Lauren, I could find no such rationalization for the Edison Group to keep her alive. Every time I opened my eyes, I expected to see her ghost standing in front of me.

Even when I managed to force myself not to worry, the only alternative was more mundane concerns and a general feeling of disappointment.

I'd found the guys. I'd brought Simon his insulin. I'd single-handedly uncovered the secrets of the Edison Group. My reward? Having Tori take potshots at me every chance she got, trying to make me look bad in front of Simon.

If there was any point in my life when I should have been anything *but* dull and boring, it was now. I could talk to the dead. I could *raise* the dead. In the last week, I'd plotted and schemed enough to win a spot on *Survivor.*

Yet all I could picture was Tori yawning.

It was nice having Simon defend me, but it wasn't any more than he might do for a little sister. I kept thinking of that—the way he'd come to my defense, the way he'd squeeze my hand, the way he'd lean in and whisper to me—and I wanted to read more into it. But I couldn't.

And so what? With everything that was going on, was I really feeling sorry for myself because a cute guy wasn't interested in me "that way"? That made me worse than boring. It made me the silly twit Derek seemed to think I was.

Speaking of Derek . . . and I'd really rather not . . . had I forgotten what he could be like? No, I'd just forgotten what it felt like to be on the receiving end. Between him and Tori, at least I'd come out of this with a thicker skin. Or lose every ounce of self-confidence I had.

A night for tossing and turning, lost in nightmares of Aunt Lauren and my dad and Rae. I kept waking up, gasping and sweating, everyone around me sound asleep. I'd gulp cold air and calm down enough to join them only to have the nightmares return.

Finally my sleeping brain found a distraction in the same place my waking brain had: thoughts of the dead body in the other room. No objective, sympathetic examination of his situation this time, though. I dreamed of dragging that poor spirit back to his shell, screaming and cursing me.

Then the dream changed and I was back in the crawl space. The musty, awful stench of death surrounded me. I felt Derek behind me, the heat of his body radiating, as he whispered, "Chloe, come on."

Come where? I was trapped in the crawl space, with those horrors crawling toward me, cold skeletal fingers touching me, the stink of them making my stomach churn.

Derek shook me, and I tried to push him away, tell him he wasn't helping—

"Chloe!"

I jerked awake, the dream evaporating. Above me, green eyes glinted in the darkness.

"Derek? What—?"

He clamped his hand over my mouth. His lips moved to my ear. "Are you awake now? I need you to do something for me."

The urgency in his voice knocked any sleepiness from my head. I squinted at him in the darkness. Were his eyes feverish? Or was that just their usual weird glow, like a cat's in the dark?

I pulled his hand away. "Are you Changing again?"

"What? No. I'm fine. Just listen, okay? Remember the body in the other room?" He spoke slowly, carefully.

I nodded.

"You're going to think about that body for me, okay? About the spirit that was in it. You need to release the—"

"Release? I—I didn't summon—"

"Shhh. Just concentrate on releasing it without waking the others. Can you do that?"

I nodded. Then I tried to sit up. Something heavy held my legs to the floor. I pushed onto my elbows. Derek lunged so fast all I saw was his dark form coming down on me, hands going to my shoulders, slamming me back into the ground, pinning me down.

I freaked. I didn't stop to wonder what he was doing. My brain just registered a guy on top of me in the middle of the night, and instinct kicked in. I lashed out, arms and legs flailing. My nails caught his cheek, and he fell back with a grunt of pain.

I scrambled up, legs still weighted down . . . and now I saw why. A corpse was crawling up me.

It was the one from the next room, little more than a skeleton, covered in clothing and strips of leathery flesh. Greasy hanks of hair patchworked its skull. Its eyes were empty pits. Its lips were long gone, leaving a skull's permanent grin of rotted teeth.

When I let out a whimper, it stopped and tried to hold its head upright, skull swaying from side to side, eye sockets searching blindly, jaws opening with a guttural *gah-gah-gah*.

I let out a bona fide "Scream Queen" shriek that rang through the room.

I kicked and fought, trying to get out from under the thing. Derek grabbed me by the armpits and yanked me out. He slapped his hand over my mouth, but I could still hear my scream, echoing around me. He growled for me to shut up and as I tried to obey, I realized it wasn't me screaming now.

"What is that?" Tori shrieked. "What *is* that?"

The flick of a flashlight. A beam shining in our eyes. And then she *really* screamed, loud enough to make my ears ring. The corpse reared up, mouth opening, screaming back, a high-pitched wail.

Simon woke up, too. When he saw the corpse, he let out a string of profanity.

"Shut her up!" Derek snarled to Simon, jabbing a finger at Tori. "Chloe! Calm down. You need to calm down."

I nodded, gaze fixed on that thing. I tried to remind myself it wasn't a "thing" but a person, yet all I could see was a skeleton held together by bits of flesh, that eyeless head swaying, those teeth clicking—

I inhaled, in and out, fast.

"Calm down, Chloe. Just calm down."

There was nothing calming about his tone, just an impatient snap, telling me to stop freaking out and get to work. I pulled from his grasp.

"You need to—" he began.

"I know what I need to do," I snapped back.

"What is that thing?" Tori gibbered. "Why is it moving?"

"Get her out of here," Derek said.

As Simon hauled Tori away, I tried to relax, but my heart was racing too fast for me to focus. I shut my eyes, only to feel something on my foot. My eyes opened to see fingers reaching for my leg.

I scuttled back. A filthy rag-covered arm reached out, finger bones scratching the newspaper on the floor as it tried to propel itself forward, too broken to lift itself. How could it even move? But it did. Just like the bats, inch by inch, coming toward me—

"You called it," Derek said. "It's trying—"

"I didn't call anything."

"Somehow you summoned it, and now it's trying to find you."

I concentrated, but at the first touch on my leg, I skittered to the side. The thing paused, skull wobbling, then those empty eye sockets locked on me as it turned in my new direction.

"You have to release it," Derek said.

"I'm *trying*."

"Try harder."

I squeezed my eyes shut and formed a mental image of the corpse. I pictured the ghost trapped inside and imagined drawing it out—

"Concentrate," Derek whispered.

"I am. If you'd shut up—"

The corpse stopped, like it could hear me. Then it reached out, blindly, searching. It found my leg and its finger started feeling its way toward my knee. I steeled myself against the urge to pull away. It needed to find me, so I let it. Ignore that and focus on—

"What did you do the last time?" Derek asked.

I glared over at him.

"I'm trying to help," he said.

"You'd help a lot more if you'd shut—"

His glare matched mine. "You need to release it, Chloe. With all that screaming, someone's bound to have heard us, and you've got about five minutes before they burst through that door and see a corpse crawling—"

"Is that supposed to *help* me?"

"I didn't mean—"

"Out."

"I just—"

"Out!"

He retreated. I closed my eyes and envisioned the skeleton, the trapped spirit—

A bony finger touched the bare skin where my shirt had twisted away from my jeans and I jumped, eyes flying open to see it right there, the skull a few inches from my face, bobbing and weaving.

The coarse scraggly hair brushed my throat and I whimpered. It went still. Then the skull moved closer still. I could smell it now, the faint stench of death I hadn't noticed earlier, churning my stomach, the thought of someone in there, trapped in that rotting—

It moved closer.

"Stop. P-please stop."

It went still. We hung there, eyeball to eye socket as I took short quick breaths, calming myself without inhaling its stink too deeply.

I waited for its next move, but it didn't make one.

I'd told it to stop, and it had.

I remembered those gruesome old pictures on the Internet of necromancers leading armies of the dead. I remembered the book Dr. Davidoff had given me about the powers of necromancers.

The power to communicate with the dead. The power to raise the dead. The power to control the dead.

"M-move back," I said. "P-please."

It did, slowly, teeth clacking. A guttural sound rose from its chest. A growl.

I knelt. "Lie down, please."

As it did, it lifted its face to me, skull moving from side to side like a snake, its growl a rattling hiss. I heard that hiss and I looked into those empty eye sockets and I felt hate. Waves of loathing rolled off the corpse. It wasn't obeying me because it wanted to, but because it had to. It was an enslaved spirit, summoned by a necromancer, slammed back into little more than a skeleton, forced to make it move to obey the will of its master.

I swallowed hard. "I-I'm sorry. I didn't mean to call you back. I wasn't trying to."

It hissed, head still moving, as if it would love nothing more than to show me what death felt like.

"I'm so sor—"

I swallowed my words. The ghost trapped in there didn't want apologies. It wanted freedom. So I closed my eyes and concentrated on making that happen, which was a lot easier when I didn't have to worry about it creeping up my legs.

As I visualized tugging the spirit out, the chattering stopped so fast I peeked, thinking I'd accidentally commanded it to be silent. But the skeleton had collapsed in a motionless heap by my feet. The ghost was gone.

twenty-two

I TOOK A DEEP, SHAKY BREATH, rubbed my face, and looked up to see Derek's figure filling the doorway.

"If you think someone might have heard, we should grab our things and go," I said, my voice remarkably steady. "We'll leave him where he is, so he'll be found and buried."

As I spoke, I had this crazy idea that Derek might actually be impressed by how I'd finally handled it. But he just stood there, fingering the scratch on his cheek.

"I'm sorry about that," I said. "I panicked when you—"

"I gave you the option of leaving earlier. I said if that"—he gestured at the corpse—"was a problem, we'd find another place."

"And I thought it wasn't a problem, as long as I didn't summon any ghosts."

"But you did."

"I was *asleep*, Derek."

"What were you dreaming?"

I remembered and went still.

"You dreamed that you summoned him, didn't you?"

"I—I didn't mean—" I rubbed my face. "Normal people can't control their dreams, Derek. If you can, then I guess you really are smarter than the rest of us."

"Of course, I can't. But it was a bad situation—you being close to a dead body. You should have known that from the crawl space."

I did know that, especially after the incident with the bats. My gut had told me to leave, but I hadn't had the nerve to admit my fear. I was afraid of being weak. Afraid of being mocked by Tori, of pissing off Derek, of disappointing Simon. In trying to be strong, I'd been stupid.

I wanted to own up to my mistake and tell Derek about the bats. But when I saw his expression—the intolerant arrogance that said he was right and I was a silly little twit—there was no way I was admitting anything.

"Everything okay?" Simon stood behind Derek, trying to see past him.

"It's . . . he's gone," I said. "The ghost."

"Good, because I think I heard someone coming."

"And when were you going to warn us?" Derek snapped.

"I wasn't going to barge in and interrupt Chloe." He turned to me. "Are you okay?"

"Of course she's okay." Tori came up behind Simon. "*She's* the one who summoned that thing. She should be asking if we're okay, after being woken in the middle of the night and totally traumatized."

"You weren't too traumatized to grab your hairbrush," Simon said.

"As a weapon, okay? I—"

I stepped between them. "Did someone mention we're in danger of being discovered? Let's grab our stuff and move."

"You're giving orders now, Chloe?" Tori said.

"No, I'm making suggestions. If you choose to ignore them, that's fine. Stay behind and explain the dead body to whoever's coming."

"Yes," said a voice behind me. "Maybe you should explain that, little girl."

A figure stood across the room, only his outline visible in the dark. I turned back to the others, but no one had moved. They were all just looking at *me*.

"Chloe?" Simon said.

A man stepped from the shadows. His long hair was only streaked with gray, but his face was so lined he looked eighty. My gaze dropped to his sweatshirt, emblazoned with a Buffalo Bruins logo. Then I looked at the skeleton on the floor, twisted just enough for me to see the same logo, faded almost to nothing on the tattered shirt.

"Chloe?" he said. "Is that your name, brat?"

"I-I'm sorry," I said. "I didn't mean to summon you."

Simon jumped in front of me. "Look, ghost, I know you can hear me. It was an accident."

The man lunged through Simon. I fell back with a yelp. Simon spun, but Derek yanked him aside.

"Who's Chloe talking to?" Tori asked.

"The ghost she summoned," Simon said.

"Grab your backpacks," Derek said. "We need to get going."

As Simon and Tori took off, Derek followed my gaze, figuring out where the ghost stood. "She didn't mean to raise you. She apologized, and we're leaving, so it won't happen again. Go on back to your afterlife."

The ghost strode over to glare up at Derek. "You going to make me?"

"He can't," I said. "And he can't hear you either. I *am* sorry. Very—"

He wheeled on me. I shrank away again, but Derek put his hand against my back, stopping my retreat.

"He can't hurt you," Derek whispered. "Stand firm and tell him to go."

"I'm very sorry." I straightened and moved forward. "I didn't mean to summon you. It was an accident—"

"Accident! That was no accident. You and your punk friends thought it would be funny to drag me back into that—that thing." He pointed at the corpse. "You think I haven't dealt with kids like you before? Drive me out of my sleeping spot for kicks. Roll me for my boots. Now you come here, conducting your satanic rituals . . ."

"Satanic? No. W-we—"

"Did you hear that?" said a distant voice. "Someone's in there."

Derek swore, then gave me a shove toward the back of the building. Simon and Tori raced in.

"Two men," Simon said. "Cops, I think. Coming up the front—"

"Back door," Derek said. "Move."

The front door banged open. Simon spun and headed for the rear. We followed.

"Hey!" the ghost yelled. "Where do you think you're going?"

A shove from Derek kept me moving.

"Oh no, you don't, little girl," the ghost said. "I'm not done with you yet. You're going to pay for that stunt. . . ."

He snarled threats right on my heels as we snuck out the back door.

twenty-three

"IS HE GONE?" Tori asked as I approached.

I nodded and inhaled. The icy night air burned my lungs. I didn't feel the cold, though—I was wearing my shirt, one of the new sweatshirts with the hood up, and the oversized jacket on top. Sweat dripped down my face as I struggled to catch my breath. I'd separated from the others a couple of blocks back, thinking that without a group, I might lose him easier. I'd been right.

We didn't know who'd come to investigate the noises. Maybe cops like Simon thought, maybe street people—we hadn't stuck around long enough to find out.

Now we stood in a parking lot, between a minivan and a pickup. Music boomed from a nearby club. That had surprised me—a packed parking lot and a busy bar so late at night on a weekday. Then I'd checked my watch and realized it wasn't even midnight yet.

"You shouldn't have taken off like that," Derek said.

"I told you what I was doing. It worked, didn't it?"

"You can't—"

"Ease off," Simon murmured. "We need to find a new place to sleep."

"Thanks to someone," Tori said.

"It isn't Chloe's fault."

"Sure it is. Even Derek said so."

"He didn't mean—"

I held up my hands. "I take all blame. Can we please stop bickering? I know everyone's on edge, but if we're going to get through this—"

"If you start a speech about how we all need to overcome our differences and work together, I'm going to hurl," Tori said.

"Well, I would, but I'm afraid this genetically modified supernatural would be eaten by a genetically modified shark."

Simon burst out laughing. "*Deep Blue Sea*." He looked at Derek. "You didn't see it. Samuel L. Jackson is giving this group of survivors the speech about how they have to stop fighting and to work together. In the middle of it, the shark comes up behind him and eats him. Best death scene ever."

"And a fitting one for anyone who makes that speech, which is why I'm not going to."

"But you're right," Simon said. "Time to call a moratorium on the bickering."

"Moratorium?" Tori said. "Oooh, big word. Showing off, Simon?"

We all turned to look at her.

"What?" she said.

"No bickering means no jabs, no insults, no snark, no baiting," Derek said. "And it means we probably won't hear another word from you for days."

"As for this situation," I said, "I take the blame, so I'll fix the problem. Stay here and I'll find us a place—"

Derek caught the back of my jacket. "You still have a pissed-off ghost looking for you and a huge reward on your head. Stay here with Tori. Simon and I will find a new spot."

Before they took off, Derek turned back to me. "I mean it, stay right here."

"Even if the owners of these"—Tori rapped the vehicles on either side—"come out?"

Derek ignored her. "She's your responsibility, Chloe."

When they were gone, Tori turned to me. "Why do you let him get away with that? He treats you like a little kid."

I said nothing, just started walking away from the spot where Derek told me to stay.

She smiled. "That's more like it."

I led her to a strip of gravel between two buildings. Then I lowered myself to the ground. "This is safer, but still close enough."

She stared at me. "You're kidding, right?"

I pulled my jacket sleeves over my hands to keep them warm.

"You actually listen to him?"

"Only when he has a point."

She towered over me. "You're going to let a guy order you around like that? Make the girls sit on their butts while the men go hunt up a cave to sleep in, maybe drag back some food for us to eat?"

"Yep."

"Well, I'm not. I'm going to show those guys that a girl can do this just as well as they can."

I leaned back against the wall and closed my eyes. She stomped off. I opened my eyes, watching her get farther away.

Derek said to stay. And he said to look after her. Conflicting requests at the moment. I know he'd tell me to forget Tori and take care of myself. But I couldn't do that.

"Hold up," I said as I jogged behind her.

"If you're going to whine at me about pissing off Frankenstein, save it."

"I'm not here to give you crap. I'm helping you find a spot. As long as we don't go far, Derek can track us." As she stepped onto the sidewalk, I made sure my hood was still on, then hurried out and caught her sleeve. "We can take quiet roads, but I need to avoid people as much as I can."

"I don't. I'm not the one with stalker ghosts and a half-million bucks on my head."

"Yes, but if the Edison Group wants us back badly enough, they might have gone public to flush us out. We both need to be careful."

We reached the end of the street. As she started turning left, I stopped her again.

"This way," I waved to the darker end of the street. "Look for a good spot in an alley. The wind's coming from the north, so we need a northern barrier. A corner or alley end or recessed delivery door would be best, so we can see anyone coming. And the worse the lighting, the better. We want dark and we want secluded."

"You're as bossy as Derek, you know that? The only difference is you give your orders nicely."

But, apparently giving orders nicely was a strategy that worked, because she made no attempt to take off or take over, just came with me as we checked spot after spot.

Behind a row of stores we found a long, narrow alley with a wall on one side and a solid six-foot fence on the other.

"This looks promising," I said.

"Uh, yeah. If you're Oscar the Grouch." She waved at a row of trash bins.

I lifted a lid and pointed at shredded paper inside. "Recycling. There aren't any restaurants around here, so the garbage won't smell."

I continued down the alley. It dead-ended at a wall.

"This is great," I said. "Three sides, the bins block part of the entrance. We can shift boxes around and put paper down to sit on."

"And maybe, if we're lucky, find a cardboard box big enough to crawl inside so we can pretend we're homeless people."

"Right now, Tori, we *are* homeless people."

That shut her up. I stopped near the end of the alley and let out a laugh.

"Come here."

She sighed. "What now?"

I waved for her to come over.

"Oh." She reached out to thaw her hands in the hot air blowing from the vent.

I grinned. "We've even got heating. How perfect is that?"

"Too perfect," said a girl's voice. "Which is why this spot is taken."

Three girls were walking toward us down the alley. All were about our age. One was blond and dressed in oversized fatigues. Another had dreadlocks. The third girl wore a battered brown leather jacket, and when she stepped into a patch of moonlight, I saw a thick scar running from her eye to her chin.

"See that?" the dreadlocked girl pointed to a tag on the wood fence. "That's our mark. That means this spot is ours."

"We d-didn't see it. Sorry. We'll go."

I started to walk away, but Tori pulled me back. "No, we won't go. You can't *reserve* an alley, mark or no mark. It's first come, first served. You want this one? Be here earlier tomorrow."

"*Excuse* me?"

The scarred girl pulled a switchblade from her pocket. It snapped open with a twang. Tori glanced at the knife but didn't budge, her gaze locking with the girl's.

"Check it out," the scarred girl said to her friends. "This chick's going to challenge us for our spot. How long you been on the streets, girl?" She looked Tori up and down. "Since about nine this morning, I'll guess. What happened? Mommy and Daddy said you couldn't see your boyfriend on a school night?"

The girls snickered. Tori flexed her fingers, preparing to cast. I caught her wrist. She tried to shake me off. I got her to notice the matching knives now in the hands of the other two, but her gaze returned to the scarred girl, and all her rage from the last twenty-four hours bubbled up. The boxes near the girls quavered and rustled. Papers swirled behind them. The girls never turned, dismissing it as the wind.

I clasped Tori's wrist tighter and whispered, "Too many."

To my surprise, her hand relaxed. Expecting a trick, I held on, but she shook me off, saying "Fine. We're going."

"Good idea," the scarred girl said. "Next time, girls, if you see that"—she pointed at the tag—"steer clear. At least until you have the hardware to play."

We started to pass, but the scarred girl's hand flew out, smacking Tori's chest and stopping her.

"Life out here isn't what you girls think it is. You've got a lot of lessons to learn."

"Thanks," Tori grunted, and tried to keep walking, but the scarred girl stopped her again.

"The thing about lessons? If they're going to sink in, they've gotta come with consequences. So I'm going to help you remember this one. Give me your jacket."

She held out her hand. Tori stared at it.

"Mine's getting old," the girl said. "I like yours better."

Tori snorted and tried to pass again.

The girl stepped in front of her, knife raised. "I said I want your jacket."

"And *her* shoes." The girl with the dreadlocks pointed at me.

"Fine, the jacket and the shoes," the scarred one said. "Take 'em off, girls."

The girl in fatigues stepped forward. "I want the little one's jeans, too. Never had a pair of Sevens." She smiled, flashing a jeweled tooth. "Gonna make me feel like a movie star."

"Yeah, if you can get them on," the dreadlocked girl said.

"Forget the jeans," the scarred girl said. "Jacket and shoes. Now."

Tori needed her jacket, and I definitely needed shoes. I bent to undo one of my sneakers, pretending to have trouble with my balance, hopping, then waving Tori over to help. To my relief, she came. I leaned against her, tugging at my shoe, and whispered, "Knock back."

Tori frowned.

I flicked my fingers. "Knock back. One, two, three." I nodded to each girl in turn.

Tori shook her head. "Binding."

"Too many. Knock back."

"Come on, girls," the scarred girl said.

Tori gave an exasperated sigh and bent, as if helping me undo my shoe. Then she shot up, her hands flying out, hitting the scarred girl with—

The girl froze. So much for my advice.

At first the other two didn't notice. They just looked at their leader impatiently, waiting for her to prod us again.

"On my count," Tori whispered. "One, two . . ."

"Hey, what's—?" the girl in fatigues began.

Tori's hands shot up, but the girl kept coming. And the scarred girl stumbled, the spell breaking. She advanced, knife raised. Her friends fell into position, flanking her. Tori tried again, but apparently she'd used up all her juice because nothing was happening.

"Whatever trick that was," the scarred girl said. "It was really dumb. You have three seconds to strip out of everything. Both of you."

"I don't think so," Tori said. "Now, back off."

Tori flicked her fingers. The girl didn't even sway.

"I said, *back off*!"

She flicked again. The girls kept coming. I spun, only to discover the problem with a blind alley—if the entrance is blocked, you're trapped. When the girl in fatigues lunged for me, I ran anyway, Tori at my side.

At the end, I deked fast, hoping to catch my pursuers off guard and dodge around them. It worked on the one in fatigues. But the dreadlocked girl saw my feint and blocked me.

I ducked her knife, but she kicked me in the back of my knee. My leg buckled, and I dropped. I scuttled out of her way. I caught sight of Tori, her hands raised as if in surrender. Then one hand shot out, grabbing for the scarred girl's knife hand. The blade flashed and laid open the sleeve of Tori's leather jacket.

Tori let out a strangled howl of outrage, as if it had sliced through her arm instead. Her hands flew up. The scarred girl jolted back to avoid a punch, but Tori's hands went straight up over her head, then slammed down.

An invisible wave smacked me, and the next thing I knew I was lying on my back. Sneakers slapped the concrete and I looked up to see Tori running over.

"Are you okay?" Seeing I was conscious, she didn't wait for an answer. "Get up!"

I wobbled partway up, my leg still throbbing from the dreadlocked girl's kick. I looked around quickly. She lay a few feet away.

Tori yanked me all the way to my feet. The girl in fatigues lay crumpled at the foot of the wall. She let out a soft moan. The scarred girl was on all fours, conscious but dazed.

Seeing the dreadlocked girl's blade on the ground, I snatched it up and ran to the girl in fatigues, telling Tori to take the scarred girl's knife as I looked for this one's. It had fallen a couple of feet away. I grabbed it. Tori was already running down the alley. I ignored the pain in my leg and raced to catch up.

"Did you grab her knife?" I asked.

"Why? You have two."

"That's not why I—"

"Hey!" a shout from behind us. "Hey!"

I glanced over my shoulder to see the scarred girl coming after us, knife in hand. *That's* why I wanted all three.

twenty-four

I SLAPPED ONE OF THE KNIVES into Tori's hand and told her to run. She did, sprinting ahead, her long legs soon leaving me behind, which was *not* what I'd meant. But we had enough of a head start. We just needed to get—

I glanced back at my pursuer and missed the curb. I stumbled and tried to recover, but my injured knee gave out and I sprawled onto a strip of grass. I dug in with both hands, ready to scramble up, but the girl landed on my back and the wind flew from my lungs.

We fought—if you could call my frantic kicking and flailing a fight. Soon she had me pinned on my back, knife at my throat. That stopped me.

"I—I—I—" I swallowed. "I'm sorry. Do you want my jacket? My shoes?"

Her face twisted in disgust. "You don't have anything I want, blondie."

She wrenched down my hood and yanked a handful of my hair. I winced and bit back a yelp.

"Red streaks?" A humorless laugh. "You think that makes you tough? Makes you cool?"

"N-no. If you want my shoes—"

"They'd never fit me. I wanted your friend's jacket, but she's long gone. Nice friend you've got there. Never even looked back." The girl eased up, knife still at my throat. "It was a taser, wasn't it?"

"What?"

"What she did to me back there. She tasered me, then my girls. I bet you thought that was funny."

"N-no. I—"

"I said I was going to teach you a lesson, and since you don't have anything I want . . ."

She lifted the knife until the point was an inch over my eye. I saw that tip coming down and went nuts, writhing to get free, but she had me securely pinned with her arm on my neck, cutting off my air as I struggled, and all I could do was watch that point coming straight for my eye. A whimper burbled up from my gut. She laughed and lowered the blade to rest on my cheekbone.

The tip pressed in. I felt the jab of pain, then hot blood trickling down my cheek.

"This is no life for pretty girls, blondie. A cute little thing like you? I'll give you a week before some player has you turning tricks. Me? I'm lucky. I don't have to worry about that." She tilted her face, showing me her badly scarred cheek. "I'm going to do you the same favor."

The knife bit in, digging deeper. I closed my eyes against the pain, then felt the girl leap off me with a snarl of rage.

As I scrambled up, I realized it wasn't *her* snarling. And she wasn't leaping off me—she was sailing up, eyes wide, knife dropping point down in the earth as Derek wrenched her into the air. He swung her straight at the wall.

I screamed "No!" I thought it was too late, much too late, but at the last moment he checked himself, so abruptly that he stumbled. The girl flailed and kicked. Her foot made contact. Derek didn't seem to notice. He looked around, saw the fence and, with a grunt, heaved her over it. She crashed onto the other side.

I was almost on my feet, unsteady, shaking. He grabbed my collar and yanked me up.

"Move!"

I found the fallen knife and snatched it. He shoved me forward so hard I stumbled. Then I started running. He got in front, leading me. We'd gone about a quarter mile when he spun, meeting my gaze with a look that made me shrink back. He grabbed my upper arm and held me still.

"Did I tell you to stay put?"

"Yes, but—"

"Did I tell you to stay put!" he roared.

I glanced around, afraid we'd be heard, but we were behind a row of stores, all the windows dark.

"Yes." I kept my voice low and even. "You did. But you also told me to watch out for Tori, and she took off."

"I don't give a rat's ass about Tori. If she walks away, let her. If she steps in front of a bus, let her."

When I looked up at his eyes, I saw the terror behind the rage and knew who he was really mad at—himself, for almost throwing that girl into the wall, just like the boy in Albany.

Saying nothing, I pried his fingers from my arm. He pulled back, clenching and unclenching his hand.

"If she takes off, let her go," he said, quieter now. "I don't care what happens to her."

"I do."

He stepped back, rubbing absently at his forearm. When he saw me watching, he stopped.

"It's an itch," he said. "A normal itch."

"Have you had any other symptoms? Fever or—"

"No," he snapped. "Don't change the subject. You need to be more careful, Chloe. Like earlier, with that body. You need to think about what could happen."

He was right. But seeing him scratching reminded me that I wasn't the only one who'd been careless, who'd ignored a potential threat.

"And what about you?" I pointed as he scratched his arm again. "The werewolf who hasn't had his first Change yet, but knows he's developing fast. Yet when you started getting restless, feverish, itchy, it never occurred to you that you might be Changing early? You let it slide . . . until it starts on the night we're supposed to escape."

"I wasn't going with you guys—"

"But if I hadn't stayed to find you, Simon wouldn't have left. You could have botched the escape because you didn't know what was happening to you."

"I *didn't*."

"Like I didn't know I could raise the dead in my sleep. But did I chew you out? Did I even mention how close I came to getting caught because I stayed to help?"

He looked away, jaw working, then said, "I tried to help you, too. And got this." He gestured to the scratch on his cheek.

"Because I woke up with a guy pinning me to the floor! I know you were trying to keep me from seeing that zombie crawling on me. A good plan, poorly executed. Then you totally lost patience and kept barking orders."

"I was trying to help."

"And what if I'd done that to you? Yelled at you to finish Changing before we got caught?"

He looked away again. "I . . . About that night. I haven't said . . ." He squared his shoulders. "We need to get back. Simon will be worried about you."

We walked about twenty steps in silence, me trailing him. When his shoulders bunched, I knew he was thinking about it again, and I prayed he'd let it go. Please just let it—

He spun on me. "Next time when I tell you to stay, I mean stay."

"I'm not a dog, Derek."

I kept my voice steady, but his jaw tensed, green eyes flashing. "Maybe not, but you obviously need someone to look after you, and I'm tired of doing it."

"Don't."

"Don't what?"

"Didn't we agree to stop bickering?"

His face darkened. "This isn't—"

"You're mad at yourself and you're taking it out on me."

I meant to be reasonable, but he exploded, coming at me so fast I backpedaled and hit a chain-link fence.

"I'm mad at *you*, Chloe. You took off. You got in trouble. I had to rescue you."

He kept coming at me. I pressed against the fence, the links whining in protest.

"And stop doing that," he said. "Backing away, giving me that look."

"Like you're scaring me? Maybe you are."

He stepped back so fast he wobbled and caught himself, and the look on his face— It vanished in a second, the scowl returning.

"I'd never hurt you, Chloe. You should know—" He stopped. Paused. Then wheeled and started walking away. "Next time? Handle it yourself. I'm done taking care of you."

I wanted to fly after him, yell that I hadn't asked him to take care of me, didn't need it, didn't want it. Not if this was the price—his rage, his guilt, his scorn.

Tears prickled. I blinked them away and waited until he was far enough that he wouldn't turn on me again. Then I followed him to Simon.

Tori was already there. She didn't say a word to me, as if mentioning what happened would mean explaining why she'd left me behind.

No one said much of anything. We were all too tired and too cold. Our new spot was a delivery bay. Safe, but the north wind blew right in. We huddled against the walls with our thin blankets pulled around us, and tried to sleep.

twenty-five

I WOKE TO THE SMELL of sausage and eggs and squeezed my eyes shut to savor the dream, knowing when I opened them, I'd be lucky to get bruised fruit and an energy bar.

"Rise and shine," a voice whispered.

A paper bag rustled. Then sausage-scented steam bathed my face. I opened my eyes to see Simon holding a familiar take-out bag in front of me.

"McDonald's?"

"Shhh."

Simon pointed at Tori, still snoring beside me, then quietly retreated from the delivery bay, motioning for me to follow.

He led me into an alley, where a fire escape ladder hung, then he boosted me onto it. We climbed up to the roof of a three-story building.

I walked to the edge and looked out. There was a park to the east, glistening with dew, the sun still rising behind it, tinting the sky pink.

"Nice, huh?" Simon said. "That park wasn't quite so empty last night or we would have slept there." He set down the bag and drinks on the rooftop. "So is this okay for breakfast? Up here?"

I looked at the view again. After last night, this was better than the fanciest breakfast in the fanciest restaurant. It might be the most thoughtful thing anyone had ever done for me.

"It's perfect," I said. "Thank you."

"Good. If it wasn't, I'd have blamed Derek."

"Derek?"

"He suggested we come up here and helped me pull down the ladder. Breakfast was my idea, though. We saw the Mickey D's last night and I thought you might like a bickering-free breakfast."

Derek picked the spot? Had he been hoping I'd be blinded by the morning sun and stumble off the edge?

"Pancakes or sausage McMuffin?" Simon asked as I settled onto the rooftop.

"Which do you want?"

"I've got mine." He lifted a wrapped sandwich. "I thought I'd buy you both and, whichever you don't want, Derek will eat. Nothing goes to waste with him around."

I took the McMuffin.

He lifted two cups. "OJ or a strawberry milkshake?"

"I didn't think you could get milkshakes in the morning."

He grinned. "I can."

When I took the shake, his smile grew. "I thought you might like that."

"Thanks. This"—I waved at the food and the spot—"is really nice."

"And well-deserved after your cruddy night. By the way, there's a cut on your cheek. We should get that cleaned up later. I know Derek gave you the gears last night—more than once."

"It's okay."

"No, it's not. Going at you about raising that zombie? That was out of line, even for Derek. He's been . . ."

"Crankier than usual?"

"Yeah. I think it's because he Changed—or couldn't Change—but that's no excuse to vent at you, not after what you did for him."

I shrugged and took a long draw of my milkshake.

"About what you did that night, staying with Derek while he was trying to Change . . ." Simon shook his head. "I don't know how you kept your cool. Finding him like that when you didn't even know he was a werewolf."

"I figured it out."

Simon took a bite of his sandwich and chewed, looking out at the sky before saying, "I wanted to tell you. Especially after he forced *you* to admit you were seeing ghosts. We argued; he won, as usual. But if we thought you could ever have stumbled on him like that, we'd have warned you. Even knowing what he is, I doubt I could have stuck around, much less helped. It took guts." He caught my gaze. "It really took guts."

I'm sure I turned crimson. I glanced away and chomped into my sandwich.

"I appreciate what you did for him, Chloe. Derek appreciates it, too, though I'm sure he hasn't said so."

I swallowed my mouthful and changed the subject. "So, about your dad . . . You never did tell me how he disappeared."

He laughed. "Enough about Derek, huh? Unfortunately, Derek is where this story starts. It was after he broke that kid's back. When it got a mention in the Albany paper, Dad decided it was time to move on. He must have known the Edison Group was still trying to find us. We should have left right away. But . . ."

Simon picked a burned piece off his muffin. "This happened a lot. At the first hint of trouble, we'd pack and move. Derek and I didn't understand why, so we'd complain." He paused. "No, *I'd* complain. After growing up in that lab, Derek was happy as long as the three of us were together. I hated moving. It always seemed I'd just made new friends, just made the team, just met a girl . . ."

"I know what that's like. Well, except the part about meeting girls."

"Yeah, but I bet you never complained. You're like Derek. You make the best of things. I bitched and moaned, so Dad always tried to make it easier on me. That day, I had a basketball game I was hyped about, so when Dad saw the article after we'd gone to school, he called Derek's cell. He told him not to mention it to me, but that he'd meet us after school and we'd take off. He never showed."

"And you haven't seen him since?"

Simon shook his head. "We got home, found the car packed, the keys in the kitchen. He'd taken his wallet or had it in his pocket when . . . whatever happened, happened."

"You think someone kidnapped him?"

"I don't know. Derek couldn't find anyone's scent in the house. It was like Dad just walked away, which he'd never do. Derek wanted to take off. Again I screwed up. I thought there was some logical explanation—maybe Derek misunderstood Dad's message. The next morning, I gave in and we left, but it was too late. They caught up with us the next day."

"The Edison Group?"

"They said they were child services. We believed them. They took us back to the house to see if Dad had returned, and when he wasn't there, they said that we had to go into a group home until they figured stuff out. Since we'd been born in Buffalo, that's where they put us. Which should have seemed weird, but we didn't know better. So that's how we ended up in Lyle House."

Simon continued, explaining that, since we'd escaped, he'd been casting some kind of seeking spell his dad taught him, but he couldn't detect him. Using library computers, Derek had searched on their dad's name and aliases, but found nothing.

"And now, with all this about the Edison Group, and Liz and Brady and Amber murdered . . ." He looked out over the parking lot. "I'm starting to think it might be a waste of time. That he's not out there. That they killed him."

"But Aunt Lauren was sure the Edison Group wasn't involved in your dad's disappearance. And she seemed certain he'd still be alive. Do you know any other place he could be? Or anyone who might know something?"

"I thought about going back to Albany, maybe talk to people he worked with, our neighbors, someone who might have seen something that day . . ."

"We could do that. We have enough money."

"Derek doesn't want to."

"He wants to stay here?" That didn't sound like Derek.

"No, he just doesn't see any point in going back—and says it's probably dangerous. But there is someone we could go to. This friend of my dad's. Andrew Carson. He lives outside New York City. Dad said if we were ever in trouble and he wasn't around, we should go to Andrew."

"Have you called him? Maybe he knows something about your dad."

"That's the problem. Dad put his number on our cell phones, but they took those when we were tossed in Lyle House. We know his name and where he lives—we've been there plenty of times. But when we tried looking him up on a computer, we couldn't find anything."

"His number must be unlisted. Or he's using an alias."

"Or he's not there anymore. It's been a few years since we saw him. He and Dad had a falling-out."

"Maybe you shouldn't contact him then."

Simon crumpled his wrapper. "I shouldn't say 'falling-out.' A disagreement. Dad and Andrew kept in touch; we just didn't go visit him anymore. He was still our emergency contact. So we *should* go see him, like Derek says. I'm just . . . not ready to give up on finding Dad. But with you and Tori here, and your picture everywhere, Derek's ready to buy the bus tickets."

"How about another solution? I need to get out of Buffalo. You need to talk to this guy. What if Tori and I go find Andrew while you and Derek look—"

"No. I don't trust Tori with you, especially after last night. Derek wouldn't go for it either."

I wasn't so sure. He might jump at the chance to get rid of me.

Simon continued, "Even if Tori's *not* homicidal, she's careless and reckless. Worse than me, which is saying a lot. We'll find another way."

twenty-six

FOR MOST OF THAT DAY, both Derek and Tori steered clear of me, like I had a bug they didn't want to catch. I didn't see a lot of Simon either. He went off with Derek to the library, still trying to find their dad or his friend Andrew. Tori tagged along. I stayed put in a lovely dank alley Derek had chosen for me. Simon left me with a movie magazine, snacks, a hairbrush and soap, and promised they'd get me to a bathroom after dark.

It was mid-afternoon when I heard footsteps tromping down the alley and I scrambled up to meet Simon. Derek might be bigger, but it was Simon who made all the noise. Derek was only loud when . . .

Derek stomped around the corner, scowling.

. . . when he was mad.

He had a newspaper rolled in his hand, bearing down on me like a puppy that had piddled on the carpet.

"Bad Chloe," I muttered.

"What?"

I'd forgotten his bionic hearing. "Bad Chloe." I gestured at the rolled-up paper and put out my hand. "Get it over with."

"You think this is funny?"

"No, I think it's tiresome."

He slapped down the paper. In the bottom corner of the front page was the headline "Missing Girl Spotted" with a picture of me. I skimmed the short paragraph, then turned to the rest inside.

It had happened last night, when Derek had been yelling at me after my run-in with the street girls. The windows around us may have been dark, but a woman had been watching from an apartment over a shop, drawn by Derek's voice. She'd seen "a girl with light hair and red streaks" being yelled at by "a large, dark-haired man." So now police speculated that I might not be a runaway but a kidnap victim.

"Well?" Derek said.

I folded the paper carefully, my gaze down. "Guess you shouldn't have yelled at me in public."

"What?"

"That's what caught her attention. You chewing me out."

"No, what caught her attention was your hair. If you'd kept your hood up like I said—"

"Of course. Totally my fault. After nearly getting my face carved up, how dare I forget my attacker yanked down my hood. Bad Chloe."

"So this is a joke?"

I looked up at him. "No, it's not a joke. It's a serious problem. The joke is this." I waved from him to me. "You've been sulking all day, brooding—"

"Brooding?"

"Just itching for me to screw up so you can rip me a new one, your favorite pastime. You couldn't just come back and calmly say we have a problem that we need to discuss. Where's the fun in that?"

"You think I enjoy—"

"I have no idea what you enjoy, if anything. But I do know what you'd like. Me, gone."

"What?"

"I've served my purpose. I got Simon out of Lyle House. Sure, you were willing to make a half-assed effort to find me, so it looks good for Simon—"

"Half-assed?"

"You showed up hours late. Left a hidden note. Came by once a day. Yes, half-assed."

"No. Ask Simon. I was worried—"

"I'm sure you faked it well. But, unfortunately, I found you and, worse, I showed up with Tori in tow and a price on my head. So it's time to activate the backup plan. Make me so miserable and unwelcome that I slink away."

"I'd never—"

"No, you won't." I met his gaze. "Because I'm not going to slink away, Derek. If I'm too much of an inconvenience to keep around, then at least have the guts to tell me to get lost."

I brushed past him and walked away.

I didn't get far. I bumped into Simon and Tori, and Derek caught up with us. And then he got his way. Not about driving me off—he still had to work at that. But this new development gave him all the ammunition he needed to persuade Simon it was time to go to their father's friend's place. The bus left at four. First, though, the half-million-dollar runaway needed a disguise.

Derek took me to a restroom in the park I'd seen from the roof. The building was locked for the off-season, but he easily broke the locks and got me in. He made sure the water hadn't been turned off, then slapped a box of hair color on the counter.

"Gotta get rid of that," he said, pointing at my hair.

"I could just keep my hood—"

"Already tried."

He walked out.

I strained to see by the bit of light coming through a row of tiny, filthy windows. It was hard to read the instructions, but it looked similar to the red dye I'd used, so I applied it the same way. I couldn't tell what color Derek had chosen. It looked black, but the red dye had, too, so that didn't mean much. I didn't think too much about it until I washed out the dye, looked in the mirror, and . . .

My hair was black.

I hurried to the door and propped it open to get better light. Then I went back to the mirror.

Black. Not sleek glossy black like Tori's hair, but dull, flat black.

Before now, I hadn't been thrilled with my latest haircut. I'd had my long straight hair chopped shoulder length in a layered style that had turned out wispy and waiflike. Still, the worst I could have said was that it made me look "cute"—not what a fifteen-year-old girl wants to be called. In black though, it was not cute. It looked like I'd hacked my hair off with kitchen shears.

I never wore black because it drained any color from my pale skin. Now I saw there was something that washed out my face even worse than a black shirt.

I looked like a Goth. A *sick* Goth, white and hollow-eyed.

I looked dead.

I looked like a necromancer. Like those ghastly pictures of them on the Internet.

Tears sprang to my eyes. I blinked them back, grabbed some tissue, and started awkwardly trying to daub leftover dye onto my pale eyebrows, praying it would make a difference.

Through the mirror, I saw Tori walk in. She stopped.

"Oh. My. God."

It would have been better if she'd laughed. Her look of horror, then something like sympathy, meant it was as bad as I thought.

"I told Derek to let me pick the color," she said. "I *told* him."

"Hey," Simon called in. "Everyone decent?"

He pushed open the door, saw me and blinked.

"It's Derek's fault," Tori said. "He—"

"Don't, please," I said. "No more fighting."

Simon still shot a glare over his shoulder as Derek pushed open the door.

"What?" Derek said. He looked at me. "Huh."

Tori hustled me out the door, brushing past the guys with a whispered "jerk" for Derek.

"At least now you know never to go dark again," she said as we walked. "A couple years ago, I let a friend dye mine blond. It was almost as bad. My hair felt like straw and . . ."

And so, Tori and I bonded over hair horror stories. We put our differences aside and by the time we were on the bus, we were painting each other's fingernails.

Or not.

Tori did try to cheer me up. For her, this situation seemed to warrant more sympathy than having a dead guy crawling over me. But the closer we got to the bus station, the lower her mood dropped, coinciding with a rising discussion of finances—how much did we have, how much would the tickets cost, should I try to use my bank card again . . .

I did use an ATM we passed. Derek figured that was okay—if they thought we were still in Buffalo, that was good, considering we were leaving. He didn't expect my card would work though. It did. I suppose that made sense. The bank or police might have told my dad to lock it, but he wouldn't cut off my only source of money, even if he thought it could make me come home.

That, of course, made me think about him and how much he must be worrying, and what he was going through. I wanted so badly to contact him, but I knew I couldn't. So all I could do was think about him, and think about Aunt Lauren, and feel awful about everything.

To get my thoughts off my family, I concentrated on my companions. I knew not having money bugged Tori. So I tried to give her a couple hundred. It was a mistake. She lashed out at me, and by the time we reached the station, we weren't talking again.

Simon and Tori bought the tickets. I wondered whether they'd catch any flak—unaccompanied teens buying one-way tickets to New York City—but no one commented. I guess we could just be traveling alone. We were old enough to do that.

Not that *I'd* ever traveled alone. Not even on a city bus. That got me thinking about who I normally traveled with—Aunt Lauren and Dad.

When I tried to stop worrying about them I only thought about someone else I was leaving behind: Liz.

Liz said she could find me, but I was sure she'd meant "in Buffalo." How long would she search for me? Could I summon her without her green hoodie . . . from hundreds of miles away? I'd need to try really hard, and that wasn't safe.

Maybe she'd move on to the afterlife. That was probably a good thing. But at the thought of never seeing her again, my mood sunk lower than Tori's until, by the time the bus arrived, it was as black as my new hair.

Simon had gone to grab sodas for the trip. Tori was already out the station door. When I struggled to get my backpack on, Derek grabbed it and threw it over his shoulder, which would have been nice if I knew he wasn't just hurrying me along.

"Stop sulking," he said as he walked beside me. "It's just hair."

"That's not—" I shut up. Why bother?

Simon jogged up to join us in the passenger line. He handed me a Dr Pepper.

"You okay?"

"Just thinking about my dad and Liz. I wish I could have told them we're leaving."

Derek leaned down to my ear. "Smile, okay?" he whispered. "You look like you're being kidnapped, and people are staring."

I glanced around. No one was paying any attention to us. Simon shouldered past his brother, whispering, "Ease off." He waved me to the first empty seat. "This okay?"

I nodded and turned in.

"There's more at the back," Derek said. "We can't sit together up here."

"No, we can't." Simon slid in beside me.

twenty-seven

I STARED OUT THE BUS WINDOW as we left the city.

"We'll be back for them," Simon said.

"I know. I'm just . . . off today."

"I don't blame you. You had a crappy night. And a crappy day before that. And a crappy week before that."

I smiled. "At least it's consistent."

"And I know that"—he pointed at my hair—"isn't making you feel any better, but if you wash it enough when we get to Andrew's place, it'll come out."

"Have some experience, do you?"

"Me? *Pfft*. Never. I'm a guy. A guy guy. We do not color our hair. We don't even use conditioner if we can help it." He ran his fingers through his hair. "This? Totally natural."

"I never said—"

"Well, it wouldn't be the first time. Or the hundredth. When a guy looks Asian and has blond hair, everyone presumes it's a dye job."

"But your mother was Swedish."

"Exactly. Blame genetics, not chemicals." He leaned over and whispered. "But I did color it once. Temporary stuff like you've got. For a girl."

"Aha."

He put his chair back, settling into it. "It was a couple of years ago. I liked this girl, and she kept going on about this other guy, how his hair went so blond in the summer, how hot that looked."

I sputtered a laugh. "So you dyed—?"

"Shut up. She was cute, okay? I bought this washout highlight stuff, then spent all weekend outside, kicking around a ball with Derek. Sunday night, I color my hair. Monday morning I go to school and, hey, look what happened from me being out in the sun all weekend."

"Seriously?"

"I couldn't admit I dyed my hair for a girl. How lame would that be?"

"I'd think it was sweet. So did it work?"

"Sure. She went to the dance with me the next weekend. Then I came home, washed my hair until the color was out, and vowed never to do that again for a girl until I knew her well enough to be sure she was worth it."

I laughed, then said, "Thanks." When he arched his brows, I added, "For cheering me up."

"I'm good at it. With Derek, I get lots of practice." He reached into his backpack. "I have something else that might cheer you up. Or scare the crap out of you."

He pulled out a new sketch pad and flipped through it. A few pages in, he turned it so I could see.

"Hey, that's me," I said.

"So it looks like you? Or does the corpse crawling toward you give it away?" He handed the sketch pad to me. "I drew it this morning when Derek was doing his computer searches. I was thinking about last night."

In the picture, I was kneeling on my blanket, the corpse in front of me. Thankfully, he hadn't opted to draw the part where I'd been screaming in mortal terror, but later, when I thought he'd been outside with Tori.

I had my eyes closed, hands raised. The corpse was rearing up, seeming to follow my hands like a cobra dancing before a flute. All I could remember was how terrified I'd been, but in Simon's sketch, I didn't look terrified—I looked calm, confident. I looked powerful.

"I know that might not be a moment you care to have immortalized," he said.

I smiled. "No, it's cool. Can I have it?"

"When it's done. I need to color it when I get some pencils." He took the pad back. "I thought it might be interesting to do a kind of graphic journal about us. What's happening."

"Like a comic?"

"I was avoiding that word, for fear of sounding like a total geek. But, yeah, like a comic. Just for us, of course. A project to take our minds off stuff. It'll be way cooler on paper than it feels when we're living it." He took a long drink of his Diet Coke, then recapped the bottle slowly. "You could help, if you wanted. You know screenwriting and scripts for comics aren't much different."

"Like a movie told in stills."

"Right. I'm not good at the writing part. I know this is a true story, so it's not like I need to make stuff up, but I suck at knowing what parts to put in and what to leave out."

"I could help with that."

"Great." He opened his pad to the page after his picture of me. There were a few rough sketches on it. "I was trying to figure out where to start. . . ."

For the next few hours, I plotted and Simon drew. When I started yawning, he closed the sketchbook.

"Take a nap. We still have five hours to go. We'll have lots of time to work on this after we get to Andrew's place."

"Will we be staying with him?"

Simon nodded. "He's got the extra room. It's just him—no wife or kids. He'll take us in, no problem." He put away the sketch pad, then slowly zipped up his backpack. "There's another thing I've been thinking. I know it's not exactly a good time, but once we get settled in, I thought maybe you and I could—"

A shadow loomed over us.

Simon didn't bother looking up. "Yes, Derek?"

Derek leaned over the seat, one hand on the back for balance as the bus swayed. He seemed distracted, almost anxious.

"We're coming up to Syracuse soon."

"Okay."

"I need something to eat. I'm starving."

"Sure. I figured we'd jump off and grab dinner."

"I can't. Not here." When Simon looked confused, Derek lowered his voice. "Syracuse?"

"I don't think they're going to be hanging out at the bus station."

"Is something wrong?" I asked.

"Nah." Simon looked up at his brother. "I'll grab some food, okay?"

Derek hesitated. He didn't look anxious, really. More unhappy. Because Simon was annoyed with him?

As I watched Derek lurch back to his seat, I thought about that. Simon and Derek weren't just foster brothers—they were best friends. From the way Simon talked, though, he obviously had other friends, teammates, girlfriends. . . . I doubted Derek had any. For him, it was just Simon.

Was that why he wanted to get rid of me? It made sense, but it felt wrong. At Lyle House, Derek had never seemed jealous of any time Simon spent with me. Derek just went off and did his own thing. If anyone followed, it was Simon.

Maybe he wasn't jealous. Just feeling ignored.

It bothered me enough that when we stopped in Syracuse, I offered to take the food back out to Derek while Tori and Simon stretched their legs.

I meant to suggest that Derek and I switch seats. When I got there, Derek was staring out the window.

"Everything okay?" I asked.

He turned sharply, like I'd startled him, then nodded and took the food with a mumbled thanks.

I slid into the empty aisle seat. "Did you used to live here?"

He shook his head and looked out the window again. I took that as a sign he wasn't in the mood for conversation and was about to suggest the seat switch when he said, "We lived just about every place else in the state except here. We can't. There are . . . others here."

"Others?"

He lowered his voice. "Werewolves."

"In Syracuse?"

"Near it. A Pack."

"Oh."

Was that how werewolves lived? In packs, like wolves? I wanted to ask, but was afraid he'd think I was mocking him.

So I said, "And that's a problem? If they smelled you?"

"Yeah." He paused, then added grudgingly, "We're territorial."

"Oh."

"Yeah."

He kept looking out the window. I could see the reflection of his eyes, still and distant, lost in thoughts he obviously didn't care to share. I started to get up.

"When I was a kid," he said, without looking my way. "When I lived in that place where you were locked up, the others were like that. Territorial."

I lowered myself into the seat again. "The other werewo—" An elderly woman approached in the aisle and I said instead, "Subjects?"

"Yeah." He turned then. "They had this pack, I guess you'd call it, and they'd claim stuff, like the sandbox, as their territory, and if—"

His chin lifted, gaze moving to the front of the bus.

"Simon's coming," he said. "He's looking for you. Better go."

I was going to say that was okay, I wanted to hear more. Chances to hear something personal from Derek were fleeting, but this one had already passed.

"You go," I said. "Sit with him the rest of the way."

"Nah, I'm good."

"Really, I—"

"Chloe?" He met my gaze. "Go." His voice softened. "Okay?"

I nodded and left.

I fell asleep and dreamed of Derek—about what he'd said, about what the demi-demon had said about him, about the other werewolf subjects. I dreamed of Aunt Lauren at the facility, saying she wanted Derek put down like a rabid dog, and of Brady saying how Aunt Lauren had tried to get him to blame Derek for their fight.

The memories and the images swirled until I felt someone shaking my shoulder. I woke up to realize the bus had stopped. Derek was in the aisle, leaning past Simon, who was asleep.

I was about to ask what was wrong. Then I looked at Derek and I knew. His eyes glittered, and his skin glistened with sweat; his hair was plastered down with it. I could feel the heat of his hand through my shirt.

I shot up. "You're—"

"Yeah," he whispered. "We're outside Albany. Truck stop. I gotta get off."

I reached to wake Simon, but Derek stopped me. "I just wanted to tell you, in case I don't get back on. I'll be fine. I'll meet you at Andrew's."

I grabbed my sweatshirt and jacket. "I'm coming with you."

I was sure he'd argue, but he only nodded, face averted, murmuring. "Yeah. Okay."

"You go ahead," I said. "I'll talk to—"

I looked at Simon, but didn't need Derek to tell me not to wake him. Better to tell the person who'd never insist on following us—Tori. So I did that, then hurried after Derek.

twenty-eight

I CAUGHT UP WITH DEREK at the edge of a wooded patch beside the truck stop.

"I need to get in as deep as I can," he said. "Follow my path. It's muddy."

I could smell the rain, the damp chill of it lingering in the night air. Dead and decaying leaves slid underfoot. A dog barked somewhere. Derek paused, tracking the sound, then nodded, like it was far enough away, and continued walking.

"If I finish this," he began. "If I seem even close to finishing, you need to take off."

When I didn't answer, he said. "Chloe . . ."

"You aren't going to turn into some bloodthirsty monster, Derek. It'll still be you, just as a wolf."

"And you know that based on how much experience with werewolves?"

"Okay, but—"

"You could be right. Dad said it would be like that—still me in wolf form—but after what those guys did? Playing with our genes? I have no idea what will happen. So you're getting out of here when the time comes or you aren't sticking around at all."

"Okay."

He glanced back at me, fevered eyes glowing. "I mean it, Chloe."

"So do I. You're right. We don't know what will happen, and we can't take chances. As soon as you sprout fangs and a tail, I'll run screaming for the truck stop."

"You can skip the screaming part."

"We'll see."

We walked until the floodlights from the parking lot barely pierced the trees. The moon was shrouded in cloud. Whether it was a full moon or a half-moon, I didn't know. It didn't matter. A werewolf's Changes had nothing to do with moon cycles. When it happened, it happened, whether the timing was convenient or not.

Derek slowed, scratching his arm through his shirt. "There's a log here, if you want to sit and wait. I'll get a little deeper in—I'm sure it's not the prettiest sight."

"I've seen it before."

"If it goes further, it'll be worse."

"I'm fine."

When we entered a small clearing, Derek pulled off his sweatshirt. Under his T-shirt, his back muscles rippled, like snakes were trapped under his skin. Having seen this before, it didn't bother me, but it did remind me of something.

"On second thought, maybe I can't watch. Unless you brought a change of clothes, you really should get undressed this time.

"Right. Hold on."

He disappeared into the brush. I turned around. A couple minutes later, the leaves crackled as he came out.

"I'm decent," he said. "Got my shorts on. Nothing you haven't seen."

My cheeks flamed at the memory, which was stupid, because seeing a guy in his boxers shouldn't be any different than seeing him in swim trunks. I'd even seen guys in their underwear, pranking at camp by running around our cabins, and I'd laughed and hooted with the other girls. But none of the guys at camp had looked like Derek.

I turned slowly, hoping it was too dark for him to see me blushing. He wouldn't have noticed anyway. He was already on all fours, his head down, breathing in and out, like an athlete preparing for a run.

I blamed the note Simon left, the image of the Terminator still lingering in my brain, but that's what Derek looked like, that scene where the Terminator first arrives, and he's crouched, naked—not that Derek was totally naked or as pumped as Schwarzenegger, but he didn't look like a sixteen-year-old kid either, with a muscular back, bulging biceps, and . . .

And that was enough of that. I looked away to scan the forest and took a few deep breaths of my own.

"Sit here." Derek pointed to a clear spot beside him where he'd laid out his sweatshirt.

"Thanks." I lowered myself onto it.

"If it gets too bad, go. I'll understand."

"I won't."

He looked at the ground again, eyes closed as he inhaled and exhaled. His back spasmed and he winced, then stretched, his breathing deeper.

"That's a good idea. Stretch and work it out—" I stopped. "Okay, I'll shut up now. You don't need a coach."

He gave a low rumble that it took me a moment to recognize as a laugh. "Go ahead. Talk."

"If there's anything I can do— I know there probably isn't, but . . ."

"Just be here."

"That I can manage." I realized his skin hadn't rippled in a while. "And we might not even have to worry about it. It seems to be passing. False start, maybe. We should give it a few more minutes, then—"

His back shot up, body jackknifing as he let out a strangled cry. He managed two panting breaths before convulsing again. His arms and legs went rigid. His back arched to an unnatural height, spine jutting. His head dropped forward. His skin rippled and his back went even higher. A long whimper bubbled from his throat.

His head flew up and, for a second, his eyes met mine, wild and rolling with pain and terror, even more than the first time because then, as scared as he'd been, he'd known this was natural, that his body would take him through it safely. Now, knowing about the mutations, he had no such guarantee.

His fingers dug into the moist earth, the tips disappearing, the backs of his hands changing, tendons bulging, wrists thickening. He let out another cry, swallowing the end of it as he tried to keep quiet. I reached out and lay my hand on his. The muscles bulged and shifted. Coarse hair sprouted and pushed against my palm, then retreated. I rubbed his hand and moved closer and whispered it would be okay, he was doing fine.

His back arched and he gulped air, and in that moment of silence, footsteps clomped along the path into the woods.

"Are you kids in there?" It was the bus driver, his words harsh in the still forest, his figure backlit by the truck stoplights. "Someone saw you kids head in here. You've got one minute to come out or the bus leaves."

"Go," Derek whispered, his voice guttural, barely recognizable.

"No."

"You should—"

I met his gaze. "I'm not going. Now *shhh*."

"Ten seconds!" The bus driver yelled. "I'm not holding up the bus so you kids can screw around in the forest."

"If he comes closer, you go in there." I pointed at the thicket. "I'll stop him."

"He won't."

Sure enough, Derek barely got the words out before the figure began retreating. A few minutes later, the bus lights receded from the lot.

"That's okay," I said. "I have money. We'll catch—"

Derek convulsed again. This time his head shot up and he spewed vomit into the bushes. Wave after wave of convulsions rocked him, each one emptying his stomach until vomit dripped from every branch and the sickly smell mingled with the sharper stink of his sweat.

Hair sprouted and retracted and he kept convulsing and vomiting until there was nothing left to throw up, and still his stomach kept trying, with horrible dry heaves that were painful to hear. I rose onto my knees and rested my hand between his shoulder blades, rubbing and patting the sweat-slick skin there as I whispered the same words of reassurance, not even sure he could hear them anymore.

His back muscles twisted and shifted under my hands, the knobs of his spine pressing against them, his skin soaked with sweat and covered with coarse dark hair that wasn't retracting, but growing longer.

Finally Derek stopped heaving and shuddered, his whole body trembling from exhaustion, his head lowered almost to the ground. I rubbed his shoulder.

"It's okay," I said. "You're doing great. You're almost there."

He shook his head and made a sound that must have been "no," but it was too guttural to be more than a growl.

"That's fine," I said. "You will or you won't. You can't rush it."

He nodded. His head was down, face averted, but I could still see the changes, his temples narrowing, hair shortening, the tops of his ears sticking out as they shifted higher onto his skull.

I absently rubbed his back, then halted. "Do you want me to stop? Move away and give you more room?"

He shook his head as he struggled to catch his breath, sides and back heaving. I massaged the spot between his shoulders. His skin stopped moving and his spine retracted. His shoulders felt different, though. Set different, the muscles bunched and thick, almost hunched. The hair felt more like fur now, like my friend Kari's husky, with a coarse top layer, softer underneath.

Derek said werewolves changed into actual wolves. I'd found that hard to believe. In fact, I'd heard that the reason the "wolfman" type of werewolf had been so popular in early Hollywood was because of the difficulty of changing a human into a wolf. If they couldn't do it with makeup and prosthetics, surely the human *body* couldn't do it. But looking at Derek, shivering and gasping as he rested mid-Change, I saw I'd been wrong. I still couldn't quite wrap even my vivid imagination around what I was seeing, but there was no doubt he was changing into a wolf.

"It seems to have stopped again," I said.

He nodded.

"That's probably it, then. For now, this is as far as—"

His body went rigid. The muscles under my hand moved, but slowly, like they were settling, preparing to reverse the transformation . . .

His back shot up, limbs straightening, head dropping and there was this . . . sound—an awful popping and snapping, like bones crackling. Then his head flew up and the crackling was drowned out by an inhuman howl. His head whipped from side to side and I saw his face then, the nose and jaw lengthening to a muzzle, neck thick, brow receding, black lips pulled back to show teeth sharpened to fangs.

One eye caught mine, and the absolute terror in it chased mine away. I could not be afraid. I could not be freaked out. I could not make this worse for him in any way. So I met his gaze, unblinking, and kept rubbing his back.

After a moment, the muscles under my hand relaxed and he went still, the silence broken only by labored heaves as he panted, the sound more canine than human. His back rose and fell with the deep breaths. Then another massive convulsion seized him, and I was sure that was the final jolt, that the transformation would finish. Instead, the fur between my fingers receded. He convulsed again, gagging, threads of bile dripping from his jaws. He shook them off, then turned his face away.

Derek hacked and coughed for a minute, his limbs trembling. Then, slowly, they slid out from under him, like they couldn't bear his weight any more, and he collapsed, panting and quivering, his fur a dark shadow of stubble, his body almost returned to a human shape, only the thickened neck and shoulders remaining.

After one more deep, shuddering sigh, he rolled onto his side, toward me, legs drawn up, one hand draped over his face as it finished the reversal. I huddled there, trying to keep my teeth from chattering. Derek wrapped his hand around my bare ankle, where my sock had slid down into my sneaker.

"You're freezing."

I didn't feel cold. The shivering and goose bumps seemed more from nerves, but I said, "A little."

He shifted, then took my knee and tugged me closer, sheltered from the bitter wind. The heat of his body was like a radiator and I stopped shivering. He wrapped his hand around my ankle again, his skin rough, like a dog's paw pads.

"How're you doing?" he asked, his voice still odd, strained and raspy, but understandable.

I gave a small laugh. "I should be asking you that. Are you okay?"

"Yeah. That must be what'll happen for a few times. A partial Change, then back to normal."

"Practice runs."

"I guess so." He moved his hand down under his eyes. "You didn't answer my question. Are you all right?"

"I didn't do anything."

"Yeah. You did." He looked at me. "You did a lot."

His eyes met mine, and I looked into them and I felt . . . I don't know what I felt. A strange nameless something I couldn't even identify as a good something or a bad something, could only feel in my gut, jumping and twitching, until I turned away and looked out over the forest.

"Yeah, we gotta go," he said, starting to rise.

"Not yet. Lie down. Rest."

"I'm"—he sat up and swayed, as if light-headed—"*not* fine. Okay. Just give me a sec."

He lay back down, eyelids bobbing as he fought to keep them open.

"Close your eyes," I said.

"Just for a minute."

"Mmm-hmm."

I don't know if they were even fully closed before he fell asleep.

twenty-nine

I HUDDLED THERE UNTIL the sweat dried from his skin and he began to shiver, still sleeping. Then I unwrapped his fingers from my ankle. He let go, only to grasp my hand instead. I looked down at his hand, so huge around mine, like a kid's clutching a toy.

I was glad I'd been here for him. Glad someone was—I don't think it would have mattered who. Even if there'd been nothing I could do, just having me there seemed to help.

I couldn't imagine what he was going through—not just the agony but the uncertainty. Was this normal for young werewolves? Starting to Change, then reversing? Or was it something the Edison Group had done? What if he couldn't ever finish it? Would his body keep trying, putting him through this hell again and again?

I knew he would already be worrying about the same thing. That didn't excuse his outbursts, but maybe it helped me understand him and not take it so personally when he lashed out at me.

I slipped my hand from his, and he shifted with a grunt but didn't wake, just tucked his hand under his other arm and shivered. I hurried to where he'd left his clothing. When I returned, I checked the sweatshirt I'd been sitting on, but it was a damp, mud-caked mess. I decided to give him my jacket instead—it had to be close to his size—but it soon became apparent I wasn't getting *any* clothes on him.

It didn't matter that they were baggy—all Derek's clothing was, like he thought he'd be less intimidating if he looked chubby instead of muscular. Still, I couldn't get his jeans past his knees and even then I was sure I was going to wake him. So I settled for draping the clothing over him. I was fussing with the jacket, making sure it was the fleece side against him, when I caught a movement in the trees. I hunkered down beside Derek and went still.

When I didn't hear anything, I peeked over Derek and saw a man through the trees. His face was rigid with anger as he walked fast. Something moved near the ground ahead of him. A truck stop visitor taking his dog for a walk?

I glanced at Derek. If the dog smelled him, we were in trouble. I pushed up to a crouch and crept forward as quietly as I could. I saw a flicker of yellow fur through the thick bushes. The man waved his hand with a flash of silver, like he was holding a chain leash. He looked furious. I couldn't blame him. It was cold and wet and muddy, and his dog seemed to be insisting on doing its business in the deepest part of the small forest.

When the man's foot flew out in a kick, though, my sympathy vanished, and I tensed, a shout of outrage on my lips. Then I saw it wasn't a dog in front of him. It was a girl with long blond hair, wearing a light-colored shirt and jeans, crawling on all fours, like she was trying to get away from the man.

He kicked her again and she twisted, scuttling forward awkwardly, like she was too badly hurt to get up and run. Her face turned my way and I saw she wasn't any older than me. Mascara raccoon-ringed her eyes. Dirt streaked her face. Dirt and blood, I realized, the blood still dripping from her nose, staining her shirt.

I sprang to my feet and as I did, the man raised his hand. Silver flashed—not a leash, but a knife. For a second, all I could see was that knife, my mind stumbling back to the girl in the alley, the knife tip over my eye. The terror I'd fought so hard to hide shot through me.

The man grabbed the girl's long hair. He wrenched her head up and that jolted me from my frozen terror. My mouth opened to call out, yell anything, just get his attention so she could escape.

The knife sliced through the air, heading straight for the girl's throat and I let out a cry. The knife passed through, seeming not to have left a mark, and I was sure he'd missed. Then her throat opened, splitting, gaping, blood gushing, spurting.

I fell back, hands flying to my mouth to stifle another scream. He thrust the dying girl aside with a snarl of disgust. She collapsed to the ground, blood still spurting, mouth moving, eyes rolling wildly.

The man turned toward me. I ran, tripping and stumbling through the undergrowth. I had to get to Derek, wake him, warn him. It seemed to take forever, but I finally made it. As I dropped beside him, I caught a glimmer out of the corner of my eyes and I turned to see the man . . . back where I'd first seen him, in exactly the same position, heading the same way.

His mouth opened, saying something, but no words came out. Why couldn't I hear him? The forest was so silent my panting breaths sounded like a train, but I couldn't even hear the man's footsteps. I realized that the whole time I'd never heard a thing.

I waited for the flash of silver I'd seen earlier, and it came, in exactly the same place. Then he kicked the girl . . . in the same spot.

I reached into the pocket of my jacket, still wrapped around Derek, and pulled out the switchblade I'd taken from the girl in the alley. I was pretty sure by now that I wasn't in danger, but I wasn't taking chances. I crept toward the silent figures moving through the woods. The man kicked the girl a second time, but again the blow made no sound, her fall made no sound, *she* made no sound.

Ghosts. Like the man in the factory.

No, not ghosts. Ghosts might not make noise moving, but I could hear them talk. I could interact with them. These were just images. Metaphysical film clips of an event so horrible it was imprinted on this place, endlessly looping.

The man grabbed the girl by her hair. I squeezed my eyes shut, but I still saw it, the memory imprinted on *me* now, replaying on my eyelids.

I swallowed and retreated. Back in the clearing, I hunkered down beside Derek, drawing my knees up, my back turned to the scene playing out in the woods. But it didn't matter that I couldn't see it. I knew it was there, unfolding behind me, and it didn't matter if I hadn't *really* watched a girl die. In a way, I *had*.

A girl my age had been murdered in these woods and I'd seen her last terrified moments, watched her bleed to death in this forest. A life like mine had ended here, and it didn't matter how many times I'd seen deaths in movies, it wasn't the same, and I wasn't ever going to forget it.

I huddled there, shivering, surrounded by darkness. I'd hated the dark since childhood. I know why now—I used to see ghosts in the dark when I was little, brushed off by my parents as bogeymen. Now, knowing that the "bogeymen" were real didn't help at all.

Every whisper of wind sounded like a voice. Every animal rustling in the forest was a poor creature I'd raised from the dead. Every creak of a tree was a corpse clawing up from the cold ground. Each time I closed my eyes, I saw the dead girl. Then I saw the dead bats. Then I saw the girl, buried in this forest, never found, waking in a shallow grave, trapped in her rotted corpse, unable to scream, to struggle. . . .

I kept my eyes open.

I thought of waking Derek. He wouldn't complain. But after what he'd just been through, it seemed silly to say I couldn't bear being out here with a murder reenactment playing behind me. I did nudge him a few times, though, hoping he'd wake up.

But he didn't. He was exhausted and he needed his rest, and even if he did wake up, what could we do? We were trapped at this bus stop until morning.

So I sat and I tried not to think. When that failed, I recited multiplication tables, which only reminded me of school and made me wonder whether I'd ever go back; and that reminded me of Liz, of how much she'd hated math, and I wondered how she was and where she was and . . .

I switched to reciting favorite movie dialogue, but, again, it only reminded me of my other life, then my dad and how worried he must be. I drove myself nuts trying to figure out some safe way to get him a message, getting more and more frustrated when I couldn't.

I finally settled on something that always comforted me—singing "Daydream Believer." It was my mom's favorite song, the one she'd sung me to sleep with whenever I had nightmares. I only knew one verse and the chorus, but I whispered them under my breath, over and over and . . .

"Chloe?"

Fingers touched my shoulder. I blinked and saw Derek crouched beside me, still in his shorts, his face dark with worry.

"S-sorry. I drifted off."

"With your eyes open? Sitting up? I've been trying to snap you out of it for a while."

"Oh?" I looked around and saw it was day. I blinked harder and yawned. "Long night."

"You've been sitting here awake all night?" He lowered himself to the ground. "Because of what happened with me? I know that couldn't have been easy to watch—"

"That's not why."

I tried to duck having to explain, but he kept pushing, and it came down to telling the truth or letting him think that watching him Change had put me in a state of shock. I told him about the girl.

"It wasn't real," I said as I finished. "Well, it was—once. But I was just seeing some kind of ghostly replay."

"And you watched that, all night?"

"No, it's"—I waved my hand over my shoulder—"back there. I didn't look."

"Why didn't you wake me up?"

"You were tired. I didn't want to bother you."

"Bother me? That is the stupidest—" He stopped. "Wrong word. Stubborn, not stupid . . . and yelling at you right now isn't helping, is it?"

"Not really."

"Next time, wake me up. I don't expect you to tough out something like that, and I'm not impressed that you did."

"Yes, sir."

"And next time you don't tell me, I *will* yell at you."

"Yes, sir."

"I'm not your drill sergeant, Chloe. I don't *like* getting on your case all the time."

I wasn't touching that one.

"I don't mean to . . ." He sighed, shook his head, and got to his feet. "Give me a minute to get dressed, and we'll head into the truck stop, warm up, and get some breakfast."

He took his clothes and headed for the thicket, still talking. "The main bus station is in the city. I'm hoping we'll have enough for cab fare. When we get inside, we'll call and get the bus rates and schedule, so we'll know how much money we have left over."

"I've got"—I pulled bills from my pocket—"eighty. I left the rest in my backpack. I don't like carrying it all around."

"Most of mine is in my backpack, too, which I forgot on the bus." He cursed himself under his breath.

"You were in no shape to be remembering anything last night. I should have thought to grab mine."

"But *you* were worried about *me*. Never mind, we'll have enough. I've got about a hundred . . ."

A pause. Then the sound of hands slapping fabric, like he was patting his pockets.

He swore. "It must have fallen out. Where did you get my jeans from?"

"Right where you left them, folded by the tree. I checked the pockets first. There was just an energy bar wrapper."

"I know I had—" He stopped and swore again. "No, I moved the money to my jacket, which I left on the bus."

"Eighty dollars should cover the bus to New York and breakfast. We'll walk, then catch a city bus to the station."

He strode from the bushes, muttering, "Stupid, stupid."

"Like I said, you had other things on your mind. We both did. And neither of us is used to playing fugitive yet. We'll learn. For now, let's get inside. I'm freezing."

thirty

WHILE DEREK WAS IN the bathroom I called the bus station and got fares and a schedule. The guy was even nice enough to tell me which city buses we needed to take to get there.

When Derek came out of the bathroom, his sweatshirt was damp and clean, and his hair was wet and glistening, like he'd wiped down the shirt and washed his hair in the sink.

"Good news first or bad—" I stopped. "Dumb question. Bad, right?"

"Yeah."

"We've got a two-mile walk to the nearest bus stop, plus one transfer to get to the terminal. The good news? The fare is sixty dollars for two students to New York, so we have enough for breakfast."

"And deodorant."

I was going to say that didn't matter, but from the set of his jaw, it mattered to him, so I nodded and said, "Sure."

We bought deodorant and a cheap comb. And, yes, we shared them. Money was too tight to get silly about that.

The smell of bacon and eggs from the restaurant set my mouth watering, but our cash wouldn't stretch to cover a hot breakfast. We grabbed cartons of chocolate milk, two energy bars, and two bags of peanuts, then headed out for our hike to the bus stop.

After about a half mile of silence, Derek said, "You're quiet this morning."

"Just tired."

Another hundred feet.

"It's last night, isn't it?" he said. "If you want to talk about it . . ."

"Not really."

Every few steps, he'd glance my way. I wasn't in the mood to share, but my silence was obviously bugging him, so I said, "I keep thinking about when I first saw that girl in trouble. When I thought it was real. I was going to do something—"

"What?" he cut in.

I shrugged. "Yell. Distract him."

"If it was real, you shouldn't have even *thought* of getting involved. The guy had a knife. He was obviously ready to use it."

"That wasn't really the point," I murmured, watching my toe kick a pebble along the roadside.

"Okay. So the point was . . ."

"I saw that knife and I froze. All I could think about was that girl in the alley, the one who held a knife on me. If last night *had* been real, I might have let someone die because I was too freaked out to do anything."

"But it wasn't real."

I looked up at him.

"Okay," he said. "Again that wasn't your point. But what happened in that alley—you still hadn't had time to slow down and . . ." He gestured, searching for a word. "Process it. You talked to Simon about it, right?"

I shook my head.

He frowned. "But you *did* tell him what happened."

Another head shake.

"You should. You need to talk to someone. You sure can't talk to Tori. Liz is probably a good listener, but she's not around." He paused. "You could talk to me, but you've probably figured out I'm not good with stuff like that. I mean, if you wanted to . . ." He trailed off, then came back firmer, shoulders hunching against the morning chill. "It should be

Simon. He'd want to know what happened, and he'd want you to be the one to tell him."

I nodded, though I didn't know whether I would. Simon had spent enough time lately on Chloe-comfort duty. I needed to start working stuff out by myself. But there was a related issue I did want help with.

"I've been thinking," I began. "After what happened, I should learn how to defend myself. Some basic self-defense moves."

"That's a good idea."

"Great, so could you—?"

"I'll ask Simon to teach you some," he continued.

"Oh. I thought . . . I guess I thought that would be more your area."

"Our dad taught us both. Simon's good. Unless . . ." He glanced down at me. "I mean, if you want, sure, I can help out. But Simon would be a better teacher. He's got the patience for it."

"Right. I'll talk to Simon then."

He nodded and we lapsed into silence again.

We reached the bus station with twenty minutes to spare. Derek had me hang back, where the agent could see I was a teenager without getting too close a look, in case my photo was circulating. He went up to the counter alone. When he seemed to be having trouble, though, I joined him.

"What's wrong?" I whispered.

"She won't give us the youth fare."

"It's not a youth fare," the woman said. "It's a student fare. If you can't produce ID, you don't get it."

"But we got tickets in Buffalo without any ID." I put my used ticket on the counter.

"That's Buffalo," she said with a sniff. "Here in the state's *capital* we follow the rules. No ID, no student fare."

"Okay, adult tickets, then."

"We don't have enough," Derek murmured.

"What?"

"It's thirty-eight each for adults. We're six bucks short."

I leaned into the wicket. "Please, it's really important. You can see on our ticket there that we already bought fares to New York, but my friend got sick and we had to get off the bus—"

"Doesn't matter."

"How about one adult and one youth? We have enough—"

"Next!" she called, and waved up the man behind us.

The bus station also serviced Greyhound, but their sign clearly stated that their student fares required a special card, which was why we hadn't bought from them in Buffalo. I tried anyway. The woman there was more sympathetic, but she explained that she couldn't issue the reduced fare tickets without entering a student discount card number into the computer. So we were out of luck.

"We'll figure something out," I said as we moved away from the Greyhound counter.

"You go. I'll give you directions to Andrew's house. He can pick me up here—"

"What if he's not there? He could have moved or could be away. Then I'd have to find Simon, use a good chunk of money for us all to come back and get you. . . ."

Derek nodded, conceding my point.

"You lived around here for a while." I raised my hands. "I know, it's not your favorite place to remember, but is there anyone you could borrow ten bucks from?"

"A friend?"

"Well, sure, maybe . . ."

A small laugh. "Yeah, you sound as doubtful about that as you should. You may have guessed I don't go out of my way to make friends. I don't see the point, especially when I'm never in one place long. I've got my dad and Simon. That's enough."

His pack . . .

He continued, "I suppose I could find someone. Simon's bound to have a friend or teammate who owed him money. He's bad for stuff like that—lends it and never asks for it back."

"On second thought, considering you vanished under bad circumstances, reappearing now might not be the wisest idea. The last thing we need is someone calling the cops."

I walked to the stand of brochures and took one listing fares and schedules. Then I went to the map of New York State and studied the two. Derek read over my shoulder.

"There," he said, pointing to a town on the map. "We can afford the full fare to New York from there."

"As for how we'll get there . . ."

That was the question.

thirty-one

OUR BEST SHOT OF getting where we wanted to go was by hitchhiking. We weren't stupid enough to thumb a ride, but we might be able to sneak one. So we decided to go back to the truck stop. I dozed for a few minutes while we rode the city bus, then we started the long walk.

We were about halfway there when Derek said, gruffly, "I'm sorry."

"About what?"

"This. You helped me last night after all the crap I put you through. And this is your reward. Stranded in Albany."

"It's an adventure. I can't remember the last time I took a city bus. I'm getting my exercise, too. After a week cooped up in Lyle House and that laboratory, I've never been more in the mood for a long walk."

We walked a while longer.

"I know you're tired," he said. "And hungry. And pissed off."

"Tired, yes. Hungry, a bit. Pissed off? No." I looked up at him. "Seriously. I'm not."

"You've been really quiet."

I laughed. "I'm *normally* really quiet. But these last couple of weeks have *not* been normal."

"I know you don't always say a lot, you've just been . . ." He shrugged.

"I thought you were mad." He shoved his hands into his pockets. "About that—being mad. You were right the other night, after what happened in that alley. I was mad at myself. It just took me a while to calm down enough to figure that out."

I nodded.

"What I did, when we lived here, hurting that kid. I didn't think it could ever happen again. I've been through it so many times, thinking of what went wrong and what I'd do if I ever got into that situation again, all the coping strategies Dr. Gill taught me."

"Dr. Gill?"

"Yeah, I know. She creeped me out even before we knew about the Edison Group. But she was a real shrink, and she did try to help. It was in their best interests to teach me to control my temper. So I was sure, if anything like that ever happened again, there was no question that I'd handle it better. And what happened? Almost the exact same scenario . . . and I did the exact same thing."

"You stopped yourself before you threw her into the wall."

"No, *you* stopped me. If you hadn't yelled, I would have done it. All those strategies. All that mental rehearsal. And when it happened, I never considered doing anything different. I couldn't. My brain just shut down."

"But it didn't take much to turn it back on again."

He shrugged.

"That's got to be progress, right?"

"I suppose so," he said, but he didn't sound convinced.

At the truck stop, our plan was to stow away in a transport. We sat in the restaurant, nursing sodas while Derek listened to the conversations around us, and picked out truckers heading our way.

The first truck was parked up front, making it impossible to sneak on without being seen. The second time, the trailer had a huge padlock on it, too big for Derek to break. The third time, as the saying goes, was the charm.

We'd followed the driver to his vehicle, which turned out to be a cube van. After he got into the cab, we snuck in the back.

The guy ran some kind of construction business. The van smelled of wood chips and oil and was full of tools, ropes, ladders, and tarps. When the truck reached the highway and the road noise was loud enough to drown us out, Derek took the tarps and made a bed on the floor.

"You need sleep," he said. "They stink but . . ."

"They're softer than cardboard. Thanks."

He handed me half an energy bar that he must have been saving.

"No, keep it," I said.

"You'll sleep better if your stomach isn't growling. And don't say it isn't. I can hear it."

I accepted the bar.

"And take this." He stripped off his sweatshirt. "Again, it might not smell great, but it's warm."

"You need—"

"I don't. I've still got a touch of fever from last night."

I took the sweatshirt. "It's okay, Derek. I'm not mad."

"I know."

I settled onto the tarp bed and pulled the sweatshirt over me, like a blanket. Then I ate the rest of the energy bar.

When I finished, Derek said, "You can't sleep with your eyes open, Chloe."

"I don't want to drift off, in case anything happens."

"I'm here. Go to sleep."

I closed my eyes.

I woke when the truck slowed. Derek was at the back, opening the door to peek out.

"Is this our stop?" I asked.

"We should be far enough. We aren't in a town, though. It's another truck stop."

"A pee break after that mega-coffee he bought."

"Yeah." He opened the door farther for a better look. "I'd rather be in a town. . . ."

"But he might not stop at one. We should get out while we can."

Derek nodded and closed the door. The truck pulled into a spot and stopped.

"Get under a tarp," Derek whispered, "in case he checks the back."

A minute later, the rear door squealed open. I held my breath. The cube van wasn't that big, and if the driver climbed inside to get something, he'd probably step on us. But he stayed at the tailgate. Tools clattered, like he was getting one from a box. Then the noise stopped. I tensed.

"I did forget the new vise grips," the man muttered. "Great."

The door shut with a bang. When I started pulling off the tarp, Derek whispered, "Wait. He's still walking away."

A minute passed as he listened, then he said, "Okay."

I got up and pushed the tarps back where we'd found them as Derek peeked outside again.

"Trees to our left," he said. "We'll head through there, then circle and grab something to drink from the restaurant before we head out."

"And use the bathroom."

"Yeah. Follow me."

We slipped out of the van and darted to the trees. Running behind Derek was worse than running behind Tori—with his long legs he barely needed to walk fast before the gap between us widened.

When he stopped short and spun to face me, I expected a scowl and an order to keep up, but his lips formed a curse. Running footfalls sounded behind me. I was about to break into a sprint when a hand clamped down on my shoulder.

Derek started to charge. I saw his expression, that telltale curl of his lip, and I wildly gestured for him to stop. He did, skidding to a halt, but his gaze stayed fixed over my head, watching my captor.

"I thought I'd picked up a passenger or two," said a man's voice.

He turned me around. It was the driver of the van. He was middle-aged with a gray ponytail and a craggy face.

"W-we didn't take anything," I said. "I'm sorry. We just needed a ride."

"Jesus," he said, shifting me into the sun for a better look. "How old are you?"

"F-fifteen."

"Just barely, I'll bet." He shook his head. "Running away from home. I'd bet on that, too." His voice softened. "That's not a road you want to take, kids. Speaking from experience, it is not the road at all."

Derek sidled closer, gaze fixed on the man, so intent I don't think he heard a word the guy said. I slid my hand into my pocket, fingertips touching my knife, not taking it out, just reminding myself it was there, that I wasn't as helpless as I felt.

I caught Derek's attention, not sure he'd notice, but he did, nodding absently, letting me know he was still in control.

The man continued, "Whatever is going on at home, it's not as bad as you think."

I lifted my gaze to his. "And if it is?"

A pause, then a slow, sad nod. "All right. Maybe that's so. It happens, more than you think, but there are other ways to deal with it. Places you can go. People who can help."

"We're fine," Derek said, his voice a low rumble.

The man shook his head. "You're not fine, son. You're, what, seventeen? On the run? Catching rides in the back of vans?"

"We're fine." Derek's rumble had gone lower, a growl now. He cleared his throat and eased back. "We appreciate your concern, sir."

"Do you, son? Do you really?" He shook his head. "I'm going to take you both inside and get you a hot meal. Then I'll make some calls. Find you a place to stay."

"We can't—" I began.

"No one's going to send you home. Now come on." His hand tightened on my shoulder.

Derek stepped forward. "Sorry, sir, but we can't do that."

"Yes, you can."

Derek waved for me to come over to him. I took a step. The man's hand tightened more.

"Let her go." The growl had returned to Derek's voice.

"No, son. I won't hurt your friend, but I'm going to take her inside and call someone who can help. I'm hoping you'll come with us, but that's your choice."

"Go," I whispered, low enough that only Derek could hear. "I'll catch up."

I was sure he'd heard, but he pretended not to.

"I'm going to ask you again, sir. Let her go."

"That sounds an awful lot like a threat, son. You're a big boy, but you don't want to take on a guy who's been in construction for twenty years and in more fights than he cares to admit to. I don't want to hurt you—"

Derek sprang, lightning fast. He had his arm around the man's throat before the guy even got his fists up. As he yanked the man down in a headlock, I stumbled out of the way, my hand flying from my pocket, knife sailing to the ground. The man stared at it. I scooped it up and put it back in my pocket.

"We don't want to hurt you either," Derek said. "But you can see"—he tightened his grip until the man's eyes bugged—"that I could. I know you're trying to help us, but you don't understand the situation."

Derek looked at me. "Run back to the van. Grab rope and some rags."

I took off.

thirty-two

TWENTY MINUTES LATER, we were a mile from the truck stop, trudging through a field. Ahead was a road that ran alongside the highway.

"You don't think we did the right thing," Derek said.

I shrugged.

"I didn't tie him too tight. He'll get out in an hour, probably less, and I left his cell phone right there, in case there's any problem."

I nodded. We walked another fifty feet.

"What would you have done?" he asked.

"You know my plan. It's the one you pretended not to hear."

We reached the roadside before he answered. "Yeah, okay. I heard. But it didn't look to me like he was going to give you a chance to escape. I knew I could take him down safely, without hurting him, before things got worse. And if I can do that, then that's the choice I'm going to make. It's how our dad taught us to handle situations like that."

I considered it, then nodded. "You're right."

He looked surprised.

"I don't have experience with this stuff, these kinds of decisions," I said. "With the girl in the alley or the Edison Group, the answer was easy. If someone's trying to hurt us, we have every right to strike back. It's just . . ."

"That guy was trying to help a couple of runaways. He didn't deserve to end up bound and gagged."

I nodded.

"Even someone like that is a threat, Chloe. Whether he means to be or not. We had to get away or his 'help' would have landed us back with the Edison Group."

"I know."

We moved to the side of the road for a passing car, tensing as it went by, making sure the brake lights didn't flash, the car didn't slow. It wouldn't matter if the driver was a psycho trying to abduct us or a grandmother offering us a lift. We had to react the same way. Run. And if we couldn't run, fight.

The car continued, speed unchecked.

"We can't trust anyone now," I murmured, "even the good guys."

"Yeah. Sucks, doesn't it?"

It did.

We continued down back roads running roughly parallel to the highway. Judging by how long we'd been in the van, Derek figured we had to be close to the next town with a bus stop, but the truth was that we had no idea. However far it was, we had to walk it—we weren't about to hitch another ride.

One problem with our quiet country stroll was the dogs. Those tied up launched into a barking frenzy when they caught a whiff of Derek. No one seemed concerned, though—out here, I guess there were so few passersby that dogs did tend to bark at them, and owners ignored it.

However, being in the country also meant that a lot of those dogs *weren't* chained. More than one came charging down a driveway. Eventually, our reaction became automatic. At the first note of a bark, we'd stop walking. I'd move behind Derek. He'd stand his ground and wait. Once the dog got within eye contact range, it would take one good look at Derek and run, yelping, for safety.

"Do they always back down like that?" I asked as we watched a yellow Lab race back home, tail between its legs.

"Depends on the dog. Big country dogs like these? Yeah. It's the fancy city ones that give me trouble. Overbred, Dad says. Makes them skittish and screws up their wiring. I had a Chihuahua attack me last year." He showed me a faint scar on his hand. "Took a good chunk out."

I sputtered a laugh. "A Chihuahua?"

"Hey, that thing was more vicious than a pit bull. I was at a park with Simon, kicking around a ball. All of a sudden, this little rat dog comes tearing out of nowhere, jumps up, and clamps down on my hand. Wouldn't let go. I'm shaking it, and the owner's yelling at me not to hurt little Tito. I finally get the dog off. I'm bleeding all over the place and the guy never even apologizes."

"He didn't think it was strange? His dog attacking you like that?"

"Nah. He said the soccer ball must have provoked it, and we needed to be more careful. When strange stuff happens, people come up with their own explanations."

I told him about the girl in the alley, accusing Tori of tasering her.

"Yeah," he said. "We have to be careful, but they'll usually explain it away themselves."

We moved aside as a pickup passed, the driver lifting a hand in greeting. I waved back, then watched until I was sure he wasn't going to stop.

"So do all animals react that way to you? I know you said rats steer clear."

"Most do. They see a human, but they smell something else. It confuses them. Canines are the worst, though." He paused. "No, cats are the worst. I really don't like cats."

I laughed. As the shadows lengthened, Derek moved us across the road to the sunny side.

"I went to the zoo once," he continued. "Fifth grade field trip. Dad said I couldn't because of the werewolf thing. I was pissed. Really pissed. Back then, I didn't freak animals out. I just made them nervous. So I decided Dad was being unfair and went anyway."

"How?"

"Forged his name and saved my allowance."

"So what happened?"

"Pretty much what Dad figured. I made the predators nervous and totally freaked out the prey animals. My classmates thought it was cool, though. They got to see an elephant charge."

"Seriously?"

"Yeah. I felt bad. So I stayed back from the pens after that. They weren't what I wanted to see anyway."

"Which was? Wait. The wolves, right?"

He nodded.

"You wanted to see if they'd recognize you as one of them."

"Nah. Nothing silly like that." He walked in silence for a moment. "Okay. Exactly like that. I had this . . ." He struggled for a word.

"Fantasy?"

A glower said that wasn't the word he'd have chosen. "This *idea* that they'd smell me and . . ." He shrugged. "I don't know what. Just that they'd do something. That something cool would happen."

"Did it?"

"Sure, if you consider it cool to watch a wolf batter itself bloody against the fence."

"Oh."

"It was . . ." His gaze went distant, staring off down the road, expression unreadable. "Bad. I got out of there as fast as I could, but he didn't stop. The next day a kid at school said they put the wolf to sleep."

I looked up at Derek.

He continued, gaze still fixed on the road. "I went home and grabbed the paper. The city section was missing. Dad had gotten to it first. He'd figured out what had happened, but he wasn't going to say anything. He knew I'd been upset about something that night, and I guess he thought that was punishment enough. So I went to the store and bought a paper myself. It was true."

I nodded, not sure what to say.

"'Sudden, unprovoked aggression toward humans,'" he recited, as if he'd never forgotten the words. "Wolves don't normally act like that. All those stories about the big, bad wolf are crap. Yeah, they're predators, and they're dangerous. But they don't want to have anything to do with humans if they can avoid it. The only time they do is if they're sick, starving, or defending their territory. I was a lone wolf invading a pack's turf. He was the alpha. It was his duty to protect his pack. And he got killed for it."

"You didn't mean for that to happen."

"That's no excuse. Dad taught me about wolves. I knew how they behaved. I'd seen it with the other boys, the other subjects . . ."

"Do you remember them? Simon wasn't sure you did."

"Yeah. I do." He rubbed the back of his neck as he walked, then looked at me. "You getting tired?"

"A little."

"It shouldn't be far now. So, uh . . ." He seemed to be searching for something to say. I hoped it was more about himself or about the other werewolves, but when he finally spoke, he said, "That special school you go to. You take theater?"

"I'm in the theater arts stream. We still take all the regular classes, like math, English, science. . . ."

And so we shifted to simpler subjects for the rest of the walk.

thirty-three

WE REACHED THE NEXT TOWN and found the bus stop—a flower shop, actually, with tickets sold at the till. We tried again for youth prices and, as in Buffalo, got them without question. Figures.

That meant we had extra cash and a little more than two hours before departure. As for what we'd do with that time and money? Our grumbling stomachs answered that question.

It was getting dark now, still early evening though, so no one paid any attention to a couple of teens walking around. We went a few blocks looking for a place that sold hot, cheap food. Derek's nose led us to a fast-food Chinese restaurant. A popular destination, unfortunately, with a huge line. I saved us a table while he went up to the counter.

The line barely seemed to be moving, and the restaurant was stifling hot. Before long, my eyelids were flagging.

"Tired, dear?"

I straightened to see an elderly woman in a yellow coat standing beside my table. She smiled at me. I returned it.

"Mind if I sit for a moment?" She waved at the empty chair across from me.

My gaze shot to Derek, still five people from the front of the line.

"I'll leave when your young man comes back," she said. "It's terribly busy in here, isn't it?"

I nodded and waved for her to take the seat. She did.

"I have a great-granddaughter your age," she said. "About fourteen, I'm guessing."

"That's right," I said, hoping I didn't sound too nervous. I shouldn't be answering questions, even incorrectly, but I didn't know what else to do. I glanced at Derek, hoping for rescue, but he was studying the menu board.

"Ninth grade?"

"Yes."

"And what's your favorite subject, dear?"

"Drama."

She laughed. "I haven't heard that one. Is it like acting?"

I explained and as we talked, I relaxed. Once we got beyond age and grade, she didn't ask anything too personal—not even my name. She was just an old lady who wanted to talk, which was nice for a change.

We chatted until Derek was second in line. Then laughter erupted at a table behind me. I turned to see two couples, a year or two older than me. The girls were sneering in disgust. One guy was red-faced with stifled laughter. The other wasn't bothering to hold his in, laughing so hard he was doubled over.

All four were looking at me.

The entire restaurant was looking at me.

It was like a nightmare where kids are laughing at you, and you keep walking through the halls, not knowing why until you realize you aren't wearing any pants. I knew I was wearing pants. The only thing I could think of was my black hair. It wasn't *that* bad, was it?

"Oh, dear," whispered the old woman.

"Wh-what's wrong? Wh-what did I do?"

She leaned over, her eyes glistening. Tears? Why would she be—?

"I'm sorry," she said. "I only . . ." She gave a sad twist of a smile. "I only wanted to speak to you. You seemed like such a nice girl."

I caught a glimpse of Derek, out of line now, striding over, glowering at the snickering boys. The woman got to her feet and leaned across the table again.

"It was very nice talking to you, dear." She put her hand on mine . . . and it passed through.

I leaped to my feet.

"I'm sorry," she said again.

The look on her face was so sad that I wanted to say it was okay, it was my fault. But before I could get a word out, she faded away, and then all I could hear was the laughter around me, the mutters of "crazy" and "schizo," and I stood there, rooted to the floor, until Derek took my arm, his grip so soft I could barely feel it.

"Come on," he said.

"Yeah," the laughing guy called. "I think your girlfriend's day pass has expired."

Derek slowly raised his head, lip curling in that too-familiar look. I grabbed his arm. He blinked and nodded. As we turned to go, the other guy at the table chimed in.

"Trolling for chicks at the psych ward?" He shook his head. "Now *that's* desperate."

As we passed the front window, I swore every eye inside followed us. I caught a few looks: sympathy, pity, distaste, disgust. Derek moved between me and the window, blocking my view as we walked.

"They didn't need to do that," he said. "Those kids, sure. They're idiots. But the grown-ups should know better. What if you *were* mentally ill?"

He led me around to the parking lot, then stopped at the back, under the shadow of the building overhang.

"You'll never see them again," he said. "And if they'd treat a real mentally ill person like that, then you shouldn't care what they think. Bunch of morons."

I said nothing, just stared out at the parking lot, shivering. He shifted in front of me, trying to block the wind.

"W-we should go," I said. "You need to eat. I'm sorry."

"For what? Talking to yourself? So what? People do it all the time. They should have ignored it."

"Would you?"

"Sure. None of my business. I—"

"—wouldn't laugh or stare. I know. But you couldn't ignore it. Maybe you'd pretend not to notice, but you'd still think about it, about the person doing it, what was wrong with her, whether she was going to freak out and pull a gun or . . ." I wrapped my arms around myself. "I'm babbling. But you know what I mean. I was sitting in a restaurant, carrying on a conversation with someone and I never even guessed she was a ghost."

"You'll figure it out."

"How? They *look* like people. They *sound* like people. Unless they walk through the furniture, there's no clue. Do I have to stop talking to strangers? Ignore every person who walks up to me? *That'll* look normal." I gave my head a sharp shake. "Babbling again. I'm sorry. And I'm sorry you got caught up in that."

"You think I care?" He put one hand on the wall and leaned down to me. "You'll work it out. Other necromancers do. You just need to figure out the tricks of the trade."

"Before I get locked up?"

"Much more of this on-the-run stuff, and you might be going into restaurants, talking to yourself on purpose, trying to get locked up someplace with a bed and a hot shower."

I managed a smile. "Right now, I'd settle for hot food."

"How about hot chocolate?"

"What?"

"On the way here I saw one of those fancy coffee places, some Starbucks knockoff. Big armchairs, a fireplace . . . Didn't look too busy. This isn't exactly a five-dollar-coffee town."

I pictured curling up in a chair, in front of a fire, sipping a huge, steaming hot chocolate. I smiled.

"It's settled then," he said. "We'll get brownies or cookies to eat. A real nutritious dinner. Now I think it was this way . . ."

We set out.

The coffee shop had been on the street with the bus stop. We tried to get there—and out of the freezing cold—as quickly as possible. After cutting through a couple of parking lots, we saw our next potential shortcut: a playground. When I started to cross the street, Derek stopped me.

"That's not always the kind of place you want to be at night."

He was right, of course. It looked innocent enough—a narrow strip of park with a line of swings and slides, a big plastic play center at the end—but between the equipment and the trees were a lot of shadows. After dark, when the kiddies had gone home, it made the perfect place for bigger, more dangerous kids to hang out.

Derek scanned the park as he sampled the breeze.

"Empty," he said finally. "Let's go."

We jogged across the road. Out in the open now, the wind got even worse, swirling around us, bitter cold. The swings twisted and creaked. As we passed, a sudden gust sent one slamming into my shoulder. I stumbled back with a yelp and caught a mouthful of sand, whirling up from the ground. As I sputtered, Derek's head shot up. I spit out the sand and turned to him. He'd gone still, face lifted.

"What do you smell?" I asked.

"I'm not sure . . . I thought I—" The wind changed and his nostrils flared. His eyes went wide. "Run!"

He gave me a shove and I broke into a sprint. In the last few days, I'd done this "running from danger" stuff often enough that my brain kicked my legs into high gear automatically, my aching feet forgotten.

Derek stayed behind me, footsteps pounding.

"Chloe!" he yelled as a figure stepped into my path.

Derek grabbed me by my shoulders, my feet flying off the ground before I'd even stopped running. He backed us up against the plastic play set. A man was sauntering our way. Another walked from the other direction. Two escape routes, both blocked. Derek glanced up at the play set, but we were against a solid wall of plastic, a crow's nest ten feet overhead. There was a fireman's pole ten feet away, but that wouldn't take us anywhere useful.

The men looked like they were in their twenties. One was tall and lean with blond hair to his collar. He wore a plaid jacket and boots, and looked like he hadn't bothered with a razor in days. His companion was shorter and beefier, swarthy with dark hair. He wore a leather jacket and sneakers.

Neither looked like the kind of guy you'd expect to hang out in a park, hassling kids for cigarettes and pocket money. Hanging out at the monster truck races, maybe, hassling girls for their names and phone numbers.

They didn't seem drunk either. They were walking straight and their eyes looked clear, glittering in the dark like . . .

I shrank back.

Derek's hands tightened on my shoulders and he leaned down, whispering, "Werewolves."

thirty-four

THE TWO WEREWOLVES STOPPED a few yards away from us.

"We're just passing through," Derek said, voice steady. "If this is your territory—"

The blond one cut him off with a laugh. "Our territory? Did you hear that, Ramon? He's asking if this is our territory."

"I know you're werewolves and I know—"

"Werewolves?" Ramon drawled. "Did he say werewolves?"

The blond lifted a finger to his lips in an exaggerated "shhh!" and jerked his head at me.

"She knows," Derek said.

"Tsk-tsk. That's against the rules, pup. You don't go telling your girlfriends what you are, even the cute ones. Didn't your daddy teach you better than that? Who is your daddy, by the way?"

Derek said nothing.

"He's a Cain," Ramon said.

"Think so?" The blond squinted, his head tilting. "Guess he could be."

"If you'd met more than one, Liam, you wouldn't be questioning. That"—he pointed at Derek—"is a Cain. Three things every Cain has in common. Big as a house. Ugly as a mud fence. Dumb as a brick."

"Then he's not—" I began before Derek shushed me.

Liam stepped closer. "Did you say something, cutie?"

"We're just passing through," Derek said. "If this is your territory, then I apologize—"

"Hear that, Ramon? He *apologizes*." Liam took another step closer. "You have no idea whose territory you're on, do you?"

"No, I don't know you. If I should, then—"

"This is *Pack* territory."

Derek shook his head. "No, the Pack is in Syracuse—"

"You think they claim one *city*?" Ramon said. "Their territory is New York *state*."

"You do know what the Pack does to trespassers, don't you, pup?" Liam said. "Your daddy must have shown you the pictures."

Derek said nothing.

"The pictures?" Liam pressed. "Of the last guy who trespassed on Pack territory?"

Still Derek said nothing.

"Your daddy didn't like you much, did he? 'Cause if he did, he would have shown you those pictures, so you didn't make the mistake you're making right now. The last time a mutt got too close to Pack turf, they carved him up with a chain saw. Then they took photos, and they passed them out as a warning to the rest of us."

My stomach lurched. I squeezed my eyes shut until the image passed. They were just making this up to scare us . . . and it was working—at least on me. My heart pounded so loudly I was sure they could hear it. Derek squeezed my shoulder, his thumb rubbing, telling me to stay calm.

"No, I haven't seen them. But thanks for the warning. I'll—"

"Who *is* your daddy?" Ramon asked. "Zachary Cain? You're darker, but you've got his look. You're about the right age, too. And that might explain why he didn't raise you right."

"Him being dead and all," Liam said. "But if it was Zack, then you should *know* to keep off Pack territory."

"Should I?" Derek said, his voice emotionless.

"Don't you know how your daddy died? Dumb ass decided to join an uprising against the Pack, got himself caught. Tortured to death, right up there in Syracuse." He looked at Ramon. "Think they used the chain saw?"

Derek cut in, "If the Pack's so bad, why are *you* on their territory?"

"Maybe we're Pack."

"Then you wouldn't be talking like you were, saying 'their' territory, what 'they' do."

Liam laughed. "Check this out. A Cain with brains. Must come from your momma."

"Do you want to know why we're here?" Ramon said. "A mission of mercy, and we're the ones praying for mercy. See, we hooked up with this kid from Down Under last year. We quickly found out why he'd left home."

"Man-eater," Liam said.

"M-man-eater?" I didn't mean to say it aloud, but it slipped out.

"It's a disgusting habit. Now hunting humans? Killing them?" He smiled. "That's always good sport. But eating? Not my style. Well, unless you count that time in Mexico—"

Derek cut him off. "So if *you're* allowed on Pack territory, I'm sure they won't bother me. I'm not causing trouble."

"Can I finish my story?" Ramon said. "So this Aussie, he's not very discreet about his bad habit. The Pack catches wind of it. Next thing you know, all three of us are on their hit list."

"The Aussie dude goes to ground," Liam said, "leaving me and Ramon holding the bag. The Pack doesn't care if we're man-eaters or not. We've had some run-ins with them before so, as far as they're concerned, we've used up our free swings. Batter out. They already caught up with Ramon once. Luckily, he got away. Or most of him."

Ramon pulled up his shirt. His side was pitted and puckered with healing scar tissue, the kind of thing I'd only seen in SFX demonstrations.

"So now you're heading up to Syracuse to talk to the Pack," I said. "Set them straight."

"That's right. Or that was the plan. But it's Russian roulette, see? We throw ourselves at their mercy, and we might never stand up again. Then we caught an amazing break."

He looked at Ramon, who nodded. For a moment, neither said a word. Liam stood there, a smirk playing on his lips, as he dragged it out.

"The break?" I asked finally, knowing Derek wouldn't.

"I had to take a piss. About two miles north of here. Pulled off the highway, got out of the car, and guess what I smelled."

"Me," Derek said.

"The answer to our prayers. A Cain?" Liam shook his head. "What did we do to get so lucky? The Pack hates Cains. Bunch of Neanderthals too stupid to keep out of trouble. If we hand them you, tell them *you* were the one snacking on humans . . ."

I felt Derek shift behind me.

"Thinking of leaving, pup? That would be rude. You bolt, we'll have to grab your girl, hold on to her until you decide to come back and hear me out."

Derek went still, but I could feel his heart thumping against my back, hear his shallow breaths as he struggled to stay calm. My hand slid into my pocket, grasping my knife. Derek squeezed my shoulder, rubbing it again.

"It's okay," he whispered. "It's okay." But his heart kept pounding, telling me it wasn't.

"Sure," Liam said. "It'll be just fine. The Pack aren't complete monsters. This poor orphaned kid just screwed up. He'll never do it again. They'll understand. He's probably got a—" He glanced at Ramon. "Fifty-fifty?"

Ramon considered it, then nodded.

Liam turned back to us. "Fifty-fifty chance of surviving. And even if he doesn't, they'll make it quick. No chain saws for you."

"Why are you telling us this?" I asked. It was like the classic James Bond scene, where the villain explains what he'll do to Bond, giving him time to think up an escape plan. Which I really hoped Derek was doing. I might not be much help—not when it came to plotting against werewolves—but I was really good at stalling.

"Good question, cutie. Why not just grab him, tie him up, toss him in our truck, and deliver him to the wolves up in Syracuse? Because the Alpha isn't stupid. If we throw him a kid who's screaming he didn't do it, he might listen. See, there's only one way this can work. If your boyfriend comes along voluntarily and confesses."

Derek snorted. "Yeah."

"You don't like that plan?"

Derek shot him a look.

Liam sighed. "All right then. Option two it is. We kill you and have some fun with your girl."

"I'll do the killing," Ramon said. "You can take the girl. She's a little young for me."

Liam grinned. "I like them young."

His gaze traveled up and down me, his look making every hair on my body rise. Derek's hands vise gripped my shoulders.

"Leave her out of this," Derek rumbled.

"Never." Liam bared his teeth. "I was almost hoping you'd say no. Sure, I'd love a scapegoat to feed the Pack. But a little cutie like that, who already knows what I am? That's . . ." He smiled. "Sweet."

He gave me a look that made me shrink back into Derek, my hand gripping the knife so hard it hurt. When Liam stepped forward again, Derek's arm shot around me, a growl vibrating up from his stomach.

Liam put his hand out toward me. When Derek tensed, he pulled back, then did it again, testing his reaction, laughing when he got one, until even Ramon started to laugh.

"Check this out," Liam said. "I think the pup's got himself a mate. Isn't that the cutest thing?" He leaned toward Derek, voice lowering. "It won't work out. It never does. Why don't you just give her to me now, let me help you get over it. Painful, but quick. It's the best way."

Derek moved me behind him. The werewolves let out a howl of laughter.

"I think he's saying no," Ramon said.

"Leave her out of this," Derek said.

Liam shook his head. "How can I do that? Look at her. So tiny and cute, big blue eyes all wide and scared." He leaned around Derek to look at me. "That hair doesn't do anything for her. I can still smell the dye. What color is it really? Blond, I bet. She looks like a blond."

His look made my insides twist.

"If I go with you, she walks away," Derek said. "Right?"

"No," I whispered.

"Course she does," Liam said.

"Derek," I whispered.

He put his hand behind him, gesturing for me to be quiet. It was a trick. He had a plan. He must have a plan.

"Here's the deal," Derek said.

"Deal?" Liam laughed. "This isn't up for negotiation, pup."

"It is if you want my cooperation. I'll go with you, but the first thing we do is get her on a bus. After I've seen her leave safely, I'm all yours."

"Uh-huh." Liam rolled back on his heels. "Is your intelligence feeling a mite insulted, Ramon?"

"Sure is." Ramon strolled up beside his friend.

"You said you'd release her—"

"And we will. Once you've done your part. Until then, she's our collateral to make sure you do. And don't worry; we'll take good care—"

Derek shot forward so fast it caught them both off guard. He grabbed Liam by the front of his shirt and whipped him into Ramon. The men went down.

"Run," Derek said.

I pulled out my knife.

"Run!"

He gave me a shove that sent me flying. I started running, but slowly, my hand on the knife as I watched over my shoulder, getting far enough so Derek would think I was safe without abandoning him.

Derek caught Ramon and whipped him against the steel fireman's pole, his head hitting with a twang.

Liam lunged for Derek. He feinted out of the way. As Ramon lay motionless on the ground, Derek and Liam faced off, circling. Liam lunged again, and Derek twisted, but Liam caught the back of his sweatshirt, yanked him off his feet, and threw him.

Derek hit the ground in a slide. Liam bore down on him, taking his time as Derek struggled to get up, wheezing and coughing, crawling along the ground. I veered to race back. Then Derek shot to his feet and broke into a run.

thirty-five

WE ZIGZAGGED THROUGH A DARK commercial district, with Liam at our heels the whole way. When we reached a town house complex, he fell back, like he didn't want to be seen chasing a couple of kids. He kept about fifty feet behind us, clearly planning to close the gap when we got to a more secluded place.

On the far side of the complex was a strip mall. When we reached it, we looked back, and he was gone. We kept going, though, until we were another two blocks away, behind a closed bakery.

I leaned against the cool brick wall, gasping for air.

"You wanted tips on self-defense?" Derek said, breathing hard.

I nodded.

"The first lesson our dad taught us? If you're up against a better fighter, the first chance you get, surprise him with your secret move . . ." He leaned down to my ear. "Run like hell."

A laugh bubbled up and my teeth stopped chattering. I took a deep breath and let myself relax against the wall.

"So he was as strong as you are?" I asked.

"Whatever those scientists tweaked, it wasn't my strength. He might have been smaller than me, but he was just as strong, and he's got a lot more fighting experience. I was seriously outclassed." He wiped off gravel embedded in his chin. "You aren't the only one who's going to need training. My dad taught me to use my strength to my advantage. Only that doesn't work fighting other werewolves."

He rolled his shoulders, then pushed sweat-sodden hair out of his eyes. "We'll catch our breath, but then we need to move. Once he figures out he lost us, he'll go back and pick up our trail."

"I'm good," I said, straightening. "Any time you want to go—"

Something moved above our heads. I looked up as Liam leaped from the rooftop. He landed on his feet right behind Derek.

"Your boy's not quite ready to leave, cutie. He has some business to finish first."

Liam hit Derek with an uppercut that sent him reeling, blood spraying from his mouth. I fumbled for my knife, but it caught in the folds of my pocket. By the time I had it out, Derek had hit Liam back and now they were both on the ground, rolling, each trying to get a grip on the other.

How many movie fight scenes had I seen? I'd even written a few. But being there, watching it, with someone I knew in serious danger, made those movie fights seem like they'd been filmed in slow motion. This was a whirlwind of fists and feet and grunts and gasps and blood. Mostly what I saw was the blood, flying, spattering, dripping, as I darted back and forth, knife in my hand.

I thought of all the times I'd been in an audience, snarking about the stupid, useless girl hovering on the sidelines of a fight, holding a weapon but doing nothing, watching the guy get pummeled. I knew I had to help Derek. I knew he was in trouble, that most of that blood and those gasps and grunts were his. I wasn't afraid to use the knife. I *wanted* to use it. But there wasn't a chance. The fists flew and the bodies flew and the kicks flew, and every time I thought I had an opening, I'd dash forward only to find Derek in my path, not Liam, and I'd pull up fast before stabbing *him*.

Then Liam got Derek on his knees, in a headlock, his free hand in Derek's hair. He yanked Derek's head back, and I saw the girl at the truck stop, her throat slashed, and I didn't stop to think whether I could do it, I ran at Liam and I drove the knife into the back of his thigh, ramming it in to the hilt.

Liam let out a howl and backhanded me. I sailed into the air, knife still clutched in my hand. I heard Derek shout my name as I hit the wall. My head cracked back against the brick. The floodlights overhead exploded into shards of light.

Derek grabbed me before I hit the ground.

"I-I'm fine," I said, pushing him away.

I got my footing, wobbled, and found it again.

"I'm fine," I said, stronger now.

I looked around. My knife had fallen beside me. I scooped it up.

Liam lay behind Derek, writhing on the ground, snarling as he tried to stanch the blood. We took off.

This time no one was chasing us, but it didn't matter. We kept running, knowing Liam would come after us the moment he was able.

"We need to get you to a bathroom," Derek said as we rounded a building.

"Me? I'm—"

"We *need* to get you to a bathroom."

I closed my mouth. Derek was obviously in shock and *he* did need a bathroom, to clean up and check the damage.

"He's going to follow our trail," I said. "We have to trick him."

"I know. I'm thinking."

I was, too, recalling every fugitive movie I'd ever seen where someone evaded tracking dogs. I slowed when I saw a huge puddle from the rain and a trash-clogged gutter. The water stretched at least ten feet across. Then, I had a better idea.

"Climb on the curb and walk along the edge," I said.

"What?"

"Just do it."

We jogged along the curb until I saw a door to a small apartment building. I led Derek over and pulled on the knob. It was locked.

"Can you break it?" I asked.

He wiped off his bloody hands, then grabbed the knob. I tried to get a better look at him to see how badly he'd been beaten, but it was too dark, and I could see only smears of blood everywhere—on his face, his hands, his sweatshirt.

He yanked the door open. We went inside, circled around a bit, then came back out.

"Now we'll follow the path we came on," I said. "Along the top of the curb. Backtrack."

When we reached the puddle, I stopped. "We're going to cut through."

Derek nodded. "So he'll reach this, keep following our trail and think we're somewhere in that apartment, not realizing we doubled back on our tracks. Smart."

Wading ankle deep through frigid water seemed to knock away the last of Derek's shock. Once we reached the other side, he took over and got us downwind so Liam couldn't smell us. Then he hustled me into a coffee shop. There were only a handful of people inside, all clustered at the counter, chatting with the server. No one even looked up as we made a beeline for the bathroom.

Derek scooted me into the men's room and locked the door. He hoisted me onto the counter before I could protest, then scrubbed his hands well, sleeves pushed to his elbows, like he was preparing for surgery.

"Uh, Derek . . . ?"

He wet a paper towel, and took my chin, lifting and wiping my face.

"Derek? I'm not hurt."

"You're covered in blood."

"But it's not mine. Honest. It's from—"

"The werewolf. I know." He picked up my hand and started cleaning it. "That's why I have to get it off."

"Derek?" I leaned down, trying to see his face. "Are you okay?"

He kept scrubbing. "There are two ways to become a werewolf. Either you're born one or you get bitten by one. If you get the saliva in your bloodstream, it's like a virus."

"Blood, too?"

"Dad says no, it's just saliva. But he could be wrong, and you've got cuts and scrapes and blood all over."

I had a *few* cuts and scrapes, and I was only flecked with blood, but I kept my mouth shut and let him clean.

As he did, I tried to check out how badly *he* was hurt. His scraped cheeks were pitted with gravel. His nose was bloodied. Broken? One eye was already darkening. Was that blood in the corner? His lip was cut and swollen. Were any teeth loose? Missing?

"Stop fidgeting, Chloe."

I couldn't help it. His injuries obviously needed more attention than mine, but there was no sense saying anything until he was done.

Finally, when he seemed to have scrubbed off every fleck of blood—and a few layers of skin—I said, "Okay, now on to you."

"Take off your jacket and sweatshirt."

"Derek, I'm *clean*. Trust me, I've never been this clean."

"You've got blood on your cuffs."

As I took off the jacket, the zipper snagged my necklace.

"It's caught—" I began.

Derek gave the jacket a tug . . . and the chain snapped, the pendant dropping. He swore and grabbed it before it hit the floor.

"—on my necklace."

He swore some more, then said, "I'm sorry."

"The girl in the alley grabbed it," I lied. "The clasp was probably weak. No biggie."

He looked down at the pendant in his hand. "Wasn't this red before?"

I hadn't taken a good look at it for a couple of days—no mirrors and the pendant had been under my shirt. I'd thought the color seemed different before, but it had changed even more now, almost blue.

"I—I think it's some kind of talisman," I said. "My mom gave it to me, to ward off bogeymen—ghosts, I guess."

"Huh." He stared at it, then shook his head and handed it back. "Better keep it on you then."

I stuffed it into my pocket, down at the bottom where it would be safe. Then I took off my sweatshirt and pushed up my sleeves. No blood had seeped through, but he still made me wash my forearms.

"Okay, *now* can we take care of the guy who was actually *in* the fight? There's a lot of blood. It seems to be mostly from your nose."

"It is."

"You got hit in the chest a few times. How are your ribs?"

"Maybe bruised. Nothing critical."

"Shirt off."

He sighed, like now *I* was the one fussing too much.

"If you want me to leave, so you can look after it yourself . . ."

"Nah."

He pulled off his sweatshirt and folded it on the counter. There wasn't any blood below his collar, where it had dripped from his nose and lip. I guess that's to be expected when you're fighting with fists, not weapons. He said his ribs on the right were sore to the touch but, to be honest, I wouldn't know bruised from broken. He was breathing fine, and that was the main thing.

"Okay, your nose. Is it broken? Does it hurt?"

"Even if it was broken, there's nothing you can do."

"Let me check your eyes."

He grumbled, but didn't resist. The bloodshot corner was already clearing, and I couldn't see any cuts. He'd have a shiner, though. When I told him that, he just grunted. I wet a fresh paper towel.

"You have dirt in your cheek. Let me—"

"No."

He caught my hand before I could touch his face. He took the cloth and leaned over the counter to wipe the dirt out himself. I tried not to wince as I watched. The gravel had gouged his cheek badly.

"You're going to need to get that checked out."

"Yeah." He looked at himself in the mirror, his expression unreadable, until he noticed me watching, then turned away and stepped back from the mirror. I handed him another wet paper towel and he cleaned his neck and collar, freckled with dried blood.

"Still got that deodorant?" he asked.

I retrieved it from my jacket pocket and set it on the counter. He kept washing.

"In the playground," I said, "when you were negotiating, you weren't serious, right? About going with them? It was a trick."

Silence stretched for way too long.

"Derek?"

He didn't look up, just reached over and got a fresh towel, his gaze averted.

"Did you hear *anything* they said?" I asked.

"About what?" His gaze still on the towel, he folded it carefully before throwing it into the trash. "Hunting humans for sport? Eating them?" The bitterness in his voice cut through me. "Yeah, I caught that part."

"That doesn't have anything to do with you."

He lifted his eyes, gaze shuttered. "No?"

"Not unless being a werewolf transforms you into a wolf *and* a redneck moron."

He shrugged and ripped off more paper towels.

"Do you want to hunt humans, Derek?"

"No."

"Do you think about it?"

"No."

"How about eating them? Do you think about that?"

He shot me a look of disgust. "Of course not."

"Do you even dream about killing people?"

He shook his head. "Just deer, rabbits." When I frowned, he went on. "For the last few years I've been dreaming of being a wolf. Running in the forest. Hunting deer and rabbits."

"Right. Like a *wolf*, not a man-eating monster."

He wet the paper towel.

"So why would you ever let these guys take you to—" I stopped. "The Pack. Is that what you wanted? Tell them you'll go, and after they release me, tell the Pack the truth and use that as a . . . an introduction? Meet them? Be with your own kind?"

"No. That doesn't matter to me. Dad says it does to other werewolves. It mattered to the other boys—they hated anyone who wasn't one of us. Me? I don't care. The only reason I'd want to meet a werewolf would be the same reason you'd want to meet a necromancer. To talk, get tips, training, whatever. Preferably from one who doesn't think hunting humans makes good sport."

"Like this Pack. They kill man-eaters and they don't seem that thrilled about man hunters. Is that what you thought? You could go to them and they'd help you? When I asked if you were listening to those two goons, that's the part I meant—about the Pack. What they'd do to you. Killing werewolves with chain saws and stuff."

Derek snorted.

"You don't believe it, then." I relaxed, nodding. "No one would do that. Cut someone up with a chain saw and pass around photos? Those guys were just trying to scare you."

"No, I'm sure there are photos. And I'm sure those guys *believe* the Pack carved up someone. But the photos must be fakes. You can do that kind of stuff with special effects and makeup, can't you?"

"Sure, but why?"

"For the same reason you just said. To scare people. Liam and Ramon think the Pack really did it, so they steer clear of its territory. Doesn't seem like a bad idea to me."

"But would you ever think of it yourself?"

That look of disgust returned. "Of course not."

"But you considered entrusting your life to people who would? Werewolves who play judge and jury for their own kind? Torture and kill other werewolves? Knowing that, you'd go to them, pretend you killed humans, and hope they'd go easy on you because you're a kid? Or were those odds okay with you? If they decided you didn't deserve to live, maybe they'd be right?"

I meant it as sarcasm. But when his answer was slow coming—much too slow—my heart hammered.

"Derek!"

He trashed the wet paper towel. "No, I don't have a death wish, okay?"

"You'd better not."

"I don't, Chloe," he said softly. "I mean it. I don't."

Our eyes locked and the panic buzzing in my head turned to something else, my heart still hammering, my throat going dry. . . .

I looked away and mumbled, "Good."

He backed up. "We gotta go."

I nodded and slid off the counter.

thirty-six

I GAVE DEREK MY JACKET and he wore it without argument—it covered the blood spatter on his sweatshirt. As we left the bathroom, the people in the coffee shop finally noticed us, but only to call out that the bathroom was for paying customers only.

The coffee shop had a post-winter clearance on promotional thermoses, emblazoned with their name, so Derek got one filled with hot chocolate, plus two paper cups. Add a half-dozen donuts and we had dinner to go.

We couldn't just waltz back to the bus station, though. Liam would still be hunting for us, maybe joined by Ramon. If they'd been following us earlier, they might know we'd gone to the bus stop and would wait for us there.

So we stayed downwind or behind buildings, then waited a half block away until we saw the bus coming. There was no sign of the werewolves. I'm sure it helped that it was just a bus stop, not a terminal—if they'd followed our trail to the flower shop, they probably hadn't figured out that we'd been there to buy bus tickets.

Yet it was only after we were on and the bus pulled away that I finally relaxed. I was on my second cup of chocolate when my eyelids started to droop.

"You should get some sleep," Derek said.

I stifled a yawn. "It won't be that long, will it? An hour and a half?"

"Close to double that. We're on the milk run."

"What?"

"The route that hits all the little towns," he said.

He took my empty cup. I shifted, trying to get comfortable. He balled up my discarded sweatshirt and put it against his shoulder.

"Go on," he said. "I don't bite."

"And from what I hear, that's a good thing."

He gave a rumbling chuckle. "Yeah, it is."

I leaned against his shoulder.

"In a few hours, you'll be in a bed," he said. "Bet *that's* a good thing, huh?"

Had anything so simple *ever* sounded so amazing? But as I thought of it, my smile faded and I lifted my head.

"What if—?"

"Andrew isn't there? Or he didn't take them in? Then we'll find Simon and we'll splurge on a cheap motel. We are getting a bed tonight. Guaranteed."

"And a bathroom."

He chuckled again. "Yeah, and a bathroom."

"Thank God." I laid my head on the sweatshirt pillow again. "What are you looking forward to?"

"Food."

I laughed. "I bet. *Hot* food. That's what I want."

"And a shower. I really want a shower."

"Well, you'll have to fight me for it. If that guy could smell my hair color, I didn't do a very good job of rinsing it out. Which may explain why it feels so gross."

"About that. The color. I didn't mean—"

"I know. You just picked something that would make me look different. And it did."

"Yeah, but it looks fake. Even those guys could tell. Wash it out, and we'll get some of that red stuff you like."

I closed my eyes. As I drifted off, Derek started humming, so softly I could barely hear it. I lifted my head.

"Sorry," he said. "I've got this stupid tune stuck in my head. No idea what it is."

I sang a few bars of "Daydream Believer."

"Uh, yeah," he said. "How'd . . . ?"

"My fault. My mom used to sing it to me when I couldn't sleep, so I was singing it last night. It's the Monkees—the world's first boy band." I glanced up at him. "And I've just lost any scrap of cool I ever possessed, haven't I?"

"At least you're not the one still singing it."

I smiled, rested my head against his shoulder, and fell asleep to his soft off-tune humming.

We got off at one of those small "milk run" stops. When Simon said Andrew lived outside New York City, I figured he meant in the Hudson Valley or Long Island, but the bus dropped us in a town whose name I didn't recognize. Derek said it was about thirty miles from the city and about a mile from Andrew's place.

Maybe it was because we knew the house was close, but that mile seemed to pass in minutes. We talked and joked and goofed around. A week ago, if someone had told me Derek *could* joke or goof around, I wouldn't have believed it. But he was at ease now, stoked even, with our destination so near.

"It's just up there," he said.

We were on a narrow road lined with trees. It wasn't really farm country. More like a rural community, with houses set way back from the road, hidden behind fences and walls and evergreens. As I squinted, Derek pointed.

"See the old-fashioned gas lamps at the end of that drive? They're on, too, which is a good sign."

We turned into the driveway—as winding and treed as the road, and seemingly just as long. Eventually we rounded a corner and the house came into sight. It was a cute little cottage, like something you'd see in an old English town, with stone walls and ivy and gardens that I'm sure would be beautiful in a month or two. Right now the most beautiful part was the light blazing from a front window.

"They're here," I said.

"*Someone's* here," Derek corrected.

When I hurried forward, he caught my arm. I looked back to see him scanning the house, his nostrils flaring. He tilted his head and frowned.

"What do you hear?" I asked.

"Nothing." He turned to survey the dark woods surrounding the house. "It's too quiet."

"Simon and Tori are probably asleep," I said, but I lowered my voice and glanced about, his anxiety contagious.

When we reached the cobblestoned walk, Derek dropped into a crouch. He lowered his head a foot from the ground. I wanted to tell him to come on, just knock on the door and we'd know whether they were here, stop being so paranoid. But I'd learned that what I would have once considered paranoia was, in this new life, sensible caution.

After a moment, he nodded and some of the tension went out of the set of his shoulders as he pushed to his feet.

"Simon's here?" I asked.

"And Tori."

He took one last slow look around, almost reluctantly, like he wanted to race to the front door as much as I did. Then we continued along the walk, the stones squeaking beneath our wet sneakers.

Derek was so busy looking out at the forest that I was the one who had to grab his arm this time. I pulled him short and directed his attention to our path.

The front door was ajar.

Derek swore. Then he took a deep breath, as if fighting off the first twitches of panic. He motioned for me to get behind him, then seemed to think better of it and waved for me to stand beside the door, against the wall.

When I was out of the way, he prodded the door open an inch. Then another. A third tap and he caught a smell, nostrils flaring. His eyebrows gathered in confusion.

After a moment, I smelled it, too. A strong bitter smell, familiar . . . "Coffee." I mouthed. He nodded. That's what it was—burned coffee.

He eased the door open wider. I pressed my back against the wall, resisting the urge to sneak a peek. I watched him instead as his gaze scanned the room beyond, his expression telling me nothing immediately caught his attention.

He motioned for me to stay put and stepped inside. Now I really fidgeted, tapping my thighs, scrunching my toes in my shoes, heart tripping. I wished I was the kind of girl who always carried a compact mirror. I could use it like they do in spy movies, to see what was happening around the corner.

When I leaned a little too close to the doorway, my inner voice piped up, telling me not to be stupid. The guy with bionic senses was better equipped for this.

Finally Derek backed out. He started to pantomime that he'd go in and look around while I stayed out here. Then, after a glance at the surrounding darkness, he seemed to think better of his first instinct. He pointed to my pocket and mimicked opening a switchblade. I took it out. He gestured for me to stay behind him, his emphatic jabs and accompanying scowl saying better than any words, *I mean it, Chloe.* I nodded.

We went inside. The front door led into a small foyer with a closet, then opened into the living room. A few pieces of mail were scattered in front of the closet door. I thought maybe it had been shoved through a mail slot, but there wasn't one, and I remembered seeing a mailbox at the end of the long drive. A small table leaned precariously against the corner, and a piece of ad mail rested on top of it.

Derek was moving into the living room. I hurried to catch up before I got "the look."

It was small and cozy, like you'd expect in a country cottage. The chairs and sofa were piled with mismatched pillows. Hand-knitted blankets were neatly folded over each back. The tops of the end tables were clear, but the shelves underneath bulged with magazines, and the two bookshelves were overflowing. One blazing lamp was the only electrical appliance—there was no TV, computer, or other techno gadget to be seen. An old-fashioned sitting room, for lighting the fire and curling up with a book.

Derek headed for the next doorway. When the floorboards creaked, he stopped short and I nearly plowed into him. He cocked his head. The house was silent. Eerily still and silent. Even if everyone had gone to bed, it shouldn't be so quiet, considering both Simon and Tori snored.

We stepped into the kitchen. The stink of burned coffee was gag-inducing. I could see the coffeemaker on the counter, the red light still on, a half-inch of sludge in the bottom, like a full pot of coffee had been simmering for at least a day. Derek walked over and turned it off.

There was a plate on the counter. On it was a piece of toast with one bite gone. An open jam jar rested beside it, the knife still inside. A coffee mug sat on the table, on top of an opened newspaper. I looked in the cup. It was two-thirds full, the cream congealing in an oily white film.

Derek waved for me to fall behind him again and he headed for the back of the house.

thirty-seven

THE HOUSE WAS BIGGER than it looked, with four doors off the rear hall.

The first led to a guest room, the bed covers pulled tight, towels folded on top of the dresser, no sign that anyone had used it recently. The next was an office with a futon couch—more room for guests, but again, no sign that any had been here in a while. Across the hall was a bathroom. It, too, looked unused, with wrapped soap and unopened shampoo on the counter, ready for guests.

At the end of the hall was the master bedroom. It was as tidy as the rest of the house, but the bed was unmade. A bathrobe lay crumpled on a chair. On one nightstand sat a half-filled glass of water and a paperback novel. There was an attached bathroom, with a rumpled bath mat and a towel draped over the shower stall. I squeezed the towel. Dry.

Back in the hall, Derek dropped again to sniff.

"They were here," he said.

"Simon and Tori?"

He nodded.

"They didn't sleep here last night, though," I said. "No one's used this room in a while.

He nodded again.

"Can you smell anyone else?" I asked.

"Just Andrew. I'll check the front again."

He walked off, apparently having decided that the house was empty, so it was safe to leave me behind. I met up with him back in the kitchen as I examined the toast. He bent to sniff it.

"Andrew?" I asked.

He nodded.

I walked to the table and looked at the newspaper. "It's like he was reading this, drinking his coffee, and waiting for the toast to pop. He puts jam on it, takes a bite and then . . ."

And then *what*? That was the question.

I picked up the coffeepot. "It's been on since at least this morning."

He walked over and eyed the pot. "Rings show it was almost full. To evaporate that much, it's been on since yesterday."

"Before Simon and Tori arrived."

Derek didn't answer. He was staring out the window over the sink, his gaze blank.

"Is this . . . like your dad?" I asked. "When he disappeared?"

He nodded.

"Were there any other scents at the door?"

He turned slowly then, his attention shifting back to me. "Yeah, but there are lots of reasons why someone would come to the door. None seem to go past it. No recent trails, at least."

"The table in the front hall looks like someone bumped into it and the mail fell off. From the looks of this place, Andrew doesn't seem the type to leave a mess like that."

"No, he's not."

"Something happened at the door, then. Someone came or someone called and Andrew left in a hurry."

Like their dad. I didn't say it again—I already knew he was thinking it.

I circled the kitchen, looking for more clues. Everything was so neat that any disruption would stick out, and I couldn't see any.

"It's definitely breakfast for one," I said. "And there's no sign that Simon or Tori used the spare bedrooms or guest bath. That would suggest that whatever happened here, it happened before they arrived."

Derek nodded, like he'd already come to this conclusion.

I opened cupboards, all perfectly ordered inside. "It seems like Simon did exactly what we did—came in, walked around, realized something had happened and then . . ."

And then what? That question again.

"If they left, there'll be a second trail outside," Derek said as he strode to the kitchen door. "I'll see if they went back to the road or—"

"Or maybe this will help." I snatched a drawing hung among the bills and notes on the fridge. "This is Simon's work, isn't it?"

It wasn't as obvious as the message he'd left in the warehouse—a comic-book character would stand out too much on Andrew's fridge. Simon trusted Derek to recognize his work even when it was a simple sketch.

"Yeah, it's his."

"It's someone swimming. I have no idea what it means but—"

"Pool house," Derek called back, already striding toward the rear of the house.

I scrambled after him, but by the time I reached the door, it was already shutting. I stepped out into the pitch-black yard, huge trees closing in on all sides, blocking the moonlight. Derek popped from the shadows, making me yelp. He waved me back inside and shut the door.

"He's not there?" I said.

"Running outside might not be such a smart idea."

He took the picture again and studied it, like he was looking for any clue that Simon hadn't drawn it willingly.

"Front door," he said. "We'll go the long way. Sneak up."

With an impatient wave for me to stay close, he started off. I took out my switchblade again and followed. It was a slow trip to the pool house. Derek stopped every few feet to look, listen, and sniff. It was too dark for me to do anything except stay as close as I could. With his dark clothing and quiet walk, that wasn't easy; and every so often I had to reach out and brush the back of his jacket to reassure myself he was still in front of me.

Finally we could see a clearing ahead and, in it, a pale building. Then came a shrill whistle.

"Simon," Derek said.

He broke into a jog, leaving me scrambling after him. Before he reached the door, it clicked open.

"Hey, bro," Simon whispered. He thumped Derek's back, the nylon jacket crinkling. "Where's Chloe?"

"Right behind—" Derek turned and saw me stumbling along. "Sorry."

"Forgot not everyone has your night vision?" Simon thumped him again and strode past, greeting me with a one-armed hug and a whispered, "Good to see you."

He squeezed my upper arm, then started to say something before Derek cut him off with a hissed, "Inside."

We stepped through the door into the glow of a lantern. Noticing that, Derek looked around sharply.

"Relax," Simon said. "No windows. You didn't notice the light, did you?"

Derek grunted and walked farther in. As he'd said, it was a pool house, filled with neatly stacked and organized pool and yard supplies. Simon and Tori had set up two lawn chairs. Wrappers and Diet Coke cans covered a nearby tabletop. I glanced around for Tori and found her asleep on an inflated raft.

"The longer she sleeps, the better," Simon said. "It's a good thing you two showed up because another day alone with her?" He pantomimed throttling.

"I saw that," said a sleepy voice. Tori lifted her head. "Believe me, the feeling is mutual."

She sat up and raked her hair back, stifling a yawn. "There's nothing like spending a whole day alone with a guy to make a girl say, 'What was I *thinking*?'"

"At least one good thing came of it," Simon murmured.

Tori looked at me. "He *left* me here. Alone. Unarmed. At the mercy of whoever took his dad's friend—"

"First, from what I hear of your spells, you're a helluva lot better armed than I am," Simon said. "Second. Left you? Excuse me? You refused to come along."

"Because I didn't see the point. Why go racing off looking for the bad guys? I'm sure if we stick around here, they'll find us soon enough. The smart thing to do would have been to get as far from this place as possible. But no, poor Derek and Chloe might not find us. Hello?" She waved at Derek. "Human bloodhound. He'll find us."

Simon leaned down to me and whispered, "It was fun."

"And then—" Tori continued.

I cut in, "And then we remembered that we called a moratorium on bickering and if we have any issues to discuss, we should wait until we're someplace safe."

"We need to discuss a game plan, too," Derek said, "in case this happens again. Right now, the important thing is Andrew." He turned to Simon. "What did you find when you got here?"

Exactly what we had, as Simon explained. The front door had been ajar, and they'd left it that way to warn us to enter with caution. They'd walked through the house, and when Simon realized it looked like when his dad had vanished, they got out of there quickly. Simon left the note, and found the keys, and they retreated to the pool house.

"Do you have the keys?" Derek asked.

Simon handed them to him.

Derek flipped through. "Looks like a full set. Is the car still in the garage?"

Simon swore under his breath. "Totally forgot to check."

"We'll look, but I'll bet it is."

"Car?" Tori walked over. "We have a car?"

"No, we do not—" Derek began.

"You're sixteen, right?" Tori said.

"I turned sixteen two months ago, locked up in Lyle House, meaning I don't have a license and even if I did—"

"But you can drive, right?" she said. "You look old enough that no cop would pull you over as long as you keep to the speed limit, don't run a yellow—"

"I'm not stealing a car from a guy who has disappeared and may be reported missing at any moment. My only point about the car was that if it's still here, Andrew didn't drive off. Someone took him. We just don't know whether it was with his permission."

"So what are we going to do?"

"Presume he was kidnapped and get as far from here as we can, in case they come back."

Tori turned to Simon. "See? We can get some sleep, then we're taking *my* advice—"

"I mean right now," Derek said.

He was right—the sooner we left, the better—but I couldn't help feeling my shoulders slump at the thought of hitting the road again. Walking again. Eating energy bars and sleeping in alleys again. I tried not to picture the house, warm and cozy, with beds, food, showers . . .

Feeling Derek's gaze on me, I straightened. "I'm good."

"Of course she is," Tori said. "Our perky little—" This time, she cut herself off. "Okay, sorry, but you know what I mean, guys. As long as Chloe can walk, she's not going to admit she needs to rest."

"I slept on the bus."

"For about an hour," Derek said. "And none last night."

"What happened last—?" Simon stopped. "Later, I know. But Tori has a point. Chloe needs to rest and she's not the only one. We're beat. It's already late. If we can rest here safely, we should all recharge our batteries. Otherwise they're going to quit when we need them most."

I could tell Derek wanted us to move out, but after a moment's consideration, he waved us to the door. "We're up at dawn, gone a half-hour later. If you aren't ready, you stay behind. Any light that isn't on, leave it off. Stay away from all the windows. . . ."

thirty-eight

WE ALL SHOWERED. Having two bathrooms made that quick. While I was waiting, I tried to tie a knot in my necklace chain—I didn't like keeping the pendant in my pocket. When that didn't work, I looked for string and instead found a piece of ribbon and tied it on that.

After the showers, we ate. Andrew had a lot of convenience food—his housekeeping skills didn't seem to extend to cooking. We found decent frozen meals, cooked them in the microwave, and they tasted so good—better than any gourmet dinner.

Simon organized our watch shifts as we ate. Derek insisted on taking the first, and the rest of us headed to bed, with Tori and me sharing the spare room and Simon on the office futon. No one felt right sleeping in Andrew's bed.

I made a bathroom stop first. When I came out, I saw the photos along the hall, and stopped at a shot of Simon and Derek. Maybe twelve, they were roasting marshmallows over a campfire. Simon looked like Simon, with his spiked dark-blond hair and big grin as he showed off his flaming marshmallow for the camera.

Derek looked different. The picture had been taken before puberty hit. His skin was clear and he had a shock of black hair, still falling into his eyes. He was taller than Simon, but not as much, and he was thinner—he hadn't started filling out yet. He still wasn't magazine cover material, but he was the kind of guy that, at that age myself, I might have stolen a glance at across the classroom and thought he was kind of cute, with really nice eyes.

"That was taken out back here."

I jumped. Simon laughed and shook his head.

"Yes," I said. "I'm still jumpy. So this was here?" I pointed at the picture.

He nodded. "The summer before Dad and Andrew had their fight, I think. There's a clearing where Derek and I camped out." He paused, thinking. "I wonder if Andrew kept all that gear. I'm sure Tori isn't the backpacking type, but . . ."

"If it means no more sleeping in rat-infested buildings, she'll go for it."

"I'll talk Derek into giving us time to look for the camping gear tomorrow. I know you're exhausted, so I won't keep you up chatting, but you will tell me about the adventures I missed this time?"

I managed a tired smile. "Sure." I started to turn away, then stopped. "You've got your watch alarm set, right? You'll get me up after your shift?"

"I doubt either of us will be taking a turn. Derek only let me organize shifts because he wasn't in the mood to argue. I'll go out at three, but he won't give up his post."

"He needs sleep, too."

"Agreed, and I *will* hassle him. But he doesn't like us being here and there's no way he'll let someone without superhero strength and senses stand guard. The best thing we can do is find those tents and sleeping bags in the morning, get him to the nearest campsite, and let him sleep then."

I got a few steps away before he said, "Chloe?"

I turned. The hall was dark, lit only by the living room light behind him, throwing his face into shadow.

"Was Derek . . . okay with you today? I know he was getting up in your face before we left Buffalo and I was worried. You guys seem fine now. . . ."

"We are."

When he said nothing, I said, "Really. We got along great, actually. A nice change."

I couldn't see his expression, but could feel his gaze on me; then he said softly, "Good." A pause and a more emphatic, "That's good. I'll see you tomorrow then. We'll talk."

We headed for the bedrooms.

Once again, sleep and I weren't on speaking terms. My brain was too busy playing in the land of nightmares.

I kept thinking of the woods surrounding the house. I'd hear a branch scrape the window and leap up, certain it was a bat and, of course, then start thinking of zombie bats, trapped in their crushed bodies. . . .

After a Disneyfied dream of prancing through the forest, leading a singing trail of undead critters, I bolted awake, sweating, and decided it was time to give up the ghost . . . so to speak. I got out of bed and checked the clock. It was almost five, meaning Simon had been right about Derek not letting us take a turn. I got up, grabbed a coat from the front closet, and headed for the kitchen.

"Chloe," Derek's growl vibrated from the forest long before I could see him. "I told Simon I want you guys to sleep—"

He stopped as the smell of sausages drifted his way. I could imagine him sniffing the air, stomach rumbling, and I tried not to laugh.

I found him sitting on the grass in a clearing. I held out a lawn chair and a plate of sausages in buns.

"I know you won't come in, so you might as well be comfortable. Unless you aren't hungry . . ."

He took the sausages. I pulled a bottle of Coke from my pocket, then shucked the coat and passed them over.

"You should be sleeping," he said.

"I can't."

"Sure you can. Just close your eyes and . . ." He studied me, then grunted, "What's up?"

I looked out over the forest. The air smelled very faintly of woodsmoke, reminding me of the photo.

"I saw a picture of you and Simon. He said you guys had a camping spot out here. Is this it?"

"So we're changing the subject?" He shook his head, set up the chair, sat, and looked at me expectantly for a moment, "Yeah. This is the spot."

"It smells like someone else had a campfire going earlier tonight. Someone burning leaves? Or kids getting a jumpstart on summer?"

"So we're definitely changing the subject?"

I paused, then lowered myself to the grass. "It's just . . . this." I waved at the forest. "I'm worried that I'm going to, you know, in my sleep . . ."

"Raise another corpse?"

I nodded.

"That's why you couldn't sleep last night, isn't it? I thought about that later, on the bus. You were afraid she was buried out there—the girl you saw get killed."

I nodded. "I was worried that if I drifted off, I'd keep thinking about her, about summoning her, like with the homeless guy. I can't control my dreams. And I figured there was a good chance she *was* buried out there, never found."

"So if you did raise her, and we left her body there to be found, that wouldn't be such a bad thing, would it?"

"Maybe . . . if I knew I could safely raise her and release her quickly. But what if I . . . What if she didn't dig her way out and I never realized I'd raised her and . . ."

I turned to look into the forest again.

"I'll get you a chair, too," he said.

I protested that I wasn't staying, but he just kept going. When he returned, he came around the other way.

"I circled the house," he said. "If there was a body on the property, I would have smelled it. The wind's good tonight. You're safe."

"It's not . . . it's not just people I'm worried about."

I finally told him about raising the bats in the warehouse.

"I didn't summon them," I said. "I didn't even know I could do that with animals, that they had a soul, ghost, spirit, whatever. If I go to sleep and dream of any kind of summoning, there's got to be a dead animal somewhere nearby. I could raise it and never know. I'd just walk away and leave it trapped in its corpse for—" I took a deep breath. "Okay, I'm freaking out, I know."

"You've got a reason to."

"It's not like I'd do it intentionally, and maybe that should make a difference but . . ."

"It's still not something you want to do."

I nodded.

He took a gulp of the Coke, then capped it, stuck it into his pocket, and stood. "Let's go."

"Where?"

"I'll hear anyone who comes near the property. So there's no need to sit here doing nothing. We might as well hunt up some dead animals for you."

I scowled. "That's not funny."

"I'm not being funny, Chloe. You're worried because you don't understand why it's happening and how it works and how to stop it. We can experiment and get some answers. It's not like either of us has anything better to do for the next couple of hours."

thirty-nine

DEREK CROUCHED BESIDE A FLAT, matted creature that had once scampered through the forest and now looked like it had been run over with a steamroller.

I tapped it with my toe. "I was thinking of something with more . . ."

"Remaining body parts?" he said.

"With more recognizable features, so I'll know what I'm summoning. But, yes, more remaining body parts would help, too."

"That was a mole. I think there's a rabbit over there somewhere."

"You can smell everything, can't you? That's cool."

He looked at me, brows lifted. "Being able to find decomposing animals is cool?"

"Well, it's a . . . unique talent."

"One that will get me far in life."

"Hey, someone has to find and clear away the road kill. I bet it pays well."

"Not well enough."

He stood and inhaled, then walked a few more feet, stooped, and prodded a chunk of rabbit fur.

"I'm definitely thinking something with more body parts," I said. "Like a head."

He gave a snort of a laugh. "It's probably around here somewhere, but I suppose you want the parts *attached*, too." He paused. "I wonder what would happen if—"

"Keep wondering, because that's one experiment I'm not conducting."

"We'll find something."

He walked a few more feet, then stopped again, shoulders going rigid as he surveyed the forest.

I moved closer and whispered, "Derek?"

Another slow scan of the woods, then he shook his head and resumed walking.

"What was it?" I asked.

"Voices, but they're far off. Probably whoever had that campfire."

Despite the dismissal, he slowed every few steps to listen.

"Are you sure it's okay?" I asked.

"Yeah."

"Should I be quiet?"

"We're fine."

After another few strides, I cleared my throat. "About the other night. When I said I didn't know that having a dead body around was a problem. Well, obviously, it happened after the bat thing so . . ."

I waited for him to fill in the blank, but he kept walking.

"I knew it was a problem," I went on. "I knew I should say so. I just didn't want to . . . overreact, I guess. When I raised that man, I wanted to admit it, about the bats, but . . ."

"You didn't need me telling you you'd done something stupid when you already knew it." He pulled back a low branch for us. "Yeah, you need to be more careful. We all do. But you don't need me making it worse by getting on your case. I know that."

He looked at me for a moment, then his nostrils flared and his face lifted to catch the breeze. He waved for us to turn left. "And about me not figuring out I was ready to start Changing? I lied. With the itching and the fever and the muscle spasms, I knew that's what it had to mean. I just . . .

Same as you, I didn't want to overreact and freak out Simon. I figured I could handle it."

"We all need to be careful. Especially now, knowing what they did, the . . ."

I trailed off, feeling the now familiar bubble of rising panic, that part of me that couldn't stop reading those words. *Genetic modification. Uncontrollable powers.* How bad it would get, how far it would go, how—?

"Chloe?"

I bumped into his arm and saw that he'd stopped, and was looking down at me.

"We'll figure it out," he said, his voice soft. "We'll handle it."

I glanced away. I was shaking so hard my teeth chattered. Derek put his fingers on my chin and turned me to face him again.

"It's okay," he said.

He looked down at me, fingers still on my chin, face over mine. Then he let his hand fall and turned away with a gruff, "There's something over here."

It took me a moment to follow. When I did, I found him crouched beside a dead bird.

"Is this better?" he asked.

I bent. The corpse looked so normal that it seemed to be only sleeping. My conscience could live with temporarily returning the spirit to this body. I started to kneel, then leaped up.

"It's not dead."

"Sure it is." He nudged it with his toe.

"No, it's mov—" A maggot crawled from under the bird's wing and I stumbled back. "Could we get one without hitchhikers?"

Derek shook his head. "Either it's going to be like this, with maggots, or too decomposed for maggots." He bent to peer at it. "They're first stage blowfly larvae, meaning the bird hasn't been dead more than—" His cheeks flushed and his voice lowered another octave. "And that's more than you need to know, isn't it?"

"Right, you did a science fair project on this, didn't you?" When he looked up sharply, I said, "Simon told me about it when I was checking out that corpse in the abandoned building. He said not to mention it to you, though, because you only came in second."

He grunted. "Yeah. I'm not saying mine was the best, but it was better than the winner's, some eco-fuel crap." He paused. "That's not what I meant. There's nothing wrong with stuff like that, but the kid used junk science. Got the environmental vote. I won the people's choice award, though."

"Because, apparently, people are more interested in checking out maggoty dead things than saving the environment."

A short laugh. "Guess so."

"Back to this particular maggoty dead thing . . . I guess I should get to work, trying to make it *un*dead."

I knelt beside it.

"We'll start with—" Derek began.

He stopped when I opened my eyes.

"Shut up, right?" he said. "I was going to make some suggestions for a, uh, testing regimen, but I guess you can do that."

"Having only the faintest clue what a testing regimen is, I'll save myself the embarrassment and graciously turn that part over to you. When it comes to the summoning, though . . ."

"Shut up and let you work." He sat cross-legged. "You said with the bats, you were summoning a ghost you couldn't see. So it was kind of a general summoning. You should start by doing a specific one. That'll tell us whether you still raise a nearby animal if you're trying to raise a specific person."

"Got it. I'll try Liz."

I figured if we were being all scientific about this, I should use some kind of control measures. I'd start with the lowest "power setting"—just mentally saying "Hey, Liz, are you there?" I did that, then checked the bird. No response.

I pictured Liz and called again. Nothing. I imagined pulling Liz through. Nothing. I tried harder, still clearly focusing on her image. I kept checking the bird and kept looking—hoping—for any sign of Liz herself.

"How hard should I try?" I asked.

"As hard as you can."

I thought of what the demi-demon had said about raising zombies in a cemetery two miles away. I was sure she'd been exaggerating. And yet . . .

"Try as hard as you're comfortable with," Derek said when I hesitated. "We can always do more another time."

I ramped it up a little. Then a little more. I was closing my eyes after checking the bird again when Derek said, "Stop."

My eyes flew open. The bird's wing was twitching. I stood and moved toward it.

"It could just be the maggots," he said. "Hold on."

He got up, took a branch and was reaching it toward the bird when his chin shot up. His eyes narrowed, and his nostrils flared.

"Der—?"

A distant crack cut me off. He lunged and hit me in a football tackle. I toppled over. Something stung my upper arm right above the bandages, then whizzed past as we dropped. It hit the ground behind us with a *thwack* and a geyser of dirt. Derek quickly lifted off me, but stayed over me, like a shield . . . or more likely making sure I didn't jump up. He glanced over his shoulder.

"You okay?" he asked. As he turned to me, his nostrils flared again. "You're hurt."

He plucked my sleeve. There was a hole clear through a fold in it.

"I think they shot a dart," I said. "It grazed me. It landed over—"

He'd already found the spot. What he dug out, though, wasn't a tranquilizer dart.

forty

As Derek held up the bullet, my heart slammed against my chest. I took a deep breath and pushed aside thoughts of the Edison Group.

"Are we on Andrew's property?" I asked.

He nodded.

"But it could still be hunters."

Another nod. He shifted off me and surveyed the forest. All was quiet.

"Crawl that way," he whispered, "into the thicker bushes. I'll get closer and take a look—"

The long grass at our feet erupted. Derek threw himself over me again with a whispered "Stay down!" like I had a choice, with a two-hundred-pound guy over me.

A horrible squawking echoed through the forest, and we looked down to see the dead bird on its feet, wings drumming the ground. I'll point out, with some satisfaction, that I wasn't the only one who jumped.

Derek scrambled off me. "Release—"

"I know."

I crawled to the other side of the clearing, far enough that I didn't need to worry about the bird trying to jump on me.

"Hear that?" a voice called between the bird's cries.

As the bird screamed, I concentrated on releasing its spirit, but all I could think was *Shut it up. Shut it up!* Another crack. We both hit the ground. A bullet zoomed over our heads, hitting a tree trunk in a rain of bark.

Still lying on my stomach, I closed my eyes. Derek grabbed my arm.

"I'm trying," I said. "Just give me—"

"Forget it. Come on."

He propelled me forward, hunched over, moving fast. Behind us, the bird continued to scream, covering the sound of our retreat. When it stopped, we did. I could hear something thrashing in the undergrowth—the bird or our pursuers, I couldn't tell. After a moment, the bird started again, its cries taking on an edge of panic that made my skin crawl.

I closed my eyes to release it.

"Not yet," Derek said.

He led me farther, until we found a cluster of bushes. We managed to get into the middle of them and hunkered down. The bird's cries subsided, but I could hear it moving.

"What the—?"

It was a man's voice, cut off by a *pfft* that anyone who watches crime movies recognizes as the sound of a silenced gun. I was pretty sure they didn't make silencers for hunting rifles . . . and that hunters didn't carry sidearms.

The bird's cries got louder. And the man's curses got louder still. A couple more silenced shots, then a crack, like he'd tried the rifle, too. The bird's screams turned to an awful gurgling.

"Jesus, what is that thing? I practically blew its head off and it's still alive."

Another man answered with a harsh laugh. "Well, I guess that answers our question, doesn't it? The Saunders girl found those boys."

I glanced at Derek, but his gaze was fixed straight ahead, in the direction of the voice. I closed my eyes and focused on the bird. After a moment, those pathetic sounds finally stopped.

When another squawk came, I squeezed my eyes shut, certain it meant

I hadn't released the bird's spirit after all. But it was only a radio. Derek strained to listen. I couldn't catch most of what was said, just enough to confirm that these men were indeed an Edison Group security team.

They'd found us. And they weren't bothering with tranquilizer darts anymore. Why would they? We were dangerous experimental subjects who'd escaped twice. Now they didn't need an excuse to do what they'd have been happy to do all along: abandon rehabilitation and "remove" us from their study. The only one who might have fought to keep me alive was Aunt Lauren, a traitor. Easier to kill us here and bury the bodies, far from Buffalo.

"Simon!" I hissed. "We need to warn him and—"

"I know. The house is through there. We'll circle."

"But we can't go back to the house. That's the first place they'll go, if they aren't there already."

His eyes dipped away, his jaw setting.

"I—I guess we have to try, don't we?" I said. "Okay, if we're careful—"

"No, you're right," he said. "I'll go. You wait here."

I grabbed the back of his coat as he crawled forward. "You can't—"

"I need to warn Simon."

"I'll come—"

"No, you stay here." He started turning, then stopped. "Better yet, get farther away. There's a road about a half mile north." He pointed. "You can't miss it. It's an easy walk—Simon and I used to do it all the time. When I give the signal, take off. Get to the road and hide. I'll find you there."

He started walking away. I wanted to argue, but knew there was no use—nothing would stop him from going back for Simon. And he was right not to want me along. I'd only be one more person to protect. Best to wait for his signal and—

Derek's earsplitting whistle cut through the night. Then he whistled again, and a third time and I knew that's what he'd meant by "signal," not just for me, but for Simon, trying to wake him up.

It was loud enough to wake *everyone* up—and to tell the whole security team exactly where—

The thought stuttered in my head. Then I started cursing him, mentally calling him every name I could think of, including a few I didn't realize I knew.

He knew his whistles would draw the attention of the entire Edison Group team. That's why he'd done it, rather than something subtle like throwing stones at Simon's window. He was drawing their attention to himself, giving Simon and me a chance to get away.

I wanted to scream at him. Those men had guns. Real *guns*. And they weren't afraid to use them. If they did take his bait—

He'll be fine. He gave you a chance to escape. Now use it. Move!

I forced myself out of the bushes and set out at a slow, crouching jog, picking my way over open area and avoiding the noisy undergrowth. When I heard footsteps, I glanced around for cover and, seeing none, hit the ground.

Two figures passed just ten feet away. Both were dressed head to foot in camouflage, like army snipers. Even their hats had net screens covering their faces.

A radio squealed, and a man's voice came over it. "Beta team?"

One of the two—a woman by her voice—responded.

The man continued. "He's over here. Head in from the east and we'll surround—"

A rifle shot knocked my heart into my throat. The crash of undergrowth sounded over the radio.

"Did you get him?" the woman asked.

"Not sure. That was Charlie team. Signing off. Get over here."

Another shot. More distant crashing. I was sure my heart was pounding loud enough for the two to hear, but they kept going, heading for that distant racket. Heading for Derek.

Beta, Charlie . . . I'd seen enough war movies to know that meant there were at least three pairs out here. Six armed security agents. Enough to surround Derek and then—

Just keep going. He'll find a way out. He's got super-powers, remember?

None of which would help him against six trained professionals. None of which would stop a bullet.

I waited until the two were gone, then I scanned the treetops. The last few summers at drama camp, we'd had Survivor days. In most athletic challenges, I'd been a washout, but there'd been one where being small seemed to be an advantage . . . that and having a few old gymnastics trophies on my shelf.

I raced to the nearest tree with low branches, grabbed one, and tested it. If Derek swung onto it, he'd crash back to the ground, but I was able to get up and onto the next, sturdier one with the branch giving no more than a faint groan of complaint.

I kept climbing until I was confident that the canopy of new leaves hid me. Then I got into a secure position and whistled—a thin, reedy screech that would have Derek rolling his eyes.

What makes you think they're even going to hear that?

I whistled again.

And even if they do, why bother with you? They know where Derek is. They'll stick with him.

The distant tramp of boots from the departing pair stopped. A murmur of voices. Then the footsteps returned my way.

Now what are you going to do? You'd better have a plan or—

I shushed the inner voice and gave another, softer whistle, just to be sure they heard me.

The radio crackled.

"Alpha? This is Beta. We think we heard the Saunders girl. She's trying to contact Souza. Do you have him yet?"

I strained to hear the reply but couldn't make it out.

"We'll swing by and help as soon as we have her."

Meaning they didn't have Derek.

Or they have him; they just need help controlling him.

The radio sounded again, another transmission I couldn't make out. The woman signed off, then said to her partner, "They want you to go back and help with the boy. I can handle the Saunders girl."

Well, that didn't work out so well, did it?

The man took off. I held still as the woman began searching for me. She passed my tree by at least a dozen feet and kept going. I waited until I was sure she wasn't going to return on her own, then knocked my foot against the tree trunk.

She turned. For a moment, she just stood there, shining her flashlight beam in a full circle. I prepared to knock again, if she walked away, but she headed toward me, moving slowly, beam skimming the ground, pausing at every bush or clump of tall grass.

When she walked under my tree, I tightened my hold and flattened myself against the branch. As I moved the foot I'd kicked with, it brushed the tree trunk. A chunk of bark fell at the woman's feet.

She shone the beam down at it.

Please, don't. Please, please—

The flashlight beam swung up into the branches.

I dropped. I didn't think about the stupidity of dropping onto an armed woman probably twice my size. I just let go and rolled off the branch, that inner voice screaming *What are you doing?!* . . . in far less polite language.

I hit the woman. We both went down, her cushioning my fall. I leaped up, ignoring the squeaks of protest from my jolted body. I yanked out my knife and—

The woman lay at the foot of the tree, her head a few inches from it. She had a net veil hanging from her hat but through it I could see that her eyes were closed, and her mouth lolled open. She must have hit the trunk and been knocked out. I resisted the urge to check, grabbed her radio, and spun, searching for the gun. It wasn't there. No rifle and no pistol . . . or not one I could see. I took a good look around to see if she'd dropped it. Nothing.

Either her partner had it or she had one hidden under her jacket. I paused, wanting to check, but was afraid of rousing her. One last look, then I snatched up the fallen flashlight and ran.

forty-one

I WAS SURE I WAS heading in the direction Derek told me, so all the security teams should be behind me. But after less than a minute, I heard the tramp of boots again. I dropped and covered my radio. I turned the volume all the way down, even though it had been silent since I'd taken it.

I crawled into the nearest patch of brush and lay on my stomach. The footsteps seemed to be going parallel to me, neither approaching nor retreating.

"Tell me how a full squad of us can lose four teenagers in less than twenty acres of woods," a man's voice said. "Davidoff is not going to be happy."

Another man answered, "With any luck, he'll never find out. We've still got an hour before daylight. Plenty of time. How far can they get?"

They continued walking and talking, their voices and steps receding. When they were gone, I started creeping out, then stopped. If all four of us were out here, should I be heading for safety? Or trying to find the others?

Um, if you go to that safe spot, where Derek expects you to be, you won't have to worry about finding them. They'll come to you.

What if they need my help?

You accidentally knocked out one woman and suddenly you're Rambo?

It felt cowardly getting myself to safety, but my inner voice had a point—if that's where Derek expected me to be, then I'd better head there and meet him.

But I *did* feel a bit like Rambo—switchblade in one hand, radio in the other, flashlight jammed in my waistband—as I stealthily crept through the thick woods.

Yeah, as long as you don't trip and impale yourself on your own knife.

I closed the blade.

"Chloe?" a female voice whispered.

I whirled so fast my foot slid on the soft ground. "Tori?"

I squinted into the night. The woods here were so dark I could only make out shapes that could as easily be trees and bushes as people. My fingers touched the flashlight, but I pulled back and kept looking.

"Tori?"

"Shhh. This way, hon."

The endearment made the hair on my neck rise.

"Aunt Lauren?"

"Shhh. Follow me."

I caught a glimpse of a figure. It was as faint as the voice, and all I could see was a pale shirt glowing ahead. I didn't move. It sounded like Aunt Lauren and the figure was her size, but I couldn't be sure and I wasn't running after her like a little kid, so desperate to believe that I raced into a trap.

I took out my flashlight and clicked it on, but she was darting between trees, and it was impossible to make out more than her shape and shirt. Then she glanced back and I got just a glimpse of a profile, a swing of blond hair—an imperfect view, but enough for my gut to say *that's her.*

She waved for me to hurry, then veered left into deeper forest. I followed, still cautious, no matter what my gut said. I was jogging past a patch of bushes when a figure lunged out. Before I could spin, it grabbed me, a hand clamping over my mouth, cutting short my yelp.

"It's me," Derek whispered.

He tried pulling me into the bushes, but I resisted.

"Aunt Lauren," I said. "I saw Aunt Lauren."

He gave me a look like he must have heard me wrong.

"My aunt. She's here. She's—" I pointed in the direction she'd gone. "I was following her."

"I didn't see anyone."

"She was wearing a light shirt. She ran past—"

"Chloe, I've been right here. I saw you coming. No one else ran—" He stopped short, realizing what he was saying. If I'd seen her and he hadn't . . .

My chest seized. "No . . ."

"It was an illusion," he said quickly. "A spell to trap you. My dad's done stuff like that and . . ." He rubbed his hand over his mouth, then said, firmer, "That's what it was."

I'd wondered the same thing, but now, hearing it from his mouth, when it should have supported my own doubts, all I could think was: a ghost. I saw Aunt Lauren's ghost. The forest blurred, and his hand on my arm seemed the only thing holding me up.

"Chloe? It was a spell. It's dark. You didn't get a good look."

All true. Totally true. And yet . . . I shook it off and straightened, pulling from his grasp. When he hesitated, hand out, ready to grab me if I collapsed, I stepped away.

"I'm fine. So what's the plan?"

"We'll wait here—"

Footsteps sounded. We pushed into the bushes and crouched. A flashlight beam skimmed the trees like a searchlight.

"I know you kids are back here," a man said. "I heard voices."

Derek and I stayed still. His shallow breathing hissed at my ear. My back was against him and I could feel the thump of his heart. The flashlight beam kept coming, cutting through the darkness. It passed over our bushes. Then it stopped, came back, and shone full in our faces.

"Okay, you two. Come out of there."

I could only see a veiled figure silhouetted behind the flashlight's glare.

"Come out," he said again.

Derek's breath warmed my ear. "When I say run, run." Then, louder, "Put the gun down and we'll come out."

"It is down."

With the light shining in our eyes and the man hidden behind it, there was no way to know if he was telling the truth.

He lifted his free hand and waved it. "See, no gun. Now come—"

The man dropped forward, like he'd been hit from behind. The flashlight tumbled to the ground, beam arcing through the air. Derek shot past me and tackled the man as he started to rise. Simon stepped from the darkness behind the man, hands raised for another knock-back spell.

"Run," Derek said, holding the struggling man. When Simon and I hesitated, he snarled, "Run!"

We took off but kept checking behind. We could hear the sounds of a fight, but it was a short one; and before we'd gone far, Derek was behind us. When we slowed, he thumped us both in the back, telling us to keep moving. The moon through the trees gave us enough light to see where we were going.

"Tori?" I whispered to Simon.

"We split up. She—"

Derek motioned us to silence. We ran until we saw the glittering light of houses through the trees and knew we must be approaching the back road. We took another few strides. Then Derek thumped us again, this one a hard whack between the shoulder blades that knocked us off our feet. He landed between us. When we tried to rise, he pushed us back down.

Simon lifted his dirt-streaked face and rubbed his jaw. "I kinda like my teeth. All of them."

Derek shushed him and twisted around to lie on his stomach, facing the other way. We did the same. I followed his gaze as it traveled over the forest, until it stopped and I heard footsteps.

Derek tensed, ready to leap up, but they were still a good distance away when they stopped, footsteps replaced by the murmur of voices. The radio in my pocket chirped. I took it out and checked the volume.

Simon looked past Derek and mouthed. "Radio?" then pointed toward the voices, asking if it was one of theirs.

I nodded.

"Sweet," he mouthed, then shot me a thumbs-up that made me blush. Derek glanced over with a nod and a grunt that I interpreted to mean, *Good job . . . as long as you didn't do anything stupid to get it.*

"I found Alpha one," a man's voice said, so low I had to strain to hear him.

Simon motioned for Derek to turn up the volume, but Derek shook his head. He could hear fine so there was no need to risk it.

"Where is he?" a woman's voice answered over the radio.

"Knocked out. Looks like he went a couple of rounds with our young werewolf."

"Get him to safety. Delta team still has the Enright girl, right?"

I shot a look at Derek, but his expression didn't change as he concentrated on listening.

"Delta two does. I'm not sure how well she'll work as bait, so I sent Delta one to get Carson from the truck."

That got Derek's attention. Simon mouthed "Andrew" to me. The voices retreated, but a moment later, the woman's came again over the radio, calling Delta two. A man answered.

"Have you got Carson?" she asked.

"I'm almost there."

"Good. Your job is to persuade him to call those kids. He's going to lure them in."

"He won't."

"I don't expect him to volunteer," the woman snapped, "but considering he's in our custody, he'll do what we say. If he refuses, shoot him."

Simon's head shot up, his eyes dark with worry. Derek motioned for him to be quiet as we listened.

Delta two came back on. "Um, did someone move the truck?"

"What?"

"The truck. With Carson. It's . . . not here."

The argument that followed was loud enough that Derek put his hands over the radio speaker, muffling it more. They spent the next few minutes making sure Delta two had the right spot and that no one else had moved Andrew and the truck. But there was no such simple explanation—their hostage was gone . . . with their truck.

"So Andrew's safe. What about Tori?" I asked when the radio went silent.

For a moment Derek said nothing, which was better than what I expected—a snapped *What about her?* As quick as he'd been the other day to say that he didn't care if Tori walked in front of a speeding car, it wasn't so easy to actually stand by, knowing she was in mortal danger.

"I'll do a sweep," he said. "If I find her, great."

He didn't say the rest, but I understood. *If I don't find her, we have to leave her behind.* As bad as that sounded, it was the right thing to do. I didn't want Derek putting himself in a bullet's path for Tori. That was an awful thing to admit. I didn't hate Tori—I didn't even really dislike her anymore. But when it came down to the cold, hard choice of putting a life on the line to save hers, I couldn't do it. Not Derek's, not Simon's, not mine. And that choice was going to haunt me for a very long time.

"Be careful and . . ." The other words that rose to my lips were "be quick," but I couldn't be that callous—even to think it shocked me. So I swallowed and repeated, "Be careful."

Derek wasn't leaving, though. We were. He made us set out first, so he could stand watch. When we were safely on our way to the back road, he'd go after Tori.

We made it about twenty paces before a figure appeared in our path. Simon's fingers flew up.

"Simon, it's—" the man said, ending in an *oomph* as the spell hit and he fell backward to the ground.

"Andrew!" Simon rushed forward.

The man rose, giving a wry smile as he brushed himself off. "I see your knock-back spell has improved."

Andrew wasn't much taller than Simon, but he was squarely built, sturdy, with a broad face and crooked nose. His crew-cut hair was gray, though he wouldn't be any older than my dad, and looked like a retired prizefighter. Not what I expected from that cozy, tidy little house.

When he looked at me, his smile faltered, the wrinkle between his brows deepening, like I looked familiar, but he was having trouble placing my face. He started to say something. Then he glanced up sharply.

"Someone's coming," Andrew said.

Simon glanced at the approaching shadow, big but moving silently. "It's Derek."

"No, that's not—" Andrew began.

Derek stepped into the light of the clearing. Andrew looked up at him and blinked. He stared at Derek, like he was trying—and failing—to find the boy he knew.

Behind the surprise in his eyes, there was something sharper, a note of worry, maybe even fear, like in that moment, he saw not his friend's son, but a big, powerful young werewolf. He blinked the fear back, but not before Derek saw it, his gaze shunting to the side, shoulders and jaw tensing, as if to say that was okay, he didn't care. But I knew he did.

"You've . . . grown."

Andrew tried for a smile but couldn't quite find it, and that, for Derek, seemed worse than the fear. He looked away completely, muttering, "Yeah."

Simon waved at me. "This is—"

"Let me guess. Diane Enright's girl."

I shook my head. "Chloe Saunders."

"It's the hair," Simon said. "She's blond, but we had to dye it because—"

"Later," Derek said, then looked at Andrew. "They have the Enright girl. Victoria."

Andrew frowned. "Are you sure?"

Simon took the radio from me and waved it. "Chloe got this from them. We heard about you escaping and them catching Tori."

"I'll go get her then. You three, get to the truck." He told us where to find it, then started to leave.

"I'm coming with you," Derek said. "I can find her faster than you can."

Andrew seemed ready to argue, but one look at Derek told him it was useless, so he took the radio from me and sent us to safety.

forty-two

WE FOUND THE TRUCK—an old SUV—hidden behind a neighboring barn. The door was open. A piece of metal had been jammed into the ignition to hotwire it. Simon was checking that out, trying to see if he could start it up, when three people ran from the woods: Derek, Andrew, and Tori.

Simon and I flung open the front doors and climbed into the back. Derek took the passenger seat. Tori sat on my other side in the rear.

"That was a quick rescue," Simon said as Andrew started the truck.

"No rescue required," Tori said. "I can take care of myself."

Derek muttered something about remembering that the next time he risked his life to help her.

As Andrew got the truck moving, I asked Tori what happened. She'd been taken captive and held under guard as the others searched. At first, she'd had two guards, but when things started going wrong they'd left her with only a single guard.

"One handy binding spell later? They lost their only remaining prisoner."

"You think they'd have taken your spells into account," Derek said.

"Well, they underestimated me," she said.

Derek grunted. Simon started asking something, but Andrew shushed us while he drove the truck over a rough field. He kept the lights off and rolled along slowly.

Simon shifted beside me, getting comfortable in the cramped backseat. His hand brushed my leg, then found my hand and took it. When he smiled over at me, I smiled back.

I expected him to give his usual reassuring squeeze and let go. Instead he seemed to take my smile as a sign of encouragement and entwined his fingers with mine and rested them on my thigh. As tired as I was—my brain reeling with questions, adrenaline still pumping—a little buzz passed through me. Silly, I guess. Making a big deal out of holding hands? So fifth grade.

I was sure, for Simon, it *was* no big deal. While he wasn't the first guy to hold my hand, let's just say my experience with boys didn't go further than that.

The buzz passed quickly, though, as we reached the road and Andrew turned on the headlights. He asked if we were all okay, and the first thing out of my mouth was, "Was my Aunt Lauren with you?"

His eyes met mine in the rearview mirror as he frowned.

"Lauren Fellows. She works for—"

"I know your aunt, Chloe, but, no, she wasn't there."

"Chloe thought she saw her," Derek said.

Simon twisted to face me. "What?"

"I—I saw someone. It sounded like her and it kind of looked like her, from what I could see in the dark. . . ."

"Did *you* see her?" Simon asked Derek.

"He didn't," I said. "And he should have, because she ran right past him."

"You saw a ghost," Tori said. "And you think it was your aunt."

"More likely a spell," Derek said. "They have stuff like that, right, Andrew?"

"Absolutely. Glamour spells and other illusions. If you didn't get a good look, that's probably intentional—whoever cast it didn't want you studying the illusion too closely."

That made sense, but I still couldn't shake the gut feeling that I *had* seen her. Not Aunt Lauren but her ghost.

Simon leaned into my ear and murmured reassurances, saying they wouldn't kill Aunt Lauren—she was too valuable.

"How's your arm?" Derek asked when I stayed quiet too long, lost in my worries.

"Did you pull your stitches?" Simon asked.

"No," Derek said. "A bullet grazed it."

"A *bullet*?"

Andrew steered to the curb and hit the brakes. "You were shot?"

"No, no. It's just a scratch."

Andrew hesitated, but I assured him—and Simon—that I was fine, and Derek confirmed that the bullet had only just passed through my shirt, grazing me.

Andrew turned back onto the road. "We'll get it cleaned up when we stop. I can't believe they . . ." He shook his head.

"Hey, I skinned my palm," Tori said. "Ground it up pretty bad."

"You need to check Chloe's stitches, too," Derek said. "She got cut with glass a few days ago. They fixed her up, but it should be looked at."

Tori waved her injured palm. "Anyone? Anyone?" She rolled her eyes. "Guess not."

"It looks sore," I said. "We should get some iodine on it."

She gave a wan smile. "I can always count on you, can't I? Guess I know who sent the cavalry back to rescue me."

"But you said you didn't need rescue, remember?" Simon said.

"It's the thought that counts."

"We wouldn't have left you there, Victoria." Andrew glanced back at her. "Tori, is it?"

She nodded.

He smiled at her. "It's good to see you and Simon together."

"Whoa, no," Simon said. "We're *not* together."

Tori agreed, just as emphatically.

"No, I meant—" Through the mirror, Andrew's gaze went from Simon to Tori. "I, uh, meant all four of you. I'm glad to see you together. That's one thing Kit and I agreed on, that the group was wrong to keep the subjects separated."

"So you worked for them, too?" I asked. "The Edison Group?"

Simon nodded. "He got out just before our dad." He looked at Andrew. "That's how they knew where to find you, isn't it? When we escaped, they figured we'd come here, so they grabbed you to use as bait."

"That seems to have been their plan. And, anyway, it was a good excuse for picking me up, something they've wanted to do for years."

"How come?" Tori asked.

"We'll talk about that later. First, let's find something to eat while you guys tell me what's been going on."

The only place we found open was a fast-food drive-thru in the next town. I wasn't hungry, but Simon insisted on getting me a milkshake and I sipped it as he explained to Andrew what had happened with us—Lyle House, our escape, the compound, the experiment, the deaths of Liz and Brady and Amber. . . .

"Rachelle is still there," Simon said as he finished. "Chloe's aunt, too, who's obviously their hostage now, like you were."

"Unless she's—" Tori began.

Simon's glare shut her up. "She's fine. But we need to get them and our dad out. Chloe's aunt doesn't think he was taken by them, but he must have been."

"I'd have to agree," Andrew said. "Nothing in my own searches has suggested any other explanation."

Derek looked over sharply. "You've been looking for him?"

"For all of you."

We drove for almost an hour and passed through only one big town. We were getting farther and farther from New York City. Finally, Andrew turned into a private drive even longer and more winding than his own.

"Where are we? A safe house for supernaturals?" Simon nudged me. "Like something out of a movie, huh?"

"Well, it certainly has played that role before, for supernaturals on the run from Cabals," Andrew said.

"Cabals?" Tori said.

"A whole other situation. But this place really serves more as a hostel for visiting members of our group. It was owned by one of our first members—an ancestral estate that he willed to us for the cause."

"What cause?" Tori asked.

"Monitoring and ultimately disbanding the Edison Group." He slowed as the dirt lane turned rough. "Or that was our original goal. We started as a band of former Edison Group employees, defectors like me who were concerned about their actions. Not just the Genesis Two project—that *is* one of our main concerns, but the Edison Group goes far beyond that. Eventually, we were joined by others, who took issue not only with the Edison Group's activities but with those of the Cabals and other supernatural organizations. Still, the Edison Group has remained our primary focus—monitoring their activities, conducting small acts of sabotage."

"Sabotage?" Simon said. "Cool."

"*Small* acts. Our main goal has been on monitoring, to the growing disgust of some of our members, myself included."

"Was Dad involved?" Simon asked.

Andrew shook his head. "I suppose you know your dad and I had—"

"A falling-out."

"Yes. And it was over this group. Your dad always stayed out of it. Too political for him. He'd been willing to help, but otherwise he didn't participate. He thought it would call undue attention to you boys. But I was pressured by the others to bring him in. As the father of two subjects from the Edison Group's most ambitious—and potentially dangerous—project, he'd be the perfect person to help attract powerful new members from the supernatural community. He was furious. All his work to keep you hidden, and now I wanted this. I'll admit, I supported the idea. But I underestimated the danger you faced from the Edison Group. I see that now."

He turned another corner, slowing more as the ruts in the road got deeper. "After your dad and you two disappeared, and we heard rumors the Edison Group had you boys, some of us began arguing for a more active stance. We were convinced you—and the other subjects—were in danger. Others with more influence insisted that the group wouldn't hurt you."

"Well, they were wrong," Tori said.

"Yes, and with your story, we'll have the proof we need to take action."

We turned yet another corner and the house appeared. For a moment, all we could do was stare. It was like something out of a gothic novel—a huge rambling Victorian, three stories tall, surrounded by forest. If there were gargoyles up there, shrouded by darkness, I wouldn't be surprised.

"Cool," Simon said. "Now this is where supernaturals should live."

Andrew chuckled. "And, for the next few days, it's where *you're* going to live. You can settle in here and rest while we make plans." He glanced back at us as he parked. "But don't get too comfortable. I'm about to ask the group to conduct a jailbreak at Edison Group headquarters, and it's been a lot of years since any of us have been there. We're going to need your help."

forty-three

I WENT TO BED AND I SLEPT. I wasn't sure I would, with the lingering excitement of the night, my fear over Aunt Lauren, my worries about the surrounding forest, filled with animal corpses waiting to be raised. But for the first time in weeks, we were safe, and that was all the encouragement my exhausted brain and body needed to shut down and bless me with deep, dreamless sleep.

I knew this wasn't the end. Not by a long shot. Even the first step—persuading the rest of this group to go back—wouldn't be as easy as Andrew hoped. And even when it was over, it wouldn't truly be over. Not for me.

I was changed. Not just the genetic modification, but me—I was different. The very thought of going home to Dad and our condo and my school and friends made my brain reel. That life was gone now. Maybe I'd go back to it someday, but it would be like replacing an actor with someone who looked, sounded, and even behaved differently. I wouldn't be the same person. I wasn't even sure I could play the role.

My old life felt like a dream—a mostly pleasant, uneventful dream. Now I'd awakened from it and realized who I was and what I was, for better or worse. There was no closing my eyes and sliding back into that blissful dream of normal. This was my normal now.

the Reckoning

BOOK THREE

one

AFTER FOUR NIGHTS ON THE RUN, I was finally safe, tucked into bed and enjoying the deep, dreamless sleep of the dead . . . until the dead decided they'd really rather have me awake. It started with a laugh that slid into my sleep and pulled me out of it. As I rose on my elbows, blinking and struggling to remember where I was, a whisper snaked around me, words indistinguishable.

I rubbed my eyes and yawned. Dull gray light shone through the curtains. The room was silent and still. No ghosts, thank God. I'd had enough in the last few weeks to last me a lifetime.

A scrape at the window made me jump. These days, every branch scratching the glass sounded like a zombie I'd raised from the dead, clawing to get in.

I went to the window and pulled back the curtains. It'd been nearly dawn by the time we got to the house, so I knew it had to be at least midmorning, but the fog outside was so thick I couldn't see anything. I leaned closer, nose pressed to the cold glass.

A bug splattered against the window and I jumped a foot in the air. A laugh sounded behind me.

I whirled, but Tori was still in bed, whimpering in her sleep. She'd thrown off the covers and was curled up on her side, her dark hair spiked across the pillow.

Another chuckle erupted behind me. Definitely a guy's laugh. But no one was there. No, strike that. I just couldn't *see* anyone. For a necromancer, that doesn't mean no one *is* there.

I squinted, trying to catch the flicker of a ghost and saw, off to the left, the flash of a hand that was gone before I could see more.

"Looking for someone, little necro?"

I spun. "Who's there?"

A snicker answered me—the kind of snicker every fifteen-year-old girl has heard a million times from jerk boys.

"If you want to talk to me, you have to show yourself," I said.

"Talk to you?" he said in an arrogant high school quarterback voice. "I think you're the one who wants to talk to me."

I snorted and headed back to bed.

"No?" His voice slid around me. "Huh. I figured you'd want to know more about the Edison Group, the Genesis experiments, Dr. Davidoff . . ."

I stopped.

He laughed. "Thought so."

The four of us—Tori, Derek, Simon, and me—were on the run from the Edison Group after discovering we were subjects in the Genesis project, an experiment for genetically modifying supernaturals. My aunt Lauren had been one of the doctors involved, but she'd betrayed her colleagues by helping us get away. Now she was being held captive. Or so I hoped. Last night, when the Edison Group tracked us down, a ghost had tried to help me . . . a ghost who had looked like Aunt Lauren.

We were supposedly in a safe house owned by a group opposing the experiments. Now a teenaged ghost showed up, knowing about the project? I wasn't about to banish him, however tempting it might be.

"Show yourself," I said.

"Bossy little necro, aren't you?" His voice slid behind me. "You just want to see if I'm as hot as I sound."

I closed my eyes, pictured a vague male form, and gave a mental tug.

He began to materialize—a dark-haired guy, maybe sixteen, seventeen, nothing special, but with a smarmy smile that said he thought he was. I could still see through him, like he was a hologram, so I closed my eyes to give him another pull.

"Uh-uh," he said. "You want more, we gotta get to know each other a little better." He disappeared again.

"What do you want?" I asked.

He whispered in my ear. "Like I said, to get to know you better. Not here, though. You'll wake your friend. She's cute, but not really my type." His voice moved to the door. "I know a place we can chat in private."

Yeah, right. Did he think I'd just started talking to ghosts yesterday? Well, close—two weeks ago, actually. But I'd already seen enough to know that while there were some ghosts who wanted to help and some who just wanted to talk, there were more who wanted to cause a little trouble, spice up their afterlife. This guy definitely fell in the last category.

Still, if he was another Edison Group subject, one who'd presumably died in this house, I needed to find out what had happened to him. But I wanted backup. Tori had no experience helping me with ghosts and, while we were getting along better, she still wasn't anyone I wanted watching my back.

So I followed the ghost into the hall, but stopped at Simon and Derek's door.

"Uh-uh," the ghost said. "You don't need to bring a guy along."

"They'd like to talk to you, too." I raised my voice, praying Derek would hear me. He usually woke at the slightest noise—werewolves have superhearing. All I could hear, though, was Simon's snores. There was no one else upstairs. Andrew, the guy who'd brought us here, had taken the downstairs bedroom.

"Come on, necro girl. This is a limited-time offer."

You know he's up to no good, Chloe.

Yes, but I also needed to know if we were in danger here. I decided to proceed with extreme caution. My subconscious voice didn't argue, which I took as a positive sign.

I started walking.

We'd gone straight to bed after we got here, so I hadn't gotten a good look at our new place. I only knew that it was huge—a rambling Victorian straight out of a Gothic horror movie.

As I followed the voice down the hall, I had the weird sense I was in one of those movies, caught in an endless narrow corridor, passing closed door after closed door until I finally reached the staircase . . . heading up.

From what I'd seen of the house as we'd driven up, it was three stories. The bedrooms were on the second floor, and Andrew had said the third was an attic.

So the ghost was leading me to the dark, spooky attic? I wasn't the only one who'd seen too many horror films.

I followed him up the stairs. They ended at a landing with two doors. I paused. A hand appeared through the door in front of me, beckoning. I took a second to prepare myself. No matter how dark it was in there, I couldn't let him see my fear.

When I was ready, I grabbed the doorknob and—

It was locked. I turned the dead bolt latch and it clicked free. Another deep breath, another second of mental preparation, then I swung the door open and stepped in—

A blast of cold air knocked me back. I blinked. Ahead, fog swirled.

A dead bolt on an attic door, Chloe?

No, I was standing on the roof.

two

I WHEELED AS THE DOOR swung closed behind me. I caught the edge, but something hit it, hard, and it slammed home. I grabbed the handle as the dead bolt clanked shut. I twisted the knob, sure I was mistaken.

"Leaving so soon?" he said. "How rude."

I stared down at the handle. Only one very rare type of ghost could move stuff in the living world.

"An Agito half-demon," I whispered.

"Agito?" He twisted the word with contempt. "I'm top-of-the-line, baby. I'm a Volo."

Which meant nothing to me. I could only guess it was a more powerful type. In life, a telekinetic half-demon could move objects mentally. In death, they could move them physically. A poltergeist.

I took a careful step back. Wood creaked underfoot, reminding me of where I was. I stopped short and looked around. I was on a kind of walkway that circled the third floor—the attic, I presumed.

To my right was a nearly flat section littered with rusty bottle caps and beer cans, like someone had used it as a makeshift patio. That calmed me down. I wasn't stranded on a roof, just a balcony. Annoying, but safe enough.

I rapped on the door, lightly, not really wanting to wake anyone, but hoping Derek might notice.

"No one's going to hear you," the ghost said. "We're all alone. Just the way I like it."

I lifted my hand to bang on the door, then stopped. Dad always said the best way to deal with a bully was not to let him know you were frightened. At the thought of my father, my throat tightened. Was he still looking for me? Of course, he was, and there was nothing I could do.

Dad's advice for bullies had worked with the kids who mocked my stutter—they gave up when they couldn't get a reaction from me. So I took a deep breath and went on the offensive.

"You said you know about the Edison Group and their experiments," I said. "Were you a subject?"

"Boring. Let's talk about you. Got a boyfriend? I bet you do. Cute girl like you, hanging out with two guys. You've gotta have hooked up with one of them by now. So which one?" He laughed. "Dumb question. The cute girl would get the cute guy. The chink."

He meant Simon, who was half Korean. He was baiting me, seeing if I'd leap to Simon's defense and prove he was my boyfriend. He wasn't. Well, not yet, though we seemed to be heading that way.

"If you want me to stay and talk, I need some answers first," I said.

He laughed. "Yeah? Doesn't look to me like you're going anywhere."

I grabbed the doorknob again. A bottle cap pinged off my cheek just below my eye. I glowered in his direction.

"That was only a warning shot, little necro." A nasty tone edged his voice. "Around here, we play *my* game by *my* rules. Now, tell me about your boyfriend."

"I don't have one. If you know anything about the Genesis experiment, then you know we aren't here for a vacation. Being on the run doesn't leave much time for romance."

"Don't get snarky with me."

I banged on the door. The next bottle cap hit my eye, stinging.

"You're in danger, little girl. Don't you care?" His voice lowered to my ear. "Right now, I'm your best friend, so you'd better treat me good. You've just been led into a trap and I'm the only one who can get you out."

"Led? By who? The guy who brought us here—" I thought up a fake name fast. "Charles?"

"No, some total stranger, and Charles just happened to bring you here. What a coincidence."

"But he said he doesn't work for the Edison Group anymore. He used to be their doctor—"

"He still is."

"H-he's Dr. Fellows? The one they were talking about at the lab?"

"None other."

"Are you sure?"

"I'd never forget that face."

"Huh, well, that's weird. First, his name isn't Charles. Second, he's not a doctor. Third, I know Dr. Fellows. She's my aunt, and that guy downstairs looks nothing like her."

The blow hit me from behind, striking hard against the back of my knees. My legs buckled and I fell on all fours.

"Don't toy with me, little necro."

When I tried to rise, he hit me with an old plank swung like a baseball bat. I tried to twist out of the way, but he got my shoulder and knocked me into the railing. A crack, and the railing gave way. I toppled, and for a second, all I could see was the concrete patio two stories down.

I caught another section of railing. It held and I was steadying myself when the plank swung straight for my hand. I let go and scrambled onto the walkway as the board hit the railing so hard that the top rail snapped and the plank snapped, too, splinters of rotting wood flying.

I ran toward the flat section of roof. He whipped the broken board at me. I stumbled back, bumping into the railing again.

I caught my balance and looked around. No sign of him. No sign of anything moving. But I knew he was there, watching to see what I'd do next.

I ran for the door, then feinted toward the flat part of the roof. A crash. Shards of glass exploded in front of me and the ghost appeared, lifting a broken bottle. I backpedaled.

Sure, that's a great idea. Just keep backing into the railing, see how long it'll hold.

I stopped. There was nowhere to run. I considered screaming. I've always hated that in movies—heroines who scream for help when cornered—but right now, caught between a broken-bottle-wielding poltergeist and a two-story fall, I could survive the humiliation of being rescued. Problem was, no one would get here in time.

So . . . what are you going to do? The superpowerful necromancer against the bullying poltergeist?

That was right. I did have a defense, at least against ghosts.

I touched my amulet. It'd been given to me by my mother. She'd said it would ward off the bogeymen I'd seen when I was little—ghosts, as I knew now. It didn't seem to work that well, but clutching it helped me concentrate, focus on what I was.

I pictured giving the ghost a shove.

"Don't you dare, little girl. You'll only piss me off and—"

I squeezed my eyes shut and gave him a huge mental push.

Silence.

I waited, listening, sure that when I opened my eyes, he'd be right there. After a moment, I peeked and saw only the gray sky. Still, I gripped the railing tight, ready for a broken bottle to fly at my head.

"Chloe!"

My knees shook at the shout. Footsteps thudded across the roof. Ghosts don't make footsteps.

"Don't move."

I looked over my shoulder to see Derek.

three

DEREK MADE HIS WAY across the flat section of the roof. He was dressed in jeans and a T-shirt, but his feet were bare.

"Watch out," I called. "There's broken glass."

"I see it. Stay where you are."

"It's okay. I'll just back up and—" The wood creaked under me. "Or maybe not."

"Just stay there. The wood's rotting. It's holding your weight as long as you stand still."

"But I walked out here, so it must be—"

"We're not testing that theory, okay?"

There was none of the usual impatient snap in his voice, meaning he was really worried. And if Derek was worried, I'd better stay right where I was. I gripped the railing.

"No!" he said. "I mean, yes, hold on, but don't put any weight on it. It's rotted through at the base."

Great.

Derek looked around, like he was searching for something to use. Then he stripped off his shirt. I tried not to look away. Not that he looked bad without his shirt. The opposite, actually, which is why . . . Let's just say friends are really better when they're fully dressed.

Derek got as close as he dared, then knotted a corner of the T-shirt and tossed it to me. I caught it on the second throw.

"I'm not going to pull you in," he warned.

A good thing, because with his werewolf strength, he'd probably wrench it from my hands and I'd tumble off the roof backward.

"Pull yourself along—"

He stopped, seeing I was already doing that. I made it onto the flat part, wobbled a step, then felt my knees start to give way. Derek grabbed my arm—the one without stitches, bandages, and a bullet graze—and I lowered myself slowly.

"I—I'm just going to sit for a minute," I said, my voice shakier than I liked.

Derek sat beside me, his shirt back on. I could feel him watching me, uncertain.

"I—I'll be okay. Just give me a second. It's safe to sit here, right?"

"Yeah, the slope's only about twenty-five degrees, so—" Seeing my expression, he said, "It's safe."

The fog was lifting, and I could see trees stretching into the distance on all sides, a dirt road winding through them to the house.

"There was a ghost," I said finally.

"Yeah, I figured that."

"I—I knew I shouldn't follow, but—" I paused, not ready for the full explanation, still shaky. "I stopped outside your door, hoping you'd hear me. I guess you did?"

"Kind of. I was dozing. Woke up confused, so it took me a while to get out here. Got a touch of fever."

I saw it now, the flushed skin and glittering eyes.

"Are you—?" I began.

"I'm not Changing. Not for a while. I know what that feels like now, and I've got a ways to go. Another day, at least. Hopefully longer."

"I bet you'll Change completely this time," I said.

"Yeah, maybe." His tone said he doubted it.

As we sat there, I snuck a look at him. At sixteen, Derek was more than a foot taller than me. Solidly built, too, with broad shoulders and muscles he usually kept hidden under baggy clothes, so he wouldn't look as intimidating.

Since he'd started Changing, Mother Nature seemed to have cut him some slack. His skin was clearing up. His dark hair didn't look greasy anymore. It still hung in his face—nothing emo, just like he hadn't bothered to get it cut in a while. Lately, that would have been the last thing on his mind.

I tried to relax and enjoy the fog-laced view, but Derek fidgeted and squirmed, which was more distracting than if he'd just been his usual self and demanded to know what had happened.

"So there was this ghost," I said finally. "He said he was a Volo half-demon. Telekinetic, but a stronger type than Dr. Davidoff. Probably the same kind Liz is. He lured me out here, locked the door, then started pelting me with stuff."

Derek looked over sharply.

"I banished him."

"Good, but you shouldn't have followed him at all, Chloe."

His tone was calm, reasonable, so un-Derek-like that I stared at him, the weird idea that this wasn't Derek creeping through my head. Before I'd escaped the Edison Group laboratory, I'd met a demi-demon, chained there as a power source. She'd possessed someone but only a ghost. Could Derek be possessed?

"What?" Derek said as I stared.

"Are you okay?"

"Yeah, just . . ." He rubbed the back of his neck, wincing and rolling his shoulders. "Tired. Feeling off. Really off. Too much . . ." He struggled for the word. "Being here. Being safe. I'm still adjusting."

That made sense. Derek's werewolf protective streak had been in hyperdrive for days, keeping him awake and on guard. Having someone else to watch out for us now would be weird. Still, not blasting me for blithely following a random ghost onto a roof was so totally not Derek that I knew there was more to it.

When I asked what was bothering him, he muttered that it was nothing. I backed off and was about to explain more about the ghost when he blurted, "It's Tori. I don't like her story about how she got away."

When the Edison Group had almost captured us last night, they'd nabbed Tori. Yet when they'd refocused their efforts on the biggest threat—Derek—they'd left the young witch with only a single guard. She'd locked him in a binding spell and escaped.

"You think they let her get away?"

"I'm not saying . . . It's just . . . I don't have any proof."

And that's what was making him uncomfortable, that his misgivings were based on nothing but a gut feeling. The math and science whiz really preferred dealing in facts.

"If you're thinking she's been a plant from the start, she hasn't." I lowered my voice. "Don't tell her I told you this, okay? When she helped me escape, she only wanted to get away from the Edison Group and run back to her dad. So she called him. Instead he sent her mom—the woman we'd just escaped. Tori was hurt, really hurt. In shock even. She couldn't have faked that."

"I didn't figure she was in on it from that far back."

"Just that she cut a deal last night?"

"Yeah."

"Would Tori turn us in for the promise of getting her old life back? It's possible, and we should be careful, but I *do* buy her story. Unless her mom told them Tori was figuring out how to cast spells—which I doubt—then, as far as they know, she just has random outbursts of power. Her binding spell could have taken out a single guard. I've seen her use it. She doesn't even need to say an incantation. It's like, if she thinks it, she can do it."

"No casting? No practicing?" He shook his head. "Don't tell Simon that."

"Don't tell Simon what?" said a voice behind us.

We turned to see Simon step out of the doorway.

"That Tori doesn't need to use incantations to cast," Derek said.

"Seriously?" He swore. "You're right. Don't tell me." He picked his way across the roof. "Better yet, don't tell her that I need incantations and weeks of practice, and I still suck."

"You were good with that knock-back spell last night," I said.

He grinned. "Thanks. Now, do I dare ask what you guys are doing hiding out up here? Or is it going to make me jealous?"

Simon was smiling as he said it, but Derek glanced away with a gruff "Course not."

"So you weren't having another adventure?" Simon lowered himself on my other side, so close he brushed against me, hand resting on mine. "It sure looks like a good spot for one. Rooftop hideaway, old widow's walk. That is what that is, huh? A widow's walk?"

"Yeah. And it's rotting, so stay off it," Derek said.

"I did. So, adventure?"

"A small one," I said.

"Oh, man. I always miss them. Okay, break it to me gently. What happened?"

I explained. As Simon listened, intent and concerned, he cast glances at his brother. Foster brother, I guess you'd say—one look at them and you knew they weren't related by blood. Simon is fifteen, a half-year older than me, slender and athletic, with dark, almond-shaped eyes and spiked blond hair. When Derek was about five, he'd come to live with Simon and his dad. They were best friends and brothers, blood tie or not.

I told him as much as I'd told Derek so far. Then he looked from me to Derek.

"I must have been sound asleep if I missed all that shouting," Simon said.

"What shouting?" Derek said.

"You mean that Chloe just told you that she followed a ghost onto a roof, and you didn't blast her all the way to Canada?"

"He's a little off this morning," I said.

"More than a little, I'd say. Aren't you going to ask her for the rest of the story? The part where she explains *why* she followed the ghost? Because I'm sure there was a reason."

I smiled. "Thank you. There was. It was a teenage guy who knew about the Edison Group and the experiments."

"What?" Derek's head whipped around, the sound more growl than question.

"That's why I followed him. There's a dead kid here who might have been another subject, and if he died here . . ."

"Then that's a problem," Simon said.

I nodded. "My first thought, naturally, was 'Oh my God, we've been led into a trap.'"

Simon shook his head. "Not Andrew. He's one of the good guys. I've known him all my life."

"But I haven't, which is why I prodded the ghost, and it was clear he hadn't recognized him. Andrew said this place was owned by the guy who started his group and was involved in the experiments. If there's a link to this kid, I think we'll find it there."

"We can ask Andrew—" Simon began.

Derek cut him off. "We'll find our own answers."

Simon and Derek locked gazes. After a second, Simon grumbled something about making things difficult, but he didn't argue. If Derek wanted to amuse himself playing detective, then fine. We'd be gone soon anyway, back to rescue those we'd left behind and take out the Edison Group . . . or so we hoped.

four

WE WENT DOWNSTAIRS SHORTLY after that. Derek headed straight for the kitchen to scrounge up breakfast. We might have gotten only a few hours sleep, but it was already almost noon and his stomach was, predictably, growling.

While he searched for food, Simon and I poked around our temporary new home. I read a book once about a girl in a huge English mansion with a secret room no one had found in years, because a wardrobe had been pulled in front of the door. I remember thinking that was ridiculous. My dad had friends with really big houses, and there was still no way you could lose a room. But with this place and a little stretch of the imagination, I could see it.

It wasn't just big. It was set up weird. Like the architect just slapped rooms onto a blueprint, with no thought to how they connected. The front was simple enough. There was a main hall connecting the doors, the stairs, the kitchen, a living room, and dining room. Then it got confusing, branching into a couple of back halls, with rooms that only joined other rooms. Most were really tiny, not even ten feet square. It reminded me of a rabbit's warren, all these little rooms going off in all directions. We even found a separate set of stairs back there, ones that looked like they hadn't been cleaned in years.

As Simon went to see if Andrew was up, I wandered into the kitchen, where Derek was eyeing a rusty can of beans.

"That hungry?" I asked.

"I will be soon."

He prowled the kitchen, flipping open cupboards.

"So you don't want me asking Andrew about that kid," I said. "You trust him, though, right?"

"Sure."

He took down a box of crackers and turned it over, looking for a "best before" date.

"That didn't sound convincing," I said. "If we're here with someone you don't trust . . ."

"Right now, the only people I really trust are you and Simon. I don't think Andrew is up to anything. If I did, we wouldn't be here. But I'm not taking a chance, not if we can find our own answers."

I nodded. "That's fine. Just . . . I know you don't want to spook Simon, but . . . If you're worried . . ." My cheeks heated. "I don't mean you need to confide in me, just don't . . ."

"Blow you off when you know something's wrong." He turned and met my gaze. "I won't."

"Is he drinking the ketchup yet?" Simon swung into the kitchen. "Ten minutes, bro. Andrew's on his way and—"

"And he's apologizing profusely for the lack of food." Andrew walked in. He was about my dad's age with really short gray hair, square shoulders, a stocky build, and a crooked nose. He clapped a hand on Derek's shoulder. "It's coming. One of the group is bringing breakfast and will be here any minute."

He kept his hand on Derek's shoulder, giving it a squeeze. It was an awkward gesture, maybe because he was a half-foot shorter than Derek, but it seemed more than that. Last night, when he'd first seen Derek after a few years, a pulse of surprise and wariness crossed his face. Derek had seen it, and I knew he'd felt it—the jab of having a guy he'd known most of his life reacting like he was some teenage thug you'd cross the road to avoid.

Like Simon, Andrew was a sorcerer. He was an old friend of their dad's, and a former employee of the Edison Group. He was also their emergency contact. Andrew and their dad had some kind of falling out a few years ago, but they'd stayed in contact, so when we'd been stuck, we'd come to him.

Andrew gave Derek's shoulder one last squeeze, then he bustled about the kitchen, getting out plates and rinsing them off, wiping dust from the counters and the table, asking how we'd slept, apologizing again for the lack of preparation.

"Hard to prepare when you don't know anyone's coming," Simon said. "Is this going to be okay? You staying here with us? I know you've got work . . ."

"Which I've been doing from home for two years now. Finally built up the seniority to start telecommuting, thank God. The daily trips into New York were killing me. I go once a week now for meetings."

Simon turned to me. "Andrew's an editor. Books." He glanced at Andrew. "Chloe's a screenwriter."

I blushed and stammered that obviously I wasn't a real screenwriter, just a wannabe; but Andrew said he'd love to hear about what I was working on, answer any questions about writing. He even sounded like he meant it, unlike most adults, who just say things like that to humor you.

"Right now, she's working on a comic with me," Simon said. "A graphic journal of our adventures. Just for fun."

"Very cool. I take it you're doing the art? Your dad told me you're—"

The doorbell rang.

"And that would be breakfast," Andrew said. "Chloe? I know Tori's probably exhausted, but she should be here for the meeting."

"I'll go wake her up."

So the mysterious resistance group was here. It didn't look like much: three people plus Andrew.

There was Margaret, who looked like a lot of the women my dad worked with—a corporate business type, tall with graying brown hair cut short. She was a necromancer.

Gwen wasn't much taller than me and barely looked out of college. As for supernatural type, with her short blond hair, turned-up nose, and sharp chin, I started wondering if there was such a thing as a pixie, but she said she was a witch, like Tori.

The third newcomer was Russell, a bald grandfatherly guy who was a shaman paramedic, in case we needed medical attention after our ordeal. With Andrew and Margaret, he was one of the group's founding members and had also once worked for the Edison Group.

Andrew said there were another half-dozen members in the New York City area, and twenty or so more across the country. Under the circumstances, though, it didn't seem safe to have them all trooping up here to meet us. So they'd sent the ones who could help us the most—a necromancer and a witch. Derek was out of luck. There weren't any werewolves in the group, not surprising given that there were maybe a couple dozen in the country, compared to hundreds of necromancers and spell-casters.

The supernaturals who joined the Edison Group weren't evil. Most were like my aunt, who offered her services as a doctor because she wanted to help people like her brother, a necromancer who'd either committed suicide or been driven off a roof by ghosts when he was still in college.

The Edison Group believed that the answer was genetic manipulation—tweak our DNA to minimize side effects and improve our control over our powers. Things started going wrong back when we were little, and three of the werewolf subjects attacked a nurse. They were "eliminated." Killed, by the same people who swore they were trying to help supernaturals. That's when Simon's dad and others, like Andrew, left.

But leaving wasn't enough for some. Concerned about what they'd seen, they'd monitored the Edison Group, making sure they didn't pose a threat to other supernaturals. Now we were bringing news of exactly what they'd feared most. For many of us, the genetic modification had backfired, producing kids with uncontrollable powers—witches who could cast without incantations and necromancers who could raise the dead by accident.

When those failures hadn't proved as easy to control as the Edison Group had hoped, they'd done the same thing they'd done to the werewolf boys. Killed them.

Now, we'd come to Andrew's group for help. We were in mortal danger and we'd left behind another subject, Rachelle, and my aunt Lauren, who were in even greater danger. We were asking this group to rescue them and end the threat against us. Were they up to it? We had no idea.

Gwen had brought the breakfast: donuts, coffee, and chocolate milk, which I'm sure she thought would be the perfect treat for teenagers. It would have been . . . if we hadn't been living on junk food for three days and if one of us wasn't diabetic.

Simon picked out a donut and a half-pint carton of chocolate milk, joking about having the excuse to eat stuff that was normally off his diet. It was Derek who complained. Andrew apologized for forgetting to warn the others about Simon and promised more nutritious food for our next meal.

Everyone was really nice and sympathetic, and maybe I was just being paranoid—Derek rubbing off on me—but behind those smiles and kind eyes, there seemed to be a touch of unease, like they couldn't stop thinking about our messed-up powers. Like they couldn't help but think that we were all ticking time bombs.

I wasn't the only one who felt uncomfortable. When we moved to the living room, Derek staked out a corner and retreated there. Simon barely said a word. Tori, who normally wanted nothing to do with us, stuck so close to me that I thought she was trying to swipe my donut.

Us versus them. The genetically modified freaks versus the normal supernaturals.

Simon and I did most of the talking. That was weird for me, the kid who always sat in the back of a group, hoping she wasn't called on to speak because she might start stuttering. But the burden of proof lay with me and what I'd seen: the ghosts of the other kids and the files on Dr. Davidoff's computer.

As we explained, I saw sympathy in their eyes but doubt, too. They believed that the experiment had gone wrong for some subjects—that was exactly the kind of thing they'd feared when they quit. They also believed us about Lyle House, the "group home" where the Edison Group had kept us. When the experiment screwed up, naturally the Edison Group would try to cover their tracks.

But the rest of it? Hunting us down when we escaped? Shooting at us, first with tranquilizer darts, then real bullets? Locking us up in the laboratory? Killing three kids who'd failed rehabilitation?

That sounded like something from a movie. No, strike that. As an aspiring blockbuster screenwriter/director, if I'd heard this pitch, I'd have dismissed it as too outrageous.

I could tell that Andrew believed us. Gwen did, too. I could see it from the horror in her face. But Gwen was the youngest, and her opinion didn't seem to count for much. Russell and Margaret couldn't hide their skepticism, and I knew convincing them to help us wasn't going to be as easy as we'd hoped.

Finally, I blurted, "Rachelle and my aunt are in *danger.* They could be killed any day now, if they haven't already been."

"Your aunt is a valuable member of the team," Margaret said, her severe face unreadable. "They won't kill her. Nor does your friend seem in imminent danger. She's happy and compliant. That's all they'll ask for now."

"But if she finds out the truth, she won't be nearly so compliant—"

Russell cut in. "Your aunt and your friend made their choices, Chloe. As harsh as that seems. They both betrayed you. I didn't think you'd be so eager to rescue them."

"My aunt—"

"Helped you escape, I know. But you wouldn't have been there if it wasn't for your friend's betrayal."

Rae had told Dr. Davidoff about our escape plans, so they'd been ready when we tried to make a run for it. She'd believed their lies about wanting to help us and thought I'd been brainwashed by the boys.

"She made a mistake. Are you saying we should let her die for it?" My voice was rising. I swallowed, trying to stay calm, reasonable. "Whatever she did, she thought it was the right thing at the time, and I won't abandon her now."

I glanced at the others. Simon agreed quickly and vehemently. Derek mumbled a gruff "Yeah, she screwed up, but stupidity isn't a capital crime."

We all looked at Tori. I held my breath, feeling the weight of the adults' gazes on us, knowing we needed consensus on this.

"Since we're already going back for Chloe's aunt, then Rae should be rescued," Tori said. "And they *both* need to be rescued ASAP. The Edison Group might not be a bunch of vindictive homicidal maniacs, but my mother is the exception, and when we left, she really wasn't happy with Dr. Fellows."

"I don't think—" Russell began.

"Now it's time to move on to the boring discussion part," Andrew interjected. "Why don't you kids go upstairs and check out the other rooms. I'm sure you'd each like one of your own."

"We're good," Simon said.

Andrew looked at the others. They wanted us out of the room so they could discuss whether they were going to help us or not.

I wanted to scream, *What is there to discuss? The people you used to work for are killing kids. Isn't this your mission—to make sure their work doesn't hurt anyone? Stop chowing down on donuts and do something!*

"Why don't you—?" Andrew began.

"We're good." It came out as a growl. That was just Derek's *I'm serious* tone, but the room suddenly went very still. All eyes turned toward him, every gaze wary.

Derek glanced away and mumbled, "You want us to leave?"

"Please," Andrew said. "It would be easier—"

"Whatever."

Derek led us out.

five

IN THE HALL, Derek turned. "You guys go see about finding a new bedroom for Tori. I'm getting more donuts."

Simon and I exchanged a look. As much as Derek loved to eat, the last thing on his mind right now would be filling his stomach. What he meant was *take Tori and get out of here, so I can listen in on the meeting.* Werewolf hearing meant he could eavesdrop from the kitchen.

"Save me a chocolate dipped," Simon said, leading Tori and me to the stairs.

"You aren't supposed to have—"

"Just winding you up," Simon tossed back. "Come on, Tori. Let's get you a room of your own."

As it turned out, Tori wanted to stay with me. Not that she said that, of course. She checked out the other options, bitched and moaned about how dusty they were and how it seemed she was stuck with me after all. I offered to take another one. She lit into me about being too nice and how I had to learn to stand up for myself. I decided it was time for a shower.

A shower would also give me a chance to wash the temporary dye from my hair. When we'd run away from Lyle House, my dad was told I'd done just that—run away. He had no idea I'd been caught almost immediately and taken to the Edison Group lab. He didn't know what the Edison Group was or what a necromancer was. To him, his schizophrenic daughter had run away from her group home and was now living on the streets of Buffalo. So he'd offered a reward. A half-million-dollar reward.

I wanted to let him know I was okay. God, I wanted to. But Aunt Lauren said he was safer not knowing the truth and Derek agreed. So, for now, I tried really hard not to think about how worried he must be. I'd get a message to him as soon as it was safe. In the meantime, his reward was a problem.

My strawberry blond hair was distinctive, even more so with the red streaks I'd added before I got shipped off to Lyle House. So Derek bought me temporary dye. Black dye. I was way too pale for black, and now I looked exactly like you'd picture a necromancer: white skin and harsh black hair. Uber-Goth. But now, thankfully, the color was fading. Or so I thought.

Tori followed me down the hall, offering tips about how to get the dye out, being Miss Helpful two minutes after calling me a wimp. These days, that seemed par for the course with Tori. She'd start inching toward friendship, then remember we were supposed to be mortal enemies.

Now she was in friendly mode. "Don't wash it more than three times or your hair will be like straw. I saw conditioner in there. Make sure you use that and let it sit."

"Right now, dry hair is better than black hair."

Simon poked his head out of his room. "You're washing out the color?"

"As fast as I can."

He hesitated, the look in his eyes telling me he was about to say something he really didn't want to. "I know you want it gone, but . . . Well, if we go out . . ."

"At this point, I'll take house arrest over black hair."

"It's not that bad."

Tori mock-whispered, "Simon's thinking the Goth girl look is kinda hot."

He glowered at her. "No. I just want—" An impatient look at Tori, telling her to get lost. When she stood her ground, he leaned down to my ear, his fingers entwining with mine. "I know you want to get rid of it. I'll ask Andrew to get you a better color. I don't care what your hair looks like; I just want you to be safe."

"That's so sweet," Tori said.

Simon moved to stand between us, his back to her. "You can check with Andrew. Maybe I'm overreacting—"

"No, you're not. I still need that shower, but I won't try washing out the color."

"Good. Oh, and Derek said you were asking about self-defense lessons. How about we try that after?"

I wasn't really in the mood for that, but he was smiling, obviously eager to do something nice for me after vetoing my hair fix. It wasn't like we had anything better to do, so I said, "Sure."

"Sounds good," Tori said. "Yes, I know, you weren't inviting me, but we could both use the training. And, no, I'm not trying to get between you guys. I'm over you, Simon. I think you and Chloe make the most nauseatingly cute couple ever. But you can gaze soulfully into each other's eyes another time. Right now, I need self-defense lessons. So I'll meet you out back."

She started for the stairs, calling, "And it wouldn't have been one-on-one for long anyway. I'm sure Derek will join in as soon as he's done eavesdropping."

I ran into Derek as I came out of the bathroom.

"Meeting over?" I asked.

"Yeah."

Simon popped his head out of their room and Derek motioned him into the hall.

"Where's Tori?" he asked.

"Outside. She's waiting for us, though, so we can't be long."

"And the verdict is?" Simon prompted.

"Gwen and Andrew believe us. Margaret suspects we may have misunderstood the situation and jumped to the wrong conclusion about Liz, Brady, and Amber being killed. Only Russell thinks we're intentionally lying."

"Jerk. Where does he get off—?"

Derek gave him a look. Simon zipped it and gestured for Derek to continue.

"They teleconferenced with a couple of the other senior members and—" Derek looked at me, and I read the answer in the way his gaze dipped from mine. "They want to slow down, get more information first. They're going to send a team to Buffalo to do recon work."

Simon glowered. "Sure, take the slow and steady path while Rachelle and Dr. Fellows could be—" He looked at me. "Sorry."

We all stood there for a minute, simmering.

I turned to Derek. "What do you think we should do?"

"For now? Play it out." His voice was gruff with frustration. "Nothing else we can do. We've got the Edison Group gunning for us. We have to stay put."

We found Tori out back. I apologized for taking so long; they didn't. Simon had barely begun showing us a wrist hold when Andrew summoned us inside.

Russell had already left. "Fled," Simon muttered, "so he wouldn't have to look us in the eye after telling the others he thinks we're lying."

Gwen was gone, too, but only to grab groceries and takeout for dinner. Yes, it was dinner time already. Having gotten up so late, we were skipping lunch.

We ate with Andrew, Gwen, and Margaret. They couched the plan in optimistic terms, of course—they were just doing a quick bout of reconnaissance work in preparation for the rescue operation.

"So, guys," Andrew said, "over the next few days, your job will be threefold. Rest up. Tell us everything you can about the lab. And get some training."

"Training?" That perked Tori up. Me, too.

Gwen smiled. "Yep. That's what Margaret and I are here for."

"And I'll be working with Simon," Andrew said, "though I know your dad's been training you for years."

"I'm sure he can use the practice," Tori said.

Simon flipped her off. Andrew pretended not to see it.

"As for Derek . . ." Andrew said.

"Yeah, I know. No werewolf teachers for me."

"True, but we do have someone. Tomas, a half-demon member who lives in New Jersey. You may remember him from when you lived at the laboratory. He was a member of the team responsible for the werewolf section of the project."

Did I imagine it or did Derek flinch? I wouldn't blame him if he did. Derek had lived in the lab until Simon's dad took him and that section of the experiment had been abandoned. The other three werewolves had already been killed. Meeting one of his "keepers" certainly wouldn't be a happy reunion.

"Tomas quit before you left the lab, primarily because he disagreed with the way you boys were treated. But he knows more about werewolves than anyone I know. Your dad used him as a resource for raising you."

Derek's shoulders relaxed. "Yeah?"

"He's away on business, but he'll be back next week. If we're still waiting to act—which I hope we won't be—it'll give you someone to talk to, answer any questions you might have."

SIX

AFTER DINNER, ANDREW WARNED us it would be lights-out at ten. Until then, he was going to get caught up on some work and we could amuse ourselves.

Problem was, we didn't want to amuse ourselves. Or get a good night's sleep. We wanted our lives back—stop the Edison Group, free Aunt Lauren and Rae, find the guys' dad, and let my father know I was safe. Sitting around playing board games would be torture . . . and that's exactly what Andrew suggested, the house being otherwise diversion free.

Tori and I were heading up to our room when Gwen popped into the hall to say good-bye.

"Can I ask you a couple of things before you go?" Tori said to Gwen as she hurried down the stairs. "I'm new to all this witch stuff and I know we're starting lessons tomorrow, but if you have time for a few questions . . ."

Gwen grinned. "Always. I'm usually the student around here, so I'm looking forward to this. Come on in the living room and we'll chat."

I felt a pang of envy. I had questions, too. Tons of them. And who did I get for a teacher? Margaret, who wasn't exactly the *let's hang out and chat* sort. Not to mention the fact that she was one of the doubters.

I trudged up the stairs and didn't notice that the guys' door was open until Derek reached out, fingers brushing my elbow.

"Hey," I said, struggling for a smile.

"You busy?" he said, voice barely above a whisper.

"I wish. What's up?"

He glanced back at the bathroom door. Light shone under it. He stepped closer, voice dropping even more. "I thought, uh, if you weren't doing anything, maybe we could—"

The bathroom door swung open and Derek jumped. Simon walked out.

"Good, you found Chloe," he said. "So what're we doing? This time, I'm not missing the adventure."

"All our adventures are accidental," I said, "and we'd be happy to miss most of them." I looked up at Derek. "You were saying?"

"Nothing. Just that we shouldn't do too much."

"Okay. So what *are* we doing?"

"Nothing tonight. Just . . . whatever." He retreated into their room.

I looked at Simon.

"Yeah, he's weird. I'll talk to him. Catch up with you in a few minutes."

I was heading into our room when Tori came up. We went in and talked, awkward conversation, thankfully interrupted when Simon rapped at our door.

"Everyone decent?" he called, and started opening it.

"Excuse me?" Tori said. "Could you at least give us a chance to answer?"

"It was a warning, not a question. I was being polite."

"Being polite would mean waiting for—"

I held up my hand. That was all it took to stop the bickering.

"I found something," Simon said as he walked in. He whipped an old-fashioned key from his pocket and grinned at me. "It was taped to the back of my dresser drawer. What do you think? Buried treasure? Secret passageway? Locked room where they keep crazy old Aunt Edna?"

"It probably unlocks *another* dresser," Tori said. "One they threw out fifty years ago."

"It's tragic, being born without an imagination. Do they hold telethons for that?" He turned back to me. "Chloe, help me out here."

I took the key. It was heavy and rusting. "It's definitely old. And it *was* hidden." I glanced up at him. "Bored, aren't you?"

"To death. So will you come exploring?"

Tori rolled her eyes. "I think I'll lie down and dream of being home, with kids who don't think hunting for a locked door is fun."

"Hey, I told you we were uncool," Simon said. "The more time you spend with us, the more it rubs off." He looked at me. "Coming?"

When I didn't answer right away, he said, "No?" Disappointment dragged down his voice before he propped it up with a forced smile. "That's cool. You're tired—"

"It's not that. It's just . . . we need to ID that kid I saw and figure out if he has a connection to this house."

"What kid?" Tori asked.

I explained about the ghost, then said, "I know Derek said we shouldn't do too much tonight, but . . ."

"But, apparently, that warning only applies to us, because he's off right now, hunting for clues about that kid. He doesn't want us pitching in. He says it'll look suspicious if we're all poking around."

So Derek was searching without me? I felt a pang of . . . I don't know, disappointment, I guess. Then I thought about earlier, in the hall. Had he been trying to invite me along? The disappointment grew.

"How about those self-defense lessons?" Tori said.

"Sure, I guess . . ." Simon said. "Better than nothing."

"Actually, there's something else I should do," I said. "You guys go on."

They looked at me like I'd suggested they swim with sharks. Not a bad analogy, really. Simon and Tori doing self-defense together was bound to result in bloodshed.

"What did you have in mind?" Simon asked.

"Just . . . Well, my aunt . . . What I saw last night . . . I'd like to . . ."

"Try summoning her," Tori finished for me. "See if she's dead, right?"

Simon shot her a look for being so blunt, but I nodded. "Right. And Liz. I want to try contacting Liz. She'd come in handy searching for clues. The problem is that, if I summon, I might call up that other guy."

"Which is why you shouldn't do it alone," Simon said. "I'll stay."

"Me, too," Tori said. "If you do summon the demon kid, maybe I can get him to talk."

She put out her hand. A ball of energy started to swirl.

"All right," I said.

seven

SUMMONINGS AREN'T NEARLY AS COOL as they look in the movies. Basically, it's the reverse of how I banish a spirit. I close my eyes and picture pulling a ghost out instead of shoving him back in.

Ideally, I'd have something that belonged to the deceased. I'd been using a hoodie of Liz's before Tori's mom confiscated it. I didn't have anything of my aunt's. So the only way this would work was if they were hovering around, waiting to make contact.

I suspected one spirit *was* hovering around—the jerk from this morning. While I was tempted to question him further, a voice in my head—which sounded suspiciously like Derek's—warned me against it. He hadn't been forthcoming before, and I'd pissed him off by banishing him. So as I sat on the floor in our room, I was careful to keep very clear pictures of my aunt and Liz in my head, alternating between them.

While I hoped I wouldn't see my aunt, I really did want to contact Liz, my former roommate at Lyle House. She had been killed the night I arrived. It'd taken time for her to believe she was dead, but once she did, she refused to go to the other side. She'd stayed and helped.

Not only was a ghost the perfect spy, but Liz was the same type of half-demon as that kid from this morning—telekinetic, meaning she was a poltergeist. So, yes, Liz would be very useful right now; but, more than that, I just wanted to see her, make sure she was okay.

"That necklace is supposed to prevent you from seeing ghosts, right?" Tori asked after a few moments of unsuccessful summoning.

Simon opened his mouth to tell her off for interrupting, but I cut him short.

"Obviously I still see them," I said. "Either it doesn't work or things would be a lot worse without it, something I'm sure I'll test eventually. I want to talk to Margaret about it."

"Okay, but if it keeps ghosts away, maybe that's why Liz isn't coming."

She had a point. And yet . . . I fingered the necklace. If it did work, what else was it keeping at bay? Something worse than that telekinetic half-demon kid?

"Why don't you take it off?" Tori began.

"Because she—" Simon snapped, then caught himself. "Let her try a bit more with it on. These things take time, and we're not in any rush. If you're bored, our room's empty."

Tori looked like she wanted to snap back, but couldn't, not when he'd said it reasonably.

"I'm good," she said, and I resumed the summoning.

Because Liz was the one I really wanted to see, she was the one I concentrated on, throwing out only the occasional calls to my aunt, praying they wouldn't be answered. Finally, when Liz didn't respond, I ramped up the appeals to Aunt Lauren. If I wanted reassurance that she was still alive, I needed to know that I'd tried as hard as I could to summon her.

"Don't," Tori whispered.

My eyes snapped open. "Don't what?"

She frowned.

"You said 'don't,' " I prompted.

"Um, no, I didn't open my mouth."

"She didn't," Simon said. "You must be hearing a ghost."

I closed my eyes and concentrated on Liz.

"Don't," the faint female voice whispered. "Please, baby."

My gut seized. That wasn't Liz. But it wasn't something Aunt Lauren called me, either. Or did she? I wasn't sure.

"If you're there, whoever you are, please show yourself."

Nothing.

"The amulet," Tori whispered. "If she can't get through, that must be stopping her."

I reached for my necklace.

"No!" the voice whispered. "Not safe."

"You don't want me to take it off?"

No answer. My hands shook so badly the amulet knocked against my neck.

"Go on," Simon said. "We're right here. Anything happens, I'll get it back on you."

I started lifting it.

"No! Please, baby. Too dangerous. Not here. He'll come."

"Who'll come?"

Silence. Then I thought I heard her whisper, but it was too faint for me to make out.

"She's trying to warn me about something, but I can't hear it," I said.

Simon gestured for me to take off the necklace. I raised it over my head—

"What the hell are you doing?" a voice roared.

Derek strode into the room and yanked the amulet back down. "You're summoning without your amulet? Are you crazy? A ghost lured you onto the roof this morning, could have gotten you killed."

Simon got to his feet. "Ease off, okay? We were trying to get hold of Liz. Then a spirit wanted to warn Chloe about something, but she couldn't hear her, so we suggested she take off the necklace, see if that would help it materialize."

Derek's trademark scowl didn't waver. "Just because you suggest it doesn't mean she needs to listen. She knows better."

"No, but the suggestion made sense," I said. "I was being careful. If you had stopped to watch instead of charging in here, you'd have seen that."

Derek kept glowering, looming over me. No one looms like Derek, but I'd had enough experience to stand my ground.

"I'll leave the necklace on," I said, "but I'm going to try again. If she's still here, then I might take it off."

"Who is it?"

"I—I—" I faltered, chest seizing. "M-maybe my aunt. I—I—don't think so, but . . . I should try again."

Some of the anger drained from his face then. He ran a hand through his hair, sighed, then nodded. "Okay. You should. If she comes back and she seems to be trying to warn you, then . . . we'll see what we can do about the necklace."

I could point out that it was really my decision, but he was calming down, and I wasn't about to crank him up again.

So I tried one more time. No luck.

"She didn't want me summoning here," I said.

"Yeah? Probably because you could call up that half-demon jerk." Derek paused, then took the sarcasm down a notch. "We'll go for a walk tomorrow, get farther from the house, and try again."

"I'll come," Tori said. "And if the idiot shows up?"

She lifted her fingers. A ball of energy appeared, whirling over the tips. She grinned and whipped her hand back, throwing it like a softball. It hit the wall and exploded in a shower of sparks, scorching the faded wallpaper.

"Whoops," she said.

Derek spun on her. "What the hell do you think you're doing?"

"Showing off. I didn't know it'd do *that*."

He strode over and wiped the wall. The marks stayed.

"No one's going to notice it," Tori said. "And if they do, they sure aren't going to blame my spells."

"I don't care. Someone could have seen you."

"So I'll get in trouble for marking the wallpaper. I'll survive."

"You don't get it, do you? We can't do things like that. They're already worried about how powerful we are. We need to tone it down or we're going to make them so nervous they might decide we really *should* be locked up in a lab."

"Now that's going a bit far," Simon said. When Derek turned on him, he lifted his hands and lowered his voice. "Look, I know why you're freaking out—"

"I'm not freaking out."

"Okay, just . . . I think we have to be careful, but they already know about the experiments. They don't expect us to be normal supernaturals. Yes, you probably shouldn't go throwing furniture and Tori should nix the fireballs, but in general . . . well . . ."

"They should know," Tori said. "If we're trying to convince them that the Edison Group messed us up, then they need to see the proof. They should know I can do stuff like that. They should know you can toss a couch across the room. They should know Chloe can raise the dead."

"No." When no one answered, Derek looked from face to face, then settled his glower on me. "Absolutely not."

"Um, I was the one keeping my mouth shut," I said.

"I'm just saying, for all of us, we need to tone it down. We can't give them any reason—" He glanced up sharply. "Andrew's coming." One last glare at the scorched wallpaper, and he hustled us out of the bedroom.

Andrew wanted us in bed, so Simon left to check his blood sugar for the night. I went downstairs for some water and was getting out a glass when Andrew popped in.

"Simon tells me you've been having trouble sleeping, so I'm going to give you this." He laid a small pill on my palm. "It's a half dose of an over-the-counter sleep aid. I'm not telling you to take it. I'm not going to ask if you did. I'm sure you got enough sleeping pills at Lyle House. I just think it's important for you to get a good night's rest. If you decide to take it, there's water in the fridge."

He left. I stared down at the pill. Taking it seemed like a cop-out. I had to learn to deal with ghosts because they weren't going away anytime soon. But he was right—I needed sleep. Being rested would help me train better tomorrow. And yet . . .

"Take the pill."

I jumped. Derek walked over to the counter and grabbed two apples from the bowl.

"You need your sleep. Toughing it out isn't going to impress anyone. It's just stupid."

Ah, Derek. Always so encouraging.

"How about you?" I said. "You thought you were close to your Change again."

"It won't happen tonight. But if it does, I'll . . ." He shrugged and bit into an apple.

"Come get me?"

"Yeah," he mumbled through a mouth full of apple.

I filled my glass from the pitcher in the fridge. "So what do you think—?"

I turned midsentence and found I was talking to myself as the kitchen door swung shut.

eight

I TOOK THE PILL AND FELL right to sleep. When I woke up, I did feel refreshed, but the room was dark. I'd left the window shade open last night, like I always did. Tori must have pulled it down. I yawned, rolled over to check the clock . . .

3:46 A.M.

I groaned, tried to sleep, and won again, only to wake to the sound of crying.

I sat up and looked around. The clock said 5:28.

At a snuffle to my right, I glanced over at Tori, curled up in her bed. Crying in her sleep? She mumbled, then resumed snoring, but still I heard the soft whimper of stifled crying. I peered at her. She was sound asleep.

I heard another wet snuffle, ending in a gasp, definitely coming from Tori's bed. I went over. Her cheeks still looked dry. I even touched one to be sure.

A long, low whimper made the hair on my neck stand up. It came from under the bed.

I backed up.

Um, what do you think is down there? The bogeyman?

Yes, a monster under the bed was a terrible cliché . . . but that didn't mean I was looking.

I thought you were going to stand up to ghosts from now on?

Maybe tomorrow . . . preferably during daylight hours.

My inner voice gave a deep, put-upon sigh.

You know who it is. Same jerk; second verse. He's trying to trick you with the crying. You can't go back to bed now or he might smother you with a pillow.

Gee, thanks. That'll help me sleep.

Open the shade. The worst thing that'll happen is you'll wake up Tori. Serves her right for closing it.

True. As I walked over, I noticed a dark oval next to Tori's bed. Figures. One throw rug in the room and she pulls it over to her side.

I had the shade halfway up when I caught a flicker of movement. Something was dripping off the side of Tori's bed, but there was no soft leaky-faucet plop—the carpet must be soaking it up.

I tugged the shade again, moonlight filling the room, illuminating—

The shade slid from my fingers, flying up with a *flap, flap, flap.* I staggered into the nightstand. The clock crashed to the floor.

The dark oval beside Tori's bed wasn't a rug; it was a pool of blood. My gaze rose to the blood-soaked sheets, then up to . . .

The body on the bed was covered in blood, the head bashed in, the face a bloody—

I tore my gaze away, stomach heaving, Tori's name coming out in a whimper. Then I saw the rest of the body: blood streaked but whole. It wore only pajama bottoms, bare chest leaving no doubt that it was male. A kid, maybe thirteen, fourteen, with dark blond hair streaked with blood and dotted with—

My gorge rose. I blinked hard, and the boy vanished. In his place lay Tori, sound asleep, still snoring. My gaze flew to the floor. Bare. No blood. No rug.

As I stared at that empty spot on the floor, I remembered the dripping blood. It hadn't made any sound. A ghostly memory, like the girl at the truck stop and the man in the factory. Horrible deaths endlessly replaying like silent films.

So it can't hurt you, right?

No, it couldn't hurt me. It could scare me. It could upset me. It could be seared into my brain forever. But it couldn't physically hurt me.

The moment I got back in bed, the sobbing started again. Then something that sounded like a laugh. I sat up, but the room went silent. I looked around. Another noise, this time somewhere between a sob and a laugh.

It might have been just the death scene replaying, but I didn't usually get a soundtrack with that. I wouldn't put it past that half-demon kid to be the director of this little scenario. If I wasn't spooked by his poltergeist stunts, maybe a gruesome death scene would work. I started to lie down again, then stopped. Derek had given me crap earlier for toughing something out on my own. I'd already let this ghost play me for a fool. I wasn't doing it again. I got out of bed and headed for the guys' room.

I stopped at their not-quite-closed door. I could hear Simon's snoring. Derek, as always, was silent. I made some noise in the hall, coughing and stamping my feet as I walked. I felt like a kid throwing pebbles at a friend's window, seeing if he'd come out and play. No answer.

I tentatively pushed the door open a few inches and stood there, waiting. Barging into the guys' room while they slept . . . well, not something I cared to do, not when I knew Derek slept in his shorts.

I coughed and shuffled a little more. When Derek still didn't wake, I peeked inside. Simon lay on the bed closest to the door, sheets tangled around him. Derek's bed was empty.

I checked the bathroom, but the door was open, the inside dark. I thought about the roof, but after the other night, I was saving that for last. Downstairs, then. First stop? The kitchen, naturally. I found an empty milk glass and a crumb-spotted plate neatly placed in the sink.

As I walked through the rooms on the first floor, I kept glancing down the hall at the rear door. He had said he'd call me if he went out to Change, hadn't he? Did he go alone? A stab of hurt zinged through me.

So what if he had? That was his right. He didn't need me to help. Except he'd seemed to appreciate having me there, and I'd liked that, being able to do something for him.

I went to the back door. Sure enough, it was unlocked. I stifled the fresh stab of disappointment and opened it. The house backed onto a tiny rear yard surrounded by forest. The sun was rising over the trees. I stepped out and peered around.

"Derek?" I called.

No answer.

I took a few more steps, then called a little louder, "Derek? Are you out here?"

A branch snapped in the woods. I pictured Derek, in the middle of a Change, unable to respond, and hurried toward the forest's edge. The noise stopped and I paused at the end of the path leading in, peering into the dark woods, listening. Another snap. Something like a groan.

"Derek? It's me."

I stepped in. It took only a few paces for the morning light to fade and darkness to envelop me.

"Derek?"

I jumped as he rounded a corner down the path. I didn't need full daylight to see the expression on his face. I didn't even need to see his face at all to know I was in trouble, just the set of his shoulders and the long strides as he bore down on me.

"I—" I began.

"What the hell are you doing, Chloe? I said we'd come out here later and try to contact that ghost. Key word? *We*. If you're here—"

I lifted my hands. "Okay, you caught me. I was sneaking out on my own, hoping no one would notice. That's why I've been calling your name."

That gave him pause.

I went on. "I had another early encounter in my room and thought, after yesterday, I'd better get backup. Tori and Simon are sleeping, but you're up, so I was looking for you."

"Oh." He rubbed a hand over his mouth and muttered what could have been an apology.

"Are you Changing?" I asked.

"Hmm? Nah. I would have come to get you if I was."

"Good. These days, the buddy system is a smart idea for both of us."

I walked back into the yard. Derek followed. The path was narrow, but he walked beside me, so close his hand brushed my elbow a few times before he mumbled something and pulled back, letting me go ahead.

"So what were you doing?" I asked. "Early morning hike?"

"Looking around. Just . . . restless."

I glanced back at him, seeing the tightness in his face, the way his gaze darted about. More anxiety than restlessness. I stepped from the forest into the yard and turned to face him.

"Something bothering you?"

"Nah." A pause, then, "Yeah. I couldn't sleep so I went up on the roof and thought I saw something down here. A light in the woods. I couldn't find anything, though."

His gaze returned to the forest, fingers tapping his thigh, like he was eager to get back in there.

"You want to keep looking?" I asked.

"Yeah, maybe."

"I'll leave you to it, then." I started for the door.

"No." He said it quickly, and reached for my arm, but stopped before he touched me. "I mean, if you're tired, sure. But you don't have to."

"Okay."

He nodded. Then we stood there. After a moment, he rubbed the back of his neck and rolled his shoulders.

"So, uh, you said something about a ghost?"

"Right." I told him what happened.

"You okay?" he said when I finished.

"Spooked, but sure, I'm fine." He kept looking at me, like he didn't believe that, and I hurried on. "So did you find anything last night when you searched the house?"

He shook his head. "I tried getting into the basement, but it was locked. There should be a key somewhere."

"Old-fashioned lock, needing an old-fashioned key?"

"Yeah, how . . . ?"

"You and Simon need to communicate better. He's already found it. Well, a key anyway. We should see if it works before everyone else gets up."

We were almost at the back door when it opened. Andrew glanced out, frowning. He didn't say anything, but the look he gave us was a lot like the one we'd gotten from the staff at Lyle House when they found Derek and me climbing out of the crawl space together. Andrew's was more uncertain, like he hoped he was wrong. Considering he'd seen me holding hands with Simon the other night, I didn't blame him for that.

The last time Derek and I had been caught together, I'd stammered excuses. He'd said nothing, and that had pissed me off. But he'd been right—my excuses only made it seem like we'd done something that needed excusing. Andrew hadn't caught us making out or holding hands or even coming out of the forest. We were in the yard together, in daylight, walking and talking. Nothing wrong with that. So why did he keep looking at us like he expected an explanation?

"Getting warmer out," I said. "Might even see the sun today."

A very mature, casual thing to say. Derek even rumbled, "Hope so." Andrew's expression didn't change.

"Are the others up?" I asked. "They were dead to the world when we left."

"Not yet. I was about to make breakfast when I noticed the back door open."

"I figured we shouldn't close it," I said. "You probably want to know where we are, right?"

He nodded and waved us through, waiting until we were inside, then turning to look out at the woods, frowning, before closing and bolting the door.

Derek went upstairs for a shower. I was going to check on Tori, but Andrew wanted my help in the kitchen, asking me to set the table while he fried bacon.

"You're a writer, so I presume you like to read," he said. "Who're your favorite authors?"

I rattled off a few names.

He laughed. "Simon was right. No society-girl princess books for you. I have something you might like, lots of action and adventure. It's still in manuscript form, but if you want a sneak peek, I'll let you borrow my laptop. I'd love to get your opinion"—he grinned over his shoulder at me—"if you don't mind playing test audience."

"No, that'd be cool. What's it about?"

He certainly made it sound good, and we talked books a bit. Then he asked me how I liked my eggs and when he was cracking ours, he said, "How much do you know about werewolves, Chloe?"

"Just what I've learned from Derek."

"Well, I'm hardly an expert myself. But Tomas told me years ago that there is one thing you always need to remember when dealing with a werewolf. They may look like you and me, but they aren't. They're only half human."

I bristled. I'd heard enough of that crap at the laboratory.

"And half monster?" I said, my voice cooler.

"No, half wolf."

I relaxed. "Derek's dad raised him to understand that."

"I'm sure Kit did, but . . . To Kit, Derek is his son, as much as Simon. There are things parents gloss over for their children. Being half wolf doesn't just make Derek a little different. Half of him is an animal ruled by instinct. There are some instincts . . ." He cleared his throat. "Derek seems very attached to you, Chloe."

"Attached?" I couldn't help laughing at that. "Sure, he feels some responsibility for me. It's like you said about being part wolf. I'm temporarily in his pack, so he has to watch out for me, whether he wants to or not. He feels obligated—instinct."

For a moment, Andrew said nothing, just flipped the eggs.

"Do you want me to start the toast?" I asked. "I can—"

"When the Edison Group first planned the Genesis project, Dr. Davidoff wanted to include werewolves and vampires."

"V-vampires?" There were *vampires*? I was still getting used to the idea of werewolves.

"The others outvoted him on that point, but he got his way with werewolves. With all of you we were messing with things we knew nothing about, but more so with werewolves."

He handed me the bread and pointed at the toaster. "Werewolves and vampires are different from the other supernatural races. They are much, much rarer and we consider them—as they consider themselves—a breed apart. You won't find a single werewolf or vampire in our group or the Edison Group. The Cabals won't hire them. Our special hospitals won't treat them. I know that sounds like segregation, but it goes both ways. Our doctors don't know enough about werewolves to treat them. And they aren't interested in coming to our doctors or working alongside us. We are as alien to them as they are to us. That doesn't mean there's anything wrong with them. They're just better off—and happier—with their own kind."

I shook my head. "Derek's happy where he is."

"Derek's a good kid, Chloe. He always has been. Responsible, mature . . . Kit used to joke that, some days, he'd rather have a dozen of Derek than one of Simon. But the wolf is coming out now, and he's struggling with it. I always told Kit . . ." He exhaled and shook his head. "The point I'm making is that I know Derek seems like a normal kid."

Normal? I could have laughed at that. I don't think anyone ever mistook Derek for a normal kid.

"But you need to remember that Derek is different. You need to be careful."

I was sick of hearing how dangerous Derek was. Different, yes, but no more than a dozen guys I knew from school, guys who stood out, didn't act like everyone else, followed their own rules. He *could* be dangerous, with his super-human strength. But how was he any worse than Tori, with her uncontrollable spells? Tori had a track record of trying to hurt me, but no one except the guys had ever warned me away from her.

Unlike Tori, Derek was struggling to control his powers. But no one even recognized that. They didn't see Derek. All they saw was the werewolf.

nine

GWEN ARRIVED FOR TRAINING after breakfast, and Margaret was supposed to show up at any moment. Simon and I were in the hall when Gwen popped in, cell phone in hand.

"Is Tori with you guys?" she asked.

"I think she's still in bed," I said. "She didn't want breakfast. I'll go get—"

"That's okay. I just got a call from work. Someone called in sick and they need me to mind the gallery. Tell Tori I'll be back around four." She started to leave, then stopped and turned to Simon. "Yesterday, when Andrew said I was a witch, you looked surprised. You couldn't tell?"

"Uh, no."

"Cool. Guess that part of the modification worked."

"Huh?"

She smiled and waved us into the parlor, then she plunked into an oversized armchair, kicked off her shoes, and tucked her stockinged feet under her, obviously in no hurry to get to work.

"I can tell you're a sorcerer just by looking at you. It's a hereditary trait. Sorcerers can recognize witches and vice versa. Andrew said they wanted to get rid of that when they tweaked your genes."

"Why?"

"Political correctness run amok. They say witches and sorcerers developed the trait as a defense mechanism." She grinned. "Know thy enemy."

"Enemy?" I said.

She looked at Simon. "What have you heard about witches?"

"Um, not much."

"Oh, don't be polite. You've heard we're inferior spell-casters, right? We hear the same about sorcerers. It's a silly rivalry, rooted back in the Inquisition. Both races are good spell-casters, with their own specialties. Anyway, Andrew says the Edison Group got the idea that if they could do away with that internal radar, we'd all just get along."

She rolled her blue eyes. "Personally, I think they made a big mistake. That recognition serves a perfectly good evolutionary purpose—to prevent accidentally interbreeding."

"Between witches and sorcerers?" I said.

"Right. It's a volatile mix and—" She stopped short, cheeks coloring. "Enough of my blathering. Work calls, however much I might like to avoid the summons." She started to stand, then stopped. "You guys like pizza?"

"Sure."

She asked us what we wanted. "I'll bring dessert, too." She looked at Simon. "Can you eat dessert?"

"I can have a little of whatever you get."

"Good." She lowered her voice. "Anything I can get you guys, just let me know. This isn't exactly a teen-friendly house, and you must be going nuts, worrying about your dad, Simon, and your aunt, Chloe. I'm really hoping—" Another glance, another notch lower on the voice volume. "They'll come around. Andrew will push them in the right direction and I'll do what I can to help."

We thanked her. She asked us what magazines we read, so she could grab some. Then Andrew called for Simon—it was time for his lesson. He told Gwen he'd love some comics, whatever she could find, and he took off. I asked for a copy of *Entertainment Weekly,* which I figured would be easy to find.

Then, before she left, I asked, "What you said about mixing witch and sorcerer blood, is it dangerous?"

"Do you mean . . . ?"

"Someone I know might have both."

She smiled. "Something tells me we're both talking about the same person, but neither wants to be the one to say it in case the other doesn't know. Is this someone named after a dead queen?"

I nodded, and Gwen breathed an exaggerated sigh of relief. "Andrew wasn't sure if you guys knew, and I didn't want to be the one caught gossiping."

I tried to tell her that Tori didn't know, but she kept going.

"Yes, mixed blood presents some challenges. It adds an extra boost, and you guys, from what I've heard, don't really need that. But the group says neither Diane nor Kit was a particularly powerful spell-caster, so—"

"K-Kit? S-Simon's dad?"

We stared at each other. Gwen's lips formed a soundless curse and she winced.

"Guess I really *am* spreading gossip. Typical." She gave a shaky laugh as she busied herself checking her cell phone. "It probably isn't true. Even the part about her dad being a sorcerer might not be true. Not like I'd know—I never worked for the Edison Group and I don't know either Kit or Diane. Anyway, sorcerer blood or not, I'm sure Tori will be just fine. I'll tell her—"

"No! I mean, she doesn't know the rumors. Any of them. Her dad being a sorcerer was just something I overheard at the lab."

"Well, then, I won't tell her. You shouldn't either."

Was Kit Bae Tori's father? He couldn't be. Kit Bae was Korean, and you could easily see it in Simon. Not so in Tori.

Sure, genetics did some wonky things—like Simon's dark blond hair. But if Diane Enright intentionally got herself pregnant with a sorcerer's child—as the demi-demon claimed—picking Kit Bae would be like choosing a red-headed father when neither you nor your husband had red hair. There was a good chance Tori's dad would know the baby wasn't his.

So, no, Tori and Simon didn't share a father. But if everyone else believed they did, Tori and Simon might hear the rumor, and that was a complication no one needed.

ten

MARGARET ARRIVED SHORTLY AFTER Gwen left. When Tori came down and heard Margaret was taking me out for my lesson, she decided to join us. Tori might be good at hiding it, but I knew she was just as anxious and restless as we were. The last thing she needed was to spend the morning in our room. Derek and Simon sure wouldn't invite her to do anything with them.

When Margaret hesitated, I said I'd be more relaxed with Tori along. Complete crap, but I can't help it. Derek isn't the only one to suffer from overwhelming instincts. I have the unshakable urge to be helpful, which I usually end up regretting. I only hoped I wouldn't this time.

Before we left, Andrew gave Margaret a bunch of tips about touring with a half-million-dollar runaway. It was clear he didn't want us to go out at all, but Margaret insisted. I was a long way from Buffalo, she said, and with my black hair, I didn't look like the girl in the poster. Besides, what kidnap victim would be driving around with a woman who could pass for her grandmother?

So we left. Margaret's car was some fancy European model, like the kind my dad always leased, which made me think about him. Dad and I had never been real close. I was Mom's baby, and after she died, well again, it was that instinct thing. Some people have the instinct to be parents and some don't, and Dad didn't, though he tried his best. He traveled a lot, which didn't help. He did care about me, though. More than I realized. After my breakdown he flew from Berlin to stay at my bedside until I went to Lyle House. He only went back when he had to, and he thought I was safe in Aunt Lauren's care.

"So this necromancer stuff," Tori said from the backseat. "Chloe doesn't know a lot about it."

She motioned for me to start asking questions. I'd fantasized about meeting another necromancer, and here I had one and hadn't asked a single thing. Worrying about Dad wasn't going to help me any.

I started by asking Margaret about the ghostly reenactments I'd seen. Residuals, she called them, but she didn't tell me anything else I hadn't already figured out. They were leftover energy from a traumatic event that played over and over again, like a film loop. Harmless images, not ghosts. As for how to block them . . .

"You won't need to worry about that for a few years. Concentrate on ghosts for now. Deal with residuals when you're old enough to see them."

"But I am seeing them."

She shook her head. "I suspect what you're seeing is a ghost reverting to his death form—how he appeared at the moment of his death. Ghosts can do that, unfortunately, and some like to do so to intimidate necromancers."

"I don't think that's what this was." I told her about residuals I'd seen—a man jumping into a saw in a factory and a girl being murdered at a truck stop.

"My God," Tori said. "That's . . ." When I glanced at her, she'd gone pale. "You *saw* that?"

"I've heard you like movies, Chloe," Margaret cut in. "I suspect you have a very good imagination."

"Okay, so can you tell me how to block them when I *do* start seeing them?"

I must have let a little sarcasm sneak into my tone, because Margaret looked over sharply. I fixed her with my best wide-blue-eyes look and said, "It helps if I know what's coming. So I'll feel ready to handle it."

She nodded. "That's a good attitude to take, Chloe. All right then. I'll let you in on the trade secret. When you see a residual, there's a surefire way to deal with them. Walk away."

"Can I block them?"

"No, but you don't need to. Simply walk away. They aren't ghosts, so they can't follow."

I could have figured that out by myself. The problem was: "How do I know it's a residual? If it looks real, how do you know it *isn't*? Before you see . . . the dying part."

"One sign is that residuals don't make any noise."

I knew that.

"Another is that you can't interact with them."

Knew that, too.

So if I noticed a guy about to jump into an industrial saw, I should stop and listen for any noise? Yell at him and see if he answered? By then, if he was a residual, he'd have already jumped, and I'd see exactly what I'd been trying to avoid. And if he was real, I could let him die while trying to spare myself an ugly sight.

If I could tell it was just a ghost—residual or not—I'd know the person wasn't in danger and I could get out of there. So, while she drove through a small town, I asked how to do that.

"Excellent question," Margaret said. "Now the real lessons begin. There are three ways to tell the ghosts from the living. First, clothing. For instance, if a man is wearing a hat and suspenders he's a ghost, likely from the nineteen fifties."

"I've seen guys wearing hats and suspenders," Tori said. "Young guys, too. It's retro."

"A Civil War uniform, then. If he's wearing that, he's a ghost."

No kidding.

"Second, as you may have noticed, ghosts can pass through solid objects. So if he walks through a door or a chair, you can be sure it's a ghost."

Even someone who wasn't a necromancer could figure that out.

Margaret turned the car onto a road leading out of town. "And the third . . . Any ideas, Chloe?"

"If they don't make noise when they walk?"

"Excellent! Yes. Those are the three ways to tell ghosts from the living."

Great. So if I saw a guy standing still, and he wasn't wearing an old uniform, I just had to ask him to walk through furniture. If he stared at me like I was crazy, then I'd know he wasn't a ghost.

I hoped that the practice part of the day would go better. When I saw where she was taking us, though, that hope faded fast.

"A c-cemetery?" I said as she pulled into the parking lot. "I c-can't— I shouldn't even be here."

"Nonsense, Chloe. I certainly hope you aren't afraid of cemeteries."

"Um, no," Tori said. "It's the bodies buried in them that worry her."

Margaret looked from me to Tori.

"Uh, dead bodies?" Tori said. "Potential zombies?"

"Don't be silly. You can't accidentally raise the dead."

"Chloe can."

Margaret gave a tight smile. "I've heard Chloe is quite powerful, but I'm sure she doesn't need to worry about raising the dead yet."

"She already has. I was there."

"I-it's true," I said. "I raised subjects of Dr. Lyle's experiment, buried in the basement at Lyle House. Then I raised dead bats in a warehouse, and a homeless guy in a place we tried to spend the night."

"Bats?" Tori said, nose wrinkling.

"You were asleep. I didn't want to wake you up."

"And I thank you for that," she said. She turned to Margaret. "I was there for the homeless guy. I saw him crawling across Chloe—"

"I don't doubt you did, but I'm afraid you girls have been the victims of a cruel trick. There are members of the Edison Group who have a very big stake in this experiment and would love to make it appear that the subjects' powers were vastly increased by the modification. One of their staff necromancers apparently wanted to make the group believe Chloe could raise the dead. That's absurd, of course. Not only do you need years of training, but it requires rituals and ingredients you don't have."

"But I raised the homeless guy *after* we got away."

"That's what they wanted you to think. Obviously, they were on your trail, which is how they intercepted you at Andrew's house. It doesn't matter. Even if you could raise the dead"—a twitch of her lips, clearly humoring me—"I'm here and I'll make sure we take the proper precautions. Learning control is the best way to overcome your fears."

When I tried to protest again, Tori asked if we could have a minute. We got out of the car and she led me to a spot under a maple tree. My stomach clenched every time I caught a glimpse of the gravestones, imagining accidentally slamming ghosts back into the corpses buried under them.

I only had to glance at the cemetery walls and I could see Derek's scowl, hear him snap, "Don't even think about training in there, Chloe."

"She's jealous, you know," Tori said.

"What?"

"You can raise the dead. If she admits that, then she has to admit you're a better necromancer than she is."

"I don't think being able to raise the dead makes anyone *better*."

"In their world it does, because it means you're more powerful. Everyone wants to be more powerful." She looked around the cemetery, her gaze going distant. "It doesn't matter if it's good power or bad. I lived with my mom long enough to see that. Margaret might not want to raise the dead, but she wants to be able to, and she doesn't want some kid to be better at it than she is. So she's telling herself you can't."

"Okay, but I'd rather *not* prove her wrong."

Tori's lips pursed. "Actually . . ."

"Uh-uh. I'm not returning any poor ghost to its rotting—"

"Only temporarily."

I gave her a look.

She sighed. "Fine. But whatever that chick's hang-ups, her job is to train you, and you need training. We all do. It'll be fine as long as you take it easy, right?"

True. While I couldn't help remembering Derek's suspicion that Tori was betraying us, I could see no nefarious advantage to encouraging me to raise the dead.

"Look, do what you want," she said. "I'll back you up. As cliché as it sounds, we're in this together. You, me, the guys. Not exactly the gang I'd pick—no offense—but . . ."

"You're stuck with us."

"My advice? Take her lesson and be careful."

I imagined what Derek would say. He wouldn't like the situation, but I think he'd eventually agree.

I went back to Margaret and said I was ready.

eleven

MARGARET LED US INTO the cemetery. There were some mourners under a temporary canopy, huddled around a casket. We steered clear of them.

The only graveyard I'd ever been in was the one where my mom was buried. Dad and I went every year on her birthday.

This one was bigger, with new graves at the front, where the mourners were. Margaret led us to the back, which had the old graves. It was empty there—the dead having been dead so long there was no one left to visit them.

As cemeteries went, I supposed it was nice, with lots of trees and benches. Take away the headstones and it would make a decent park, especially with the sun warming up the cold April morning. I tried to focus on the sun and the scenery, not on what lay under my feet.

Margaret stopped at one of the more recent graves in the old area. It was of a woman who'd died in 1959 at the age of sixty-three. Margaret said that was ideal—someone who hadn't died so long ago that she'd be spooked by our modern clothes, but long enough ago that she wouldn't have a lot of loved ones left and want messages passed on.

She told us to kneel like we were the family of this woman—Edith—come to pay our respects. Most necromancers avoided daytime summoning, but Margaret thought that was silly. Coming at night only called more attention to yourself. In the daytime, if you brought a friend—a supernatural of course—it was easy, because you could kneel at a grave and talk and no one would look twice.

"Or you could use a cell phone," Tori said.

"That's hardly respectful in a cemetery," said Margaret with a sniff.

Tori shrugged. "I guess. But she *could.* And she should probably have a cell anyway, for when a ghost tries talking to her in public."

Margaret rolled her eyes. I thought it was a good idea and appreciated it.

It would be great to think Tori was starting to like me, but, as she said, she'd realized how alone she was. Everyone needs an ally and I was the only choice.

I sighed. I'd never realized how good I'd had it, back in my normal life, where if a popular girl talked to me, the worst thing that could happen was she was planning to mock my stutter to get a laugh from the popular guys.

Margaret opened her briefcase and took out baggies of herbs, a piece of chalk, matches, and a little saucer. Ritual material to help necromancers summon, she explained. Tori suppressed a snort, as if to say I didn't need that. I said nothing.

"Should I remove this?" I asked, pulling my pendant from under my shirt.

Margaret blinked. "Where did you get that?"

"My mother, when I was little. I was seeing ghosts, and she told me this would keep them away. So it's for real?"

"Real, yes—real superstitious nonsense. I haven't seen one since I was about your age. Necromancers don't use them anymore, but they were once quite the hot fashion item for our kind. It's supposed to reduce a necromancer's glow."

"Glow?" Tori said.

"That's what ghosts see that marks us as necromancers, right?" I said.

Margaret nodded.

"And if this necklace makes it dim," I said, "then the necromancer won't attract ghosts."

"Well, then Margaret's right," Tori said. "It's definitely not working. But that's not the same one you were wearing at Lyle House. That was red and on a chain."

"It *was* red." I fingered the blue stone. "The chain broke. But if it is real, then changing color could mean it lost its power."

Margaret stared at the pendant. "It changed color?"

I nodded. "Does that mean something?"

"They say—" She shook it off. "Superstitious nonsense. Our world is full of it, I'm afraid. Now let's get started. The first thing I need you to do, Chloe, is read the woman's name, and keep that in your mind. Then, aloud, you'll repeat what we call an entreaty. Say the spirit's name and respectfully ask her to speak to you. Try that."

"Edith Parsons, I'd like to speak to you please."

"That's it. Next we light the . . ."

As Margaret explained, a plump woman in a blue dress appeared behind the gravestone, her wrinkled face frowning as her bright blue eyes peered around. When those eyes swung my way, the frown vanished in a wide smile.

"Hello," I said.

Margaret's gaze followed mine and she jumped.

Tori snickered. "Guess Chloe doesn't need that stuff after all."

Margaret greeted the woman, who glanced her way, but her gaze—and smile—swung back to me.

"Aren't you a sweet little thing," she said. "How old are you, doll?"

"Fifteen."

"And you can see ghosts. I can tell by the glow. I've never met one of you, but I've heard the others tell of such things. They call you a . . ." She struggled for the word.

"Necromancer," I said.

Her face screwed up, like she'd bit a lemon. "In my day, they called people who talked to ghosts spiritualists or mediums. Much nicer words, don't you think?"

I agreed.

She looked from me to Margaret and laughed. "All these years of not believing folks when they talked about you people, and here I meet two in one day."

She reached out and tapped the air around me, my glow, I guess.

"So pretty," she murmured. "It draws the eye . . . Yours is so bright, dear. Much brighter than hers. I suppose that's because you're younger."

I'd heard that the stronger the glow, the stronger the necromancer, and it must be true, because Margaret's lips tightened.

"C-can I try something?" I asked.

"Of course, doll. No need to be shy. This is a special day for me." She lowered her voice. "It can get a bit dull on the other side. This will be a lovely story to tell my friends."

"I'm going to take off my necklace, and I'd like to know if it changes my glow."

"Good idea," Tori murmured.

Margaret harrumphed, like it was a waste of time, but didn't stop me. I lifted the ribbon over my head and handed it to Tori.

The old woman gasped. "Oh my."

I turned to see her staring, eyes like saucers. Then there was a shimmer to my left . . . and one to my right.

Margaret let out an oath. She lunged over, snatching the necklace from Tori and pressing it into my hand. The air continued to shimmer, shapes taking form as I yanked the necklace back on.

Edith vanished and in her place appeared a young woman in a pioneer outfit. She knelt in front of me, sobbing.

"Oh, praise God. Praise *God*. I have been waiting so long. Please, help me, child. I need—"

A young man in a ripped and filthy denim jacket grabbed her by the shoulder and yanked her back. "Listen, kid, I've been stuck here since—"

A heavyset man gave the young guy a shove, sending him flying. "Have some respect for your elders, punk."

"Thanks." I looked past him to the pioneer woman, cringing and sobbing. "How can I—?"

"I was talking about *me*," the man said. "I was here first."

"No, you weren't. I'll get to you." I tried leaning around the man.

"You want me to take a number? Fine." He grabbed the pioneer woman and threw her. She disappeared. "Whoops. Guess she left. My turn."

I leaped to my feet. "Don't you—"

"Don't I what?" He lunged forward. His face went purple, swelling to twice its size, eyes bugging out, black tongue lolling. I reeled back. The guy in the dirty jacket jumped behind me. I spun out of his way.

"Sorry, kid." He smiled, showing rows of rotting teeth. "Didn't mean to spook you. Spook you. Get it?" He laughed. I backed away, but he closed the gap between us. "Got a problem you can help with, kid. See, I'm stuck here in limbo, on account of a few things I didn't do. Bum rap, you know? So I'm trapped here, and I need you to do something for me."

"And me!" a voice behind me shouted.

"And me!"

"Me!"

"Me!"

I turned slowly and found myself surrounded by ghosts of all ages, at least a dozen of them, pressing closer; eyes wild; hands reaching for me; voices rising, shouting, demanding, snarling. The heavyset guy who'd flashed his death mask planted himself in front of me.

"Don't just stand there, brat. This is your job. Your duty. To help the dead." He shoved his face down to mine, purple and swollen again. "So start helping."

"We will," said a voice to my left.

I turned. The mob of ghosts parted. Margaret stood there, a saucer filled with dried plants in one hand, a burning match in the other.

"You're scaring the child," she said calmly. "Come over here and speak to me instead. I can help."

The ghosts swarmed her. Then they screamed. They howled. They cursed. And they began to fade, fighting and struggling and cursing some more, but continuing to vanish until only Margaret was standing there, blowing smoke from the burning plants in the saucer.

"Wh-what is that?" I asked.

"Vervain. It banishes ghosts. Most of them, anyway. There's always a stubborn one."

She strode past me and I turned to see a grandfatherly old man backing away.

"No, please," he said. "I wasn't bothering the child. I was only waiting my turn."

Margaret kept advancing. Tori scuttled out of her way, looking around in confusion, only able to see and hear us.

"Please," the man said. "This might be my only chance. It's just a message."

He looked past Margaret to me and his eyes glistened with tears. "Please, dear. Just one moment of your time."

A creepy, queasy feeling snaked through me. This felt so wrong—a grown man begging me for a favor.

"Hold on," I said to Margaret. "Can I hear what he wants to say? Please? He wasn't one of the ones scaring me."

Margaret hesitated, then waved for the man to continue quickly.

He took a moment to compose himself, then said, "I died two years ago. I fell asleep in my car and it went off a cliff. They never found it and they said . . . they said I took off, left my wife, kids, grandkids. All I need for you to do is send them a letter. Just tell them where they can find the car."

"I have to write this down," I said, turning to Margaret. I was sure she had paper in the car. Even a cell phone would do—I could text in a message—but she shook her head.

"Wait," Tori said. She pulled a few pieces of folded paper and a pen from her pocket. "I was going to make a list of stuff we need. Andrew said someone would go shopping for us later."

I took down his wife's address and the location of the car. It didn't make sense to me—roads and landmarks I wouldn't know—but the ghost said his wife would understand. He said to add a note from him, that he loved her and would never have left her.

"She might not believe I sent a message from the grave, but she'll look anyway. I won't take up any more of your time. Thank you."

Before I could say a word, he disappeared.

"Now that was cool," Tori said, taking the pencil and extra paper from me.

As I folded the page with the information, Margaret reached for it.

I handed it over. "I guess it'll have to be mailed from someplace far from here, huh? Just in case."

"It's not being mailed."

"What?" Tori and I said in unison.

"You never promise to deliver a message for a ghost, Chloe. *Never.*"

"But—"

Her hand cupped my elbow, voice going gentle. "You can't. If you do, then what you saw today will be only the beginning. Word will get out that you're willing to help, and while there are perfectly good requests, like this one, you heard some of the others. Most of those ghosts were in limbo. *Sentenced* to limbo. You can't help them, and you don't want to, but that won't keep them from hounding you day and night. So you have to ignore both: the good and the bad."

I looked up into her face and briefly saw someone else there, a younger, sadder woman. I realized that what seemed like cold efficiency was self-preservation—the tough, no-nonsense necromancer, her heart hardened to the pleas of the dead. Was this my fate? Toughen up until I could throw that note in the trash and never think of it again? I didn't ever want to be that way. Ever.

"Are you okay?" Tori whispered.

Margaret had moved away and was dumping out the ashes of the vervain. Tori touched my arm. I realized I was shaking. I wrapped my arms around myself. "I should have brought a sweater."

"It's still chilly when the sun goes in, isn't it?" Margaret said as she came back to us.

She held up a baggie of dried stuff.

"Vervain," she said. "I'll give you some back at the house. Obviously you could use it."

She tried to smile, but she was out of practice and only managed a twist of her lips.

"Thank you," I said, and surprised myself by meaning it.

"Are you up to some more work?" she asked.

I glanced down at the bag she held, like it was a prize for a lesson well done, and as much as I wanted to quit, that eager-to-please part of me blurted, "Sure."

twelve

"IT'S EASY TO SUMMON ghosts who want to be called," Margaret said, "but sometimes you need to speak to a reluctant one. While we try to respect the wishes of the dead, you've just seen the importance of maintaining the upper hand in the necromancer-ghost relationship. Some really believe we exist only to help them, and we must quickly disabuse them of that notion. Being firm in your summoning is one way to establish the proper reputation."

Margaret took the lead, going from grave to grave. We visited four ghosts, chatting with them for a minute, before she found one that didn't want to answer her summons.

She let me try. The ghost didn't answer me either.

"Do you know how to increase the power of the summons?" Margaret asked me.

"Concentrate harder?"

"Exactly. Slowly increase your concentration and sharpen your focus. Start doing it now. Gradually, gradually . . ."

We kept on like this for a while, Margaret getting frustrated by how slowly I was ramping up the juice. Finally, I felt an inner twinge that said "that's enough," and I said so.

She sighed. "I understand you're nervous, Chloe. Whoever raised those bodies has frightened you."

"*I* raised—"

"That's not possible. Yes, you are clearly a powerful young necromancer, but without the proper tools and rituals, you just can't do it. I don't even have the ingredients with me."

"But what if that's one of the modifications they made? Making it easier for me to raise the dead?"

"There would be no reason to—"

"Why not?" Tori interjected. "Raising the dead must have some use."

Armies of the dead, I thought, and tried not to remember the old pictures I'd seen, crazy necromancers raising undead hordes.

"All right," Margaret said. "You girls are worried because you don't know what's been done to you. But the only way to overcome that fear is to understand the extent of your powers and learn control. I'm not asking you to give it everything you have, Chloe. Just a little more."

I did, and caught the first shimmer of an appearing spirit.

"Wonderful. Now, just a little more. Pace yourself. That's it. Slowly, but firmly."

That inner alarm clanged louder now.

"No more," I said. "It doesn't feel right."

"But you're making progress."

"Maybe, but I'm not comfortable with going further."

"If she doesn't want to—" Tori began.

"Victoria?" Margaret held out the keys. "Please go sit in the car."

Tori stood. "Come on, Chloe."

I got to my feet. Margaret's fingers wrapped around my leg. "You can't walk away and leave a spirit like this. Look at him."

The air shimmered. An arm poked through. A face began to take form, then faded before I could make out any features.

"He's caught between limbo and the world of the living," Margaret said. "You need to finish pulling him through."

"Why don't *you*?" Tori said.

"Because this is Chloe's lesson."

Tori started to argue again, but I silenced her with a shake of my head. Margaret was right. I had to learn to fix this problem. I wouldn't be responsible for trapping a ghost between dimensions.

"I'll push him back," I said.

"Banish? That doesn't work on trapped spirits."

I shook my head. "I mean *push* him. Like summoning, only in reverse. I've done it before."

The look she gave me reminded me of when I was seven and I'd proudly informed our housekeeper that I'd donated half my clothing to a charity drive at school. It had seemed perfectly sensible to me—I didn't need so much stuff—but she'd stared at me like Margaret was now, with a mix of horror and disbelief.

"You never, ever push a ghost back, Chloe. I've heard it's possible, but—" She swallowed, like she was at a loss for words.

"I think it's a bad thing," Tori whispered.

"It's a terrible, cruel thing. You have no idea where you're pushing them. They could be lost in some—some . . ." She shook her head. "I don't mean to alarm you, but you can never take that risk again. Do you understand?"

I nodded. "So I keep tugging this one . . ."

"That's right."

I knelt and kept at it until sweat trickled into my eyes. I went past the mental alarms and finally the ghost began to materialize.

"That's it, Chloe. You're almost there. Give him one last—"

Tori yelped. My eyes flew open. She was staring at a nearby oak tree, her eyes wide. Something was moving under the tree—a shapeless mat of blackish gray fur stretched over bone.

"Send it back," Tori whispered. "Quick."

"Ignore that and finish summoning this spirit," Margaret said.

I turned on her in disbelief.

"Are you nuts?" Tori said. "Can you see—?"

"Yes, I can," Margaret's voice was eerily calm. "Apparently I was mistaken about the extent of Chloe's powers."

"You think?" Tori said.

I stared at Margaret. Her face was expressionless. In shock? She had to be. While she didn't seem like the type to freak out, she'd just seen me raise a dead animal—without rituals, without ingredients, without even trying. Gaping in horror like Tori would be a perfectly reasonable response. But she only watched the thing, creeping toward us, pulling its mangled body along.

Its head lifted, as if it could sense me watching. It had no eyes, though, no snout, no ears, just a skull covered in bits of tattered fur and skin. Its head bobbed and wobbled, like it was trying to see who had called it forth.

"Chloe," Margaret said sharply. "As horrible as that thing is"—did her voice quaver a little?—"your priority is this human ghost. Pull him through quickly."

"B-but if I—"

She clasped my arm, panic edging into her voice. "You need to do this, Chloe. *Quickly*."

The creature was closing the gap between us. It was a squirrel; I could see tufts of long, gray fur left on the ratlike tail.

It started to chatter, a horrible squeaking, rattling sound. It lifted its head, then turned its empty eye sockets my way and continued creeping forward, leaving a trail of fur and bits behind, the wind bringing the stink of rotting flesh.

Tori clapped her hand over her mouth. "Do something," she whispered.

I shored up my nerve, closed my eyes, and plowed forward, throwing everything I had into one massive pull, imagining myself yanking the ghost—

The ground under us shook. Tori shrieked. Margaret gasped. My eyes flew open. The earth quavered and groaned and then, with an earsplitting crack, ripped open right in front of us.

Tori grabbed my arm and yanked me to my feet. We backpedaled as the ground yawned open with a thundering roar, dirt spilling into the crevasse and flying up, the musty stink of it billowing out.

The chasm split wider and deeper, an avalanche of dirt rushing in from all sides, tombstones swaying and rumbling. One toppled in, and still the earth split, until the top of a coffin appeared, shaking and rattling.

"Oh no," Tori said. "No, no, no."

She grabbed my arm again and tried to yank me backward. I brushed her off, walked to a place far enough away to be safe, then closed my eyes and concentrated on releasing the spirits. And if that sounds incredibly calm of me, let's just say the earth wasn't the only thing shaking. I had to drop to my knees before they gave way.

I squeezed my eyes shut and kept at it even when Margaret grabbed my shoulders. She shouted for me to get up, but I concentrated on releasing. Release, release, release . . .

Someone screamed. Then someone else. I leaped up and looked around, but there was no one near the crack in the earth, now at least twenty feet long, a half-dozen coffins exposed.

The ground had gone still. All I could hear was the rustling of leaves. I looked up. The tree branches were covered in tiny, new buds. That wasn't what was making the noise.

I followed the sound to the coffins. Not a rustling, but a scratching, nails raking the inside of the caskets. Then came the faint, muffled cries of ghosts trapped in those bodies, trying to claw their way—

I dropped to my knees again.

Release them. That's your job now. Your only job. Release those spirits before the zombies—

Another scream, this time from behind me. A group of newly arrived mourners was coming our way, the pallbearers carrying the casket toward an open grave on the edge of the old section.

They'd stopped and were staring down at the casket. I started toward them, slowly, cautiously, gaze fixed on that coffin, telling myself they'd stopped because of the earth tremors.

A gasp from the crowd. Then I heard what they did—a *bump-bump* from inside the casket.

Relax. Relax and release. Release, release, re—

A low moan came from the casket, and every hair on my body rose. Another moan, louder. Muffled. Then a strangled cry from within.

Two of the pallbearers dropped their handles. Their end of the coffin tipped and the other four, startled, let go. The casket plummeted, hitting a gravestone as it fell, lid popping open with a crack.

The knot of mourners blocked my view, everyone grabbing the person nearest them—some for support and others to push them out of the way as they ran.

When the throng cleared, I saw an arm on the ground, the rest of the body still hidden behind the gravestone. It just lay there, hand palm downward, arm encased in a suit sleeve. Then the fingers moved, curling clawlike, gripping the ground as the corpse pulled himself forward, turning my way, toward the one who'd summoned him and—

And the one who'll send him back. Now!

I squeezed my eyes shut and imagined the man, a vague figure in a suit. I imagined setting his soul free, sending up an apology with it, releasing him—

"Good," Tori whispered beside me. "It's stopped moving. It's— No, wait. Keep going. Keep— Okay, it stopped." A pause. "Still stopped." Her voice was breathless with relief. "You did it."

Maybe so, but I didn't open my eyes to check. As Tori went to assess the situation, I kept releasing spirits, picturing people in suits, people in dresses, people of all ages, animal spirits, spirits of every kind; and while I did, I listened, not just for the shouts and shrieks of the living, but the thumps and cracks and scratches of the living dead.

When I opened my eyes, Tori was coming along a path toward me, keeping back from the edge of the crevasse. People lined both sides now, eyeing it warily, waiting for the earth to move. But it didn't.

"The dead are dead again," Tori murmured as she came up beside me. "Everything's quiet."

Margaret stood along the chasm with the others. When I called to her, she turned slowly, eyes meeting mine, and in them I saw fear. No, not fear. Horror and revulsion.

You aren't like her. She sees that now, what you are, what you can do, and it scares her. Scares and disgusts.

She waved us back to the car, but didn't move herself, like she couldn't bear to walk with me.

"Stupid bitch," Tori muttered. "Oh, let's take the necromancer with superpowers to the cemetery. Of course you aren't going to raise the dead, you silly girl."

"I'd say I showed her, but I really would have rather not."

Tori's laugh quavered. "We should probably get out of here before anyone starts asking questions."

"Not too fast," I said. "We don't want to look like we're running from the scene."

"Right."

As we walked, we gawked—it would seem weird if we didn't. We gaped at the crevasse. We squinted up at the sky. We pointed at the fallen casket and whispered, all the while walking as fast as we dared, trying to look like we were as shocked and confused as everyone else.

"Girls!" a man called. "Hold on."

I turned slowly and saw a middle-aged man bearing down on us. I tried to get Margaret's attention, tell her we might have trouble, but she was looking the other way, leaving us to deal with it.

thirteen

"ARE YOU GIRLS OKAY?" the man asked.

Tori nodded. "I think so."

"Wh-what was that?" I said. "An earthquake?"

He nodded. "Seems so. We haven't had even a tremor in twenty years."

A young woman in a long leather coat came up behind him. "And we wouldn't have had one now, if it wasn't for the quarry reopening last summer."

"We can't go pointing fingers until we're sure," the man said.

"Oh, I'm sure. There's a reason those environmentalists wanted to keep it closed, and a reason it shut down in the first place . . . after the *last* tremors, twenty years ago. Do you think that's a coincidence? All that digging, knocking around the Teutonic plates. Now look—" She gestured at the chasm and scowled. "The quarry's going to have to pay for this."

"Is everyone okay?" I asked. "I thought I heard a scream."

"Oh, that was just—" She waved at the casket, still upended on the ground, surrounded by mourners who were all hoping someone else was going to volunteer to return the body. "My great-uncle was being buried today; and when the ground shook, he started bumping around in the coffin, scared the guys, and they dropped it."

The man cleared his throat, warning her that we didn't need the gory details, but she carried on.

"The coffin busted open, Uncle Al fell out, the ground shook again, and—" She tried to suppress a snicker. "They thought he was, you know, moving."

"Eww," Tori said. "I'd have screamed, too."

"Anyway," the man cut in, "I see your grandmother wants you girls in the car. I don't blame her. Mother Nature might not be done with us yet."

We thanked them and headed to the parking lot, Margaret still keeping pace twenty feet behind us.

"Teutonic plates?" Tori said. "Do they bury German pottery with the dead around here?"

I had to laugh at that, but it was a bit shaky.

She continued, "To cause an earthquake the *tectonic* plates need a fault line, which are, like, on the other side of the country."

"It sounded good. And that's all that matters. Derek and Simon say that's what people do if they see supernatural stuff—make up a logical explanation. If you didn't know about necromancers and you saw what just happened, what would you think? A freak earthquake? Or someone raising the dead?"

"True. Still, Teutonic plates?"

This time I sat in the back with Tori. When we reached the highway, Margaret finally spoke.

"Who taught you to do that, Chloe?" she said.

"What?"

Her eyes met mine in the rearview mirror. "Who taught you to raise the dead?"

"N-no one. I—I've never even met another necromancer before you." Not exactly true. I'd briefly met the ghost of one, but he hadn't been much help.

"Did the Edison Group give you books? Manuals?"

"J-just a history book that I—I skimmed through a bit. Th-there wasn't anything on rituals."

A moment of silence as she studied me through the mirror. "You were trying to make a point, weren't you, Chloe?"

"Wh-what?"

"I said you couldn't raise the dead; you proved you could. You visualized returning a soul—"

"No!" My stutter fell away. "Return a ghost to a rotting corpse to make a point? I'd *never* do that. I was doing exactly what you asked—trying to pull that spirit through. I was summoning. But if I do that with bodies around, I can raise the dead. That's what I tried to tell you."

She drove for a minute, the silence heavy. Then her gaze rose to the mirror again, meeting mine.

"You're telling me you can raise the dead simply by summoning?"

"Yes."

"My God," she whispered, staring at me. "What have they done?"

Hearing her words and seeing her expression, I knew Derek had been right last night. I'd just done something worse than raising the dead—I'd confirmed her worst fears about us.

When we got to the house, Andrew was the only one around. Margaret called him into the kitchen, closing the door behind them.

There wasn't much point in shutting that door. Margaret didn't yell, but her voice took on a strident note that echoed through the house.

The upshot of her tirade was that I was the devil's spawn and should be locked up in a tower before I unleashed hordes of the living dead to slaughter them all in their sleep. Well, maybe that's an exaggeration, but not by much.

Tori smacked open the kitchen door and marched in, with me close behind. "Excuse me. Who took the genetically modified necromancer into the cemetery?"

Andrew turned to her. "Tori, please. We don't need—"

"Chloe didn't want to go there. Did Margaret tell you that? Did she tell you we warned her that Chloe could raise the dead? That I'd seen it? That she didn't believe us?"

I swore I could see sparks flying from Tori's fingertips as she waved her hands.

"Did she tell you Chloe asked over and over to stop? That Margaret *made* her keep going? Even after Chloe raised a dead squirrel, Margaret forced her to keep summoning."

"I did not force—"

"You told her she'd trapped a ghost between dimensions."

"All right," Andrew said. "Clearly, we need to discuss—"

"Oh, we need to discuss a lot of things," Margaret said.

Andrew shooed us out. As soon as we were gone, the fight started up again. Tori and I listened outside the door.

"We weren't prepared," Margaret said. "Not at all."

"Then we need to *get* prepared."

"She split open the ground, Andrew! The very earth opened to free the dead. It—it—" She took a deep, ragged breath. "It was like something out of the old stories my grandfather used to tell. Terrible stories that gave me nightmares about necromancers so powerful they could raise entire cemeteries of the dead."

I remembered what the demi-demon said. *You called to your friend and the shades of a thousand dead answered, winging their way back to their rotted shells. A thousand corpses ready to become a thousand zombies. A vast army of the dead for you to control.*

"She can raise the dead at fifteen," Margaret continued. "Without training. Without ritual. Without intention."

"Then she has to learn how to—"

"Do you know what Victoria told Gwen? She's never learned a single spell, but she can cast them. If she sees it, she can do it. No training. No incantations. Naturally, we thought she was telling stories, but now—"

She sucked in air. "We can't handle this. I know they're just children, and what has happened to them is terrible and tragic. But the greater tragedy would be to tell them they can expect to lead normal lives."

"Lower your voice," Andrew said.

"Why? So you can keep assuring them everything will be all right? It won't. Those children are going to need to be monitored for their entire lives. It's only going to get worse."

Tori tugged me away. "She knows what happened was her fault, so she's covering her butt as fast as she can. We don't need to listen to this."

She was right. Margaret had screwed up and she'd been scared. She wasn't the kind of person who could easily accept either, so she had to lay the blame elsewhere—make us out to be so bad that she couldn't have been expected to control the situation.

And yet . . .

These were our allies. Our only allies. We knew that Margaret and Russell had already been second-guessing Andrew's decision to take us in. Now I'd given them exactly the ammunition they needed.

fourteen

TORI AND I WERE heading for the stairs when I heard the thud of heavy footfalls. I hoped it was Simon. Prayed it was. But I knew it wasn't. I turned to see Derek bearing down on us, scowling.

"I'll handle him," Tori said.

"I've got it." I raised my voice as he drew near. "We had a problem—"

"I heard." He parked himself three feet in front of me, like he was trying not to loom, but it didn't matter. Derek could loom from across a room.

"Then you also heard it wasn't her fault," Tori said.

He didn't even glance at her, the full weight of that scowl pinning me. "Did you summon in a cemetery?"

"Yes, I did."

"You knew that was a problem?"

"Yes, I did."

"She didn't have a choice," Tori said.

"She always has a choice. She can say no."

"I tried," I said.

"You can't *try* to say no. Either you do or you don't." He lowered his voice, some of the fury evaporating, but the hard edge lingering. "It's not enough to say the word, Chloe. You need to follow through and that's the part you can't seem to manage."

"Whoa," Tori said. "You're out of line."

"He has a point," I murmured.

"What? You—" She struggled for a word. "Don't put up with that, Chloe. I don't care how big or how smart he is, he has no right to talk to you that way. You did your best."

I'd allowed myself to be pushed into something I'd known was wrong.

"What do you think they're talking about in there?" he said. "How to help us control our powers?"

"We know what they're talking about, Derek. And I know what I did. Exactly what you warned us against last night. I gave everyone who doesn't want to help us a reason not to."

He opened his mouth. Closed it. You'd think that I'd get some credit for realizing this before he told me. But he had a point to make; and all I'd done was throw up a temporary obstacle, one that barely checked his speed before he barreled right through it.

"The word is *no*, Chloe. *No*, I will not do that. *No*, I don't think it's safe. And if you push me, well, sorry, but I just can't seem to summon right now."

"I—"

"What if they asked me how strong I was? Do you think I'd walk in there and pick up the sofa for them?"

"That's not what I was trying—"

"But it's what you did. You gave them a full-out demonstration of just how powerful you are, and now they're going to be wondering if the Edison Group had the right idea, locking us away—even killing us."

"Oh, come on," Tori said. "They wouldn't—"

"Are you sure?"

I shook my head. "If you believed that, Derek, you wouldn't still be here. You'd be upstairs with Simon, packing his bag for him."

"Yeah? And where would I go? The Edison Group tracked us to Andrew's cottage and we still have no idea how they managed it. And what did they do to us there? Ask us to come along nicely? Fire a few tranquilizer darts? No, they shot at us. Bullets. We're stuck here, Chloe."

"Whatever happened today, she didn't do it on purpose," Tori said.

His jaw worked, then he spun on Tori. "Why are you suddenly defending her? Trying to win her over for a reason?"

"What's that supposed to mean?"

"I don't trust you, Tori."

"Um, yeah, I got that message loud and clear long ago."

Simon appeared in the doorway behind Tori and Derek. He waved to me and mouthed "run while you can."

Not a bad idea. I snuck around them and zipped out the door to where Simon waited. Then I glanced back at Tori.

"Don't worry about her," he said. "Probably the most fun she's had in days." He led me into the next room. "Sadly, I can't say the same for Derek, and as soon as he stops arguing long enough to notice you're gone—"

"Hey!" Derek called. "Where are you two going?"

Simon took my elbow and steered me at a jog through the house as Derek's footsteps pounded behind us. Simon kept going until we were outside.

He led me to a garden bench and we sat. I glanced toward the house.

"Relax. He won't pull that crap in front of me."

He eased back on the bench, arm going around my shoulders, gaze slanting my way, checking to make sure of his welcome. I moved closer and he smiled.

"Okay, so what happened with your lesson?" he said. "I know it wasn't good, but I missed the details."

I told him, and when I was done, he shook his head. "What was she *thinking*? Taking you to a cemetery for necromancy lessons?"

That was exactly what I wanted to hear, but I knew this was the easy way out. Blame someone else, like Margaret had done. Yes, she'd played her part, but so had I.

Derek was right. I should have refused. I had to take responsibility, even if it meant saying no to an authority figure, because I was the authority on me.

"Do you like ice cream?"

"What?"

Simon smiled. "That got your attention."

"Sorry, I was just—"

"Worrying. Which is why I'm taking you out for ice cream. Derek and I went for a jog earlier and saw a service station about a half-mile that way." He pointed. "There was a sign for ice cream in the window, so that's where we're going after dinner."

"I don't think they're going to let me go anywhere now."

"We'll see. So . . . ? Yes? It's not exactly what I had in mind for a first date, but we're kinda stuck here and I'm kinda tired of waiting."

"D-date?"

He glanced over. "Is that okay?"

"Sure. Yes. Definitely." My cheeks heated. "Okay, let's try that again, with a little less enthusiasm."

He grinned. "Enthusiasm is good. It's a date then. I'll talk to Andrew."

I was about to go on my first date. Not just my first date with Simon. My first date ever. I wasn't telling him that of course. Sure, he'd be cool with it, probably joke about the pressure. Being fifteen before my first date wasn't that weird, but it felt weird, like being fifteen before my first period, and I certainly hadn't told anyone about *that*.

A date, with Simon. I'd agreed quickly enough, but after we went inside for lunch, I realized what I'd done.

It felt like standing at those cemetery gates again: my gut was telling me this was a really, really bad idea. Dating while on the run for our lives? Dating one of the guys I was on the run *with*? What if it went badly? How would we—?

But it wouldn't go badly. It was Simon and everything would be okay. I just had to relax. Unfortunately, lunch didn't help with that.

Margaret was gone, but she must have told Russell what happened, and he'd swooped in like a vulture, hoping to catch us in some terrible display of uncontrollable power.

Andrew should have shown him the door. He didn't, probably thinking it was better to let him see that we were just normal kids. But it made all of us miserable, me most of all, feeling Russell's gaze on me as I struggled to eat, that faint look of distaste on his face. The kid who can raise the dead. The necromancer freak.

After lunch, I fled to my room. Simon tried to lure me out, but I said I was tired and joked that I didn't want to fall asleep on our date. Around three, Derek rapped on the door, calling a gruff "You should come out. Simon's worried." When I said I was napping, he went silent and I thought I heard him sigh and scuff his feet, like he wanted to say something else, so I got up and went to the door, planning to walk out and say, "Oh, I didn't know you were still here."

I'd hoped he did have something to say. Not an apology for chewing me out—that would be expecting too much—but an excuse to talk to him about what had happened at the cemetery, consider our options if things got worse . . .

Mostly I just wanted him to stop being mad at me and go back to being the other Derek, the guy I could talk to, could confide in. But when I opened the door, the hall was empty. I went back to bed.

fifteen

TORI CAME IN AT FOUR and seemed surprised to find me still in bed.

"You've been in here all afternoon?" she said. "I thought you were outside with the guys."

"What'd I miss?"

"Me mopping floors."

That made me smile.

"You think I'm kidding?" she said.

"No, I guess we'll have to pull our weight around here. We can't expect Andrew to clean up after us."

She rolled her eyes. "Can you really see Andrew assigning us chores? The guy apologized for the place not already being cleaned and ready for guests. I offered to clean for him, just to be nice."

When I didn't say anything, she shook her head. "That last part *was* a joke, Chloe. Andrew's paying me the same amount he would for the housekeeper, though it'll probably take me twice as long. Not like we're overscheduled, I figured, and I could use the money. So now I'm the official housekeeper, and if I find wet towels on the floor, I'll hide them between your sheets."

Two weeks ago, if someone had told me Tori would willingly clean a house—even for money—I'd never have believed it. I couldn't imagine her wielding a mop. But I'd also seen how hard it had been for her when we'd been on the run, not having any cash of her own. While I was sure this wasn't her ideal way to earn it, apparently she'd rather scrub toilets than ask for handouts.

That made me realize something. What would happen to Tori when this was over? Did she have relatives she could live with? Was she thinking the same thing? Frantically making money just in case?

"Gwen's back," she said. "She's talking to Andrew first. Gotta admit, though, I was looking forward to this lesson a whole lot more before you got yours."

"You'll be fine. Just don't get mad at her."

She smiled, and I could see nervousness there, but excitement, too. She wanted to learn how to use her powers properly. We knew we were a danger and we didn't want to be. Why didn't anyone else see that? Why did they keep treating us like thoughtless, careless kids?

"You okay?" she asked.

"Sure."

She reached into her back pocket and pulled out folded sheets of paper.

"This might make you feel better."

I opened it. Blank paper, left over from the cemetery, after I'd taken down the ghost's message.

"I'm sure there's a pencil around someplace," she said.

"A pencil?"

"Uh, yeah, movie buff. What do they do in films when someone writes a note on a pad of paper and takes the top sheet?"

I smiled. "Use a pencil to bring up the impression of what was written."

"I doubt they'll be taking us to a post office anytime soon, but you can send a letter when we get a chance."

"Thanks."

She left. When I heard footsteps in the hall a little later, I thought it was Derek coming back, but Tori pushed open the door, walked to her bed, and thudded onto it.

"No lessons for me," she said.

"What happened?"

"Andrew's version? The group has decided to postpone training until they better understand our abilities. In other words, we've totally freaked them all out." She shook her head. "Andrew's a nice guy, but . . . too nice, you know?"

"Like me?"

"You're a different kind of nice. I know Andrew's trying to help, but I really wish he had more . . ." She struggled for a word.

"Backbone?" I blurted, then felt my cheeks heat. "I—I don't mean—"

"See, there's your version of 'too nice.' You don't want to hurt anyone's feelings, even behind his back. *Backbone* is exactly right." She reclined on her bed. "Anyway, enough of that. Simon's looking for you, as usual. Go play, Chloe. I'll keep your brooding spot warm."

Sure enough, Simon was looking for me. Apparently, the guys had been unable to try getting into the basement that morning—Andrew had insisted on hanging out with them, kicking a ball around outside.

Now Andrew was locked up with his laptop in the study, so Derek had slipped into the basement. Simon was keeping watch, which was easier to do unobtrusively if he had someone to hang out with. We were in one of the unused rooms, checking out a wall of photos, when Andrew passed by. He saw us looking at the pictures.

"They're from the previous owner," he said, coming in. "None of us, as you see."

"Gotta fly under the radar," Simon said.

Andrew nodded. "Supernaturals always need to be thinking of that, Chloe—all the ways we can accidentally expose ourselves or call attention to ourselves. Even publicly associating with other supernaturals can be a danger. That's not to say you won't have supernaturals as friends. You will, and that helps. But we're always careful."

I said I understood.

"Now these are family photos of the man who owned the house. Todd Banks. The founder of the Genesis project. Dr. Lyle had the original idea, but he died before genetic modification was a possibility. It was Todd—Dr. Banks—who took his ideas and began the experiment. He was also the first to sound the alarm about the potential pitfalls. He warned the Edison Group, but they were too enamored with the possibilities to admit they'd made mistakes. Dr. Banks left and founded our group of concerned ex-employees. He bequeathed the house to us on his death a few years ago."

As Andrew talked, I noticed a photo of Dr. Banks . . . with a dark-haired boy off to the side. He looked about thirteen in the shot, but I still recognized his face. It was the Volo half-demon ghost.

"Is that Dr. Banks's son?" I asked as casually as I could.

"His nephew. That would be . . ." Andrew's brow wrinkled. "I can't remember his name. I never met him. I know he lived here for a while, with his cousin and his uncle. That's the older boy, which I only know because the younger one was blond."

I remembered the body in the bed. The horribly beaten body . . . of a light-haired boy a few years younger than the half-demon I'd met.

"You said Dr. Banks left this house to your group. What happened to the kids?"

"They went to live with another relative. A grandparent, I think."

Both boys were dead, and I knew it. The question was, did Andrew? Or was this a story he'd been told?

Were the boys part of the Genesis project? It seemed like it. Yet the kid I'd seen had been older than me. Even if he'd survived his uncle, he had to have died a couple of years ago, given his age in the photo. That meant if he was alive today, he'd be a few years older than Derek, who was supposed to be one of the first subjects.

"Was there a woman living here with them?" Simon asked.

"Hmm?" Andrew said as he waved us from the room.

"Chloe heard a woman's voice last night, and we thought it might be a ghost. Was there a woman living with them?"

"Not as far as I know. I could be mistaken, though. Now, I should get dinner going. I know you're supposed to eat at regular times, Simon. And I know you two have something special planned afterward." He winked at me and I'm sure I blushed.

As Andrew headed for the kitchen, Derek snuck up from the basement. The three of us went upstairs, ducked into the guys' bedroom, and closed the door.

"It's storage," Derek said. "Two big rooms full of stuff and one locked room."

"Locked?" Simon perked up.

"I busted it open. It's a workshop. Nothing but tools."

"So why would it be locked?" I asked.

"I'd love to say it's suspicious," Simon said. "But if this Banks guy had kids around, then I'm not surprised. My dad isn't exactly Mr. Handyman, but he kept a lock on his toolbox. You know parents. Paranoid."

"Yeah," Derek said. "Especially after their son flattens his finger trying to nail a drawing to the wall."

"Hey, I'm not the genius who suggested it." Simon glanced at me. "Tape wouldn't hold it, and Science Guy explained that the paper was too heavy for the adhesive. So I got some nails."

Derek rolled his eyes.

"So that's it?" I said. "Storage and a tool room? No clues at all?"

"Didn't say that. There are labeled boxes of clothes and stuff. Three names: Todd, Austin, and Royce. Todd's stuff is adult."

"Dr. Banks," Simon said. "The guy who owned this place. And let me guess, the other boxes were for teenage boys."

When I explained what Andrew said, Derek nodded. "Royce is your half-demon's name, then. His clothes are bigger. So Andrew said he moved away after Banks died? Maybe he was killed later and came back."

"I don't think so. I'm pretty sure it was Austin's body I saw last night."

A family, dead. Including two teenagers. All with connections to the Edison Group, maybe to the Genesis project. And we were taking refuge in the same house.

"We can't go anywhere," Derek said.

That's what we were all thinking, of course. Run. But where? None of us thought Andrew was secretly aligned with the Edison Group, holding us here while going through this elaborate ruse of plotting an attack on them. But what had happened to Dr. Banks and Royce and Austin? Did it have anything to do with us?

"I'll keep looking," Derek said. "Maybe ask Andrew a few things. You guys—"

"We'll be gone for a while after dinner," Simon said.

"Oh. Yeah. That's right." Derek's gaze flicked my way, but before I could meet it, he'd turned to Simon. "So, uh, Andrew was good with that?"

"Yep. You lose that bet, bro. Sure, he gave me a whole bunch of warnings—gotta walk through the woods, not on the road, Chloe can't go into the store, blah-blah. But we can go."

"Huh." Derek looked over his shoulder, like he'd been hoping Andrew would say it wasn't safe. After a moment, he nodded and said, "Okay, then."

"We've got some time to kill before dinner," Simon said. "How about picking up those self-defense lessons?"

"Sure," I said. "I'll get Tori . . . and don't make that face. I'm getting her. Derek, you joining us?"

"Nah." He turned and headed down the hall. "You guys go on."

Simon gave us a self-defense lesson in the backyard, teaching some basic holds, which Tori, with her binding spell, thought was kind of useless. But she only whispered that to me and didn't rub it in with Simon.

There was a moment during that lesson, when Simon was trying to show Tori a hold and they were standing side by side, me sitting on a patio chair watching them, and . . . For a second, I thought *Maybe they could be related.* I don't know what it was, the angle of their faces, I think, something about the cheekbones, the mouth. Dark eyes, same height, same slender build.

Then Simon stepped away and whatever I'd seen disappeared. I decided I was taking a few superficial similarities and letting my imagination fill in the rest.

Dinner came. Dinner went. I headed upstairs to get ready.

I always thought I wasn't the kind of girl who gave a lot of thought to stuff like this—first date, first kiss. Don't get me wrong. I wanted those things. But I didn't fantasize about the big day and what I'd wear and how I'd act. Or so I thought.

But I guess I still always had this image of my first date. I'd buy a new outfit and maybe get a haircut. I'd definitely wear makeup and I'd probably paint my nails. In short, I'd look better than I ever had, and when I opened my door to that first guy, I'd see it in his eyes, in his smile.

When Simon knocked at my bedroom door, I'd brushed my hair and found Vaseline for lip gloss. I couldn't even shower because Tori was running the washing machine. As for clothes, I wore the same jeans and shirt I had been in since escaping the laboratory, though I had managed to get the pizza sauce stain off the shirtsleeve . . . most of it, anyway.

Still, when I did open the door and he smiled at me, it was just like I'd always imagined, and I knew everything was going to be okay.

sixteen

ABOUT FIFTY FEET INTO the forest, Simon stopped dead and swore.

"What?" I said.

He waved at the woods. "I should have checked with you. Is it okay? Being out here?"

I assured him it was fine.

"Derek warned me the woods made you nervous, that you were worried about raising dead animals." He glanced at me. "And you weren't even thinking about that until I brought it up, were you?" He cursed again, more imaginatively now.

"It's okay," I said. "As long as I don't summon or fall asleep, I'll be fine."

"And if you *do* fall asleep, I need some serious work on my conversation skills."

We walked a little farther.

"Speaking of conversation, how, umm . . ." He made a face. "Sorry, I'm a bit nervous."

"Did you have a lesson with Andrew today?"

A dramatic whoosh of relief. "Thank you. Yes, I did. Boring, boring, boring. No sudden surge of power for me. I'm just a regular—" He paused.

"Okay, that was incredibly insensitive. Did I mention I'm nervous? I should be happy to have normal powers. And I am."

"But still, it must be annoying, seeing Tori casting new spells right away when you've been training for years."

"Yeah. It wouldn't be so bad if it wasn't Tori."

"So what spells *can* you do?"

"Nothing useful. You need to master the basics first. I get that, but right now, all I care about are spells that will help us, and perfecting my fog spell isn't going to do that."

"That knock-back one is good."

He shrugged.

"Maybe Andrew can teach you the binding spell Tori casts."

He shook his head. "It's witch magic."

"That's different?"

"Do you want the quick answer or a lesson on the spell-caster races?"

"Option two please."

He smiled, hand tightening around mine. "There are two major spell-casting races. Sorcerers are male and have sons, all of them sorcerers. Witches are female—same deal, but with daughters. Sorcerer magic uses hand gestures along with incantations, mostly in Greek, Latin, and Hebrew. And, no, I don't speak Greek, Latin, *or* Hebrew—I can just recite the spells. Knowing the languages would help, but memorizing spells is tough enough right now. Sorcerer magic is offensive—used to attack. Witches use the same languages for incantations, but they get to skip the hand gestures. Their magic is defensive."

"Used to stop an attack."

"Or escape one, which would be useful these days."

"You can't learn witch magic?"

"We can, with a whole lotta effort, because it's not our natural kind. Right now, I need to stick to my own, though I'd like to learn a few witch spells someday. Just not from Tori."

When we reached the service station, Simon bought the ice cream, then we went back out to a log and sat down.

"I would have been fine with a single scoop," I said.

"Too bad."

"But—"

"I've been diabetic as long as I can remember, Chloe. I've never had double scoop ice creams so I don't miss them. If it bothered me, I'd never eat with Derek, would I? And since I'll be done first, I can give you a spell demonstration as snack-time entertainment."

He did that, goofing around and making me laugh. Then we walked back, holding hands and talking some more. It was getting dark. When we could see the lights of the house through the trees, he stopped and tugged me in front of him. My heart hammered in what I told myself was anticipation, but felt more like terror.

"Was it okay?" he asked.

I smiled. "Better than okay."

"So I won my pass to date two?"

"You did."

"Good."

His face lowered toward mine and I knew what was coming. I knew it. But when his lips touched mine, I still jumped.

"S-sorry, I—I—"

"Skittish as a cat," he murmured. His hand slid to the back of my neck and he tilted my face up. "If I'm moving too fast—"

"N-no."

"Good."

This time, I didn't jump. I didn't flinch. I didn't gasp. I didn't do anything. Simon kissed me and I just stood there, like someone had cut the cord between my brain and my muscles.

Finally, the connection caught and I did kiss him, but awkwardly, some part of me still holding back, my gut twisting, like I was doing something wrong, making a huge mistake, and—

Simon stopped. For a moment, he hovered there, face above mine, until I had to look away.

"Wrong guy, huh?" he said, his voice so soft I barely caught it.

"Wh-what?"

He eased back, and his eyes went blank, unreadable.

"There's someone else," he said. Not a question. A statement.

"S-someone . . . ? A boyfriend, you mean? From before? No. Never. I wouldn't—"

"Go out with me if there was. I know." He took another step back, the heat of his body fading, the chill of night air moving in. "I don't mean a guy from before, Chloe. I mean one from now."

I stared at him. *Now? Who else . . . ? There was only one other guy—*

"D-Derek? Y-you think—"

I couldn't finish. I wanted to laugh. *You think I like Derek? Are you kidding?* But the laugh wouldn't come, just this thundering in my ears, breath catching like I'd been smacked in the chest.

"Derek and I aren't—"

"No, not yet. I know."

"I—I don't—"

Just say it. Please let me say it. "I don't like Derek."

But I didn't. Couldn't.

Simon jammed his hands into his pockets and we stood there in that awful silence until I managed to say, "It isn't like that."

"It wasn't. Not at first." He stared out at the woods. "It started to change after the crawl space. You guys hanging out together, the . . . vibe changing. I told myself I was just imagining it. When you and Tori escaped from the lab, it seemed like I was right. But then, after the truck stop, when you guys came back . . ." He went quiet, then looked over at me. "I'm right, aren't I?"

There was a note of pleading in his voice. *Tell me I'm wrong, Chloe. Please.* And everything in me wanted to say it. This was Simon. Everything I'd ever dreamed of in a boyfriend and here he was, mine for the taking. I only had to say the words, and I tried. I *tried.* But all I could manage was another weak, "It's not like that."

"Yeah, it is."

He started to walk away, back in the direction we'd come. Then he stopped and, without turning, he reached into his jacket and held out a rolled-up paper, murmuring, "This is for you."

I took it, and he continued walking.

Fingers shaking, I unrolled the paper. It was the picture he'd drawn of me, now colored. It looked even better than it had in the sketch. *I* looked better. Confident and strong and beautiful.

The picture blurred as my eyes filled with tears. I quickly rerolled it before I ruined it. I took a few steps after him and called out. I could see his figure in the distance, still walking, and I knew he heard me, but he didn't stop.

seventeen

I WATCHED SIMON WALK AWAY, then wiped my eyes with my sleeve and headed for the lights of the house. I'd just passed the edge of the woods when the rear door opened, light spilling into the nearly dark yard. Then a hulking figure blocked the light.

"No," I whispered. "Not now. Just go back inside—"

The door slapped shut, sound echoing as Derek marched across the yard, dead on target.

I looked around, desperate for an escape route, but there was none. Go forward and deal with Derek, or run back toward Simon and have to deal with both of them. I kept walking.

"Where's Simon?" he snapped.

Relief washed through me. I didn't trust myself to speak, so I just pointed back to the woods.

"He *left* you? Out here? At night?"

"He dropped something," I mumbled, trying to get past him. "He isn't far."

Without a sound, he was right in front of me, blocking my path.

"You're crying?" he said.

"No, I—" I tore my gaze away. "Just dust. From the path. Simon's that way."

I tried to pass him, but he stooped, trying to get a look at my face. When I wouldn't let him, he caught my chin. I jerked back, flinching at his touch, heart thudding at it, too.

I told myself Simon was wrong. I'd never be dumb enough to fall for Derek. But I had. With him so close, my stomach kept doing weird little flips. It wasn't fear. It hadn't been fear for a while.

"You *have* been crying," he said, voice softer. Then his breath caught, the growl coming back as he snapped, "What did Simon—?" He bit off the words, cheeks reddening like he was embarrassed even to think Simon might be responsible.

"What happened?" he said.

"Nothing. It just didn't work out."

"Didn't work out?" He spoke slowly, like he was processing a foreign language. "Why?"

"Talk to Simon."

"I'm talking to *you*. What'd you do to him?"

I stiffened. Only he was right. I *had* done something to Simon. I'd hurt him. And for what? Some stupid crush on a guy who barely tolerated me most of the time? Was *that* the kind of girl I was? Pick the jerk over the nice guy?

"I screwed up. Again. You're shocked, I'm sure. Now, let me go inside—"

He blocked me. "What'd you do, Chloe?"

I sidestepped. He sidestepped.

"You like him, don't you?" he said.

"Yes, I like him. Just not . . ."

"Not what?"

"Talk to Simon. He's the one who thinks . . ."

"Thinks what?"

Step. Block.

"Thinks what?"

"That there's someone else," I blurted before I could stop myself. I took a deep, shuddering breath. "He thinks there's someone else."

"Who?"

I was going to say "I don't know. Some guy from school, I guess." But Derek's expression said he already knew the answer. The look on his face . . . It'd been humiliating before, having Simon accuse me of liking Derek, but that was nothing compared to how I felt when I saw Derek's look. Not just surprise, but shock. Shock and horror.

"Me?" he said. "Simon said he thinks you and I are—"

"No, not that. He knows we aren't—"

"Good. So what *does* he think?"

"That I like you." Again, the words flew out before I could stop them. This time, I didn't care. I'd completely humiliated myself, and now I was just empty and ashamed. All I wanted was to get him out of my way, and if telling him that made him run in terror, then good.

But he didn't run. He just stared at me, and that was worse. I felt like the biggest loser at school, admitting to the coolest guy that she liked him. He stood there gaping like he must have heard me wrong.

"I don't," I said quickly. Those words came easily now, because at that moment, they were true. "I *don't*," I said again, when he just kept staring.

"You'd better not." His voice was a low rumble, the scowl settling into place as he finally eased back. "You'd better not, Chloe, because Simon likes you."

"I know."

"Simon's had girls calling him every day since he was twelve. They follow him at school. They even talk to me, trying to get to him. Cute girls. Popular girls."

"So I should be thrilled that a guy like him even *looked* my way, right?"

"Course not. I didn't mean—"

"Oh, I know what you meant. I should count my blessings that I happened to be around when his choices were, well, none, really, because otherwise I'd never have stood a chance."

"That's not— I never said—"

"Whatever."

I wheeled and headed the other way. He cut me off.

"Simon likes you, Chloe. Yeah, he's dated a lot of girls. But he *really* likes you, and I thought you liked him back."

"I do. Just not . . . not like that, I guess."

"Then you shouldn't have let him think it *was* like that."

"You think I led him on? For what? Kicks? I don't have enough excitement in my life, so maybe I'll tease a nice guy, get his hopes up, then laugh and skip away? How could I know how I felt until we went out and—?" I stopped. I couldn't win this fight. No matter what I said, I'd still be the evil bitch who'd hurt his brother.

I turned and started walking along the edge of the woods.

"Where are you going?" he called.

"You won't let me go into the house. I'm sure Simon doesn't want me around him either. So it seems like I'm going to take a moonlight stroll in the forest."

"Oh, no, you're not." He jumped in front of me. "You can't go wandering around alone at night. It's not safe."

I looked up at him. His green eyes glittered in the dark, reflecting the moonlight like a cat's. His scowl had vanished. The defiance was gone, too, replaced by a tightness around the mouth, a worry that clouded his eyes; and seeing that quicksilver change, I wanted to . . .

I didn't know what I wanted to do. Kick him in the shins seemed like a good option. Unfortunately, bursting into tears seemed more likely, because here lay the root of the problem, the contradiction in Derek that I couldn't seem to work out, no matter how hard I tried.

One second he was in my face, making me feel stupid and useless. The next he was like this: hovering, concerned, worried. I told myself it was just his wolf instinct, that he had to protect me whether he wanted to or not, but when he looked like this, like he'd pushed me too far and regretted it . . . That look said he genuinely cared.

I turned toward the woods and resumed walking. "I'll be careful. No dead will rise tonight. Go back inside, Derek."

"You think that's all I'm worried about? The Edison Group—"

"Could be camped out there right now, waiting for us to venture into the deep, dark woods. If you believed that, you'd never have let Simon go out."

"I didn't like it. But he promised you'd be back before dark, which is why I was at the door, getting ready to come find you two." He caught my arm, quickly releasing it and grabbing my sleeve instead. "Just—"

He stopped. I turned to see him staring into the forest, chin lifted, nostrils flared, face tense.

"Don't pull that," I said.

"Pull what?"

"Pretending you smell something out there. Someone."

"No, I thought—" He inhaled again, then shook his head sharply. "Nothing, I guess. Just—" He rubbed the back of his neck, wincing slightly, and I noticed the sheen of sweat on his face, shimmering in the moonlight. His eyes glowed brighter than usual. Fever bright. The Change was coming.

Not now. Please not now. That's the last thing I need to deal with.

He released my sleeve. "Fine, take a walk."

I set out, staying in the yard. I wasn't foolish enough to march into the woods to spite him. I'd gone about twenty feet when I glanced around to see where he'd gone. He was five paces behind, following soundlessly.

"Derek . . ." I sighed.

"I need some fresh air. Go on."

Another twenty feet. He kept following me. I turned and glowered up at him. He stopped and stood there, face impassive.

"Fine," I said. "I'll go in the house. You can track down Simon before the Edison Group snatches him."

He followed me to the door, then waited as I went in before heading out to round up his brother.

eighteen

TORI WAS IN OUR ROOM, reading an old leather-bound book from the library downstairs.

"So, how was the big ice cream date?" she asked, without looking up.

"Okay."

She lowered the book. I quickly looked away and opened a bag that was sitting on my bed.

"Oh, that's your new clothes," she said. "Margaret bought them. Apparently Gwen wanted to, but the old bat insisted. Payback for this morning, I think."

It was bargain store stuff. From the children's department. At least it was for *girls*, unlike the ugly boys' sweatshirts Derek had bought me. Still . . . I unwrapped the pajamas. Pink flannel covered in rainbows and unicorns.

"Hey, you think that's bad?" Tori said. "She shopped in ladies wear for me, and got a granny nightgown with lace. *Lace*. I'd trade you if those would fit me." A thump, as she tossed the book onto the floor. "So how'd the date go?"

"It didn't."

She hesitated. "Well, love to say I'm surprised, but don't forget, I'm the girl who was crazy about Simon until she was forced to spend twenty-four hours alone with him. That cured me, fast."

"Simon's fine."

"Sure, he is. Or he will be when he grows up a little."

"He's *fine*. It was me. I screwed up. I—"

I didn't continue. I could only imagine Tori's reaction if I said I might have a crush on Derek. I'd lose every ounce of her respect I'd earned.

I wished I could talk to someone, though. A girl with more dating experience, preferably one who wouldn't think I was a complete loser for liking Derek. Rae would be good. She didn't care for either of the guys, but she'd listen and give advice. Liz would be even better—always helpful, never judging. As for my school friends, it was like they belonged to another life, friends of another Chloe.

"Were you crying?" Tori peered at my face. "You were."

"I–it's nothing. I—"

"Simon pulled something, didn't he? Got you out on that walk, and the next thing you know, it's not your hand he's holding." Her eyes blazed. "Guys. They can be such—"

"It wasn't like that."

"If he pulled that crap, you can tell me. I've had a few surprise first dates myself. Wish I'd had my spells then. Especially the binding one."

"It wasn't like that." I met her gaze. "Really. Simon was fine."

She eyed me. "You sure?"

"The only thing he did was kiss me, and he asked first. He was fine. I—I froze up."

"Ah." She settled onto my bed. "First kiss?"

"N-no. Of c-course not."

"You know, it's hard to lie convincingly when you stutter, Chloe. So it was your first kiss. Big deal. My first one was last year, and I made him wait until the third date. I don't let a guy push me into anything I'm not ready for. They think because I'm popular I must put out. I don't, and by the end of the first date, they know it." She reclined on the bed. "So he kissed you and you froze up, and he thought that meant you weren't into him. It happens. He should have expected that—everyone knows how jumpy you are."

I glared at her.

"Well, it's true. Just tell him he surprised you, and ask *him* out. Try again."

And what if I didn't want to try again?

I finished gathering up my stuff. "You're getting the room to yourself tonight."

She sat up. "What?"

"I'm going to sleep in the next one. I just— I'm not really good company."

I could see that hurt her feelings. I was getting good at that. At the door I paused. "Thanks. For . . . everything today. I appreciate it."

She nodded and I left.

I should have stayed with Tori.

Being alone meant I had nothing to do except curl up under the covers and cry about how horribly wrong my life had gone, then despise myself for wallowing in self-pity.

I'd screwed up everything. I couldn't control my powers, even when our future depended on it. No one was talking about freeing Rae and Aunt Lauren and finding the guys' dad anymore. We'd be lucky if my cemetery summoning didn't turn *us* into prisoners.

The only people I could count on were Derek, Simon, and Tori. After they'd all apparently forgiven me for my cemetery screwup, now I'd hurt Simon, pissed off Derek, and rebuffed Tori.

I wanted to go home. If I had real guts, I'd pack my bag and leave before I made things worse. I couldn't even manage that, though. I hated, hated, *hated* myself for being so weak. I couldn't seem to do anything but cry until at last I fell into an exhausted sleep.

A rap on the door woke me. I squinted at the nightstand, looking for the clock, only to remember that I'd changed rooms.

"Chloe? It's me." After a pause, he added, "Derek," like I could mistake that deep rumble for anyone else, like I could mistake that little part of me that perked up like an eager puppy saying, "It's *him*. Quick! Go see what he wants."

God, how had I been so blind? It seemed so obvious now.

Sad and pathetic.

Par for the course these days.

I pulled the covers up and closed my eyes.

"Chloe?" The floorboards creaked. "I need to talk to you."

I didn't answer.

Another creak, this time the door itself, and I shot up in bed as he slipped in.

"*Hey*!" I said. "You can't—"

"Sorry," he mumbled. "It's just . . ."

He moved into the moonlight. That was no accident. He wanted me to see his eyes burning with fever, his skin flushed, hair sweat soaked. He wanted me to say, "Oh, you're Changing," leap out of bed, and insist on going outside with him, help him through it, as I had the last two times.

I looked at him and I lay back down.

He stepped forward. "Chloe . . ."

"What?"

"It's . . . It's starting again."

"I see that."

I sat up, swung my legs out of bed, and stood. He breathed a sigh of relief. I walked to the window.

"Head down that path about thirty feet, and you'll find a clearing to the left. That should be a good place."

A spark of panic ignited in his eyes. After how he'd treated me today, I should have said "good." But I didn't. Couldn't. It took everything I had just to crawl back into bed.

"Chloe . . ."

"What?"

He scratched his arm. Scratched hard as the skin bubbled, his muscles writhing. He glanced at me, and the look in his eyes was so miserable that I had to clamp my jaw shut against the impulse to say, "Fine, I'll come with you."

"*What?*" I said instead.

"I—" He swallowed. Licked his lips. Tried again. "I—"

Even asking me to come with him was too much. He'd never had to before.

"I . . . I need—" He swallowed again. "I want . . . Will you come with me?"

I lifted my gaze to his. "How can you even ask me that? How many times did you chew me out today? Make me feel like everything's going wrong and it's all my fault?"

His eyes widened in genuine surprise. "That's not what I meant." He brushed his sweaty bangs back. "If I hurt you—"

"How could you not hurt me? This morning, after the cemetery, I needed your help. Your advice. All you could do was make me feel worse than I already did, which, believe me, wasn't easy. Then tonight, with Simon, you acted like that was all my fault, too, even when you could see how upset I was, how bad I felt." I took a deep breath. "After the truck stop, after our trip back . . . I thought we were friends."

"We are."

"No." I met his gaze. "Obviously we're not."

The look on his face, confused and miserable, made me feel awful, which only made me madder. He had no right to come in here and expect help, then make me feel guilty for refusing.

"Chloe, please." He rubbed his hand over his throat. The veins and tendons pulsed. Sweat beaded on his forehead. "It's coming faster this time."

"Then you should go."

"I c— I ca—" He swallowed hard and looked at me, fever making his eyes so bright they seemed to glow. "Please."

It wasn't the "please" that did it. It was the absolute panic in his eyes. He was terrified of the Change, of not knowing whether he could complete it, if the genetic modification had done something to him and that's why he kept suffering through this, only to fail before he reached the end.

He'd never actually said that, and maybe I'm a pushover, but I couldn't send him off to do it alone. So I grabbed my jacket and sneakers.

"Thank y—" he began.

I brushed past him to the door. "Let's go."

nineteen

WE KEPT TO THE SHADOWS in the yard in case anyone looked out and saw us heading for the forest. Once we reached the path, Derek stayed beside me, sneaking glances my way, giving me that dejected look that only made me madder, because I didn't want to feel guilty, yet I did.

I wanted to set this aside and get back to normal. But when he looked at me, I had only to think of that other look—the horrified one when I said Simon thought I liked Derek—and that shut down any impulse to make up.

"You wanted to talk about what happened at the cemetery," he said finally.

I didn't answer.

"We *should* talk," he said.

I shook my head.

We picked our way along the path. I tried to hang back, letting him take the lead with his better night vision, but he stayed at my side.

"About the other day, when I yelled at you for summoning without your necklace . . ." he said.

"It's fine."

"Yeah, but . . . I just wanted to say that testing without it is a good idea. We should try—"

I turned to him. "Don't do this, Derek."

"Do what?"

"I'm coming along for your Change, so you feel obligated to help me in return."

He scratched hard at his arm. "I don't—"

"Yes, you do. Now, let's find a place before you start Changing in the middle of the path."

He kept scratching, blood welling up in lines down his arm. "I just want to—"

I caught his hand. "You're making yourself bleed."

He stared down, struggling to focus. "Oh."

"Come on." I turned off the path, heading for the clearing I'd spotted earlier.

"I heard what Andrew said this morning," he said. "About me."

"I figured you did," I said, softer than I meant to, then cleared my throat, trying to find the anger again.

"He's got a point. I'm not—"

"You're fine. Andrew's an idiot," I snapped. Great. I'd found the anger and sent it in the wrong direction. "He's wrong, okay? You know that. Let's just drop it."

"When I blew up at you about the cemetery, I . . . I didn't mean to. I'm frustrated and I—"

"Please," I said, wheeling on him. "Just stop, okay?"

He did, for about five paces. "I was frustrated with the situation. Being stuck here. The Change coming on makes it worse. I know that's not an excuse."

I glanced up at him. He watched me, expectant. He wanted me to say maybe it did explain things. Cut him some slack. The problem was that *I* wanted to. And if I did, then the next time he felt like venting on me, he would.

"Chloe?"

I stopped at the edge of a small clearing. "Is this okay?"

He said nothing and I thought he was checking it out, but when I turned, he'd gone still, his chin up, staring into the forest. "Did you hear that?"

"What?"

He shook his head. "Nothing, I guess."

He stepped into the clearing and looked around, murmuring, "Good, good." Then he stripped off his sweatshirt and set it on the ground. "You can sit here." He glanced over at me. "Remember the other night at Andrew's? When you came out to keep me company, and we tried doing some training with you? We should do that again."

I sighed. "You aren't going to quit, are you? You think if you can just say the right thing, it'll all be okay."

His lips twitched in something like a smile. "I can hope, can't I?"

"Sure. And if it works, what does that make me? You get to treat me any way you want and as soon as you decide to play nice, all is forgiven."

"I *am* sorry, Chloe."

"For now." I turned away. "Forget it, okay? Let's just—"

He caught my elbow. His skin burned even through my jacket. "I mean it. I'm really sorry. When I get mad like that, it's not— it's not—" He released my arm and rubbed the back of his neck. Rivulets of sweat ran down his face. The skin on his bare arms rippled.

"You need to get ready."

"No. I need to say something. Just give me a sec."

He took a second. Then another. Then another, just standing there, rubbing his arm furiously, gaze fixed on that.

"Derek, you need—"

"I'm fine. Just give me—" He took a deep breath.

"Derek . . ."

"Just one sec."

He started scratching again. When I moved forward to grab his hand, he stopped.

"Right, right," he murmured. He flexed his hand, then made a fist, as if to keep himself from scratching. "I tell you not to be scared of me. I snap at you when you back away. But sometimes . . ."

He reached around to scratch his shoulders, wincing as his nails dug in.

"Derek, you have to—"

"Sometimes that's exactly what I want," he said. "That's what I'm trying to do—scare you off."

"So you don't accidentally hurt me." I sighed. "You aren't going to—"

"No, it's not that. It's—"

His hand went to his forearm, then he stopped short as dark stubble sprouted.

"You're Changing, Derek. We'll talk later."

"Right. Yeah. Later. Good." The words rushed out in a whoosh of relief.

He looked around, blinking as sweat streamed into his eyes.

"You need to get down," I said gently.

When he still didn't budge, I caught his hand and tugged. He lowered himself with some difficulty, then got up on all fours, in position to begin the Change.

"Unless Margaret brought you a lot of new shirts, you might want to take that one off," I said.

"Right."

He pulled at the hem, tugging it up, but his arm wouldn't twist the right way to get the shirt up over his head, like his joints were already repositioning, fusing. So I helped. I drew the line at removing his pants, though. Luckily, he'd pulled on sweats to sleep in, and he was able to fumble them down to his knees, and I was okay with taking it from there. His shorts were staying on. If they ripped during the Change, I just hoped the transformation was far enough along that . . . well, whatever.

He barely had his clothes off before the full body spasms hit, his back shooting up, his spine bending at a seemingly impossible angle, wrenching a gurgling whimper from him as his face contorted in agony, the cry cut short as he spewed dinner into the bushes.

It went on like that for a while. The spasms, the convulsions, his skin and muscles rippling like something out of a horror movie. The gasps and moans and stifled cries of pain between retching and dry heaves. The stink of vomit and sweat.

You'd really think this would cure any romantic notions I had about the guy. But I'd seen it three times now, and I watched every time, knowing if I looked away, moved away, let him think I was horrified and disgusted, I'd only make it worse.

I wasn't horrified and disgusted. What I saw wasn't some guy puking and grotesquely contorting. I saw Derek, in unbelievable agony and scared out of his mind.

It took only that first awful spasm to chase away the last of my anger. There would be time for that later. Instead, I knelt beside him, rubbing his shoulders, telling him he'd be okay, he was doing fine, just keep going.

Finally, the retching stopped and he crouched there, head down, hair hanging, hiding his face, his body covered in short, black hair, his shoulder muscles hunched, arms and legs straight, clawlike fingers half buried in the earth. He panted, drawing deep, ragged breaths.

"You're getting there," I said. "It's coming faster this time." True or not, it didn't matter, only that he accepted it, nodding and relaxing a little.

Another spasm hit. His body convulsed in wave after wave. His legs and arms kept changing, thinning and shortening, his hands and feet doing the same. The hair on his head retracted as the hair on his body lengthened from stubble to thick fur. As for his face, I knew that was Changing too, but he'd averted it.

His body continued spasming until he had to stop again, heaving as he struggled for breath. I rubbed his back and he leaned against me. I could feel his muscles trembling, like he could barely hold himself up on all fours. I moved closer, letting him rest against me, my head on his shoulder, feeling his heart beating hard and fast as his shudders gradually slowed.

"You're almost there. Keep going. You're going to finish this time. Just—"

He tensed. Then his back flew up, knocking me aside. His body went rigid, head still down, back lifting higher and higher, like someone was pulling it up, head sinking lower still, black fur gleaming in the moonlight.

Bones crackled. Derek gave a deep moan that made me move closer again, rubbing his back, telling him it would be okay. Then, with a final shudder, it was. He lifted his head, turned to look at me, and he was a wolf.

twenty

THE LAST TIME DEREK had tried to Change, he'd made me promise to go someplace safe as soon as he seemed close to finishing. When I saw that wolf in front of me, a lead weight dropped in my gut telling me I should have taken his advice. But as soon as his eyes met mine, the dread evaporated. I might be looking at a massive black wolf, but in those green eyes, I still saw Derek.

He tried to take a step, but his legs slid out and he hit the ground with an earthshaking thud. I scrambled over to him as he lay there, eyes closed, flank heaving, tongue lolling.

"Are you okay?"

His eyes opened and he gave an awkward jerk of his muzzle, as if he was trying to nod, then his pupils rolled up and his eyes closed again.

He was fine, just exhausted, like the last time when he'd been too tired even to dress before he fell asleep. I stood and started for the path, wanting to leave him in peace. I made it two steps before he snorted. I turned to see him lying on his belly, ready to jump up. He jerked his muzzle, telling me to come back.

"I thought you'd want to be—"

He cut me off with a snort. It was hard for a wolf to scowl, but he managed a good glower.

I took the switchblade from my jacket pocket. "I'll be fine. I'm armed."

A snort. *I don't care.* A head jerk. *Get back here.*

When I hesitated, he growled.

"Well, you've got the growling part down pat already. Must be all those years of practice."

He began to rise, legs wobbly.

"All right, I'm coming back. I just didn't want to be in your way."

A grunt. *You're not.* Or that's what I hoped he meant.

"You can understand me, can't you?" I said as I returned to sit on his discarded sweatshirt. "You know what I'm saying."

He tried to nod, then snarled at the awkwardness of it.

"Not easy when you can't talk, is it?" I grinned. "Well, not easy for you. I could get used to it."

He grumbled, but I could see relief in his eyes, like he was glad to see me smile.

"So I was right, wasn't I? It's still you, even in wolf form."

He grunted.

"No sudden uncontrollable urges to go kill something?"

He rolled his eyes.

"Hey, you're the one who was worried." I paused. "And I don't smell like dinner, right?"

I got a real look for that one.

"Just covering all the bases."

He gave a rumbling growl, like a chuckle, and settled in, lowering his head to his front paws, gaze on me. I tried to get comfortable, but the ground was ice-cold through his sweatshirt, and I was wearing only my new pajamas, a light jacket, and sneakers.

Seeing me shivering, he stretched a front leg toward the sweatshirt, pawing the edge and snarling when he realized he couldn't grab it.

"The lack of opposable thumbs is going to take some getting used to, huh?"

He motioned me closer with his muzzle. When I pretended not to understand, he twisted and gingerly took the hem of the sweatshirt between his teeth, lips curled in disgust as he tugged it.

"Okay, okay, I'm just trying not to crowd you."

That wasn't the only reason I was uncomfortable getting too cozy with him now, but he just grunted, again seeming to say it was fine. I moved over beside him. He shifted, his torso making a partial wind block, the body heat from the Change still blasting like a furnace.

He grunted.

"Yes, that's better. Thanks. Now get some rest."

I had no idea what would happen now. I doubted Derek did either. He'd been focused on getting *through* the Change. What I did know was that this was only half the process. He had to Change back, and he'd need time and rest for that.

And how would it happen? Did he have to wait until his body was ready, like he did with the Change to wolf? How long would that be? Hours? Days?

Feeling his gaze on me, I forced a smile and pushed back my worries. It would be okay. He *could* Change. That was the important thing.

When I relaxed, he shifted closer, fur brushing my hand. I tentatively touched it, feeling the coarse top layer and soft undercoat. He leaned against my hand, as if to say it was okay, and I buried my fingers in his fur, his skin so hot from the Change it was like putting my numb hands on a radiator. My cool fingers must have felt just as good, because he closed his eyes and shifted until I was leaning on him. Within minutes, he was asleep.

I closed my eyes, meaning to rest for just a moment, but the next thing I knew, I was waking up, curled on my side, using Derek as a pillow. I jumped. He looked over at me.

"S-sorry, I didn't mean—"

He cut me short with a growl, telling me off for apologizing, then bumped my leg, knocking me back onto his side. I lay there a moment, enjoying the warmth. He snarled a yawn, flashing canines as long as my thumb.

Finally, I sat up. "So, I suppose you should do something wolfie. Hunt, maybe?"

A grunt, the tone saying *no*.

"Run? Get some exercise?"

Another grunt, less decisive, more like a *maybe*.

He pushed to his feet, wobbly, still adjusting to his new center of gravity. He gingerly moved one forepaw, then the next, one rear paw, then the other. He picked up the pace, but still slow as he circled the clearing. A snort, like he'd figured it out, and he broke into a lope, stumbled and plowed muzzle-first into the undergrowth.

I stifled a laugh, but not very well, and he glowered at me.

"Forget running. A nice, leisurely stroll might be more your speed."

He snorted and turned fast. When I fell back, he gave a growling chuckle.

"Still can't resist throwing your weight around, can you?"

He lunged again. This time I stood my ground and he checked his leap at the last second . . . and toppled sideways. I didn't hide my laugh that time. He twisted fast, grabbed my pajama leg and wrenched, and down I went.

"Bully."

He growled a chuckle. I fingered an imaginary tear in my pant leg.

"Great. I finally get some pj's and you rip them."

He walked over for a better look. I tried to grab his foreleg, but he darted out of my reach and tore across the clearing. Then he stopped, looking over his shoulder as if to say *how'd I do that?* He turned and tried racing across it again, but his legs tangled and he fell in a heap beside me.

"You're thinking too much, as usual," I said.

A dismissive snort as he got to his feet. He tried running again, and didn't fall, but did more lurching than loping, his legs threatening to tangle at every step.

"Apparently this could take a while, so how about you practice and I'll head back to the house—"

He darted past me and veered to block my path.

I smiled. "I knew that'd work. So am I right? It's better when you act, not think?"

A sigh whistled out of his nostrils, condensation hanging in the frigid air.

"You hate that, don't you? We should keep a scorecard, see who's right more often: me or you."

He rolled his eyes.

"Not a chance, huh? You'd never live it down if I beat you. But I am right this time. Your body knows how to move as a wolf. You just need to shut your brain off and let your muscles do their thing."

He dashed at me. When I didn't move, he tore around me, circling wide, head lowered, picking up speed until he was a blur of black fur. And I laughed. I couldn't help it. It looked so . . . amazing. To be in another form. To experience the world that way. I was happy for him. Finally, he threw on the brakes, skidding to a halt, each leg shooting out in a different direction.

"You're going to need to work on that part," I said.

He growled and gave a head shake that I couldn't interpret until he got to his feet, muzzle lifting to catch the wind, ears swiveling forward.

"Someone's coming?" I whispered.

He grunted. *Shhh, I'm listening.*

I listened with him, straining to hear what he did. Then came a sound I didn't need werewolf hearing to pick up—a long, eerie howl. The fur on Derek's back rose, adding inches to his already huge frame.

"Dog?" I whispered. But I'd heard enough dogs in my life to know that wasn't what this was.

Derek dashed behind me and bumped the back of my legs. *Run.*

I raced to the path. Derek stayed behind, the thumping of his paws barely even betraying him, and I finally understood why he always moved so quietly. Predatory instinct. An instinct—and a skill—I lacked, and as we ran that became painfully obvious.

I might be half Derek's size, but I was the one who sounded like a two-hundred-pound beast plowing through the woods. My breath chugged like a locomotive. My feet found every stick on the path, each snap as loud as gunfire. I tried to be quieter, but that meant slower. When my pace dropped, Derek bumped me from behind, telling me not to bother, to keep moving.

I could see the lights of the house ahead. Then, from somewhere between it and us came an earsplitting whistle. I stopped. Derek did, too, in a skid that knocked me to my knees.

He grunted an apology. As I rose, he'd already recovered and was in front of me now, muzzle raised to sample the wind. The breeze was coming from the side, though, and he paced, trying to catch a whiff of whoever had whistled. When he did, his body went rigid, ears back, growl bubbling up. Then he wheeled, almost slamming into me.

"Who—?"

He answered with a snap of his jaws, catching the hem of my jacket. *Just run.* I did.

twenty-one

WHO WERE WE RUNNING FROM? I'd seen enough horror flicks to know that howl had come from a wolf, and there were no wild ones left in New York State. That meant werewolf.

Liam and Ramon, the two who'd tried to grab Derek the other day, had said all of the state was the territory of the Pack, who'd hunt and kill any trespassing werewolves. Obviously they weren't that thorough—Derek had lived here all his life. But had they finally found him?

If it wasn't the Pack, then who had whistled? Andrew said the Edison Group didn't hire werewolves. Was he wrong? If they wanted someone to track their missing subjects, a werewolf would be the best supernatural bloodhound around.

Right now, it didn't matter. Derek knew who'd whistled; and even if he couldn't tell me, his actions said we were in trouble, and all we could do was hope to outrun it.

"There's a creek over there," I said, pointing. "If it's a werewolf that we're trying to lose, water will hide our trail, right?"

He answered by veering that way.

The creek wasn't much more than a trickle, but it was enough to swallow our trail. As we ran, it cut deeper into the earth, banks rising to small cliffs on either side. If we kept going, we might find ourselves trapped.

Derek took the lead, scrambling up the creek bank with me following, soaked sneakers sliding in the dirt as I grabbed roots to pull myself up. I moved as quietly as I could, knowing any werewolf would share Derek's keen hearing.

We ran along the embankment until we reached a thick patch of woods. Derek herded me into a clearing in the middle of it. He crouched in the center, his front legs stretched out, his head and tail down. Trying to Change back to human form. After a few minutes of straining and snarling, he gave up.

"We can't stay here," I said. "If it's a werewolf—"

He grunted, confirming that.

"Then he's eventually going to find our trail. These woods aren't that big."

Another grunt. *I know.*

"I think the house is that way."

He shook his head and pointed his muzzle a little more to the left.

"Okay, good," I said. "So we just need to—"

He went still again, nose rising, ears turning. I crouched beside him. He kept sniffing, grumbling deep in his throat, like he'd caught a scent he couldn't seem to find again. Finally, he prodded me toward the mouth of the clearing with a noise that I thought meant *run*, but when I shot forward, he caught the back of my jacket between his teeth.

"Go slow?" I whispered. "Quietly?"

A grunt. *Yes.*

He slid in front of me and took a step. Then another. A cloud rolled over the moon and the forest went black. We stopped. A twig cracked to our right. Derek spun so fast he crashed into me, pushing me back as I stumbled, snapping at me when I didn't move fast enough.

As I retreated into the clearing, I could make out a dark shape at the edge. At another twig crack, Derek slammed into the back of my legs, pushing and jostling me until I was at the far side of the clearing, then prodding me into the thick brush.

"I can't—" I whispered.

He snapped and growled. *Yes, you can.*

I got down on all fours and pushed into the brush, hands in front of my face to clear the way. I'd gone only a few feet when I hit a tree. Thick bushes blocked either side. I twisted to tell Derek that I couldn't continue, but he'd stopped at the edge of my hole, his backside blocking the entrance.

The cloud cover thinned, and a figure materialized in the path. It was another wolf, as black as Derek. It seemed to roll toward us, silent as fog, slowly and steadily drifting our way.

The clouds finally passed by the moon, but the wolf was still black as night from his nose to his eyes. I noticed pale stripes along one flank. When I squinted, I saw that they were strips of missing fur, the uncovered skin pink and puckered with recent scar tissue. I'd seen those scars just a few days before.

"Ramon," I whispered.

Derek snarled, fur rising, tail puffing, fangs flashing. But the other wolf kept coming at us, steady and relentless. Finally, with a roar, Derek rushed at him.

Ramon stopped. He didn't back up. Didn't even growl. He just stood his ground until Derek was almost on him, then feinted to the side and ran straight at me.

Derek tried to stop, but he'd put too much momentum into the charge and he skidded into the brush.

As Ramon barreled toward me, I scrambled to get away, but the brush was too thick. Fortunately, it was too thick for him, too, and he couldn't get any farther than Derek had, just close enough for me to smell the stink of his breath as he tried to shoulder his way deeper into the undergrowth.

Then he yelped and flew back with Derek's teeth embedded in his haunch. Ramon yanked free and lunged at him. Derek ducked and tore past Ramon to block the mouth of my hiding place.

For a moment, all I could see was Derek's tail. Then I glimpsed Ramon off to the side, backing up, peering around Derek, like he was assessing the situation.

He lunged to the left. Derek sprang that way, snapping and snarling. Ramon feinted right. Derek blocked. Left again. Blocked again. It was like that evening in the playground when Liam kept pretending to grab for me, taunting Derek, laughing as he reacted every time.

"He's teasing you," I whispered. "Trying to wear you down. Don't fall for it."

Derek grunted. He tensed, like he was locking his legs. But it didn't help. Every time Ramon made a move my way, Derek jumped, snapping and growling.

Finally Ramon tired of the game and ran full out at Derek. They hit with a bone-cracking thud and went down, biting and growling, grunting and yelping when fangs sank in.

My hand tightened around my switchblade. I knew I should do something. Leap into the fray. Protect Derek. But I couldn't. The other day, seeing Derek and Liam fighting in human form, they'd moved too fast for me to interfere. That was slow-motion compared to this, a frenzied ball of fur and fury rolling across the clearing, one indistinguishable mass of black fur and flashing fangs and spattering blood.

I *had* to do something, because Derek had a serious handicap: me. He couldn't seem to forget I was there, and every time Ramon rolled my way, Derek stopped fighting to get between us again.

I wanted to tell him to forget about me. I was fine, burrowed deep in the undergrowth and armed, and there was no sign of Ramon's partner, Liam. But I knew it wouldn't do any good. That protective instinct overrode reason.

I stood, reached as high as I could, and grabbed the bottom branch of the tree behind me. My stitched arm complained, but I ignored it. I clambered up. Climbing was easy. The tough part was not looking down every time I heard a grunt or a yelp.

Finally I was too high for Ramon to reach. I called to Derek, telling him I was safe. He still had to check, of course, glancing up and getting a hunk of fur ripped out of his neck. But once he saw where I was, he threw himself fully into the fight.

Still, as big as Derek was, he was no match for an experienced adult werewolf. When faced with Liam, Derek had run the other way, admitting he was outclassed. There might be a streak of arrogance in Derek, but there wasn't any bravado. If he couldn't win a fight, he had no problem running.

This time, though, he couldn't run.

I clutched the knife and wiggled out along the branch until I was over the fighters.

Speaking of bravado . . .

I stopped, feeling a prick of guilt at even thinking of something so stupid. If I dropped onto them, I'd be lucky if I didn't get Derek killed trying to protect me.

I hated cowering there like a helpless heroine. Yet I *was* helpless against Ramon. I didn't have superhuman strength or superhuman senses or fangs or claws or magical powers.

Stop whining about what you don't have. Your brain still works, doesn't it?

Under the circumstances, I wasn't too sure.

Just use it. Think.

I stared down at the fight, racking my brain for a plan. As I watched, I realized I could tell which one was Ramon by the scars. If I could—

The scars.

I leaned down as far as I dared.

"Derek! His side! Where he's scarred . . ."

I struggled for a way to explain without giving away the plan to Ramon, but I didn't need to say another word. Derek twisted and clamped down on Ramon's flank. Without fur for protection, Derek's teeth sank in easily. Ramon yowled. Derek wrenched his head back, ripping out a big chunk of Ramon's flank.

Blood gushed. Derek pranced back out of the way and dropped the hunk of flesh. Ramon charged, but his rear leg faltered. Derek dodged around Ramon and bit his flank again.

Ramon roared in pain and fury, and wheeled, tearing himself from Derek's grip. Blood spattered as he tore around fast and grabbed Derek by the scruff of the neck. They went down, Derek struggling and clawing until one of those claws scraped across Ramon's opened flank. A yelp from Ramon, and Derek was free. Derek backpedaled toward the stream bank. It was at least a fifteen-foot drop and I called to warn him, but he kept backing up.

Ramon lunged at him, bristling and snarling. Then a whistle cut him short. Liam. Ramon checked his charge, threw back his head, and began to howl. Derek leaped on him. Ramon cut the howl short and threw Derek off, then kept advancing on him, driving him back toward—

"Derek! The cliff!"

This time, his gaze swung up, meeting mine. But he didn't stop, just kept going, gaze once again locked with Ramon's.

At the last second, Derek veered left, circling and hitting Ramon square in his wounded flank. Ramon sailed off his feet. Derek pounced on him. His fangs sank into that mass of shredded flash. Ramon let out an unearthly howl of agony.

Ramon managed to scramble up, his back to the cliff. Derek lunged at him. Ramon backpedaled. At the last second, he saw the looming drop and started to twist out of the way, but Derek head butted him in that wounded flank, sending him flying over the edge of the embankment.

I climbed down and ran over to Derek, poised on the bank, looking at Ramon, who was still conscious, struggling to get up, one foreleg twisted at an ugly angle.

The whistle came again. Derek turned sharply, banging my legs, then prodding me with his nose, telling me to get moving.

"Is it Liam?" I asked.

He dipped his muzzle in a nod.

As for why Liam would be in human form, I wasn't stopping to wonder. He was still a formidable threat. The only advantage was that if he wasn't a wolf, tracking us would be slower.

"It came from near the house," I whispered as we ran. "We should head for the road. Do you know where—?"

He answered by barreling past me. We ran for a few minutes, but I kept falling behind. He raced back to take up the rear.

"I'm sorry," I whispered. "I can't see and I keep tripping—"

He cut me off with a grunt. *I know. Just go.*

I took the lead, letting Derek tap the back of my legs whenever I started heading off course. Finally, I could see lights through the trees. Derek prodded me toward them and—

"Making a helluva racket, ain't ya, pup." Liam's Texas drawl echoed through the forest.

Derek knocked me flying. I hit the ground hard, chin scraping the earth, dirt spraying into my mouth. I tried to rise, but Derek was standing over me. I ran my tongue over my teeth, making sure I hadn't lost any.

Derek chuffed and prodded the back of my neck. I was going to interpret that as an apology, whether it was or not.

"Come out, come out, wherever you are," Liam sang.

Derek nudged me into a thicket so small we had to crowd in together and I got a mouthful of fur. When I tried to give him more room, he growled at me to be still. I sat down and he pressed against me, getting the rest of his bulk into the thicket, until he was practically on my lap.

He lifted his head to sample the wind. It was coming from the same direction as Liam's voice, meaning he couldn't smell us.

I closed my eyes to listen better. I could feel the pounding of Derek's racing heart. Mine must have been beating just as hard, because he nudged my arm until I opened my eyes and met his, dark with concern.

"I'm okay," I whispered.

He shifted, trying to take more weight off my legs. As he moved, my hand brushed a patch of wet fur. I drew back to see my fingers sticky with blood.

"You're—"

He cut me off with a grunt. *I'm okay. Now, shhh.*

I tried to see how badly he was hurt, but he shifted again, this time keeping me down.

We sat there, silently listening. His ears swiveled, and every now and then they'd twitch, like he'd caught a noise. But instead of tensing, he began to relax.

"He's moving away?" I whispered.

He nodded.

I settled in. It was hard to be afraid for your life when there was a two-hundred-pound wolf on your lap. It was oddly comforting. Between the heat of his body, the softness of his fur, and the beat of his heart I found myself blinking to stay awake.

"Is he gone?" I whispered.

Derek shook his head.

"How long should we stay—?"

Derek stiffened. I peered into the night, but when I glanced at Derek, he didn't have that pointer-on-a-scent look. His head was still down. His eyes were wide, and he held himself completely still.

Then I felt it. His muscles were twitching.

"You're ready to Change back," I whispered.

He grunted, tense, worry seeping into his eyes.

"No problem. It always takes a while after the first sign, right? We'll have time to get you back to the house. You can Change there—"

He convulsed, his front legs shooting out. He collapsed on his side, all four legs going rigid, head jerking back, eyes rolling wildly.

"It's all right. This is better anyway. Just let it happen."

Not like he had a choice. I crawled over him, getting out of the way of those flailing claws. Crouching behind him, I rubbed his shoulders and told him he was doing fine, everything was okay.

His head lowered, then flew back with a bone-cracking snap. He let out a yelp, ending in a snarl as he tried to be quiet, but the convulsions kept coming faster and a whimper escaped with each fresh spasm. When he finally stopped, everything around us stayed silent. But I knew Liam had heard.

I leaned over Derek, whispering encouragement, hoping to block any sound of Liam, keep him from panicking. Soon, though, Derek's head shot up and I knew Liam was coming.

Derek was well into his Change now, his muzzle shortening, ears moving to the sides, hair growing as his fur retracted. I leaned down to his ear.

"Just keep going, okay? I'll look after it."

He stiffened and made a noise that I knew was a *no*. I rose. He tried to do the same, only to be hit with another convulsion.

"I'll be okay," I said, pulling out my knife. "I won't do anything stupid. You're almost finished. I'll distract him until you are."

"*No,*" his voice was garbled, guttural.

I turned to go. He grabbed for my leg, but his fingers were still knobby stubs and I easily pulled away. Without looking back, I ran from the thicket.

twenty-two

I RAN, GETTING AS FAR from Derek as I could. Finally I saw the figure of a tall, lean man with light hair, limping through the forest, cane in one hand. Liam. The limp explained why he wasn't in wolf form. If Changing was as painful as it seemed, I could only imagine how bad it would be if you were injured. That injury also meant he had a grudge to settle. With me.

I took a deep breath, trying to calm my galloping heart. It didn't work. Too bad. I couldn't let him get close enough to see or hear Derek Changing.

I ran as close as I dared, then pulled up short in his path. He stopped and smiled.

"Hello there, cutie," he drawled. "I thought I smelled you."

"How's the leg?"

His grin turned a little less friendly, more bared teeth than smile. "Hurts like a son of a bitch."

"Sorry about that."

"I bet you are."

He stepped closer. I stepped back.

"Don't worry," he said. "I forgive you for the leg. I like a little spirit in my fillies." His look sent a shiver through me. "Makes them more fun to break. Now where's that big ox of a boyfriend?" He raised his voice. "This is a coward's ploy, pup, sending the girl out to distract me. About what I'd expect, though, considering how fast you ran away last time."

He listened, seeing if the taunt would bring Derek out.

"He's busy," I said. "With Ramon. He figured I could handle you."

Liam threw back his head and laughed. "You *do* have spunk. We're gonna have fun, just as soon as I take care of your boyfriend."

He moved toward me. I sidestepped, leading him away.

"You wanna play chase, cutie? I'm real good at it. How about we let your boyfriend and Ramon have their fun while we have ours and—?"

Something buzzed. Liam sighed, reached into his pocket, and flipped open a cell phone.

"Kinda busy," he said. He paused, listening. I could hear a man's voice on the other end and thought I caught Derek's name. "Yeah, yeah. You keep calling, we're never going to catch him for you."

If Liam said "we," then it wasn't Ramon phoning. Someone from the Pack? Had Liam already promised them Derek and now had to deliver?

"Quit your moaning," Liam said. "I told you we'll have him by sunrise. We just hit a minor complication. There's a reason he came out into the woods tonight—messing around with his girlfriend."

Liam looked at me. "Cute little thing. Dyed black hair. Big blue eyes." He paused. "Chloe? Yeah, she looks like a Chloe."

The Edison Group? Had to be. Right now, though, all I cared about was that whoever it was, he was keeping Liam occupied, giving Derek time to Change.

"Well, see, that's the problem," Liam continued. "We can't seem to separate the two. So, taking him in might mean taking her, too." He paused, listening. "Of course, we'll try to leave her alone, but . . ." Another pause. "I understand. Getting rid of the pup—one way or another—is your main concern. So you accept the risk of collateral damage?" As he listened to the answer, he smiled at me. "Absolutely. If we can't separate them, you won't need to worry about the girl again. I'll make sure of that. Now, if you have anything else to say, how about texting me? I'm kinda busy."

He hung up. "Seems some people consider you expendable, Chloe."

"Who?"

He lowered his voice to a mock whisper. "Bad people. It's a hard lesson, but the world is full of—"

A distant cry stopped him short. He turned in the direction of the thicket.

"Speaking of bad people, seems someone's been telling me fibs. Your boyfriend's not playing with Ramon, is he?"

I stepped in front of him.

He started to brush past me. "I know you're eager to have some fun, but I need to get your boyfriend out of the way first. Don't you worry, though. It sounds like he's Changing, and, if so, this is going to be quick."

I jumped in his way again.

His smile turned brittle. "Save that spunk for later. Right now, it's only going to piss me off, and you don't want to do that."

I let him pass but stayed on his heels, struggling to think up a plan. I could hear Derek moaning. The Change might have come on fast, but it was taking time to finish.

Derek's defenseless. If Liam finds him like that, he'll kill him.

I know, I know.

Then do something.

I took out my switchblade, opened it, and crept forward, closing the gap between us, gaze fixed on Liam's back. He glanced over his shoulder. I hid the knife. He stopped.

"How about you walk in front of me?" he said.

"I'm okay."

His face hardened. "Get in front of me, where I can see you."

As I passed him, my gaze went to his cane. Like Ramon, he was wounded.

Use that.

"Y-you said you'd take Derek to the P-Pack," I fake-stammered. "That's still the plan, right?"

He just waved me on, gaze locked on the distant spot where Derek was.

"P-please d-don't—"

I lunged and grabbed for the cane, but he whisked it out of reach, then swung it around, hitting me in the back so hard it knocked the air from my lungs and the ground from under my feet.

I hit the dirt, gasping, injured arm burning. I lifted my head, struggling to focus as Liam continued bearing down on Derek's thicket. Every breath felt like a white-hot knife stabbing my lungs.

Do something.

Like what? I was powerless. I—

No. I wasn't powerless. There was something I could do. The thought of it made bile rise in my throat, but it was nothing compared to what I felt at the thought of Liam finding Derek before he finished his Change.

I had to buy him more time.

I closed my eyes and concentrated, pushing past the warning alarms. I poured everything I had into the summons . . . and nothing happened. All those genetically enhanced powers and, when I needed them, they failed.

Then you're going to have to do this the old-fashioned way.

I tried to rise. Pain ripped through me and the forest seem to tilt, my gorge rising again. I gritted my teeth and crawled to a nearby fallen branch. I wrapped my fingers around it, steeled myself against the pain, then pushed myself up. Once I was standing, I ran at Liam. He wheeled out of my path, but I managed to swing and hit his thigh in the same place I'd stabbed him three nights ago.

He howled and staggered. I hit him again. He went down. As he fell, he grabbed for me, but I danced back, stick raised. When he tried to get up, I swung again. This time, he caught the stick and whipped me off my feet. I let go of the branch, but I was already sailing through the air. I crashed down a few feet from him, then scrambled out of the way as he twisted to grab me.

I managed to get to my feet. He started pushing up, then stopped, staring at something behind me.

Please let it be Derek.

I turned to see a partially decomposed rabbit pulling its mangled body toward me. Its ears were shredded strips of leathery skin. Its nose was a crater, lips gone, big front teeth protruding. Its eyes were shriveled raisins. The back half of its body was flattened and twisted, hind legs to one side as it dragged itself forward.

"Stop," I said, my voice eerily calm.

The rabbit stopped. I turned to Liam. He looked at me, face screwed up. Slowly, he rose, still staring at me.

"Forward," I said.

The rabbit lurched toward Liam. He stumbled back.

I got to my feet. The rabbit stood beside me, gnashing its teeth.

I mentally commanded it to advance on Liam. It hesitated, then it swung its head in his direction and started toward him.

He let out a string of curses, backing away slowly. Then a growl sounded behind him.

Liam turned. A dark shape moved between the trees, hidden in their shadows. I could see only the outline—the pointed ears, bushy tail, and long muzzle. Had Derek reverted to wolf? As the beast crept forward, though, I realized it was barely half Derek's size.

It stopped under a tree, almost hidden there, only its teeth visible, lips pulled back, growl vibrating. When it stepped into the moonlight, I braced myself for a hideous undead beast. But it was only an ordinary, living dog, probably from a nearby home.

The dog advanced on Liam, still growling. Werewolves and dogs didn't mix—I knew that from Derek.

Liam locked gazes with it and gave a growl of his own. The dog kept coming at him.

"Shoo, pooch."

Liam drew back his foot to kick it. Then he caught sight of the rabbit drawing alongside him. He backed away. The undergrowth behind him erupted in a flurry of breaking twigs and squeals. I couldn't see what it was, but Liam let out an oath, almost backing into the snarling dog.

The dog lunged. Liam kicked it. As it flew back, moonlight caught the dog's flank, and I saw a hole the size of my fist, squirming with maggots.

Liam saw it, too, and he cursed and backed away. The dog threw itself at him. Liam swerved out of its path.

"Stop," I said.

The dog did. It stood there, teeth bared, eyes blazing, every hair on end, growling at Liam.

The rabbit lurched toward him. He kicked it, and it flew into the undergrowth, only to come back out again. Something else came out with it, some kind of rodent, mostly skeleton, rattling and gnashing its tiny teeth.

"Stop," I said.

They did. Liam looked at me.

"Yes, they're dead," I said. "Yes, I control them. And you can't kill them. You can try, but you can't."

"Well, then, I guess I'm going to have to fight the one I *can* kill."

He charged at me.

I commanded the dog to attack, but my brain stuttered, seeing Liam bearing down on me. I dove to the side. He grabbed my pajama leg and yanked. I fell onto my stomach, scrabbling to get up, fingers digging into the ground, nails tearing. I wrenched and his grip slid to my foot. I gave a tremendous heave and flung myself forward, leaving him with my sneaker.

As I scrambled to my feet, I heard a smack. I spun to see Derek—in human form—on Liam's back. Liam bucked and threw him off. Derek grabbed him, and they went down fighting.

The dog raced toward the two. I commanded it to be still, and it slid to a stop, snarling and straining like a rabid dog on a chain. I closed my eyes and gave it another order—to leave its body.

I kept releasing it and the other spirits, desperately trying to ignore the grunts and gasps of the fight. When I opened my eyes, the animals had collapsed, their souls freed.

Liam and Derek rolled on the ground, locked in combat, Liam's hands in Derek's hair, trying to yank his head back, Derek's hands around Liam's neck, neither one able to get the grip they needed to throw the other off.

I yanked out my switchblade as I raced forward. I hit the button . . . and felt the blade sink into my palm. I let go. The knife fell into the undergrowth. I dropped to my knees, digging for it.

A crack like the snap of a tree branch. I shot up. Derek lay on his back, Liam over him, Derek's hands still around his neck. Both had gone still. Derek stared up, wide-eyed. Liam's eyes were just as wide, but they saw nothing, fixed in an empty look of final shock.

twenty-three

"I—I DIDN'T . . ." Derek began.

He scrambled out from under Liam. The werewolf's body fell, limp, to the side, his head twisted, neck broken.

Derek swallowed. The sound echoed in the silence.

"I didn't— I just— I was trying to stop him."

"You didn't mean it," I said softly. "But he did."

He looked at me, eyes refusing to focus.

"He would have killed you," I said. "Killed both of us, if it came down to it. You might not have meant to do it, but . . ."

I didn't finish. I could have said the world was better off without Liam, but we both knew the point wasn't whether Liam deserved to die, but whether Derek deserved the guilt of killing someone. He didn't.

"It wasn't a fight to the death for you. But it was for him."

Derek nodded and rubbed the back of his neck, wincing as his fingers hit a scrape.

"Are you okay?" I asked.

"Yeah. Just a few cuts and bruises. I heal fast. Might need a stitch or two here—"

He glanced down at the blood-smeared cut on his side . . . and realized he wasn't wearing any clothing. I'd be lying if I said *I* hadn't realized it already. Kind of obvious. It wasn't like he'd been going to take time out to find his clothing before stopping Liam.

Fortunately, under the circumstances, I hadn't had time to dwell on the lack of clothing. With the fighting and, now, as he crouched, I hadn't seen any more than I had when he was in his shorts. That didn't keep him from turning bright red.

I peeled off my jacket and wordlessly handed it to him, and he tied it around his waist with a mumbled, "Thanks." Then, "We should get going."

Only we didn't get going. We lapsed into silence, with Derek still crouched beside Liam's body, his head down, hair hanging around his face, his back and arms covered in a sheen of sweat. He shivered.

"I'll go get your clothes," I said, pushing to my feet.

He caught my elbow. "Ramon."

"Right."

I blinked hard, feeling fuzzy—from shock, I guess. One of us had to kick-start their brain, and Derek seem stalled, unable to stop staring at the man he'd killed.

"We need to move him," I said. "At least into the brush for now, to cover the body. Then we'll have to come back tomorrow and bury him."

I couldn't believe what I was saying. Hiding a body? A *body*?

And what's the alternative? Leave him lying in the path and hope none of the neighbors ever walks through here?

Body disposal might be something I never expected to do outside a screenplay, but this was my life now. Adjust or give up.

I stood and took Liam's arm, giving it a tentative tug.

"I've got it." Derek rose. "I'll carry him. We can't leave drag marks or anything, and we'll need to bury him right away, so no dogs find him."

"Bury who?" said a voice beside me.

I jumped so high, my heart rammed into my throat.

"Chloe?" Derek said.

I turned to see Liam walking toward us.

"Chloe?" Derek said again.

"It's L-Liam. His ghost."

Liam stopped. "Ghost?" He looked at me, then at his body, on the ground. He swore.

"You're dead," I said.

"So I see. That must make you one of those people who can talk to the dead and"—he glanced at the bodies of the dog and rabbit, lips curling—"raise the dead."

His gaze returned to his own corpse, and he swore again.

I cleared my throat. "As long as you're here, I have some questions."

He looked at me, brows lifting. "You're kidding, right?"

"No." I knelt beside his body and reached into his pocket.

"Chloe?" Derek moved closer, frowning.

I took out Liam's cell phone. "Someone called him. Someone who seems to have set the whole thing up, someone who knew me, my name." I looked at Liam's ghost. "Who is it?"

He choked on a laugh. "Seriously? I just *died*. Your boyfriend there killed me. You really expect me to stick around and chat? Love to, but I'm a little traumatized right now. Maybe later."

He turned to leave. I raced into his path.

"You're about to go to the afterlife," I said. "This is your last chance to do something good."

"Huh, well, since you put it that way . . ." He rolled his eyes. "I'm not interested in second chances. I didn't do a thing that I regret. If you want answers . . ."

He stepped up, towering over me. I resisted the urge to back away, but I must have stiffened, because Derek moved closer and whispered, "Don't let him harass you."

"Harass her?" Liam said. "She's the one who can't get enough of my company." He looked down at me again. "As I was saying, if you want answers, find them yourself. And try to have some fun while you're at it, because I have a feeling I'm going to be seeing you again real soon . . . over on this side."

Derek's hand tightened on my arm. When I tried to pull away, he leaned down and whispered, "Let him go. It's not worth it."

"Listen to your boyfriend, cutie," Liam called as he strode away.

I pulled myself up straight. "What did you think of my zombies?"

Liam stopped, turned slowly.

I waved at the dead dog. "Do you know how I did it?"

"Do I care?"

"You should. Necromancers raise the dead by sending a spirit—a ghost, like you—back into a corpse, where it's under my control, as you saw. It works the same for animals and people. So either you answer my questions, or I'm shoving you back in there." I pointed at his dead body.

He laughed. "I'd say you've got balls, but that'd be kinda inappropriate."

"Do you think I'm kidding?"

He answered by turning his back and walking away. I closed my eyes and imagined tugging him toward his corpse, just a little pull.

"Hey," he said. "*Hey*!"

I opened my eyes to see him straining against an unseen force.

"Did you think I was bluffing?"

I ramped it up a notch and he stumbled. I gave another tug. His ghost shot a few feet toward his body.

"Okay, fine," he spat at me. "What do you want to know?"

"Who hired you?"

"You've got the phone. Figure it out."

I told Derek what Liam said, then asked, "Was it the Edison Group?"

His face screwed up. "The electric company?"

"Was it a man named Marcel Davidoff?"

"Who?"

"Diane Enright?"

"He's right," Derek whispered. "You've got the phone. Ask something else."

"When you found us the first time, in the playground, you said you'd pulled off the road and picked up Derek's scent. That was a lie, wasn't it?"

"Everyone lies, sweetheart. Get used to it."

"Someone hired you to get rid of Derek."

"You've figured it out. So you don't need me—"

"Why?"

"Why what?"

"Why do they want him gone?" I asked.

"Because I'm a werewolf," Derek said. "Like Andrew said, no one wants us around."

"Bingo, pup. It's a lesson best learned early. They're all afraid of us." He strolled over to Derek. "You're trying to be a good kid, aren't you? You think that'll show them they're wrong. So, how's that working out for you? Guess what? They don't care. To them, you're a monster, and nothing you do—or don't do—will change their minds. My advice? Give 'em what they want. It's a short, brutal life." He smiled. "Live it up."

Derek stared straight ahead, patiently waiting.

"He can't hear a word I'm saying, can he?" Liam said.

"Nope."

He swore. "Here I try to impart some final pearls of wisdom to the next gener—"

Liam disappeared. I jumped, startled, then looked around.

"Chloe?"

"He's gone."

"Left?"

"No, he just—" I kept looking, but couldn't see any ghostly shimmer. "He was talking and then he vanished, like someone yanked him over to the other side."

"What did he say?" Derek asked.

"Nothing we didn't already—"

Derek wheeled. A man appeared twenty feet down the path. Ramon. Derek stepped in front of me.

Ramon raised his hand, palm out, showing he wasn't armed. His broken arm hung at his side. As he walked toward us, I could see bruises on his jaw and blood soaking the side of his shirt. With every step, he winced.

"I'm not here to fight you, kid," he said. "If you insist, I'll give it my best, but I'd really rather call it a draw."

Noticing Liam's body, he stopped and shook his head.

"It was an accident," I said.

"Yeah, well, I'm sure he had it coming." Another head shake, but there was genuine grief in his eyes. After a moment, he tore his gaze from the body and looked up at Derek.

"So now what?" Ramon said.

"We call it a draw, like you said. But if you ever come after either of us again . . ."

Ramon gave a tight laugh. "Do I look like I'm in any shape to hunt you? Nah, this was Liam's scheme. Crazy son of a—"

"Someone hired you two. Who was it?"

"Ask him." He hooked his thumb at Liam. "He's the man with the plan. Always was. I just go along for the ride."

"So you have no idea who hired him?"

"Some supernatural. A healer guy."

"Sorcerer?" I said. "Shaman?"

"No clue. I'm not into that stuff. Anyway, someone put Liam in touch with this guy who wanted a werewolf to track you down"—he nodded at Derek—"and hand you over to the Pack. Just so happened we were already in trouble with the Pack—on account of Liam, as usual."

"And this was the perfect solution," I said. "Give Derek to the Pack, blame him for the man-eating, and get paid for your trouble. If you couldn't take him in alive, that was okay, too."

"Not at first. The guy wanted you handed over to the Pack, seemed to think that would be okay. Or pretended to, anyway."

"And if the Pack turned out to be killers, that wasn't his fault," Derek said.

"You got it. After we lost you the first time, he started getting antsy. Just wanted you gone one way or another. You want my advice?" He looked at Derek. "Take your girlfriend and start running. Whatever you're trying to do here—live with other supernaturals, pretend you're one of them—it won't work. They'll always be watching you, expecting you to lose control." Ramon shook his head. "You know much about wolves, boy?"

"A bit."

"There's a reason they live as far from humans as they can. Centuries of experience. People don't like other predators around. Makes them nervous. When they get nervous, they try to eliminate the threat. Now, I'm going to say good night and take my buddy there."

"And give him a proper burial?" I said.

A sharp laugh. "We don't get luxuries like that. I'm going to take the down payment on the job, then I'm going to take his body to the Pack, settle up with them. And, yes, it's a helluva thing to do to a friend, but out here, it's survival of the fittest." He met Derek's gaze. "For us, it's always survival of the fittest."

With Derek's help, Ramon managed to get Liam's body over his shoulder, teeth gritted against the pain of the extra weight. Then he hobbled off into the night.

twenty-four

WE RETURNED TO WHERE Derek left his clothes before his first Change. As he dressed, I checked Liam's cell phone. Derek walked up behind me and looked over my shoulder.

"He used initials for the name. RRB. But it's a 212 area code. That's New York City, so it could still be the Edison Group, using a local contact for the job."

"Yeah."

"You don't sound so sure."

He looked in the direction of the house.

"You think it's one of them?" I said. "But we met Liam on the way *to* Andrew's place."

"They could have known I was on my way, sent Liam to stake out the bus route."

"How? At the time, Andrew was being held by the Edison Group. He didn't know we were coming, meaning no one in his group did either."

"They could have been watching his house, seen Simon and Tori, figured out we were on our way, made a few calls to the bus companies, found out two kids got off in Albany the night before. It's a stretch. But . . ." He shrugged.

"It's a possibility." I checked the initials again. "Did you catch Russell's last name? Ramon said the contact was a healer. Russell's a shaman. Unless Ramon meant a sorcerer."

"Sorcerers aren't healers. Witches are, kind of, but if it's a guy, he's a shaman."

"We need proof. And I know how to get it." I raised the cell phone.

Derek shook his head. "Too risky. I'm no good at imitating voices."

"You won't have to. Liam said if the guy wanted anything else, he should text him. So, presumably Liam might also text *him*."

"Good idea." Derek reached for the cell phone. "I'll tell him—"

I pulled the phone out of his reach, and I looked at him. He got the message, rubbing his chin and nodding.

"Go ahead."

As I typed, he stepped back and tried not to watch over my shoulder. It wasn't easy—he kept rocking forward to peek. But he managed to resist the urge to take over, and I appreciated that. Afterward I let him read what I'd typed and he approved.

According to the message, Liam had Derek and the girl cornered. He might be able to take them alive, but if he tried, he could lose them again. What did the boss want Liam and Ramon to do?

Whoever was on the other end must have been poised over his cell phone, waiting, because the reply came back in seconds. Five words. *Just take care of them.*

I sent back another, to be absolutely clear, saying if he wanted us to dispose of the bodies, that'd cost an extra 10 percent. Again, a quick response, one word this time. *Fine.*

I looked over to see Derek staring at the message. Just staring, like he still believed Liam and Ramon had only been trying to scare us and their orders were to leave me alone and deliver him to the Pack.

"Are you okay?" I asked.

He nodded. But he didn't look okay, face pale, eyes fixed on the screen.

"Derek?"

The phone vibrated. Another message, from the same sender, wanting to clarify that the extra 10 percent covered disposal of *both* bodies. And if they did take Derek alive, I had to disappear.

"Because if I go back, I can tell Andrew what happened," I said. "It's better if we both vanish, and it looks like we ran off together."

I glanced at Derek. He'd gone an odd greenish shade, like he was going to be sick.

"I'm so sorry," he said finally, the words little more than a whisper. "They were going to kill you because you came out here with me. To help me. I asked you to come."

"And how's that your fault?" I didn't mean to snap, but I was mad. Not at Derek, but at *them*—everyone who made him feel like this. Before I could apologize, he blinked hard, the shock falling away, and I knew my anger had worked better than any words of reassurance.

"They targeted you because you're a werewolf," I said. "That's it. It's nothing you did, and nothing you can change. It's their problem."

"But if I know it's a problem, I shouldn't endanger anyone else."

"So you should have come out here alone? That's—"

"Not just that. I put you and Simon in danger just by . . ."

"By being here? And what's the alternative? Take off? Give up on finding your dad? Leave Simon behind?"

He blinked. "No, I wouldn't leave . . . but I feel like . . ."

"Feel like what?"

He shook his head, looking away. I walked around in front of him.

"Feel like *what*, Derek? Like you should leave? Like we'd be better off if you did?"

He rolled his shoulders in a half shrug, then looked away again. I was right. He just didn't like hearing the thought voiced; it sounded too close to self-pity.

"No one is better off if you leave," I said.

"Yeah." He mumbled the word, unconvinced.

"Simon needs you."

He nodded and stared into the forest.

I need you. I didn't say that, of course. How could I, without it sounding weird? But I felt it, heart hammering against my ribs, and it wasn't some romantic *I can't bear to be without you* nonsense. It was something deeper, more desperate.

When I thought of Derek leaving, the ground seemed to slide under my feet. I needed something to hold on to, something solid and real when everything around me was changing so fast. Even if there were times I thought it would be easier without Derek there, ready to tear a strip off me at my every misstep, in some ways I relied on that—someone to keep me thinking, keep me striving to do better, keep me from burying my head and praying it all worked out.

When he turned my way, he must have seen it on my face. As fast as I tried to cover it up, it wasn't fast enough, and when he looked at me, the *way* he looked at me . . .

Panic. I felt panic, like I suddenly wanted to be anywhere but here, and nowhere but here, and I wanted, I wanted . . .

I tore my gaze away and opened my mouth to say something, anything, but he beat me to it.

"I'm not going anywhere, Chloe." He rubbed the back of one shoulder, scowling, like he was working out a knot. "I don't mean to get all . . ."

"Angsty?"

A short, sharp laugh. "Yeah, I guess. Way too much call for angst lately. I'm really better with action."

"I hear you." I lifted the cell phone. "And maybe with this, we can kick-start that action. Ready to go talk to Andrew?"

He nodded and we headed for the house.

It wasn't until we got back that the full impact of the night hit. Someone wanted Derek dead. That same someone had been willing to let me die because . . . well, I guess just because it didn't matter. *I* didn't matter. I was just an obstacle to the goal.

How could someone look at kids who'd never done anything wrong and see only a threat best eliminated with murder? Whoever did this was no better than the Edison Group.

Someone wanted Derek dead because he was a monster. But when he'd accidentally killed Liam, Derek had suffered and he'd continue to suffer, however justifiable the act.

So who was the real monster?

The house was quiet. That was weird. It was like we'd woken from a nightmare and could just crawl back into bed as if nothing had happened.

I let Derek get Andrew.

They found me at the kitchen table. Derek said, "There's something we need to tell you," and from the look on Andrew's face, I think he expected Derek to say he'd gotten me pregnant. It seemed to come as something of a relief to discover we'd only been hunted by killer werewolves—or at least until he realized it wasn't the Edison Group that had sent them. Once he saw that text message and confirmed it was Russell's number, things changed, and Andrew finally became the kind of guy we needed him to be.

He was furious, pacing the kitchen, vowing if not vengeance, at least answers. And safety. He promised us that nothing like this would happen again, even if it meant he had to take us away from the others and handle the Edison Group alone.

He called Margaret and told her to get over to the house. He didn't care if it was four A.M., this wouldn't wait until morning. He couldn't get hold of Gwen, but he left the same message.

Next, we got Simon and Tori up, me talking to Tori, Derek to Simon. I was quite happy not to have to face Simon just yet.

I told Tori what happened. Or a version of it, balanced between conveying the seriousness of the threat and not freaking her out. Derek and I also hadn't told Andrew everything because we didn't want to freak *him* out. In our version, Derek hadn't completed his Change. Everyone was already worried enough about him without us admitting he was now a full-blown werewolf. We also hadn't admitted that Liam was dead, saying Derek had just knocked him out, then Ramon called it a draw and carted his friend away.

Derek wanted all of us to pack our bags and run. I knew that's what he wanted because it's what I wanted, too. It wasn't an option, though. Not yet.

If anything, tonight had only opened another window on the danger lurking beyond our castle walls. I suppose it's dramatic to say we were under siege, but that's how we felt.

In a movie, we'd set out, braving Ramon and Russell and the Edison Group assassins. Those who refused to leave the castle would be branded wimps and cowards. But there's a reason people do stupid things in movies—no one wants to watch a bunch of kids pace and bicker and angst as they wait for the adults to come up with a plan. We didn't much like it either, but for now, we were stuck with it.

twenty-five

ONLY MARGARET SHOWED UP. While Andrew said Gwen must be at her boyfriend's, cell phone off, I could tell he didn't like that. Had she been in on the scheme to get rid of Derek? I hoped not.

If we expected the same outrage from Margaret that we'd gotten from Andrew, we were disappointed. But she was upset and concerned. Good enough for now.

When I came out of the shower, I found a piece of paper shoved under the door. It was a pictogram message from Simon, like the one he'd left at the warehouse. It started with a ghost as the salutation—meaning me—and closed with a cloud of fog and lightning bolt—meaning him. As for the message itself, it was a little more complicated than the last one, and it took me a while to work out.

The first symbol was a piece of paper with "I bequeath . . ." across the top. The second was the letter U. Then the number 4. Then two hands, one putting something in the other's palm. Then the musical note "mi." *Will you for ___ me?*

I stared at the two hands, trying to figure out the missing word until a loud sigh came through the door.

"Either the answer is no or my drawing sucks."

"Hold on." I quickly dressed and opened the door. Simon was leaning against the wall.

"So?" he said.

"I'm having trouble with one part." I pointed to the hands.

"Give," he said.

"Ah." I read the note. "Will you for . . . *forgive* me?" I looked up at him. "I think that's supposed to be my question."

"No, you did the right thing. You realized it wasn't what you wanted, and you said so. I'm the jerk who stomped off and left you alone in the forest. I'm sorry. Really sorry." He paused. "So . . . are we okay?"

Relief made my knees wobble. "We're okay. But I *am* sor—"

He held up a hand to cut me off. "I can't get mad at you for confirming something I already suspected. I gave it a shot. It didn't work out. I'm not going to say I'm fine with that, but . . ." He shrugged. "I like you, Chloe. And it's not a girlfriend-or-nothing kind of like, so I'm hoping we can skip the we-tried-dating-and-it-blew stage and jump straight back to where we were, if you want that."

"I want that."

When we got downstairs, Andrew was gone. We figured he went to confront Russell, but Margaret, left behind on babysitting duty, wouldn't confirm that. Was this how it would be? Left on the sidelines while the grown-ups took action? I hoped not.

Simon and I found Derek in the kitchen. Simon wanted to grab an apple and head someplace so we could plan our next move, out of range of the adults, but Derek handed him his blood tester and insulin pouch, then got bacon and eggs out of the fridge. Simon sighed and Derek gave him a look.

"I hope you don't expect me to make that," I said.

Now it was my turn to get the look.

"I'm just saying . . ."

"Not all of us grew up with live-in housekeepers," Derek said.

"I don't need breakfast," Simon said. "We have to talk."

"About what?" Derek said.

"Um, getting out of here?" he said. "Someone tried to *kill* you. Both of you."

"And the only thing new about that is that it wasn't the Edison Group," Derek said, "who are probably also on our trail, waiting for us to do something stupid like run away again." He put bacon strips in the frying pan. "We're staying. At least until we know what they plan to do next."

"I want to summon Royce," I said.

Derek jerked his head around fast enough to cause whiplash. "*What?*"

"I want to contact Royce. If I'm lucky, I'll get his uncle or cousin instead, but it's more likely that it'd be Royce, and we'll have to deal with that. We need to know what happened here, and we need to know it fast."

"She's right." Simon met his brother's gaze. "You know she is."

Derek's jaw worked as he chewed that over. Finally he said, "On one condition. No Tori. The last thing we need is her whipping a fireball at Royce."

"All right."

I went upstairs to get Tori down for breakfast. I took her into our confidence and asked for her help by keeping Margaret busy and letting us know if Andrew showed up. She'd have rather come to the summoning, but she seemed okay with that.

After breakfast, we decided to do the summoning in the basement—far from Andrew, without the dangers of the roof. And, I'll admit, Simon and I were eager to get a look down there.

For the first time in my life, I walked into a basement and shivered only from an actual draft. It was exactly as Derek had described it—two big rooms full of stored stuff and a small workshop. Simon joked about secret passages, but Derek squelched that idea.

I did my usual thing—closed my eyes and knelt. I could imagine Dr. Banks from his photo. Austin was tougher, because I kept seeing his bloodied body, and that didn't help me relax. So I mainly focused on Dr. Banks, concentrating to the point where I could sense that inner alarm ready to go off, saying it wasn't safe to go farther.

"Nothing," I said.

"Are you sure?" Simon said. "You twitched."

"Try it again," Derek said.

I did, and still nothing happened, but Simon said, "Yeah, that was a definite twitch. Your eyelids moved, like you saw something."

The next time I tried, I *did* feel it, a little spark that made me flinch. I sighed and shifted.

"Take your time," Simon murmured. "No one's going anywhere."

I summoned, fighting the urge to crank it up another notch. There *was* a spirit present. I felt that same hyperawareness that I did with bodies, like I was straining to hear a voice too faint for my ears to detect. Goose bumps speckled my arms.

"I want to take off my necklace."

I braced for a fight, but Derek only nodded. "Lift it over your head slowly, and keep it in your hands for now. See if that makes a difference."

I closed my eyes and grasped the necklace.

"No!"

I jumped, then looked from Simon to Derek, but I knew it wasn't one of them.

"She's back," I said. "The woman."

When I summoned again, the sensation returned, stronger now, and it took all my willpower not to ramp it up and yank the spirit through.

"Careful," the voice whispered.

My goose bumps rose higher.

"C-can I see you, p-please?" My voice wavered. I cleared my throat and tried again, but still stammered through it.

"Chloe?" Derek said.

I followed his gaze to my hands. They were shaking. I clenched the necklace and took a deep breath.

"Is it your aunt?" Simon asked.

I shook my head. "No. I—" I was about to say I didn't know who it was, but I couldn't get the words out. I knew who this was. I just didn't dare believe it.

"Listen, baby . . . Have to listen . . ."

Listen, baby. I knew who called me that. I knew this voice.

"Mom?"

twenty-six

"WHAT?" SIMON SAID, SHIFTING FORWARD. "Your mom's here?"

"No." I shook my head sharply. "She's not. I—I—I—"

I took another breath and clenched my shaking hands. "I don't know why I said that."

"You're exhausted," Derek said.

"What if it is?" Simon said.

I caught the look Derek shot him, telling him to be quiet. Still, he asked me, "If there's a ghost there, do you want to keep trying?" He met my gaze. "It probably isn't her."

"I know."

I closed my eyes. I wanted this to be my mom. From the day I'd learned I could speak to the dead, I'd been pushing this possibility from my mind as hard as I could. Even thinking about talking to her made my chest tighten.

But I was terrified, too. My mom was a distant, cherished memory. She was hugs and laughter and everything good about my childhood. Thinking of her was like being three years old again, curled up on her lap, completely safe and loved. But I wasn't three anymore, and I knew she wasn't the perfect mom of my memory.

My mother had put me in this experiment. She'd wanted a child so badly that she'd enrolled in the Edison Group's study. Yes, they'd told her they would fix the side effects that led to her brother's death. But still, she'd had to have known she was taking a risk.

"Chloe?" Simon said.

"S-sorry. Let me try again."

I closed my eyes and forgot all of that. If it was my mother, I wanted to see her, no matter what she really was, no matter what she'd done.

So when I summoned, I allowed myself to picture my mother, to call her by name.

"—hear me?" Her voice came again, so soft I could catch it only while I was concentrating. I pulled a little harder.

"No! . . . enough . . . not safe."

"What's not safe? Summoning you?"

Her answer was too weak to make out. I opened my eyes and peered around, searching for any sign of a ghost. To my left, I caught a shimmer, like heat rising off the floor. I held my necklace out for Derek.

"No!" the voice said. ". . . put it . . . not safe."

"But I want to see you."

". . . can't . . . Sorry, baby."

My chest clenched. "P-please. I just want to see you."

". . . know . . . can't . . . necklace . . . safe."

Derek gave it back. I lowered it over my head, but resumed summoning, stronger now, pulling—

"Chloe!" Her voice was so harsh my eyes flew open. "Not so hard . . . bring him."

"Royce? I've dealt with him before. I want to talk to you." I summoned again.

"Chloe! . . . keep . . . I'll leave . . . shouldn't be here . . . not allowed."

"What's not allowed?"

"You aren't allowed to speak to her," Derek murmured. "Necromancers aren't supposed to be able to contact their dead relatives. I've heard that. I didn't want to say anything, because I wasn't sure. Obviously, you can contact her, just not very well. And she doesn't want you to try harder, in case you bring Royce."

"But I *need* to—"

I didn't even get the sentence out, and the air began to shimmer, a shape taking form. My mother's shape, so faint I could barely see it, but enough so I knew. I *knew.* The tears started. I blinked them back, and she disappeared again.

"It was you that night at Andrew's," I said. "In the woods. When they were chasing us. You tried to help. You've been following me."

"Not always . . . can't . . . tried to warn . . . oh, baby . . . run . . ."

"Run?"

" . . . not safe . . . no place safe . . . not for you . . . so many lies . . . get away . . ."

"We can't run," I said. "The Edison Group found us that night at—"

"No . . . that's . . . tried to tell . . ." Her voice started to fade. I strained to hear, but it kept moving away. I held out my necklace.

"Um, Chloe?" Simon said. "If your mom said to leave that on—"

"She was trying to tell me something, and she's disappearing."

"Summon her again," Derek said, taking the necklace, "but carefully."

I gently pulled as I called for her. Derek stayed poised beside me, necklace stretched between his hands, ready to drop it over my head at the first hint of trouble.

"She's gone," I said finally. Tears prickled again. I blinked them back and cleared my throat.

"What'd she say?" Simon asked.

"That it's not safe for us anywhere, which we already knew. But there was something else. Something she wanted to tell me about that night at Andrew's."

"If you want to keep trying, go on," Derek said. "If you pull through Royce, you can send him back, right?"

I nodded. Margaret said it wasn't safe, but I wouldn't feel bad about shoving that particular ghost into the wrong dimension. So, still kneeling, I cranked up the power, trying to summon—

"Looking for someone, little necro?"

I jumped, losing my balance. Simon and Derek both grabbed for me, Derek catching me with one hand while awkwardly dropping the amulet ribbon over my head. I pulled it down and looked around.

"Royce," I said. "Can I see you? Please?"

He chuckled and appeared partway, like he had before. "Liked what you saw, huh?"

They say you can't fake a blush, but I sure tried. That was the way to deal with this jerk. Flattery, as painful as it was.

"You were right," I said. "We need your help. Things are going wrong."

"Surprise, surprise."

"Were you . . . one of us? Part of the Genesis project?"

"I'm genetically modified, but I'm not one of you imitations."

"Imitations?" I said.

"Of the original model. Me. Well, Austin and me."

"I thought we were the first subjects."

"They called it Genesis *Two*," Derek murmured. "I thought they meant two as in second to the biblical one. They meant the second study. They must have done one before us."

Royce laughed. "You kids really are idiots. Do you really think this is their only experiment? Yeah, you're the second wave . . . of the Genesis project. Then there's the Icarus project, the Phoenix project . . ."

Dr. Davidoff had hinted that the Edison Group was involved in other experiments, but I acted like this was all new. "How do you know all this?"

"I'm smart."

And his uncle was one of the group leaders.

"What went wrong?" I asked.

"Wrong?"

"You're dead. Austin's dead. Dr. Banks is dead. . . . Did that have anything to do with you? You and Austin?"

Anger flickered across his face.

"Something went wrong," I pushed. "With you two. That's how he knew—"

He feigned a yawn. "Anyone else finding this conversation really boring? Let's liven things up with a game." He walked over to Simon. "You joked about a secret passage earlier."

"He can't hear you, remember?" I said.

"Do you want to make your boyfriend happy, little girl? I'll tell you where the secret passage is. You know there *is* one. In a house this big, the basement has to be just as large."

I told the guys what Royce had said.

"Not necessarily," Derek said. "It was common in that period not to build full basements—"

"Boring. There is a passage to another room—one they don't want you to find. Especially you, little necromancer. They wouldn't want you to bring those bodies back, get their stories."

I hesitated. Simon asked what he'd said and I told them.

"I think he's full of it," Derek said. "But I'll bite. Where's the passage?"

Royce pointed and I relayed it.

"The workshop?" Derek said. "There's nothing in there. I already checked."

"Why do you think the door's locked?" Royce said.

"Because you're a genetically altered half-demon with telekinetic powers," I said. "As a prototype, they wanted you under careful supervision, but in a normal environment. So instead of the laboratory, you lived here with your uncle Dr. Banks."

"Really bored . . ."

"And your power, being telekinesis, means you can move objects with your mind, right?"

"Um, yeah. Want another demo?"

"No, just making a point. You lived here. You can move objects with your mind. Over there"—I pointed at the workshop—"is a room filled with tools. Why is it locked? I think that's kind of obvious."

Simon laughed. The ghost spun on him, but the scare was lost on Simon.

"Open that door," Royce said.

"Why? So you can bring out some toys? I don't think so."

Simon snorted another laugh.

A broom flew from the wall, coming straight at me like a javelin. An unwieldy javelin, I might add. I easily ducked out of the way, and Derek just as easily caught it in midflight.

"Good reflexes, big guy," the ghost said.

He strolled over to a bunch of plastic bins stacked against the wall and flipped open the top one.

"Oh, look, Uncle Todd kept my old stuff. He's so sweet, packing my things away after he murdered me."

"M-murdered you?" I said in spite of myself.

He rummaged through the box.

"Get ready to send him back," Derek whispered, then to Simon, "Go upstairs."

Simon shook his head. "I—"

Royce spun like a shot-putter, whipping something at us. I dove out of the way. Derek caught it—a bowling ball—then snarled at Simon, "Upstairs!"

"Oooh, good reflexes, superhuman strength, and a very convincing snarl. I think we have ourselves a werewolf." He got right in Derek's face. "How about a little one-on-one, wolf-boy? Battle of the superpowers?"

I shut my eyes and pictured Royce sailing backward. But he just kept taunting Derek.

"Maybe we should all go upstairs," Simon said. "Get away from this creep."

"He'd follow us," Derek said.

"Oh, don't listen to him," Royce said. "Sure. Go on upstairs. There are lots of fun things to play with up there. Razors. Scissors. Knives." He smiled and whispered in my ear. "I really like knives. There's so much you can do with them."

I glanced at Derek. He looked anxious, shooting glances from me to Simon, like he couldn't decide between letting me finish banishing Royce and getting us out before we were hurt.

"I'm trying," I said. "I'm really—"

"I know. Take your time." He shot an arrogant look of his own in the ghost's direction. "He's not dangerous. Unless you can talk someone to death."

The ghost spun and whipped a barbell. It came at us, but awkwardly, like he'd fumbled the shot. Derek moved mockingly slow and caught it before it crashed to the floor. I continued banishing Royce.

Royce started rooting around the box again. "Where's that other dumbbell? . . . Oh, that's right. I used it already." He got in Derek's face again. "To bash my brother's brains in while he slept. Do you sleep, wolf-boy?"

My brain stuttered, flashing images of Austin's body, the blood, blood everywhere . . .

"Chloe?" Derek said.

"I-I've got it."

"She doesn't have anything," Royce said. "She pulled me through and I'm not going back."

"Simon?" Derek whispered. "Upstairs. Now."

I had to stay here to banish Royce and Derek had to stay to protect me, but Simon was a bystander, one Royce would eventually target.

Simon left. I heard him stop on the stairs, unwilling to go too far in case we needed him.

A crash. My eyes flew open to see Derek on his feet, Royce picking up a piece of a smashed plate from the concrete floor.

"Oh, look," Royce said, running his finger along the broken edge. "Sharp. I like sharp."

Derek moved in front of me. I stared at his back and emptied my mind of everything except the image of Royce, sailing backward through the dimensions, through *any* dimensions. I concentrated until my temples throbbed. Still nothing.

You can't do it. Stop trying and get someplace safe.

But there was no safe place. Not from this ghost. I had to get rid of him.

"How much do you know about werewolves?" Royce was saying, pacing as he turned the shard over in his hands. "We grew up on that crap, Austin and me. All part of our cultural training, my uncle said."

"What's he saying?" Derek asked.

"I'm trying not to listen."

"Go ahead," Derek said. "Tell me."

Royce lunged at Derek, swinging the shard like a blade. Derek sidestepped out of the way, then kept going, circling wide around Royce, luring him away from me, motioning for me to resume banishing.

Royce charged. The china shard came a little too close to Derek, giving my mental shove a little panicky oomph, and Royce's half-materialized form wavered.

Again, Royce swung too hard. This time the shard sailed from his hand. He scrabbled after it. Derek got there first, stomping the piece under his sneaker.

Royce raced for the rest of the plate. Derek managed to step on the biggest piece, but Royce snatched up another. I gave him another big push. Again he wobbled.

Royce walked backward, eyeing Derek. Derek's gaze stayed glued to the new shard—tracking Royce.

"You like science, don't you?" Royce said. "Well, I'm going to try an experiment of my own. Like I was asking before, how much do you know about werewolf legends?"

Again, I repeated his words. Derek still said nothing, only backing up, keeping Royce's focus on him, letting me work at banishing the ghost.

"I don't remember many of them," Royce went on. "It was pretty boring stuff, at least the ones Uncle Todd told us. But he had others—books he didn't want us to read. There was this one about werewolf trials. Seemed every medieval serial killer tried to get off with the werewolf defense. There was this one cool story about a guy who told the court he was a werewolf. Only problem was, they'd seen him kill someone—and he looked human. So do you know what he said?"

Derek motioned for me to relay the message. I did, as best I could.

"He said, my fur is on the inside," Derek replied.

Royce laughed. "Guess I'm not the only one who likes the gory old stories. All right then, tell the little necro how it ends. What did the court do?"

I hesitated to relay the question, but Derek insisted on getting the message, then said, "Cut off his arms and legs and dissected them to check for fur inside the skin."

Royce looked at me. "Sadly, there wasn't any. But they'd saved themselves the fuss and bother of a trial."

He wheeled and ran at Derek. Derek's hands flew up to shield himself. The shard sliced the back of his hand, blood spurting.

Royce danced back. "I don't see any fur, do you? Guess we'll just have to keep going, to conduct a thorough experiment."

I saw the blood dripping down Derek's hand, shut my eyes, and gave one rage-filled shove. The shard clattered to the floor. Royce was still there, faint though, teeth gritted, tendons popping, struggling to hold on.

I walked toward him, mentally pushing, watching him fade until he was only a glimmer, and then—

"What have you done?" roared a voice behind me.

twenty-seven

I SPUN, EXPECTING TO SEE Andrew, but no one was there.

A ghost popped out in front of me, so close I fell back. Derek grabbed my arm to steady me.

"I think he's gone," Derek said. "Did you hear something?"

I looked up into the bearded face of Todd Banks, contorted with fury, eyes wild and red rimmed.

"I-it's Dr. Banks."

"Do you think this is a game?" Dr. Banks shouted. "Who told you about Royce? Did you think it would be amusing? Call him forth and see if he's as crazy as they said?"

Derek leaned down to my ear.

"Release him. Whatever he can tell us, it's not worth it."

I shook my head. Derek didn't like that, but settled for scowling and keeping his grip on my arm, like he'd yank me out of the room by force if things went bad.

Some of the anger seeped from Dr. Banks's eyes as he studied me.

"Chloe Saunders," he whispered. "You must be Chloe Saunders." He looked at Derek. "The werewolf boy."

"Yes," I said. "Derek. That's Derek."

The rage surged again, his eyes going crazy wild. "You must not summon here, girl. Leave my nephew in peace. Remember him, though, because that is your destiny. The power will grow until it consumes you and leaves a monster in your place. It will make you do things you could never imagine, things so horrible that—"

He teetered, as if fighting the memories. Hands closed around both of my arms, and I realized Derek had moved behind me. I could feel him there, strong and solid, his warm hands rubbing the goose bumps on my arms.

"Let him go, Chloe," Derek murmured. "Whatever he's saying, you don't need to listen to it."

"Yes," Dr. Banks said. "Yes, you do. You don't understand. Everything went wrong. We made mistakes. An error in the calculations—"

"With the genetic modification?"

"Yes, yes." He waved aside my interruption. "I told them. I *told* them. But they ran the tests and everything seemed fine. Only it wasn't. They manipulated the data."

"Manipulated the data?" I said.

That got Derek's attention. "What data?"

"For the modifications," I said. "What does that mean?"

"They changed the data so it gave the proper results," Derek said.

"Yes," Dr. Banks said. "Correct. See? Even a child can understand. But they couldn't."

"So Dr. Davidoff manipulated the data—" I began.

"Davidoff?" Dr. Banks snorted. "A fawning puppy who does whatever he's told."

"So who manipulated the data?"

Dr. Banks continued like he hadn't heard. "The experiments. Oh God, the experiments. Testing this and testing that, pushing the boundaries to discover what he could create and what he could sell. Such dreams. Mad and grandiose dreams of knowledge, power, and the fantasy of a better life for our kind. Fools that we were, we believed, and gave him free rein. He didn't care about us. And he doesn't care about you. That's why it's critically important that you—" He started to fade. "The magic in this place. You need to pull me back."

I did, gently at first, but he kept disappearing.

"Harder. Chloe. I need to tell you—"

He faded before I could catch the rest. I summoned again. He flickered in and out, and I caught only words, none meaning anything out of context.

"He's being pulled away," I said.

"Let him go," Derek said. "We've got enough."

"He was trying to tell me something."

Derek snorted. "Aren't they all? Must be a rule in the ghost handbook—if in danger of evaporating, make sure you're in the middle of a dire pronouncement."

I tugged off my necklace. I handed it to Derek, but he tucked it into my pocket.

"Keep it on you, okay?"

Dr. Banks came through easier now, but he wouldn't stay. When I ramped up the power, he said, "No, Chloe. You'll bring Royce." He faded, his voice pulsing in and out. ". . . else . . . try . . . Clear your mind . . . focus on me . . . don't pull . . . just focus."

I did. He kept talking, telling me to relax, focus not on yanking him through, but welcoming him.

The back of my skull began to throb. I kept going until a sharp, sudden pain made me gasp. I waited for Derek to ask what was wrong, but he just sat there, watching me.

Another stab through the back of my skull. Then a flood of ice-cold water rushed through my veins and I tried to scream, but I couldn't. Couldn't move. Couldn't make a sound.

"Chloe?"

I heard Derek, but couldn't even move my eyes his way.

"Do you want my help?" Dr. Banks whispered. "You need to welcome me in."

Welcome him in? In where? I'd barely thought the question when I realized the answer.

He was trying to get inside me.

I fought, mentally trying to shove him out, shut my brain down, block him, but that ice kept spreading through me. Derek's hand closed on my shoulder as he reached to grab the necklace from my pocket. I toppled over backward like a statue.

I caught a blur of motion, like Derek had lunged for me, but everything was fuzzy. Even his voice was distant and muffled. The only words I could hear were Dr. Banks's, crooning inside my head.

"Just relax," he whispered. "I won't hurt you. I'm only going to borrow your body. I need to fix this. I took the easy way out, killing myself before I'd put an end to the horrors I began."

My mother had been warning me about Dr. Banks, that he'd been driven mad by what Royce had done, by his role in it. And now he was inside me.

I felt the floor scrape my back, saw the ceiling whoosh past, like Derek was dragging me by my ankles. The room flickered and went dark. When it popped back, I was staring at the ceiling.

"Wha-what happened?"

I felt my lips move and heard my voice, but no one answered. I got to my feet.

"Chloe, come on," Derek said behind me. "Say something."

"Say what?"

I turned. He was crouched across the room. A pair of legs stretched out, sneakers pointing to the ceiling. My sneakers. My legs.

I raced over. There I was, lying on the floor as Derek fumbled to get the necklace over my head. I lifted my hand. It was my hand—still covered in scratches from the forest last night.

"Derek?"

He didn't answer. I reached for his shoulder.

My fingers passed right through it.

I was a ghost.

My eyes opened then—the eyes on my body, lying on the floor. The lips curving in a small smile that wasn't like mine at all.

"Hey, there." The voice coming from those lips was mine, but the tone, the inflection, were wrong.

Derek frowned, and tried getting the necklace on me again.

The other me batted his hand away. "I don't need that."

"Yes, you do."

"No, I don't."

Derek smacked my hand away and yanked the necklace over my head. The pendant hit my skin and I *felt* the slap of it, hot as a burning brand, and I gasped—me and my body, gasping in unison. A flash of darkness. Then I was staring at the ceiling again.

Derek's face appeared, green eyes dark with worry.

"Chloe?"

I breathed. That was all I could do. Inhale. Exhale. I felt Derek's hands around mine, and I focused on that.

"What happened?" he asked.

"I—I—I—"

A voice behind Derek laughed. "Do you think I can't get back inside you? I will. Then I'll help your friends stop the Edison Group." Dr. Banks loomed over me, face in mine, eyes flashing with madness. "We'll hunt down the other subjects and I'll end their suffering, and then I'll end your friends'. Once they're gone, you'll follow, and you can all be together . . . in the afterlife. I *will* finish this."

"No, you won't," I said, getting up.

He smiled. "You might have the power, Chloe, but you have no idea how to use it."

"Oh, yes, I do."

I reached out and shoved him—with my mind and with my hands, pouring all my rage into it, and for a second, I swore I actually felt him. Then he flew off his feet, sailing backward, screaming as he disappeared.

"Chloe?"

Derek touched my shoulder and I wanted to turn around, collapse against him, and tell him everything. I steeled myself against the urge and took a deep breath.

"We need to get out of here," I said. "As soon as we can."

———

As it turned out, we'd be leaving sooner than any of us dared hope. Andrew had returned, alone. Russell was gone. He'd packed and left his apartment before Andrew had got there.

We could hear Margaret and Andrew on the speakerphone with other group members. It was clear, Margaret said, that we were indeed more than they could handle, and the best way to relieve themselves of the burden was to hand us over to someone else—namely Aunt Lauren and, if they could find him, Simon's dad.

I didn't care that Margaret's motivation was purely selfish—I could have run in there and hugged her.

We were leaving tomorrow, heading to Buffalo. That meant it was time to start planning in earnest. Andrew asked me to provide details of the laboratory. I tried—this was the moment I'd dreamed of—but every word was a struggle. It was like someone cut my energy cord. I was completely drained and numb.

The guys helped. Simon drew the lab floorplan as I explained. Derek got me a glass of ice water. Even Tori murmured "Are you okay?" at a break in the conversation. Only Margaret seemed oblivious, grilling me until she finally had enough and dismissed us. I made it into the parlor, walking only until I found an armchair, then curling up in it. I was asleep the second my eyes closed.

When I woke up, I was still in the chair, a blanket tucked in around me, my glass of water waiting on the table. Derek sat a few feet away on the sofa, lost in thought as he stood watch. Stood watch for what, I didn't know. It didn't matter. Threat or no threat, it felt good to wake up and see him there.

And as I watched him, I realized *how* good it felt. All my denials were just that—denials—because it would be easier if we were just friends. But it wasn't like that, not for me.

I wanted to walk over there. I wanted to curl up beside him, lean against him, talk to him. I wanted to know what he was thinking. I wanted to tell him everything would be okay. And I wanted him to tell me the same thing. I didn't care if it was true or not—I just wanted to say it, to hear it, to feel his arms around me, hear the rumble of his words, that deep chuckle that made my pulse race.

He turned my way, and I was so engrossed in my thoughts that I didn't notice for a second. Then I realized I was staring at him, and looked away fast, cheeks flaming. I could feel him looking at me. Frowning slightly, like he was trying to figure something out. Before he could, I gulped my warm water and said, "Must be almost lunchtime," which was a stupid thing to say, but all I could think of. It took him a moment before he answered, shrugging and saying, "Maybe." Then, "You okay?"

I nodded.

"You want to talk about what happened downstairs? With Banks?"

I nodded again.

"I should get Simon," he said. "He'll want to know."

Another nod, but he didn't move, just watched me as I kept sipping the warm water.

"Chloe."

I took my time looking up, certain he'd figured out what I'd been thinking and was about to let me down gently. He wouldn't say "Sorry, I'm not interested," because that wouldn't be Derek—too presumptuous—but he'd find some way to convey the same message, as I had with Simon. *I like you. I just don't like you that way.*

"Chloe?"

I looked up then, and what I saw in his eyes— My hands fumbled the glass, and I dropped it, water splashing over me, soaking my jeans. I scrambled to catch the glass before it hit the floor, barely making it, on one knee, prize gripped firmly in my hand. And I was still there when I felt the glass being tugged from my fingers. I looked up to see Derek crouching in front of me, his face inches from mine. He leaned forward and—

"What'd you lose?"

Simon's voice came from the doorway, and we shot to our feet so fast we collided.

"What were you looking for?" Simon said, walking in. "Not your necklace, I hope."

"N-no. I—I just dropped my glass." I gestured at my wet jeans. Then I glanced at Derek, who stood there, hands stuffed in his pockets.

"I was just about to . . ." I was going to say I'd been about to explain what happened with Dr. Banks. Only I didn't want to. Not now. I wanted to rewind the tape, go back to that moment on the floor, pray Simon didn't show up for another minute, just long enough to find out if what I thought was going to happen *would* happen. But it wouldn't. Not now. The moment had passed.

"I—I should change my pants."

"Sure." Simon thumped onto the sofa.

I made it to the door, then Derek said, "Chloe?" and I turned, and it looked like he was trying to think of something to say, maybe find some excuse to come with me, and I wanted to help, to offer him one, and I think if I could have, he'd have taken it, but I couldn't. God knows, I tried, but I couldn't, and he couldn't either, so he just mumbled, "You want an apple or something? I'll grab it while you're getting changed," and I said sure, and that was that.

twenty-eight

HOW LAME DOES IT SOUND if I admit I stayed upstairs longer than necessary, combing my hair, washing my face, using a blow dryer on my jeans when I realized my new ones didn't fit well, then brushing my teeth.

Considering Derek had seen me in ugly pink pajamas, dirt on my face, my hair full of twigs, having minty-fresh breath wasn't going to make him go "Wow, she's really cute." But it made me feel better.

When I left our room, I went looking for Tori. She'd taken off after the planning meeting, saying something about cleaning, so we hadn't had time to update her on Royce and Dr. Banks. On the main level, I followed the vacuum cord in the hall and found her in the library, at the bookshelf, dusting off the old, leather books.

"I don't think you need to do that anymore," I said. "We're leaving tomorrow."

"I don't mind."

She pasted on a smile, and I don't know what tipped me off—that smile or Tori claiming to enjoy dusting. I stepped in and looked around. A light flickered as the kaleidoscope screensaver started up on the open laptop.

"That's Margaret's computer," I said, walking over to it. "Were you on it?"

"Just trying to email some friends and let them know I'm okay, but there's no internet."

"Uh-huh."

"You don't believe me? Check. No wireless and I can't find an outlet, not surprising when this place doesn't even have the phones hooked up."

"That's not what I meant." I turned to her. "Endangering us by emailing your friends? No way."

She settled on the edge of the desk. "See, now that's progress, because a week ago, you would have totally bought it."

I jiggled the mouse. It brought up a file system window. I looked at her.

"It's not what you think," she said.

"What do I think?"

"That I'm a spy for the Edison Group, gathering intelligence. Or trying to contact them, let them know where we are."

"You aren't a spy."

A wry smile. "I don't know if I should thank you for the vote of confidence or blast you for being too nice to accuse me to my face. I know that's what the guys think. Especially Derek. And I bet I know why they think that, too."

"Why?"

"Because I got away too easily at Andrew's house. They're right. I *did*." She eased back on the desk. "I didn't think so at first. When I escaped, I was all, like, 'God, I'm good. Those idiots didn't know who they were dealing with.'" She laughed, but it wasn't an easy laugh. "Once things cooled down, I thought, 'Yeah, I'm good, but not that good.' They knew I had magical outbursts when I got mad. So they knew I wasn't some helpless teenage girl. If I got away that easily, maybe it was because they let me."

"Why?"

"That's the question, isn't it? At first, I thought they'd planted something on me. I was shaking out my clothes, washing them. I even ironed them, to be sure."

"That was a good idea."

"No, it's nuts. I've been hanging around you guys too long. But I also figured, if the Edison Group could catch only one of us that night, planting a GPS and releasing me *would* be a good idea. I wasn't about to be the one who led them to us. So I went overboard making sure there was no transmitter."

"And there wasn't."

"As far as I could tell. That leaves option two: they released me because I'm the small fish in the pond. I wasn't worth keeping."

"I can't imagine—"

"Think about it. They get word that werewolf boy is on the rampage. Then they hear that Andrew has escaped. Suddenly, I'm not double-guard worthy. They leave me with one and hope he can keep me. He couldn't."

"Okay, so"—I waved at the computer—"what are you doing?"

"Trying to prove I'm not a spy. By spying." She turned the computer toward her. "Doing some intelligence work of my own is the best way to show I'm not a complete waste of space. When Andrew said they couldn't get in touch with Gwen that got me thinking."

She typed as she talked, fingers flying over the keyboard. "Russell obviously didn't act alone. Maybe Gwen was in on it, but I don't think so. She didn't like him."

"No?"

"He thought she was a ditzy blonde. The only time he got near her was when he was trying to look down her shirt. He's not evil genius material, either. Someone else masterminded the scheme to capture Derek, and they're also behind the plan to get rid of the rest of us. I nominate Margaret. I've gone through her files and email. Now, I'm digging into the stuff she deleted—or thought she did. Even after you empty your deleted folder or recycle bin, it's still there, if you know how to find it."

She started typing, flipping through folders so fast I got dizzy watching.

"You really are a computer—" I began.

"Say 'geek' and I'll use you for spell practice. I'm a software designer. But, yes, I know a few things about hacking, courtesy of a loser ex-boyfriend who used his talent to change his grades so he could spend more time gaming. Like World of Warcraft is going to help you through college. I had him teach me the basics, though, before I dumped him. You never know when it might come in handy."

I'm sure it had come in handy before now. I remembered how Tori had blackmailed Dr. Davidoff into letting her leave the lab.

"Okay, I've got some deleted emails. I'm searching on all our names and Simon's dad's. Who were those werewolf guys Russell hired?"

"Liam and Ramon, but Liam was the contact. That's L-I—"

She gave me a look. I shut my mouth and let her type. Nothing came up.

"Are there any to or from Russell?"

"Yep, he's MedicGuy56. I found him in her contact list. I'll take a look."

She was flipping past one sent to Russell when I caught a word that made me tell her to stop. Syracuse. Home of the werewolf Pack. The note gave instructions for finding a house outside a town called Bear Valley, near Syracuse.

I read on.

> Tomas says not to go to the house. Wait and approach them off the property, preferably in a public setting, and definitely when the children are not present. If possible, approach the Alpha or the woman. Tomas says he cannot stress these things enough. Do not go directly to the house. Do not approach when the children are there.

"Alpha?" Tori said.

"It's a wolf term. It means the pack leader. These were instructions for turning Derek over to the Pack."

"Well, then, we've got our evidence."

"Keep looking. The more we can find, the better. Search on Alpha, Pack, Bear Valley, Tomas . . ."

"Yes, ma'am."

At a sound in the hall, I scurried to the door. It was Margaret, but she was heading the other way. Behind me, Tori murmured, "No, that's . . ." She trailed off, then swore under her breath.

I hurried over. She was staring at an email with only a few terse lines from Margaret, assuring the sender that she'd conveyed Tomas's instructions to the "person Russell has hired to resolve the situation."

"Great, more proof," I said. "So what's the problem?"

She just pointed to the recipient's email address: acarson@gmail.com.

"A-Andrew? No, that can't be right. Is there another Carson?"

"That's Andrew, Chloe. I checked her contact list and other emails. And there's a response, too."

She flipped to a second email. Another short one, basically an "okay, thanks" from Andrew.

"Check the date," she said.

It'd been sent the day we'd first met Liam and Ramon. A day when Andrew had, supposedly, been in the Edison Group's custody.

twenty-nine

TORI KEPT SEARCHING. There wasn't much more—just enough to confirm what we'd already figured out. Andrew had been part of the plot to turn Derek over to the Pack. And he hadn't been anyone's hostage.

"So Andrew is part of the Edison Group?" Tori said. "That doesn't make sense."

"No, it doesn't." I pushed the laptop back and sat on the desk. "You were with me at the laboratory. Between the two of us, we saw a lot of staff members. Did you recognize any of them that night at Andrew's?"

"That was a security team. We never got a chance to see them before."

"Sure we did. Simon, Derek, and I did on the night we escaped Lyle House. You and I did after we escaped the Edison Group. What we saw, both times, was mainly staff with only a couple of guards. If they had some high-powered security team, wouldn't they have called them in for that?"

"Maybe it *was* the staff and the guards. How would we know? They were wearing . . ." She looked at me. "They were wearing things on their hats, covering their faces. They didn't do that at the warehouse when they were chasing us."

"Or the night Derek and I escaped Lyle House. Why hide their faces when we'd already seen them?" I thought back to that night. "You weren't the only one who got away too easily."

"Andrew, you mean."

"Not just him. I was hiding up in a tree. One of the women found me. I dropped on top of her. Stupid thing to do, but it worked—she was knocked out cold. Or so I thought."

"See, we're both just that good."

"Apparently not."

We tried to exchange a smile.

"The Edison Group didn't track us to Andrew's," I said. "That's what my mom was trying to tell me."

"If you guys are going to talk about that, you might want to go up on the roof," Derek rumbled from the doorway. "Or be a little quieter. I could hear you from down the hall."

"Because you've got bionic hearing," Tori said.

I started to say something, but Derek beat me to it.

"Simon had to go talk to Andrew. I thought maybe you . . ." He glanced at Tori, annoyed, like she was eavesdropping. "I thought there might be old files in the attic. You want to come up and see? Maybe get some more info on Dr. Banks?"

I had to stifle the urge to say "Sure!" So what if we'd just discovered that the people giving us refuge were the same ones who tried to kill us three nights ago? Finding out whether Derek liked me was *so* much more important.

"I can't," I said. "We—"

"That's okay," he cut in, starting to retreat.

I stepped forward to stop him. "I would. But—"

"But Chloe can't come out to play right now," Tori said. "She's in the middle of helping me unravel a conspiracy, a matter of life or death. *Our* life or death."

"The Edison Group didn't attack us at Andrew's place," I said. "He did. Andrew and the others."

I told Derek what we'd found. For once, I hoped he'd say I was wrong, that my logic was flawed and there was a perfectly reasonable alternate explanation.

But when I finished, he swore. Then he paced, swearing some more, until he stopped and shoved his hair back.

"We're wrong, aren't we?" I said. "We misinterpreted the data."

"No, you didn't."

It was my turn to swear then, making Tori arch her brows.

"I'm just mad at myself," Derek said. "I saw the possibility. I wondered whether we all got away too easily that night at Andrew's. I wondered why they shot at us when they used darts before. I wondered why they covered their faces. I just never thought it could have anything to do with Andrew. I *did* think he might be behind the kidnapping attempt last night, though."

"But you said—"

"That I trusted Andrew. I did. But he thinks I'd be better off with my own kind, so I wanted to see his reaction. That told me he wasn't involved. Or so I thought."

"He seemed genuinely surprised," I said. "Furious, even."

"Guess he's a good actor," Tori said. "Okay, so am I the only one who's wondering why they went through the trouble of that fake Edison Group attack when we were already going to Andrew's place?"

"Going doesn't mean staying," Derek said.

"Huh?"

"We might not stay with Andrew," I said. "If things didn't quite go our way. We've already run away twice."

"So if they convinced us the Edison Group had tracked us down and was lurking out there, prepared to shoot to kill . . ."

"That would trap us better than guard dogs and barbed wire."

I quickly looked at the door. "You said Simon was with—"

Derek swore. "Right. He's with Andrew. I'm sure whatever's going on here, hurting Simon isn't part of the plan, but I'll go get him. I'll remind him it's past his snack time. He needs to have morning and afternoon snacks for his blood sugar, so that won't sound suspicious."

I nodded. "We need to be careful."

"Screw caution," Tori said. "I'm outta here."

We looked at her.

"Well, I am. As long as someone comes with me."

We kept looking at her.

She sighed. "Fine, but when everything goes to hell, just remember, I get to blame you guys, because I wanted to leave right away."

"We are leaving right away," Derek said, "just as soon as we know as much as possible about their plans. You said that was Margaret's laptop, not Andrew's, right?"

I nodded. "But I know a way to get Andrew's, if you want Tori to search it."

"Good. Do that. I want to know exactly what they have in mind."

thirty

"ANDREW?" I PEEKED INTO the kitchen, where he was getting a snack with the guys.

"Hmm?"

"That book you were going to let me read . . ."

"Oh, right. My laptop is in the office. Should be all powered up."

"Is there a password?"

He smiled. "Nope. As valuable as I think unpublished manuscripts are, there's not really a black market for them. There's a link to the book right on the desktop for you."

He gave me the title.

"Tori wanted to take a look, too, if that's okay?"

"Absolutely. The more feedback I can get from the target audience, the better. If anything sticks out—problems with the characters, the plot, the language—let me know."

Tori rolled her eyes at the lack of security on Andrew's laptop. Like most people who weren't tech-savvy, he presumed if he deleted stuff, it was gone. Or maybe he knew traces remained, but figured we wouldn't know how to find them. And he'd have been right . . . if we didn't have Tori.

We started with an email search and found the ones he'd exchanged with Margaret, removing any doubt it'd been him. There were also a few between him and Tomas, where Andrew seemed determined to ensure a safe transfer of Derek to the Pack. Had he really been that concerned for Derek's safety? Liam clearly had orders to kill if necessary. Was that decision made behind Andrew's back? That would explain why he'd seemed so genuinely shocked when he'd found out what had happened to Derek and me.

Or maybe I just wasn't ready to see Andrew as one of the bad guys yet. I'd liked him. I really had. Yet it only took one more email for those feelings to evaporate, one that had nothing to do with Liam and Russell or the Edison Group. When Tori found it, we both read it and read it again, neither of us saying a word until I managed a shaky, "I-I'd better get the guys."

"I'll see if there's more," she said as I raced off.

I finally tracked down Derek. He was alone in the library, thumbing through a book.

"Found you," I said on a sigh of relief.

He turned. His lips curved in a quarter smile, gaze softening in a way that did something to my insides, made me pull up short, momentarily forgetting why I was there.

"I-Is Simon around?"

He blinked, then turned back to the shelf.

"He's upstairs. He's really pissed about Andrew so that's probably the safest place for him until we're ready to go, or he'll say something to him we don't want said. You need him?"

"Actually, m-maybe I should show you first."

He glanced over his shoulder, frowning.

"We found something."

"Oh." He paused, like he was mentally shifting gears, then nodded and followed me out.

Tori swiveled in her seat as we came in.

"There are more," she said. "He sent one every couple of weeks. The last one was only a few days ago."

"Good," I said. "Would you mind keeping an eye on Andrew?"

"Sure." She took off.

"Wait." I grabbed Derek's sleeve as he headed for the chair Tori had vacated. I wanted to say something. I didn't know what. But there was no way to tell him that wouldn't be just as much of a shock, so I ended up stupidly murmuring, "Never mind."

When he read what was on the screen, he went absolutely still, like he wasn't even breathing. After a few seconds, he yanked the laptop closer, leaning in to read it again. And again. Finally, he pushed back the chair and exhaled.

"He's alive," I said. "Your dad's alive."

He looked up at me and, I couldn't help it—I threw my arms around his neck and hugged him. Then I realized what I was doing. I let go, backing away, tripping over my feet, stammering, "I-I'm sorry. I'm just—I'm happy for you."

"I know."

Still sitting, he reached out and pulled me toward him. We stayed there, looking at each other, his hand still wrapped in my shirt hem, my heart hammering so hard I was sure he could hear it.

"There's more," I said after a few seconds. "More emails, Tori said."

He nodded and swiveled back to the computer, making room for me. When I inched closer, not wanting to intrude, he tugged me in front of him and I stumbled, half falling onto his lap. I tried to scramble up, cheeks burning, but he pulled me down onto his knee, one arm going around my waist, tentative, as if to say *Is this okay?* It was, even if my blood pounded in my ears so hard I couldn't think. Thankfully, I had my back to him because I was sure my cheeks were scarlet.

I hadn't misunderstood his look earlier. This was something. Or it would become something, I hoped. God, I *hoped.* Right now, though, there was too much else going on. I hated that, but I was kind of glad of it, too, giving my brain time to stop spinning.

After a second—still perched on Derek's knee—I forced my attention back to the screen.

I read the first email again. Dated two months ago, it was a chain of three messages, the first, short and to the point.

> It's Kit. Got myself in some trouble. Do you know where the boys are?

Andrew answered.

> No, I don't. What kind of trouble? How can I help?

The reply was longer.

> Nasts caught up with me. Saw an article on D. Tracked me down before I could run. Went with them to distract them from the boys. Kept me a few months until I finally gave them what they wanted. The boys are long gone. Thought EG, but no sign at the lab. Maybe Nasts? Child services? No idea. I need help, buddy. Anything you can do. Please.

He signed off giving a phone number and saying both it and the email address were temporary, but he'd be in touch again in a couple of weeks.

I flipped to the next email as Derek read over my shoulder. There were three more of the same—Mr. Bae begging for news, Andrew saying he was looking for Simon and Derek, but his Edison Group contacts swore the boys weren't there.

The last one from Mr. Bae was dated three days ago, when Andrew had supposedly been held hostage by the Edison Group. That meant he'd gotten this *after* he knew where Simon and Derek were.

"There's one more on the list," Derek said. "It must be a reply."

It was, sent the night when Andrew and the others had been staking out his cottage, waiting to make their fake SWAT team swoop and gather us up.

> Still nothing. I might have a lead, though. A guy who works for the Cortezes says there's a rumor they're holding a couple of teenage boys. I'll call as soon as I have more.

"Cortezes?" I said.

"A Cabal, like the Nasts. Corporations run by sorcerers. Rich and powerful. More Mafia than Wall Street, though."

"So Andrew was lying."

"Not just lying. Trying to send Dad on a wild-goose chase when he knew exactly where we were."

"This changes everything."

He nodded.

"We need to get out of here."

He nodded again, but didn't move. I leaned forward to grab a pen and paper from Andrew's desk, then jotted down the latest email address and phone number. When I handed it to Derek, he took a second to even notice my outstretched hand.

"You okay?" I said, twisting to face him.

"Yeah, just . . . Andrew. Getting rid of me, I could see. But keeping Dad away . . . Dad trusted him."

"And now we can't," I said. "Which sucks, but the main thing is that your dad's alive."

He smiled, hesitant at first, then a blazing grin broke through that made my heart stop. I recovered and grinned back and went to throw my arms around his neck, then stopped, blushing. Before I could pull back, he caught my elbows and put my arms around his neck and pulled me into a hug.

Then he jumped, chair swiveling so fast I nearly went flying. I heard footsteps in the hall and I scrambled off his lap just as Simon swung in, breathing heavily, like he'd come running.

"Tori said you wanted to see me? Something about Dad."

I moved aside so Derek could show him the emails, then stepped into the hall to watch for Andrew and to leave them alone. This was the news they'd been waiting for and they'd gone through hell thinking it might never come, so I tried not to eavesdrop.

"Chloe?"

Derek stood in the doorway. He motioned me back in. Simon was at the keyboard, control panel open.

"There's no Internet connection," I said, "if that's what you're looking for. No phone either."

"Andrew has a cell," Simon said.

"Too risky," Derek said. "There was a pay phone at the service station. We'll call on our way out, set up a place to meet him."

Simon's eyes lit up at the thought of finally talking to his dad. Then they clouded with anger, the thrill of seeing news from his dad warring with the pain of Andrew's betrayal.

"So we're going now, right?" I said.

"Yeah," Derek said. "We're going."

thirty-one

BY NOW, WE WERE EXPERTS at this escaping thing. We filled Tori in, then split up to gather what we needed—clothes, money, food. We took turns, two packing while the other two hung out, talking so Andrew didn't wonder why he had a house with four teenagers in it and sudden silence. Thankfully Andrew spent the whole time in the kitchen. I don't think any of us could have faced him.

Tori and I were on make-our-presence-known duty when Derek slipped in with an armful of ski jackets.

"Found these in the basement," he said. "It got cold last time." He passed me a red one and gave Tori a blue one. "Simon's finding one that fits, then coming up. We'll head out the back door. You three will go on ahead. I'll stay inside and make sure Andrew doesn't come out until you're safe in the woods."

"And if he does?" I asked.

Derek rubbed his mouth, meaning he'd rather not plan for that possibility.

"Don't tell me you'll have any problem taking him out," Tori said. "After what he did to you? I say we handle him now, save us all this sneaking around. I'll use the binding spell. You guys tie him up."

"Works for me," Simon said, coming up behind us. "I still remember my knots from Scouts."

Derek hesitated. Then he looked at me, which surprised me a little, and I said, "I—I agree," not really sure he was looking for that, but he nodded, and I said, more firmly, "It's the best way. Otherwise, once he figures out we're gone, he'll—"

The doorbell rang. I wasn't the only one who jumped. Derek grabbed our bags, ready to bolt.

"Guys?" Andrew called. "Can someone get that? It's Margaret."

"That makes things a little tougher," Tori murmured. "But not much. She's old, and she's just a necromancer." A glance at me. "Sorry."

"Guys?" Andrew's footsteps tapped down the hall.

"Got it!" Simon called.

"We'll take out Margaret first," Derek murmured. "Tori can bind her. Simon can tie her. I'll go for Andrew. Chloe? Move the coats and bags into the closet, just in case."

Move the coat and bags? Sometimes I really wished my powers were a little more, well, powerful. I hefted two backpacks as Derek headed for the kitchen and Tori and Simon went to the front door.

I was coming back for the second load when I heard Margaret's voice. Had Tori's binding spell failed?

"This is Gordon," Margaret was saying. "And this is Roxanne. With Russell and Gwen gone, we thought it was safe to bring a few more of our members in to meet you. Now, let's all go review our plans."

Tori wanted to take on all four, but suggested it only halfheartedly. Four adults versus four kids meant bad odds, especially when we had no idea what supernatural types Gordon and Roxanne were. Our plan, then, was to sneak out as soon as they started their meeting. Except they wanted us in on that meeting. Simon opted out—he couldn't face Andrew—so Derek and I covered for him. I was the one they most wanted to talk to anyway, asking more questions about the Edison Group laboratory and staff.

I had to call on all my years of drama training to pull off that performance. That, and not look in Andrew's direction any more than absolutely necessary. I seethed the whole time, knowing they didn't care what I said, that they weren't planning on going back. I had no idea what they *were* planning, only that we weren't sticking around long enough to find out.

Finally, they released us.

"Get Simon," Derek whispered to Tori as we hurried down the hall. "I'm going to move the bags out to the woods. Chloe? Cover me."

It would make more sense for Tori—the girl with the spells—to cover him, but I didn't suggest it. Derek still didn't trust her enough for that.

Tori didn't even make it as far as the stairs, when a voice called, "Kids? Are you back here?"

Derek swore. It was Gordon, the new guy.

"Over here," I said, walking to where he stood in the hall. Derek followed.

Gordon was about Andrew's age, average height, with a potbelly and graying beard, the kind of guy who'd be recruited to play the office Santa.

"Do they need us again?" I asked.

"No, they're busy making plans, so I thought I'd say hi. We didn't get much of a chance to chat in there." He walked over to Derek and beamed a wide smile, shaking his hand. "You don't remember me, do you? I'm not surprised. You were just a little guy the last time we met. I used to work with your dad. We played poker on Tuesdays." He clapped a hand on Derek's shoulder and steered him into the living room. "Andrew tells me you're quite the science whiz. I teach physics over at . . ."

Gordon kept talking, leading Derek into the next room. Derek shot me a look, annoyance mingled with frustration. When I opened my mouth, though, he shook his head. We were stuck. Again.

"Are we going?" Tori whispered, returning with Simon.

"Not yet."

Gordon eventually called us all in. He'd known my aunt and Tori's mom, so now he wanted to get to know us a little better, too. Yesterday, we'd all have been thrilled with the chance to make a good impression and prove we were normal kids. Now, it was just creepy, giving our life stories to a guy who might be ready to kill us if our powers proved as uncontrollable as he feared.

After the meeting, they all decided to stay for dinner, and there was no way for us to get out, not all four of us with our backpacks.

"Can we leave them behind?" I asked. "We've got money. What if—?"

"Tori?" Andrew called. "Could you give me a hand with dinner?"

"Um, actually . . ." she began.

Andrew popped his head around the corner. Seeing all four of us clustered in the hall, he frowned, then forced a smile.

"Am I interrupting something?"

"Just making plans for a breakout," Tori said.

My gut twisted, eyes widening.

"We were hoping to sneak off for ice cream after dinner," she explained.

"Ah." Andrew ran his hand through his hair, looking uncomfortable. "I know you kids are tired of being cooped up here—"

"Developing serious cabin fever," Tori said. "Plus, my housekeeping wages are burning a hole in my pocket. We'll be careful, and we'll be back before dark."

"I know, but . . . No, guys. Sorry. No more going out." He tried for a smile. "We'll be leaving for Buffalo tomorrow and I promise we'll stop for ice cream on the way. Now, if I can get your help, Tori . . ."

He led her away.

"He knows," Simon said as we sat in the games room, pretending to play Yahtzee.

"It sure feels that way," I said. "But maybe we're just paranoid?"

We both looked at Derek.

He shook the dice onto the table a few times, deep in thought, then said, "I think we're okay. We're just nervous."

"We want out so it feels like they're blocking us." Simon exhaled and tried to settle into his seat, fingers drumming his leg.

"We should wait until tonight," Derek said. "Head to bed, then go after Andrew when he's asleep. The others will be long gone by then, and that'll buy us more time—no one will realize he's in trouble until morning."

"Makes sense," Simon said. "Question is, are we going to make it that long without going nuts—"

He stopped as Derek cocked his head, then pivoted toward the door.

"Trouble?" Simon whispered.

"Cell phone."

"Um, yeah, they've all got them. So—"

"They're that way." Derek pointed left. "I'm hearing a muffled ring from the front door, where they left their coats."

"Okay, still not—" Simon shot up straight. "Cell phone. Dad." He scrambled up. "Where's the number?"

Derek held the paper with the number just out of his reach. "Cool it."

"Okay, okay." Simon took another deep breath, forcing himself to relax. "Cooled?"

Derek handed it over.

I hung back, again reluctant to intrude, but Derek motioned me along. As we neared the front door, he waved Simon ahead, whispering that we'd stand guard while he called.

"So what'd you think of that book Andrew is editing?" Derek asked.

I gaped up at him. Very attractive, I'm sure.

"Talk to me," Derek whispered.

"Right. Sorry. It's . . . good so far. I—"

"No signal," Simon hissed, peeking around the corner.

"Move around," Derek whispered back. "Andrew's been using his."

While Simon did that, I pretended to talk about the book, which wasn't easy when I hadn't read so much as a single line. So I blathered on with general comments about pacing and style, until Simon peeked again, waving frantically, phone at his ear as he mouthed "It's ringing!"

Derek motioned him back behind the corner, then told me to keep talking. I did, though I couldn't help hearing Simon.

"Dad? It's me. Simon." His voice cracked and he cleared his throat. "Fine. Well, okay." Pause. "He's right here. With me. We're with Andrew." Pause. "I know. We're trying to—" Pause. "No. Not Andrew's. It's a safe house. Belonged to a guy named Todd Banks. Big old— Dad? Dad?"

Derek strode off, motioning for me to stand watch.

"Signal," Simon whispered.

Derek started to say something, then swung around the corner, gaze fixed down the hall. Sure enough, a second later, I heard footsteps.

"Guys?" Andrew. "Dinner."

"Coming!" I called.

"Let me try—" Simon began.

"No," Derek said. "I need to erase the outgoing call. Get in the kitchen with Chloe. We'll phone again from the service station tonight."

Everyone picked at dinner, forcing down only enough to make it look good. Derek kept whispering for us to eat, fill our stomachs, but he barely finished himself, too busy straining to hear the ring of the cell phone, worried his dad might call back and expose us.

He didn't. From what I'd heard of their dad, Derek got his cautious streak from him. Where a normal person would automatically call back after being disconnected, I suspected their dad would look up the number first and something about it—like Gordon's name attached to the listing—had stopped him.

He wouldn't try calling Andrew, either. The fact that Andrew hadn't told him we were with him spelled trouble. He wouldn't make contact. He'd just come looking for his boys.

Had he heard the part about us being in Dr. Banks's house? Did he know where that was? If so, would he come for us too late, get captured trying to save his sons after they'd left?

I reminded myself that the service station was only a fifteen-minute walk away. We could warn Mr. Bae before he tried anything. Unless he was close enough to the house to come for us *before* we left . . . A nice thought, but I knew we couldn't count on it and probably shouldn't even hope. We had a plan. We'd get out safely, find Mr. Bae, and with his help rescue Aunt Lauren and Rae.

thirty-two

I RETREATED TO MY ROOM at nine. Tori was there, engrossed in *The Count of Monte Cristo.* She didn't do more than wave until she finished her chapter. We talked for a while. Nothing important. Just talk, struggling to stay calm as we prayed for time to speed up. We were almost there, though. Just a few more hours . . .

Derek said Andrew never went to bed before midnight. If we wanted to get him after he was sound asleep, that meant waiting until two.

To my surprise, I fell asleep, so soundly that I didn't hear the alarm on the watch Derek had given me earlier. I woke to Tori shaking me with one hand, while trying to shut off the alarm with the other.

I yawned and blinked hard.

"Running away after you've barely slept in a week isn't a great idea," she said. "Luckily, I anticipated this."

She popped open a can of Coke and handed it to me.

"Not as good as coffee," she said. "But I bet you don't drink coffee, do you?"

I shook my head as I gulped it.

"Kids," she said, rolling her eyes.

The door flew open, Simon rushing in.

"Excuse me?" Tori said.

"It's Derek," he said to me. "I can't wake him up."

We ran from the room. Derek was still in his bed, sprawled, the sheets draped onto the floor. He lay on his stomach wearing only his boxers.

I shook his shoulder. My fingers were cool from the soda can, but he still didn't move.

"He's breathing," Simon whispered. "He just won't wake up."

Tori walked toward the bed. Out of the corner of my eye, I saw her give Derek a once-over.

"You know, from this angle, he doesn't look too bad," she said.

I glared at her.

"I'm just saying . . ."

I leaned over Derek, calling him as loudly as I dared.

"Personally, I'm more a running back girl myself," Tori said. "But if you like the linebacker type, he's—"

My glower shut her up.

"You're in my light," I said, waving her aside.

"Do you know first aid, Chloe?"

I shook my head.

"Then you're in *my* light. Scoot."

I let her through. She checked Derek's pulse and his breathing, saying both seemed okay, then leaned down to his face.

"Nothing weird on his breath. Smells . . . like toothpaste."

Derek's eyes opened, and the first thing he saw was Tori's face inches from his. He jumped and let out an oath. Simon cracked up. I madly motioned for him to be quiet.

"Are you okay?" I asked Derek.

"He is now," Simon said. "After Tori jump-started his heart."

"We couldn't wake you up," I said. "Tori was making sure you were okay."

He kept blinking, disoriented.

"I have a Coke in my—" I began.

"I'll grab it," Tori said.

I turned back to Derek. He was still blinking.

"Derek?"

"Yeah." He mumbled, like he was talking through marbles, then made a face and cleared his throat.

"How do you feel?" I asked.

"Tired. Must have been sleeping hard."

"Like a rock," Simon said.

"Do you feel groggy?" I asked.

"Yeah." He made a face again. "What'd I eat last night?"

A chill ran through me. "Does your mouth feel fuzzy?"

"Yeah." He swore and pushed himself up.

I grabbed the Coke from Tori as she came back. "He's been drugged."

"Drugged?" Simon paused only a second, then said, "Andrew."

"I'll grab our bags," Tori said. We'd taken them to our rooms last night, worrying they'd be found in the closet downstairs.

I got Derek's as he chugged the rest of the Coke.

"Andrew brought us sodas last night, before bed," Simon said as he took his bag.

"And he said which one was Derek's?"

"He didn't need to. Mine's always diet."

I looked at Derek as he wiped his hand over his mouth. "Are you going to be okay?"

"Yeah. Just let me get dressed."

Why would Andrew drug Derek? Were they coming for him tonight? Or had our paranoia been well placed and the group knew exactly what we were up to? Either way, our best fighter was out of commission.

"I'll stay with Derek," I said. "Simon, can you cover Tori and get to Andrew's room?"

He glanced at Derek for confirmation. Derek blinked hard, focusing, then managed a slurred, "Yeah. Do that."

"But be careful," I said. "There's a good chance Andrew's not in his bed."

They came back ten minutes later.

"He's not here," Simon whispered.

"What?"

"There's no sign of him anywhere," Tori said. "The truck's outside, but there aren't any lights on in the house."

"And his shoes are gone," Simon said.

"Meeting someone," I whispered. "Someone must be here to take Derek, and Andrew's outside with him, trying to figure out how to do this."

"Or he's been taken," Tori said.

Derek rubbed his face, then gave his head a sharp shake. "Forget Andrew. Let's just go and be careful."

Simon threw Derek's arm over his shoulders, despite his brother's protests. I carried Derek's bag as well as my own; Tori had Simon's.

We peered down the dark hall. Derek sniffed. The last trace of Andrew was old, meaning he hadn't come upstairs since delivering the sodas. Derek stood at the top of the main staircase and listened, then shook his head. No sounds from below.

We headed for the stairs at the back of the house, the narrow ones we'd found earlier, probably for servants once upon a time. It was one area Tori hadn't cleaned—nor had anyone in years, apparently, and I had to cover my nose and mouth so dust didn't set me sneezing.

When we reached the bottom, I was in the lead, Tori right behind me, and Simon helping Derek at the rear. The stairs ended at a door. I turned the knob slowly, trying to be quiet. It twisted partway, then stopped. I pushed. The door didn't budge.

Tori shouldered past me and tried. "Locked," she whispered. "I thought you guys—"

"Checked all the doors last night," Simon said. "We did. It was open."

"Move," Derek mumbled, his voice still thick.

We squeezed aside. He wrenched the knob and the lock snapped, making me wince at the noise.

The stairs opened into a dark, low ceilinged room. An old pantry or something. Tori flicked on her flashlight. The room was filthy and empty—another reason no one used these stairs. This time, she was first to the door. I knew what she'd find even before she announced it.

"Locked."

"Seriously?" Simon whispered.

Derek strode past, awake now. He twisted the knob and, again, the lock snapped. He yanked the door. It didn't budge. He pulled harder, making the hinges groan.

"It's spell-locked," said a voice behind us.

We turned as Andrew stepped through the stairwell doorway. Simon's fingers flew up for a knock-back spell. Derek wheeled to charge. Andrew swung his hand toward me. Sparks flew from his fingers. Simon and Derek both stopped.

Andrew gave a wry smile. "I thought that might work. Simon, you know how this goes. I've got a spell all set to launch. It only takes a word to finish it."

"Wh-what kind of spell?" I whispered, hypnotized by those sparks jumping at me.

"Lethal," Andrew said.

Derek growled. A real growl, so wolflike it made the hair stand up on my neck.

Off to the side, Tori mouthed something at me. I couldn't make it out, but guessed she was warning me she was going to cast.

"No," Derek said, the word still almost a growl. His gaze was fixed on Andrew, and I thought he was talking to him, but then his eyes slid Tori's way. "No."

"Listen to Derek," Andrew said. "If he thought there was any way of getting to me before I launched this spell, he'd do it himself. Tori, move in front of me, please, so I can see your lips. Simon, sit on your hands. Derek?"

I glanced over at Derek. His gaze was riveted on Andrew, eyes blazing, the muscles in his jaw taut. Andrew said his name again, but he didn't seem to hear, fists clenching and unclenching at his sides.

"*Derek*," Andrew said, sharper.

"What?" Another growl passing as a word.

Andrew flinched, then caught himself and squared his shoulders. "Turn around."

"No."

"*Derek.*"

Derek only glowered. Then he tilted his head and I couldn't see his expression, but something in it made Andrew draw back, just a little. His Adam's apple bobbed. He tried to straighten again, tried to meet Derek's gaze, but couldn't quite manage it. His fingers flexed, sparks jumping as they faced off.

"Derek?" I whispered. "Please. Don't do this."

He started at the sound of my voice, breaking eye contact with Andrew, and the second he did, his expression changed, the wolf drawing back, Derek returning.

"Do as he says," I said. "Please."

He nodded and slowly turned to face the wall.

"Thank you," Andrew said. "I'd hoped to avoid this, but I guess I underestimated the dose. I don't want to hurt you, Derek. That's why I knocked you out. I don't want to hurt any of you. I'm here to protect you. I always have been."

Simon snorted. "Yeah, sure you don't want to hurt Derek. You asked those werewolves to kill him painlessly, right?"

"I didn't try to kill Derek."

"No, you hired someone to do it. You're too big a coward to look him in the face and pull the trigger. Or maybe it was the mess you were worried about. I know how much you like your clothes. Bloodstains are such a bitch to get out."

"I didn't—"

"We found the emails!" Simon jumped to his feet, then at a look from Derek, stopped and lowered himself to the floor again. "We know you were in on it."

"Yes, I was in on the plan to hand Derek over to the Pack. That's what you found, isn't it? Nothing about me giving them permission to kill him. That was entirely Russell's doing. Our plan was to turn him over to the Pack. Tomas and I learned everything we could about them until we were satisfied they wouldn't kill a sixteen-year-old werewolf. They're like any other organized group of supernaturals—a place for their race to learn how to control their powers and live in the human world. A place where they can be with their own kind."

I looked over at Derek, bracing myself to see a glimmer that said that's what he wanted. But he only stared at the wall, his gaze empty, emotionless.

"That's what I think is best for you, Derek," Andrew said. "Werewolves belong with werewolves."

"And sons belong with fathers," I said quietly.

Andrew stiffened. His gaze shot to mine, wary.

"We found those emails, too," I said. "You kept their dad away from them."

A pause. Then, "Yes, I did. And there's a reason."

"Sure there is," Simon said, his voice dripping with sarcasm. "Let me guess. Our dad is really an evil Cabal sorcerer. Or an Edison Group double agent. Take your pick. He's a bad, bad guy who'd kill us if he got the chance."

"No, Simon," Andrew said, his voice softening. "Your dad is the best father I know. He gave up everything—his career, his friends, his life—to go on the run to protect you. He refused to join our group because it could endanger you. His priority is you two, not taking down the Edison Group. He would never let me take you back to that lab to help stop them. If I called, he'd take you—all four of you—and run. He'll tell me to stop the Edison Group without you."

"Not a bad idea," Tori said.

Andrew shook his head. "If Kit takes you kids, then you're safe. If you're safe, then my people have no motivation to disband the Edison Group. I've been trying to convince them to do this for years, and now they're ready to act, but only if there's an immediate threat. If you're gone, they'll return to monitoring. And that's if they decide to *let* you go with him."

"Why wouldn't they?" Simon said. "Takes us off their hands."

"For many of them, that's the least of their worries, falling far behind their concern over the threat you pose to the supernatural world at large. If your dad comes . . ." He shifted, hand flexing, the spell wavering for a split second before surging again. "I hope that Russell acted alone when he told those werewolves to kill Derek and Chloe, but honestly . . . I don't know."

"Nice friends you've got there."

"Yes, some of them are my friends, Simon, but most are like other members of a club. We share one interest, nothing more. That interest is protecting our world. For me, that means shutting down the Edison Group. For some of them—"

"It means shutting down us," I murmured.

"Don't listen to him, Chloe," Simon said. "He's a liar and a traitor. If these people are so worried about us, why are they leaving us alone with just you to watch us?"

"They aren't. That's why I had to stop you before you set foot out that door."

Simon laughed. It wasn't a nice laugh. "Right, because they're lurking in the dark, waiting to slam us with energy-bolt spells. No, wait, that's you, isn't it?"

Andrew lowered his fingers just a fraction, like he wanted to retract the threat. "Yes, they're there, Simon. Not right outside the door, but close enough, guarding the escape routes. Because that's exactly what they fear most. That you'll escape. That you'll run to humans and expose us. Or you'll lose control and expose us. You ran from Lyle House and you ran from the Edison Group. What's the first thing you'll do if you get a whiff of trouble? You'll run and—"

Derek lunged. He hit me in the shoulder and knocked me to the floor, landing on top of me. His body jerked, like he'd been hit with the spell, and I let out a yelp, struggling to get up, but he held me down, whispering, "I'm okay. It's okay," until the words finally penetrated.

I lifted my head to see Andrew caught in a binding spell as Simon hurtled to his feet. Simon tackled him and wrenched his hands behind his back. Derek got up to help. He pinned Andrew.

"Y-you're okay? He didn't hit you with a spell?" I said, walking over, knees wobbly.

"Yeah, he did."

Andrew lifted his head. "And, as you can see, it was the *nonlethal* energy bolt. I said I don't want to hurt you, Derek. I wouldn't have hurt Chloe, either. I only needed you to listen to me."

"We listened," Derek said. "Simon? I think I saw rope in the workshop. Chloe? Stay here. Tori? Cover Simon, in case there's anyone else in the house."

thirty-three

DEREK HAD MORE QUESTIONS for Andrew. He asked about that night at Andrew's cottage. Andrew admitted he'd been part of the plan to stage his kidnapping and impersonate the Edison Group. The whole thing had been a setup—even giving us the opportunity to snatch a radio so we could hear about his "escape." They'd set themselves up as our rescuers, so they could take us into protective custody.

Simon came racing in and threw down a length of rope. "His cell phone. We can call Dad. Check his pockets."

"It's in the nightstand by my bed," Andrew said. "And it's useless. Reception has been cutting in and out and it's been out all night. I think someone's using a blocker on the house."

"I'm not taking your word for it," Simon said.

"I don't expect you to."

Sure enough, we couldn't get reception. Even sneaking onto the roof didn't help.

So Andrew was telling the truth about that. But what about the rest of it? Were his people really out there, waiting and watching? Or was this just another lie to keep us from running?

We bound and gagged Andrew and put him in the basement. Then we talked.

Not surprisingly, Tori wanted to make a break for it. Simon agreed. Neither wanted to be stuck here a moment longer than necessary. We should run and, if caught, as Tori said, "What are they going to do? Shoot us?" Problem was, that might be exactly what they'd do.

We didn't think Russell had acted alone. Had it been him and Gwen? Or more? How many people in this group secretly would be happy to see us dead—a convenient solution to the dilemma of our inconvenient existence.

Even if they didn't want us dead, if all four of us were caught sneaking through the woods with our backpacks, there'd be no question of what we were doing. We'd lose our chance to get away.

So, one of us should go. But who? Derek was the most likely to be killed if caught. Tori might roll her eyes at the suggestion we were in mortal danger, but she wasn't volunteering either. And Derek wouldn't entertain the idea of either Simon or me going.

We argued. Then we split up, Derek and Simon going downstairs to try to get more information from Andrew, and Tori deciding to keep searching Andrew's laptop, to see if there was anything there that we'd missed, something that might support or refute his claims.

As she searched, I knelt and tried to summon Liz. She'd be the perfect solution to this problem—she could zip out unnoticed and see if anyone was guarding the house. I was careful to picture her clearly and call her name, so I wouldn't accidentally summon Royce or Dr. Banks. There was someone else I'd love to contact—my mom—but I couldn't think about that. Even if I got her, I doubted I could hold her here long enough to search for us.

So I called Liz. And called and called, and didn't feel so much as a twitch.

"Derek with you guys?"

I jumped. Simon walked in. I got to my feet.

"I thought he was with you," I said.

"Nah. He made me test my blood sugar, and I grabbed a snack, but when I came back, Andrew was alone."

"I'll help you look."

I found Derek on the roof, looking, listening, and sniffing for signs of anyone guarding the house.

"Oh, this is a great idea," I said. "The guy they're most likely to shoot is standing on the roof, giving them a perfect target."

"They won't see me up here."

When I gave him a look, he sighed, like I was making a huge deal out of nothing, then sat and said, "Okay?"

"I don't think it's safe for you to be up here."

"Just a few more minutes." He took off his coat and held it out beside him. "Sit down here, between me and the chimney. It's safe."

"It's not me I'm worried about."

"I'm fine."

"How do you know that? They could have night vision goggles, sniper rifles . . ."

The corners of his mouth twitched and I braced myself for "You watch too many movies." He didn't say it, but I knew he was thinking it.

"You're not coming inside, are you?"

"I will. Just sit down. I want to talk to you."

"And I want you to come in. We can talk there."

"I don't smell anyone out here. I think Andrew's lying."

"Please, Derek? Come inside?"

"In a minute."

I turned and walked away.

"Chloe . . ."

I hoped he'd follow. I knew he wouldn't. He didn't.

"Found him," I said, meeting Simon in the upstairs hall. "On the roof."

"The *roof*? I suppose you told him he's an idiot."

"I asked him to come down. He won't."

"Because he thinks it's the right thing to do. The right thing for everyone *else,* that is. One day he's going to get himself—" Simon ran his hands through his hair. "I can talk to him. I can yell at him. It just doesn't get through. He's not suicidal. It's not that he doesn't care if he lives or dies. It's just—"

"Not a priority."

"Not if it interferes with protecting us. He can argue that's the wolf, but those two werewolves you met weren't throwing themselves in the line of fire to save each other, were they?"

"No."

He exhaled. "I might know a way to get him down. But don't hold your breath."

"I won't."

After Simon left, I knew what had to be done. There were only a few hours until daylight and we were sitting around like headlight-stunned deer, waiting for the car to hit us. We needed to know if there was really someone guarding the property, and there was only one way to do that properly.

thirty-four

I STEPPED OUT THE BACK door and edged along the house, where Derek couldn't see me from the roof. The wind blew at my back, meaning my scent wouldn't carry to him. Good. I slipped into the woods.

The best way to find out if there was anyone watching the house was to send out a decoy. Of the four of us, I was the best choice. I didn't have Derek's strength or Tori's and Simon's spells. I was the smallest and the least able to defend myself; and as much as I might hate that, right now it was an advantage because I posed the least threat.

There was only one problem. The property was huge. That meant there was a lot of perimeter to cover. So how were they doing it? When Derek had asked that, Andrew said they were using spells. Simon wasn't convinced that was possible, but admitted he didn't know for sure.

And what about last night? It made sense that they hadn't been guarding the property when I was out with Derek—they had Liam and Ramon to do that. But what about earlier, when Simon and I had gone for ice cream? Andrew said they'd been tracking us and hadn't been concerned, knowing Simon wouldn't leave Derek behind. Still . . .

Did I really think we were under guard? No. Andrew was setting up imaginary bogeymen to keep us in the house until his friends showed up in the morning and rescued him. So all I had to do was prove I could make it to the service station.

To reach it, I needed to cut through the woods. As I walked, the lights from the house faded, and it got dark—"can't see my hand in front of my face" dark. I'd brought a flashlight, but once I was in the woods, I'd realized that wasn't my cleverest idea ever. I might as well stick a neon arrow over my head.

Without the flashlight, I'd be just as likely to alert someone by stumbling and crashing around in the dark. So I used it—with my hand over the light, letting only a faint glow seep through.

The forest was dark, but it was far from silent. Twigs and leaves crackled. A mouse shrieked, its cry cut short by a sickening crunch. The wind whispered and wailed overhead. Even my feet made noise with every step. I tried to concentrate on that, but the more I did, the more it sounded like a heartbeat, *thump-thump, thump-thump, thump-thump.* I swallowed and clutched the flashlight, plastic slipping under my sweaty fingers.

Just keep walking. Stay on the path. One foot in front of the other.

An owl hooted. I jumped. A snort, like a stifled laugh, and I spun, fingers slipping from the lens, the beam spinning in an arc, revealing nothing.

Who did you think was there? One of Andrew's group? Laughing at you?

I released my death grip on the flashlight and switched it to my other hand, wiping my damp palm on my jeans, then covered the beam again. I took a deep breath, breathing in air that smelled of rain. Rain and damp earth and the faint stink of decay. Dead things. Rotting things.

Another deep breath, then I started walking again, trudging along, shoulders hunched, burrowing as far into the ski jacket as I could, the bitter wind freezing my nose and ears.

I peered up, hoping for moonlight, seeing only patches of gray sky through the thick trees, branches entwined over my head like long, crooked—

I looked down, but the view wasn't any better. Endless trees stretched out on all sides, dozens of thick trunks, any of which could be a ghost, standing there, watching me, waiting . . .

The ground was softer here, and each step made a creepy, sucking sound. Undergrowth rustled to my left and I caught a whiff of decomposing flesh. An image flashed—the zombie dog and zombie rabbit and whatever else I'd raised last night. Had I really released them all? Or were they still out here, waiting for me?

I walked faster.

A wordless whisper sounded behind me. I wheeled, fingers tightening on the flashlight. The voice kept whispering, the sound rippling around me. I followed it with the wavering light beam, but saw nothing.

Something hit my bandaged arm. I yelped and jumped. The flashlight flew from my hand, hit the ground, and went out.

I dropped and fumbled around until I found it. I flicked the switch. Nothing.

I knocked the flashlight against my knee, but it stayed off. I blinked hard, and gradually I could make out the squatting lumps of bushes and the gnarled trunks of trees.

"Afraid of the dark?" a voice whispered.

I knocked the flashlight again. Harder. Still nothing.

"That's a pretty red coat you're wearing. Little Red Riding Hood, all alone in the woods at night. Where's your big, bad wolf?"

A chill crept through me.

"Royce."

"Smart girl. Too bad you aren't smart enough to know what happens to little girls all alone in the woods at night."

I remembered the residual of the girl I'd seen at the truck stop, bloodied and beaten, crawling through the undergrowth, trying desperately to escape her attacker, only to have her throat slashed, to bleed out in the forest, be buried there.

Royce laughed, a deep laugh, rich with pleasure. He enjoyed my fear. Fed off it. I sucked it in, shoved the flashlight in my pocket, and started walking again.

"Do you know whose coat you're wearing? That's Austin's. His ski jacket. The color of blood. Fitting, isn't it? He died in a coat of red. Blood and brain and little bits of bone."

I walked faster.

"When I saw you coming, for a second, I thought it was Austin. But you don't look like him. Not at all. You're a pretty little girl, you know that?"

I tried to block his voice, concentrate on the thump of my footsteps instead, but they were softer now, too soft, and there was nothing else, just this dark, silent forest and Royce's voice. He'd materialized now, walking beside me. My skin crawled, and I resisted the urge to rub my arms.

"I like pretty girls," he said. "And they like me. Just gotta know how to treat them." His grin flashed in the darkness. "Would you like to meet one of my girls? She's not far from here. Sound asleep under a bed of leaves and dirt. You can wake her up, have a nice girl-to-girl talk, ask her what I did." He leaned over, whispering in my ear. "Or do you want me to tell you?"

I stumbled a little, and he laughed. I looked around, getting my bearings, but all I could see was the endless black forest. Something scampered across my path. Royce laughed again.

"Jumpy, aren't you? That's not good for a necromancer. Your nerves will be shot long before the madness gets you."

I kept walking.

"Did they warn you about the madness?"

"Yes, your uncle told me how we'll all go crazy like you." Hearing my voice calmed my racing heart.

"Me? I'm not crazy. I just like hurting things. Always have. Uncle Todd just wouldn't see it. Told himself Austin's puppy had an accident, the neighbors' cats were killed by coyotes . . . You know how grown-ups are."

I walked faster. He kept pace beside me.

"When I said madness, I meant the curse of necromancy. They did tell you about that, didn't they? Or maybe they're afraid to. You're such a delicate little thing."

I said nothing.

"See, after a lifetime of seeing ghosts, necromancers—"

"I'm not interested."

"Don't interrupt me." His voice chilled.

"I know all about the madness," I lied, "so you don't need to tell me."

"Okay, we'll talk about the girl, then. Do you want to hear what happened to her?"

I veered left.

"Are you walking away from me?"

That cold edge slid into his voice again. I made it three steps, then something hit the side of my head. I staggered. An egg-sized rock bounced on the ground and rolled into my path.

"Don't ignore me," Royce said. "Don't interrupt me. Don't walk away from me."

I stopped and turned. He smiled.

"That's better. Now, what do you want me to talk about? What I did to that girl? Or the curse of necromancy? Your choice."

I gave him a mental shove. He flickered, then shot back, face screwed up with fury.

"Are you trying to piss me off? Because that's really a bad idea."

He disappeared. I spun, trying to find him. A rock hit me in the back of the head, so hard I blacked out for a second, coming to on my knees, blood trickling down my neck.

I leaped up and ran. The next stone hit my shoulder. I kept going, trying to envision him flying into the next dimension, but I couldn't focus, didn't dare shut my eyes even for a second, the undergrowth grabbing at my feet, branches whipping my face, path long gone.

A rock hit the back of my knee and I stumbled. I managed to keep my balance, staggering forward, then breaking into a run again. A branch poked my eye. Then my foot snagged in a vine and down I went, sprawling face-first on the ground.

I pushed myself to my hands and knees. Something whacked me between the shoulder blades, and I was knocked flat again, face in the dirt. A half-buried stick jabbed my cheek hard enough to draw blood.

I didn't try to get up this time. I lay on my stomach, head down, eyes closed, trying to send Royce back to the other side.

"I told you to stop . . ." His voice trailed off as the blow struck—a light, glancing blow. The stick fell beside me, as if he'd weakened too much to hold it.

I pushed harder. The stick rose. I counted to three, then rolled out of the way. He materialized then, face a mask of rage. I leaped to my feet. He swung again, wildly now, and I easily ducked it. He flew at me, wielding the stick. I mentally hit him with everything I had. He flew clear off his feet, landing flat on his back, stick falling.

He grabbed for the stick, but it rolled away. He tried to snatch it. It jumped off the ground, spinning into the air. He glowered at me, like I was doing it. I wasn't.

The stick dangled above his head. He jumped for it. It swung sideways, out of his reach. He jumped again. It dropped to the ground.

Royce glared at me, and when he did, a figure appeared beside him—a teenage girl with long blond hair, dressed in a Minnie Mouse nightshirt and orange giraffe socks.

"Liz!"

"What?" Royce followed my gaze, but she'd disappeared.

I backed away. Royce grabbed for the stick. It rolled away from his fingers. He snatched it up—and it snapped in two.

When he glared my way, Liz appeared, wildly gesturing for me to banish him.

I closed my eyes. It was a struggle to keep them shut and not brace against a blow, but I trusted that Liz had it under control. I pushed him as hard as I could, envisioning all kinds of helpful scenarios—Royce falling off a cliff, Royce falling off a skyscraper, Royce falling out an airlock. It wasn't hard to come up with ideas.

Royce raged. He cursed. He threatened. But if he threw anything, it never reached me. His words surged and faded, growing weaker each time, until finally there was silence and Liz said, "He's gone."

thirty-five

LIZ STOOD THERE, GRINNING. "We did it."

I laughed, a shaky two-seconds-from-crying laugh, my knees weak with relief.

She walked over. "So, I'm going to guess that loser is a telekinetic half-demon like me. From the experiment?"

I nodded.

"That doesn't mean I'm related to him, does it?"

"I don't think so."

"Whew, 'cause I've got enough nuts in my family tree already. And speaking of nuts, you have some kind of radar for them, don't you?"

"Apparently."

"It worked on me, though my crazy quotient must not be high enough yet, because it took me forever to find you. I could hear you calling, but answering was another matter."

"Thank you."

My voice wobbled. Liz hurried over, arm going around my shoulders. I couldn't feel her hug, but I could imagine it.

"Your poltergeist bodyguard is back on duty. Between the two of us, we can handle all the big, scary ghosts. I trounce 'em and you bounce 'em." She grinned. "Hey, that's pretty good."

I smiled. "It is."

"And speaking of big and scary, I'm going to guess you're out here with Derek, helping him Change into a wolf. You'd better grab him, because there's more in these woods than losers throwing sticks and stones. There are losers with spells and guns." She studied me. "And why do I get the feeling that's not a surprise?"

I explained, as quickly and quietly as I could.

"That Andrew guy is telling the truth," she said. "There are four people out here, dressed in black, carrying radios and rifles. That's not a lot, but they've got some high-tech gadgetry on their side—normal and supernormal. They've set up trip wires and those infrared laser things, and I heard them talking about something called perimeter spells."

"We need to get back, then, and—"

"Shhh. Someone's coming."

I crouched.

Liz whispered in my ear. "I don't think it's our poltergeist pal, but wait here. I'll go check."

She took off. I huddled as close to the ground as I could get. When a huge figure reared up in front of me, I let out a yelp. It sprang forward.

"It's me," whispered a familiar voice.

"Der—"

Thwack. He stumbled, Liz behind him, a sturdy branch raised.

"Liz, it's—"

She hit him again, a home-run swing between the shoulders, and he went down with an *oomph* and an oath. She recognized the voice—or the curse—and leaned over, getting a look at him.

"Whoops."

"I'd say he deserved that, always sneaking up on people." Simon appeared from the direction Derek had come. He glanced around. "Hi, Liz . . ." I pointed and he turned her way.

"Hey, Simon."

I relayed her greeting as Derek got up, muttering.

"Did someone say Liz is here?" Tori stumbled out of the forest.

When I pointed at Liz, Tori smiled the brightest smile I'd seen from her since . . . well, I don't know when. Liz had been Tori's friend at Lyle House, and they said hello, me playing go-between.

"What are you guys doing out here?" I asked.

"We're your official search party," Tori said. "Complete with bloodhound."

She waved at Derek, who was brushing off his jeans.

"I left you a note," I said to Derek. "I told you where I was going and what I was doing."

"He got it," Simon said. "Didn't matter."

Derek glowered. "You think leaving a note makes it okay to do something—"

"Don't say stupid," I warned.

"Why not? It *was* stupid."

Simon winced and murmured, "Ease off, bro."

"That's okay," I said. "I'm used to it."

I looked up at Derek. He wavered for a second, then crossed his arms, jaw setting.

"It was stupid," he said. "Risky and dangerous. Those guys could be out here with guns—"

"They are." I turned to Simon and Tori. "Liz saw them. Andrew was telling the truth. We need to get back inside before they hear us fighting."

It was a silent walk back. At the rear door, Liz stopped. She reached, palm out, and it was like pressing against a pane of glass.

"I think there's a spell to keep ghosts out, like at Lyle House," I said. "You might be able to get in the basement or the attic, like you did there. Other ghosts have. I'll go—"

"I'm fine out here, Chloe. You go do your thing."

I hesitated.

She smiled. "Seriously. I'm not going anywhere. When you need me, I'll be here, okay?"

I barely got through the door before I was wishing I'd stayed outside with Liz.

"You were mad at me for staying on the roof," Derek said, bearing down on me.

"So I took off to spite you?"

"Course not. But you were mad at me for taking a risk. So you did the same, to prove your point."

"No fight with you is ever worth risking my life, Derek. And I wasn't mad at you. Upset, yes. Worried, definitely. But if I thought my opinion counted more with you now, it's a good thing you straightened me out fast."

He blanched at that. "I—"

"I went out there for the very reason I said in my note. Because we had to know and I was the best suited to get the answer."

"How? Do you have night vision? Superhuman strength? Superhuman senses?"

"No, but the guy who did wouldn't come off the roof, so the next best choice was the person *without* all that. The one they know isn't a threat."

"She's right," Simon murmured, coming up behind us. "You don't like what she did, but you know it needed to be done."

"Then we should have decided that together."

"Would you have listened?" I asked.

He didn't answer.

I continued. "I couldn't talk to you, because you'd have stopped me. I couldn't talk to Tori because you'd blame her for letting me leave. I couldn't talk to Simon because he'd *know* you'd blame him, so he'd stop me, too. I don't like sneaking around, but you didn't leave me a choice. It's black-and-white to you. If Simon or I take a risk, we're stupid and reckless. If you do, we're stupid for worrying."

"I never said that."

"Did you listen to me up on the roof?"

"I said I was coming in."

"When? I left twenty minutes later, and Simon was still up there, trying to talk you down." I shook my head. "Enough. We don't have time to bicker. We need to make plans."

thirty-six

WE CONSIDERED HAVING LIZ scout for safe passage, but we were dealing with spells and high-tech alarms—things a ghost wouldn't trigger. We had to presume the perimeter was locked tight.

We also had to presume it wouldn't be locked as tight during the day, when they had Andrew and Margaret and the two new people to keep an eye on us. That's when we had to escape.

Until then, we needed to play along with their plan. Andrew had used us; now we'd use him. That meant setting him free, though. We racked our brains to come up with another solution, but there wasn't one. To escape, we had to convince them everything was okay. To do that, Andrew had to be right where they expected him to be.

We weren't letting him in on our scheme, of course. We'd leave him in the basement until morning, then announce that we'd decided the only way to take down the Edison Group was to follow his plan.

Come morning, when Margaret and any others arrived, they'd find us eager to get going. So, we hoped, they'd let their guard down and that's when I'd send Liz out to make sure the exit route was clear.

If that failed, we'd fight our way out. Then we'd call Mr. Bae.

It was almost six when we finished our plans, meaning we still had at least a couple of hours before Margaret showed up. Tori kept working on Andrew's computer. By this time, we didn't expect to get anything more from it, but it gave her a purpose. The guys watched Andrew. That gave them a purpose. And me? I was lost. Scared and lost and frustrated. And hurt. As much as I tried not to think about Derek, I couldn't help it.

I found a pad of paper and a pen, and went into the parlor to turn tonight's walk through the woods into a movie scene. I hadn't written a single line since first arriving at Lyle House. Right now I desperately needed that escape.

I was sketching out the scene when the door opened. I looked up to see Derek standing there.

I kept my expression neutral. "Hmm?"

"Got something for you." He held out an old eight millimeter video camera. "I found it downstairs. It's not working, but I think I can fix it."

A video camera? What would I use it for? Recording our great escape? I didn't say that, because I knew it wasn't the point. This was a gift, a way to say "I know I screwed up and I'm sorry."

His eyes begged me to take it. Just take it. Forgive him. Forget what happened. Start over. And that's what I wanted to do—accept his gift and smile and see that spark in his eyes and—

I took the camera and set it on the table.

"It's cold in here," Derek said. "Is the radiator working?" He walked over and put his hands on it. "Not very well. I'll grab a blanket."

"I don't need—"

"Just a sec."

He took off. A minute later, he came back and handed me a folded blanket. I laid it on my lap. He looked around, then crossed the room and sat on the couch.

After a few moments of silence, he said, "Why don't you come over here? More comfortable than that chair. Warmer, too, closer to the radiator."

"I'm fine."

"Hard to talk to you over there, across the room."

He moved down to the end of the couch, though there'd already been plenty of room. He put his arm along the back. He tried for a smile and didn't really manage it, but my heart still did a little flip.

He's sorry, Chloe. He really is a sweet guy. Don't be a bitch about this. And don't screw it up. Just go over there. Give him a chance and, in no time, you'll forget everything else.

And that's exactly why I stayed in my chair. I didn't want to forget everything else or the next thing I knew, he'd be back on that roof, putting his life in danger.

"You don't get to do this," I said finally.

"Do what?" He asked the question innocently enough, but his gaze dipped slightly. "I'm sorry. That's what I'm trying to say, Chloe. That I'm sorry."

"For what?"

He looked up, confused. "Making you mad."

I didn't answer, just got up to leave. I made it as far as the door. Then he was there, behind me, hand on my elbow. I didn't look back at him. I didn't dare. But I stopped and I listened.

"When I got mad about you leaving," he said, "it wasn't because I thought it was stupid or I didn't think you'd be careful."

"You were just worried about me."

An exhale, relieved that I understood. "Yeah."

I turned. "Because you think I'm worth it."

He put his fingers under my chin. "I absolutely think you're worth it."

"But you don't think you are."

His mouth opened. Shut.

"That's what this is about, Derek. You won't let us worry about you because you don't think you're worth it. But I do. I absolutely do."

I lifted onto my toes, put my hands around his neck, and pulled him down. When our lips met, that first jolt . . . It was everything I hadn't felt with Simon, everything I'd wanted to feel.

His hands went around my waist, pulling me closer—

Simon's footsteps thudded through the hall. We jumped apart.

"And he says *I* have lousy timing," Derek grumbled. Then he called, "What's up?"

"Andrew says he needs to go to the bathroom," Simon said, walking in. "I'm all for saying too bad, but . . ."

"Fine. I'll handle it," Derek said. "Chloe? Wanna come—"

"I need to talk to Simon."

He gave me a weird look at that, but only for a second, like he wasn't jealous, just maybe a little hurt that I wasn't jumping to come with him.

"It's important," I said. "Grab Tori, though. She can help with Andrew."

He nodded and left.

thirty-seven

"SO," SIMON SAID. "Looks like you and Derek are getting along again. What happened? Did he give you the look?"

"Look?"

"You know. The one that makes him look like a whipped puppy, and makes you feel like a jerk for doing the whipping."

"Ah, that one. So it works on you, too?"

He snorted. "It even works on Dad. We give in, we tell him it's okay, and the next thing you know, he's chewing up slippers again."

I laughed.

Simon slumped into a chair. "The problem is, you know he's trying to do the right thing. So what if he doesn't think about himself enough? Would we rather he was a self-centered jerk?" He shook his head, then said, "You wanted to talk?"

"There's something I need to suggest, but . . . Derek's not going to like it."

"Spill."

I told him what I had in mind. When I finished, he swore.

"Bad idea?" I said.

"No, good idea. But you're right—he'll never go for it. If you even suggest it, he'll think it's a test and either get mad or do it to humor you, which won't help, because if he's just humoring us, he won't stay there."

"Stay where?" a voice asked.

We looked over as Tori walked in.

"I thought I heard Derek calling me," she said. "What's up?"

I told her my idea.

"We should have done that the minute we knew they were gunning for him," she said. "Why would he complain? It's not like you're telling him to get lost—just hide out for a few hours, make them think he's gone." She sat on the sofa. "You've got my vote, not that it counts for anything."

"It does," I said. "You're part of this. We need to start acting like you are."

I looked at Simon.

He shrugged. "I guess so."

"Gosh, I've never felt so wanted," Tori said.

"I trust you not to stab me in the back for fun," he said. "But if it's in your best interests? I'm not turning around. Just in case."

"So I've gone from evil incarnate to ordinary bitch. I can live with that." She stretched out her legs. "So who's telling Derek?"

"No one," I said. "That's the problem. He won't do it and even by suggesting—"

"You want me to lie low?" The deep rumble from the doorway had us all look up. Derek stepped in. "Pretend I took off?" He turned to Simon. "Is that what you want?"

"It is," Simon said.

"Chloe?"

"It's not about what we *want*," I said. "Who was the one Andrew knocked out last night? Who's the one they're all watching? They want you gone, Derek, and I honestly don't think they'll make a move until you are."

He met my gaze, searching it, like he was looking for something there. He must have seen it, because he nodded. "Okay. You're right. We need them to relax, and they won't do that with me around."

Not exactly the rationale I hoped for, but I took it.

We decided the best place for Derek was the attic. There were windows that Derek could jump out of easily, so it was safer than the basement. Dirtier, but safer.

While Simon helped Derek gather food and blankets, I went outside and called Liz.

"I need to know if you can get in the attic," I said.

"I'm one step ahead of you. I can get on the roof, in the attic, and kind of in the basement, but not so well."

I told her about our plans for Derek.

"You want me to keep him company?" She grinned. "We can play tic-tac-toe in the dust." She saw my expression and stopped smiling. "That's not what you need, is it?"

"I'm worried about him. He's not very good at looking after himself."

"And he could use a poltergeist bodyguard?"

I nodded. "Take care of him for me. Please."

"I will."

Next we released Andrew. We told him that Derek had decided it was safer for everyone if he left. We'd tried to stop him, but he'd snuck off into the woods, where he was presumably going to hide until he found a way to get off the property.

We didn't tell Andrew that *we* planned to find a way off the property, too. As far as he knew, we were going along with his plans.

Margaret showed up while we were having breakfast, and we discovered another advantage to Derek's disappearance—it gave us an excuse for being anxious and quiet.

As we were finishing, the doorbell rang. All three of us jumped, Simon dropping his spoon into the bowl with a clatter.

"I guess Derek wouldn't be ringing the bell, huh?" I said.

"He might." Simon pushed back his chair. "I'll answer."

I knew what he was thinking—hoping. That it was his dad. The chances of Mr. Bae ringing a bell at a house where his sons might be captives seemed pretty remote, but I followed, if only as an excuse to get away from Andrew and Margaret.

I got to the door as Simon was swinging it open. There stood Gwen.

"Hey, guys," she said with a strained smile. She held up a box. "No donuts this time—I learned my lesson—but I brought some amazing muffins. You can eat those, right?"

"Uh, sure," Simon said.

Simon backed up to let her in. He shot a glance at me, a clear *What's she doing here?*

"Andrew's b-been trying to get in touch with you," I said.

"I know. Work. You know how it is." A forced laugh. "No, I guess you don't, lucky kids. Enjoy it while you can because the truth is"—she leaned over and whispered—"grown-up life sucks. But I'm here now and ready for action. Andrew's message said we're leaving for Buffalo today."

I nodded.

"Great. I'm just in time, then. Come on in and let's chow down on these muffins. They are amazing."

When we showed Gwen into the kitchen, I tried to gauge Andrew's and Margaret's reaction. Both seemed surprised. For Andrew, it was pleasant surprise. For Margaret, not so much. She didn't seem angry, just annoyed at the flighty girl zipping in and out at whim.

They adjourned to the living room. The three of us made excuses and took off.

"She's lying," Tori said. "I don't care how ditzy she is, no one ignores a half dozen urgent calls, then sails in with blueberry muffins."

"Russell sent her to spy," Simon said. "He's up to something."

"It doesn't matter," I said. "Whatever their scheme, we'll be gone soon enough. Just keep an eye on her until then. I'm going to send Liz out looking for escape routes."

thirty-eight

I WAS NEARING THE STAIRS when Simon hailed me.

"Can you give something to Derek?" he whispered. "It's in my room."

We went up. He pulled his bag from its hiding place, took out his sketch pad, folded a page in quarters, and handed it to me.

"Give him that. And tell him it's okay."

"Okay?"

Simon's gaze dropped and he shrugged. "He'll understand." After a moment's pause, he looked up again and forced a smile. "Now let's do this and get out of here."

Simon walked me to the stairs leading to the attic and roof.

"Chloe? Simon?" It was Margaret, downstairs.

Simon swore. He glanced at me.

"Can you go?" I said. "I really need to send Liz out or we'll never get away."

He nodded. I slid into the nearest room and shut the door as he called, "Right here!"

"I need to speak to you two."

Margaret's pumps clicked up the stairs underscored by the thump of Simon's feet, running toward her. I leaned against the door to listen.

"Have you seen Chloe?" she asked.

"Mmm, no," Simon said. "She was trying to find a quiet place to do some writing. Did you check the sunroom, around back? She likes—"

"I'll look. I need you to go to the basement and help Tori bring up extra chairs for lunch."

"Lunch? We just had breakfast. And we have plenty of chairs—"

"No, we don't. The rest of the group is arriving to make final preparations. Andrew's gone to the airport to pick them up, so I need you kids to help with the chairs."

"Tori can handle—"

"I asked *you*, Simon."

"All right," Simon said, raising his voice to be sure I heard. "I'll get the chairs from the basement. I wouldn't bother Chloe with it, though. Those chairs are bigger than she is."

Margaret sent him on his way, saying she'd be right down to supervise. Simon's sneakers pounded down the steps. Then Margaret called Gwen, who answered from downstairs.

"I need to speak to Chloe," Margaret said when Gwen got there. "I brought a necromancy book for her. Simon said she's up here. You look at the front of the house, and I'll take the back."

Simon had said I was probably in the sunroom . . . on the main level.

I looked down at the door handle. There was a lock, with an old-fashioned key on the inside. I turned it as slowly as I could.

I glanced around. I was in one of the unused bedrooms. There weren't any closets, but the wardrobe across the room looked big enough to hold me. As I stepped toward it, my sneakers squeaked. I considered pulling them off, but the floor was filthy, and it'd be just my luck to step on a rusty thumbtack and yelp loud enough to bring everyone running.

I picked my way across the room. I was halfway to the wardrobe when a thump stopped me midstride. I looked up. Derek?

I listened. Silence. I took another slow step. Then another.

"Chloe?"

It was Gwen's voice, a stage whisper from just outside the door. I froze.

"Chloe? Are you up here?" Then lower, under her breath. "Please, be up here. *Please.*"

I looked at the wardrobe. It was too far for a silent dash.

"Chloe? I know you're here."

I looked around. There was a huge dresser beside me, draped in a sheet. I backed up alongside it and crouched.

The door is locked, silly. She can't get in.

I didn't care. If I was found hiding in a locked room, they'd be suspicious, and we couldn't afford that. I should have just gone with Simon.

"Please, Chloe." Her voice sounded like she was inside the room.

You're imagining things.

"Why did I come back?" Gwen whispered. "What was I thinking?" Then, louder, "There you are. Thank God."

My heart slammed into my ribs. I looked at the dresser, but I was completely concealed, the sheet right down to the floor, hiding even my feet.

She's bluffing. She can't see you. She can't possibly—

Gwen stepped in front of me, her short hair wild around her pale face, makeup streaked, eyes huge.

"Come on, Chloe. Quickly!"

I rose. "I—I was l-looking for—"

"It doesn't matter. You need to find Simon and Tori. Do you know where they are?"

"In the basement, but—"

"Hurry!" She reached for me, then stopped short, and pulled back. "You have to warn them."

"About what?"

She shook her head. "Just come on!"

She waved me to the door. I grabbed the knob and turned. It stopped. Locked. The door was still locked.

"Open it, Chloe. Please."

I reached for Gwen. She backpedaled, but not fast enough. My fingers touched her arm . . . and passed through. I clamped my hand over my mouth.

"Don't scream, Chloe. Okay? Please, please, don't scream."

I nodded.

Oh God! She's a ghost. She's dead.

She couldn't be. I just heard her a minute ago, heard her footsteps when she headed down the hall to search. And that was the last time I'd heard them.

I remembered Margaret's words: *Simon said she's up here. You look down there, and I'll take this end.*

Then a thump. The sound of a body falling.

Margaret killed Gwen? That was crazy. Impossible.

Sure, she just happened to fall and break her neck while searching for you.

I swallowed. "Margaret," I whispered.

"Seems that old bag is a whole lot nastier than I ever gave her credit for," Gwen muttered. "I didn't like the way things were going. I . . . I'd heard things. Margaret and Russell. That's why I took off when Andrew called. I didn't want to get involved. But I couldn't do it. I had to come back, thought I should warn Andrew, help him watch out for you kids. Bad idea, obviously. Never even got to the warning part."

I wheeled toward the door. "Derek."

Gwen stepped in front of me. "Is he someplace safe?"

I walked through her.

"Chloe, is he someplace safe? Because if he is, then you have to leave him there. You need to warn Simon and Tori. You said Margaret sent them—"

"To the basement for chairs. For the others coming this afternoon."

"No others are coming, Chloe."

I raced to the door. As I unlocked it, Gwen slipped through the wall.

"Careful," I whispered. "Margaret—"

"Can see me. I know."

Gwen came back and waved me out, motioning for me to dash into the next room and wait again. That's how we did it—me darting from room to room, heading for the rear stairs as Gwen scouted the way.

I did as she said, but inside I was a panicked mess. All I could think was: *Gwen's* dead, *and now Simon and Tori are in the basement, and Derek's in the attic, and am I making the right choice, and will I get to them in time, and oh my God,* what *is going on?*

I was nearly at the back stairs, when Gwen motioned for me to hide. I scooted under a bed, covering my mouth to keep from breathing in dust.

Margaret's heels clicked in the hall. They seemed to be receding. *Please. Please, please— Yes!* She marched down the main stairs as she called a name—Russell. Russell was here?

Oh God, I had to warn Derek. I had to get up to the attic—

And if he finds out Simon's in danger, he'll barrel down there and get himself killed. He's better off where he is, thinking everything is okay.

I closed my eyes and breathed in and out until my heart slowed to a gallop. Gwen checked to make sure the coast was clear, then I hurried to the servants' stairs.

With Gwen watching, I made it to the bottom of the stairs. From there I could see the basement door, ajar. I listened for Simon and Tori—for once I'd have loved to hear the sound of their bickering—but instead I heard Margaret and Russell's muffled voices coming from behind a closed door . . . a door between me and the basement.

Gwen led me forward, step by careful step. I listened for a break in the conversation or the sound of footsteps, but they kept talking.

I was three steps from the basement when Margaret's pumps clicked against the hardwood.

I looked toward the basement, but it was too far. I wheeled and pushed open the nearest door.

"No!" Gwen whispered.

I turned. She madly waved me out. Then, in mid-gesture, she disappeared. I froze for a second—just long enough to hear Margaret turning the doorknob—then spun to find a hiding place. I stopped short. Andrew stood on the other side of a coffee table.

He was looking at me, frowning.

"Chloe?" he said, my name coming slowly, carefully, like he wasn't quite sure.

"Hold on," Margaret said as the door creaked open. "I thought I heard someone."

Andrew's eyes widened. He motioned me over, gesturing for me to hide behind the table—it was long and solid, so I wouldn't be seen. I hesitated only a second, then ran for it. My sneaker slid in something and I tried to keep my balance, but my other foot slid, too, the floor slick, and I crashed onto the coffee table, hands smacking the top of it, knees cracking against the edge.

"We've found Chloe," Margaret said from behind the doorway, her voice completely calm.

I looked up to see Russell coming at me, a syringe in his hand. I backed away, scrambling over the other side of the table.

"Andrew?" I said, looking up. "Help—"

Andrew was gone.

A needle jabbed into the back of my leg. I kicked Russell, hearing him grunt as my foot made contact. The room swayed. I blinked hard, fighting to stay conscious. I tried to get up, get off the table, but my arms gave way and I toppled over the other side.

I hit something soft and rolled off it, landing in a warm puddle. I struggled to focus and lifted my hands. Blood. I was lying in a pool of blood.

I tried getting up, but my muscles refused, and I slumped to the floor. The last thing I saw was Andrew's face, inches away, dead eyes staring into mine.

thirty-nine

COLD METAL VIBRATED AGAINST my cheek. A car roared past.

"How's his blood sugar?" A distant woman's voice. Margaret.

"Low." A man's voice, closer. Russell. "Very low. I can give him a glucose shot, but we really should—"

"Do that."

"Derek." Simon's voice now, the name coming out as a moan.

My eyes fluttered open. We were lying on the floor of a van. Simon was a few feet from me, still asleep, face screwed up, like he was in pain.

"And give him more sedative," Margaret called back from the driver's seat. "I don't want them waking up."

"He really shouldn't get too much—"

"Just do it."

I closed my eyes to slits, so they wouldn't realize I was awake. I tried to look around without moving my head, but all I could see was Simon and, over his head, Tori's sneaker.

Derek. Where is—?

My eyelids closed again.

The van stopped moving. Cold air rushed over me, exhaust fumes blasting in. The engine rumbled, then died. Another rumble, like a closing garage door. The wind disappeared and everything went dark. Then a light flicked on.

Simon retched beside me. The stink of vomit filled the van. I pried my eyes open to see him, sitting, supported by Russell, who held a plastic bag for him.

"Simon." My voice came out thick.

He turned. His eyes met mine and struggled to focus. His lips parted and he rasped, "You're okay," then he gagged and hunched back over the vomit bag.

"What did you give him?" a man's voice snapped.

I knew that voice. Cool fingers wrapped around my bare arm. I looked up. Dr. Davidoff's face hovered above mine.

"It's all right, Chloe." He smiled. "You're home."

A guard rolled me through the halls in a wheelchair, my arms and legs strapped down. Tori rode beside me, also restrained, pushed by another guard.

"It's a temporary measure," Dr. Davidoff had assured me when the guard bound me to the chair. "We don't want to sedate you again, so this is our only alternative until you've had time to reacclimatize."

Dr. Davidoff walked between the guards. Behind them, Margaret and Russell walked as they talked to Tori's mom, who hadn't said a word to her daughter since we'd arrived.

"We decided this was the best place for them," Margaret was saying. "They need a level of control and supervision that we just can't provide."

"Your compassion and consideration are overwhelming," Diane Enright said. "And where did you want us to deposit your finder's fee again?"

I could feel the chill in Margaret's tone when she answered. "You have the account number."

"We aren't leaving until we've confirmed the deposit," Russell chimed in. "And if you get any ideas about not paying us—"

"I'm sure you've taken precautions against just such a possibility," Mrs. Enright said drily. "A letter to be opened in the event of your sudden disappearance, exposing us all?"

"No," Margaret said. "Just someone waiting for our call. A colleague with a direct line to the Nast Cabal and all the details of your operation. I'm sure Mr. St. Cloud wouldn't want that."

Dr. Davidoff only chuckled. "Threatening a Cabal with a Cabal? Clever. But that won't be necessary." The good humor drained from his voice. "Whatever Mr. St. Cloud's interest in our organization, we remain an independent operation, meaning we do not operate under the auspices of his Cabal. You made a deal with us—a sizable payment in return for our subjects and the disbanding of your little rebel group. You have earned that payment and you will get it without treachery or threat of violence."

He glanced back at them. "However, considering it is, ultimately, Mr. St. Cloud's money that is paying you, I would suggest that when you leave the safety of our walls, you get as far away as you can, as fast as you can."

When Tori's mom led Margaret and Russell away, I asked about Simon. I hated giving Dr. Davidoff the satisfaction of hearing the tremor in my voice, but I had to know.

"I'm taking you to see him now, Chloe," he said in that condescending fake-cheerful tone I knew too well. *Look how good we are to you*, it said. *And look how you treat us. We only want to help.* My fingernails dug into the arms of my wheelchair.

Dr. Davidoff strode ahead and opened a door. We went up a ramp and found ourselves in an observation room overlooking an operating room. I looked down at the shining metal operating table and the trays of gleaming metal instruments, and I gripped the chair tighter.

A woman was in the room, off to the side of the observation window, so I could only make out a slender arm in a lab coat.

The door to the operating room opened, and a gray-haired woman entered. It was Sue, the nurse I'd met last time I was here. She wheeled a gurney. Simon lay on it, strapped down.

"No!" I flung myself against the restraints.

Dr. Davidoff chuckled. "I don't even want to know what you think we have in mind, Chloe. We're bringing Simon in to hook him up to an IV.

Being diabetic, he's easily dehydrated by vomiting. We don't want to take any chances, not while that sedative is still upsetting his stomach."

I said nothing, just stared down at Simon, my heart thumping.

"It's a precaution, Chloe. And what you're looking at is simply our medical room. Yes, it's equipped for surgery, but only because it's a multi-purpose room." He bent and whispered. "If you look closely, I bet you'll see dust on those instruments."

He winked, the genial uncle humoring the silly little girl, and I wanted to— I don't know what I wanted to do, but something in my expression made him flinch and just for a second, that genial uncle vanished. I wasn't the docile little Chloe he remembered. It would be safer if I was, but I couldn't fake it anymore.

He straightened and cleared his throat. "Now, if you'll look down there again, Chloe, I believe you'll see someone else you recognize."

I turned toward Simon, still lying on the gurney, pale as the sheet pulled over him. He was listening to the woman in the lab coat, but I could only see her from the back. She was slender, below average height, with blond hair. And it was that hair, the way it swung as she leaned over Simon, that made my breath catch.

Dr. Davidoff rapped on the window. The doctor looked up.

It was Aunt Lauren.

She shaded her eyes, like she couldn't see anyone through the tinted glass. Then she turned back to Simon, talking as he nodded.

"Your aunt made a mistake," Dr. Davidoff said. "You were so upset when we brought you here that she panicked. She was under a lot of stress and she made some bad decisions. She sees that now. We understand and we've forgiven her. She's a welcome member of the team once again. As you can see, she's back to work, happy and healthy, not chained in a dungeon or whatever horrible fate you'd imagined befalling her."

He looked down at me. "We aren't monsters, Chloe."

"So where's Rachelle?" Tori's voice made me jump. Her chair was next to mine, but I'd forgotten she was here. "She's up next on the happy-friends reunion tour, I suppose."

When Dr. Davidoff said nothing, the sneer fell from Tori's face.

"Wh-where's Rae?" I asked. "Sh-she is here, right?"

"She's been transferred," he said.

"T-transferred?"

He forced a jovial note into his voice. "Yes. This laboratory is hardly the place for a sixteen-year-old girl to live. It was only temporary lodgings, which we would have explained if you'd stayed long enough to let us. Rachelle has been moved to—" He chuckled. "I won't call it a group home because, I assure you, it's a far cry from Lyle House. More like a boarding school. A very special boarding school, just for supernaturals."

"Let me guess," Tori said. "You can only get to it by a magical train. How stupid do you think we are?"

"We don't think you're stupid at all. We think you're special. There are people, as you've discovered, who think *special* means dangerous, which is why we've designed a school for your education and protection."

"Xavier's School for Gifted Youngsters," I said.

He smiled at me, completely missing the edge in my voice. "Exactly, Chloe."

Tori twisted to look at him. "And if we're all very, very good, we'll get to go there and live with Rae and Liz and Brady. Is Amber there, too?"

"As a matter of fact—"

"Liar!"

The venom in Tori's voice made him flinch. The empty chairs rattled and the guards glanced over at them, and fingered their sidearms. I barely noticed. All I could think was: *Rae. No, please, not Rae.*

"Liz is dead," Tori said. "We've met her ghost—seen her throwing stuff, using her powers. Even my mother saw it. She knew it was Liz. Or didn't she mention that?"

Dr. Davidoff unclipped his pager and pressed a button, undoubtedly summoning Tori's mom, while using the delay to find the right expression—regret and sadness.

"I wasn't aware you knew the truth about Liz," he said carefully. "Yes, I admit it. There was an accident the night we brought her in from

Lyle House. We didn't tell any of you because you're all in a very fragile state—"

"Do I look fragile?" Tori said.

"Yes, Victoria, you do. You look angry and distraught and very vulnerable, and that's completely understandable if you think we killed your friend. But we didn't."

"What about Brady?" I asked.

"Chloe saw his ghost, too," Tori said. "Here. At the lab. He said he was brought in to talk to you, saw her aunt Lauren, and then *poof*, game over."

His gaze flicked from me to Tori, assessing the chances that Tori somehow had proof of Brady's death as well.

"Chloe was still experiencing aftereffects from her sedatives," he said. "She had also been on a regimen of drugs to keep her from seeing ghosts, either of which may have caused hallucinations."

"How did she hallucinate a boy she'd never met? Do you want her to describe him, because he sounded an awful lot like Brady to me."

"I'm sure Chloe saw a photo of him, whether she remembers it or not. Brady was close to Rachelle. She probably described him—"

"You have an explanation for everything, don't you?" Tori said. "Fine. Brady, Rae, and Amber are all living happily ever after in your super-special boarding school. You want to calm us down? Get them on the phone. Better yet, set up a video conference. Don't tell me you can't do that, because I know Mom has the equipment."

"Yes, we do, and we will let you speak to them just as soon—"

"Now!" Tori roared.

Sparks fizzled at her fingertips. The empty chairs wobbled. One crashed over backward. Her guard pulled out his sidearm.

"I want to see them now! Rae and Brady and Amber—"

"You can *want* all you like, Miss Victoria." The door opened and Tori's mother walked in. "But your wants no longer matter. You lost that right when you ran away."

"So you still recognize me, Mom? Whew. I thought maybe I'd changed so much that you'd forgotten who I was."

"Oh, I recognize you, Victoria. You're still the same spoiled princess who ran away from her responsibilities last week."

"Responsibilities?"

Tori's fists clenched and her restraints snapped open. My guard lunged forward, but Dr. Davidoff waved him back and motioned for the other to put away his gun.

Tori got to her feet. Her hair bristled, popping and sparking.

"Sedate her," Mrs. Enright snapped. "If she can't behave herself—"

"No, Diane," Dr. Davidoff said. "We need to learn how to handle Victoria's outbursts without resorting to medication. Now, Tori, I understand you're upset—"

"Do you?" She wheeled. "Do you really? You locked me up at Lyle House and told me I was mentally ill. You shoved pills down my throat. You murdered my friend. You made me into this genetically modified freak, and yet you tell me it's my fault!"

She slammed her fists against her sides. Tiny bolts sparked off them, making her guard step forward.

"Does that make you nervous?" she said. "That's nothing."

She lifted her hands. A ball of energy spun between them, barely bigger than a pea at first, then growing and growing. . . .

"That's enough, Victoria," Dr. Davidoff said. "We know you're very powerful—"

"You have no idea how powerful I am." She tossed the ball of energy in the air, where it spun, shooting sparks. "But I can show you."

Behind Tori, her mother moved out of everyone's sight as they all stared at Tori. Mrs. Enright's lips moved in a spell. As I opened my mouth to warn Tori, a bolt shot from her mother's fingertips, whipping past Tori and hitting the advancing guard in the chest.

The guard dropped. Dr. Davidoff, Mrs. Enright, and the other guard rushed to his side.

"He's not breathing," the guard said. He looked up at Dr. Davidoff, eyes wide. "He's not *breathing*."

"Oh my God." Mrs. Enright slowly turned to Tori. "What have you done?"

Tori jumped, startled. "I didn't—"

"Get Dr. Fellows," Dr. Davidoff snapped to the other guard. "Quickly."

"I didn't do that," Tori said. "I didn't."

"It was an accident," her mother murmured.

"No, I did not do it. I swear to God—"

"She's right." Everyone looked up sharply at the sound of my voice. I twisted to face Mrs. Enright. "Tori didn't cast that spell. You did. I saw you cast—"

A sudden smack against my cheek, like an invisible slap, so hard my wheelchair rolled back. Blood spurted from my nose.

"Tori!" Mrs. Enright said. "Stop that!"

"I didn't—"

Tori froze, caught in a binding spell.

Mrs. Enright turned to Dr. Davidoff. "Now do you see what I mean? She's completely out of control. She lashes out at enemies and friends alike and she doesn't even realize she's doing it."

"Restrain her," he said. "I'll take Chloe to her room."

forty

AND SO, AFTER A WEEK on the run, I ended up exactly where I began. In the same cell. Lying on the same bed. Alone.

Dr. Davidoff had hustled me out before Aunt Lauren came for the guard. I thought he might want her to check my bloodied nose, but he'd just brought me a wet cloth and a clean shirt from my closet at Lyle House, telling me I could see my aunt as soon as I was calm and ready to listen. As rewards went, spending quality time with my aunt who'd turned traitor—again—wasn't really the incentive he thought.

For the past week, I'd dreamed of the day I'd come back here and rescue Aunt Lauren and Rae. Now I was here and there was no one to save. Aunt Lauren had returned to the fold. Rae was dead.

I squeezed my eyes shut, but tears rolled down my cheeks anyway.

I should have tried harder to persuade Rae to come with me. I should have come back for her sooner.

Rae was dead. And Tori was next. Her mother had murdered that guard to frame her. I couldn't comprehend the evil of that, but I knew what it meant. Diane Enright wanted her daughter dead. She'd become a liability, a threat.

Tori would die and I wouldn't be far behind. And what about Simon?

And Derek? I wiped away the tears and sat up. I had two choices: escape or accept my fate. I wasn't accepting it. Not now, not ever.

I took stock of my surroundings and what I could use. As for the room, nothing had changed. As for me, all I had were the clothes I wore—the new shirt and my jeans, still stained with Andrew's blood. I tried not to think about that.

I patted my pockets, hoping for my ever-present switchblade. Gone.

One pocket crackled, though. Paper. I tugged it out and unfolded it. When I remembered it was the picture Simon had made for Derek, I started to refold it, but I'd already seen what he'd drawn—a sketch of me, crouching beside a black wolf, my arm around its neck, and I remembered Simon saying "Give him that. And tell him it's okay."

My eyes stung. I shakily refolded the message, and tucked it back into my pocket. Then I straightened and gave my head a sharp shake. I still had one very big trick up my sleeve. I pulled my legs up onto the bed, closed my eyes, and called the demi-demon.

I'd barely finished summoning her when warm air tickled the top of my head.

"Well," whispered her tinkling voice, "this looks very familiar."

"I need your help."

"Now that's new. And quite welcome, I might add. The first thing you need to do is free me. Then we'll rain down hell on all who have wronged us."

"I'll free you *after* you help me. And we'll skip the raining-down-hell part."

"Oh, but it's so much fun. All that fire and brimstone and rivers of lava. Demons beating their ragged wings and fanning the flames." A pause, then a deep sigh. "Sarcasm is lost on the young and gullible, isn't it? I meant it figuratively. Wreak havoc, if you will. Smite our mutual enemies."

"No smiting."

"You're going to ruin all my fun, aren't you? Fine. Free me and—"

"*After* you help me."

"Details, details. I suppose you want to escape again. I'm not quite sure why, given that you seem rather fond of this place. You keep returning."

I glared in her direction. "Yes, I want your help escaping, but we're also going to free Simon and Tori and, if Derek's here, he comes, too."

"Presuming you mean the werewolf boy, he hasn't passed through those doors since he left years ago. But if they do bring him in, I will include him in the plan. I am nothing if not fair in my dealings with mortals."

I'd seen enough demonic-pact-gone-wrong horror movies to know I needed an iron-clad agreement. The problem was that I didn't know exactly what I needed her to do. Get me out, sure. But how?

Not surprisingly, she had an idea. Also not surprisingly, I didn't like it.

"Isn't there another way?"

"There's always another way. Personally, I would prefer that witch Diane Enright. I'm quite fond of witches, as I believe I've mentioned. True, she's still alive, but that's an obstacle easily overcome. Tell the guard you wish to speak to her and I'll guide you through the rest. Breaking her neck is the simplest method, but you are rather small for that, so—"

"No."

"Then it's back to my original suggestion, isn't it?"

A minute later, I was kneeling on the carpet, doing something I'd sworn I'd never even consider. Return a human ghost to his corpse. Right now, though, it was the only way I could see to keep from becoming a corpse myself.

I focused on the memory of his face, commanding him back.

"A little more," the demi-demon murmured. "Yes, that's it. Now call him to you."

I did. And I braced myself for screams.

"They're all in the meeting room," the demi-demon said, as if reading my mind. "Just bring him quickly."

A minute later, the card lock clicked. The door swung open. And there stood the guard Mrs. Enright had killed.

Earlier, he'd just been "the guard." I didn't know his name. Didn't want to. I'd had to struggle to recall his face for the summoning. He'd just been an anonymous minion of the Edison Group. And now, when I desperately wanted to depersonalize him again, instead I saw a man. Young. Short brown hair. Freckles. Traces of acne on his cheeks. Was he much older than me? I swallowed, and made the mistake of lifting my eyes to his. Brown eyes, dark with rage and hate. I dropped my gaze.

He still had the card key in his hand, raised, and I fixed on that. Another mistake. A wedding band sparkled on his finger.

Oh God, he had a wife. Kids? A baby maybe? One who'd never see—

I squeezed my eyes shut.

You had nothing to do with his death.

But I'd done something that felt just as bad. I'd brought him back to life. And when I glanced at his face, I saw how terrible that was—the hate, the fury, the disgust.

"Close the door," the demi-demon whispered.

I did.

The guard watched me, eyes narrowed, card still raised, like he'd love to shove it down my throat. Watch me choke on it.

When he spoke, his words were garbled. "Whatever you want me to do, I won't."

The demi-demon chuckled. "Then you don't know much about necromancers, particularly this one," she said, though he couldn't hear her.

"I don't want anything," I said. "I'm sorry—"

"Sorry?" He spat the word and stepped toward me. His coat swung open, showing a charred hole in his chest. The stink of burned meat wafted out. I gagged, and my mouth filled with bile. He stepped toward me again.

"Stop," I said, voice quavering.

He did, and stood there, skewering me with those burning eyes.

"I might suggest you take his gun," the demi-demon said. "To be safe."

I looked down. His fingers rested on the butt of his pistol.

"Don't move," I said.

I tugged out the gun.

"You're going to use me to escape, aren't you? You won't. You belong in here. They were right. You're monsters. I hope they kill you all." He sneered down at me. "No, actually, I hope they don't kill you. I hope they lock you up and experiment on you. Poke and prod and test until you wish you were dead."

A week ago, I'd have shivered at those words. Today, I wasn't going to cower under his threats and name-calling, and I wasn't going to shy away from what I had to do.

I told him to sit. He did. He had no choice. Then I freed his soul, envisioning not a release but an exchange. Eyes shut, I sat cross-legged, necklace on the floor, inches from my hand. I willed this to work. Please work. Just—

"Well, that's better," the guard said, his mumble replaced by a weirdly musical lilt. He cleared his throat. "No, *that's* better," he said, in his normal voice.

I snatched the necklace back. The guard gave a girlish laugh. His eyes glowed orange. He blinked and rolled his shoulders, then cleared his throat again and the laugh deepened. His eyes went black, then brown.

"Will I pass?" the demi-demon asked from inside the guard's body.

I picked up the gun from the floor.

The demi-demon laughed. "Do you really think I'd shoot you and doom myself to eternity in a rotting mortal shell? I am as much your slave as the mortal, and I promise, I shall obey with far less unseemly whining."

I rose, the gun still in my hand.

"I would suggest you keep that," she said. "But you'll need to find a place to hide it."

I tucked it into the back of my waistband. Whenever I'd seen that on the big screen, I'd rolled my eyes, thinking "one wrong move and you're going to shoot yourself in the butt." But, right now, it was the only place I could think of.

As I adjusted my shirt over it, my fingers trembled. I took a deep breath.

"Yes, I know," the demi-demon said. "That experience was far from pleasant, but at least he was angry about it."

When I glanced over, her brows arched. "Would you rather he'd been grateful? Happy to be resurrected? Pleading for a few final minutes with his family?"

She had a point. I pulled the shirt down one last time, then finger-combed my hair.

"You look marvelous, my dear," she said, and fluttered her fingers at the door. "Shall we?" She paused. "Let's try that again." Her voice went gruff. "Ready to go, kid?"

I was.

forty-one

AS THE DEMI-DEMON HAD SAID, all the major players were in a meeting. Given how loath they were to admit to problems, we hoped they hadn't rushed to tell all the other guards about the death of their colleague, so anyone we encountered wouldn't find it odd to see him escorting the prisoners through the building.

As it turned out, the halls were empty. We made it to the security office without seeing or hearing anyone. The door was unlocked. The demi-demon opened it. A guard sat inside, his back to us as he monitored the screens. I stayed behind the demi-demon, but when the guard turned, I caught enough of a glimpse of him for my heart to sink. It was the one who'd been with us earlier.

I jerked back out of sight, and I plastered myself to the corridor wall.

"Hey, Rob," the demi-demon said.

"Nick?" the guard said. His chair scraped the floor, as he scrambled out of it. "I thought you were—"

"So did I," the demi-demon said. "Seems it takes more than a witch's spell to kill me. Whatever mojo that shaman Phelps uses, it's good stuff."

"They called in Phelps?" The guard exhaled. "I didn't think they would. Dr. Fellows is good, but . . ."

"She's no shaman healer. A lot easier on the eyes than old man Phelps, though."

They both laughed at that.

"Anyway, I'm back in action, and apparently, almost dying doesn't even earn me the rest of the shift off. They want you up front, manning the door. Trudy's nervous with those kids back."

"I don't blame her. Personally, I don't know why they keep trying to rehabilitate them. After what that brat did to you, I'm ready to lock them up and throw away the key. I'll go keep Trudy company, though." The squeak of shoes, then a sniff: "What's that smell?"

"Smell?"

"Like something burned."

"Yeah. I think Trudy burned popcorn in the microwave again."

"No, it's not popcorn." Another shoe squeak. "It's coming from—"

A gasp. Then the thump of a falling body. I raced into the room. The demi-demon was tugging the guard into the corner.

"Do you see a ghost, child?" she asked without turning.

"N-no."

"Then he isn't dead, is he?" She arranged him, mostly hidden behind the chairs. Then she took my hands and pressed them to the guard's neck where his pulse beat strong. "You're giving me the first chance at freedom I've had. Do you think I'd spoil that?"

She looked at the guard, then slid a sly glance my way. "Still, this would be an excellent opportunity to obtain a far more suitable body for me, one that *no one* thinks is dead."

I glared at her.

She sighed. "All right then. Find your friends."

I scanned the monitors while she watched the door. There was no sign of Tori, but I'd expected that—it only meant she was in one of the camera-free cells. I found Simon, still in the surgery, still strapped down, an IV in his arm, no sign of a guard.

I checked the other screens. Dr. Davidoff was in a meeting room with Mrs. Enright, Sue, Mike the security guy, and the two others. They were deep in debate.

The rest of the rooms were dark, all except one that wasn't any bigger than my walk-in closet at home, crammed with a twin bed, small desk, and chair.

Someone sat at the desk, writing, chair pulled as far from camera range as possible. I could see only a shoulder and arm, but I recognized the dark purple silk blouse. I'd been with Aunt Lauren when she bought it this winter.

The woman stood, and there was no doubt. It was Aunt Lauren.

I brought the demi-demon in and pointed at the screen. "What room is that and why is my aunt in there?"

"Because she was naughty. Apparently, distaste for imprisonment runs in the family. She was scarcely confined to a regular cell for a day before she tried to escape. They decided she needed more direct supervision."

"So she's a captive?"

"She helped you escape. Did you think they'd throw a feast in her honor? Sacrifice a goat or two?"

"They said she'd changed her mind and admitted she made a mistake."

The demi-demon laughed. "And you believed them? Of course you did, because they've never been anything but perfectly honest with you."

My face heated.

"Yes, they tried to make her see the error of her ways," the demi-demon said. "They offered immunity and forgiveness and feather pillows. She's a very valuable member of the team. But she refused." She looked at me and sighed. "I suppose you want to rescue her, too."

I nodded.

"Then let's get on with it."

I grabbed her arm before she walked away. "Rae. The fire half-demon girl. They said she was transferred. Is she here, too?"

The demi-demon hesitated, and when she spoke, there was a softness in her voice. "No, child. She's not here. And I don't know what became of her, so don't ask me. She was here one evening, and come morning, she was not."

"They killed—"

"There's no time for that. Your friends await and they"—she pointed at the Edison Group meeting—"will not be in there forever."

We freed Tori first.

I tried to prepare her for the shock of seeing a dead man walking by going in first, but she caught a glimpse of him, and after a split second of surprise, said "Good idea."

I was going to explain that I hadn't created a zombie guard slave, but the demi-demon was already at the next door, checking the third cell, Tori right behind her. I decided that if Tori was fine with me raising the dead for personal use, then there was really no reason to tell her I'd actually made a deal with a demon.

That didn't work so well with Simon, who knew I wouldn't be nonchalantly controlling dead people. And I couldn't use the no-time-to-explain excuse because we had time—undoing his restraints, getting out his IV, bandaging him, and looking for his shoes, while the demi-demon guarded the door.

So I told them the truth. Tori took it in stride. I was beginning to think Tori would take anything in stride.

Simon said nothing for a moment, and I braced myself for *Are you nuts?* but this was Simon. He only slid off the bed, crouched beside me while I checked under a table for his shoes, and whispered, "Are you okay?" I knew he meant the part about raising the dead, and when I nodded, he searched my face and said, "All right." I assured him I'd been careful with the demi-demon and he said, "I know, and we'll keep being careful." And that was that.

forty-two

"NEXT STOP, DEAR AUNTIE LAUREN," the demi-demon trilled. "Then straight to the nearest exit and"—she smiled—"freedom for all."

"Not all." Tori glanced at me as we walked. "We need to download the project files. There are other kids out there thinking they're mentally ill, like Peter and Mila. Plus others who might not have come into their powers yet."

Peter had been at Lyle House when I arrived, and he'd been released before we escaped. I hadn't known Mila, only that she'd been there before me, and had been "rehabilitated" and sent back into the world.

"I would love to get those files," I said. "But we don't have time to access and print—"

Tori pulled a thumb drive from her pocket. I wasn't even going to ask where that came from.

"You have Dr. Davidoff's password," she said. "We have access to his office. I can download the files while you're getting your aunt."

"And there's got to be a phone," Simon said. "I can try my dad again."

They were right. I'd regret it if we left without those names. And I'd regret it even more if we got locked up again and had passed up the chance to tell Mr. Bae where we were.

We got to the office. It needed an additional code, but the demi-demon knew it. Then I said the demi-demon and I would get my aunt and come back.

"So the sorcerer is staying with his sister?" the demi-demon asked.

"Sister?" Simon said. "She's not—"

"Sister spell-caster," I said to him quickly. "She talks like that."

When we were far enough away, I whispered, "So Simon's dad really is Tori's father?"

"The worst-kept secret in the building." Her singsong tone jarred with the guard's gruff voice. "And that, my child, is saying a lot."

"Guess that explains why her mom freaked out when Tori admitted she liked Simon."

"Oooh, that would be awkward. A lesson to you in keeping secrets. They will come back to haunt you in the most uncomfortable ways. Whether that one feels any guilt, though, is quite another matter. She has the morals of a succubus. I must admit, it was quite amusing, watching her attempt to seduce the sorcerer. Quite a blow to her ego when she failed."

"Failed?" I said as we turned the corner. "But if Tori is his daughter, then obviously—"

"Obviously nothing. What do they teach children in school these days? Sex is hardly the only way to reproduce. Arguably the most fun, but if that fails, and you have access to a complete laboratory, with every excuse to procure the necessary bodily fluids . . ."

"Eww. That's—"

An alarm bell clanged right over my head.

"Time's up, it seems," the demi-demon murmured.

She opened the nearest door with the card and propelled me inside, slipping through after me.

"My aunt—"

"Is fine. She's only a few doors down, safe for now. You're the pigeon who's not in her coop."

The demi-demon led me across the room to a second door, opening into a big closet. She ushered me inside.

"Simon and Tori—"

"Are, I presume, in possession of functioning ears and brains. They will hear the alarm and take cover, which is what we need to do."

As I stepped into the closet the guard's body collapsed. I fell to my knees beside it.

"I believe you'll find he's still quite dead." The demi-demon's voice came from above my head. "As useful as that mortal form was, this one is better equipped for sneaking about."

"I thought you said you couldn't get out of there without my help."

"*Implied*, never said. I'm a demon. We know all the loopholes. Now, I'm going to take a look around. You still have that gun, don't you?"

"Yes, but—"

"Take it out and hope you don't need to use it. I'll be right back."

A rush of warm air. Then I was alone with the guard's body.

The alarm continued to whoop.

Did I hear the pounding of running feet? A shout? A shot?

Relax. There's nothing you can do.

That was the problem. I was stuck cowering in my hidey-hole, shaking hands wrapped around a gun that I didn't know how to fire, knowing there was nothing I could do, nothing that wasn't so reckless Derek would have reason to yell at me if he were here, and God how I wished he were. I'd take the yelling just to know he was safe—

He is safe. Safer than if he was *with you.*

If he'd been left at the house then, yes, he'd be fine. He had Liz to watch out for him, and he had no idea where we'd gone and no way to come after us. He'd be furious, but safe.

I glanced over at the guard. He lay in a heap, dead eyes staring up at me. I thought about him, wondered—

Don't think about him. Don't wonder anything. Or you'll get your wish and you won't be alone in this closet.

I looked away quickly and erased his image from my head. I checked out the gun instead. I'd written shoot-outs in screenplays but, to my embarrassment, had no idea whether the gun was loaded or if there was a safety on it. Stuff like that doesn't matter in a screenplay. You just say "Chloe fires the gun" and leave the rest to the actor and the props department.

It looked like a Glock, though, and from what I remembered, they didn't have safeties. Just point and shoot. I could manage that if I had to.

See, you're not helpless. You have a weapon. Two weapons.

Two? My gaze slid to the guard and I swallowed hard. No, I'd never—

Sure you would, if it came down to it.

No, I—I . . .

Can't even finish the denial, can you? You'd do it if it was the last resort. Controlling the dead. That's your power. Your greatest power.

I squeezed my eyes shut.

"You can't see anyone coming like that."

It took a moment to realize that the voice hadn't come from inside my head. The demi-demon was back.

"What set off the alarm?" I asked.

"I haven't a clue, but your friends are safe. They've retreated to Davidoff's reading room. The group realizes you've escaped, but, shockingly, they presume you actually tried to get out of the building. Fortunately, you're nowhere near an exit. Unfortunately . . ."

"We're nowhere near an exit."

"I can get you out. I may even be able to rescue your aunt on the way. But your friends are in the opposite direction, and I can't possibly—"

"Then I don't go. Not until it's safe for all of us."

"A noble choice. However, there's only one alternative and I fear you'll like it even less than my last suggestion."

"Free you."

As I said it, my inner voice screamed that I'd been tricked. But I could hear the shouts of the Edison Group. They really *had* been alerted and there was no reason for the demi-demon to do it herself, not when she could have easily escorted us out the door and claimed her reward.

"Free me and you will cripple the magics cast on this place," she said.

"Great. That'll help end the experiments, but how does it get us out? It's not the magic I'm worried about. It's the alarms and guys with guns. What I need—"

"Is a distraction. And that's what I'm offering. My magic permeates this place. The disruption will affect far more than their spells. You will get the distraction you need."

Our plan had failed and she had every reason to lie now and convince me to free her, before I realized I was trapped.

"I made a bargain," she said. "A demon's bargain is binding. Free me and I am bound by my word as tightly as these bonds."

Did I trust her? Of course not. Did I have another option? Not one I could see.

"Tell me what to do."

forty-three

FREEING THE DEMI-DEMON WASN'T much different from freeing a ghost. I suppose that made sense, since she'd gotten here by a type of summoning.

"Almost there, child," she said, her warm breath swirling around me. "I can feel the shackles falling. A quarter century of servitude and finally I will be free. The very walls will tremble with my leaving, and they'll scurry like frightened mice. Just a little more. Can you feel it?"

I couldn't feel a thing, just wished she'd shut up and let me concentrate.

She let out a cry that made me jump, and the closet filled with whirling hot air. I braced myself. The wind whipped around me, then gradually subsided to a pleasant breeze before disappearing altogether.

Silence.

"Is that . . . it?" I said.

"Hmm. Do you feel anything else? A vibration, perhaps?"

"No." I glowered in the direction of her voice. "You promised a distrac—"

The closet shook. A dull rumble sounded overhead, like a train chugging across the roof. As I looked up, a sudden tremor knocked me off my feet.

A ceiling tile hit my shoulder. Then another. The tiny room creaked and groaned and crackled, walls splitting, chunks of drywall raining down.

"Out, child!" The demi-demon shouted to be heard above the din. "You need to get out!"

I tried to stand, but fell back to all fours. The room kept shaking and creaking, walls groaning as they ripped open. Drywall dust filled my nose and stung my eyes. I crawled blindly, following the demi-demon's voice as she led me.

I made it out of the closet and into the main room. It was shaking just as much, the floor tiles buckling beneath me. A chunk of falling plaster hit my back. Another the size of a fist glanced off my injured arm, shattering as it hit the floor, bits flying into my mouth.

As I spat out the plaster, I smelled something other than drywall dust. A sweet scent, strangely familiar.

"*Faster*," the demi-demon said. "Keep moving."

As I crawled, the shaking stopped. The groaning stopped. The room went completely silent and still.

I looked around. Dust still filled my eyes, making them water. The floor was carpeted in plaster. The walls were a patchwork of cracks and hanging chunks of drywall.

The room groaned again, softer now, like it was settling, and all that remained was the sweet smell.

The demi-demon kept urging me on. I got to my feet. Outside, I could hear the distant shouts and cries of the Edison Group. Overhead the light flickered like a strobe, throwing the windowless room into darkness.

"You have your distraction," the demi-demon said. "Now take advantage of it."

As I stepped toward the door, something brushed my leg. I jumped and looked down. Nothing was there. Another step. Warm fingers stroked my cheek. Hot breath whispered wordlessly in my ear, blowing strands of hair, tickling my neck.

"I-Is that you?" I asked.

"Of course," said the demi-demon . . . from across the room.

I looked around. I couldn't see anything except debris. The light continued to flicker. Distant voices shouted about finding the computer tech.

"Their systems are down," the demi-demon said. "Perfect. Now go."

I started forward. At a giggle to my left, I spun. A growl sounded behind me and I spun again.

"The *door*," the demi-demon said. "Get to the door."

A blast of hot air knocked me off my feet, flat onto my back.

A giggle erupted above me. Then a low voice, speaking in a foreign language. I pushed up. Another blast slapped me down. Hot air whirled around, drywall dust flying like a sandstorm, filling my eyes, my nose, my mouth.

I crawled toward the door. The wind buffeted me from all sides. That sweet smell—sickly sweet now—made my stomach churn. Invisible hands stroked my head, my back, my face. Fingers plucked my shirt, pulled my hair, pinched my arms. Voices whispered and growled and shrieked in my ears. But the only one that mattered was the demi-demon's, urging me on, guiding me to the door.

My head struck the wall. I patted around until I found the doorknob, pulled myself up, and turned it. Yanked. Turned. Yanked.

"No," I whispered. "Please, no."

Seems those electrical failures might not be so convenient after all.

Fingers ran through my hair. Warm breath caressed my cheek. Hot wind whipped around me. The light flickered.

"Sweet child," a voice whispered.

"What is she?" another asked.

"Necromancer."

A giggle. "Are you sure?"

"What have they done to her?"

"Something wonderful."

"Get away from her," the demi-demon said. "She's not yours. Shoo. All of you."

"Wh-what's going on?" I asked.

"Nothing to worry about, child. It's simply a bit of fallout from the liberation ritual. There are usually precautions taken against such a thing, but we didn't have the time. Or the materials."

"Precautions against what?"

"Well, when you free a demon, you open a . . ."

"Portal into the demon world?"

"*Portal* is a strong word. More like a teeny tiny tear."

The voice continued as we talked. The unseen fingers touched me, poked me.

"These are demons?" I said.

"Hardly," she said with a sniff. "Minor demonic spirits. Little more than pests." She raised her voice. "Who are going to be in serious trouble if they don't heed my commands."

The spirits hissed and spat and chortled. And stayed where they were.

"Ignore them," she said. "They can't do more than touch you, and they can barely do that. Think of them as an infestation of otherworldly insects. Annoying and inconvenient, but hardly dangerous. They can't manifest in this world without a dead body—"

She stopped short. We both looked at the closet door.

"Quickly," she said. "Send me back to that guard. If his corpse is occupied, they can't—"

A thump sounded from the closet. Then a low hiss. I spun and yanked on the exit door. Growls erupted from the closet. As I whaled on the door, I heard a scratching, like nails scraping wood. The click of a knob. The squeak of the door hinges. I spun toward the closet. The lights went out.

forty-four

FINGERS BRUSHED MY FACE, making me jump back from the door. Across the room, nails scraped along the floor.

"He's coming," a voice whispered. "The master is coming."

"M-master?" I said.

"They lie," the demi-demon said. "It's just another—"

A wail at my ear drowned her out. I jumped back, knocking over a chair and falling hard. A blast of desert wind whipped my hair in my face, twisting my clothing, binding me. I heard the sounds of struggle, the curses of the demi-demon barely rising over the gibbering and shrieking of the spirits.

Then, as suddenly as it had begun, it ended. The wind died and the room went silent.

Completely dark and completely silent.

"A-are you there?" I called.

She didn't answer. Instead, I heard the scrape of nails, then the whisper of fabric as it slid across the floor. I leaped to my feet only to tangle in the fallen chair and topple over it, bashing into another piece of furniture. The back of my head cracked against something and the wound from earlier reopened, blood streaming down the back of my head.

The scratching stopped, and I heard sniffing. Sniffing and the smacking of lips.

I wiped the blood away and scuttled back, thumping into the wall. A chattering, then a hiss, and it went quiet again. I could pick up the distant voices of the Edison Group, and I clung to that, a reminder of where I was, in the lab, not locked away in a basement crawl space with dead bodies crawling toward me.

Umm, actually, yes, there is a dead body—

But it wasn't a rotting corpse.

True, it's a nice fresh one . . . possessed by a demonic spirit.

The scraping started again. I wrapped my arms around myself and squeezed my eyes shut.

Oh, that'll help.

No, but *this* would. I concentrated on freeing that spirit. I kept at it, as hard as I dared, but that whispering of fabric and scratching of nails kept coming closer, so close now I could hear the scrape of buttons against the floor. I scrambled to a new spot, hit another chair, and crashed down on top of it.

Just release it. Stop worrying about getting away. Release it.

I closed my eyes. Not that it mattered. The room was so dark I couldn't see a thing, couldn't see the guard's body slithering across the floor, couldn't see how close it was, couldn't see it—

Focus!

I released and released and released, but it still kept coming, the whispering and the scratching, the hissing and the chattering. I could hear more now—teeth clicking and grinding. And I could smell that sweet demon odor mixing with the stink of burned flesh, making my stomach heave.

Concentrate.

I did, but no matter how hard I tried, the thing didn't pause, didn't growl or hiss, gave no sign it felt anything.

Hot breath seared my ankles. I yanked my knees in and hugged them, blinking hard, desperately trying to see even a shape, but the room was completely dark. Then the scratching and whispering and chattering all stopped, and I knew it was right in front of me.

A sharp rip, like fabric tearing. Then another kind of rip, a dull, wet sound that made the whimper die in my throat, and I huddled there, knees drawn tight, listening to that awful wet tearing sound, punctuated by popping, like bones crackling and snapping.

I squeezed my eyes shut. Dismiss, dismiss—

Something wet and cold flicked across my ankle. I pulled my foot back, hands flying to my mouth, stifling my scream. I leaped to my feet, but icy fingers grabbed my legs and yanked me down. It held me tight, hands climbing up my legs as it pulled itself onto me.

I went wild, kicking and punching, but it held me down with superhuman strength and then it was on me, crouched over me, pinning me, hissing, sickly sweet breath blasting in my face. I felt something cold and wet on my neck. It was licking me, licking the blood.

I punched and kicked and imagined releasing it and for a second felt that iron grip loosen. I heaved and rolled, and managed to get free, scrabbling backward until I hit the wall.

I pushed to my feet and tried to run, but tripped over the chair I'd toppled earlier. I caught myself before I fell, then scurried back, expecting any moment the thing would pounce and knock me down. But it didn't, and when I listened I could hear a wet rasping noise where I'd left it. I backed away slowly.

With a click, the lights came on, and I saw the guard crouched on all fours, arms and legs bent . . . wrong, bent where arms and legs shouldn't bend. It looked like some kind of monstrous insect, limbs broken and twisted, bones sticking through fabric. Its head was down and it kept making those wet rasping noises.

I stepped to the side and saw what it was doing—licking my blood from the floor. I backed up fast, and it turned its head—completely turned it, the flesh on its neck ripped through, the head swiveling freely. It curled its bloodied lips back, bared its teeth, and hissed. Then it skittered toward me, those broken and twisted limbs moving so fast they seemed to skim the floor, body held only inches above it.

I ran for the closet door. With lightning speed it raced into my path. Then it reared up, hissing and spitting.

"Release it, child," a familiar voice whispered at my ear.

"Y-you're back." I looked around, bracing against the pokes and pinches. "The others . . ."

"Gone, and staying gone. Only this one remains. Release it and you'll be done."

"I've tried."

"And now I'm here to distract it while you try again."

A gust of hot air whooshed between me and the thing, and it reared again, gaze following the wind as the demi-demon whipped past.

I closed my eyes.

"Your necklace," she said.

"R-right." I tugged it off and looked at it, reluctant to put it down.

The thing spun on me again. The demi-demon said something in another language, getting its attention. I set the necklace on a chair, within grabbing distance, then closed my eyes and worked at dismissing it.

I felt the spirit slipping away, snarling. At a click, my eyes shot open, gaze following the sound to the door.

"Yes, it's open," the demi-demon said. "And not a moment too soon. Now finish this."

Knowing the door was open gave me the extra boost I needed, and the next sound I heard was a thump as the guard's broken body fell to the floor.

"Excellent," the demi-demon said. "Now retrieve your trinket and—"

A furnace blast of hot air hit me, so strong it made the others seem like a gentle breeze.

"Wh-what's that?" I said.

"Nothing, child," she said quickly. "Now, *hurry*."

forty-five

I GRABBED MY NECKLACE AND pulled it on as I raced for the door. I was about to veer around the guard's body when it rose, pushing to its feet as if its bones weren't broken in a dozen places. I started around it.

"Stop!" it thundered.

I did. I have no idea why. It was just that kind of voice.

I turned to see the guard's body standing straight, chin up, eyes blazing an unearthly green. I could feel the heat radiating off it even from a half-dozen feet away.

"Diriel!" it roared, peering about the room.

"Um, over here, my lord," the demi-demon said. "And may I say, it's a pleasure to see you—"

He spun in her direction, and when he spoke, his voice was weirdly melodic. Like the demi-demon's, only deeper, masculine, hypnotic even. I stood there, rooted to the floor, just listening.

"For over two decades you have not answered my summons. Where have you been?"

"Well, you know, it's a funny story. And I'll be happy to tell you just as soon as I—"

"Are you asking me to wait on your convenience?" His voice was low, but it made me shiver in spite of the heat.

"Certainly not, sir, but I've made a bargain with this—"

"Mortal?" He wheeled, as if seeing me for the first time. "You made a bargain with a mortal *child*?"

"Like I said, funny story, and you are going to love—"

"She's a necromancer." He stepped toward me. "That glow . . ."

"Isn't it pretty? There's such charming variation among these mortal supernaturals. Even the weakest among them gets something, like that lovely glow."

"A necromancer's glow is indicative of her power."

"Quite right, and it's a good thing, too, because being such a weak necromancer, she needs a very strong glow to attract any ghosts."

He gave a dismissive snort and walked over to me. I didn't flinch—but only because I was frozen with terror.

This was a demon. A full demon. I knew that with a certainty that made my legs quiver.

He stopped in front of me and tilted his head, sizing me up. Then he smiled.

"So," said the demi-demon—Diriel. "I'm just going to help this poor, defenseless necromancer child . . ."

"Out of the goodness of your heart, I suppose."

"Well, no, it seems the silly chit freed me. Completely accidental. You know children, always playing with the forces of darkness. So it seems she's done me a favor, and if you'll let me complete the contract, sir, I will be right with you—"

"How powerful does a child necromancer need to be to free a demi-demon?" he mused. "I can feel your power, little one. They've done something to you, haven't they? I have no idea what, but it is wondrous."

His eyes gleamed, and I felt them slicing through me as if he were peering into the heart of my power, and when he did, he smiled again, and it made me shiver.

"Perhaps, but she's a child, my lord. You know what the Berithian Treaty says about wooing youths. Quite unfair, I agree, but she will be an adult soon enough, and if you allow me to cultivate the child by completing my contract . . ."

He glanced in her direction. "Whatever deal you've made with the child can be completed another time. I'm not letting you slip away again so easily. You have a penchant for disappearing."

"But she—"

"Is powerful enough to summon you when she wishes." He turned back to me and before I could move away, his hand was under my chin, holding it, the guard's dead fingers oddly warm. He tilted my face up to his and murmured, "Grow up strong, little one. Strong and powerful."

A blast of hot air. Diriel whispered, "I'm sorry, child." And then they were gone.

I jumped over the guard's fallen body and raced to the door. The handle turned before I touched it. I looked around, ready to run, but there was no place to run *to.* I took out the gun and backed against the wall. The door opened. A figure peeked in.

"A-aunt Lauren," I whispered.

My knees wobbled. There'd been a time when I'd chafed under Aunt Lauren's constant mothering, but after two weeks of relying on myself and other kids who were as scared and lost as I was, her look of concern was like a warm blanket on a freezing night, and I wanted to throw myself into her arms and say, *Take care of me. Fix this.*

But I didn't. She was the one who ran over and hugged me and as wonderful as it was, that feeling of wanting to be rescued passed, and I felt myself pulling away and heard myself saying "Come on. I know the way."

As we hurried out, she glanced back in the room and saw the guard's body.

She gasped. "Isn't that—?"

Without missing a beat, I cut her off, stammering, "I—I don't know what happened. I g-got scared and he just walked in here and—"

She hugged me, whispering, "It's okay, hon."

She believed me, of course. I was still her little Chloe who'd never *think* of raising the dead.

As we slipped into the hall, she saw the gun and took it from me before I realized what she was doing. When I protested she said, "If we need to use it, I'll be the one who pulls the trigger." I knew she was trying to protect me from having to shoot someone. I didn't *want* to shoot anyone, but there was something about giving up the gun that chafed, the feeling of being shoved back into a role I no longer fit.

"Simon and Tori are in Dr. Davidoff's office," I whispered.

"We'll go this way. It's longer, but we're less likely to bump into anyone."

We turned a corner and a balding guard stepped from a room. I tried to tug Aunt Lauren back, but he'd already seen us.

"Don't move, Alan," Aunt Lauren said, raising the gun. "Just step back into that room and close—"

"Alan," said a voice behind him.

He turned. A shot fired. The guard dropped. Mrs. Enright stood there, lowering a gun.

"I really do hate these things," she said, lifting the gun. "So primitive. But I thought it might come in handy."

I glanced at Aunt Lauren. She was frozen in a binding spell.

"Look what your aunt did, Chloe." Mrs. Enright waved at the guard, motionless on the ground. "Such a shame. They won't let her off with house arrest this time."

I looked from Aunt Lauren to the dead guard.

Mrs. Enright laughed. "You're thinking of raising him, aren't you? Such a resourceful girl. I suppose we have you to thank for all this." She waved her free hand at the cracks in the walls. "That's what I like about you. Resourceful, clever, and, apparently"—she motioned at the guard again—"getting more confident in your powers each time we meet. I'd almost like to let you raise him, just to see what you'd do."

"Let us go or—"

"I'm the one with the gun, Chloe. Your weapon takes longer to activate. If he so much as twitches, it's good-bye to Aunt Lauren. Any bargains come from me, and I'm still quite willing to deal with you. I think we could—"

A dark shape leaped on her back. As she fell, she twisted to see a huge black wolf pinning her. She opened her mouth to cast, but Derek grabbed her by the back of the shirt and whipped her against the wall. She recovered, rolling aside and reciting words in a foreign language. He grabbed her and flung her again. She hit with a crack, then lay still.

I raced forward.

"Chloe!" Aunt Lauren shouted, freed from her binding spell.

"It's Derek," I said.

"I know. Don't—"

I was already there, dropping beside him as he panted, flanks heaving, fighting for control. I grabbed handfuls of fur and buried my face against him, tears threatening.

"You're okay," I said. "I was so worried."

"You weren't the only one," said a voice.

I glanced up to see Liz and smiled. "Thank you."

"I just went along for the ride. After that happened—" She waved at Derek. "You know how blind people need Seeing Eye dogs? Well, apparently werewolves could really use Opening Door poltergeists."

Derek rumbled deep in his chest and bumped me.

"We need to go. I know."

I started getting to my feet, but he leaned against me. I could feel his racing heart. He pressed his nose against my neck, breathed deeply, shuddered, and his heart slowed. When he sniffed again, his nose went to the back of my neck, finding the blood and grumbling with concern.

"It's just a bump," I said. "I'm fine."

I wrapped my hands in his fur one last time, holding him tight, then pushed to my feet. I turned to Aunt Lauren. She stood there, staring. Just staring.

"We have to go," I said.

Her gaze lifted to mine and she stared some more, like seeing someone she didn't recognize.

"Liz is here," I said. "She'll scout the way."

"Liz . . ." She swallowed, then nodded. "All right."

I gestured at Tori's mom. "Is she . . . ?"

"Still alive, but it was a hard blow. She should be out for a while."

"Good. Derek? We need to get Tori and Simon. Follow me. Liz, can you go ahead and make sure the way is clear?"

She smiled. "Yes, boss."

I took a few steps, then realized Aunt Lauren wasn't following. I turned. She was still staring.

"I'm okay," I said.

"You are," she said softly. Then firmer, "You really are."

We set out.

forty-six

WE COLLECTED TORI AND Simon just as they were heading out to rescue *me*. After a very brief explanation about the earthquake and the wolf by my side, I asked if Simon had gotten hold of his dad. His face darkened, telling me the answer wasn't good.

"Voice mail," he said.

"Seriously?"

"It said he was unavailable and switched to voice mail. I left a message. He could have been out of range or on the phone or . . ."

He didn't finish, but we all knew what he meant. *Unavailable* could mean a lot of things, not all of them as innocent as being stuck between cell towers.

"We'll call again as soon as we're out," Aunt Lauren said. "Which should be soon."

We headed for the nearest exit. We'd gone about twenty feet before Liz came racing over.

"Three of them," she said. "Coming this way."

"Guns?" I asked.

She nodded.

If it was three unarmed staff—even with supernatural powers—I'd be willing to take them on. But guns were another thing. I told the others.

"There's an unused wing to the west," Aunt Lauren said. "They won't guard that exit because it's through a secured door."

I followed her and used the key card to get us into the wing. As soon as we were through, Derek stopped short, the hair on his back rising, lips curling in a silent growl.

"Do you smell someone?" I whispered.

He shook his head sharply, with a grunt, as if to say *sorry*, and we started forward again, but he was wary now, gaze flicking from side to side.

"I know this place," Simon murmured. "I've been here."

"Your dad used to bring you to work sometimes when you were little," Aunt Lauren said.

"Yeah, I know, but this place . . ." He looked around, then he rubbed the back of his neck. "Creeps me out, whatever it is."

"The exit is around the corner and down at the end," Aunt Lauren said, ushering us on. "It leads into a yard. We'll need to climb the wall, but that's another reason they won't guard it."

We continued along. Simon and Derek weren't the only ones getting chills. It was so quiet. An empty, dead place. Shadows hunkered along the walls, out of reach of the security lights. It stunk, too, reeking of antiseptic soaked right into the floors, like an abandoned hospital.

I glanced in the first open door and stopped short. Desks. Four tiny desks. A wall of faded posters of alphabet animals. A blackboard, still showing the ghosts of numbers. I blinked, certain I was seeing wrong.

Derek nudged my legs, telling me to get moving. I looked at him, and I looked at the classroom.

This was where Derek had grown up. Four tiny desks. Four little boys. Four young werewolves.

For a second, I could see them—three boys working at the three clustered desks, Derek alone at the fourth, pushed slightly away, hunched over his work, trying to ignore the others.

Derek nudged me again, whining softly, and I looked down to see him eyeing the room, every hair on his neck on end, anxious to get away from this place. I murmured an apology and followed the others. We passed two more doors, then Liz came running back.

"Someone's coming."

"What?" Aunt Lauren said when I relayed it. "From down there? That can't be. It's—"

The clomp of footsteps cut her off. She looked each way, then waved to the nearest door.

"The key card, Chloe, quickly!"

I opened it and we all tumbled inside. As I closed the door behind us, the lock whirred shut. I looked around, squinting to see with only the glow of an emergency light.

We were in a huge storage room packed with boxes.

"Lots of places to hide," I whispered. "I suggest we find one."

We split up as footsteps echoed down the hall. I turned, nearly tripping over Derek. He hadn't moved, just stared into the room, fur bristling.

I looked around. I saw boxes, lots of boxes, but over along the far wall, something else—four beds.

"T-this was—" I began.

"Where is everyone?" boomed a voice from the hall.

Derek snapped out of it, grabbed my sleeve between his teeth, and tugged me deep into the sea of boxes. We found a spot in the back corner where boxes were piled three high, leaving a small space for us to hide. Derek nudged me toward it. I whispered for the others as he went back to gather them up.

In a minute, we were all wedged in that space, crouched or sitting. Derek stood at the opening, guarding it, ears swiveling. As the steps drew closer, I didn't need his hearing to pick up the voices.

"Scientists." A man snorted. "They think they can hire a few rent-a-cop half-demons and they're ready for something like this. Arrogant sons of . . ." His mutters trailed off. "How close is Mr. St. Cloud?"

"His flight will arrive in seventy-five minutes, sir."

"Then we have an hour to clean this mess up. How many kids was it again? Four?"

"Three were recaptured. The fourth—the werewolf—wasn't, but there was a report that he'd entered the building."

"Great. Just great." Their footsteps sounded outside the door. "All right, here's the plan. I need two survivors. If you can get me two, Mr. St. Cloud will be happy. And that doesn't include the werewolf."

"Naturally, sir."

"We need a place to set up a base of operations. The team will be here in five minutes."

"It doesn't look as if they use this wing, sir." A door creaked. "This room even has desks and a blackboard."

"Good. Start setting up and get Davidoff on the radio. I want him down here now."

I waved for Liz to go check things out.

We all strained to listen, praying they'd find some problem with the room or be offered a better one. It didn't happen.

"At least they're on the other side of our escape route," Tori said.

"It doesn't matter," Simon said. "We've got a Cabal SWAT team setting up down the hall. We're screwed."

Liz came running back in. "There are two guys in suits and one wearing what looks like a soldier's uniform. Plus four more like him marching up the hall."

The clomping of boots echoed her words.

"We'll hold tight," I said. "They'll send those guys searching—hopefully somewhere else. When we get a chance, we'll run."

Derek chuffed and slid in behind me, letting me rest against him, so warm and comfortable that I started to relax, and when I did, so did he, muscles softening, heart rate slowing.

"So you two came on your own?" I said to Liz. "How?"

"Drove."

"But Derek doesn't have his license."

Simon laughed. "Doesn't mean we don't know how to drive. Dad let us start last year, bombing around empty parking lots."

"That's a few minutes at the mall, not eight hours on the highway."

Derek grunted, as if to say it'd been no big deal, though I'm sure it couldn't have been easy.

"We took Andrew's truck," Liz said. "After we found . . . After Derek found his . . . Well, you know. We probably weren't far behind you. I helped navigate."

"How'd you communicate?"

"Paper and pen. Amazing inventions. Anyway, once we were in Buffalo, I led him here. We couldn't figure out a way in and he got stressed and apparently that"—she waved at him—"is what happens when a werewolf gets stressed. By then, the garage door was open, some staff guy bringing in a car. He took one look at Derek and decided it was time for a new job."

Noises sounded in the hall. Liz went to check it out. Behind me, Derek's flank twitched. I rubbed it absently, the muscle jumping under my fingers. Then I asked the question I'd been dreading since Aunt Lauren first found me.

"Rae's dead, isn't she?" I said. "Dr. Davidoff said she was transferred, but I know what that means. The same thing it meant with Liz and Brady."

The look on Aunt Lauren's face at that moment . . . I can't describe it, but if I had any doubt about how much she regretted the role she'd played in all this, I saw it as I mentioned their names. For a second she said nothing. Then she jumped, like she'd been startled.

"Rae? No. Rae isn't dead. Someone broke in and took her. They think it was her mother."

"Her adoptive mom?"

Aunt Lauren shook her head. "Her birth mother. Jacinda."

"But Dr. Davidoff said she was dead."

"We said a lot of things, Chloe. Told a lot of lies, telling ourselves it was better for you all, but really, just because it was easier. If Rae thought her mother was dead, she wouldn't ask for her. From everything I heard, though, they think that's who—"

Derek's flank twitched again. I glanced down to see a muscle spasming. Another started in his shoulder. When he caught me looking, he growled, telling me it was nothing, just ignore him and pay attention.

As Aunt Lauren talked, I rubbed the muscle in Derek's shoulder and he leaned against my hand, relaxing. I knew it wouldn't help. He was ready to Change.

"We need to get going," I said. "I'm going to call Liz."

She raced through the boxes before I even finished summoning her. Tori's mom had joined the SWAT team in the next room. Apparently, Derek hadn't hurt her as much as I might have hoped. She was nursing a killer headache . . . and a killer grudge. Derek was to be shot on sight—shot dead, not tranquilized.

Reinforcements from a Cabal satellite office were on the way to help sweep the building with manpower and spell power. They were determined to find us before this St. Cloud guy arrived.

"We're going to have to make a run for it," I said. "As soon as it's quiet—"

Derek convulsed, nearly throwing me off him.

"Someone doesn't like your plan," Tori said. "And just when I was thinking how nice it was that he doesn't have a voice. Won't keep him from arguing apparently."

"That's not it," I said as Derek convulsed again. "He's Changing back."

"Can it wait, because—?"

Derek's whole body spasmed, all four legs shooting out, a back claw nicking Simon, a front paw swatting Tori. They both leaped out of the way.

"I think that's a no," Simon said.

"We need to clear out," I said. "As you can tell, this requires room. And it might not be something you want to see."

"Tell them I second that," Liz said. "I caught a glimpse, and that was enough." She made a face and shuddered.

I shooed them out, then turned to Derek, lying on his side, panting. "You've done this alone now, so I guess you don't need—"

He caught my jeans leg between his teeth, pulling gently, his eyes asking me to stay. I told the others I was, and said if they heard any sign that the SWAT team was searching this hall, they were to get out—all of them.

"We aren't leaving you two," Simon said.

Derek growled.

"He's agreeing with me," I said. "For once. You have to go. With any luck, they'll presume that means Derek and I are someplace else."

Simon didn't like it, but he only grumbled for Derek to hurry.

Aunt Lauren stayed after they'd gone. "If anything happens, you're coming with us, Chloe. Derek can look after—"

"No, he can't. Not like this. He needs me."

"I don't care."

"I do. He needs me. So I stay."

We locked gazes. Again, a look passed through her eyes, surprise and maybe a little bit of grief. I wasn't her little Chloe anymore. I never would be again.

I walked over and hugged her. "I'm fine."

"I know." She hugged me back, fierce and tight, then left to join the others.

forty-seven

DEREK'S CHANGE CAME FASTER now and maybe a bit easier—no vomiting this time. Finally it was over, and he fell onto his side, panting, shaking, and shivering. Then he reached for my hand, holding it tight, and I entwined my fingers with his, shifting closer and using my free hand to brush sweaty hair from his face.

"Whoa," a voice said, making both of us jump. Simon stood in the entrance to our corner, a pile of fabric in his hands. "You really need to get dressed before you start that."

"I'm not starting anything," Derek said.

"Still . . ." He held out the stack in his hands. "Dr. Fellows dug up some hospital greens for you. Get dressed and then . . . whatever."

"We weren't—" I began.

"Have you still got my note?"

I nodded.

"Give it to him."

I pulled the folded page from my pocket and handed it to Derek. When he was busy with it, Simon let the smile fall from his face as he studied his brother.

"Is he okay?" he mouthed.

I nodded. I passed Derek the scrubs as he refolded the note, then turned away to let him dress.

"We good?" Simon asked.

"Yeah." Derek lowered his voice.

A squeak of shoes as Simon turned to go. Derek called him back, grunting with effort as he rose, his bare feet padding over. A short, murmured conversation. Then the slap of Simon smacking Derek's back, and his footsteps retreated.

A whisper of fabric as Derek dressed. Then a hand on my waist, a light touch, tentative. I turned and Derek was right there, his face above mine, hands sliding around me as I tilted my face up—

"What the—?"

We both jumped—again. Tori stood there, staring at us, Simon behind her, grabbing her arm.

"I told you not to—" Simon began.

"Yeah, but you didn't say why. I sure didn't expect . . ." She shook her head. "Am I the last one to know everything around here?"

Liz raced in. "What's going on?"

"Derek's ready," I said. "We need to move."

We had one gun, one werewolf, one poltergeist, one supercharged spell-caster, one not-so-supercharged spell-caster, and one perfectly useless necromancer, though Liz was quick to remind me that she needed me to relay her words.

Our plan, though, involved something much simpler than a supernatural showdown. We were falling back on the advice Derek's dad had given him for dealing with a significantly stronger opponent: run like hell.

While Liz watched the operations room, we'd try to make it to the exit door. If we failed? That's when the gun, werewolf, poltergeist, and spell-casters would come into play.

According to Liz, there were five people in that room—Mrs. Enright, Dr. Davidoff, the head suit, his assistant, and one SWAT guard. They seemed to be staying put, manning the war room while the employees searched. Every now and then, one of those employees would pop in for an update or orders. We just had to pray that didn't happen during the few minutes it'd take us to get to the door.

As we coordinated a what-if plan of attack, Derek stood beside me. Aunt Lauren kept giving us weird looks. We weren't doing anything to earn them, but she kept glancing over and frowning.

Finally she said, "Derek? Can I speak to you?"

He stiffened and glanced at me, as if to say, *What does she want?*

"W-we don't have time to—" I began.

"It'll just take a second. Derek? Please?"

She waved him across the room. Tori and Simon were arguing about spells and Liz was in the hall, so no one else noticed. Aunt Lauren said something to Derek. Whatever it was, he didn't like it, his gaze shooting to me as he scowled and shook his head.

Was she telling him to stay away from me? I could hope that today she'd seen he wasn't dangerous, maybe even seen how I felt about him, but I guess that was too much to hope for.

I wanted to march over and interrupt, but before I could, Derek stopped arguing. He eased back, head bent, hair hanging forward, deep in thought. Then he gave a slow nod. She reached out and took his arm, leaning in to say more, her face taut with urgency. He kept his gaze down, nodding. I told myself he was just saying whatever she wanted to hear so we could get out of here, but I'll admit I felt a lot better when he walked straight to me, rumbling, "You ready?"

We stepped aside as Aunt Lauren got Simon and Tori.

"Was she telling you to stay away from me?" I asked.

He paused, then said, "Yeah." He squeezed my hand out of Aunt Lauren's sight. "It's okay. We're good."

We headed for the hall.

Our biggest worry had been the loud click of the door lock, but Derek listened and motioned for me to open it while the men were talking. Then Derek took the lead, in case anyone came in through the exit door.

I was behind him, Simon behind me, Tori and Aunt Lauren following.

Those thirty feet seemed like thirty miles. I longed to bolt for the door, throw it open, and be gone; but we had to move silently, which meant excruciatingly slowly.

We'd gone about ten feet when someone in the war room said, "We have a breach, sir. A perimeter spell."

"Where?"

Derek picked up speed, just a little.

"Hold on," the man said. "It seems to be right outside—"

"Chloe?" Aunt Lauren's loud whisper floated through the halls.

I spun to see her jogging the other way—toward the room where the Edison team and the Cabal guys were. She called my name again, like she was searching for me.

My mouth opened. A hand clamped over it, an arm going around my chest, holding me still, Derek's voice in my ear, whispering, "I'm sorry."

"I think I hear them," Dr. Davidoff said.

"Chloe?" Aunt Lauren ran full out now, shoes slapping the linoleum. "Chloe?"

She wheeled into their room and let out a yelp.

"Hello, Lauren," Tori's mom said. "Lost your niece again?" She cast a binding spell, freezing my aunt. "I see you still have that gun. Let me take that, before you kill someone else."

As I struggled, Derek waved for the others to keep going. I vaguely saw Simon and Tori pass me as Derek scooped me up and started for the exit, and I knew *this* was what Aunt Lauren had told him to do, what he'd tried to argue against. If there was trouble, she'd sacrifice herself to save us. His job was to get me out of there.

I twisted my head to see Mrs. Enright holding the gun on Aunt Lauren, still frozen.

"Time to rid ourselves of a very inconvenient—"

"A gun, Diane?" a man's voice called. "Guess your charm isn't the only power you underestimate."

A man stepped around the corner. He was about my dad's age, a couple of inches shorter than Mrs. Enright, slender, with silvering black hair. He was smiling—and it was a smile I knew well, even if I'd never seen this man before.

"Dad!" Simon shouted, skidding to a halt.

forty-eight

MR. BAE LIFTED A HAND, waving casually, like he'd walked in on us sitting around chatting. I struggled and Derek released me.

"Hello, Kit," Mrs. Enright said. She turned the gun on him.

He tsk-tsked. "Is that really the impression you want to make, Diane? Prove to everyone here that a witch needs a gun to fight a sorcerer?"

She lowered the gun and raised her hand instead, fingers sparking.

"There," he said. "That's better. Now come on over and show me how much you missed me."

She cast an energy bolt. Mr. Bae's hand flew out and her bolt stopped short, exploding in midair. The guard advanced on Aunt Lauren, gun pointed, now that the binding spell on her was broken.

Simon lunged forward, but his father motioned for him to run. Simon kept going. Derek caught his shoulder. He looked down at me, then from the door to his father, caught between the impulse to protect him or protect us.

"Fight," I whispered, and it was all I needed to say. Derek released Simon and pushed me toward the door. Tori locked the guard in a binding spell and yelled for Aunt Lauren to follow me. My aunt sprang up and grabbed the guard's gun and hit him in the head with it as Derek plowed into Dr. Davidoff, sending him flying.

Tori cast another spell, then another. I don't know what they were, only that the walls started to shake. The cracks from earlier yawned wider. Plaster rained down.

I wanted to do something, anything, but Derek saw me and shouted for me to get back. Then one of the men in a suit hit him with a spell, knocking him forward before his dad slammed an energy bolt into the guy. I stayed where I was, knowing that as much as I wanted to help, I'd only put everyone else in danger trying to protect me.

The building continued to shake, weakened walls and ceiling cracking. White dust rained down, enveloping everyone, and I could catch only glimpses through it, snapshots of the action.

Tori facing off with her mom.

Liz running toward Mrs. Enright, a broken plank in her hand.

The guard lying unconscious under everyone's feet.

Derek tackling the main suit, his dad and Simon taking on the other.

Aunt Lauren standing over Dr. Davidoff, gun at the back of his head.

Then, with an earsplitting crack, the ceiling gave way. Huge chunks of plaster and broken wood crashed down. Boxes and crates and filing cabinets toppled through from the attic. The ceiling kept ripping and cracking, and I looked up to see it splitting right over my head. Derek shouted. He hit me, knocking me to the floor and pinning me beneath him as the rest of the ceiling collapsed.

When the hall finally stopped rumbling, I heard Mr. Bae calling for Derek.

"Here," Derek said. "With Chloe."

He moved off me and helped me up. I rose, coughing and blinking. I could make out Simon and Mr. Bae safe in the room where we'd hidden earlier.

"Tori?" I heard Liz saying. "Tori!"

I squinted and moved toward her voice; Derek still gripped my arm, staying close. Liz was hunched over Tori.

"Tori!" I yelled.

She lifted her head, brushing a hand over her face. "I-I'm okay."

As she got up, I looked around frantically for Aunt Lauren. Then I saw her, stirring under a pile of rubble between me and Tori. I leaped forward, but Derek pulled me back.

"Stay there, guys," Mr. Bae said. "Tori—" He paused and when I looked over, he was staring at her, like he'd only just seen her now, *really* seen her.

"Dad?" Simon said.

Mr. Bae shook off the surprise and said, slowly, "Tori? Head toward me. That ceiling doesn't look good."

I glanced up. Broken timbers and huge pieces of plaster swayed overhead. Boxes teetered on the edge.

Tori looked around. The guard and two guys in suits were almost buried under the rubble. Dr. Davidoff lay on his stomach, not moving. Beside her lay another body—her mother, her eyes open, staring up.

"Ding-dong, the witch is dead," Tori said. She swayed. Then she made a weird, strangled hiccupping noise, shoulders hunching. "Mom . . ."

"Tori? Hon?" Mr. Bae called. "I need you to come over here, okay?"

"Aunt Lauren," I said. "She's caught—"

"I've got it," Tori said, wiping her sleeve over her face. She bent and started pulling pieces off my aunt.

A plank flew up from the pile behind Tori. Dr. Davidoff's eyes were open, mentally guiding it. I opened my mouth to scream a warning and Liz raced to grab it, but it swung down, hitting Tori in the back of the head. She fell face-first to the rubble. Aunt Lauren scrambled up, pushing the last pieces of plaster aside. Then she stopped. Dr. Davidoff rose behind her, gun pressed to the back of her neck.

Liz grabbed the plank he'd hit Tori with, but he saw it move and said, "No, Elizabeth." He swung the gun toward Tori. "Not unless you'd like some company in the afterlife."

Liz dropped the wood.

Dr. Davidoff moved the gun back to Aunt Lauren. "Pick that board up again, please, Elizabeth, and move in front of me, so I can see where you are."

She did.

"Now, Kit, I'm going to give you five minutes to take your boys and go. The modifications appear to have succeeded with Simon. As strong as Derek is, he seems normal for a werewolf. Another success. Chloe and Victoria are the problems, but I assure you, they'll be well cared for. Take your boys and—"

"I'm not going anywhere," Derek said. "Not without Chloe."

He stiffened, like he expected me to argue, but I barely heard them talking. My blood roared in my ears, stomach churning, knowing what I had to do, fighting to get past every instinct that screamed against it.

Dr. Davidoff's eyes lifted to Derek. He frowned, assessing, then nodded. "So be it. I won't turn down the opportunity to keep our only werewolf subject. Take your son, then, Kit."

"I'll take *both* my sons," Mr. Bae said. "And Victoria and Chloe and Lauren."

Dr. Davidoff chuckled. "Still don't know when to cut your losses, do you? I'd think ten years on the run would have taught you a lesson. Think of everything you gave up, just because I wanted Derek back. I'm sure Simon would have been a lot happier if you hadn't been so stubborn."

"Stubborn's good," Simon said. "And it runs in the family. I'm not leaving until you give them up, too."

Derek rubbed the back of my shoulders, mistaking the tightness for fear, not concentration. Simon cast an anxious glance my way as sweat poured down my face. I closed my eyes and focused.

"Go, Chloe," Aunt Lauren said. "Just go."

"That's not how it works," Dr. Davidoff said. "I can shoot you and Tori before Kit or Derek can take me down. Make up your mind, Kit. There's a Cabal team on the way, if they haven't already arrived. Cut your losses and go."

A shape rose behind Dr. Davidoff. Derek sucked in a breath, then slowly released it and whispered under his breath, encouraging me. Simon and Mr. Bae quickly looked away so Dr. Davidoff wouldn't turn around.

"You only have a few minutes, Kit," Dr. Davidoff said.

"Pick up the gun," I said.

He laughed. "Your aunt knows better than to dive for a gun ten feet away, Chloe."

"Dr. Davidoff," I said.

"Yes?"

"Shoot him."

He frowned, mouth opening. Mrs. Enright's corpse swayed. Her eyes met mine, rage-filled eyes.

"I said—"

She fired. Dr. Davidoff hung there, mouth working, hole through his chest. Then he dropped. I squeezed my eyes shut and released Mrs. Enright's soul. When I opened them, Aunt Lauren was crouched beside Dr. Davidoff, fingers to his neck. His ghost stood beside her, staring, confused.

"He's gone," I said. "I—I see his spirit."

Someone shouted. Boots clomped in the distance.

"We have to go," Mr. Bae said. "Lauren—"

"I'm fine."

"Derek, grab Tori and follow me."

We raced out the door just as shouts echoed behind us. Mr. Bae yelled for Simon and Aunt Lauren to get over the wall, as he boosted me and Derek carried Tori. I got to the top, then crouched beside Simon, the two of us helping Derek as Liz ran ahead, shouting the all clear.

As we climbed down, Mr. Bae stood atop the wall, ready to shoot spells at anyone who came out. But no one did—the rubble and the bodies slowed them down long enough for us to get away. By then, Tori was conscious and we ran, all of us, as far and as fast as we could.

forty-nine

MR. BAE'S VAN WAS PARKED a mile away in a shopping mall. He'd bought it a month ago, using faked paperwork, so it couldn't be traced back to him, and it looked like he'd been living in it. He threw his sleeping bag and a cooler into the back, and we all climbed in.

I don't know where we ended up. Pennsylvania, I think. No one asked. No one cared. It was a really long, really quiet drive. I was in the back with Aunt Lauren, and even though I noticed Derek glancing back at me anxiously every now and then, I soon fell asleep to the murmur of Simon and his dad in the front seat.

I woke up when Mr. Bae pulled into a roadside motel. He got two rooms and we split up, guys going in one, girls in the other. Mr. Bae said he'd order pizza for us all and then we'd talk. Aunt Lauren said not to rush. No one was hungry, and I'm sure the guys wanted some alone time with their dad.

Liz and Tori seemed to figure I needed alone time with Aunt Lauren, too. Liz took off, saying she was going to wander and she'd be back by morning. Tori said her stomach was queasy from the long drive, so she was going to sit outside for a while to get some fresh air. Aunt Lauren asked her to go behind our unit, so no one driving past could see her.

That's when it really hit me: we weren't going home, not yet anyway.

And we'd have to get used to always thinking about stuff like that, about who might be watching.

I sat beside Aunt Lauren on the bed, and she put her arm around my shoulders.

"How are you doing?" she asked.

"Okay."

"What happened back there . . . At the lab . . ."

She didn't finish. I knew what she meant—killing Dr. Davidoff. And I knew that if I mentioned it, she'd tell me I hadn't actually killed him. But I had. I wasn't sure how I felt about that, only that Aunt Lauren wouldn't be the person I'd talk to about it, because she'd only try to make me feel better, not help me work through it. For that, I'd need Derek, so I just said, "I'm okay." Then, "I know I can't go home right now, but I want Dad to know I'm okay."

"I'm not sure that's—"

"He has to know. Even if he can't know about the necromancer stuff and the Edison Group stuff. He has to know I'm safe."

She wavered for a moment, but seeing my expression, she finally nodded. "We'll find a way."

When I found Tori out back, she was just sitting there, like that night at the warehouse when her dad betrayed her. Sitting there, staring into space, hugging her knees.

This had to be so hard for her. The guys got their dad back, I got Aunt Lauren back. And Tori? She'd watched her mother die. No matter how horrible Mrs. Enright had been, no matter how much Tori had come to hate her, she'd still been her mother.

Tori wasn't alone here. She still had a parent, a biological one anyway, but I was sure Mr. Bae wouldn't be too quick to tell her. That would be too weird, like saying, "Sorry you lost one parent, but here's a replacement."

I sat down beside her.

"I'm sorry about your mom," I said.

A short, bitter laugh. "Why? She was an evil, murdering bitch."

"But she was *your* evil, murdering bitch."

Tori gave a choked laugh, then nodded. A tear slid down her cheek. I wanted to put my arm around her, but I knew she'd hate that, so I just moved closer, bumping against her. She tensed and I thought she was going to move away, but then she relaxed, leaning against me. I could feel her body shaking as she cried. She didn't make a sound, though, not even a whimper.

A huge shadow rounded the corner. Derek stepped out, head tilted to catch the wind. His lips twitched when he saw me, curving into a crooked smile.

"Hey," he said. "I thought I—"

Tori lifted her head and wiped her eyes on her sleeve, and Derek shut up.

"Sorry," he said gruffly and started to retreat.

"That's okay," she said, getting to her feet. "My pity session is over. You can have her now."

As she walked away from us back to our room, Derek stood there, looking uncertain again. Anxious again. I waved for him to sit beside me, but he shook his head.

"Can't right now," he said. "Dad sent me to find you."

I went to get up, but my foot was asleep and I stumbled a bit. Derek caught me and didn't let go. He bent, like he was going to kiss me, then stopped.

Was he always going to do that? I almost teased him about it, but he looked so serious, I didn't dare.

"Your aunt," he said. "Did she say anything about your plans?"

"No."

Once more he leaned down to me, then stopped again.

"Didn't she say *anything*? Like whether you're going home or not?"

"I'm not. As long as that Cabal is still out there, we can't. I suppose we'll stay with you guys, if that's what your dad has in mind. Probably safest."

He exhaled, like he'd been holding his breath, and I finally understood why he was so anxious. Now that we'd escaped the Edison Group and were back with our families, he thought that meant we'd go our separate ways.

"I'm definitely *hoping* we'll stay with you guys," I said.

"Me, too."

I slid closer, feeling his arms close around me, tightening. Our lips touched—

"Derek?" his dad called. "Chloe?"

Derek let out a growl. I laughed and backed up.

"We seem to get a lot of that, don't we?" I said.

"Too much. After we eat, we're going for a walk. A *long* walk. Far from every possible interruption."

I grinned up at him. "Sounds like a plan."

Speaking of plans, Mr. Bae had plenty. Over pizza he confirmed what I expected—we needed to go on the run again, this time from the Cabal.

"So everything we did back there, at the lab . . . it didn't do any good?" I said.

"Probably only pissed the Cabal off," Tori muttered.

"No, it helped," Mr. Bae said. "The Edison Group won't recover from this anytime soon, and it'll take some time for the Cabal to sort through everything and plan a search. Fortunately, being a Cabal, they've got a lot on their to-do list, and we won't be at the top. You're valuable, and they'll want you back, but we'll have some breathing room." He glanced at my aunt. "Lauren? Living on the run may not be what you had in mind, but I'm going to strongly suggest you and Chloe come with us. We should stick together."

Derek looked at me, tensing, like he was ready to jump in with arguments if Aunt Lauren disagreed. When she said, "That would be best," he relaxed. So did I. Simon grinned and shot me a thumbs-up. I looked over at Tori. She seemed to be holding herself as still as she could, her face rigid, not giving anything away.

"And Tori will come with us, right?" I said.

"Of course." Mr. Bae smiled at her. "I suppose I should make sure that's okay with her, though. Will you stay with us, Tori?"

She nodded, and slid a half smile my way.

"We'll need to lie low for a while," Mr. Bae said. "I have a few ideas of places we can go. Simon says Tori got a list of the other subjects. We'll make contact with them. They have to know what was going on . . . and what happened. We'll look for Rae, too. If she's with her mom, that's good, but we'll want to make sure of that. We don't want anyone left behind."

It was overwhelming, but it felt weirdly good, too, knowing we weren't alone, knowing we could help the others. We had a lot of work ahead of us, but a lot of adventures, too. I was sure of that.

Derek and I went out for our walk after dinner. Alone.

There was an open field behind the motel and we headed there. Finally, when we were far enough from the motel, Derek led me into a little patch of woods. He hesitated then, unsure, still just holding my hand. When I stepped in front of him, though, his free hand went around my waist.

"So," I said. "Seems you're going to be stuck with me for a while."

He smiled. A real smile that lit up his whole face.

"Good," he said.

He pulled me against him. Then he bent down, breath warming my lips. My pulse was racing so fast I could barely breathe. I was sure he'd stop again and I tensed, waiting for that hesitation, stomach twisting. His lips touched mine, and still I kept waiting for him to pull back.

His lips pressed against mine, then parted. And he kissed me. *Really* kissed me—arms tightening around me, mouth moving against mine, firm, like he'd made up his mind that this was what he wanted and he wasn't backing down again.

I slid my arms around his neck. His tightened around me and he scooped me up, lifting me off my feet, kissing me like he was never going to stop, and I kissed him back the same way, like I didn't *want* him to ever stop.

It was a perfect moment, one where nothing else mattered. All I could feel was him. All I could taste was his kiss. All I could hear was the pounding of his heart. All I could think about was him, and how much I wanted this, and how incredibly lucky I was to get it, and how tight I was going to hold on to it.

This was what I wanted. This guy. This life. This *me.* I was never getting my old life back, and I didn't care. I was happy. I was safe. I was right where I wanted to be.

Meet sixteen-year-old Maya and her best friend,

Daniel—two ordinary teens with extraordinary

abilities—in this exclusive *SNEAK PEEK* at

The Gathering,

the first book in a thrilling new paranormal trilogy by

***New York Times* bestselling author Kelley Armstrong!**

THE CAT HAD DANIEL pinned face-first to the ground. Daniel lay still, playing dead, as I shouted at the mountain lion and my parents shouted at me. The cat snarled again and I braced myself, ready to run if those powerful hind legs bunched for flight. But it made no move to come after me, just snarled and spat and stayed over Daniel.

Rage boiled up in me. Maybe it was shock, but it felt like rage, pure fury coursing through me. I screamed at the cat, and I looked it square in the eye and when I did it was like everything else disappeared. I met its gaze and the world seemed to dip and darken and I smelled wet earth and thick musk and fresh blood. The wind whipped past, like I was running. Running so fast the ground whizzed beneath me, the wind cutting across my skin. Exhilaration filled me.

the Darkest Powers trilogy